...The EMP was just a first blow, opening the door for further strikes that will finish the job throughout the rest of the country. I am speculating, of course, but from our figures and the readings we gathered back at the base, I'd say the warhead was detonated high over eastern Ohio. We'd be totally guessing if we tried to declare a yield, but I'd say that more than 95% of the electronics, computer, and technological infrastructure on the eastern seaboard – from Maine to most of Florida, and from the Atlantic to as far as Nebraska, will have been fried. There are probably fires burning out of control in every major city in that area, and the fires will get worse as time goes on because there'll be no water to dowse them. The trucks that put out fires won't work, and the communications that control emergency response is now gone, and probably forever. The damage done will make the work of Mrs. O'Leary's cow look like child's play...

"An Epic Story of Hardship and Survival"

Praise for W1CK

"...WICK has rocked my world and shaken everything inside me..."

"Michael Bunker goes way beyond writing a popular thriller: he clearly has a literary agenda, making the W1CK series so rich and so deep you could analyse each and every page and write a whole book about it. I guess you'd have to call it W1CK1P3D1A."

"...The writing is excellent. We need more Indie writers like this ... Michael's writing changed my perception of this life quite a bit. I hope it does the same for you."

" ...The characters are richly constructed .... The prose is easy to read and the story develops smoothly. I can't wait to find out what happens but I don't want the story to end! "

"...combines the best of Sinclair Lewis and James Howard Kunstler in a truly great read that will both engage you and challenge you to think- and choose wisely."

"...Mr. Bunker has managed to write a carefully crafted and extremely, disturbingly believable piece of fiction about the modern human condition."

"Exciting, riveting and compelling story... Highly recommended reading..."

" ...So glad I took the plunge and got hooked on this thrilling series! Characters that are personable. Settings in vivid detail. Couldn't wait to move on to the second book!"

"...I was kept guessing at every turn of this book. I love how this story becomes rich and alive in my mind without being tedious or over-written. He tells you just enough to keep you engaged, but doesn't overwhelm with detail."

"...It had me fully engaged from page one."

"...Great fiction with a lot of realistic probabilities. Not your typical end of the world doomsday thriller."

"I love Michael's way of writing and the subjects he writes about....
"

"... packed with great characters, suspense, philosophy, and thought-provoking ideas."

"...will have you reading non-stop into the wee hours of the night and will leave you gasping for air."

"Ok, this book has me on the hook... I very rarely read fiction but this outing by Michael Bunker has been terrific. ... Buy it for yourself and your friends."

"This was the most intriguing book I have ever read. It started out to be a journey and ended up with nail biting, edge of your seat conclusion. ...What a rush this was."

" ... The writing is gorgeous, tactile, vivid, with a plot yarn that unfolds a landscape beautiful and terrifying."

"I was engaged in the story from the start - something I've missed from many other authors from this genre recently. Nice to see some real literary talent and wit in this genre."

"A compelling story that is beautifully written. Each sentence simply melts into the next. Michael Bunker has a gift for awakening the imagination. ..."

"You can't go wrong when you have fiction with excitement for the brain AND heart. Combine that with the lurking knowledge that

many elements of this story could be off the fiction backburner and onto full heat reality very soon, and, well, it all adds up to one I could not put down."

"I found it to be a captivating use of the English language. Packed with well written, thought provoking mental imagery."

"...I could hardly put it down. Read in two sittings. Like eating a beautifully prepared, delicious meal when you are really hungry, eating so fast, scraping every speck and morsel from the plate..."

"... Michael Bunker draws you in with his beautiful imagery and storytelling. I have a feeling I'll be following this author for some time!"

"The twists and turns keep coming. This is an excellent read. And the kindle version is so inexpensive that you would be foolish not to read it."

" ... Entertaining and thought-provoking. Can't wait to get my hard copy because you never know if the power will go out."

"...I literally read it in one sitting because I could NOT PUT IT DOWN. I wish I could give it more than 5 stars."

MICHAEL
BUNKER

WITH CHRIS AWALT

WICK: The Omnibus Edition

Cover Design by Jason Gurley

For information on Michael Bunker, or to read his blog:
http://www.michaelbunker.com

To contact Michael Bunker, please write to:

M. Bunker
1251 CR 132
Santa Anna, Texas 76878

ACKNOWLEDGEMENTS

Our sincere thanks go out to Stewart, David, Jason, Kate, Melonie, Hanna, all the beta readers, and everyone else who has played such a huge part in getting this series out to its audience. We never could have done it without you all.

Chris Awalt would like to thank those who provided support and encouragement during the writing of this book, particularly Dick and Dorothy, Anne, Vinnie, and Michael.

As we close this opening series in *The Last Pilgrims* story, we want to thank all of our awesome readers. Your enthusiasm and support has encouraged us, and has lifted us up during the writing of this epic tale.

We now present to our friends the completed WICK story. It has been a wild ride, and a wonderful collaboration with all of you.

Thank you all.

Michael Bunker and Chris Awalt.
June, 2013.

For a limited time, get the sequel to *the Wick Omnibus* for **free** right now! Go to: http://bit.ly/FreeLastPilgrims to get the full novel for free!

CONTENTS

KNOT ONE

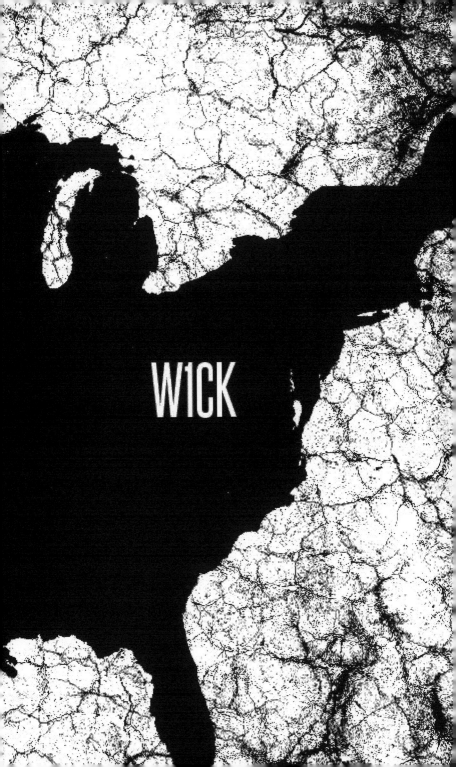

CHAPTER 1

People aren't meant to live in cages. Though their first sensate experience comes from inside the warm enclosure of the womb, that is not their natural state. Their first true experience of the world begins the moment they are pushed out of that embrace. It is in that adrenaline-fueled rush into the open air of freedom that they gasp their first breaths and begin their lives anew.

It is odd, then, that individually they yearn for freedom, but in numbers they seek control. From the moment of their birth - that moment when they open their eyes and look up with blurry focus into the faces of their mothers - humans find a world that is hostile to their freedom. Their natural curiosity is checked as soon as they gain language. When they take their first tentative steps, they are curbed on all sides. Even when this is done for their benefit, it carries the seed of authority. "Don't touch that, it will burn you" becomes "because I said so, that's why." Guidance piles into guidelines. Structure morphs into stricture.

This is not a new story; there is nothing new under the sun. Though it is recreated in each generation, the formation of social sensibilities in the hearts of individuals is the well-worn path upon which societies tread, and on which Empires rise and fall. If the world does its job well, if the masses of individuals learn their places, then young children grow into youths and then become adults who not only accept artificial and arbitrary restraints but, joining the teeming crowds, are pleased to impose these shackles on themselves and others.

Good sense and benevolent law, designed to promote peace and freedom from without and to gently nurture from within, are subtly replaced by systems of power and control, imposed for the benefit and propagation of what can only be called *The Hive Mind*. It's a tale as old as time.

Regret. Missed opportunity. Doubt and loss. Failure and limitation. In the end, people lovingly polish the silvered bars and oil the locks and chains of their own prisons. Sitting inside their cages, both those of metaphor and reality, they look out between the bars and imagine what they might have been. Everywhere men are born free, the philosopher says, and everywhere they are in chains.

It is difficult to see this in the machinations of a city, where each individual acts freely—or believes himself to do so. It is comforting to think that there is a qualitative difference between the choices one makes regarding which fashions to follow and which products to buy, and the stampede of a herd of cattle. Yet, Tolstoy wrote that, even in those historical moments when men look back and see patriotism and sacrifice as the driving forces of history, "the majority of the people paid no attention to the general course of events but were influenced only by their immediate personal interests." In the stream of time, as cultures and societies stampede to destruction, so few are willing to identify their prisons or recognize their chains.

Clay Richter had decided he'd had enough of that.

* * * *

Tuesday

People aren't meant to live in cages, he thought, as he locked the door of his Brooklyn brownstone for the last time. He was standing at the head of a stoop, his back to the world on the morning after the worst natural disaster around here since anyone could remember. As he pushed the key in the lock and turned it to the left, the motion in his wrist and the anticipatory swivel in his hips and the turning in his shoulders felt good on the balls of his feet. His body was fluid and light. A cool, pervasive wetness hung in the stirring air and he felt, for the moment, as if he were one with the natural elements, and this feeling made him smile.

Clay turned and paused to look around. He felt like he was making a prison break. Was anyone watching his flight? Would anyone notice the tangled sheets he'd tossed and turned on the night before as the storm raged outside his window? Upon waking, he'd simply stripped the sheets from the bed and balled them up, tossing them out the window, where they now lay on the curb among the branches and leaves that had fallen from the sky as Sandy roared her way through the tri-state area. They lay there like a rope, knotted and tangled among the debris.

You make your bed, you lie in it, he thought. For the first time in years—since the day that he'd received the call from Cheryl that had changed his life forever—he was done with lies. When his feet touched the floor that morning, the cool grainy texture of the hardwoods pressing against the soft pink flesh of his soles, he knew that he would have the courage to tell himself the truth. He had to get out of his cage if he was going to have a life.

He took a deep breath of the thick moist air and stepped down to the gate. The world was numbly bustling about, surveying the damage, as he lifted the latch and stepped onto the sidewalk. People were haltingly filing past in gauzy disbelief. Some whispered in hushed tones, others were nervously sharing bits of news. "Did you see the tree that fell across Bond Street? My God, have you ever seen anything like this?" Others simply walked and stared, too dumbfounded to do anything else.

The streets were not full now like they had been just two days earlier, when passersby talked in excited tones, daring the forecasters to be right. Then, they'd been almost celebratory as they walked by in pairs along the sidewalks, carrying their cases of bottled water and their bags of batteries and flashlights. "They always hype these things you know..." they'd said. "I remember during Irene they told us to stay indoors, and they closed down the subways, and even cancelled schools, and for what?" Now, the damage was done and they knew the answer to that question.

Clay stood for a moment and fingered the key, rubbing its smooth, worn face, as he felt the mist form droplets on his face and liked it. He was tempted to simply hang the key on the spires of the black wrought iron fence and walk away. He thought of Otis, the town drunk from Mayberry—how he'd stumble into the jailhouse after a bender and reach for the key on the hook for a cell that he had designated as his own and let himself in and out as he pleased. *Otis.* I won't be coming back but maybe some other sucker could use it, he thought. Then he changed his mind. He preferred to throw the key in the Hudson—a solemn and solitary protest against the willful confinement of urbanism. He felt the key fall heavily into his coat pocket as he stepped into the street.

If anyone was worried that one of their fellow inmates was escaping they didn't give a visible sign. Not even Mrs. Grantham, that inveterate snoop, was peeking through the curtains of her cell. She was probably sitting on the edge of her couch, rubbing her hands together in that way she did, watching her cats eat their breakfast. Clay had sat with her on many mornings, locked in the interminable stillness behind a door laced with chains and deadbolts. Only moments ago, passing her door he'd thought, "Should I check to see if she's OK?" but then he'd thought better of it. *No way would that conversation have gone for less than thirty minutes.* Even now, with the storm, he'd have had to hear about how one of the neighbors had committed some imaginary wrong, or how her daughter hadn't called. For years he'd watched her hobble up the steps of the brownstone they shared on Dean Street, hunched over by the weight of her cares but unwilling to do anything about them. He'd always liked her in an odd way, in that way one humors a crank, but now as he made his break for freedom, he felt nothing but a vague sense of pity. Like Otis, she was the warden of her own confinement, drunk on the wine of the world's expectations and neglect, and unable to put down the glass. *She's a prisoner,* Clay thought, *everyone around here is.*

* * * *

The boots on his feet felt tight and fine as he walked along Dean and turned north onto Court, which he would follow until he reached Borough Hall. He congratulated himself on his prescient cleverness, having bought the boots used (therefore already broken in) at a thrift store down the street a few weeks before anyone had ever even heard of Sandy. They were purchased on a whim along with the hiker's backpack he now had strapped to his back, on a day when an ill-defined sense of foreboding that had haunted him for weeks had suddenly caused him to scratch an itch.

On that day, while walking home from work, he'd stopped in front of the shop's window, halting out of spiritual necessity as much as any real physical need. In the shop he found both items neatly shelved in separate sections and was drawn to each for reasons that he couldn't fully explain. Probably some hipster had used them on a summer trek across Europe, only to sell them when the rent was due. Both were high-quality items, with rich, supple leather, and they were exactly what he would have bought for himself if he'd gone in search of new ones. Now, making his way uptown, Clay liked the feel of their weight as he stepped around the debris scattered along the street.

His impromptu plan was to cut across Brooklyn Heights to the Promenade and walk along it to its end merely to see the damage from that elevated perspective. Then he'd make his way due north, over the bridge into Manhattan, into Harlem, and, if all went well, he'd just keep going. Out of the city. Away from this prison. *Far from the Madding Crowd.* He was ultimately headed home to the farmhouse in Ithaca. Home. The place where he'd shared life with Cheryl and his beautiful girls before the accident.

Despite the certainty of his goal, a feeling of foreboding still gnawed at his stomach as he weaved around the odd fallen tree or nodded to the occasional passerby. He chalked the strange feeling up to a claustrophobic sense of needing release from the city. He breathed in the morning air and kept moving.

He thought about that word... *home.* Home was where there was a certain tree at the edge of the field across the road that led to the front porch. That lovely tree was the first thing he and Cheryl saw as they rounded the sweeping curve of the country road on the day they first viewed the property. She'd taken one look at it as they drove into the driveway and said she was ready to buy if he was.

In a forest thick with trees, that single, solitary tree had always been his favorite. In it he'd hung that lazy tire swing, which had taken him much longer than it should have to accomplish. The branches reached so high that his rope would not loop over them no matter what angle—or how hard—he threw it. He'd finally succeeded by tying a bucket to the end of the rope to give it weight so that he could launch it over a branch and then lower it slowly to the ground. Then, reveling in this victory, he and Cheryl had sat on the lawn and watched the girls play in the sprinklers and push each other in wide arcs under the broad, shading limbs. Now as he made his way through Sandy's wake, he wondered if that tree was still standing.

* * * *

Clay was struck by the almost *usualness* of it all as he moved through the street. Shopkeepers were busily sweeping their sidewalks, pushing the debris into the curb, then arching their backs to relieve the tension from the motion. Women in slickers walked their dogs, stopping to talk in little groups as their children toddled along after them.

Of course, there was the occasional limb, twisted and broken from the terrifying winds of the night before, but he was surprised that his neighborhood had not suffered more damage. Sometimes in the midst of the tempest a leaf lays still and is not tossed and therefore suffers, as we all do, from a lack of perspective.

He had listened to the radio through the night as winds howled and lights flickered but had not yet seen any proof of the kind of apocalyptic damage the reports were describing. He had long since given up television in an effort to cut himself off from the endless assault of technological input, and thus had not seen the images of houses pushed from their foundations and fires burning out entire city blocks. The reports had stopped just short of saying that the world had come to an end, but what they did not say they always implied. Here, however, he found that life was creeping onto the streets. There were occasional cracked windshields on occasional cars, and street signs and shingles and leaves tossed about, but nothing like what he had expected to find. The winds were still gusting and the rain came in sheets as he cut between Boerum and Cobble Hills, and he found himself glad that he had been on higher ground when the storm hit.

From the Promenade he could begin to make out the reason for the heated reporting. Sea trash lay down along the waterfront greenway, and trees were uprooted on the paths. From the height of the visible waterline, he imagined—though he could not see from his vantage point—that other low-lying areas of Brooklyn were crushed by the weight of the water. Sure enough, as he walked, he heard conversations from people huddled in groups. Red Hook, Gowanus, and DUMBO had been submerged in water and debris. Rumors and rumors of rumors were shared about the devastation and its aftermath. People talked of water rushing into homes as fast as the inhabitants could gather their things and rush out.

It was disconcerting to hear the flurries of conversation and watch the waves that had now receded back within their banks. The surge had sent six feet of water flooding onto the street during the night, but now, the waters were roiling past, and the murmurs of the people silenced the water's burblings. Clay did not join the conversations. He merely wove in and out of the scattered groupings and watched the people watching. He stopped only occasionally to take a picture or to look out over the East River, but he had not come to dawdle and gawk, or, as so many of the others around him had, to lament the destruction of their city and gird themselves to rebuild it once again. He had merely come to witness nature's powerful force firsthand and then walk into the wilderness to join it.

At the end of the Promenade he stood along the railings and took a final view of the New York City skyline. It was beautiful in its graphic simplicity, its skyscrapers formed like architectural representations of the ups and downs of stock market shares that were so closely tracked just over the river. Still, as he stood and took it all in, Clay couldn't help feeling that the concrete and steel rising into the dense grey clouds rushing overhead were more dangerous than the storm that had just passed. The storm spent its fury in the space of a single night, but the weight of the oppressive city had strangled men since the days of Cain, and would, it seemed, go on doing it forever.

Turning on his heel, Clay headed west and cut along Orange Street on the northern end of the neighborhood he'd just circled. He wound his way back through the grid of streets and passed along Pineapple Walk to the Cadman Plaza and then through the great lawn of the War Memorial. Trees and branches and leaves littered the streets, mixed with odd bits of siding and shingles that had come slicing down from the sky. The cumulative effect of the damage began to make an impression. Trees that had been young when Henry Ford was scratching out ideas for assembly lines had toppled over to crush the products of his imagination. Buildings that had been built before Coolidge took office were pock-marked with evidence of windfalls.

Clay stepped around and over and through the storm's fingerprints like a cop who had no respect for a crime scene. Thick wet foliage clung to the soles of his boots, but he shook it off as he kept moving. He was walking with a purpose now.

He walked into Whitman Park – nestled, perhaps ironically, perhaps not, in the shadow of New York's Emergency Management office. He snapped the clip around his waist meant to hold some of his backpack's weight off his shoulders, and slid his arms out of their straps. He dropped the pack to the ground and spun it around and unzipped a front pocket. He reached inside and took out an energy bar and sat down on a bench nearby. He had come to pay respects to the poet who had written in a time when Brooklyn could still be called rural. It was not just a passing indulgence. When he had packed his bag several days before, he put in only the items he felt he'd need for the journey—a change of clothes, a small box of matches, a few small bottles of water, and a Walkman radio with an extra pack of batteries. He didn't bring any food except a few energy bars, figuring that he had money and could buy whatever he needed along the way. He wasn't survival camping in the outback after all, and he wanted to minimize the weight he'd have to carry. He'd been forced to make a decision about which books he wanted to bring. A well-worn copy of *Leaves of Grass* had been one of only two to make the cut, the second being Hemingway's *The Sun Also Rises*. The former was to remind him to live life, the latter that, even if he failed the first, the earth would still abide. He was serious about traveling lightly. He hadn't even brought his cell phone.

It was Cheryl who had taught him to love Whitman. Before the girls came along, they would sit out under the stars on a blanket at the farmhouse and she would quote *When I Heard the Learn'd Astronomer*. It was partly those moments, the biggest part, that had brought him to Brooklyn in the first place after she and the girls had died.

He'd moved into the city because he had grown tired of wandering around the farmhouse, watching the dust motes drift through the early morning light, listening for the stirrings that would never come again. He had moved to the city to experience firsthand what she'd always admired from afar, in the hope that, by losing himself in the blur of faces, he could somehow lose his memory. Try as he might, though, he'd not been able to love Brooklyn, perhaps because, try as it might, it had not been able to make him stop loving her.

He thought back to the day that the call had come in. Frightening silence—all but the labored breathing of his beautiful wife. Cheryl and the girls had been in Boston visiting her parents when they'd driven back through the tunnel on their way to Logan. Clay had stayed behind to lay new tile in the kitchen, and he was just putting the finishing touches on the grout when he heard the phone ring. Seeing her number pop up, he had cheerily picked up and made some crack about their sleeping late and missing their flight. There was dead silence on the other end, except for the sound of his wife wheezing and slowly pushing out that she loved him. She whispered that there had been a terrible accident. Something had crushed the car. She didn't know what and didn't know if they would make it. He gripped the phone in confusion and desperation and began to cry into it helplessly. Baby? Baby? Oh, God... Baby?! Are you there? The noises of chaos eventually rose to overtake his wife's whispers and then the line had gone dead in a horrible screech of metal.

The next hour, the longest of his life, was spent on the phone with area hospitals, and police and fire departments. No one could tell him anything. Eventually, he got a call from Mass General, an Officer Somethingorother. "Mr Richter..." The tone in the voice told him all that he needed to know.

The rest had been a blur of details. A concrete panel had come loose from the ceiling in the Big Dig tunnel just as his wife had passed underneath it. The resulting blow had caved in the driver's side compartment and sent the car careening into the walls of the tunnel. His wife had survived the initial crush, but his two daughters had been thrown from the vehicle. All were now gone. He would need to come to Boston to identify the bodies.

Clay thought of that moment a thousand times since that day, but it never stopped leaving an ache. It was a still-opened wound. It left a pang now as he took the last bite of his energy bar and stood up and slipped on his backpack. He knew it was foolish to wish that it had happened to him, as though the wishing could somehow alter the hands of fate. It was the kind of thinking that led to a comment he'd heard a man make while walking along the Promenade. The man had been walking with a friend and shaking his head in disbelief, when he stated, "I was watching the news on CNN about New Jersey, and I almost feel guilty that those poor people got hit so hard when we didn't." Clay thought this was exactly that kind of death wish thinking that life in the city promulgated and that he was now escaping.

He came out of the park and jogged quickly north to Prospect where he ascended the stairs to the opening of the Brooklyn Bridge walkway. Looking up at the thick, twisted cables that formed a warp and weft like a net in the sky, he thought they looked as much like a snare as they did a support. The granite and limestone towers rose in their neo-Gothic austerity across the span of the two shorelines. The waters swirled past in their still dangerous attitude that, even at that moment, had shut down the tunnel servicing the subways and the ferries offering conveyance.

The bridge stood massive in its impact and arrogance, having just laughed off Sandy like she was a bad joke. Untold "Wonders of the World" had come and gone like so many flowers in a summer field, only to disappear into the dusts of history. Some, like the Lighthouse of Alexandria, had lasted millennia, while others, like the Colossus of Rhodes, had lasted but the blink of an eye. In the modern age, the bridge had done better than most, outlasting other suspension bridges due to its deck and truss engineering. It had even housed, during a time when the Cold War was raging across the land, a bunker intended to outlast a nuclear bomb. Now, as Clay stood before it on the morning after the storm, he couldn't decide whether its towers looked more like watchtowers seeing out into the future, or guard towers of a prison.

Always leave yourself a way out. His father had told him that one day, a lifetime ago, when he'd watched the old man playing cards with a group of his buddies. He had watched his father draw hand after hand of bad cards and yet, at the end of the night his old man hadn't lost any money. "Life doesn't owe you anything, but you don't have to take it lying down, son. Sometimes, the only thing you can do is to walk away, but always leave yourself a way out."

The lesson had stuck. Though Clay didn't know what was ahead of him, he was certain that he no longer wanted what was behind. Frost wrote that the best way out is always through. Clay was thinking something like that as he turned up his collar against the cold, whipping winds, and set out across the bridge.

CHAPTER 2

The rich, deep voice of Johnny Cash came blasting out of an old school boombox. It was one of those black-cased, dual deck affairs with the chrome rimmed speakers and thin sliding buttons. Made it look like a '65 Plymouth. Heightening the effect, the box was strapped, with a variety of hooks and multicolored bungees, to the handlebars of a broken-down bicycle that was slowly weaving in and out of pedestrian traffic. Johnny Cash's voice asked how high the water was, echoing a refrain heard throughout the area on that day.

The man on the bicycle wore bright orange pants and a long trailing coat made from a textured fabric that might have looked better on a vintage couch. It was mostly green, the coat, but it was hard to tell for certain with its sun-faded pattern and the fact that much of it was covered by the man's long red hair and a beard that was graying on the ends, spilling out of his neck.

Something in the cool misty air made Cash's voice ring out with an otherworldly clarity. It amplified the gospel choir hum underlying the voice and the dum-thwacka-dum of the guitar's choppy train strokes. When the key shifted higher, the voice might have been in the room, if it had been a room.

The red-haired man moved in meandering undulations past the people who were turning to watch him. He was barely even pedaling, merely turning the handlebars and letting the natural momentum of the bike carry him forward, until he came to a stop at the foot of the brownish grey tower. Clay watched him as the man squinted his eyes and peered up at the sky to the clear patch of grey that was framed by the parallel lines of the cables. A helicopter came into the space and circled around and then headed back up the river.

Clay had always loved the city's misfits, even if he preferred to take them one at a time. The man leaned his bicycle against the tower's sides and reached in a pocket and pulled out a handful of balloons. *Balloons?* Then he knelt down next to a small, curious boy, whose mother was busy talking to another man as they looked out over the river. She didn't notice the boy reaching for her hand.

"What's your name, little man?"

"Gareth."

"Were you scared last night in the storm?"

The little boy began to nod, but Clay could see his heart wasn't in it. He didn't like the implication, even at his age, but he was mesmerized by the man's beard and the colors in his clothing.

"Or maybe... You were brave?"

The boy's eyes lit up. This was more like it. "Bwave."

The man took a balloon and pumped a lungful of air into its long curved shape, then began twisting it into a circle. Then he took another and asked the boy what was his favorite animal. Puppy. He twisted the balloon into a zig-zag shape that rose up from the circle and curled up at the end. It looked nothing at all like a puppy. If anything, it looked like one of those graphic blue waves found on a surf shop door. The little boy didn't mind, though, and the man reached up and placed the balloon like a crown on the boy's small head.

As he did so, the woman looked down and smiled, and another young boy, older than the first, came up and asked for an elephant. The man quickly fashioned the exact same hat. He handed it to the boy.

"Hey... That's not an elephant," the boy said, in obvious disappointment.

"Little fella, if you'd seen what I saw last night, you'd think that everything looks like a wave, too," the red bearded man said, and he reached up and patted the boy on the head.

He stood up, and Clay, who had stopped to watch the show, laughed out loud, causing the man to turn and bow. As he did so, his hair poured out onto his chest. "Pat Maloney, at your service," the man said. The song on the boombox, which had repeated at least once, maybe twice, while Clay stood there, wound down to its final thrum.

Clay reached into his pocket and pulled out a dollar. He extended it to the man but was waved off. The man told him he wouldn't know what to do with it, that he lived by the seat of his pants. "Consider the lilies, my friend. They neither toil, nor spin..." Clay found the man charming and believed him. They stood for a while and talked as the clouds and the waves and the people rolled by.

The man told Clay that he had passed the storm in a shelter at a nearby high school. He'd wanted to stay in the streets, just for the experience, but he'd gone down to Battery Park in the afternoon ("To see if our lady was still standing...") and the water washed up over the barricades and came up to the bench he was standing on. "I decided it didn't make sense to die yet."

They began to walk and, as they did, they talked about everything under the sun. Clay was surprised at the man's knowledge. He quoted Russian poets as easily as he did the stock pages. Clay found him intriguing, and asked if he had a secret, if he was actually some trust fund millionaire in hiding or maybe a journalist on undercover assignment. The man shook his head and said no. "You are assuming that I am homeless," he said. "And in that you'd be correct. But who isn't? In fact, there are a lot of people who are going to be homeless now. This storm is going to wake people up." Clay didn't tell him that it had already done so for him. "Do I have a secret? No. I celebrate myself and sing myself. And what I assume, you shall assume, for every atom belonging to me as good belongs to you." Again, Clay didn't tell him that he knew Whitman well and appreciated the sentiment, and the man, in turn, didn't seem to care what Clay knew or didn't know. Not once as they walked over the bridge to Manhattan did he ask Clay where he was going. He didn't have the need to find out. Nor did he explain why he was walking with Clay in the direction he'd just left. He just walked and talked, pushing his bicycle along, simply passing the time with a friend.

Clay had met such people before, but never one quite so lucid. They seemed to live in the shadows of the city, just biding their time, willing to drop everything and follow where life leads. Clay had wondered how people like this man made it, somehow able to string along with nothing in a city that taxed you in the morning when you stepped out your door. He himself had struggled to bring the ends together, even with the settlement he had received from the contractors responsible for the death of Cheryl and the girls. Clay imagined that the man with the red beard had simply decided the world of material reality could do nothing to help or harm him.

Clay once had a college professor tell him, as they walked across a parking lot next to a McDonald's, that with the knowledge he carried around in his head he could flip burgers and be happy. Clay decided that this man had made much the same decision.

They came to a box for the exit that drops down over Park Row. Clay told the man that he was getting off there and the man reached down and fiddled with the buttons on his boombox. The voice of Johnny Cash began to sing about how he kept a close watch on his heart, how he kept his eyes wide open.

"I like your tunes, by the way," Clay said.

"Oh, you like Cash?"

"I do. I especially like his prison stuff."

Clay paused for a moment, wondering if he should share any more with the man, and the man took the pause as a sign. "Yeah, I wonder whether those guys over there still like it or if they have switched to Jay-Z." He motioned with his thumb over his shoulder to the Metropolitan Correctional Center, just visible over the barrier of the walkway, nestled in among a jumble of buildings down the street. "I don't know," Clay said, "I guess a little of both." The man laughed. "I noticed you didn't have to ask me what I meant... that's OK. I like a guy who has done a little time. I think it does something to clean out the soul."

Clay didn't tell him that he was right, that he once had a few unsavory days after Cheryl was gone when he turned to drink a little too hard and got tired of some guy running his mouth. Nor did he tell him what he'd been thinking about the city, or why he had to get out. All that was behind him now, and he didn't feel the need to talk about it.

"You know," Red Beard said, "many of those people are political prisoners, jailbirds of circumstance who just happen to find themselves on the wrong side of whatever 51% of the people have decided is wrong at a particular time in history. Walk around drinking laudanum on the streets in 1850 and you'd fit right in. Get caught with some Vicodin not prescribed to you in 2012 and you'll likely get to see the inside of a jail cell." The man went on, seeming not to notice that Clay was fidgeting with his hands in his pockets. "Even some of the most violent prisoners are sometimes prisoners of circumstance and epoch. Rats in cages will turn on each other violently... for no other reason than they have nothing better to do. And stealing? Ha! Well, that, too can be relative when bankers are handed trillions in bailout dollars—money printed for the purpose by the government—to patch up the hole left after they lost trillions on risky speculation in derivatives." The man stopped and looked at Clay intently. He wanted Clay to pay attention, to *hear* him. "You can be the little Dutch Boy and stick your finger in the dam, or you can lay back and watch the dam burst, learn to swim, get baptized in the wash. Me? I got my floatin' shoes on. I'm going to learn to walk on water."

Clay wanted to hug him, but didn't. He reached out instead and put his hand on the man's shoulder, feeling the frayed textures against his hand and gave the shoulder a squeeze. The man looked at Clay and, for the first time since they had begun to talk, flashed a hint of some vulnerability. Something in the eyes.

"I wish you well, my brother." Red Beard smiled at Clay and looked down. He stepped onto the pedal and pushed himself up and over the seat. Steadying himself, he steered the handlebars toward the city he'd just come from and began to roll slowly down the hill... and was gone.

* * * *

Clay took a quick detour through Wall Street. It was an extra bit of walking, but he didn't mind. He had heard on the radio the night before that downtown had been destroyed, and he wanted to see it for himself. Not that he had any love for the place, or had spent any real time there. It was more like a morbid curiosity. Wall Street was the engine that generated the city, one of them anyway, the most powerful, and he liked the idea that the money centers that the man with the red beard had just spoken about would now have to fix a few leaks of their own. He imagined the headline in the dailies over the next several days: *Manhattan Annoyed. Queens Destroyed. Quick! Fix Manhattan.*

There was something else out there in the city that he was trying to identify. Worry. Maybe not worry. Concern. It was a taste in the air, palpable but light and airy, like the smell of ink and leather in the lobby of a nice hotel. You could barely make it out, but it was growing.

Not that any of the hotels smelled like ink and leather at the moment. In fact, they smelled like seaweed. Wet sea trash spilled across the sidewalk, pushed up the streets four and five blocks in, when water that would drown a man had poured across downtown. It had settled into the cracks of the cobblestones, reminders of an earlier age, salty and toxic and rank. Vegetation, where it existed among the concrete and steel, bent over and clung to the earth, already beginning to turn yellow from the chemicals.

Clay watched the men work in their bright yellow jackets and orange helmets and bulky police and fire gear. He stepped around the occasional yellow tape and bright orange cones, walking as if he meant business. He passed like a ghost among the men who were too busy stringing hoses from the buildings out into the street to notice him. Generators purred, pumping the water that had flooded the buildings onto the sidewalk where it splashed in fan shapes onto the concrete and poured over the curb and ran down the street and into the drains and back towards the sea.

Carpets on floors of banks and insurance companies steamed and fogged the insides of windows, making it impossible to see out into the street, into the future. Con Edison men stood drinking coffee, waiting for their turn in the buildings. *Where did they get the coffee? There isn't a shop in sight open.* Police sat in cars or on the hoods of cars, watching the men do their work.

Italian and Arab men picked through their stores, lifting the thick wet boxes that had washed across the floors, spilling out their contents, and carried the boxes, dripping and coming apart, out into the street where they piled them in asymmetrical heaps. Chinese women swept the floors of their taco stands.

Clay walked through the wet steamy mess with an economy all his own, cutting down side streets, dipping in alleys, winding through the maze of trucks lining the curb. When he'd seen enough, he came out on Broadway and headed toward midtown.

The city was quiet in a way that made him feel like he might be in the middle of a Twilight Zone episode. Here and there a siren would chirp and out of a radio somewhere—*battery powered?*—a news reporter talked about the election, how the candidates for president would deal with the aftermath of the hurricane. Altogether the city sounded quieter. Muffled. Different.

Clay felt good. Not emotionally, maybe, but physically. His joints were loose and the gear on his back felt light, and lightly carried. The walk was invigorating, and he felt a small bead of sweat run down his chest in the space between his skin and the fabric of his shirt.

A small delivery truck rumbled by, and a distinctive squeal came from the brakes as the driver drove two-footed—simultaneously pressing the gas and the brakes. Clay heard a shop owner comment that power wasn't the only problem, but that gasoline was about to be really hard to come by.

As he made his way uptown, he shifted his path back and forth like a ship captain tacking to follow the stars. There were avenues that were closed off here and there, and as the chaos of downtown resided, there were police officers who wouldn't allow passage. He stopped for a moment at one point and looked back down 5th Avenue towards the Flatiron Building that stood as a timeless waypoint emphasizing the city's rigidity. He kept moving, a fish swimming upstream through the now fluid events and persons.

A woman in a business suit, looking out of place today for some reason he couldn't quite pin down, asked Clay if he had a cell phone she could use to make a call. She explained that her battery had died, that she couldn't find power, and held the unit up to him like a defunct passport. It was her lifeline. It was her life. He shook his head no and shrugged apologetically. She looked at him as if he were an alien.

Had he heard that a building had collapsed in the West Village? Had he heard that the subways might be out of service for months? Did he know where you could get some coffee? Strangers who would normally pass him on the street without looking up now stopped him and sought information. *Was it the backpack that made them think that he might know?* As they passed, they shared their own news. Bits of gossip reached him on the air, some of it trivial, some of it ludicrous, some of it frightening with bluster.

Sidewalks could tell tales that would make men blush on any normal day. There was something about walking through the city after the storm that made Clay feel like a voyeur. People were out in the streets, stripped of their pretensions. It was like when the city gets hit by a snowfall and everyone comes out in community, but now they had a slight helplessness in their eyes. A homeless man passed Clay and asked for a cigarette. He was used to despair.

Tree branches were down in the park, and leaves, many of them still green, stuck to the damp sidewalk in clumps and lay thick in the gutters and along the foundations of buildings. Across the occasional street lay a fallen tree snapped at the trunk, the roots still buried under concrete. Workers were climbing over the debris like ants, carrying it away to some field somewhere to be stacked and mulched.

After disasters, people usually come together. It happened after 9/11, and Clay could sense it happening today on a smaller scale. There wasn't the terror that had been present on that day, with its overwhelming reality of the apocalypse hanging in the air in dust and cancer and ash and death. 9/11 had been huge and monumental and devastating. It had fundamentally changed the world, and this was nothing like that. Still, Clay could sense the beginnings of an inkling that something was in the air. He just couldn't identify it quite yet.

A few more blocks up 5th Avenue and there on his left as he passed by was an ice cream vendor who had just opened up his cart and was giving away his ice cream for free. Maybe he couldn't keep it frozen, or maybe this was his way to lift spirits, but a sign lettered by hand with a thick, black Sharpie simply said FREE. People stopped and talked and licked their cones and shivered in the damp.

Walking faster now, block after block disappeared behind him, and above 34th Street, just past the Empire State Building, he noticed that the power was up. It became apparent first by the street lights, and the traffic plugging the avenue. Life seemed almost, but not quite, normal. Normal. *A funny word. What is normal anyway?* Clay had recently read a UN report that claimed that over 1/2 of the world's population now lives in cities, and cities are almost inevitably located on coasts, along fault lines, in areas where major disasters are most likely to occur. *Is that normal?* He'd spent some time thinking about the implications of this. It was one reason for his flight. Millions of people living on top of one another in an artificial system, supported by a crumbling and unsustainable infrastructure, provided for by criminally deficient food grown on industrial farms and shipped thousands of miles on government roads. *This is not civilization. It is madness.* He watched the cars, piled up like toys in the streets, emitting their fumes into the fast rushing clouds, carrying their overheated toxins into the atmosphere, readying the next storm. If this is going to be normal, he thought, where does one go to hide from it?

A sign said, "Free Juice, We'll Share." But it was not fruit juice that was being given away. A power strip ran from an extension cord somewhere inside a coffee shop, and every empty outlet was filled with plugs and cords leading to phones and devices. One man was sitting at a laptop, trying to check his Facebook page. The life-blood of modern society. People had walked up from Downtown looking for power and news and normal. A woman asked the man if he was almost done and then walked inside to tell the owner that he ought to limit how long people can hog the power.

Mid-town. Here some business was going on, and there was a whole lot less damage. A yellow cab pulled over to the curb just north of 42nd Street, opposite the library. Its doors opened and passengers spilled out onto the sidewalk. They looked like clowns piling out of a Volkswagen. Four, five, six fares, squeezed into a single cab. More fares piled in, and the Jamaican driver smiled at him and said, "You want to ride in this cab, mon, you got to get on top!" Clay laughed a little, smiled, and just shook his head. He was walking out of Gomorrah.

At the end of the block on east 43rd, Clay stepped into Little Italy Pizza. It was clean and bright and open, and he bought a slice so he could use the bathroom, which was something he'd increasingly needed to do. He set his backpack on the ground and felt his shoulders roll in their sockets. Pausing to eat his slice, he listened to voices and stories for a moment, and as he did, the veneer came off of everything. Clay realized that he was living one of those moments in time when an entire society or culture experiences some event at the same time. Like the bombing of Pearl Harbor, or VJ Day, or Kennedy's assassination. Or 9/11. Maybe this wasn't that big. Maybe it wasn't even as big as Katrina. But it was big in a way that mattered. A kind of widespread ground zero had been slung across the city; and beyond that, the state; and beyond that, the tri-state; and beyond that, the nation. It was the nature of such things. The farmer in Iowa pays for the recovery in New York through his taxes and his grain. As the government has increasingly turned to the declaration of 'national' disasters, and as the course of societal events has increasingly led to the likelihood of disasters, both natural and man-made, there is a kind of shared experience that attends to these things. And nature had outdone herself here in providing reason for the focus. The enormity of the timing of his escape really began to occur to him for the first time.

One very energetic woman in a bright red jacket was telling her husband that the HMS *Bounty* ("a by-god, full-on 18th century sailing ship") had sunk off the Carolinas, and that a freighter was now in the middle of Staten Island, and that the Boardwalk in Atlantic City had floated out into the ocean. Clay thought about news that was occurring elsewhere during the storm, as people were focused on their immediate locations. Being cut off from the world, how would people deal with the world at large? Or would they care to? What would happen in the upcoming elections? He wondered about news that would slip through the cracks in this moment, how nations would prepare for war against other nations, how children would be snatched from their parents, how celebrities would shill for their causes. He wondered how he would know these things without the woman in the bright red coat to tell him.

* * * *

Outside again, Clay started to walk, and for the first time he began to feel tired. Even in his well-broken-in boots his feet were starting to hurt a little. Noon was moving into afternoon, which would then slide into evening, and it occurred to him that he wasn't making good time. If he kept on walking at this pace, he was going to be in Harlem at dark fall, and he wasn't sure how he felt about that. He wondered if looting or riots might start, and if they did, would they be confined to the areas currently without power? Things have a way of falling apart, and Clay wasn't sure he wanted to be out in the street if and when they did. He lengthened out his stride and made an effort to put the city behind him.

CHAPTER 3

Clay walked into Harlem in the late afternoon. He was tired in his bones and began to feel a chill. He'd walked the last several miles along the avenue deep in thought, past St. Patrick's Cathedral on his right and NBC Studios on his left, past the long stretch of glitzy stores with their high-end commercial excess, past the high-rise mansions of Central Park East with their celebrity tenants and media moguls, and past the row of museums housing the world's great treasures. None of these worlds felt real to him in their religion of consumerism and stilted aesthetic tastes. Even Central Park, with its languorous urban sprawl, felt false in comparison to the experience of sitting on the front porch swing at Ithaca in the early light of fall and listening to the green frogs greet the sunrise. He was feeling alienated and tired. He needed to find rest.

As he came around the northernmost end of the park, he walked into the small, circular amphitheater where Duke Ellington's statue stands as a testament to the meeting of two worlds, and sat down on the concrete risers. He undid the straps of his backpack, shook himself out of the harness, and flexed his feet inside his boots, feeling the tension in his calves tighten and then release.

He looked up at the sky and tried to estimate the hour, then figured how much further he could go before he'd have to find shelter for the night. He had hoped, when he started out in the morning, to make it to the George Washington Bridge, but he'd badly overestimated himself and he'd spent too much time sightseeing. He was just over halfway there—maybe three-fifths—and it would be dark soon. He didn't relish walking through Washington Heights late at night, particularly without knowing exactly what he would find when he got there. He was flying mostly blind, and the area was known to be questionable, even on a good day. No need to turn this into a suicide mission. *Maybe I should just stop at the Y*, he thought, and start again fresh in the morning.

As he sat and caught his breath, a young black man, somewhere around 14 years old, Clay guessed, came rolling up 5th Avenue from the direction Clay had just come. He was riding a longboard skateboard, and the syncopated sounds of the wheels striking the cracks of the sidewalk were deeper than one might have expected. Kerthump, kerthump... kerthump, kerthump. Clay watched him as he stepped off the board at the curb and flipped the end up to his hand, carrying it like a cane into the small park. He walked to the foot of the statue and looked up as if he was trying to peer over the open lid of the grand piano the composer was standing at and into the heart of the strings. He was tall, with thin hands and sharp cheeks, and had the earliest beginnings of what might eventually become dreadlocks, his hair twisted in tiny knots at the roots. The earbuds in his ears were obviously playing some song with deep syncopation like the kerthumps of the skateboard wheels, but it sounded, from where Clay was sitting, like jazz rather than hip-hop. He drummed his fingers on his skateboard and then became self-aware and noticed Clay looking at him, causing him to flash a sheepish smile and set his board on the ground and push off in a running start. Clay turned his head to watch him as he moved across the walk between the tree lines and jumped over the curb and crossed the street and headed west along 110th.

Clay scratched his face and felt the beginnings of a beard, just the hint of stubble from this morning. He lifted his arms above his head, felt his shoulder pop and his back muscles ache, then he stood and shook out his legs.

* * * *

Clay walked up Malcolm X Boulevard and into the heart of Harlem. He was tired of cataloguing trees and fallen branches. There weren't even that many around here. For once, it seemed, nature had spared those who were often hardest hit by the problems of the city. The electricity was running, people were going about their business, and life seemed as close to usual as possible. He was glad to be walking under a broad expanse of sky, even if it was turning to a bluish hue as dusk began to settle behind the still grey clouds.

As he came to about 120th Street, he dipped into a small bodega. He walked through the store towards the back to get a bottle of water from the cooler, and he could hear a conversation over the racks, near the counter, between two flirtatious youths.

"Oh, come on, you know you want to... give me your number, baby..."

"I'll tell you what I'm going to give if you don't leave me alone, Papi... the back of my hand!"

"There, see, you called me Papi. Come on, baby. Give me your number."

Clay came around the aisle and saw the young man from the statue leaning over the counter on his elbow, flashing his most confident smile. The girl blushed and noticed Clay and turned away from the young man to help him. "Oh, don't mind him. He's just trouble, that's what he is," she said.

"With a capital T," the youth chimed in, and then, noticing Clay from the statue, seemed to straighten up a little.

"You're the guy from Duke Ellington."

"Yes. I am indeed, that very same guy. How are you?"

"Good, I'm just trying to get a little notice here. Hey, where're you walking with that backpack?"

"Home. Where are *you* going with your skateboard?"

"The same, and I guess I better be off. Where's your home, mister?"

"Mister? Now, don't be calling me mister. I'm not ready to be called mister just yet. I'm going to Ithaca. Upstate. Ever been there?"

"Nah, but my mom has a friend in Woodstock. Is that anywhere close?"

"Ehh. Not really, about a 150 miles."

"Oh, I'm sorry. I don't get out of the city much."

"Well, you should, there's a whole big world out there."

"Yeah. That's what I hear. Maybe I'll get a backpack and head out myself one day."

"Well, there are worse things to do."

With that, Clay paid the bill, smiled, and walked out. As he did, the youth, too, gave up his flirting and grabbed his board where he'd left it leaning against the door.

He walked out just as Clay opened the top to his bottle of water and leaned his chin up and back to take a swig. He gave Clay a little wave that made him seem much younger than the conversation they'd just shared, and then turned back up the street.

He dropped his board and took a running start, landing thick on the deck, then he rolled across the sidewalk. (Kerthump... kerthump.) He gave his board a little jump as he rolled off the curb and out in the street, where he was promptly hit by a car.

* * * *

Clay had been the first one to reach him. The car itself had come to more or less an immediate stop, but the driver was so stunned by the body flying onto her hood that she'd been paralyzed into inaction. The boy, for his part, had rolled up onto the windshield and had come sluggishly to a stop before jumping down from the hood and trying to act as if nothing had happened. The board was broken under the wheel of the car, and the boy's painful grimace as he hit the ground showed that more than his pride was hurt. He hopped on one foot as Clay reached him and lifted him up to support him while helping him onto the curb. A small crowd gathered of a few straggling pedestrians who stretched their necks to see if anything was worth seeing, then moved on when it became apparent that no blood had been spilled.

Clay sat the boy down on the ground and inspected his foot. It appeared as if the ankle had been sprained badly, but there didn't seem to be any broken bones. The ankle was tender when he offered resistance and already it was beginning to swell and turn slightly blue. The boy wouldn't be able to walk.

"Oh, my mom's going to kill me," the boy said. "She just bought me that board."

"Oh, I'm certain that she won't do that. That would be murder. Up you go, come on," Clay said. "Let's go, I'll help you walk. Lean on me."

"But mis-" the boy caught himself.

"Clay."

"But Clay, I don't want to stop you from going home."

"I'm going that way, anyway - "

"Stephen."

"Stephen... I might as well stop a murder."

* * * *

They hobbled along the street, this odd pair, like two soldiers escaping the front. Never leave a man behind, Clay smiled to himself. Always leave yourself a way out, and never leave a man behind. He wondered what others around them thought. Normally, he was a believer in what Eleanor Roosevelt once said: you wouldn't worry what other people thought of you if you only knew how seldom they do. But, in this case, from the looks they received as they straggled along, he felt it safe to make an exception.

Turning west on 132ⁿᵈ, they limped for half a block before coming to a narrow space between two buildings that opened through a gate. "She'll be in here," the boy said as he left Clay's shouldering support and tried to make his way into a garden. Clay followed closely, with his arms out extended as though he were carrying some gift to meet a queen.

"Mom?"

Clay saw the woman stand up from the edge of a flowerbed where she'd been kneeling and pruning, and turn around with an attitude that she'd obviously rehearsed before. She was tall and thin, like her son, with an angular face, and hair bundled up in a knot till it spilled down her back in long ropy twists. She was, despite her initial look of perturbation standing there among the still blooming fall flowers, beautiful.

"Mom, I had an accident. This man here, Clay, helped me get home." The woman's face softened, and her features dissolved into concern. Only then did she notice Clay standing there behind the boy, sticking out like a thread on a homemade sweater.

"Wha' happened?" the woman said as she moved toward the boy, not hurriedly, but deliberately, and with tenderness. She smiled at Clay, and he wondered about her accent. It was obvious and surprising, made more so by her son's lack of the same.

"I got hit by a car. I'm OK!" he quickly added. "I wasn't watching where I was going."

She moved toward him and took him in her arms and held him like she wouldn't let go. Clay stepped backwards and glanced down before looking up into the woman's face as she opened her eyes and took him in.

"Mister..."

"Call me Clay."

"Thank you. I don't know who you are or why you were in the right place at the right time, but thank you for helping my Stephen."

"It was no problem ma'am. He needs to get off that foot though. He sprained the ankle pretty badly."

"Yes, of course," the woman said and then helped the boy out of the gate and up the stairs of the adjacent house. "Where you going?" she said as Clay turned on his heel, as if to leave. "I've got to get on," he said, noticing the dark in the sky.

"Nonsense, you'll stay and have dinner." Clay didn't know whether it was something she'd seen in his eyes or the fact that he carried the backpack, but she'd summed him up in the space of a glance, and he could tell that arguing would be futile. He was hungry. That settled the matter.

He undid the slips of his harness and dropped his pack to the ground, picking it up by a handle on top, and followed them up the stairs.

* * * *

The room was clean and bright, warm and warmly designed, with numerous books lining shelves that extended the lengths of the walls. Clay stood and examined them as the woman disappeared in a room down the hall with the boy. The titles were those you don't normally find on an American bookshelf, with names like *The Female Poets of Great Britain*. Many of them were old; all of them were worn. In the spaces between the books, there were also odd little eclectic items. Fossil samples, butterflies in cases, the exoskeletons of insects, and the like. Sprinkled through the displays were black and white photos of the woman and her son, neatly-framed, showing them in various poses in mostly unidentifiable locations, each more lovely than the others. The walls were lined with impressionist renderings, some with warm blotches of color seemingly haphazardly arranged to create an effect of chaos, others carefully, meticulously set with parallel lines and grids of intricate color. Clay seemed to recognize something in them that he couldn't yet make out, and he was trying to decide what it was when the woman came back into the room.

"Oh, that boy is such a naughty one. Lord knows I love him, but he does know how to give me a headache."

"I know," Clay said, "I had girls of my own..."

The woman heard his voice trail off and seemed to immediately understand. "I'm sorry," she said. Clay waved her off, as is if to say, Thank you, but no need to be sorry.

"Who's the artist?"

"Those are mine. You like them, eh? They are meant to represent the lines you find in nature in the smallest detail. I was a painter before I became a landscaper. My first love, however, is botany. It seems a nice way to combine both."

"Oh, wow. These are nice."

"Thank you. I studied at the Cooper Union. It was the reason I came to this country."

"From?"

"I'm a Trini. And I hope you like Trini food. Stephen tells me that you're on a journey?"

"Yes, ma'am, I'm going back to my farmhouse in Ithaca."

"Oh? To inspect it for damage from the storm?"

Clay nodded his head no. "To live. I'm going home for good."

"Ahhh. A fugitive. Or is it a refugee? I'm going with fugitive. Well, Mr. Fugitive, take your pack and go down the hall to the second door on the left. You'll find a clean towel and you can make yourself at home."

"Oh, I appreciate it, and I'll certainly eat your food, but I couldn't—"

"Nonsense. You can, and you will. You're not going to make it to Ithaca tonight, and you don't want to be out in these streets."

Clay could tell that it would be better to save his breath with this woman. "Well, thank you."

"No thanks needed. You took care of my boy. It is I who should be thanking you. My name, by the way, is Veronica. Dinner will be ready in half an hour."

Clay walked into the bedroom and lifted his pack onto the bed. Unzipping its large front pocket, he began pulling the items out one at a time. The small water bottles he'd brought were all gone. He still had the matches and three of the energy bars. The rest of the things he pulled out, organizing them on the bed. The last of these items, a small stack of papers he had rolled up like a telescope, was crinkled from the trip. He slid the rubber bands off the ends and straightened the papers with his hand. It was a small, typed manuscript of poems that he'd once written to his love. He'd spent many hours writing poems, both before and after Cheryl and the girls had gone. Not all of them were 'love poems' per se, but all were, in some way, sincere declarations of his undying devotion. Some of them were about things he saw, or thoughts that he'd had, but all of them were motivated by his loss and his love for his wife and children. At one point he'd considered having them published, but had never had the courage to submit them. They were really just exercises in adoration—of life, of love, of the home he'd once known with his family. Now as he caressed the pages, standing there in this home where a mother and son were still together, still able to touch each other's faces and hear each other's voices, he smiled as he thought about how his daughters might have sassed some boy like the girl in the bodega had. He yearned for Cheryl and the brush of her hand against his cheek, remembering the way she sang when she cooked dinner.

* * * *

The warm water felt good on his body after the long day of walking, and soothed his tired muscles. Clay stood under the stream and pushed his hands across his face and through his hair. Steam filled the air with fog, and he wondered whether this would be the last shower he'd have for a while. There was simply no telling once he got back on the road, but he liked the uncertainty. That was part of the adventure, walking out into the world without knowing what would happen next. He reached and twisted the knobs, feeling the warm spray slow to a trickle and then a drip and then he stepped out into the softness of the towel.

Coming back to the room after having dressed in a fresh pair of blue jeans and a t-shirt, Clay found that Veronica had gathered his clothes from the floor, and he heard the machine in the hallway filling. *Thoughtful.* He'd have never asked, and if anyone else had done it, he might have found it intrusive, but something in her way made him feel comfortable with the gesture. He was glad to be in this home at this moment rather than walking in the dark toward God knows what. He came out of the bedroom and passed through the hall and made his way again into the living room.

The house was filled with a warm, tempting aroma of food and life, and he felt the hunger in his stomach tumble, and that feeling pleased him too. He looked across the room and saw Veronica with her back turned to him, her long twists of hair flowing across her back as she moved around her kitchen.

"I appreciate this. I really do."

"No worries. It'll be nice to have company for dinner. I took the liberty of washing your clothes. I hope you don't mind. I tried not to be too snoopy."

"No, not at all. And thanks. I'm afraid I am putting you out."

"Hmmph," she said, and went back to cooking. She told him it'd be ready in a minute.

Clay had once heard that the best way to tell if you'll get along with someone is to question their tastes in music. He walked across the room to a small stereo, where the woman had CD's lined along the window.

"You like The Mountain Goats?"

"Yes, I like John Darnielle's passion, and his lyrics. I even like his religious album." When she said this, she made quotes in the air around the word "religious," and Clay knew exactly what she meant—that the album had not really been religious, and that anyway, all his music was suffused with a kind of respect for such sensibilities, and that anyway, one man's religion was another man's folly. He understood her meaning as certainly as if they shared a secret language, which as fans, they kind of did.

"I saw him in October at the Bowery Ballroom," Clay said.

"Yeah? Yudehdedaedadiwahdehdowndeh?"

"Ummm. What?"

"You deh... de day... dad I... wah deh... down deh?"

"Oh, yes, I guess I was. Wasn't it great? It's a surprise I didn't see you." He blushed because he realized that he had just as much as said that she was hard to miss with her long black hair and her striking features. His blushing made her blush, and she smiled, reaching up with her hand to cover the smile.

"Yes, well it's a surprise that I wasn't seen."

* * * *

The meal consisted of something she called "buss up shot" which was a light, flaky dough cooked in ghee butter ("because it looks like a busted up shirt," Stephen said, as if that somehow explained everything.) Veronica set out three separate bowls with each having a separate dish of chickpeas and spinach and curry chicken. "Just tear off a piece of the bread and wrap it around a bit of these and put it your mouth," she told him, "and if you're feeling brave, try a little pepper sauce." She pushed a small bowl of some condiment across the table, from which extended a spoon.

Clay was feeling brave although Stephen apparently wasn't, and after his first bite he realized why. He reached down and gathered a bite of chickpeas in the dough and poured a bit of the sauce from the spoon and ate it. His mouth was set aflame with a sensation he hadn't quite felt before. His eyes and nose and mouth began to water. Veronica and Stephen began to snicker and then finally busted out laughing as Clay wiped his face. "I told you that you'd better be brave, Mister, but I didn't say be stupid! Just a drop, Clay. Just a drop."

"Yeah, well you left that part out, Veronica." He choked for a moment and then felt the taste of the food kick in, and reached in for another bite.

It was the best meal he'd had in months. The company, the food, the warm cup of coffee afterward – Clay found himself thoroughly enjoying the whole experience. They sat and talked about the storm and how Veronica had come to this island from another island, from a small town outside of Port-of-Spain.

"There was a hill there you could drift down forever," she said. "Just get on your bike in the morning and begin rolling downhill, never once pedaling, and not stop until the sun was setting. Of course, then you had to walk back up!"

Clay told them that he'd once climbed a tree in his forest in Ithaca to see the sunrise, and as he was watching it come over the horizon, it had been so beautiful that he lost his balance and fell out of the tree and hadn't landed until evening. "Of course, most of that I'm making up," he said, "but, hey, what good is a story if it is entirely true?" They all laughed and the bowls slowly emptied.

After they finished, Clay helped Veronica clear the dishes from the table and Stephen went into the living room to turn on the TV. The news of Sandy's devastation was on every channel, and they gathered around for a moment to watch. The video of destruction was sobering—of roller coasters falling into the sea and smoke rising up from cinders and waters rushing over streets and sand piling up on the barriers or being washed out to sea. It seemed like a million miles away now even if some of it was right outside the door.

"You sure you want to go back out into that?" Veronica asked.

"That's exactly what I am leaving," Clay said.

"Yes, I see your point. Well, then you better get some rest, Clay." With that, she got up and excused herself, and as she turned to leave, she looked back over her shoulder and asked, "You a Republican, Clay?"

"Tonight, ma'am, after that meal... I'm whatever you want me to be."

"I'll put you down as a political agnostic, which is good enough for me," and with that she said that she had to go out to run a few errands. She went back into the hall and came out with a bag and told Stephen to watch over their guest. Then she let herself out, and the two of them sat for a bit, watching a few minutes more of TV.

In between the reports from the storm, the talking heads were already looking for the next big story. The election dance was playing itself out in real time, and both sides seemed to be wondering how to best use the destruction and death and suffering to insure their ascension to power. Vladimir Putin in Russia was strengthening his hold on the former Soviet Republics, and political dissidents were joining the press in accusing his government of killing or silencing his opponents. A video showed Secretary of State Hillary Clinton trying to thread the needle between these two storylines, saying that Russia was secretly moving to rebuild the former Soviet Union, and that the incumbent candidate leading America would not sit idly by and let that happen. After just a few moments of politics and world news, the scenes shifted back to local destruction and loss and calls for the government to help those who found themselves in dire need.

After a while, shaking his head thoughtfully, Stephen stood up and walked towards the television. "Do you mind if I turn this off?"

"Not one bit," Clay replied.

"Listen to some music?"

"Sure," Clay said, as the boy walked over to the stereo and pulled out a CD, slid it into the player, and pushed the button. The somber, soulful cry of Ellington's *Harlem Nocturne* came plaintively out of the speakers. The music stood in sharp contrast to the day's events with its peaceful, swinging somnambulism.

"I figured you liked Duke Ellington."

"I do," Clay said.

And the two of them listened to its end.

* * * *

Wednesday

Clay slept like a rock.

When he woke in the morning, he was feeling refreshed and happy, the weariness of yesterday's travels washed away by peaceful rest. He put his feet over the bed and dropped them to the floor, then put on his jeans and shirt. He pulled a lambswool sweater on and then his socks and boots. He stepped out into the hall and smelled eggs, and the heavenly scent of coffee in the air. Veronica was standing at the stove tending the eggs, humming to herself, doing a lazy sway while she did so. As she heard him enter, she turned around. "Good morning, Mr. Fugitive."

They sat and ate in a silence—more out of respect for the memory of the night before than for sorrow at their imminent departure. After the meal, they spoke. Clay talked of tending his garden in the spring. Veronica told him that she couldn't wait that long and that she had to get some newer plants covered in her garden that day. At the end of the meal, Clay began to return to his room to pack for his trip, and Veronica stopped him by holding out the bag that she'd left with the night before.

"I hope you don't mind. I said I didn't snoop *too* much, but when your stuff was out on the bed yesterday I saw that your gear is entirely unsuited for the journey ahead of you, you foolish man." She winked. "Even with the stuff I got for you, your supplies are insufficient for such a journey," she hesitated, "...if... if things were to go bad, you see?"

Clay nodded his head. He didn't want to interrupt, and he figured she was just concerned with his welfare.

"I would hazard a guess that your skillset probably is insufficient as well, Clay, and a stranger should be forgiven for thinking that you've embarked on your journey hastily, and ill-prepared...," she smiled, trying to soften the blow, "...but with the things I've added to your pack, I'm hoping that you'll get home alright."

Clay nodded again, and returned her smile.

"I like the books you've chosen to carry with you, Hemingway in particular. He got at the notion that the earth is more powerful than we imagine. We've seen evidence of that recently. But because of that, you can't go traipsing off into the woods with a single change of clothes and some energy bars and books and nothing else. Take these. I got you some bottles of water for your thirst and a Mylar blanket to keep you warm and a fishing kit to keep you fed. I keep a bunch of wool military blankets on hand for emergencies and cold nights, so I rolled one up for you and put it in your pack with your clothes. You never know what you will find out there, Clay. In case you find something dangerous, here is a knife that belonged to my husband. I put a flashlight in your bag too, and oh, and something else... it's in the small blue box. Don't open it until you get home. It won't do you any good 'til then, so I wrapped it to keep it dry."

Clay looked down in the bag and suddenly felt a wave of emotion for this woman who had done so much for him. All he'd done was what should be expected from a man, but she'd really extended herself in hospitality and courtesy. Clay was moved.

"What's this?" He reached into the bag.

"Oh that. Yes. Well, I have probably overstepped my boundaries. I saw on your bed the stack of poems. I shouldn't have looked, but I did, and I'm not sorry. I have a friend who once owned the Huemanity Bookstore here in Harlem. One of the last great independent bookstores in the city. The kind of place that, were he around today, you might find Langston Hughes reading his poems to a group of young toughs. A beautiful place. Anyway, she closed the shop down because she realized people wanted to drink coffee more than they wanted to buy books. She's now opening a café, but she's still trying to find a way to have both. So, she bought an *Espresso Book Machine*, the first one in Harlem. It binds your books right on the spot. She's planning to open in the spring and we were talking about the machine the other day, and then I saw your poems and... she hopes to have people come in and write their books over her coffee and then bind them and go back out into the street. I called her last night and asked her if she minded if I used it. This is the first book bound on it."

Clay looked at the cover. *The Poems of C.L. Richter.* A tear formed in his eye.

"I hope you don't mind. I read a few. I know..."

Clay choked back a tear. "No. I don't mind," He looked at her and realized that what she really meant to say was: I know. I've lost someone, too.

He put the book back in the bag and stood there for what seemed like the beginning of forever. He smiled and told her that if she ever got to Ithaca, she and Stephen had a home in his forest. She reached out and gave his hand a squeeze, and then they both turned away, him to his packing, her to her gardening.

* * * *

The rest of that day was spent in a blur, as if in a dream. Clay bid Veronica and Stephen good-bye and made his way to the bus line that would carry him up to the George Washington Bridge. He walked across the expanse and, as he had planned, he threw his key in the river, watching its slow mournful arc until it disappeared behind the webbing of girders and concrete and fell through space to land with a splash that no one could hear.

Once he was in New Jersey, he walked for hours and hours along what passed for the back roads, 4 and then 17, past the slow-changing landscape that morphed from urban to suburban. He passed fields and farms and golf courses and shopping malls and industrial wastelands and streams.

At the end of the day he checked into a small hotel just outside of Suffern. He found his room and lay down on his bed and rested his weary feet. Just before he dropped off to sleep, he reached into his bag and pulled out the copy of his book that Veronica had made for him. Opening it to the first page, he noticed that she'd placed in it a folded slip of paper. He opened it up and read the following poem just prior to slipping away.

Bound No'th Blues, by Langston Hughes

Goin' down the road, Lawd,
Goin' down the road.
Down the road, Lawd,
Way, way down the road.
Got to find somebody
To help me carry this load.
Road's in front o' me,
Nothin' to do but walk.
Road's in front of me,
Walk...an' walk...an' walk.
I'd like to meet a good friend
To come along an' talk.
Hates to be lonely,
Lawd, I hates to be sad.
Says I hates to be lonely,
Hates to be lonely an' sad,
But ever friend you finds seems
Like they try to do you bad.
Road, road, road, O!
Road, road...road...road, road!
Road, road, road, O!
On the no'thern road.
These Mississippi towns ain't
Fit fer a hoppin' toad.

CHAPTER 4

Cheryl was twenty-three when he first experienced her in the cafeteria at TC3. TC3 was what everyone called Tompkins Cortland Community College, and so Clay had learned to call it that too. He'd tried, for a while, to get his friends to call it The Cube, and he still liked that nickname, or maybe "TC-cubed" was a better one, but it hadn't really caught on, so he went along with the flow.

Anyway, Cheryl was working part-time in the cafeteria as a cashier. After four years spent running around Europe with Bohemian girlfriends, staying in hostels and photographing everything in sight, Cheryl had only started college a year earlier at the ripe young age of twenty-two. She caught Clay's attention one day near the beginning of the fall semester when she was on her first day of work and he was going through the line to pay for his lunch. He always had the same lunch, consisting of one roast beef sandwich (extra mustard), one bag of chips, and a single chocolate chip cookie. He was a creature of habit, but not of stone, and so that day, to mix things up, he'd decided to go through the pay line with the pretty young girl at the cashier counter.

Most love stories start in one of two ways. There is the "Hollywood" way wherein two polar opposites are forced to work together on a job, say, or a bank heist or an unavoidable outing with children. It can be anything really. It doesn't have to involve a job or a bank or children. It could involve planning brunch for a friend's wedding party, or setting out on a mission to Mars. The point is the two people involved initially hate one another. With a passion. Until somehow and one day the tension is too much (and too obvious) and they share an awkward kiss. After the kiss, sometimes accidentally achieved while both are specifically trying to avoid having anything to do with each other, they are forced to realize that they are mutually attracted. That's when the music cues and a love story begins.

The "real world" way that lovers meet, the second kind, usually starts with a shared look from across the room. There is nothing of loathing or hatred in it. In fact, usually, the look is followed by the man being immediately and lethally struck down by the woman's ethereal beauty. Slayed by Cupid, he can do nothing else, from that point on, but pursue the woman until he captures her heart. There is no soundtrack, save that one in the heart, but in this kind of story, the man's heart skipping and the woman's cheek blushing give hint of the music to come.

Or something like that. Either way the story is familiar.

Neither one of these well-worn paths was the route to romance trodden by Cheryl Woolsey and Clay Richter. Instead, it came down to the cost of a roast beef sandwich.

The total price for his meal on that blessed Monday—his first day with Cheryl in his life—was $6.25, and he paid for it with a crisp, new $10 bill. She did her magic with the cash register and promptly handed him his change. $2.75. Looking him directly in the eye and smiling innocently.

He looked at the pile of money in his hand—fully $1.00 short of what he was owed—squinted his eyes threateningly at her, harrumphed, and then moved silently on to a table to eat his meal in defeat. He did not once look back at this thief, this grifter, this circus con-woman with her big floppy Burberry and her skinny long legs and her dark heart hidden behind a too-ready smile. *Who wears a Burberry hat,* he thought, *in-doors?* And he ate in a kind of plotting silence.

The next day, Clay, seeing Cheryl perched on her wooden stool at the register on the far end of the lunch line, purposefully placed on his tray the exact same items that he always had and went through the line as he had the day before. Reaching the register, he placed his food before her and, once again, Cheryl smiled at him sweetly while blatantly and fearlessly stealing a dollar from him. He looked down at his $2.75 in change, grimaced indignantly, thrust it into his pocket and went to his table to eat his meal.

It was all he could think about. He was obsessed. He didn't study that night at all.

The following day, the pattern continued, only this time, after receiving his change minus the dollar Cheryl had again stolen from him, he smiled back at her sweetly, pocketed the change, then reached over and picked up a roll of mints (priced at $1) and stuck them in his pocket with his change. He winked. At that, her eyes narrowed a bit and they shared a long and knowing stare before he finally retreated to his luncheon table.

The fourth day of this unique courtship with Cheryl, Clay loaded his tray with the identical lunch items, and she rang up the sale on the register. He noticed that the bin of mints had been removed from the counter, an obvious sign of one-upsmanship. He could see it behind the counter, just beyond his reach, almost as if someone had calculated his height and the stretch of the fabric he would be wearing that day, and had gone through the motions to calculate the lean of his body, the inclination of the packaging. The mints had been put... just... beyond... his reach.

Without so much as a pause, he reached into his pockets and pulled out the exact amount he owed. $6.25. Nothing more, nothing less. He counted it out quite deliberately making a show of each bill, then slowly dropped the change in the center of the bills, letting the last quarter drop dramatically from his hand and roll slowly in a lazy circle on the formica before it began to spin, increasing its speed as it collapsed, dying slowly and dramatically and rhythmically on the countertop. Clay smiled, nodded his head in victory, and then began his triumphant walk towards his table. It was then that, without warning, he was struck in the back by a hastily thrown roll of mints. He turned around slowly, and balancing his tray in one hand, he casually bent down and picked up the mints. Snapping a single mint out dexterously with one thumb, he popped it into his mouth, winked again at Cheryl, and went to the table to eat his lunch.

Not long after what became known as The Mint War, he met Cheryl in the campus bookstore. He smiled at her and she smiled back and the first word she ever said to him dropped from her lips.

"Jerk."

"Thief."

"Meanie."

"Reprobate."

They stood and smiled at each other. Smiles of shared affection. The rest, as they say, is history. Not even a year later they were married, and they had a hard and fast rule after that. No stealing. Even if she was only doing it out of psychological curiosity—to see who would notice.

* * * *

Thursday

Twenty years had passed since that meeting, and here he was, a lonely widower, staring up at a filthy, water stained popcorn ceiling in a cheap motel room. The weight of the last few days suddenly hit him. God, or Fate, or inertia or chaos—whatever ruled the world—had led him to this place in a conspiracy of silence, simply standing by and watching as his life transpired. He suddenly felt melancholy, sad, and alone, like he was moving to an end, but the purpose of that end suddenly seemed less clear.

He knew that getting *home* would help everything. Having just been in a real home with Veronica and Stephen had reminded him of what he was missing. But, he also knew that without the people in the house to make it a home, he would still be wandering the rooms like before, listening for the sounds of others.

He put this thought out of his head. Sometimes giving in to thoughts makes them become self-fulfilling prophecies. He willfully meditated, instead, about what he would do when he got to Ithaca. Maybe he would get a milk cow—he always liked Jerseys—and some goats and chickens. *I could do that*, he thought, as he finally began to stir from his reverie, to shake the morning cobwebs from his head. He had no real sense of freedom yet, but the idea that there was a future for him, and that the future involved home and peace, made him smile. *Still a bit of a journey*, he thought, *but the only way to get there is a step at a time.*

He took stock of his body, particularly his legs. Tight. Muscles sore, but in a good way. His feet hurt. *I should have done this six years ago rather than lock myself away in that urban prison. But, I can still do this. I can. Man, it would be so beautiful to have Cheryl and the girls with me... but I don't.*

He knew there would be no water in the tiny bathroom, but he couldn't help trying the rusted faucet anyway. After check-in, the managers had brought in a couple of buckets of dirty, rusty water to be used only—they had carefully explained several times—to flush the toilets. He still had the three bottles of water Veronica had given him back in Harlem, so he used a judicious amount out of one bottle to splash water on his face and brush his teeth. There were three energy bars left in his side pocket, so he ate one of them, and for some reason that he couldn't rightly identify, he wasn't able to get himself to throw the metallic wrapper away. He folded it carefully and stuffed it into one of the side pockets of the backpack. *Why did I do that?* He couldn't really say. There was some need to conserve now, to make everything count, as if whatever materials had come his way had done so for a reason and he had a responsibility to make them count. Or perhaps he was just getting nervous. Maybe what had happened with Sandy was not the end, but just the beginning. Maybe things were going to spiral downhill in the aftermath. He remembered the Christmas blizzard of a few years back, how some of the stores had run out of food in an astoundingly short amount of time, making shopping in them like walking through a Soviet-era bread line. After that storm, you had to be happy with whatever could be found on the shelves and not ask questions—just pay for whatever was available, and be glad you got it.

The long walk out of New York had affected him, and the cheerful optimism of the morning before had fled. Seeing the blank and fearful faces of people he'd passed in the gas lines yesterday replaced the optimism with a feeling of—what was it? Dread? He'd watched a man throw hot coffee through the open window of a van at a woman with her children in tow who had tried to cut in a gas line. He had seen police cars and fire trucks and ambulances rushing down country roads, and National Guard helicopters flying overhead. He had heard the words "war zone" used far too frequently to describe too many places along his route. It felt like the eye of the storm had passed and the winds were now reforming, only this time they were driven by people's hot air and their ungracious impatience. "Blow, blow thou winter wind," Shakeapeare wrote, "thou art not so unkind as man's ingratitude." Clay worried that if that ingratitude turned nasty, things could go downhill fast.

After packing up his things and tightly lacing his boots, he strapped on his backpack and stepped out into the bright sunlight of Day 3 of his walk. He stretched a little and took in his environment, noticing the cars in the parking lot and even a couple of tents on the greenbelt leading into the motel. *I'm not the only one on foot,* he thought.

Despite the sunshine, the day was cool and brisk and portended change. Maybe it was the warning that Veronica had implied ("Not everyone is as nice as you are..."), but he got the sense that something was out there, something dangerous, or at least something with that kind of potential.

Thinking this as he stepped outside, Clay didn't want to get caught up in chit-chat or to engage with any of the assorted characters that were milling about outside of his motel room as he stepped across the parking lot toward the lobby to return his key. There was a man who looked like he could have been a travelling salesman, wrapped up in tension and angst and jargon, talking in loud tones on a phone with someone who didn't show sympathy for the fact that he might not get to his next appointment, and if he didn't that he might not make his number, and if he didn't that he might not keep his job. There was a man who walked around his eighteen-wheeler, flexing his tattooed arms and checking the cables to see if his load had loosened in the night and that his tires were all inflated, all the while glancing across the lot to the window of a diner where a waitress stood taking orders. Neither of these men, nor any of the other people who were milling about, were dangerous in themselves. Rather, it seemed that the environment, the system, the whole machine made up of the sum of its parts, was the problem. It was like an engine knocking but you couldn't really tell from where or what piece needed replacing.

Clay couldn't help noticing, despite his general unwillingness to put up with any foolishness this morning, the guy two doors down from his room. He was sitting on the tailgate of a pickup, cutting up fruit with a pocketknife and sticking the pieces of apple in his mouth. It would not be an exaggeration to say that he looked out of place.

The man was possibly in his 50's to early 60's, but fit, trim, wearing starched and faded blue jeans and cowboy boots. Wherever he was, Clay thought, this man was there *on purpose.* He wore a dark brown cowboy hat and a starched, blue dress shirt, and he smiled from under his heavy mustache and waved at Clay. He indicated with his pocketknife as pretty and matter-of-factly as you please that Clay should come over there and eat some fruit. Even as he did so, he had a look of indifference on his face, as if to say, "Suit yourself. If you want some, it's sitting there waiting for you." In some odd way this indifference was reassuring.

Clay couldn't imagine why he would be responding affirmatively to a man waving a knife at him, but almost without any conscious thought or hesitation he strolled over to the back of the pickup and stood there uncomfortably with his hands in the pockets of his coat. He shifted in the backpack and looked at the man, and then at the fruit, and then at the dust on his boots.

"Get you some fruit," the man said, smiling in a way that you could only really identify because of the wrinkles near his eyes. It was impossible to see the smile itself because a mustache extended down over the man's mouth, obscuring it from view. Clay stared at him for a few seconds. The man looked like Sam Elliot, he decided, although, even as he decided this, he wondered why every cowboy in the world somehow looked like Sam Elliot. Still, the impression was unmistakable. He sounded remarkably like him too, with his deep gravelly voice and his as-yet-unidentified southern drawl.

"Go on. You look like you could use some, and fruit might get hard to come by here pretty soon."

Clay hesitated for a moment, like a dog that's not sure whether a man is going to kick him or pet him, and then he moved forward and took a chunk of apple. He stepped back to his safe spot and took a bite and started to chew.

Sam Elliot looked at him and smiled with his kind blue eyes, mindfully chewing on his own piece of apple. The two strangers awkwardly continued in this manner for what seemed like a very long time. In reality it was only a minute or so, but it seemed like it took forever, the two of them sitting around eating apples together like strangers who've met in the parking lot of a cheap motel after the worst natural disaster in memory. Breaking the moment of profound silence, the older man looked around and motioned to nowhere in particular with his pocketknife. "I'm Clive Darling."

Clive Darling then looked around and nodded towards the tents on the greenbelt. "Things seem peaceful and serene now, but they probably won't stay that way for long." With that, he narrowed his eyes and wiped his mustache with his thumb and forefinger. "Most everyone here is out of gas. Even the stations that still have power are plumb out, and the last few stores I stopped in have been nearly stripped bare."

He looked back at Clay and sighed deeply. "This is that moment when things could go either way. If things go bad, some of these folks might get right desperate and things could get ugly."

Clay didn't tell him that he'd had some of the same thoughts.

"I give it 48 hours or so, and then it probably won't be safe on the roads after that. Least, not if things get worse."

Savannah, Georgia. That's how Clay pegged him. His accent was right out of *Midnight in the Garden of Good and Evil*. It was that slow, but exceedingly proper southern drawl, the one that made people sound rich but not stupid and caused anything they said to come across as critically important and wise no matter what it was they were saying. With a Savannah accent, one could say, "I do believe I'll go pick a peach from that tree over yonder," and it would sound as important and fascinating and even historical as, "Why don't we all gather together and just open fire on Fort Sumter?" It was the kind of accent that had *import*.

Clay took in more of the picture. Clive was rich, or at least he looked it. You could tell from the way he handled the knife, the way his shirt was tucked, the angle of his hat. Very particular, like a man who had leisure to worry about such things. Despite the fact that he looked like he was used to having money, Clive seemed comfortable eating apples from the tailgate of a $50,000 pickup truck. Maybe he made his money in cattle, say, or corn or lumber. Maybe he was used to watching from a ridge, up high somewhere along a look-out, as the workers in some valley below pushed the livestock or the produce or the timber into trucks that would haul them away to market. Maybe he sat and ate apples as he figured out profit margins and devised economies of scale. Maybe, or maybe not. Sizing people up isn't a science if you don't get paid for it, Clay thought. Nevertheless, the man was impressive in a way that could not be denied.

"Clay. Clay Richter," he said, smiling back and nodding his head. He wasn't ready to shake hands with the man, mostly because of the knife, but he was ready to make conversation.

"Richter?" Clive said, smiling. "Hmm... Kraut?" Seeing Clay's eyes narrow a bit, he added, "Oh, don't mind me. I'm one of those old fellas that just blurts out whatever he thinks without passing it through some filter. What I meant to say is—are you of German extraction, sir?"

"Way back," Clay answered, showing that he wasn't offended at all. "My grandfather on my father's side came here in 1929 to escape... things going on in Germany."

"He a commie?"

Clay laughed this time. "No. He was a Republican, in the Charles Lindbergh mold of Republicanism. He may have been a fascist, but he certainly didn't like or approve of Hitler."

"My kind of guy," Clive said, laughing at his own joke. "Where you headed?"

"Upstate. Not far from Ithaca. Escaping the city," and before he could stop himself he added, "and not because of the storm." For some reason, Clay, who had been so reserved in his interactions with people along his journey—even with Veronica, despite her kindness—found it easy to talk to this cowboy.

"Hmmm... a mystery. I like it. So you're the grandson of a fascist and you are starting off on your Luddite life in the wake of the worst hurricane to hit New England in recorded memory. Interesting, to say the least."

Clay looked down at the ground and kicked a pebble with the toe of his boot. He watched as the pebble rolled across the pavement and came to rest under the treads of one of Clive's brand new tires. "Maybe it's not quite like that," he said through a grin. He didn't know why he felt the need to open up to this old guy and spill the beans, but he did. "I'm just heading home. I've been gone a long time, and I've had enough of cities and consumerism and the whole charade of progress." He paused for a second. "And if I hear another word about this election, I'm seriously going to snap. In fact, that's been one of the few benefits of the storm... it has changed the subject off the horse race."

"Like I said – a Luddite!" Clive nodded and laughed straight from the belly, "and an anarchist to boot!"

"I haven't thought it out that far yet, but maybe I'm heading in that direction."

"Well, maybe you should have said that when I asked you which way you were headed," Clive said, folding the knife and putting it back in the front pocket of his jeans.

"Maybe I should have," Clay nodded and shifted the backpack on his back, nervously pretending to adjust the straps. "Oh, and thank you kindly for the apple." He hesitantly turned to leave still feeling like he shouldn't, or maybe it was that he didn't want to.

"Well, hold on there a minute, Ned Ludd," Clive said, wiping his hands on his jeans and tidying up the tailgate. "I've got enough gas to get us down the road a bit. I know you're not an axe murderer because, well, I just know, that's all, and because you were willing to take an apple from a guy with a knife. That makes you either stupid, brave, or insightful, and I don't think for a minute that you're stupid. So that leaves brave or insightful. Either of those makes you better company than most of these jokers on the road. I like a little conversation when I drive. So what I'm saying is... are you up for a ride?"

Clay hesitated.

"I don't know how much gas I have left in the tank, but hopefully it will get us to Liberty, which should cut your walk down quite a bit. It'll save you two to three days of walking, at least, maybe more. I've got another—well, let's just say—another form of transportation picking me up in Liberty. But I might be able to get you that far. And anyway, at one of the stores I stopped at last night they were saying that there's another storm coming. Don't know nothin' about it, but they said it could be bad. So what do you say, young Mr. Ludd. Would you rather hoof it than keep an old man company?"

Clay looked around. Maybe Clive was right. He'd heard about things turning south really fast after a natural disaster, and Clive seemed like a nice enough guy, even if he was peculiar.

Clive looked at him, shrugged, and said, "Well Ned, if you insist on walking, let me give you some more fruit for your bag."

"I'll ride, Clive."

"Well, then! Good. Let me get my gear and we'll saddle up."

* * * *

The ride was smooth and nice, and the pickup truck was plush and comfortable. The conversation was as peculiar as Clive but in a way that Clay was growing used to. Clive was a regular fountain of information, and he seemed to know more about disasters and psychology and the ins and outs of social disintegration than a cowboy from Georgia should. He wasn't exactly sure how much cowboys *should* know about such things, but he was pretty sure that Clive knew more.

Just outside of Sloatsburg they passed a couple of cars on the side of the road with the hoods lifted. The flashing hazard lights on both of the cars said they had been recently abandoned. "Probably out of gas," Clive said matter-of-factly. "When they write the epitaph on this civilization it will read, 'They Ran Out of Gas.' And speakin' of, we're getting low on petrol ourselves," he added, "but this ol' truck'll go a long way on empty."

As they drove, they passed occasional walkers and hikers, and Clay turned to look into their faces and tried to read their thoughts. *Where are they going? How far do they have to go? What are they leaving behind?* He wondered whether people had thought the same things about him yesterday when he'd been walking on the long road. His mind visited memories of news clips about refugees in war time in places like Rwanda and Sudan. Displaced and fleeing. He thought that he just as easily might be a refugee on this same road, and he wondered whether catching a ride could mean the difference between life and death for some of these people. He wondered to himself if maybe they should stop and pick some of them up.

Clive answered his thoughts, as if he had heard them. "We can't pick them up, Ned Ludd," he said, sadly. "I know I picked you up, and it seems the neighborly thing to do and all, but we're going to float into Liberty on fumes, if we make it at all. Besides, like I said, some of these folks ain't gonna be nice to be around starting pretty soon. You don't have time to eat an apple with each one of 'em and size 'em up on the side of the road."

"I understand," Clay replied, and he really did. He liked to think of himself as the helpful and friendly kind, but he really just wanted to get home. And anyway, if they couldn't find more gas, the truck wasn't going much farther. They'd be refugees themselves soon.

"Listen Clay," Clive said, all of the sudden speaking very seriously, "this whole world exists in a hologram of civility. If you don't mind an ol' cowboy quoting Thoreau... Thoreau said that 'the mass of men lead lives of quiet desperation', and that was more than a hundred and fifty years ago." Clive waved his hand outward, indicating everything. "This is all pretty simple, even for an ol' horseman, and I hope I don't bore you with my opinions, but this world has a long history of empires rising, followed closely by empires falling. Believe me, they make a bigger mess falling than they ever made rising."

Clay looked at him and thought for a moment about the red-haired man on the bike and how he had not recognized the resemblance before, but he sure did now.

"Do you mind me waxing philosophic, Clay? We've got some time to pass, and I've got this speech memorized, and perhaps I can put words to some thoughts you've had yourself.

Judging from what you said earlier, I mean, about the city and consumerism and such."

Clay looked over at Clive and just rolled his left hand with his forefinger extended in a small loop like he was rolling the tape forward, indicating that Clive should continue. Clive smiled, and did.

"Man always starts simply. He works the ground, raises his crops, tends his animals, and loves his family. His children, who probably didn't work too much to build the farm, don't generally recognize the same value in it, and they work it only begrudgingly. His grandchildren hate the farm, and either they or their children move to the city and end up automating the world. They can't be blamed much. It's in the nature of things. They build up a system of *just-in-time* delivery of goods made widely available and priced cheaply through the coercion of economic power and the largesse of wars of conquest and mechanization. They think they're building on the family legacy when really what they are doing is destroying."

Clive smiled at Clay, and continued, "You with me? What I'm saying is: that's the history of America, brother. I don't mean to speechify even though I do, but this ain't the first time we've seen this rodeo. Man's been down this little trail before. Just go ask the Greeks and the Romans. Folks that think we're on to something new ain't been paying attention. Rome wasn't built in a day, but when it was built, it was built on the back of the countryside, and it sucked out the life from the country to feed its appetites. Your politicians, be they Democrats or Republicans, fight over the fumes of the excess once built up by the hard work of families and the labor of farmer poets. The bankers and factories eventually sell everyone weapons so they can kill one another because there's good money in that, no denying it. Then one day, after the fires go out and the stench of death wafts over the planet, the survivors start over, and a man works his piece of ground, raises his crops, tends his animals, and loves his family. Then we're off running to the next go-round. You got me?"

Clay sat silently for a minute, thinking and looking forward through the windscreen then back to Clive at last. "You have given this speech before. Go on," he said.

Clive reached forward and tapped on the gas gauge, shaking his head. "Oh no, I'm not really trying to convert you or anything. Don't think that. Besides, I have the feeling we are already on the same page. This ain't a recruitment. I'm just sayin' that there's some things coming down, Clay. Real soon. Maybe even now, today, this minute. And when these things come down, you don't want to be in the city. You don't want to be in this truck on this highway neither. You want to be far away from the masses of people living their lives in quiet desperation. Anyone whose life is dependent on the *system*—what did you call it? 'Cities and consumerism and the whole charade of progress?'—you just want to be as far away from that person and that charade as possible. Especially when those people live in bunches, stacked on top of one another in those cities and suburbs like a house of playing cards set to tumble."

Clay nodded his head, thinking. He looked out the window and watched a hawk swoop across the sky in a long lazy circle, coming to rest in the top of a barren pine, his large wings dropping and turning in a way that made his tail turn under him, sending his body upright. "I can't say I disagree with you much Clive, but then, you somehow already know that about me. These are things I've thought for some time now. In fact, some of that is the reason I'm heading home."

"Well," Clive said with a smile, "I kinda did know that about you. That's why I called you 'brother'."

They rode in silence for a time, noticing aloud to one another the increase in foot traffic on the sides of the highways. It was going in both directions now, and there was a look of urgency on the faces of the passing strangers. Every now and then they'd come upon a fallen tree or a collapsed billboard or some other damage from Hurricane Sandy, but all-in-all things seemed remarkably peaceful, considering.

It was becoming painfully obvious that gasoline was going to be a huge problem. Every station they passed was lined with cars and people holding gas cans. Many truck stops and filling stations had large 4' x 8' pieces of plywood out by the road that read, "No Gas!" in bright-colored spray paint. Clay thought that there ought to be no reason for stations that have electric power to be out of gas.

Clive looked over to him and shook his head. "Pumped dry by thousands and thousands of scared folks and profiteers along with a few intelligent folks who see that things might go bad. They're all getting every drop of life-blood they can get. You can tell what people love and need the most when you see what they rush to get or save when bad things happen. This society is hooked on gasoline and electricity. It is the vital drug of this culture. Crack cocaine isn't even as addictive to the wide world of people grown dependent for their very lives on stuff like cellphones and video games and other gadgets. Stuff that hadn't even been invented when Thoreau wrote *Walden*, or when the first bridge was built across the Mississippi up in Minneapolis." He paused, letting that sink in.

Clay rode along silently, watching a handful of refugees sitting on a fallen tree on the shoulder of the road smoking cigarettes and cutting up. He wondered whether they had just met, or if they'd been traveling together. He was thinking about what Clive was saying, but didn't know exactly what he thought about it... or even what Clive wanted him to think about it.

Clive glanced over again, noticing Clay's pensive look, and said, "Oh, I know! I know! I'm a hypocrite. We all are. I use the tools that are available to me, even while my mind and my heart wars against 'em." He leaned forward, stretching his back and re-adjusting the seat belt across his chest. "But what I'm saying is no less true whether I'm a hypocrite or not. This age-old social experiment in empire building and civilization is heading for a very big crash—just like Athens and Rome before it—and I have to tell you brother, it's coming really soon. There ain't nothing new under the sun."

As he finished this last sentence, Middletown, New York appeared, and Clive pulled the truck off at the next exit. He was going downhill, so he cut the engine off and coasted for almost half a mile before pulling into the parking lot of a small, family restaurant with a sign out front that said, "Sorry. We're Open".

Inside they sat down in a wide booth covered in maroonish pleather, and were met there quickly by a woman in an apron upon which the name "Madge" had been embroidered in thick green thread. A waitress in a hurry with a pen and paper at the ready. "We have turkey sandwiches and coffee. No water. That's what we have," she said. Madge looked at them impatiently and was already walking away when Clive said, "We'll each take two of everything that you just said."

When Madge showed up ten minutes later with the food, Clive asked her if anyone in town had any gas. Madge just shook her head negatively and said, "Twenty-five for the sandwiches and coffee, and exact change will be appreciated if you got it," and she was gone before either of the men could say a word.

Clive pulled out his wallet before Clay could even reach for his own stash of money, and threw a fifty down on the table. "I got this, Brother Clay. And she can keep the change because that paper money will be worthless in a week anyway." Clay thought the comment was strangely specific, but the two were back on the road before he could ask Clive about the tip or the comment on the impending worthlessness of cash. Just as he was about to do so, the old man started up the conversation where he had left it off.

"I'm a self-made man, Clay, and I don't mind sayin' that I'm rich by worldly standards. I made most of my money in cattle and land over thirty years ago, and I've had those thirty years to learn about money and what it will buy and what it all means. I made my money honestly, or as honestly as a man can make money in this system."

"I'm sure you did," Clay remarked, not really sure, but wanting to keep Clive talking.

"But I'm also something rare in this system, and I don't mind sayin' that either." Clive continued while intently studying the gas gauge and, for a moment, comparing what he saw with some figures he had scratched on a notepad he kept in his front shirt pocket. "I'm reflective... that's what I am. What I mean by that is that I don't just take life as it comes floating along without thinking, like Thoreau's 'mass of mankind'. You get what I'm saying, Clay? I think about things, and I study, and I read. That's why I say that it didn't have to be this way. We could have learned from every other empire in the history of the world. We could have avoided the pitfalls that were inevitably going to follow industrialism and urbanism." He banged his knuckles lightly on the steering wheel, emphasizing his point, before returning to it. "We didn't have to give in to the silent rule by an oligarchy of bankers and politicians and corporations. We could have avoided the dialectical thinking forced upon us by statists of every stripe, Clay, but we didn't. And when this is all over—and I mean to say it will be real soon—but when it's all over, there will be some obvious bad guys. And the people who still live will want to blame them. But Clay, here's the point—the blame is in ourselves. That's where it is. In ourselves, Ned Ludd."

"Ok," Clay responded, stunned a bit by the seriousness and solemnity of Clive's tone. "I can see that you are a pessimist, and in some ways I am too. So maybe we are brothers of a sort. But I have to ask you why you say that paper money will be worthless *in a week*. The rest of that... that moving monologue... it was all kind of general and philosophical, but the part about greenbacks being worthless *in a week*. In a week? That's pretty specific."

Clive smiled. "Well, Ned Ludd, perhaps I was being dramatic. And sometimes rich people make the mistake of being reckless and profligate in order to make a point. I apologize for that, although I hope, even if I'm wrong, that I was still able to help ol' Madge out a little bit."

The sound of the gasping of the motor interrupted the conversation, and Clive guided the truck over onto the shoulder, coasting as long as he could before throwing the truck into Park.

"I reckon that's it, Clay," Clive said, opening his door to climb out. "We're on foot from here."

* * * *

The two gathered their belongings. Clive already had everything he needed stuffed into a large, army green duffel before Clay met him at the back of the truck and reached in the bed for his own backpack.

"Looks like we're five miles from Liberty, where I catch another ride, Ned," Clive said, smiling with his eyes as he threw the duffel onto his back, the strap stretching across his ample and muscular chest. "I'd love to give you a ride all the way to Ithaca, but I can't, but if I could I would. I may be rich, and I may come off as a freebird, but I do have places to be and in some way I am responsible for people who don't always appreciate my freebird tendencies."

"No problem, Clive," Clay said. "I'm just glad for the company."

The two walked silently for a few minutes, before Clay broke the silence. "So, what do you think is going to happen next, Clive?" he asked. Clive was a great guy, and a deep thinker, but Clay didn't believe for a minute that this man had made all of his money *just* on cattle and land. Nor did Clay think that Clive had gained all of his knowledge and information *just* reading books. He didn't know why he felt this way, but there was something about the man that made Clay think that his travel partner knew even more than he was letting on.

They took a few more steps before Clive spoke, and when he did, his accent seemed to have disappeared, and he spoke with clarity and purpose and intent. "I think we're about to get hit, Clay. Hit real hard. There's more to this than you can possibly know, and it is likely you will think that I'm crazy after I say it, but what have you got to lose in listening to an old man? We've only got five more miles together, it seems."

The two men watched a lady walk past them in the other direction, pulling two small children in a large plastic wagon. Clive tipped his hat to the lady, but she didn't notice, or maybe she just ignored the gesture. "I'm heading to Canada," Clive continued. "My people have a place in Nova Scotia that we've been preparing for a dozen years. We're set up there to ride out what comes next. Got another place—a farm—down in PA. May end up there, we'll see. We've been expecting this for a while."

"Expecting what?" Clay asked, half afraid of the answer. Up 'til now he'd thought that he and Clive had in common a kind of rejection of urban life, but this sounded like something more, something like one of those crazy survivalist things where people move off into the woods and build bunkers. He had certainly felt a weird aggression in the last several days, but Clive was talking like there was something much bigger than just social unrest in store.

"Well, there's a theory, Clay—and it's way more than a theory, let me tell you—but there is a theory, held by a lot of people that know things in this world, that the Soviets faked their collapse back in '92." Clive paused and looked at Clay for effect. Clay swallowed his tongue and said nothing. He simply walked in silence, as if in invitation for the old man to continue, which he did.

"Now, I can't expect you to believe that based on the mere utterance of a sentence by a stranger on the side of the road, but believe me. There is a lot to it. I could go into reasons, but I'll just give you one. Did you know that just a couple of days before Sandy hit, the Russians ran a nuclear submarine off the east coast of the USA?"

Clay thought of the woman in the red dress. "No, I didn't know that, but what does that have to do with anything?"

"Well, it's just an anomaly that makes you wonder. Why would a country that long ago gave up its dreams of empire risk a high cost naval instrument in such turbulent seas? Why then?

Why there? Why do it at all, in fact, if you've given up dreams of empire?

"Anyway, according to the theory, they gave themselves 20-25 years to accomplish an important task. Prior to the 'collapse' they couldn't import a speak-n-spell from the west, and their economy was in tatters, and their whole system was a joke. They've now had twenty years of receiving Western aid and technology, all the while letting America lash about as the lone superpower, exhausting her resources, her economic and moral strength, and the good will of the rest of the world. The theory says that once the right confluence of events comes to pass; when America is weakened and divided and suffering from losses abroad and disasters at home; when she is at her most vulnerable—well that is when the old guard of communists in Russia will strike."

Clive waved outward with his left hand then brought the hand back to rub his mustache and readjust his hat. "I'm assuming it will be some kind of EMP strike, but it could be anything from that all the way up to a full nuclear attack."

Clay stared out at the road as they walked. Cars seemed to be going by faster, and the drivers avoided eye contact as they sped on their way. "And you believe this attack is imminent?" he asked.

"No, Clay," Clive said matter-of-factly. "I *know* it is imminent."

"You know it is imminent – like when my grandmother knew it was going to rain—or you *know* it is imminent, like in... you have absolute knowledge that this is going to happen, that it is *about to happen*?"

"Let me ask you a question, Clay," Clive said, stopping for a moment and looking Clay in the eye. "When your grandmother said it was going to rain, not when she just kind of wondered aloud, but when she said to come inside because it was about to rain... was your grandmother ever wrong?"

"No."

They walked on in silence for another mile before Clay could find the words to say something, anything, about what he had heard. "I guess we'll know soon enough, won't we Clive?"

"Yes, we will Ned Ludd."

Clay looked at the old horseman who seemed to strain not at all against his heavy burden. More miles washed by as they walked in silence, and the older man didn't tire in the least. Clay wondered how anyone could be so certain about anything in this life and after a while he didn't care if Clive was right or wrong. It was refreshing to meet someone who plowed forward and who was certain of his direction and goal. There was a kind of inspiration merely from being in the presence of certainty.

Clay finally broke the silence. "So you're saying I shouldn't get that hybrid car I've been wanting, and that maybe I shouldn't depend on my electric stove?"

They both laughed, and Clive winked at him, his eyes smiling like before. "I'm saying y'all don't even call the power company to get the power back on!" The Savannah accent was back.

* * * *

Just outside of Liberty, they left the highway, and Clive led with purpose through a copse of trees that brought them to the entrance of what looked like a Golf Course. Looking around, Clay saw the sign that read *Grossinger Country Club* and noticed that Clive seemed to know the grounds.

The place was eerily abandoned, and Clay figured that no one was playing golf with everything else that was going on in the world. They sat down near the driving range and talked and rested, and after about thirty minutes of chit-chat about things less important than the end of the world, Clay heard the thump-thump-thump sound of a helicopter coming towards them from the north.

The helicopter landed out in the open on the driving range. The chopper was a big one and expensive, a play toy of the rich and famous and of top-level bureaucrats. Clay had seen choppers like this on television shows—usually landing on some rooftop in Manhattan to ferry billionaires to airports and distant garden parties.

Clive held his hat down from the wash of the rotors and turned to Clay while he threw his bag over his shoulder. "You can come with me Ned Ludd. We've always got a place for our brothers."

Clay looked at the helicopter just as a man in some kind of uniform got out and opened the rear door. Looking back to Clive, Clay shouted through the storm of noise, "I appreciate the offer Clive, really I do, but I've got to get home. That's been my plan for some time now, and I want to see it through. Besides, I don't want to be in that thing when the EMP hits." He smiled at Clive as they shook hands.

"Well, neither do I, Ned Ludd, but I'm praying I'll get home safely too." As he said this, he reached into his pocket and pulled out a business card and handed it to Clay. "When you get home... if things haven't crashed before then, give me a call and let me know you made it safely." Once again, the accent seemed to have vanished, but it was hard to tell with the whirr of the rotors. Clive turned to walk away, then turned back and said, "I like you Ned Ludd. I hope you do alright."

Clay was going to answer him, but he was gone, and in seconds the helicopter lifted into a sky that had grown cloudy and gray in just the last few minutes. He waved instead, and Clive, looking out through the window, gave him a sharp salute as the chopper pulled away and headed north into the lowering clouds.

CHAPTER 5

Two and a half hours later, as he walked alone northward on the highway, the sun was dropping into the western sky, and the temperature, which had been moderately cool throughout the day, sank with the sun. The weather had begun to turn right about the time that Clive had climbed into his millionaire copter, and the clouds had slowly lowered until they almost seemed to brush the tops of the trees.

Clay thought about that strange encounter as he walked along. Before flying off to his apocalyptic retreat, Clive had mentioned in passing that another storm was coming. He had, of course, spoken in those strange tones about a storm of political intrigue, but there had been something more, an actual weather report of a blizzard or something. Clay had taken out his radio from a side zipper pocket in his backpack, but he'd not been able to get any reception from the few radio stations that still seemed to be transmitting. For a very brief moment, he'd locked onto an AM station from the city, but all they talked about was the upcoming election and the damage on Breezy Point. Nothing of value to him now, nothing of storm movements and forecasts. The station bled away and he was left with scratchy silence.

He flipped up his collar and wiggled his toes inside his boots. It was getting cold now. His very thoughts were getting cold. The smooth, languid restfulness of the walk through the city, the warm seclusion of Veronica's house, the heated intrigued of the luxurious cabin in Clive's truck—all that was gone now. His thoughts became sluggish and brittle. He felt his blood move slowly to his extremities and back again to his heart, the movements growing shallower with each successive circuit. He felt the cold first in his fingertips, then his knuckles, then his digits, then his hands.

After Clive's departure, he walked back to the highway from the Golf Course, heading north-northwest again along the eastern bank of the highway, passing walkers and worried hikers carrying gas cans and sacks and sometimes children. He passed more and more people along the highway. *Where were all these people coming from?* Some nodded a lukewarm greeting, but most just kept their head down, walking purposefully, their breath pouring out before them like spirits.

As the temperature dropped, and coinciding with the change of the weather and the impending darkness, the number of people on the road—in cars and on foot—had diminished as well, until only now and then did he see anyone else on the road. "I'm going to be cold tonight," he said aloud, though there was no one around to hear him.

* * * *

The animals are acting funny. The thought occurred to him, and he didn't even know why he had the thought, or what it meant. He remembered having this thought a few days before Sandy hit, watching a group of swallows range through the sky, then land in a tree overhead and screech. Now he didn't hear any birds at all. He could not even hear a dog bark anywhere in the distance. *Maybe another storm IS coming.*

He passed what might have been a very small hamlet on his right off the access road and, as he did, he hearkened back to Clive's warning about how people were going to get edgy and dangerous on the roads as time went on. Veronica had said as much to him too, without all the political context. He knew that this was probably true, and not just because Clive and Veronica had said it. He had watched what happened in and around New Orleans only days after Hurricane Katrina, and many of the books he'd begun reading lately, books that fed his discontent with the city, had talked about what might happen in any urban society when people started getting restless after a major event. The line between order and chaos in society could indeed be a very fine one, and the threads that made up that line seemed increasingly strained already. If a blizzard did more to cut off access to gas and groceries and electricity and normal, it could put that social fabric near the breaking point.

Clay had never been a doomsday survivalist, or a doomsday anything, but he was interested in alternative viewpoints. As he had explored a number of these different viewpoints online, and in a bookstore around the corner, he'd been surprised at how many of them actually made some sense. Even Clive, with his apocalyptic vision, had said some things that seemed to resonate. Clay wondered why he was drawn to these kinds of outsider visions. For example, one particular book he'd read in the weeks before the storm had been written by a neo-Amish separatist. He knew that this was a stretch for a guy in Brooklyn. How could he have explained to his friends at the coffee shop that he was reading a book by this guy in Texas named Jonathan Wall who had suggested that a major disaster would eventually strike that would be the straw that would break the camel's back? Wall stated that such a disaster could begin the precipitous tear in what he believed was an 'artificial veil of civility' that perilously held Western Society together. How could Clay even explain to his friends that he was reading a book that dared question the industrial and cultural foundations of the modern society?

No matter. He would be home soon in his farmhouse in Ithaca, and the world could crack open and swallow the city whole, using Texas for desert, and he would be secluded in his forest. He watched his breath form in front of his face and felt his brain congeal around this thought.

Clay decided that he should get off the road, if only to be removed from the possibility of meeting strangers that might be unpleasant. Walking on the back roads might take him several more days to get to his destination, but, in the end, his goal was to actually *arrive* at that destination, and now he figured his odds of doing so increased in direct negative proportion to the number of people he would encounter on the way. *Leave yourself a way out,* he thought, that lesson still in his mind. *Don't get trapped!*

He walked another mile past the hamlet, then veered to his right to cut through a wooded greenbelt. As he did so, the cold wind began to blow more forcefully, and darkness fell around him like a cloak. He crossed over the northbound access road and headed into some woods that ran alongside the road.

He began to shiver. He wasn't a survivalist by any stretch of the imagination, but he did know a few things he'd picked up here and there by watching survival shows on the Discovery Channel. He suddenly found himself thankful for those long hours he'd spent sitting in front of the television after Cheryl and the girls had died. He had never been out in the wilderness much, but he had imagined it happening, and he thought that this was half the battle.

In the backpack, he still had the rolled up woolen blanket that Veronica had stuffed in there, and the Mylar survival blanket, folded tight into a small square, still in its plastic wrap, was safely stowed in the side pocket of his pants.

His coat was supposed to be rain proof, and his boots were excellent for hiking. They should keep his feet dry, even if the weather did turn bad. He sent up a little thank you to the heavens for bringing the strange confluence of events to this point. He was truly out in the wilderness now, and he felt ready to face whatever came.

After another thirty minutes of walking northward and away from the highway, the darkness deepened as the heavy clouds dropped down and became fog. No light made itself available to assist him in his efforts to navigate the woods. He stopped, and reaching into his backpack he pulled out the small flashlight Veronica had thought to pack for him. He was so very grateful to have met her and to have talked with her. He made a mental note to send her a letter or postcard upon reaching home, to thank her for her kindness, and now—for likely saving his life.

* * * *

The woods have been frightful for millennia. When Hawthorne wrote, he made them the seat of mysterious evil. Children's fairy tales often take the protagonists deep into the forest to teach them a moral lesson in goodness. Thoreau went into the woods to redeem them, but he was only a stone's throw from civilization and had a cleaning woman come round once a week to do his laundry. Now, as Clay walked deeper into the dark of the forest, he thought through the cold in his feet and the chill on his face that the forest could frighten as well as comfort. He held onto this thought as the cold made his thinking disjointed and his actions more mechanical and instinctive.

He looked around for some high ground and found some in a close growing copse of pine trees and figured that the bed of pine needles under them would make as good and comfortable a bedding as he might otherwise have concocted.

At that point, he got to work making a shelter, working mainly with scattered memories from books and television shows he'd read and seen over the last couple of years. From pine branches he built a shed roof lean-to, open to the south, covering the north wall thickly with more branches that were heavy with needles. When the lean-to roof was dense enough to block the breeze, he built another wall, this one straight up and down, about three feet from the open front of his little hut. He started with two stout branches, pounded them into the ground about four feet apart, and then wove thinner branches between them like wicker. Against this wall he leaned more greenery and branches to make it both a heat reflector and wind break should the wind shift around to the south.

Next he began digging a small trench with his hands and his pocket knife, and eventually a small scoop that he quickly carved from the wide end of a fatter branch with Veronica's knife. The trench ended up being about ten inches deep, and almost a foot across, and it ran parallel to, and within eight inches of, his heat reflector wall.

Despite the dropping temperatures, he began to sweat from the exertion, and he reminded himself not to let himself get too wet. Hypothermia was now his most immediate enemy and could start very easily were he to get damp in these temperatures. By about eight or nine o'clock, he had the trench finished, and he figured it must be in the high 30's Fahrenheit outside, and the air was damp and thick and the fog obscured anything from his view that was more than fifteen feet away. A stiff breeze began to pick up from the north as he walked around the campsite picking up rocks to fill in his trench.

He'd learned most of this method from reading the story of a survivalist (he could not recall the man's name) who had been traveling in the mountains of Turkey during a winter storm. The survivalist had nine or ten locals with him who knew the area and who constantly laughed at him and ignored his warnings when he told them that a blizzard was going to come through the mountains overnight. The survivalist built what he called a "fire bed," while the Sherpas (for lack of a better word to call them) laughed at him and called him names in their own language. The story ended with the man waking up in the morning after the blizzard and finding all of the Sherpas frozen to the ground and dead. While Clay didn't expect it to get that cold on this night, he wasn't taking any chances. It was November, and who knew what kind of storm might be heading his way.

Using the small box of matches he had put in his backpack and some lint pulled from the wool blanket, along with some dried leaves and pine needles, Clay soon had a roaring fire going in his fire bed on top of the rocks he'd spread in the trench. The fire would heat up the rocks, and eventually, when the coals were ready and spread over the whole trench, he would bury the lot again with six to eight inches of soil, pack it down, and on top of this warm ground he would make his bed.

He was pleased with himself and smiled and even laughed a little when the whole exercise of building the fire bed actually worked. As the fire crackled and snapped, causing one of the rocks to explode from the heat, Clay huddled in the wool blanket and warmed himself by the fire.

Despite the fact that he had walked a good portion of the day, he wasn't overly hungry. He'd eaten the two turkey sandwiches in Middletown, which, though it seemed to be too much at the time, served him well to get him this far. He decided to bed down with the little hunger he felt from not eating supper, saving the two remaining energy bars for tomorrow.

After covering the trench with soil, he had packed it down, stomping it with his boots, feeling the heat from his soles come up into his toes. He took off his jacket and his pants (that's what the books said to do), wrapped himself in the Mylar blanket, covered that with the woolen blanket, and then carefully placed his coat and pants over the top of that. Figuring that the more layers he had the better, he put his spare set of clothes (the set that Veronica had washed for him) on top of the whole pile to complete his heated cocoon. Twenty minutes later he was surprised by how warm he was. The night would grow colder, he was certain of that, but now he felt happy and content that he would make it through the night no matter how cold it got. If a guy can make it through a blizzard in the mountains of Turkey, surely he could make it through a gentle freeze in mid-state New York.

He closed his eyes and listened to the wind. It whistled through the treetops like a siren's song.

* * * *

He woke up during the night and didn't have any idea what hour it was. He was still comfortable enough, but it was definitely getting colder and everything around him was damp. He couldn't see in the darkness except to make out the shape of his shelter and the nearby wall of his heat reflector, but he could hear well enough. Only occasionally he would pick up the growl of a car going by on the distant highway, or the low rumble of a faraway train or truck. Once or twice he thought he heard an animal prowling around his camp, and for that reason alone he was glad he had not eaten anything for supper before lying down to sleep. The smells of his camp shouldn't attract any predators.

He lay there for what seemed like an hour in the blackness thinking about Cheryl and the girls and camping trips with them up near Saranac Lake, or that one summer that they spent a miserable, rainy week in a campground near Niagara Falls when everything went bad and he and Cheryl had quarreled incessantly. He felt the familiar pang of loss and thought through the many things he should have said to her, and what he would give for just a moment of her telling him he was wrong.

As a boy, he'd camped and fished as much as most people his age, and once, at about ten years of age, he'd accompanied his parents on what was intended to be a long hike down the Appalachian Trail. The rugged adventure part of the trip had come to an abrupt end when he had haphazardly tossed a crab apple core at a distant tree, only to have a bear cub drop out of the tree, scaring them all nearly to death. His father had bravely and calmly backed the family slowly towards the car, all the while praying aloud that the cub's mother wouldn't show up looking for her offspring. She didn't, and they spent the rest of the vacation playing "spoons" and "hearts" from the safety of a cabin overlooking the river. The cabin was close to the woods, but closer still to an old store where he'd convinced his mom and dad to take him to buy Dr. Peppers and Moon Pies. He imagined the taste of Moon Pies and wondered if they still made them.

Clay lay there in the dark and considered whether he'd already reached the extent of his camping and survival know-how. Maybe he'd blown his whole compendium of knowledge on the fire bed. He felt pretty confident that he could fish with the little survival fishing kit he'd found in the backpack (another thing for which he intended to thank Veronica), and he might be able to snare some dumb animal with his shoelaces (something else he'd learned on television), but his best bet was to find a backwoods store somewhere where he could use his ready cash to stock up on food. One fire bed did not make him *Jeremiah Johnson*. He tried to remember the plot of that movie but kept getting it mixed up with the one about Grizzly Adams.

His thoughts drifted over to his meager water supply, and he remembered that of all of the issues and categories of survival needs, water was always supposed to be the first and most important. Just as this occurred to him, he noticed that there was moisture covering the lean-to (and everything else), and he saw several places where, near the corners of the lean-to, water was dripping in constant drops. He pulled back his covers and reached into his backpack for the two empty water bottles he had stored there. *Boy is it cold!*

After setting the empty bottles to catch the drips, he decided to drink the third bottle of water completely down, since he felt sure the three bottles would fill up overnight, provided the thick, moist air didn't freeze before morning.

With all three bottles emptied and catching water, he climbed back under his covers and pressed his body down as hard as he could against the warmth radiating up from the fire bed. *What time is it?* He didn't know, and before long he was asleep again.

* * * *

Friday

Morning came and he was up just as soon as the gray of daylight replaced the black of night. He figured it to be sometime between six and seven o'clock, but he couldn't be sure. The air was clear of fog again, though the clouds were thick and threatening, and he noticed that the temperature must have turned freezing, or very near it. There was a thick frost on everything, and his water bottles had a paste of fog building on the inside. They had ceased to catch water. Of the three bottles he was able to combine them to fill two completely, with a swallow left over for breakfast. His work had netted him 32 full ounces of good drinking water. He was satisfied with that.

Everything was wet. Even his coat, pants, and his spare set of clothes were soaked completely through. He spent the next hour trying to start a fire but was unsuccessful due to the damp. Many of his now precious matches had simply crumbled as he struck them against the box, and the wooden sticks had torn along the strike side, leaving a dangerously small patch of grit. He knew there had to be a trick to starting a fire in the wet, but he had wasted half of his matches, and nothing he carried or could find would catch fire in the thick, humid air of the morning. Even the sticks of the matches wouldn't burn, and when they did, he'd held them under a piece of wool or a corner of a leaf, until they'd burned down to his fingers. *If only I knew more about survival...*

His first plan was to put on the damp clothes and hike back to the road, but, deliberating on this idea, he talked himself out of it. He'd made a decision to leave the road for a reason, and that reason was still viable. It was likely that the highway would become increasingly unsafe as time passed, and he didn't want to go back there. While he could not know what conditions were actually like back on the main highway, the logic of his original decision hadn't changed. Clive had rambled on about other, less natural, disasters, and while he was skeptical of these, they'd left an ominous feeling in the pit of his stomach. He decided that his trajectory should be away from, and not towards, other people.

Next, he decided that he would just stay put awhile, hoping that the day might clear up and that his clothes and coat and blanket would dry more as the day wore on. He shivered as he thought this. He wasn't sure how much patience he would have if, after some time, the sky and weather showed no positive changes. As he pondered his situation, and, seeking any warmth he could find, he instinctively put his hand down onto the dry earth under where his bed had been, and he felt the faint heat still radiating from the ground.

A light went on in his head, and he began to dig, first with his hands and then with his wooden scoop, until he had reached the layers of ash and burnt material left over from the fire. Pushing around in the charred remains with a stick he found some coals, still red hot, and now that oxygen was available, they were glowing— even more so every time a breeze blew by. Some of the other lumps of wood, having been starved of oxygen in the covered trench, had become perfect little pieces of charcoal.

Clay jumped to his feet and began to look around for anything... *anything...* that would burn. On the leeward side of a small hill, he found a place where leaves had swirled and had stacked up quite deep. He pushed off the upper damp layers and found drier leaves underneath. He grabbed a handful of these and rushed back to his shelter as fast as he could. Using the red coals and the dry leaves, he was finally able to kindle a fire, and, after adding successively larger pieces of twigs and branches and the charcoal from the fire bed, soon his fire burned warm enough to dry some of the firewood he'd collected. Before long he had a good and warm fire by which to dry his clothing and his blankets.

Two hours later, his clothes were dry and he was hiking again. As close as he could figure, he was going nearly due north. The weather had not gotten any better, and he was so thankful that he had been able to start a fire, feeling that perhaps he had saved his own life this morning. Whether that was true or not, it made him feel good to think it to be true. After forty-five minutes of walking among the trees, he was warming up and feeling strong, despite his lack of food.

He passed between two farms that looked to be a half mile apart and noticed that there was a minor state road running by the farms in what he hoped was a northerly direction. He revisited his internal debate about staying off the highways but rationalized that this was a little-used paved road and that it would be much safer than the highway he'd already fled. He wasn't sure he still believed in luck, but he thought he should be able to gain a mile or two quickly traveling by road and that it was less likely that he would run into troublemakers this far into the Catskills. After arguing with himself and the spirit of Clive Darling for a good five minutes, he gave in to his need for speed and started walking along the highway.

* * * *

An hour later, Clay stopped next to a pond to the east that was within sight of the roadway. In the distance, he could see what appeared to be a farm or some habitation or business — he couldn't be sure — on the far north side of the pond. The day was dark and gray enough, and he was hungry enough, so he decided to stop and fish awhile along the southern edge where the forest came up to the edge of the water. If trouble appeared or anyone was coming his way, he knew he could disappear quickly into the stand of trees. He wondered at his creeping paranoia and suspicion. What was the reason for this caution? But then he went back to what was becoming for him first principles. It made sense while hiking across strange terrain in a place where hunters or farmers might carry guns to leave himself a way out.

Clay took a few moments to rest and felt the hunger clawing at his belly. He decided to eat the two remaining energy bars, but saved a chunk from the second bar, rolling the doughy material into hard balls to use for bait. Again, he saved the metallic wrapping from the energy bars, but tore off a small section that he then shredded into smaller pieces to serve as something of an eye-catching lure to go along with his bait.

He tied one of the hooks from Veronica's fishing kit onto the small roll of fishing line, and then threaded a piece of the metallic wrapper from the food bars onto the hook. On went the little ball of energy bar, and then another piece of the metallic wrapper. Clay had no idea if this little experiment would work. The drab grayness of the day might keep the metallic paper from catching any light or the attention of any hungry fish, but it was all he could think of, so he set himself to the task.

Looking around the edge of the pond, he found a small piece of wood, about three inches long, which would serve as a float or bobber for his line. He tied this bobber about two feet up on his fishing line and then, letting out more and more of the line, he threw the hook, line, and bobber out into the pond, holding tightly to the small roll of line. Clay sat quietly for maybe ten minutes, holding the line almost breathlessly. Before long, though, the cold of the day gripped him, and his patience for holding the line grew thin, and he wrapped his end of the line around a heavy rock and stepped into the trees to lay down for a rest.

He found a good straight tree along the edge of the pond that would block him from view if anyone were to look this way from the road. He was still within sight of his line as he collapsed against the tree, tired from the exertions of the morning. The air was really starting to bite with the cold, and he felt the moisture level rising in the air, and he began to sense a wicked cold coming his way. His eyes were closed for what seemed like seconds when suddenly the air was filled with a fine mist, and he grimaced and furrowed his brow hoping that he wasn't about to get the worst of his current dreads—any combination of rain, sleet, or snow. His earlier good mood and self-satisfaction degraded along with the weather.

He closed his eyes for a moment, silently crying out for wisdom to the spirit of Clive Darling, or the gods of chance and fortune, or even the blessed God of Heaven, anyone who might hazard to hear. Receiving no response, he blasphemed the lot of them and peeked through one eye and saw that his bobber was no longer visible. Crawling to his feet in the mist, he rushed over to his line, pulled it in, and saw that he had indeed snagged a fine fish.

The little ten-inch brown trout was wiggling gamely on the ground, and Clay reached over and picked it up by its jaw, holding it out to inspect his catch. He had never even heard of anyone catching a trout on an energy bar, figuring that they usually ate flies and things that were on the top of the water. *But hey, why look a gift fish in the mouth?* He chided himself for making such a silly joke but then forgave himself because he was hungry and slightly delirious. Then he looked the fish in the mouth and removed the hook.

He knew enough to gut and scale the fish, which he did with his pocketknife on the flat rock he had used to weigh down his line. After this task was finished, he wrapped the fish in the plastic wrapping from the Mylar blanket—*You see, it makes sense to hold onto everything!* he thought—and slipped the fish into the side pocket of his pants. He'd cook it when he could get to a place where he could start a fire.

Despite the damp and cold, Clay made sure to carefully wrap up his line and put it and the little hook back into the little emergency fishing case. All of his stuff stowed again in his backpack, he washed his hands in the pond and then headed into the forest to find a place to build a fire and warm himself.

* * * *

Sometimes errors of judgment—whether from ignorance, pride, or even stupidity—pile themselves on top of each other until they are left to be catalogued and surmised only later by the people who find the bodies. Other times, men's lives are spared by luck, or chance, or divine providence, and they live to compile and analyze their errors themselves. In either case, when individuals reckon themselves lost, lacking a map, they often turn inward for the answers. They stumble forward with limited information, having finite senses and reason, and the hope that springs eternal in their breast either leads them further into, or out of, the wilderness. They attribute everything behind them to happenstance and everything before them to be subjects for their cunning and skill. And, all the time, the world spins on. We, of all people, can forgive honest strivers their mistakes and blunders, but nature and reality are often less forgiving. Some mistakes you only get to make once, and most of us are too limited to know exactly which of our own errors might turn out to be fatal.

* * * *

The ground Clay traversed grew increasingly rugged, and the fine mist turned first to tiny sleet pellets, and then into snow as he trekked through the forest. He was looking for something—he knew not what—but some kind of natural shelter of rocks or trees wherein he could hide from the wind and snow. He didn't like his chances of building another lean-to and fire bed in this weather, and he knew he felt better and warmer when he walked, so head and face down he trudged into the forest looking up now and then to see if his place of rest had been found.

All of this time, Clay had thought he was walking north, but he was actually walking east-northeast—away from his goal, and deeper into the forest. The snow started to stick and his thoughts stuck together too, but he had a fresh fish in his pocket and water in his backpack, and he believed that all he needed was shelter in order to find his happiness again.

A couple more miles and he crossed a snow covered road of some sort. *Small, probably a logging road or a fire road*, he thought. It didn't seem to head anywhere better than where he already was. He guessed (wrongly) that the road headed back west so he just crossed over it and kept walking back into the forest on the other side, maintaining what he thought was his northerly route. After a while, walking as straight as he could manage in the conditions, the wind died down and the flakes turned into the big wet kind. The Inuit have a name for this kind of snow, but Clay didn't.

The whole country began to look beautiful and peaceful to him, and he paused for a moment to look at it more closely. The hills rose around him, more sharply here, and he marveled at the charms of the place. He recalled, very vividly, a memory of the distinctive and poignant quiet he had known in the winter, in the woods, in Ithaca. Cheryl had been at his side as they watched the flakes fall and one caught on her nose as he bent forward to kiss it off. Now, Clay looked out over the countryside and saw the snow settling in the branches in their beautiful crystalline purity and grew lost in the moment even as God looking down from his heavens would have seen him lost in the white of the world.

He saw a remarkable hill a hundred yards to his right, and it struck him that this might be just what he was looking for. As he got closer, he made out at the top of the hill some huge rocks and boulders, and he ran toward it and shouted into the sky. He skipped most of the way with his hands thrust into the air in victory, like Rocky ascending the steps of the Philadelphia Art Museum.

Coming up to the low hill, he climbed it quickly and confidently and found a small, somewhat sheltered area behind a large rock. He clumsily attempted to cross himself in celebration—not even knowing why or what that genuflection really meant. He wasn't religious, but if he got through this and found his way home, he promised to praise Clive and Veronica and all of the other gods for the rest of his life.

He rested for a few minutes, tasting the cold with his tongue and embracing the vitality brought on by adrenaline and the chill now bracing his back, then he pulled off his backpack and set himself the task of trying to start a fire. He gathered together some twigs and a few scattered needles and leaves and piled them along the base of the rock. Then he pulled off some lint from his wool blanket, just as he had done the previous night, and confidently arranged everything in order so that all would be at hand when it was needed. He fished the matches out of the pack, noting that he only had seven or eight left. "This ought to be easy," he said to himself aloud and immediately regretted it. Though he was confident after the previous successes that all should go well for him again, he'd already learned not to take that success for granted.

Striking the first match, he had barely touched it to the small roll of wool fibers when the breeze, swirling around the rock, blew the match out. Clay cursed, and then tried again. This time the match blew out immediately, never even reaching full flame before it was snuffed out by the wind. Clay turned his back from the direction he thought the wind was coming and struck the third match only to have it blow out when a stiff, frigid blast snuffed the flame again.

He never started the fire. His hands were too cold to fully cup around the flame and his fingers too stiff to do anything more than the perfunctory motions of striking. He tried every possible combination of wind blocks with the remaining matches, but each, in turn, was blown out by the wind. Clay slumped back against the rock, cursed loudly once again, then huddled into himself trying to think of what to do next. His stomach ached in response to his hunger and his mind was muddled by the cold.

He went through his options. Back to the forest road... but where did it lead? That road seemed (to him) to be heading in the wrong direction, and what if it just went on interminably into the forest preserve? There was no "pro" except that it was a road and that the walking might be easier. *Look for another answer.* Back the way he came? All the way back to the pond? There was a house or something there! But what were the chances he could find his way back? He looked over the low rocks in front of him and couldn't even see the footprints that had followed him the last few yards up the hill. He'd come miles, and if he did find his way back (which was doubtful), who says that he'd find any help there? Besides, Clive had infected Clay with an onset of paranoia, and in his cold and cloudy thinking he figured he'd just as likely find trouble going backward as forward. Keep walking? That seemed to him to have the greatest promise. The geography was getting more rugged, which meant he could find a good shelter or a cave. To his thinking, he might find a home or cabin or safety and warmth by accident walking towards home and Ithaca as easily as he would find it going in any other direction.

Climbing back down from the hill, he was a much different man than the victorious one who had taken it by infantry charge only minutes earlier, and he was met with the enormity of his defeat upon clearing the base of the hill by a frozen gale of snow and cold that caught his breath away with its intensity. For the first time the words formed in his brain, and the reality of it crystallized before him. *I might die.*

The next few hours were away and beyond all that Clay had ever imagined a blizzard could be, and lightly clothed and almost past shivering, he struggled forward against the wind and piercing snow, step by frozen step. His mind was not functioning properly, and he heard voices around him but could not find the strength to search for them. He heard Clive say "Nor'easter," but some part of his mind knew that Clive had never said "Nor'easter" to him, and that Clive was somewhere in Nova Scotia drinking cocoa by a hot fire. He heard Veronica lecturing him about fleeing and cowardice, and he knew that, too, had not happened, but in his mind the manifestation of this lecture was as certain as the blizzard, and crueler and infinitely angrier. He heard Cheryl, but could not make out her words, and his mind visited Jack London's books and Andy Taylor's Mayberry, and tales of political intrigue and philosophies of the imminence of death. His mind seemed to swirl out of control and rise up from his being and surround him on every side.

He did not know, and had no way to figure, how long he had been walking, and he began to keep time by how far down he still had feeling in his legs, and how much of his face and hands still reacted to stimuli from his brain. Still, he kept struggling forward. Once, he discovered that the thing that always seemed to happen in the books about blizzards or climbers on Mt. Everest was actually true. Without knowing how he had gotten there, he was lying down. He began to feel warmer and sleep started to steal through him. His mind was of two parts—the one side against the other— arguing in his head that he should both go to sleep and get the hell up and start walking. The dreamlike state that was stealing upon him made everything light and beautiful even as the small voice in his head screamed that his body was shutting down and that if he went to sleep he would never wake up.

Struggling to his feet was like pressing against frigid death, and he noticed through the snow that the day had grown darker and that night was falling. How long had he lain there in the snow? *Doesn't matter now, keep walking or die*, the man with the red beard on the bike had said. Dusk and then night fell like a weight, and his mind started to slip in step with his feet, and coming upon a particularly steep decline, he tumbled forward, rolling head over heels down a slope, where he came to rest against something that his brain had trouble identifying. Looking up to the sky and darkness, he saw in what may have been a single, blue shaft of moonbeam what seemed like an infinite regress of netting. Was it the bridge? No, it was lighter in texture, in weight, and it held him as he leaned against it. Not cables, but what? Chain-link. Rising into the heavens and curving out over his head in a series of barbed-wire overhangs. Chain-link, and a sign hanging on it. It took him a few seconds to realize that he had stumbled into a fence and that maybe he was saved.

Crawling to his deadened and icy feet with the help of the chain-link savior, he got himself upright and tried to read the sign but could not manage it through the snow and ice and dark. He tossed his backpack to the ground and found that he had not the dexterity to open it with his frozen hands so he managed it with his teeth and then reached in and took hold of his flashlight in his paw of a hand, and, struggling to get it to come on, he finally achieved it and shone the bright light at the sign...

STAY AWAY!
Military Facility
Stay 500 Yards From This Fence!
Trespassers May Be Shot

He looked again and saw that the fence was topped with loops of razor wire, and looking around now with an increase in attention born of adrenaline and fear and the possibility of salvation, he noticed that there was no light in any direction. There was only the faint gray-blue light that snow gives off when there is some moon to be seen. He could not see the moon and he could barely see at all. There! Maybe he imagined it— in the distance the outline of a building maybe a hundred yards away inside the fence. *Something institutional.*

He started to stumble down the fence line and tried to shout but found it difficult. After fifty yards or so he came across another sign that repeated the warnings and the threats of death and worse if he did not stay five-hundred yards from the fence. Another fifty yards and he came upon a section of fence that had obviously been demolished by a succession of falling trees—damage from Sandy or maybe the Nor'easter, if that is what this was.

Disregarding the warnings, because being shot, at this point, seemed to him like a deliverance, he stumbled through the opening in the wrecked fence provided by the toppled trees, and steadying himself against one of these trees, he bowed his head, trying to gather together the strength to make it to the building he could now see in the distance.

Don't get trapped! His father called to him through the cold. He squinted and looked into the shadows. How could he consider, even in this moment of delusion, crippled by fear and terror, a suggestion to turn back? The irony. Those who would find the body would write down in their notebooks that their investigation had shown he had eschewed the salvation of one

prison while fleeing from another. He was hysterical in his panic
for his life.

Adrenaline and hope and fear will only get you so far, but
together these forces were enough to get him across the battlefield
of blowing snow and frigid winds, and when he blinked again he
was huddled up against the building and struggling to clear his brain
enough to think of what to do now. His victories had come in
steps. First he had made it to a fence he did not know was there.
From there, he had made it to a threshold in the fence that he
could not have even imagined would be there. Now he had made
it to the building. Could he find an entrance? Blind luck had
gotten him this far, why give up on it now?

He placed his left hand against the building, and as he
struggled forward, he kept his frozen fingers in contact with the
structure so that his mind wouldn't forget where he was and would
remind him that warmth and salvation were somewhere within that
wall. Struggling through drifts and the swirling snow, he collapsed
twice, but will and the touch of the wall kept him going as he
resumed his trudging. After a few minutes, he noticed a break in
the endless expanse, and hurried to the breech as best as he was
able. He fell forward and flung himself into an enclosure of heavy
cinder blocks and came face to face with an unmarked steel door,
painted black—all but for a window placed 2/3 up its height.

He was out of the wind and snow now, and the blessed relief
washed over him for a few seconds. Hope began to spark, ever so
lightly in his breast, and he shouted out towards the window, not
knowing what he said. The window was made of glass, thick and
foreboding, crisscrossed with chicken wire and probably shatter
proof. *Is this a prison?*

He shouted again and banged on the glass with his hands, and
then screamed even louder with the pain that shot through him into
his brain from the impact of his frozen hands on the glass. "HELP
ME!" he screamed again and again, as tears, unbidden, began to fall
down his face.

The hope that had burned brightly for a mere moment began
to dim again after several minutes of banging and screaming. His
head slipped down towards his chest, and he noticed for the first
time, incongruently, that he now had a beard. He hadn't shaved in
a week. *Had it been a week?* He noticed because his tears and
snow and ice had frozen into it. He closed his eyes. He was under
shelter and out of the worst of the weather, but it was well below

freezing, and again the specter of death seemed to darken his thoughts. He thought about praying but gave up on the idea. *Why start now?* He opened his eyes again and looked up, and he saw a light fixture in the ceiling of the entranceway. He looked at it, and as he did, the thoughts only murkily working their way through his brain, he knew he was going to die, but he hoped his last hope that that singular light would come on... and when he did—or as he did—inconceivably, the light blinked on.

CHAPTER 6

Clay pounded on the door, screaming. With his face frozen, his shouts sounded mostly incoherent, even to himself. *Somebody here? Somebody hear me!* The meaty side of his fist felt dead as it landed with cold steel thuds. He gasped for air. Ceasing his struggles for a moment, he leaned on the door, catching his breath. *It is so cold. My being is cold.* His thoughts felt like gel in his skull.

There was a small sign next to the door that he missed before but now, with the light, he could see it. It was written in what looked like Russian. *Russian?* He looked again. *Really?* Really. There it was. It was unmistakable. There were letters that seemed to be backwards, and others that were clearly not English. *Brain freeze.* People suffering from hypothermia often report confusion in their thinking. That *has* to be it. He blinked and tried to refocus. *What was he doing? Oh, yeah.*

He returned to the futile pain of pounding his fists on the door. He kicked it with his boots, feeling the dead vibrations of the cold shimmer through his leg. He screamed as loud as he could and kept screaming and kicking until, from somewhere—some interminable distance away—he thought he heard a faint sound. *Shussle. Click.* There it was again. *Shussle... Click.*

The sound grew closer. It grew closer still. He could hear it through his own pounding and the kicking but the command from his brain to cease his protests had not yet reached the rest of his body. Seconds later, he saw light through the window and watched an inner door open into the small vestibule behind the window. He heard a faint, unrecognizable noise, and then a face appeared at the small, square opening, looking out at him. The face stared at him awhile, squinting its eyes and shaking its head. No voice could be heard, but he could tell from the round and exaggerated syllables the face made with its mouth that it was shouting, "Go away!"

Clay pleaded to the face. It was a man's face, and a man should have compassion, shouldn't he? His thoughts marched through the muck of his mind before spilling out of his mouth in his cold and frozen language. "Hypothermia," his tongue spat out. Somewhere in his brain he thought that this should be enough, but he forced his face to form more words. "C'mon! Dying! Need Help! Nowhere... to... go. Can't go! Need to warm up, that's all. Don't leave me out here, man!" He didn't know if the words were intelligible or not. He didn't know if they could be heard, but this is what his brain told him he was saying.

The face of the man in the window refused. It shouted back, and Clay could now hear a voice, although the sound was muffled and distant. "This is a secure facility! No one is allowed in here. You *need* to go away! You can be arrested or shot. Just go away!"

Clay laughed. He was hysterical. "Arrest me then! Or shoot me," he shouted, laughing heartily through his weakened state. He hoped that the face could hear him. He had to will himself to concentrate. "Arrest me! Please." Then his voice dropped to a whisper, and he leaned his head on the glass. "I'm dying. I'm as good as dead anyway."

That's it, he thought. *I'll just die right here.* Yelling again, he made his closing plea. "If you don't let me in, I'll just die right here in the doorway. Then you'll have to deal with my body in the morning!" Each word was exaggerated in elongated, shallow syllables. "If you don't open up right now, I am going to lie down here and... I'll die, man. I'll just go to sleep..."

As he said those words he felt a bone-aching tiredness wash over him like he had never felt before. Sleep. He looked at the face in the window, and a Whitman quote streamed forth out of him before he could even think of why he remembered it: "I will show that nothing can happen more beautiful than death." He shouted the line at the face in the window and the face looked back, as if it was considering how beautiful death might be, how lovely it would be to see it. Then the face dropped out of the window and disappeared.

Clay felt his whole body slump and suddenly recognized the tension that had gripped him while he had been pleading for his life. He strained his eyes in the mix of dark and light and shadow, looking around for the best place to lie down and die. Going painfully to one knee on the frozen concrete, he was just about to sink into the snow when there was a rattle of keys at the door. The lock turned and the door slowly opened. Clay turned to look behind him but was instantly blinded by the light as he stood to his feet. He heard the voice that had just been shouting from behind the door.

"Get in here. Quickly."

* * * *

"Thank you," Clay muttered, stumbling through the doorway before the body of the man at the doorway. "Thank you."

"Listen, pal," the man said, dipping his head in an attempt to look Clay in the eye. "I don't know what you're doing out in this mess, and I really don't care. Don't ask me for anything, don't ask any questions, and only speak when you're spoken to. You got it? I can get in big trouble for letting you in here. You got any weapons?"

"No."

"You have any warrants?"

"Any what?"

"Warrants. You wanted for anything?"

"Ummm. No, sir. Nothing I know of."

"Don't be cute. You do or you don't."

"No. I don't."

"Well, that's good. At least that's something. OK," the man said, pointing to a chair across the tiny vestibule. "Sit over there and be quiet." Clay stumbled to the chair, almost falling from the weight of his burden as the heat from the room rushed into his body. The man lifted Clay by the arm and helped him out of his backpack.

The man was tall, solidly built, and clearly not very happy. His hair was thin and wispy and brown and he spent a good deal of time trying to cover that fact, if the swirls on his head were any sign. He wore black fatigue pants and a black windbreaker with the word SECURITY printed on the back in yellow. He looked Clay up and down, then unzipped the backpack and rifled through it for a minute.

"Anything in your pockets?" the man asked, brusquely.

"A fish," Clay replied without thinking, only then remembering that he still had the brown trout in his pants pocket.

"A fish?"

"One brown trout, sir. Gutted and scaled. Possibly frozen." Silently he got permission to pull out the fish. Clay extracted the fish, still wrapped in the plastic bag.

"I won't even ask what that is all about."

The man looked at Clay from head to toe again, then did a quick and cursory pat down before shaking his head again. "A brown trout. Now I've seen everything. Ok, man, here is the deal. I've got a holding cell here by my office. You can use it for tonight, but you'll be unceremoniously kicked out of here in the morning. And I mean it. I can get you some coffee and a little bit of food. Maybe I'll cook your fish. I might even be able to dry your clothes. But you are out of here in the morning even if hell itself has frozen over, you understand?"

"Yes, sir. Out in the morning."

"Ok, then. My name is Todd, Todd Karagin, Officer Karagin, but you can just call me Todd," he said. He turned and walked back through the second door, indicating that Clay should follow him. He continued talking as he walked. "This place is a juvenile detention facility, but don't let that make you think you're in a day care. This facility is for long-term, hard-core criminals. Murderers. Rapists. That sort of thing. This ain't Oliver Twist. Some of the people in here will cut you up like you cut up that fish."

Clay tried to look around as he shuffled after Todd, but he shivered so much that his teeth ground together and his vision vibrated and was cloudy and dark.

"I am... Cl.. Cl... Clay. Sorry. I'm very... cold."

"Ok, Clay," Todd said, leading him down a small hallway before stopping to open a series of locks on a door. He motioned Clay through and Clay walked along the hallway feeling the thaw in his face as he worked his jaw to get back his feeling in it. "Here we are. In here." He felt a hand on his shoulder as Todd guided him into a lighted cell to his left. "Let's see if we can get you warmed up. We call this place 'The Tank'. It's your standard temporary holding cell. There's a heavy blanket in here and a pillow. Strip your clothes off and wrap yourself in the blanket. I'll go get you some warm clothes you can wear. I hope you don't mind prison orange."

"No...no... no, sir. I don't mind," Clay said, though something in him did mind just a little.

He looked around the cell. It had a large, thick, reinforced glass window that ran the length of the hallway, and the cell itself was approximately eight feet long on each wall. The bed was a concrete slab built into the opposite wall, and there was no sink. There was a small stainless steel toilet built low to the ground. No mirror. The mattress was a thin foam pad, covered in cloth, and stained from who knows what. On the mattress were a folded army blanket and a pillow in a clean pillow case.

"Listen, Clay," Todd said sharply, "I have to run and get you some clothes from supply. Here is the way this works. I'm not going to lock you in, but you need to know that I'm helping you out at huge risk to myself and my own future. I like my job, so until you walk back out that door, I'm God to you. I am the law and the testimony in this place." He stopped speaking for a minute, and looked at Clay shivering before him.

"You a Democrat, Clay?"

"Man," Clay shook his head, stomping his feet and shaking his hands from the cold and shivering uncontrollably, "I'm... I'm whatever you say I am until I leave here, Officer Todd."

"Just Todd. Good. The election's in four days. Could go either way, don't you think? It don't matter much to me who wins, though. We'll still be here doing our thing." His voice trailed off, causing Clay to wonder whether he might have some deeper meaning. Then the man snapped to and said, more in command than suggestion, "Alright, get out of those wet clothes and I'll go find you something dry."

"Thanks again, Todd," Clay said to the man's back as he sat on the bed and watched the word "SECURITY" in bold yellow walk out of the cell and then turn to the right, only to take an immediate left and disappear down a darkened hallway.

A split-second later, just as Clay started to clutch at his clothes and the pain in his fingers shot through with warmth, Todd re-appeared in the light, the circular orb in the ceiling making his face look ominous and shadowed. He raised his voice to call Clay from the hall, through the window. "Listen, Clay. I'm serious. There're some bad actors in here. Don't go nosing around. Stay put. Don't make me sorry I let you in."

"No problem, Todd," Clay nodded, even as he wondered why Todd felt it so necessary to stress the point.

Why so much security for children?

Clay stripped off his cold, wet clothing, and when he was naked he wrapped himself in the wool blanket. It felt good to have something against his skin that was not frozen and wet. He began to shiver again, and some of the shivers went down the whole length of his body and even hurt as his lower back shook furiously.

He sat for a moment and felt his heart pump and tried to inspect his fingers and toes for frostbite. As he did so, some faint but transient insight blinked on in his brain... *what was it? What was that thought?* His mind struggled against the cocktail mix of senses and emotions that churned inside him. Confusion, on the rocks, but with a warm radiant buzz, shaken, not stirred. He felt drowsiness and apathy and a strange sense of pain, comfort, and victory. Groggy, almost as if he had a concussion, and his brain hurt when he tried to focus too hard on one thing. He felt thrilled to be alive, but he was overwhelmed with worry and fear. Looking around again, he heard a small voice scream silently inside himself as the flash of insight clarified for him again. *This is a cell! Don't stay in here! You might be locked up, trapped, with no way out!*

He dismissed the thought as quickly as it formed. He wasn't here as a criminal or some offender. He was a guest. *Even Dad would understand that.* He pressed his fingers through his newly-grown beard. He could leave right now if he wanted to. *Can't I? Sure I can.* But he didn't want to. Not yet. He had almost died in that storm.

The room was of cinderblock construction, painted institutional white with light green trim that looked like someone had painted it in a hurry. Or maybe the workmen had painted it with their feet. That was something his dad always said when he'd done subpar work... *Did you do that with your feet?* It was sloppy in its lines and drips of paint were scattered along the edges of the floor. It made him feel claustrophobic so he moved over into the doorway and from there he took a step out into the hallway.

Across from him stood another locked doorway—like the exterior door through which Todd had brought him into the facility. The window on the door was also crisscrossed with chicken wire. The hallway adjacent, which Todd had walked down before disappearing into another set of locked doors, was dark except for some very low emergency lighting inset into the ceiling about every ten feet. The hallway was about twenty yards long. The hallway where he stood as he stepped out of his cell continued another twenty feet or so to the right, where it was bisected by another, similar door. *Was this the door he had just walked through?* He suddenly found himself disoriented. Through the glass he could see the hallway continued about twenty feet, where it terminated at a third door, from which light poured forth.

Ten feet from Clay's cell, on the left, looked to be an office, the kind you could pass right through into another part of the building. Clay listened down the hallway but heard no noise emanating from there. He had presumed (with a cloudy head and very little real information) that Todd must have disappeared into a security office, and passing through it there must be a hallway that opened into another part of the facility. Standing in the hallway, the facility reflected and multiplied eerie silence. There was no sound, save the sound of his breathing.

Standing barefoot on the highly polished floor he tried to focus his thoughts, choosing for the moment to think of warm things—the sun on his face through the bay window in the old farmhouse, Hemingway at a bullfight in Madrid eschewing the more expensive "la sombra" (shade) seats, to sit in "el sol" (the sun)... his fire bed last night... *was that just last night?* When had he seen Clive? Yesterday? *Was that yesterday? It seems like a week ago, now.* His brain hurt and confusion overwhelmed him again.

Hypothermia was funny, in an unfunny way. He could remember some things, things he didn't even try to think of, with alarming clarity, and others were all scrambled up like eggs in his brain. He heard his father saying, "You have to play the cards you are dealt, but leave yourself a way out." He tried to remember what Clive looked like. A moment later, after a struggle, he said, "Sam Elliot," but no one was around to hear it.

He walked forward, unthinking, just moving in order to create some modicum of warmth. Unconsciously he started to jog in place, but doing that made him feel precariously balanced and he feared he might slip on the shiny surface of the floor, so he stopped and just rocked back and forth, trying to use his thighs to produce some element of heat for his blood. He looked up into the window across the way, and then his eyes focused for a second and he moved forward again, looking down the hall and through the second door towards the bright light in the distance.

As his eyes focused, he noticed that the emergency lights in the hallway were a little brighter than he had first thought, and as he focused his eyes on the distant light coming through the third door there was a slight modulation in the light and Clay thought to himself that the lights overhead had blinked, but then he stood and watched the modulation and suddenly became aware of a slight electrical hum coming from a light overhead.

Some faces appeared in the window in the distance. They had been there before, but he hadn't seen them in the light. Now, as his senses returned, they came into focus and he could see, but not hear, that they were shouting and beckoning to him. His heart jumped. He felt the cold of the floor on his feet. He could not read their lips or hear their shouts, but he could see that a few of the faces seemed to be red from crying. Their hands were clawing at the window in exactly the same way that he had cried out and clawed at the window outside the facility only moments ago. This connection, though unidentified in his conscious mind, tore at his heart and soul. He blinked in incomprehension.

The people behind the glass motioned to him, and in his short-term memory he heard, conformed to the movements of their lips, his own voice screaming out for someone to hear him and save him. But, in reality, he could not hear the voices at all. He thought of the face staring out at him through the glass, and wondered if that is the way he had looked, pawing and beating on the glass to be let in. The juxtaposition of the wild gesticulations of the faces and the utter silence of the hallway was jarring, and his thoughts remained jumbled and confused.

Whoever was locked up in that distant room was motioning to him, and as he focused his eyes again a sign was held up, written crudely on paper. Clay narrowed his eyes to try to read it, and his squint blocked some of the light, but the light from behind the faces shone through the paper and he could make out some letters. It was only, maybe, forty feet to the end of the corridor, but it was through windows crisscrossed with chicken wire and his brain was still fuzzy as he struggled to solve the puzzle.

Focusing his eyes intently the chicken wire disappeared and he noticed that the sign was written in Russian. *Russian again?* He felt his knees buckle slightly and his head grew light and, shaking his head at the faces he motioned helplessly and wondered if this was another of his recent delusions. *Sorry. I don't read Russian,* he pantomimed. He tried to communicate with his eyes, but that didn't work any better. *I'm just a man on a walk... a beautiful walk out of the prison of my old life.*

Different faces appeared in the window and also made wild pleadings for help. He blinked and Cheryl appeared in his memory and was transported to the other side of the glass. He was jolted for a second, then shrugged. "Sorry, Cheryl," he gasped, surprising even himself at the words. *I can't help you.*

* * * *

Try to warm up, Clay said to himself, and began to pace back and forth down the short hallway, stepping back into his cell after a moment to sit on the bed again. Todd had told him not to snoop around. He suddenly wondered whether there might be cameras watching him, and he did his best to appear unconcerned about the faces he'd just seen down the hallway. This wasn't, in the end, all that difficult. He did not want to encourage anyone who might be looking to him as a way of escaping their own prison. He thought of Mrs. Grantham and the doll-eyed walkers that he and Clive had passed on the roadside. *I have a prison of my own that I'm busy escaping, thank you very much.*

He thought of the door that led back out into the cold blizzard, telling himself that he could leave anytime at all, and that he was perfectly free, and saying it firmly, out loud, he mostly believed it. *Isn't that what we all tell ourselves?* But he had just come within a hair's breadth of freezing to death in a blizzard the likes of which New York had never seen and the muting and silencing of his compassion was a momentary need brought on by his reason. He decided that it would be best for the moment to do precisely as Officer Todd had asked.

He did not know how long he waited. Time seemed to have disappeared since he'd begun his walk through the mountains. *Was it now Friday night? Or was it Saturday night?* He got up and paced the floor. He sat down on the edge of the bed. He looked down the hallway again, noticing signs here and there, all written in Russian. *What is this place?* Shaking his head, he turned and walked back into the cell.

He thought to squeeze out his socks so they would dry faster, so he did that to all of his clothes, ringing them into the toilet and then stretching them out on the concrete bunk. He remembered Clive's business card so he pulled it out of his pants pocket and blew on it for a second before sticking it into the zippered pocket of his pack. *The memory is a funny thing.* He was unsure of exactly what day it was, but he remembered Clive's business card.

His body and his mind slowly reconnected. If he'd been asked, he would have said that the period from his entry into the facility until now had taken hours. In actuality, it had only been minutes. As he sat on the bed and his core temperature came up, Clay suddenly became aware of a noise in the hall. Keys turning. Clay heard whistling and a moment later Todd returned with steaming hot coffee, some garish prison clothes, blue slip on shoes, and a few more blankets.

"Alrighty Clay my-boy, here're some temporary clothes and warmth for you. Be glad you aren't being in-processed into this facility permanent-like. You wouldn't like it in here." Todd set everything down on the end of the bed and handed the coffee to Clay, who took it gratefully and with copious thanks.

"Bring those over into the office when you're done getting dressed. I'll throw them in the dryer for you. Oh, and bring your fish too."

Todd turned to leave again and, as he did, Clay thanked him again profusely, but Todd just waved his hand at him dismissively. As he stepped out of the cell, Clay asked, "What is this place, Todd?"

"I told you. It is a juvenile detention facility. In layman's terms it's a juvie prison run jointly by the state of New York and the Federal Government for hard-core juvenile offenders."

"Then why are all the signs in Russian? I... I didn't stumble into Siberia did I?" Clay asked, smiling at his joke and trying his best to be polite.

Todd smiled but the smile seemed forced. "Well, Clay, generally when someone saves your life and offers to cook your fish for you it is best not to ask too many questions. That was part of our deal. This is a secure facility, after all, so let's be clear about that." He looked at Clay as if the matter was settled, slightly jutting out his chin and narrowing his eyes. Then he relaxed and added, "Listen, I figure your brain is still a little frozen from your hike and the details may be a little cloudy. Drink your coffee and put on these dry clothes and I'll talk with you in the office when you're done."

* * * *

Five minutes later, Clay walked into the office, feeling sheepish and embarrassed in the jail clothing, but refreshed nonetheless. He had the blanket around him and carried the wet clothes wrapped up in his shirt. Todd took the clothes from him and dropped them into a plastic mail basket next to his desk. Clay smiled to him and handed Todd the fish.

"Here in a minute I'll go get you some supper," Todd said, looking down at the fish, "and this will be most of it." He slid out from behind the desk. "We're shorthanded due to the storms, and our supplies are way down. Do you want another cup of coffee? We've got plenty of coffee." Clay nodded, and Todd took his cup over to the coffee maker and filled it to the top.

"You still have power, I see. Sandy didn't knock it out around here, I guess?" Clay asked, taking the coffee from Todd and nodding his thanks.

"Sandy was only the first blow, man. Power has been sketchy since she went through four or five days ago, but it's looking like this nor'easter is going to do most of this area in BIG-TIME." He really laid emphasis on those final words and Clay noticed to himself how quickly the memory of Sandy had faded. Already it was "four or five days ago" and he could relate, having lost his own sense of time in the aftermath. Todd continued, "Power's out all over the eastern seaboard and some people are saying that it might be out for a long time. Radio called it a cascading blackout, and it's more serious than it sounds. Last I heard they're shutting down the nuke plants. We're on a generator right now. As you probably saw out there, fuel was a problem even before the Nor'easter hit. Now it's near impossible to get. That's why some of the areas and hallways in this place only have emergency lighting levels right now. As is, though, we've got enough fuel for a week, maybe more if we really cut back our usage. In a serious emergency, we can get some more backup fuel from nearby, and if the stuff really hits the fan, I'm sure the National Guard would have us pretty high up on the list to get gasoline. One way or another, it looks like it's going to be a long month or so before things get back to normal."

There was that word again, Clay thought. *What is "normal"? Seriously? Was it 'normal' in the millennia before his great-grandparent's generation, or in the state that almost a quarter of the world's population still live in today, where people have no concept of readily available electrical power? No running addiction to fuel?*

Who gets to define that? He didn't say this to Todd. He simply shrugged his shoulders and sipped his coffee. It felt good to be back in his body.

"How long are they saying this storm might last?" Clay asked, hoping beyond hope that the nor'easter might blow through quickly and that he could really get back on the road in the morning.

"I don't know. It looked bad last time I checked. Could be a couple of days," Todd replied, "why? Where're you headed?"

"Up near Ithaca. I got out of the city on Wednesday." He stopped himself. "Or was it Tuesday? Man, are the days just running together for you now?" Todd nodded in agreement. "Anyway, caught a ride up yesterday, and then..."

"... then you got lost in the worst blizzard up here in modern memory? Yep," Todd grinned, "that sounds about right. You were lucky to make it anywhere out there, man. Counting Sandy and now this storm, they'll be stacking up bodies like cordwood after this is over."

"I hope not," Clay said, narrowing his eyes, uncomfortable with the word picture.

"You can bet on it," Todd said, nodding his head and indicating 'outside' with his coffee cup, "one thing I know is that in this world today, people die when things aren't running absolutely perfectly. One glitch, people die. Ninety-five degrees in Chicago for five days? They're hauling bodies to the morgue, man. The worse the disruption, the more bodies pile up."

And this we call normal? Clay thought, then took a drink of coffee and tried to change the subject. He wasn't as subtle as he might have hoped.

"What in the world are you doing with a Russian prison here, Todd?" he asked, raising his eyebrows and trying to look innocent.

"I thought we agreed you were going to practice your manners, Clay," Todd said, with a condescending smirk on his face.

"Ok, Todd. It's your *dacha*. I'm just here drinking coffee, trying to warm up."

Seeing that Clay was not at all satisfied with his evasion, Todd grimaced, took a deep breath and then offered an explanation. "There are a lot of immigrants from the former Soviet Union—you know, Mother Russia, the Ukraine, all of those old republics over there. My little wing of the prison houses juvenile prisoners from the former Soviet bloc who don't speak much English. It's as simple as that."

Clay thought the explanation sounded rehearsed. And something in the back of his mind kicked at the thought that this man still used the term "former Soviet Union." It had been so long since he had heard that term, even the maps and school textbooks rarely mentioned it at all. And now, out of nowhere, in the midst of the weirdness of his journey, he was hearing it used everywhere. He'd heard it on the television at Veronica's, then from Clive Darling in his big, expensive truck, and now from Todd. It didn't sit right, but he didn't want to irritate his host so he smiled and said, "You don't have to explain anything to me, Todd, I'm just here for the coffee... and some food?"

Todd smiled back. "Now you're talking! I'll take your clothes to the dryers and then get us some grub. Why don't you go lay down in your cell and I'll holler at you when it's all ready?"

"Can we call it my 'room' instead of my 'cell'?" Clay asked, grinning.

"Oh yeah, Clay, whatever makes you happy, bud... now you run on back to your *guest room*, and hotel manager Todd will get you some supper."

* * * *

As soon as Todd was gone from sight, and when he heard the double doors slam shut in that awful way that jail and prison doors always seem to shut, Clay walked back into his cell, lying out onto his bunk, feeling incarcerated again and thinking about closing his eyes and getting some sleep. But the coffee was doing its warm work in him and his mind was busy, though not yet working altogether right. He could still feel the disembodied faces of those young men down the hallway who cried and clawed at the door for freedom. *What was their crime?* Clay wondered.

He reached into his backpack, shuffled some things around in it, then pulled out his copy of *The Poems of C.L Richter* and looked at its clean blue cover, already familiar. The caffeine was finally starting to clear his mind somewhat and, stretching his neck to each side to relieve some of the stress, he turned to one of his poems randomly and read...

Who are they, who never loved us?
Generations gone and faded!
Seated high in freedom's ample chorus,
Heedless, broad, and died ne'er sated.
Your buildings reach up to heaven!
Streets with traffic ring,
Sacred markets sing,
Burdens hefted mixed with leaven.
We sip the cup of your greatest failings!
Tread the paved earth and polish the railings!
Sense the grave fabric you tore.
Glance sadly at great hope's dismissal,
Sublimity of your war,
On your children who grant you acquittal.
We walk now, cursed upon the earth,
And reckon not how our parents bequeathed us dearth.

He closed the book and shook his head. *Wow.* He'd been in a dark place when he wrote that. He wondered what Cheryl had thought of his glaring indictment of all of their ancestors. This distrust and dislike of modernity had been with him longer than he'd thought. Maybe he was just a Luddite anarchist, like Clive said.

He put the book back into the pack and zipped it closed.

Standing up again he considered for just a moment what it would be like to actually be locked in this cell, and then he laughed, figuring that it would feel kind of like the last six years of his life felt. Wasn't his Brooklyn apartment his most recent jail? Wasn't this what he was escaping? Back to comparing physical and metaphorical prisons again. *If only I were tired enough to fall asleep.*

He walked back out into the hallway, figuring it would be some time before Todd would return. He struggled within himself for a moment, hoping to keep from looking through the door that led down the hall to *the others.* But the window, crisscrossed with chicken wire, drew him in like a moth to flame.

The faces were still there, and when they saw him appear a struggle broke out, some pushing and shoving, and then he could see that they held up a new sign. He had to strain his eyes again, lean really close to the window and allow his eyes to get used to the extremes of dark and light.

This is not prison. Students! Help we! Dying! Starve!

Another paper was thrust against the window...

No food 1 week since Sandee. Hungered. Help we!

What? He shook his head, showing the faces that he didn't understand. *How can that be?* Todd seemed to be fed well enough. The place had emergency power. Why wouldn't they be feeding the inmates? Was it a labor problem? Had people stopped coming to work? That could certainly be true. Clay couldn't imagine anyone making it to work in the past several days.

His mind worked feverishly now as the faces once again begged him. Tear streaked faces, pleading for help. *What if they are trapped. What if they are telling the truth? Could it be?* He suddenly put his finger on something that had bothered him about the conversation with Todd. He'd never in his life heard of a prison facility for a particular people speaking a specific language. Not in America. Not in 2012. As he watched the faces he noticed that several among them seemed to be pushing the others out of the way. Those faces mouthed the word "No" and "Go" and waved him away, but in a way that was subtle, not aggressive or obvious. He couldn't decide whether they were afraid for the others, or for him, but he decided he ought to do *something.*

Clay walked back into his cell and looked around. He had a flash of inspiration and reached deep inside his backpack and pulled out the small pocket camera he'd carried with him since he left. He had intended to use it to document his trip and had made some small efforts to do so early on. One can only shoot so many pictures of downed trees, however, and he'd simply pushed the camera deep inside the pack and forgotten about it. He saw now that he had several exposures left on the digital dial and he stepped out into the hall and quickly snapped some picture of the faces in the window.

Mindful that Todd could walk through the office at any moment, Clay didn't give much thought to what he was shooting. He simply raised the camera and listened behind him as he rattled off the last of the camera's memory. He was vaguely aware that there was a scuffle in the light of the window as the youths—*were they youths?*—began pushing their way into the window. He then walked quickly back into the cell and hid the camera in the deep recesses of his backpack and turned around and sat on the bed. He was vaguely proud of himself. *If nothing else*, he thought, *I can show it to somebody when I get out of here.* Maybe some news organization would be interested in the story. He tried to fight it, but he couldn't help it—his mind drifted back to the moment when Cheryl was trapped in that car, the girls dead, their lifeless bodies ruined on the cruel pavement. No one had been there to help them. *What if these young people are trapped?*

He heard Todd return into the office, so he joined him, breathing deeply and trying to look pleased and excited at the thought of a meal.

"I cooked up your brown trout, Clay, and I didn't have any tartar sauce, but I do have the bottom scrapings from a jar of mayonnaise and an ounce or so of dill pickle relish if you want to make something of that. I also found a half a packet of Saltines and a tomato."

Clay nodded to him and said "Thanks." He wasn't sure if he could eat now that he thought there might be children starving only fifty feet away from him. He nibbled some on his fish, and he could feel Todd's eyes on him as if the guard expected him to offer some kind of critical review of the meal.

"Do you all eat pretty well here, Todd? I mean... is prison food as bad as they make it out to be?" He snapped off a piece of cracker and choked it down before taking another sip of coffee.

Todd looked at him, amused, and then shrugged, "Well, usually we do alright, but things have been a bit tight this week. What with the storm and the lack of power and the disruptions and all. We're a little low on manpower and most of our deliveries haven't made it." He rocked back in his chair, trying, and failing, to look nonchalant. "I suppose with this nor'easter, it might stretch on a little longer, but it's not like we're freezing and starving out in the blizzard like you were an hour ago."

Clay took a larger bit of the fish, and he felt his stomach growl and he felt guilty for it, but he chewed with some intensity now. Todd took a long drink of his coffee then got up to pour himself another cup. "So what's it like out there, Clay? How bad is it from what you've seen?"

Clay was happy for the diversion, and between bites of fish, filled Todd in on what he knew, at least all of the basics. He related his trip across the bridge, but left out the part about Veronica, offering only the parts that he had seen on her television. He told Todd about his ride with Clive, leaving out any details about Clive the man but sharing what he knew about the stores stripped of products, and about the gas lines, and about how the people walking on the highway seemed to be like zombies, their eyes dead like shark's eyes... doll eyes.

"They weren't zombies or undead or vampires or anything like that, they just looked like it, you know?" he said. This, he supposed, was the veil of civilization peeling back, the line of civility stretching ever thinner.

Just as Clay was finishing his story, and his fish, he heard a muffled sound coming from down the hall. THUMP. The sound seemed heavy, as if a body had been thrown against a wall or a bird had flown into a window. It was jarring. It reminded him of a tree falling in the woods in winter, after the crack, in that long, slow moment before the top slams into the snow.

THUMP.

Clay looked up at Todd, and he saw the guard's countenance fall. Fear, mixed with anger and confusion marched across the tall security officer's face, and he seemed to be frozen in place, unable to move.

"Todd? Um... What was that?" Clay asked, sitting up straighter in his chair.

THUMP. Louder. Somehow closer.

There seemed to be a loud clatter, off in the distance, like a car wreck a dozen blocks away on a foggy day in his Brooklyn neighborhood, and Clay could barely make out voices and screaming. The sounds were as if they were in a freezer or a coffin buried deep someplace and the vibrations were deeper than the clatter.

THUMP... Closer.

The last one was loud, and Todd jumped to his feet, finally motivated to action. He spun around to the cabinet behind him and pulled out a large bat, a stun gun, and a handful of handcuffs.

THUMP. Louder. The sounds of breaking glass and screams.

"Todd?"

"Get in the cell and close the door! I'll lock it behind you!"

THUMP. The sound of wood splintering.

"What is this, Todd?"

"GO! NOW! Into your cell! They're trying it! It's a jailbreak! RUN!"

Clay hopped up from his chair, his tray spilling onto the ground and the coffee, thankfully cooled, landed down the front of his bright orange prison jumper, drenching him. He sprinted down the hall, his mind reeling, and as he turned towards his cell he could hear that the inmates had breached the second door with a loud crash of what sounded like wood and steel and glass, and now voices could be heard, yelling Russian words, and there seemed to be fighting and shouts and yelps.

Todd pushed him from behind and Clay landed hard on the concrete bunk, his shoulder smashing painfully into the cinder block wall. "Gonna turn out the light and lock you in, Clay! Don't make a sound! They'll kill you, man!"

The light snapped off.

He heard the lock click into place and the keys rattle in Todd's hands and Todd's panicked footsteps as he raced back towards the office. Clay stared up at the extinguished light, and the bulb, clad in heavy metal mesh, was visible now as the element faded to black. His mind connected it with the light in the entry vestibule that had clicked on to herald his safety and salvation and he heard the door across the way splinter and complain as the weight and pain of hunger and despair and freedom crashed against it.

CHAPTER 7

For some men, the world is an autoclave. A steam engine bearing down upon them. A tumbling aerial swan dive into a lake of uncertain depth. There is no society that stands behind them, no motion to follow their leadership, no positive reviews in the daily papers. Life is merely, as Hobbes said, solitary, nasty, brutish, and short. Life for such men—for (perhaps) most men throughout history—varies little in substance from that of the animals. Cattle in their stampede, sharks in their chum-fueled frenzy, armies of driver ants with their smothering razor-sharp jaws lined in charging columns... each of these bears a striking resemblance to the worst expressions of human nature in its unbridled chaos. And in the long catalogue of such expressions, from war to neglect to terrorism, little compares to a prison riot.

Sitting in the darkness, back pressed hard against the cold concrete bunk, Clay felt a terror well up in him that he had only felt once before in his life. His mind, still addled from the sense of displacement brought on by the effects of hypothermia and shock, flashed back to that moment when he was on the phone with Cheryl after the crash. It was the only thing he could hold on to, and it was also the worst. That infinitesimal micro-second when he just absolutely knew that everything he loved had just been taken from him. That was it. That was the moment. Sheer terror. Helplessness. Fear.

The sounds of violence punctuated the air and he closed his eyes wanting to wish himself invisible amid the pandemonium of Hurricane Sandy crashing outside his cell. *What? No. This is not Hurricane Sandy. Sandy's gone. Cheryl's gone. Back in prison now.* No, this was not the hurricane. Sandy was merciful.

Now there was loud shouting—sounded like Russian—and he could clearly hear Todd, though the words were in a language he did not understand, pleading as if for his life. Clay understood the language of pleading fluently. He had practiced it and was attuned to its inflections and lexicon, the nuances of its verbiage. He had pleaded with Todd to be let in; the inmates had pleaded with him for help; and now Todd was pleading for his life. He heard a shriek amidst shouts and what could only be described as a gurgling noise as he searched through his mind for some escape route. He hadn't left himself one. He waited and held his breath.

More commotion now and the sound of upturned furniture and a turbulent ruckus as another door somewhere relented, pummeled into submission. *Maybe they'll just go.* If they would just go out the same doors Clay had come in, they could get away. The entrance vestibule was right there. The fence was down. *Is the blizzard still raging? Are they smashing in the doors to my left, or to my right? Can't tell.* His heart was pounding in his chest, and he could feel his elevated pulse in his eyelids.

And then there was silence. Blessed relief. *Are they gone?* He tried to calm his breathing and slow his heart rate and he took several deep diaphragmatic breaths trying to force himself to calm down. Panic never served anyone. He swallowed and listened and waited. Then he heard the jingle of keys. Panic. His heart racing again. *Please let it be Todd. Please let it be Todd.*

The key was in the lock now and before this fact had time to register, the reinforced wooden door to the Tank flew open and Clay was seized in the grip of a mass of humanity. There was shouting and anger, violence and the smell of unwashed bodies in the air, and he was enveloped in dark color and dragged out of the cell by his hair and his arms and feet. The lights in the hall had been extinguished and glass lay on the floor and as he was dragged down the hall his skin slid across it in dark, jagged slices. He kicked and tried to rise but he was thrown to the ground and fists and elbows began to fall on him like rainwater. Clay moved to cover his face and tasted blood in his mouth as a boot stomped his head against the cold concrete. His ribs were crushed by shadows and his feet were held down and someone stood on his arm and ground a heel in.

The beating lasted for an eternity. In reality it was only a moment but the brain fills in the spaces of such moments and the fluidity of sensory overload becomes a kind of infinite regress. The electrical impulses in his brain fired their neurons like scattershot in slow motion replay and then, as quickly as it had begun, it was over. He heard spit fly out of the shadows, felt the saliva in his beard, and there was a final kick... that was the one that hurt...

landed next to his right eye and he saw stars—not stars but fireworks, firing upwards like rockets—and he felt like he was about to lose consciousness.

Criminals.

For a moment there was silence. The storm passed along the shores and the calm was felt, and there was more Russian spewed at him, angry and vicious, but it was only the lapping of waves on the banks. He collapsed against the cold of the floor for a moment then was dragged back into his cell.

The shuffle of shadows left the room and the door closed behind them and he was left alone in darkness and pain.

* * * *

Clay laid in the dark with his eyes closed. He listened for the sound of movement but heard none. After a moment or two, convinced he was temporarily safe, he raised himself from the ground and stumbled onto the bunk. Feeling for his pack on the end of the bed, he was overwhelmed by a need to protect it. He quickly stuffed it under the bunk and draped one of the blankets over the lower end of the bed so that the pack could not easily be seen from the doorway. Then he reached inside his jumper and ran his hand along his ribs feeling the tenderness under his touch. He reached up to touch his eye and felt blood dried on his face, but couldn't seem to find any cut. The marks on his body from the glass were superficial scratches, but his jaw ached and his eye was on fire.

Having taken inventory of his body, he now leaned back onto the bunk and tried to lift his legs to lie down but was unable to manage it for long because of pain and soreness coming from his back and kidneys. Not knowing exactly why, he pushed the thin mattress off the bed onto the floor and lay down flat on the cold concrete bunk and the icy smoothness on his back and his bruises immediately started to numb the pain. He laid there for a moment, embracing the numbness.

Turning over to his side, he tried again to imagine all of this away, and, thinking clearly now for the first time in a very long time, he began to count the stupid mistakes he had made since leaving Veronica's place there in Harlem. *That,* he thought now, *was the first and biggest of them.*

* * * *

After what may have been five minutes, or an hour, or three, Clay heard the lock turn again and the light flicked on and a head looked in, then a few more.

"You alright, man?" one of the heads asked. *Hard to see faces, even with the light on.* Clay looked at them through the only eye he could open. The flood of light in his dilated pupil caused his eye to water.

"Um... no," He responded, trying to push himself up with his hands. He felt his body ache at this new demand, but he grimaced through the pain and sat up to look into the faces of his captors. The three young men all had sheepish looks on their faces, almost as if they were embarrassed. It was something in their manner. He couldn't decide exactly what it was.

They were dressed in standard prison garb, and their faces looked wan and thin. They looked hungry and they smelled of sweat, fear, and elation. The lack of depth perception caused him to see them only partially. He wasn't sure how to size them up. They looked almost familiar.

"So... ok, good," one of the faces said in a friendly and almost apologetic way, nodding toward him. He was the short, stocky one with close-cropped hair, black. He had the look of a bulldog. He was small, but muscular, with a barrel chest, despite the evident loss in weight he had suffered. His voice was surprisingly high for a man, soft-spoken, gentle, and airy. After a pause, he continued, "good that you can communicate and that you're not dead."

Clay looked up into the young men's faces and then, unconsciously, his hand rose up to his lips and examined them to make sure they were not badly split or swollen. He didn't think that he'd lost any teeth. For the most part, his mouth was fine, but as his hand withdrew it migrated to the lump above and to the right of his right eye, and he noticed the eye was closed and that the lump stuck out far enough that the skin over it seemed foreign and unconnected to his face.

"You broke my face," Clay said, trying to open his right eye unsuccessfully.

The bulldog shook his head, sadly. "Well... technically it wasn't us who broke your face," he indicated with his hand to the three young men in the room. "In fact, we tried to warn you off, or at least I did, when I saw you looking down the hallway." *That* was why the face looked familiar, Clay thought.

"You could have tried holding up a sign that said *'get out of here now'* or *'run for your life'*," Clay said, with not a little bit of hostility in his voice. He looked down at his feet and noticed that the bridge of his foot had a large, blue welt.

"We'd have gotten it far worse than you did if we tried to alert you in any way," Bulldog said. "But I did try to warn you as best as I could under the situation."

"And what was the situation?" Clay asked.

"Well, no one in that cell block has eaten anything in a week, and we were on half-rations before that," Bulldog replied, matter-of-factly. "The leaders in there decided, when they saw you walk in, that maybe you'd be of some help, but instead you took pictures. After they couldn't get you to help them, they decided to do just what they did. To be truthful, I didn't think they'd do it. But, as you can imagine, they aren't particularly... pleased... with your participation or help. Frankly," he said almost sorrowfully, "I'm surprised you aren't dead."

Clay hung his head down and felt the tightness in his neck. "I was going to show those pictures to somebody in order to get you help, you know? I came in out of the blizzard half dead myself, and was trying to figure out how best to handle it."

"Ahh, yes. Well, they couldn't have known that, I guess."

It occurred to Clay that these men—at least Bulldog here—spoke absolutely perfect English. Not a trace of any accent. Not from Russia, not even from New England. Not from anywhere. He spoke perfect accentless English.

"Anybody want to tell me what's going on here?" Clay asked, painfully arching his back and testing to see if he felt any serious organ or bone injuries. He was pretty sure he had a couple of broken ribs. Couldn't know if there was bleeding somewhere on the inside.

"Well," Bulldog said, hanging his head and shuffling his right foot against the concrete floor and pushing on the mattress, "I just told you. It seems you got caught up in a riot."

"That part I had figured... ummm.... what is your name?" Clay asked.

"I am Mikhail. This tall one here is Vladimir Nikitich and the other one by the door is Sergei Dimitrivich. You can just call us Mikail, Vladimir, and Sergei."

"Your English is impeccable," Clay responded, icily.

"Why wouldn't it be? We're Americans," Mikail shot back.

"None of this makes any sense," Clay said, continuing to feel with his hands down the length of his legs, engaging in an extended medical self-examination as they talked.

"You don't know the half of it, Comrade," Sergei sneered, looking toward Vladimir and laughing.

"Listen," Mikail interjected, "what's your name, anyway?"

Clay looked up to Mikail, straining to see anything—any light at all—through his swollen right eye.

"Clay."

"Well, listen, Clay. For the three of us, I am really sorry that this has happened to you. I know that you may not believe that, or you may not care, but it is true. I really didn't want any innocents to get caught up in what's going down here right now." As he talked, his right hand found his own rib cage, and he seemed to unconsciously press against his ribs one at a time as though he was counting them. "You're in a bad spot. So are we. None of us asked for this."

"Ok, so you're sorry," Clay said, looking Mikail in the face with his one good eye. "So, why don't you guys let me out of here and I'll just be on my way."

Mikail shook his head. "That's impossible, for two reasons. One," he held up one finger to illustrate his point, "is that there is one hellacious blizzard going on out there. No one could go anywhere even if they wanted to. Two," another finger popped up, "is because we're not in charge. In fact, we're probably the worst allies you could have right now... except, of course, for all of the other maniacs in this place."

Mikail turned and began to tap the wall with his hand, then looked back at Clay with a worried look on his face.

"It's not possible for you to understand the politics of this place, Clay. You don't even know where you are. But," he indicated 'out' by making a circular motion with his hand, "the rest of these guys are real criminals. Some of them are the worst kind of criminals. Whereas we," he indicated the three there in the room with Clay, "are *political* criminals. They think we're spies. Listen." He stopped and walked toward the cell door, looking out for a moment before poking his head back in. "Forget all of that. None of that is going to make sense to you. I just say all of that to tell you that we are not your enemies, and those guys out there are not your friends. They're rifling through the place as we speak, looking for food. That's all they can deal with right now. Todd is dead, and if they find any other guards around here, those guys will be dead, too. I'm thinking that the back to back storms basically doomed the place. I'm not sure that any of the other guards even made it out here after the Hurricane. I'm thinking Todd's been manning this place by himself. So, when no food showed up and things ran low in the cafeteria, he just decided that no one would care if we starved to death."

Clay stared for a moment, trying to take it all in. Mikail looked at Sergei and Vladimir, "Well, I think that's about it, Clay. An unnecessary chain of unfortunate events and now, shall we say, things have gone a little haywire."

Clay just looked at Mikail, not sure what to think about anything he was hearing. He slipped off the bunk onto the mattress on the ground and sat there, pulling his legs up to his chest. Mikail crouched down, looking at Clay face to face. He whispered conspiratorially, "The new bosses, those thugs out there, they sent us in here because we speak good English, which is exactly why they hate us. That is why they suspect us of being spies. They don't trust us. But they use us, you see, because our English is good. We're here to find out if you can help them. To find out what you know."

Clay shrugged, wordlessly. What could he tell them? He knew nothing. He showed as much in his face, as a way to answer.

"These young men and boys will kill you, Clay. That's a fact. They almost did it before, but we were able to stop them. So, we're supposed to find out just who you are and if you have any value to them."

Clay shook his head, slowly. Strangely, the effects of the hypothermia had worn off, but the world he'd stepped into seemed to have shifted. It was as if the beating—perhaps it was the adrenaline—had served to heighten his awareness and his thought processes were back to normal, but the world had gone sideways in the bargain. He felt like he'd walked off the edge of the earth. He believed that Mikail wanted him to tell him something but he had absolutely nothing to tell him. He was a guy who had hiked out of the city and into the mountains and seemed to have wandered into a world not of his making. The only thing he knew for sure was that his only way out of this was going to be to convince someone, somewhere, to let him leave.

"Well," he said, after some thought, "I'm Clay... I told you that. I am a hiker and a traveler that got lost in the storm. The second storm, not the first one. I was fine after the first one. I'm from upstate but I've been living in Brooklyn for the last six years. I got out of New York because of the storm, and because I just want to get home. I'm trying to get home to Ithaca. Then the nor'easter hit. I got completely turned around. I was unprepared. I made stupid decisions. Blah, blah, blah. Anyway, I stumbled into this place. One whole section of the external fence is down, by the way. That's how I got in. Anyway, I stumbled into this place about half dead and frozen and I was able to plead with that security guard named Todd to let me in to warm up and dry out. That's all that I know, but it's the truth."

"Yes," Mikail said, "well, the truth shall set you free, I suppose." He stood up and looked at the others.

Vladimir, the tall one, speaking for the first time, said, "Stumbling into this place was probably a bad deal for you. Might have been better if you died out there in the cold."

"Maybe," Clay said.

"No maybe," Vladimir said. "This place eats people. It doesn't spit them back out."

Sergei interrupted. "What Vladimir Nikitich is saying, Clay, is that you need to work with us. Think of something to give them. If they don't need you, you're dead. Right now they're probably at the cafeteria ripping it apart for packets of ketchup or rotten fruit. But they won't be down there forever."

Mikail picked up where Sergei left off, almost without missing a beat. "Just so you know, those guys aren't geniuses. They're not all idiots, but most of them are. They're in here for being sociopaths, psychopaths, and rejects, your social castaways. Warwick has those things just like any other place in the world. Maybe even more so. You ever been in jail, Clay?"

"Yeah. Nothing too serious, though. You call this place Warwick?" Clay asked.

"That's where you are. Not the prison here. The prison is *part* of Warwick. Warwick is the whole damned town."

"What do you mean the whole town?"

"Clay," Mikail continued, "Focus. What you've stumbled into is too big to get in your head, so you're just going to have to get your head into what's going on right here and right now. Everything else... you don't need to know. What you need to know is that here in a bit—maybe in an hour, maybe in five minutes—those guys that wrecked this place and killed Todd are going to come back here, and you will need to give them something. We don't have time to mess around."

"Give them something? What can I give them? I don't even know what's going on," Clay said in something approaching despair.

"If you're working for someone, Clay—CIA, some faceless government agency, a joint task force, anything like that—you'll need to tell them. That'll keep you alive. You'll have value to them then."

"But none of those things are true!"

"Do you want to live, Clay?" Mikail asked, with an intense look on his face that seemed to mask a motive that Clay was not able to discern.

"Of course."

"Then what are you *really* doing here?"

"I told you."

"You told me nothing!" Mikail shouted angrily, before thinking better of his outburst and lowering his voice, "I'm trying to help you, Clay. That's all. No one else needs to die. Who are you?"

That was it. Right there. That was the moment when Clay knew. Looking Mikail right in the face, he knew... and Mikail knew too.

"I'm just a guy who's had a very bad day. I obviously ended up in the wrong place at the wrong time. I'm just trying to get home."

Mikail nodded at the other two and they slowly moved toward the door, but before Mikail turned to leave, he knelt down and touched Clay on the shoulder, "I don't think you're going to make it home, Clay, not if I can't tell those guys something other than that you're just a tourist who stumbled into prison. That story doesn't fly, so just think about it."

With that, the three young men shuffled out of the Tank and the door closed softy behind them and Clay heard the lock turn and engage and the light clicked off bathing him once again in inky blackness.

* * * *

Outside, somewhere, the blizzard still raged, if Mikail was to be believed.

Inside, the questions swirled through Clay like a tempest in their fury. How would a prisoner have even known all of this, Clay wondered, especially one who was an outcast among outcasts? If Mikail was under suspicion as a spy, how would he have known their motives, and his own role in carrying them out?

Clay sat on the floor in the dark and went over the conversation in his mind, trying to grasp at any straw that would help him solve the puzzle in a way that would allow him to give the three visitors the benefit of the doubt. He could find none.

He didn't know what kind of place this was, this place called Warwick, but he knew that whatever storm was raging outside was nothing compared to the storm raging in here. Further, he knew that if he was so foolish as to allow himself to think for a moment that the three young men were being straight with him, he would certainly end up dead. Perhaps it was the weirdness of the encounter with others who, like him, were aliens in their own homeland, or maybe not that, exactly, since he'd experienced several such encounters over the course of the last few days. But it was something along those lines. He'd grown sensitive to the nuances of such meetings. Out of all of his uncertainties and confusions, Clay was absolutely sure of one thing...

Mikail had the keys.

These three young men were not innocent victims of circumstance, like he was. They were not "political prisoners" either. In fact, he was certain that these three were the ones really running this place.

* * * *

Saturday

He didn't know when he fell asleep, but he figured it must have been way after midnight. He was so exhausted, though, that he eventually slipped into a very deep and fitless sleep. It was the kind of sleep that only attends to a man whose waking life is falling apart. When he awoke he could not remember tossing and turning at all.

Clay's eyes (or was it "eye", singular?) opened slowly when he heard a commotion in the hallway outside his cell. He sat up in his bunk and it took him some time to get his bearings on where he was. The dull aches in his body reminded him that things had not gone well the night before and his right hand found the lump near his eye and probed it, noting that he still didn't have any feeling there at all. It was dark in the room, so he didn't know if he'd regained any sight in that eye. A thought crept into his mind and slowly formed until it joined with memory and he realized that somewhere out there, according to Mikail, the prisoners were supposed to be deciding his fate. Apparently they were in no hurry.

Along with his pains and a dull ache coming from his lower back, he felt a gnawing hunger that reminded him that he had not eaten much at all since the turkey sandwiches at the restaurant just off the highway back in another life. The little bit of fish he'd swallowed right before the riot hadn't amounted to much, and he felt the growl in his gut and the faintly pleasant tightness that reminded him of day three of a fast. *Does the condemned man get a last meal around here?* He suddenly remembered that food may not be the best topic of conversation with prisoners who have been starved for a week.

After an hour or so sitting quietly in the dark the light flipped on and he saw a face look in at him through the tiny window. With his one good eye and the crisscross of chicken wire he didn't recognize the face at all. Clay sat up on the bunk and pushed his way along it to the far wall, not knowing if this was to be another interrogation or if they were actually coming to kill him.

The lock turned and the door swung open and a face looked in at him and smiled. It was the face of a boy who looked to be about sixteen or seventeen, and then the rest of the boy came through the portal carrying a faded green plastic meal tray. The young man approached slowly, with some hint of fear on his face, and he tried to smile bravely as he handed the tray to Clay.

Clay looked down and he was startled at what he saw. For a starving people they surely ate well around here. His tray was loaded with four or five thick slices of some kind of rye bread slathered with butter. There were two hard-boiled eggs, peeled; a bowl of some kind of hot cereal grains (also slathered with butter); some sliced apples; a hunk of whitish cheese; and a mug of hot, black coffee.

"Wow," Clay said, looking over the veritable feast. "Good thing I still have my teeth."

The young boy nodded, smiled politely again, and then turned to leave.

"Wait... you," Clay sputtered, not knowing what to call the youth, "what's your name?"

"I don't speak the English," the boy said, shyly and with a very heavy Russian accent.

"Someone forgot to tell your mouth," Clay responded.

"Vasily," the boy replied, again with a very thick accent, looking over his shoulder as if he were doing something very wrong. He stepped back out into the hall, and then quickly returned back to the cell with a case of water in plastic bottles, still in the plastic wrap. The writing on the water bottles was, he assumed, in Russian.

Clay grabbed one of the bottles of water and twisted off the cap and took a long swig of water. "Where'd you get the food, Vasily? I thought you guys were all starving to death." Indeed, Vasily did look slightly thin, though not in any way approximating starvation or even some kind of malnutrition. His eyes were clear and bright, and his hair had been cut recently and he looked strong in a sinewy kind of way.

Vasily did not reply, but something in his eyes tried to communicate with Clay and he wrapped his hands nervously in his faded orange prison shirt not knowing if he wanted to flee or stay and talk.

"Are they going to kill me today, Vasily?" Clay asked, taking a bite from the toast, his good eye rolling back in pleasure at the taste of the salty, melted butter and beautifully toasted rye bread. When he looked back to Vasily, he smiled at the boy again, just waiting for a reply.

Vasily did not reply, he just nodded his head and walked back out of the cell. The lock ticked closed but this time the light was left on.

* * * *

The next two meals that day were the only other interruptions to Clay's somewhat welcomed solitude. Lunch was as bountiful as breakfast had been, though Clay could not be sure exactly what each of the dishes were or what they contained. There was a cold, sour soup that Vasily called "Okroshka" which had some green leafy vegetable, large pieces of potato, and chunks of fish. It was delicious. There was actually a small dab of some white caviar with small crackers which he did not enjoy, but then there was a heavy pancake topped liberally with butter and sour cream which was perfect. There was more coffee to drink, along with a shot of vodka. The only things he left on his tray after lunch was the caviar and the vodka. He laughed to himself as he looked at the un-tasted vodka. *Last time I had vodka, I got thrown in jail!*

Supper was a bowl of what looked like beet soup with ample pieces of meat (he could not tell if it was beef or venison or some other meat) and heavy dollops of sour cream on top. This was served with thick chunks of black barley bread with butter and a couple of sliced cucumbers.

"Maybe they're getting me ready for my execution," he told Vasily, "fattening me up so they can eat me." The boy, who either did not understand or did not appreciate gallows humor, simply paused at the door as if to say something, but decided better of it and then disappeared again.

He was left alone without visitors for a few hours after his supper, and then, about the time that he figured it might be starting to get dark outside, he heard a knock at the door and recognized the tall figure of Vladimir peering in. *Why knock?*

Mikail led the procession into the cell and Vladimir and Sergei came in behind him. Both leaned up against the walls with arms crossed affecting a youthful position of arrogance and unearned power, like thugs who had just taken over the playground. It had become evident to Clay that Mikail was the man in charge and it didn't seem that he minded letting Clay know that either.

"Good evening, Clay," Mikail said with a cold smile of mock friendliness.

"Hello," Clay responded unemotionally. It was apparent to him that the façade of good cop had been dropped. Mikail had apparently decided to now deal with him as who he really was, whatever that could be. With the better lighting and some minimal use of his right eye, Clay now noticed that Mikail was probably in his early 20's, older than Clay had originally thought, though youthful enough to pass for an older teenager. Sergei and Vladimir did not look to have reached their 20th year yet and were maybe in their late teens.

"I hope you have enjoyed the food. Things improved for us radically once we'd taken the town," Mikail said, with just a hint of pride.

"So there is a Russian town around here?" Clay asked.

The three young men started to laugh, Mikail laughing the hardest, and it took a moment for him to return to his more serious demeanor.

"Yes, Clay, there is a Russian town around here. Right here in America. Warwick, as we informed you earlier. And like a wick draws up oil, so Warwick has drawn you into itself. It is our town, and now we run it."

"Congratulations. Ok, so what does that have to do with me? Why am I still here? Why are you still acting like I should know something I don't? Why was I beaten? What comes next?"

"Easy, Clay" Mikail said, "You are still here because we have not yet decided what to do with you. You are a hostage. The rest can wait for now."

"Do I get a phone call?" Clay asked sarcastically.

"Maybe you could if the phones were working, or if anyone else in the tri-state area had electricity. But..." Mikail paused, taking a deep breath. As he did so, Clay could sense the bravado drain out of him, replaced by a level of stress and weight that the young man was not entirely used to. *The crown weighs heavy on the head of a king.*

"But," Mikail continued, "it seems that the fortuitous duet of storms that has plunged this part of America into utter darkness, has had—is having—some serious effects. We were able to take this prison—and all of Warwick—because the guards and many of the employees either couldn't make it here to work, or chose not to come in for some selfish reason of their own. As we mentioned last night, the prison didn't even have a ghost staff on duty when we took over. The town fell just as easily."

"I don't know Warwick, and I don't know Russian, and I don't know you, and I don't have any idea what any of this is all about, Mikail," Clay stated, frustrated and starting to get angry.

"We're pretty sure that you are telling the truth, Clay. Unhappily, whether you knew it or not, whether you were a spy or not, whether we took over the prison or not, you probably were not going to make it out of here alive," Mikail said in a matter-of-fact tone. He showed that he was not particularly concerned one way or another with what Clay thought about what he was saying. "You see, you've stumbled into a very secret compound, Clay. Once you got into this building, you were not getting out alive. This place doesn't exist. Warwick doesn't exist. As of last night, man, you don't exist."

"What is all of this, then, Mikail? Why are you telling me any of this? Do you think that you are some movie villain, some brilliant psychopath who has a soundtrack playing everywhere he goes and likes to talk his victims to death? Why not just do whatever it is you're going to do?" Clay asked.

"We've come to take you to a meeting, Clay," Mikail said, smiling. "We're waiting on word that a 'high value target'—is that what you people like to say?—has been captured, then we're going to have a little town meeting in the gymnasium. Nothing so sinister as you imagine. We're just filling time, being neighborly. I am glad you liked the food."

As Mikail finished talking, Clay saw another young man enter and some words were shared between him and Mikail, and then the young man exited again without having looked at Clay at all.

"Time to go to the meeting, Clay, are you ready?" Mikail asked, smiling.

"What do you want me to say, Mikail?"

"You don't need to say anything. Just put your hands behind your back. We're going to take a walk." Mikail pulled out a set of handcuffs and before Clay could even think of some plan to fight or escape or shout, the handcuffs were clamped on to his wrists behind his back, and he was gently pushed toward the door. Mikail and Sergei walked before him, Vladimir walked next to and somewhat behind him, holding him lightly by the handcuffs.

The first thing Clay noticed was that the door to the hallway down to the cell clusters, the hallway down which he had first seen the prisoners, was completely intact. There was no damage to it at all. In fact, as he walked toward the office and followed Sergei into it, he saw no damage anywhere. No wood particles, no pieces of glass, no blood. There wasn't a single clue that there had ever been a riot. Of course, he thought, he'd only heard it. He hadn't seen any of it.

Rounding the corner into the security office, as soon as Sergei and Mikail had moved to the right and cleared from his vision he saw, sitting at his desk, completely unmarred, unbeaten, and fully alive... Officer Todd Karagin. The man smiled like the cat that ate the canary, the smile of the magician who was savoring his lifelong best reveal.

"Good morning, Clay," Todd said with a wink in his voice, if not exactly in his eye. "Good to see you. Welcome to the Charm School."

CHAPTER 8

Never, in the long history of humankind, at least since Plato wrote of The Cave, had a man appeared so surprised and confused as Clayton Richter did in that moment. He stood in the prison office, handcuffed, before the man that had, he had thought until this very moment, died in an effort to save him. *And now it turns out to be a con? But... why the charade?* Clay wondered.

For his part, Officer Todd was, for the moment, enjoying the surprise. He was acting like he'd just won a prize fight. He stood up and cracked his knuckles, and sucked his wind in and did one of those shadow-boxing dances, before raising his arms in mock triumph. "What's the matter, Clay? Cat got your tongue?"

If Clay had been a bit more clever and if this new shock hadn't stolen his breath, he might have replied, "Yes, Schrodinger's cat," and while these Russians tried to figure out what he meant by that, he might have rushed headlong into the officer or straight through the office, down the hall, trying to find a door, *anything,* any way that might lead to *out.* But none of that happened, because he was surrounded by captors, deep inside a locked prison and sometimes cowardice and fear are the things that keep endangered men from engaging in heroic stupidity.

As it was, he stood there like someone about to be administered a test he knew he'd flunk. No. It was worse... It was that he felt so overcome by a sense of helplessness and disgust that his knees buckled slightly and he turned pale. *Too many weird things. Too much to handle. Best to just observe my right to remain silent.* He caught his balance with a shuffle of his feet and then straightened, but he didn't answer.

Todd reveled in the obvious reaction. Clay wasn't sure whether the man couldn't, or wouldn't, wipe the smile from his face, but he knew instinctively that there was a difference. The officer reached down and snapped the black holster on a service pistol, patting the gun with his right hand and winking at Clay as he saw Clay trying to remember whether he'd been armed when he first met him.

"My real name is Fedya Leonivitch Karaganov," the officer said. "My friends call me Teodor, or just Todd. You are in Warwick, but I guess you know that already. It is the place of our birth. It will be the place of your death. We call it Novgorod among ourselves. Perhaps you'll get to see some more of our little town before your short visit with us comes to a close." He smiled at this, pleased with himself, and Clay wondered why. Then he leaned over Clay and made a sweeping gesture with his arm. It was the kind of gesture that you make when you make an obvious bow, like that one the servant makes before the throne. Todd made *that* kind of gesture, then he stood up and said in his best mock British, "And might you have any bags, Guv'nuh."

Clay looked at him and all of the throbbing pain and discomfort from the recent beating intensified and he could feel his broken ribs expand and strain with his breath, and as a man he just wanted to punch Todd in the face. But, he didn't. He was still processing the fact that Todd was not dead and here the man was before him, and in the seriousness of the moment and with all that had happened, Todd was playing the clown as if life and love and hate and tragedy and comedy were all the same thing and that there was no proper place for each.

"And might you have any bags in yuh guest quarters, sir, or will you just be traveling with what's on your person? Have we advised you of our check out policy?" Somewhere in that last sentence he had lost the accent, probably about the word "sir."

Clay just stared. He didn't know what to think. Was this just Todd's weirdly aggressive finale in acting out a too-scripted end to the little production they'd just so obviously put on for his benefit? Or was it an actual, honest-to-goodness threat.

Clay looked at the other men in the room and noticed that none of them carried weapons or made stupid jokes. He wondered now if he had been wrong in his assessment that Mikail was in charge, and Mikail seemed to notice his doubt. He'd been standing to the side, watching, like the others, for Clay's reaction, but now he stepped forward into the center of the men. "Enough, Todd," Mikail said sharply. He barked out what sounded more like an order than a question. "Has Volkhov been captured?"

"He's being brought to the gymnasium as we speak. They found him hiding like a coward in his basement. Everyone else is being assembled according to your instructions. We can go whenever you're ready." Mikail looked around the room, then looked at Todd, then at Clay, and motioned with his hand toward the hallway.

* * * *

Todd took Vladimir's place escorting the hostage, and the whole entourage walked through the office, past an unlocked door, then moved into a long hallway that was dark and only faintly lit by the emergency lighting recessed in the ceiling. As they passed under evenly spaced orbs of light they went into and out of the light and the darkness in regular succession, occasionally stopping or slowing to open doors or turn down hallways as they wound through the maze of the prison. Clay found himself, for no apparent reason, beginning to shuffle his feet, as though he had leg irons. *Dead man walking,* he thought. It was an eerie and frightening feeling and he could not help thinking that he was a condemned man, walking to his execution.

The others, the youths, were practically stoic in their quiet, as though they were going over something in their minds, mulling some decision. Only Todd seemed unable to stand the silence. He nervously fidgeted with his hand on Clay's arm before he began speaking a little too boisterously. "You're probably a little freaked out right now, aren't you? That's OK. I would be, too. Imagine how I felt, for example, when you showed up at our door in that storm. We'd already been planning our little takeover for a long time when you showed up, you see. And here you came, just in the nick of time."

Clay heard the implication but hadn't yet figured out whether they had come to believe him. He turned his head to look at Todd for some clue, but he couldn't make out the guard's features in the dark with only one good eye.

Todd gave him a clue. "I was pretty sure that you were a spy sent by American intelligence. It was just a matter of deciding which outfit you were with."

Clay decided to press his case, but cautiously. "I was with me," he retorted blandly. "Only me."

"Yes, maybe. But how could we have known that? A man who takes pictures... he could be anyone, couldn't he? And besides, it didn't matter. It's not like you're innocent, Clay. The sign did say you'd be shot if you didn't stay five hundred feet away. I even told you that myself, and you agreed. You even asked for it! Remember? Either way, of course— "

"The pictures were innocent, a stupid mistake, and I was *dying*," Clay intoned.

"Well, you still are, Clay," Todd shot back, laughing at his own wit. "I guess, in the end, we *all* are, but some sooner than others." Clay buckled again, causing Todd to have to stop and shake him violently, as a warning to keep moving.

Todd went on, "Anyway, the whole world is about to go bottom-side-up and you're getting a ringside seat, at least for the opening bell... aren't you excited?" Clay looked at him. Layers of incomprehension were turning into utter confusion. The pieces of fact and truth that he thought he held were being scattered one by one. He wondered to himself if this might be, perhaps the moment when he stepped off into the abyss.

"Is there any way we can do this," Clay asked, "without the chit-chat?"

"I doubt it," Todd replied dismissively. "You see, we weren't expecting the main event until Tuesday. Didn't you say you were a Democrat, Clay? I forget... Oh yes, I remember... you said you were whatever I wanted you to be. It probably would have been better if you were CIA. I mean, you probably would have lived longer. You would have had some value then,"

Still no real comprehension.

"Anyway, Tuesday and your ringside seat... We were planning for it all to happen later, but the storms happening together as they did, well, that pushed up our plans considerably."

No comprehension.

"But then we had to take over the town, and that took a moment, so—"

"Enough, Fedya Leonivitch," Mikail snapped, and then leaned into two double doors which he'd just unlocked, revealing what in the utter darkness appeared to be a very bright line of light at the place where the two doors met and which grew larger as the doors swung outward into a courtyard where Clay saw, once the bright moonlight had washed over him, laid out in the valley, tucked in the hollow of a range of mountains that rose up and shielded it on all sides, a hamlet that for all the world seemed as if it belonged in the Caucasus Mountains.

Warwick, Russia, America.

Comprehension.

* * * *

The cold hit them like an icy frozen wave and the snow was still falling, only not as violently as before, and their boots (his shoes) crunched on the frozen snow and ice that had been trampled down by the weight of many feet.

They passed through a gate set in a heavy chain link fence like the one he'd seen when he first stumbled upon the prison, and heavy razor wire reflected the moonlight and the beams from the flashlights. Then they headed down a slight hill on a well-traveled path through the snow and eventually they were on a sidewalk that was packed hard in trampled down snow and ice and Clay had to slow a bit because his prison shoes had no traction.

Arriving at what appeared to be an old school gymnasium, Clay looked around and decided that this was exactly what this structure was. It was the only building in the hamlet that was lighted, but the snow and the moonlight gave the whole town a beautiful, blue shade and the buildings and the town folk could be seen clearly as they moved toward the gym. People were going in, chatting nervously in Russian, and Clay could see armed men—boys actually—all around the place and directing the people into the building.

Once inside, Clay saw that the gym was set up for an assembly with chairs arranged in neat rows covering the floor and there was a small stage to the left but it was dark and the deep red curtain was drawn closed. Clay glanced around and saw that the gym looked like any old American gymnasium built anytime between, say, the 1940's and 1960's, with a hardwood floor deeply worn by thousands of feet, and the smell of All-American high school sweat hanging in the air. The main difference between this gym and any other that he'd been in throughout his life was that the signs in this gym were all in Russian lettering, and the scoreboard also seemed to be sprinkled with Russian figures as well. There was an old banner hanging limply on the far wall and Clay wondered what it said. Probably something like "Go Bears! Beat the—" *who? Who would these Russians play in a basketball game? The Chinese? Latvia?*

Mikail's entourage lined up in front of the stage on a low podium as more chairs were brought in. Todd, a little too roughly, forced Clay into a seat and then sat down in the empty seat beside him. Todd seemed to be absolutely loving every minute of this bizarre pageant, as if he had waited for it all of his life.

Clay watched as hundreds of people filed in—the citizens of Warwick, he presumed—and he noticed that they were an interesting mix of young and old, mostly middle class, it seemed, and neither expensively nor shabbily dressed. There were some Asians and what looked like Arabic people among them as well. The crowd resembled what Clay would assume any small town in rural Russia might look like, though their faces showed signs of strain and worry and it was obvious that they were not used to having men with machine guns everywhere.

Clay heard a noise start from somewhere within the crowd and the noise grew outward exponentially like a wave. At first it was just a whisper and then it became a general gasp, slowly growing into loud murmuring as the back door to the gym was thrown open and a cold air rushed in along with four heavily-armed boys dressed all in black who pushed before them in chains an old man with a thick gray beard. The man had evidently been severely beaten during his 'capture.'

The man looked old and wise and his condition readily discomfited the crowd as he passed along a makeshift lane that formed in the standing room only crowd that had formed at the back of the gymnasium. The old man proceeded to walk into the crowd and the lane continued forming before him, giving off an impression of Moses parting the Red Sea by walking into it one belabored step at a time. Women put hands over their mouths to stifle gasps and men had looks of outrage on their faces, but none were brave enough or outraged enough to do anything other than gape and murmur and then slink slowly back into their seats.

The old man had trouble walking and stumbled to the ground several times as he was pushed rudely and disrespectfully from behind by the armed boys. As he fell to his knees, his head drooping low, one of the boys snatched him up roughly, pushing him forward once again until the group had joined the "leaders" at the front of the assembly. Volkhov (Clay assumed this must be the one they had called Volkhov, and it turned out that he was right) was thrust down into the empty chair next to Clay, and his head hung down so that Clay could not see his face.

A deathly silence finally overtook the crowd. The tall young man named Vladimir stood and walked forward and indicated with his hand upraised in the ancient style of the Romans that he had something to say, as if he were Cicero about to address the Assembly.

The general din in the room died down, as all eyes were turned to him.

Clay suddenly felt someone behind him, slightly at his side. He felt the person put a hand on his shoulder and lean over and whisper into his ear. "I am to be your interpreter. I am called Alyona," He tried to turn his head to see who it was and then realized to his surprise that it was a young woman who was maybe eighteen years of age. She, too, turned her face, so that she could look him in the eye, and he saw that she had the slightest smile and sadness in her eyes.

Vladimir began speaking. Alyona translated into Clay's ear as quickly as Vladimir spoke. She spoke English well, but not perfectly, and this accent for the first time gave Clay the impression of Vladimir's, and even Mikail's, *Russian-ness*, which was something they had lacked in his mind until now.

"As most of you know, or have heard, the town of Warwick is now in our hands. You may not believe it is so, but we are sorry for any trouble that this necessary action has caused you and your families. It was something that had to be done. Comrade Mikail Mikailivitch Brekhunov has assumed command of this town—if it may be called a town—and has graciously organized this meeting to inform you of the situation and the details of what must soon come to pass. I will endeavor to be brief.

"This place—which the Americans call Warwick—is not a 'town' at all, though you may think that it is because you have lived in it all of your lives. It is a prison, and a place of slavery, owned and operated by billionaire capitalists on American soil. It is the Dachau of the American Experience and when we write its history, as we shall, the thousands upon thousands of human deaths will be catalogued for the rest of the world to know. The people who live here did not choose to be born here, did not invite or approve of their own slavery, and have committed no crimes against either America or Russia.

"Most here may not even know that this town—this spy factory we ourselves call Novgorod—has not been a part of the federal government of the United States since 1992. To the contrary, after the so-called 'collapse' of the Soviet Union, the American government, ashamed of what it had done to thousands of free U.S. citizens born on its soil, desired to shut this place down and sweep their crimes under a rug. Those who lived here twenty years ago may remember that time. Even today we call it "the Great Confusion." If the American government plan had been completed in 1992, most of you would have either been killed or deported to Russia, a foreign country to you, where you were not born. Those sent to Russia would have been given false passports and would have been expected to spy for the Americans in your new country. Most of you, though, would have met with some unfortunate accident, because it would not do to release you all into freedom in America, a place you do not know, cannot understand, a place where—by their accounting—you do not even exist.

"Every one of us, who is over the age of ten years old, knows what this place is because that is when they tell us. And we know, even if we do not admit it or consciously understand it, that we were born into slavery in a spy school, and that we have been incarcerated here against our will for all of our lives. Every one of us knows by heart the Declaration of Independence, and the Constitution of the United States, yet, for some reason, we do not acknowledge that our very existence here, and our continued enslavement here, is a patent violation of those rights supposedly guaranteed to all citizens of America.

"At ten years of age, we were tested by our captors, and those who tested the highest for intelligence and the necessary characteristics requisite for dishonesty and lying, were set aside for extensive training so that, eventually, we would be sent to Russia to live among the peaceful people there to be traitors to our own culture and identity.

"Over the last fifty years, thousands of our friends and neighbors have been shipped to Russia to live there as Russians and to spy for America, and that is the truth of this place. But we are not Americans! We are not citizens of the United States of America, for if we were citizens we would have the basic rights afforded to all American citizens. We have been born Russian, and our lives have been lived as Russians, despite whatever soil happens to have been under our feet for all of our lives. We are Russians!"

Both Vladimir and Alyona stopped speaking for a moment, as the crowd began to become very animated at this last point. Many of the older villagers began shaking their heads and booing and hissing, while some of the younger residents were nodding their heads and clapping. Vladimir seemed to want this reaction and he allowed the turmoil to continue until it rolled across the entire crowd of people assembled inside the gymnasium. It gave Clay a moment to catch his breath and wonder at what he'd just heard. He felt light-headed. *Too much information...* He didn't understand *any* of it.

Vladimir raised his hand, and then raised his voice so he could continue.

"In 1992, this town and facility, slated to be closed by the American government, was purchased...." (murmurs and heated shouts from the crowd) "Yes.... It's true! You were bought as chattel property by American capitalists! This town and facility was purchased by American billionaires and has since operated as a private security firm with special contracts with the American government to provide human agents, information, intelligence, and scientific research to the intelligence infrastructure of America! Comrades! You are property! You are cattle! You are owned by companies, and you belong to them!"

The crowd was now in turmoil and a general buzz began to grow into an angry din until Vladimir quieted them again with the raising of his hand.

"Comrade Mikail Mikailivitch is in the process of freeing you from your slaveholders, and that process may take some time. You have been used as weapons against the free and peaceful people of Russia who have done nothing to deserve your hatred or your enmity. Comrade Mikail has come to save us all, and to free us from the bondage under which we have lived our whole lives!" Again the crowd became very animated and loud, and Vladimir had to raise his voice even louder to quiet the crowd once again.

"I said I would be brief, and I will be brief. With us today, we have some prisoners who deserve your attention. On my right, you will see two men who are with us in chains. Some other guards and employees of *Warwick, Incorporated* were, unfortunately, killed during the liberation of this Dachau, this prison camp, this death camp of lies, or they would be here in chains before you as well.

But these two men have been captured according to the revolutionary laws we have implemented in order to insure safety and peace while the next events unfold."

Vladimir stopped. Clay noticed the theatrical quality of his pivot as he turned to regard the two men, and now the entire crowd did as well, and Clay found everyone in the gymnasium looking straight at him. He blushed, he did not know why, to be there under the gaze of the crowd. Vladimir walked over to Clay and, reaching down, pulled him to his feet.

"This man calls himself Clay, and he is one of two things, Comrades: He is either a spy employed by American intelligence to thwart our work toward your liberation and freedom... or, he is what he claims to be; an innocent wanderer, who, during the most sensitive part of our revolution, just *happened* into the Warwick Prison. He is one or the other, and to us it matters not. He is a prisoner all the same, and has violated our laws and thus is a criminal and a representative of arbitrary abuse and of the wickedness of the capitalist powers. He is held now so that we can ascertain whether he has any future value to the Revolution."

Vladimir pushed Clay back down into his seat, and then tried, struggled, and eventually succeeded, to haul the injured and weak old man to his feet.

Clay's face paled and his head seemed to drain of blood as he sat and watched Vladimir lift the old man, and as he did so Clay's equilibrium failed a bit and he almost lost his balance, almost slid off his seat into the floor...

Uugghhh...! He had to come up for air... What was this freaking place?! He was sitting here, going under water in a freaking Russian prison camp in the Cascades... Or was it the Caucasus... Whatever! He was sitting here before a crowd of people who seemed unfriendly and who spoke Russian and who were in the path of his freaking homestead farm in Ithaca! He thought of the Superstorm and the aftermath. And the Walk. And the Almost Was. And the "What is that!" He was feeling overwhelmed and shell-shocked. He was thinking of the talk with Clive, and the firewall. And His Cheryl's Face. And the sweet, precious faces of his daughters... His Daughters! His beautiful, artful daughters...

...and then he blacked out.

* * * *

After a brief moment in which the crowd sat and watched the group of men at the podium bend to the aid of the collapsed man near the podium, life in the crowd began to stir. A man stepped out of the crowd, a woman cleared her throat, two stomps of a foot, a shift of a grocery bag across the floor, conversations about hairdressers and 'when do we find out what is going on?' and 'God when is this going to be over?', and whispers while children run on the floor and start playing... and all of it is in Russian.

* * * *

Vladimir spoke again. "Every one of you here knows who this man is."

The crowd reassembled themselves and fell into silence again. They were taut. At attention. The man at the podium began to speak as Clay slowly, groggily opened his eyes...

"Lev Volkhov is known to everyone in Warwick..."

Spinning. He was going under again. He steadied himself and began to breathe deeply and the spinning slowed and then stopped. The man at the podium was standing, and talking, and his words began to wash over him and Clay calmed himself and listened.

"... unhappily, as some sort of wise sage—an ancient seer and prophet of forgotten times. At one time or another he has taught everyone here, and he is called The Professor by most of you who still cling to him as your honorable teacher and grandfather. But who is Lev Volkhov really? He is a traitor, many times over! In fact, not one person in this gymnasium could tell me positively which side Lev Volkhov is on today. Do you know? Of course you don't. It has been a long day, and perhaps he has switched sides again since he woke up this morning?

"Volkhov was born in Soviet Russia in 1937 but came to America in December of 1956 after the failed Hungarian Uprising. He came to America in the guise of a Hungarian college student seeking asylum, supposedly having fled the so-called 'Soviet crackdown.' But that is not who Lev Volkhov was or is.

"Let's see if we can unravel it. By his own admission—and we all know this from his own stories in our classes—he was a Soviet spy, and the Hungarian college student cover was designed to infiltrate him into the American society. But wait, it gets better! –"

> *Clay sat.*
> *And waited.*
> *For any of this... any of it... to get better.*

"In 1962 Volkhov was exposed to the Americans as a Russian spy by Golitsyn and other traitors to the Soviet Union. That is the risk, isn't it Professor?" Vladimir spit on the floor as if to say that the title of Professor was offensive to him. "Isn't that the risk, that no matter how well you do your job, that some weasel or coward or double is going to get caught and then give you up to your enemy? Isn't that what has happened to most of our friends and parents and loved ones in Russia? Aren't many of them dead now for this same reason?"

Vladimir turned back to the crowd.

"Rather than take a free ticket of expulsion back to his homeland, we are informed that Volkhov switched sides! We all know the story because he has told it to us enough times that we know it by heart. He became a traitor to Soviet Union, and began working for the Americans. Eventually, afraid for his life—because he is by nature a dishonorable coward—Volkhov agreed to come here to Warwick and be an instructor, to train other spies to infiltrate and harm his own people. That is how most of you know him. But is that all we know about Lev Volkhov? No! Still No! Some of you know, as do many of us standing here before you, that—according to Lev Volkhov—he never did switch sides! Over the years he recruited many of us to secretly work for the Russians, and to do harm to the American intelligence plans. How can we keep it all straight? Well, to those of us who knew that Volkhov was actually, and had always been, a Soviet spy, we loved him for that and he became to us like a father—even while he was betraying you. He taught us English and how to put away our Russian accents so that we might better serve our Mother Russia. Some of you today, your hearts go out to broken Volkhov because you know him as grandfather and teacher. To you, he was a traitor to Russia and a lover of America, and you loved him for it. To us, he was faithful to Russia, and we loved him for it.

"Let me pause now and clear the air. So many faces! So much switching of sides! What can we believe? Right? But, in reality, it is all very simple. Volkhov was sent to the U.S. as a spy. He was unwittingly exposed by Golitsyn and served his country by allowing himself to be recruited by U.S. intelligence so that he could infiltrate this place for his home country. He has switched sides only once, and that most recently. For all intents and purposes, Volkhov has been a faithful employee and servant of his former Soviet masters... until just over a year ago."

The gasps started up again in the audience. And Vladimir let it go on for a minute and then he began, again, his speech.

"Just over a year ago, Lev Volkhov informed his superiors here in Warwick, and their handlers in American intelligence, what he has been doing all of these years. *That* was when he became a traitor. He exposed the names of hundreds of your neighbors, your parents, your friends as double-agents. He gave them everything. The damage wrought by what he has done spirals outward, even now.

"I have spoken long enough. Now it is time for our new leader, our liberator Mikail Mikailivitch to speak to us."

There was some applause and a lot of general noise, and a smattering of boos, and hisses, and even a few sounds of spitting as Vladimir bowed to Mikail and went to take a seat.

Mikail stood up and looked over the crowd. His eyes were piercing. While the crowd looked on and at one another and wondered whether anyone would tilt at windmills, or hoist themselves, you know, on their own petard, Mikail's eyes gripped the whole town and everyone began to wait, in absolute silence, for whatever he had to say.

When he spoke, there were no interruptions. There was no applause, and no booing. The gymnasium, as a single entity, embraced the voice of Mikail with utter and soundless attention.

"Comrade Vladimir Nikitich has spoken well. I do not plan to wear out your patience, so I will speak only briefly.

"I am a young man. But I believe that actions speak louder than words.

"I know what you may think, but you are wrong. I do. I believe that *actions...* speak *louder...* than words."

Full Stop.

"I think you all have some idea now as to what is happening. In here, and out there.

"As we gather here tonight, forces beyond your reckoning and your imaginations are gathering together to right many of the wrongs of the world. As you in Warwick now know, all of this part of the country is without power, and the Americans have announced that voting in Tuesday's elections for the Presidency of America has been delayed in all of the areas affected by both Hurricane Sandy and the blizzard that we have all just suffered.

"Oh, how we all have suffered, and we have also persevered. But, because of the blizzard, all over America tonight, riots and disturbances have greeted this announcement about the election. Societal upheaval is underway. It is nothing that was not expected. But still, perhaps, not entirely to be welcomed, because it can be worked into the plan.

"Of course, we," he indicated to the men standing at the front and the others with guns, "did not plan the Hurricane or the Nor'easter, but they could not have happened at a more opportune time for all of us. For well over two decades, for my whole life and for the entire lives of many of you young people here, our cultural and national brethren in Russia have been planning an event. Some say that the spark of the idea of that event was birthed as far back as 1960, and that very event, so long in the planning, is soon to come to pass.

"I will have more to say on that in the future, but I wanted to mention it because some of you might believe that this action of ours in taking the prison and then Warwick has been rash and unplanned. You might be saying to yourselves, 'Hey, as soon as the Americans learn of it, they will raid this place and destroy all of us.' But you would be wrong if you were to believe that. There is no help—or intervention—coming from the Americans, and if it does come, it will be destroyed.

"So tonight—and I hope you don't mind if I just do away with all pretense—is all about the necessarily brutal assumption of power."

He looked at the crowd. They looked at him.

"In several days, you will thank me. In the meantime I will expect you all to behave yourselves and to obey all commands and laws given to you, and to wait patiently for your liberation from this American Gulag. In the end, I am sure, you *will* thank me.

"But I am not a Pollyanna. I am not a sanguine dreamer just hoping that things will go right. Some of you, unhappily, feel affinity for your captors and you want to see America win. So old is the Stockholm syndrome... older than Stockholm. So to display to you my determined intention to maintain power and peace and security among us, we are going to have an execution. Right here. Right now."

The crowd stirred, inhaling deeply for the first time, and there was conversation as each man or woman or child seemed to need to gain balance or understanding or perspective by whispering to a neighbor or parent or friend.

The word "execution", in a general sense, hit Clay in much the manner that such a thing should hit a man, but the mental churnings and the snap-snap of puzzle pieces coming together in his brain prevented him from clearly analyzing just what the word meant *to him*.

"I apologize to those of you who are of a temperament that is too sensitive for what you are about to see. It is a necessary evil. The murders and deaths of thousands of your brethren and hometown friends have escaped your notice, but this death will not. Believe me, it is a necessitous act to insure order. We have brought before you tonight a few criminals, and one of them will now face execution as a sign of our determination.

"I am not a terrorist or a tyrant. I am a patriot, of sorts, for a nation I have never seen, and likely never will see. I, like you, am Russian. And so that we will not seem to be unfair, I have determined to let these two prisoners speak to you on their own behalf if they so wish."

Vladimir walked over to Clay and lifted him up by his upper arm and pushed him forward toward the crowd. The people murmured and whispered, and he wondered what they were thinking. His heart pounded in his chest and his mouth was so dry that he could only swallow with difficulty.

Clay looked over and near the wall closest to the entrance he saw Vasily. The young man's eyes were closed as if he were praying or wishing himself to be anywhere else in the world than here.

Clay's legs moved only with reluctance, and he did not know if he could trust them for long.

"I have nothing to say," Clay began, "other than that I am not a criminal. I have broken the laws of neither the United States nor Russia. I am an innocent man, just trying to get home to my old farm in upstate New York. In this, I am like you. I have been in a prison, and only hope to be free. I know nothing of Warwick, nothing of spies or intrigue or wars or traitors. I only want to go home." He turned slowly and walked stiffly back to his seat.

Vladimir bent down to lift up Volkhov, but as he did, the old man began to rise to his feet under his own power. His head was still drooped over onto his chest as he began to rise, and Clay wondered whether he had been that way since he had first arrived— as if he were unconscious the whole time. As he stood to his feet, though, his head rose as well and, eyes ablaze, he stepped confidently forward before the people of his town.

"I don't need to introduce myself. You all know me. Every one of you. I taught you, and I probably taught your parents. What young Vladimir has said about me is mostly true, and the things that are not true are things about which I will not quibble. All of my adult life I have been a Russian spy, and for most of that time I have lived in America. Now, for a short time, I have also been an American spy, living in a little piece of the world that, for all intents and purposes, is Russia.

"This place. Our place. Warwick.

"In reality, though, I have no country, for I am a citizen of nowhere." He paused for a moment, and his legs seemed to grow unsteady. He attempted to wipe his face with his arm but was unsuccessful, the chains preventing any such movement.

"I am an old man," Volkhov continued, "and old men learn things, and these things I will tell you." He looked over the crowd and captured the audience with his steely gaze.

"It is true. I did tell the Americans about the plans to destroy her; plans I have known about for twenty years or more; plans that existed even before I knew about them. I did so because I believe that a surprise attack on America, which is what we are talking about here after all, is a foolish plan, and a murderous idea.

"It is the *governments* of America and of the Soviet Union that have been at war throughout this last century, and not the peoples of those two countries. Ideologies are at war, and not individuals. But ideologies do not suffer and die in wars. People do. And I have learned, because I have been on both sides, I have lived in both worlds. I have lived in both worlds and have been accepted in both worlds and have been rejected by both worlds, but mostly I have found a home. Like here, among you."

Lev Volkhov paused to let the crowd bathe in that thought. Clay knew that Alyona was still speaking into his ear and translating the old man's words, but that reality faded and another, higher, reality emerged and he heard the man speak and as his mouth moved, Clay understood him and heard his voice and it was as if Alyona disappeared as Volkhov spoke directly to him.

"...But there are no differences between the sides. We are talking here about a Cold War grown hot that most of the rest of the world has already forgotten. They've just forgotten it existed. America has never been at war with the Soviet Union, except by proxy... in Vietnam, and Afghanistan, and Nicaragua, and Korea, and a hundred other places around the world. Everyone is trained to think of these opposing forces as two sides, good and evil, light and darkness, right and wrong. However, as an old man I have learned that there are actually three sides. One side is always pitted against another, so that the third side wins.

"Did you hear that? The third side always wins.

"How do you know which is the third side? The third side is always made known by what *actually happens*. We are dealing with the age-old dialectic that everyone knows about and no one heeds and all of you were my students, and you should all know who you are..."

He waved his cane at the crowd. They watched him.

"... and what that means."

Silence.

"In America, as we speak, Republicans and Democrats are at war, and neither side will ever win because they want the same things, only at different speeds and with different details. The third side will win, because there is not a dime's worth of difference between Republicans and Democrats. Both sides will accept annihilation and totalitarianism because neither side truly wants freedom.

"They are all statists. Do you know the meaning of this word? Yes, those of you who were my students...

"I have learned this, so listen to me. The Russian and American people do not want war, but they will have it. Why? Because the third side wants it! The third side always wins!

"I will give you a most poignant example. Black separatist Malcolm X and white separatists heading the KKK were both controlled by the CIA in the 1960's."

Stomp.

"Malcolm X admitted this in his autobiography! Why? Because democratic socialists in the government and around the

world did not want fascism or communism, they wanted Martin
Luther King."

Cough.

"And if you want Martin Luther King—who would never have
even been *received* by Americans willfully—you use The Nation of
Islam and the KKK to frighten people into embracing MLK."

Wheeze.

Aaahhrrggh. Clay felt as if he was going over. He felt himself
dipping. He was sitting watching this old man seem to draw
strength from the crowd and he began to feel as though the man
drew even his own vital energy. He was growing woozy.

"If you want democratic socialism in America, you do not just
propose democratic socialism! You produce a far left Democrat
party and a far right Republican party who both want statism
regardless of what they say!

"Do you know the word? Do you know *that* word?
Statism?" He stuck out his chest and rose to the crowd. An angel
floating over head at just that moment might have seen a giant
magnet in the center of a box with a million tiny metal marbles
spread around the walls of the box, just vibrating, ready to make
their break. To run to the man. To freedom.

Clay wondered how, if they did, if the crowd did surge
forward toward Volkhov, he might swim through the crowd,
through the chaos, to the door to the valley and make a break of
his own.

The man continued, but in a quiet, more reasoning tone,
"They are all statists, only with different winners.

"And the people will embrace democratic socialism! *All* of
them will. Both sides. They already have. But you can never tell
the people that, can you, because you see their lusts and their drive
for comforts... you see... all of them are statists."

He let the word sink in.

"They are all against real freedom."

He let that sink in.

"Your political pundits, your crazy activists, your radio show
hosts are all successful *precisely* because they do not uncover the
real and simple truth. Do you hear me? The truth. As long as
they stay away from the truth, and play their audience into the
hands of the dialectic, then the money flows and they get to keep
their seats in the game.

"But the truth, perhaps that is too big to swallow entire. Let's begin with a bite.

"Every false conflict is precipitated. Think about it... Every false dialectic is put forth by someone... *someone...*"

He let the statement hang in the air.

"... because the third side wants something that the people will not freely give. If people wanted freedom, they'd turn off their televisions and move from the cities and grow their own food and just say 'NO.'"

"Did you hear that? *No.*"

The crowd sat in silence.

"No, to everything that is contrary to their freedom. No. Simply... Not marching, or petitions, or voting, or organizing, or gathering signatures... Just *No.*

"It is hard to believe, but sometimes just saying 'No' is a revolutionary act."

Absolute silence.

"But they do not want freedom. The crowd. They want peace and safety and comforts without cost.

"In America tonight people are fighting one another in the streets, and people are burning down businesses, and people are shooting one another at the gas pumps, and the economy has plummeted into the abyss. Why? I will tell you why. Because in the last century or more, so-called 'patriots' and so-called 'communists' have whipped the people into a frenzy and given them the false idea that 'voting' is the only arbiter and guarantee of their peace.

"And now... now... now some of them believe that 'voting' has been taken from them. Their only hope. Their great 'god'."

Clay wondered at the oddness of the talk for a moment. He was beginning to come back to his senses after the fainting spell and he was listening to the man enough to have picked up that many of the things he said sounded familiar, but in a far off kind of way.

"We all only have one inalienable right. Only one! It is not the vote. It is not. It is, instead, the right to say 'NO' to all of this manipulation.

"And then we must be prepared to accept the consequences of that singular, valorous, and revolutionary act.

"But that is the one thing that modern people just *will* not do."

He let that word sink in. *Will.*

"We are enslaved by our possessions, and imprisoned by our wants.

"I am just an old man. I've lived my life without a country. I have made a lot of mistakes, and I've caused a lot of pain and even death no doubt. But I have learned something. I believe that all of this, every bit of it, is about power. Power is the ability to coerce others to do what they would not otherwise do.

"All of history is a lesson in the third side using lies and wars and manipulations to get what they want. The Russian people do not want war."

The crowd shuffled their feet on the floor. They looked at him.

"But the third side does. So we will have warfare.

"The American people do not want war, but the third side does, so we will have warfare.

"The powers-that-be finance both sides of every conflict, and the third side profits, and the people don't care as long as they are comfortable and well fed and have some neighbor to hate."

He paused again and let that sink in.

"Let me ask you a question, those of you who condemn me for switching sides—which I did not do, by the way—but if you say I did, well... there is always the public's opinion. But let me ask you a question. Why, if I switched sides as you say I did, isn't America moving to stop what I told them is going to happen? Or why didn't they listen to Golitsyn, or Stanislav Lunev, or Vladimir Bukovsky, or any of hundreds of other men just like them. You know these names. I have taught you all of them.

"Defectors. Dissidents. Refuseniks. Risking life and limb, leaving family and home, to go off into the wilderness of public opinion... and to freedom. Why, if I have switched sides, do the Americans treat us defectors as defective?

"I told them that my country planned to destroy America within a quarter century of 1992. And to what end? Did they listen?

"If the-powers-that-be in America had *wanted* it stopped, then they could easily have stopped it. Could they not? But why, then, did they not?"

He swallowed, and let the crowd wonder.

"Just Golitsyn's testimony alone ought to have been enough to convince them. It has been estimated *very* conservatively, and yet, even in that tentative suggestion, it has been argued persuasively that almost all of his predictions, *almost* all, have been fulfilled. And most of them by 1993!

"Trotsky, in *The Revolution Betrayed*, predicted that just such a thing may have to come to pass in order for the worldwide revolution to take place. Are you telling me that the American leadership never read Trotsky!?"

Not since Marc Antony stood before the Romans, had a crowd been more receptive, more quiet and attentive, more thriving with pent up energy.

"But I am not here to say that Russia is our enemy! No! WE are our enemy. We who will not unplug from the dialectic and refuse to participate are the enemy. No! *Refuse*. Never again. Not anymore! No. Simply, No.

"I did not betray my country. I betrayed a handful of wicked men—some Russian, some American—who want to annihilate the world...

"...so that they can have their worldwide revolution.

"America has always been the only bulwark against that worldwide revolution. And whatever side we are on we must admit that. So, no, I did not betray America. I told them the truth about what was about to happen, not because I love America—"

He paused.

"—but because I love truth."

Volkhov looked around, worn out from speaking, and his eyes seemed to close as he glanced at faces he knew around the room. "I'm tired," he said, "and I don't care if these young boys shoot me now. I've said what I had to say."

The old man slowly moved back to his seat and sat down, ignoring the thunderous applause and some boos and hisses from the gathered villagers. Mikail stood and once again froze the commotion with his icy stare.

"Nice speech old man," he said with no hint of affection or emotion. Then he raised his voice to silence the crowd. "I wanted everyone to hear his confession from his own mouth, and he did not disappoint me. Now, I told you that one of the men up here will die, and I am a man of my word."

He turned on his heel and walked over to where Clay was sitting, right beside Officer Todd Karagin. He stood over Clay and indicated to the officer with a wave of his hand that he wanted him to hand over the pistol from its holster, snapping his fingers at Todd as though he were a dog. Even Pavlov couldn't have asked for a faster reaction, and Todd complied, handing the pistol, butt first, to Mikail who made a display of examining it to make sure it was loaded. He checked to see if there was a bullet in the chamber and that the safety was released and then he walked around Clay ominously, peering into his eyes and looking into his soul.

Clay's pulse had been racing dangerously ever since Mikail had repeated his statement that one of them would die. But now, as he looked into the eyes of the man who was menacing him, he suddenly felt a calm come over him. He felt at one with his surroundings. He looked into the tough exterior Mikail was putting out and he saw a pitiful vulnerability. He thought of the look in the eyes of the red haired man on the bicycle as they'd parted, and the eyes of the young man named Vasily from his cell when they first met. He then watched as the sad vision of Mikail turned around and confronted the room full of peasants, by waving his loaded gun. The impotent threat of the thing. Clay had decided that such a threat could have no long-term hold over his soul anymore. He watched and he felt a surreal sense of calm flood through his body. *Is this it?*

He tried to think of everyone he loved, but now, with death staring him in the face, he could not. He really could only think of what Volkhov had said, and that he had also been a pawn and a prisoner in a system of lies that his own lusts had enabled. All of this, this microcosm of world conflict and agitations playing itself out in a gymnasium in a little town in New York, was all engendered by his own lust for comforts and stuff, and air-conditioning, and cheap gas, and gadgets, and the soul-killing desire for *more*. That was the root and the base of it. That was the prison he'd tried to escape when he left Brooklyn. Everything else was just theater. *Perhaps dying is the only real freedom.* His interpreter had moved away from him and, after pausing for a moment, had returned to her seat. *Poor girl. She doesn't want to get shot by accident. I don't blame her.* He saw her looking at him and he nodded his 'thank you' to her.

Mikail spoke again to the assembled villagers, but Clay could not understand him. Suddenly Mikail was walking very rapidly towards him. Clay closed his eyes and bowed his head and he heard the deafening shot from the pistol.

But he didn't feel anything,

His heart raced again and his eyes opened and his breath caught in his chest.

Looking up, he saw Mikail walking by him and out the door with the pistol still in his hand.

* * * *

What happened? He looked up and saw the crowd and they were all frozen in shocked disbelief and there were screams and a few people fainted. Clay looked out over the crowd, his ears still ringing from the blast, smoky confusion rising in the air.

He scanned the crowd with his eyes and suddenly felt the thick, wet, fluid seeping into his prison jumper. He thought it might have been urine at first, but then he reached down with his hand and wiped the viscous stuff from his arms, and realized he was soaked in blood. He instantly came into awareness of the people rushing to the figure beside him and he looked to see if Volkhov had been shot, then saw the blood seeping underneath the old man's chair. Without any particular notion of volition in doing so, Clay stood up to see where Volkhov had been shot.

But Volkhov's eyes met his and they both looked down into each other's souls and they confirmed in that look that they each were still alive.

* * * *

The body of Officer Todd Karagin was writhing on the ground. He had been shot in the head.

It looked like the old man was going to collapse, and Clay motioned to him and Volkhov stood up and they both backed away from the body as it kicked and twitched there on the ground. A young boy came up—he could not have been more than fifteen—and he pulled the trigger on his machine pistol hitting Todd's body three or four more times and eventually, after an agonizing few seconds, the writhing stopped and Todd's blood ran into the hardwood of the gymnasium in Warwick.

The crowd watched the frenzy at the podium in silence and no one even noticed the weary, haggard traveler helping the old bearded saint off the podium and into a chair at the edge of the crowd.

CHAPTER 9

An hour later Clay and Volkhov were locked in a cell together. Not the cell Clay had been in earlier, not the Tank, but one of the cluster cells where the young boys had been held prior to Clay's arrival at Warwick Prison.

Clay and Volkhov talked, but only after a moment or two of silence. Upon entering the cell, they'd sat quietly, collecting their thoughts and breathing. *Then* they had talked. Clay heard more of the old man's story and he told a bit of his own. They clung to one another in the exhaustion and euphoria that grips two people who have temporarily escaped death together.

Clay did not know Lev Volkhov, but in a strange way, he felt a kinship with the old man. Somehow he even had affection for him, this man he did not know. Like everyone else in America, Clay had been trained to call every idea that flew in the face of the collective talking points a *conspiracy theory*. But he'd identified with Volkhov's speech to such an extent that, except for the details about spying and such, the old man could have been reading the text directly from Clay's heart. This is not merely to point out that Clay felt at peace with *the man*; it is to notice the more important fact that Clay felt at peace within himself in the man's presence.

He knew that both he and Volkhov had been on a long journey that had led them here. His own journey had not started on the steps of that Brooklyn brownstone the day after Sandy. He'd been traveling all of his life. Clay thought of friends and loved ones—the ones still alive, and the ones he'd lost—and he imagined telling them the story of this journey. Would they believe it? Who knows. Everyone carries their own baggage into a story.

Some people would hate the things that they'd heard and would reject this old man and his ramblings, and would curse the things that Clay now thought about the world and his countrymen and this life and the way of it. Some might want to lock Volkhov up and others would want to embrace him or stone him or ignore him with the hope that he would just go away. After all, the dialecticians had done their work. Journeys, in the end, are individual things no matter how many people come along on them. His journey had led him to this place and time, and he accepted where he was despite the danger, and he saw in Volkhov a fellow pilgrim on the pilgrimage of truth. Perhaps they had just started too late. Procrastination tends to be the genesis of almost every journey.

This old man with him in his cell had carried burdens and had walked a path that, prior to meeting him, Clay had only read about in books. He'd lived a life of adventure and danger. More importantly, perhaps, the man had lived a life of the mind. He had lived within himself and within his worlds, whichever one he found himself in, in a search for knowledge and truth. His face was lined with intrigue and despair and excitement and frightful loss. He wore a beard that most, even those who lived in a Russian village today, would consider "unkempt" or wild. Despite his higher learning and his brilliant mind he could easily be mistaken for a homeless drunk or an insane philosopher-poet.

Clay could imagine Volkhov as Diogenes lying in the sun when Alexander the Great rode up and said something akin to "I am the great King Alexander!" to which Diogenes had replied, "I am the great dog Diogenes." Alexander had promised Diogenes anything he wished in the whole world, to which Diogenes had only replied, "I wish you'd get out of my sun."

He had the look of that. The face of Lev Volkhov aged in wisdom and worry and want, had had enough of king's shadows.

* * * *

In the fullness of time, Volkhov wanted to talk, so Clay let him.

"Clay, what I said in that gymnasium was the truth, but it didn't matter. In the grand scheme of things it was just an old man railing against the darkness of a life lived by lies. Solzhenitsyn, my honored countryman, said 'Live Not By Lies' and it took me way too long to heed him. I should have read more Solzhenitsyn and Tolstoy and less Marx and Lenin.

Had Clay been in the *other* world he would have thought about the books in his backpack, of his own influences, of the writers who gave him hope, but he was not, and he didn't.

"America is more divided than it was before the Civil War... why? Because the third side has presided over a century's long plan to dumb down the people and to colonize them into thinking that the only answer to every problem must come from government. In my last ditch effort to save a system that really doesn't want... no more... it doesn't *need* saving, I tried to tell the Americans the truth of what is coming. But, like Golitsyn before me—"

"Stop." Clay interrupted. "There's that name. I don't know who he is..."

The old man waved him off and kept talking.

"The Americans believed everything—bought the whole story—except the most important part! They claimed not to believe what is called *The Long-Term Deception Strategy.* I told my new masters that the Sino-Soviet split in the 1960's had been faked. I told them that the Perestroika and Glasnost were faked. I told them that the plan was—" he stopped, as if searching for a word, "—that the plan *had always been*, to break up the Soviet Union and feign a collapse in order to rake in Western aid, weaken the capitalist west, and to eventually destroy America.

"Golitsyn told them this in his book *New Lies for Old*, written before the collapse in '92, and they believed everything but *that.* So many other defectors told them this, but they would not believe it."

The old man looked at him, sadly and spread his hands, holding them palms upward as if in prayer.

"Volkhov told them this too, and they could not accept it."

Clay looked at him and continued to listen.

"But I've learned that there are some in the halls of power who are one with those who are in the halls of power everywhere. They are the ones who forced America's leaders to disbelieve the truth. Because the third side wants the war.

"They want the planet to lose six and a half billion of its inhabitants. They want to save the environment by destroying it, or they want all of the gold, or they want to continue to be the masters of history... I don't pretend to understand the *why* completely. I don't understand why, but in just a couple of decades from now what once was America will be a collection of independent fiefdoms, a balkanized mess of warring kingdoms like medieval Europe. That is what comes next."

As Volkhov paused, the door opened and Vasily came in slowly with another case of bottled water. Though this cell had a sink, the water system was not currently operating due to the power outages. Clay smiled at him, and Vasily smiled back weakly.

* * * *

Just before Volkhov and Clay were ushered into the cell they'd been standing in the cluster day room when Mikail came in to give instructions on their care. Mikail, speaking in English, probably out of habit more than anything, had ordered Vladimir to have Vasily oversee the two prisoners as their caretaker. He had given Vladimir specific instructions that no one else should be admitted to the room to see them.

"Vasily is young and stupid and doesn't speak English," Mikail had told Vladimir.

They smiled and nodded but Clay had seen a change in Vasily's face. It was subtle, so subtle that no one else noticed it. His jaw had tightened and his eyes had narrowed only slightly and his gaze had met Clay's. There had been an invisible communication between them. Vasily understood English. He was a book that had been judged by his cover, but they had misread him. He was not stupid, although he was indeed young. Clay had decided that perhaps he had an ally.

* * * *

Now, in the cell, as Vasily dropped off the water, Clay looked at him and pointed to the ceiling and then to his ear asking Vasily silently if the room was being monitored. Vasily shook his head 'no' then spoke in perfect English, "The whole electronic security apparatus is down right now. The entire facility is on minimum power, and since you two are the only prisoners, they have shut down everything but the emergency lighting."

His words hit Clay like a rocket. What *is* this place, where even those who seem the meekest are so competent? To the two adults in the cell, the boy had just summed up a mountain of information in the most efficient way possible. He was like a co-conspirator or... a spy.

He went on. "They've 'appropriated' several homes in town for themselves, and there are only four guards placed at the entrances of this building for security."

Volkhov looked at Vasily with concern and care on his face and asked, "What will you do, Vasily Romanovich?"

"What would you have me do, grandfather?" Vasily asked affectionately.

Clay wondered whether this term was a sign of respect or an indication of lineage. He was finding it hard to see, in the big picture, who was on which side in this vast game of chess, but he knew in his heart, as well as he had ever known anything, that the three of them in this cell were of one mind in that moment.

"You must escape here, Vasily. The attack, if it comes as planned, will start in three days and if you are still here, things will get very bad very fast."

Volkov turned to the cinder-block wall and drew a map of the east coast with his finger. "It will start in the areas currently blacked out, and the attack will focus first on Washington D.C. and the rest of the eastern seaboard. News will be sketchy, and any government information will be lies. The rest of the country will just hear about the continually plummeting stock market, and the major power outages. They will say that information is unreliable because of the lack of power and fuel."

He paused and looked at them. "Turmoil and confusion."

"It's already gotten pretty bad out there, grandfather. It has been bad since the first storm hit, but in the last two days everything has just gone haywire. You haven't heard the news. We've been listening in on the radio pretty much whenever we have free time. The world is spiraling into chaos even now."

The boy paused. Clay heard in the pause, as the old man did, the boy asking, "How will I escape? And where will I go?"

Volkhov offered a way out.

"Clay here says that the fence is destroyed on the south side of the facility. If you can get out that way, you could escape. I don't know where you can go in the long-run. Go to the Amish, if you can. We've talked about that."

Clay looked at him, surprised.

"Or just find someplace away from the cities to hide out. There may not be a good solution out there, but being in here would be the worst solution of all,"

Volkhov shook his head. He tried to be secretive about it, but Clay saw him wipe away a single tear that had welled up in his eyes.

"They have guards posted on all of the exits," Vasily said. "If I leave through the north door, towards Warwick, I will not be noticed, but if I attempt to leave out of any of the other doors, they won't open them to me and they'll ask questions. Besides, what about you grandfather? And Clay? What should *we all* do?"

Clay looked at Vasily intensely. He really did hope that the boy would escape, but Vasily didn't seem to have much hope for himself. Clay grabbed a bottle of water and took a long drink, and then he handed one to Volkhov.

The old man received it with a nod, as a way of thanks. Clay offered one to Vasily, who refused, saying that he had plenty and that he didn't want to drink theirs.

"Where are you staying, Vasily?" Clay asked.

"Most of us who are considered 'worthless'—we who do not have homes and families to go to—are sleeping on cots in the gymnasium."

Clay looked at Vasily and decided that he had to trust him. "Vasily, I need to tell you that I have a backpack hidden in the Tank. They never thought to look for it, at least as far as I know. I think mostly because they killed the only man who ever saw it. Why they never searched the Tank for the camera is beyond me, but with so much going on, I think—once they realized that I was just a lost hiker—they just forgot about it.

"Anyway, the backpack is stowed under the bunk in the Tank, hidden under a blanket."

"What should I do with it?" Vasily asked.

"Do you think you can get it out of here?"

"I can. I can walk it out the north entrance and tell the guard there, if he asks, that I am taking it to Mikail. They all think I'm stupid, so they don't suspect me of anything. They don't think I'm capable of trickery, lying, or subterfuge."

"That makes you the best spy ever in a whole town of spies, Vasily," Clay said, smiling.

"They could eventually figure it out if the guard thinks to ask Mikail about it later, but that won't happen for some time, if it happens at all. Most of the people think of me as an ignorant automaton and I do my best not to rid them of the notion."

He smiled at Clay. "It made my life easier in here for them to think that I was stupid and that I didn't speak English."

"What in the world were you locked up in here for, Vasily?" Clay asked.

"I got drunk," Vasily replied. "I was tired of all of the abuse and I stole some vodka from the store and sat out behind the church in the cemetery drinking. Some students from school came by and started in on me, so I set into them like a windmill in a hurricane. It's the first time I ever did such a thing, but I think it had built up in me for a long time."

Clay smiled at Vasily and replied, "Well, I've been there, brother. Got locked up for it too! Ok? So listen, the backpack isn't immediately critical, but if any one of us can escape, it has things in it that might keep us alive," Clay said. "There is at least one clean change of clothes in there too. I think Todd stole my other clothes, thinking they were the only ones I had. But there are some other things in there that might be useful as well."

Volkhov stood up and took a long swig from his bottle of water. He looked at the bottle intently.

"This reminds me, both of you, starting tomorrow, if we are still alive, do not drink any municipal or public water supply," he said.

"Why?" Vasily asked.

"Just don't."

"Ok."

Volkhov continued, "Vasily, when you leave here you need to find Pyotr Alexandrovitch, my nephew. He knows the whole story. There is another way out that he will show you."

"Yes, grandfather, I'll do it, but what about you two?"

"Well—"

Clay interjected. "All I can think of is that we can try to make a break for it. This place has never been weaker than it is right now. It has almost no security and only four guards. Mikail carries the keys. We can just jump him or something and try to make a break through the south fence."

"It won't work, Clay," Vasily responded. "I have the room key, which also fits the cluster doors, but it only fits the rooms in this cluster. Vladimir is head of security now, and I think only he carries the external door master keys. I have to knock on the door to get out, so that means the guards carry a door key as well."

Clay paused and thought. He trailed his hand along the cold concrete before slapping it in delight. "That's it! So you have a key to this cluster, and the guards at the exits have a key to the external doors?"

"Yes, that's true."

"And if you were to try to exit the south door, which is only a brisk run from the collapsed fence, they wouldn't let you out because you're not authorized to go out that exit, is that correct?"

"Yes."

"Beautiful! And they'd never let you through, because you only speak Russian. Right? At least that is what they think! Right?"

The boy looked at him, waiting.

"Right now there is only one man with a key and a gun between us and freedom! So you could speak in perfect English and they would assume that it was either Vladimir or Mikail! They'd open the door to either of them, would they not?"

"They would!"

Clay and Vasily smiled broadly and started to give one another a high-five, but then they looked over at Volkhov who was frowning. "We shouldn't try to all get out the same way," he said, "What if something goes wrong? They'd kill us all." He looked at Clay. "You and I, we are as good as dead already to Mikail and his people. Not Vasily. He can get out cleanly."

"What do you recommend, grandfather?" Vasily asked.

"We mustn't underestimate Mikail. He is a brilliant young man, and I don't mean that he is just 'smart'. He tested off the charts in every category. He is a phenomenon."

Volkhov looked at Clay as if to ask if he knew what they were up against. Clay nodded his head and took another drink from his bottle.

"Why wasn't he sent to Russia to spy? He's old enough isn't he?" Clay asked.

"Some people are not sent because they fail the tests, or because they are not adept at being dishonest, or because they have a skill or ability that is valuable for the village here. Some people are not sent because they lack some critical mode of thinking that is required for the job they are being sent to do. Mikail was not sent because he has a gloriously beautiful mind and is a completely unpredictable sociopath."

"You'd think that would be a plus in the spy game," Clay said, smiling.

"They don't mind 'sociopath' so much, but 'unpredictable' is what gets you disqualified. His whole attitude—his anger, bravado, and even his danger—comes from being rejected for service by the Americans. The Russians accepted him, because they had nothing to lose. He is expendable if he fails, and if he doesn't..." Volkhov said, sighing.

"Ok, so back to this plan. So you and I bust out the back, Volkhov, while Vasily goes out the front. Then he can meet up with—what is your nephew's name, Pyotr?"

"That's it," Volkhov said, nodding his head.

The old man took Vasily by the shoulders and smiled at him affectionately for a moment. "Vasily, you will take the bag because you can surely get it out without being stopped. You must get to Pyotr. Whatever the cost. Tell him what we are doing. If we get out, tell him we will meet you at the pumping station. He'll know what that means."

Vasily nodded, and gave the old man a hug. When the embrace was broken, Volkhov added, "Let me tell both of you something. If anything goes wrong during this ill-advised and quixotic jailbreak, anything at all, you are to leave me behind. I will not go with you unless you promise me that. I am an old man, and I really don't want to live through what is coming anyway. If the attack comes, it will be on Tuesday. That was the plan from the beginning. It will begin on the evening of the election."

Both Clay and Vasily nodded. Something in the back of Clay's mind should have noted that he was making a plan for escape with a young boy and an old man who had just stated that there was to be some sort of apocalyptic attack due on the day of an election, but he did not make that connection in that moment. The tension between his old world and this new world had snapped. He was simply a man fighting for his life in a cell with two other men who were doing the same, and who were offering to watch his back.

* * * *

The excitement of making a decision had trailed off and an aura of sadness now permeated the cell. They stood silently for several moments before Volkhov again broke the quiet. "Come Tuesday, you guys have to really step it up a notch. Everything will change dramatically, even as it has already begun to change.

"Don't drink municipal water anywhere on the Eastern Seaboard. Stay away from any areas where masses of people are gathered. Don't trust anyone in uniform..."

He paused to let that sink in.

"Don't try to fight it out, because that is a loser's game. The Soviet plan, or should I say, the plan of those on the third side, will be to foster instability and chaos and panic. The primary purpose of government in an advanced civilization is to prevent or minimize panic. That is it. Everything else is window dressing. You don't have to invade a country to destroy it. The people will do that for you when their comforts evaporate."

"Sounds ominous," Clay said.

"You have no idea," Volkhov replied. After a moment he said, "People who know such things will expect the bombs to start dropping immediately, but that won't happen. They will want to maximize the damage from confusion and riots before they use bombs. You'll have some time to get somewhere safe."

"You mean *we* will have some time," Vasily said.

"If I am alive, then yes. Anyway, as I mentioned during my boring speech, the higher-ups on both side know what is coming. It's been planned all along. But the law of unintended consequences will come into play. No plan survives contact with the enemy.

"They'll intend to launch missiles soon enough, but subordinates, and some free agents, and others throughout the system will have war-gamed that. The initial launches will be thwarted by massive EMP attacks in all of the critical places.

He paused and looked at the farmer-poet and the errand boy standing before him, his generals. He felt not a single bit, not even the scintilla of the slightest bit, of irony.

"We don't have time for me to explain it all. Anyway... *two weeks*. That's how long you'll have. Then, the law of human ingenuity will kick in. Despite key cards and codes and fail-safes and guarantees it will only take two weeks before some brilliant minds on every side figure out a workaround. And they *will* figure out a workaround, you can bet."

He stopped and let the word *will* sink in.

"Two weeks," Clay said, nodding his head. "That's *if* we get out of here."

Vasily looked at Clay and said, "So, now you will have to be the one to imitate Vladimir's voice. Can you do it?"

"I can," he said, and Clay was pretty sure he could.

* * * *

They went back over the plan quickly, noting that the guards would be expecting Vasily to exit at any time now. There was no benefit in making them suspicious. So after they had all agreed to the plan, Vasily shook their hands and departed. He was to grab the backpack, and head out the north door. His job was to not get caught, and to meet up with Pyotr.

"Do not turn back, no matter what happens," they told him. They'd give him five minutes, then head out the south vestibule— the one through which Clay had entered this nightmare.

Five minutes passed like an hour. The air was so thick with expectation and fear and excitement and terror that Clay wanted to scream in order to cut through it - if only so that he could breathe.

Moving through the unlocked cluster doors, Clay and Volkhov tiptoed as silently as they could manage. All went well and they passed through the final door and turned to the right and Clay could see that the Tank's door was open but the light was off and he assumed that Vasily had successfully removed the backpack.

Listening for a moment, they heard no sounds and that was a good sign because it meant that Vasily had made it outside without the guards being alerted or suspicious.

Clay and Volkhov had agreed that when they heard the lock in the inner door snap and when the door started to open outward, they would rush through the door and do their best to overwhelm the guard. There was supposed to be only one man standing guard, but he would be armed. Clay and Volkhov looked at each other with a shared agreement that they would see each other on the other side.

* * * *

It was very dark and the overhead emergency lights provided little assistance, but the darkness should give them cover. Clay wondered for a moment about the mechanics of his body, how he should hold his voice out, just so, in order that his much smaller body could emit the same force of sound as the huge beast of a man.

He stepped to the door and felt the urgency in his belly. He cleared his throat silently and swallowed.

* * * *

When they were ready and in place, Clay knocked on the door and with an authoritative voice commanded the guard to open up. He thought he did a pretty good job of it. He looked at Volkhov in the dim light and could see that the old man's head was nodding approval.

The outer door opened and they heard the guard grunt and then they heard the key slip into the lock on the inner door, but then the sound stopped.

"Who is it?" the voice asked in heavily accented English, "say again who it is!"

"It's Vladimir Nikitich, stupid! Open the damn door!"

They heard the grunt again and then the lock turned and the door began to pull outward and that is when they rushed through the door.

* * * *

Clay slammed through the portal violently and felt the guard collapse into the vestibule wall as the door unexpectedly hit him across the face. He felt Volkhov rushing behind him, clasping on to the thin fabric of his prison jumper, and he saw the faint outline of the stunned guard with the machine pistol and he rushed him and put his hand on the gun, pushing it downward as he brought the full force of his body crushing downward against the darkened figure.

He was surprised when the guard recovered so quickly, and he felt the gun being ripped from his hand and a booted foot came upward and caught him in the chest and he was brutally kicked across the vestibule. He expected bullets to rip into his body at any moment, but Volkhov had responded like a man half his age and he crashed into the guard before he could raise the gun. With both hands the old man grappled with the gun and his head turned toward Clay, who had regained his feet...

The old man shouted "GO!" at the top of his lungs.

* * * *

Time, in such moments, telescopes outward. Every moment, every motion becomes an infinity, an eternity. The reasons before you and behind you come into sharp focus in your being and you know what it is you are made of. Such moments are, perhaps above any other moments in one's life, clarifying.

Clay was able to see in the darkness and he rushed forward to help Volkhov but it was too late and the gun fired and both Volkhov and the guard crashed to the ground.

Clay froze and heard Volkhov yell "GO!" again. This time it was weaker, less in bravery than in finality. He immediately knew that he did not want to waste the man's sacrifice, and he pushed his way out the outer door and began to sprint along the south wall of the prison.

* * * *

His right hand brushed lightly along the wall and the cold gripped him and he realized he was just in his prison garb. He could feel the cold assaulting his fingers through the cracks in the bricks where the mortar lines had crumbled and were now filled with flaking snow.

The gun fired again and when Clay looked back he saw the guard was backing out of the outer door and Clay felt himself sprinting as fast as he could run through the snow and down the gentle incline that led to the fence line. He lost one of his slip-on shoes in the snow, and then the other came off, and he fell down in a small snowdrift, but he clawed his way back up and kept running. He could see his breath rush out of his body like a spirit.

He ran for his life.

He broke towards where he knew the gap would be in the fence and was now running across the open field, struggling in his bare feet through the snow and from this point on things could only be called 'surreal.' He saw what looked like huge gray balloons floating all around him toward the ground and though he was confused he picked up his speed and looked over his shoulder to see if the guard was gaining on him.

He didn't see the guard coming and thought perhaps that he had made it, and he ran toward the grey balloons floating beautifully out of the sky and he listened intently in the distance for a gunshot. But he didn't hear any.

He didn't hear any gunshots.

* * * *

When he came up over the last rise where he expected to see the fallen trees, he noticed that there were no trees at all. He ran toward the nothingness. In fact, any clue that would tell him that the storm had destroyed any section of the fence *at all* was now gone completely. The fence that stood now was shiny and new, and the ground was disturbed around it evidencing the new construction, then his vision of the new fence was obscured by one of the gray balloons and then another and another.

* * * *

Clay Richter stopped and stared in the middle of the pristine field of glowing snow and watched the forms fall downward in the crisp moonlight. His eyes focused intently on the billowing orbs as they hung in the sky and just gently swayed in the reflective glow of the nighttime. They contrasted sharply with the clear, black sky, filling up with air and glow from the snow's bright light. They were beautiful and wondrous... and then Clay realized what they were.

Parachutes.

As he watched one of them down while it fell silently through the cold, he realized that hanging from the bottom of the round parachute was a paratrooper with a rifle.

His heart raced, and then he knew he was saved.

* * * *

Clay ran in the direction of one of the men, waving his arms like a drowning man in the sea of snow. Collapsing into a snow bank, he struggled to move on all fours, shouting that he was an American and that he had been captured by escapees from the prison. Rising to his feet he stumbled forward thinking that the man was too far away for him to see Clay clearly, but the soldier looked around and noticed him, anyway. He heard the sound of Clay's yelling and he started toward him, raising his weapon as he did.

* * * *

What's going on? Clay struggled in his mind to ask that question. Then he suddenly realized they could not know who he really was because he was wearing prison garb. They could not know him.

He put his hands above his head and dropped to his knees. He showed them he meant no harm. He repeated his story loudly as a soldier walked across the snow toward him. Another was making his way through the distance and Clay could almost see them, could almost read their faces.

Then his heart sank. He looked back up into the paratrooper's eyes, and followed the intent gaze. Off to the left. The paratrooper was not looking at him at all.

Clay looked across the field of snow and saw his tracks leading backward, toward the prison, toward the figure of a man standing in the doorway.   The man stepped into the light underneath the overhang and then was followed by another, and another, and Clay followed the paratrooper's eyes to see Mikail and Vladimir and Sergei walking towards them.

* * * *

He saw the paratrooper raise the gun and he wondered if the soldier was going to shoot the three unarmed young men right there in the snow.

The man shouted to the trio approaching on foot, but—and this fact took time to penetrate Clay's mind—the soldier spoke in Russian.

He spoke in Russian?

Clay saw his life flash before his eyes. He saw the tree swing and the cabin, and the inside of his brownstone, and Veronica. And Cheryl. Lovely Cheryl. He swallowed and looked up into the nighttime sky.

* * * *

Clay heard the shouts in Russian and saw the waving angry menace of the bulldog Mikail.   The gun moved slowly, lazily towards Clay and then Clay...

...heard its bark and felt its bite.

He saw the flash at the muzzle and thought how beautiful it was, how much it looked like fireworks. He felt bullets ripping into him and sensed a jerking in his body. The breath ran through him and then out of him and he noticed the beautiful fog it made against the clear night air, rising up like a spirit.

He collapsed on the snow.

* * * *

The last thing Clay Richter saw was his own blood in sharp contrast with the whiteness of the pristine snow. It ran in little rivulets along the fresh packed snow where his body had fallen and then sank into the white and beyond that into the ground he loved so dearly and from whence he'd come. The last thought he ever formed, which slowly gripped his fading mind, circling in and around his consciousness like a vise until it held in him for an instant like a thin point of light or like a star in relief against the midnight sky, was a sentence that never had its own chance to find its period.

Always leave yourself a way o

* * * *

Vasily Romanovich Kashporov heard the gunfire, and then he heard it again, and then once again. Looking over his shoulder and up the hill he saw the outline in the dark sky of the silent paratroopers gliding down in and around the prison walls and its fence and its fields.

A half-dozen came down in the street, drifting past the grocery between the Church and the shops and the houses. Some others looked as though they might have landed on top of the gymnasium.

He shivered just a bit in the cold wind and ducked his head as he pulled the shoulder straps up on the backpack and tightened them slightly across his chest.

He set his square face towards Pushkin Street and the light brown house on the end which even at that very moment had a candle showing through the window.

He knew the house well. He'd often passed it on his errands in and around the village and many times he had stopped to admire its many raised gardens and unique landscaping.

That was where he knew he'd find Pyotr Alexandrovitch Bolkonsky.

From The Poems of C.L. Richter:

Lullaby for My Daughter

Little one, your hair undone,
Your legs all full of flying
You saved me from the Me, Myself,
and with so little trying.
Before you came, life's endless game
was won when worlds were winning.
And then life's toils and chase of spoils
was stopped, and worlds stopped spinning.
You spin upon the needles head
and, needless, heed my pleading
that all life's cares be plowed to shares
of bounty for thy needing.
The night comes strong as day grows long
and sunrise preps her entry.
Now sleep, dear one. The moon, the sun,
and nature be thy sentry.

KNOT TWO

THE CHARM
SCHOOL

CHAPTER 10

Warwick was a nice enough town, if one were merciful enough to forget, even for a moment, its purpose in the world. Nestled deep in a thick forest, in a sleepy little hollow shielded on all sides by ancient mountains cut through by dissecting rivers and grinding glacial ice, the town was beautiful in its way, like many New England towns.

In the spring and summer, its verdant plateau was adorned with the delicate purple blooms of the deadly nightshade and the brief yellows of lady slipper orchids. In the fall, the leaves of its towering canopy of yellow birch, black cherry, red oak, and white pine trees drifted lazily through the crisp mountain air and piled along the streets and in the forest bed in heaps of luscious reds and golds. It was a quaint place, shrouded in antiquity, despite its relative youth.

One might easily have found resting in those piles of leaves, for example, on a normal autumnal evening, a man who by dress and mannerisms resembled (if one didn't know better) the image of a colonial Rip Van Winkle. Or a man looking like that mad monk Rasputin might have been found raking those leaves, gathering them into neat little piles to be composted as he nodded to the women passers-by, or watched the children playing Cossacks and Robbers in the street.

All in all, Warwick (often called Novgorod, as a nickname, by the locals) had the quality of a foreign town in a foreign land, as if the inhabitants had come from some other country and brought the bricks and stone and wood of their ancestral homes with them, along with their clothes and language and customs. It was the kind of place one rarely sees in the landscape of American modernity. This, in the particular case of Warwick, was especially convenient, since almost no one had ever seen it.

There was only one road leading into and out of Warwick and, in the recent twin natural disasters—the raging superstorm called Sandy and the even more powerful blizzard that followed in its wake—even that route had been cut off.

Where the town had drawn its sustenance, beyond the ample and well-worked vegetable gardens and the livestock that dotted its streets and lay hidden in its valley, had always been something of a mystery, even to those who lived there.

There had been no convoys of trucks along its lone corridor, no planes flying low and touching down on a secluded runway. Somehow the town had simply, since its inception in the late 1950's, in a time when two superpowers were engaged in a cold war, been re-supplied through capillary action from some unknown source or sources. The Spar grocery and the smaller specialty markets—the butchers, the bakers, and the candlestick makers— seemed to remain perpetually well stocked, though the selection was probably more limited than one might find in a land where competition thrived.

Most American towns, villages, and even tiny hamlets either grew or they died. Warwick, by contrast, just maintained. The same forces that multiplied or diminished growth in small town America were not at work in Warwick. Competition for labor from nearby cities, children escaping small town life for college or for excitement in the Metropolis, young adults fleeing the staid and boring village for... well... for anything else, even for war, these were not defining factors in Warwick.

Other American towns either provided a boon for encroaching modernity, enticing new and bigger businesses to come and build and supply the needs and dreams and lusts of modern life, or they suffered a drain of the young and dull or best and brightest. Because of the centuries-long culture war against the traditional home and multi-generational families, modern American small town life had become a fleeting thing for all but the old-timers, and this reality—outside Warwick—meant that the market forces that feed or starve a town were usually pretty evident to anyone who cared to look. By contrast, somehow Warwick lived and breathed and regenerated itself almost invisibly.

There had been rumors once of an underground passage, something like a Moscow Metro-2, but these rumors (like those about the very existence of Warwick) had never been confirmed by anyone who had ever been there and made it out alive. Sure, trucks delivered goods and supplies, just like in any other town. This isn't, after all, a fairy tale; the shelves are not stocked by elves at night. But the trucks that carried the lifeblood of urban life to Warwick came from warehouses within town, and where those warehouses got their goods and supplies, very few people actually knew.

The town was a closed loop, but it had not always remained completely hermetically sealed. Alumni existed... somewhere. There had been such people, for example, a rare and storied few souls who had escaped the town during what was known as the Great Confusion in 1992 - when the Soviet Union had collapsed and the town's nominal reason for existence had come into question. Later however, with guards and dogs patrolling its surrounding forest, and that forest extending out to a distance of five football fields and sometimes more, crisscrossed with listening and heat detection devices, the town's topographical subterfuge had served its purpose well in keeping the residents in, and hikers or other curious onlookers who might stumble onto the place out.

Before the twin storms, even airlines didn't fly over the area. Instead, they followed the dictates of the jet stream and the regulations for air traffic set down by military and intelligence planners. Like other strategically cloaked areas—one thinks of Area 51 or RAF Menwith Hill—the town of Warwick had been established and maintained in absolute secrecy, with every effort made to ensure that prying eyes were kept out. Any eyes that had crept in, and there had been a very few, were pried out, which is to say that any intruders that actually saw the town, and were caught, usually disappeared or met with some unfortunate accident in the forest. Electronic prying was equally difficult. Satellite photos and maps showed only an endless expanse of trees.

There was, in fact, in the same region of New York State, another Warwick - another village by the same name. However, even this was a diversion. That other Warwick, around since the beginning of American Independence, served as a convenient placeholder for anyone who ever had a question about rumors, or who made an inquiry concerning whereabouts.

This Warwick, this hamlet built during a war that was always expected but, like Godot, never seemed to arrive, was an anachronism. It was a wick, the archaic name for community, built for a war that was never a war.

War-Wick.

Like its sister village, its twin, it was an American city built in a year of freedom, but following the blurring of its purpose—as the conflict which threatened that freedom seemed to disappear—this Warwick had become an inscrutable enigma. It was a camouflage for a freedom, a force seeking purpose in shadows.

Contrary to the age-old wisdom, those who were responsible for the place had decided that this was good and proper enough. Therefore, despite its long-lost mission, Warwick had become, it seemed, a light kept discreetly under a bushel.

To be clear, and to remove any poetic obfuscation, Warwick had been, for many decades, a Cold War era spy school, or, as it was referred to by those who lived there, a *charm school.* This was its raison d'être, its reason for being. And while its purpose as a school was in some ways sinister, the town itself had maintained much of its charm.

Thousands of individual Americans had been born, raised, and trained in Warwick, all with the explicit purpose of eventually being sent to the Soviet Union to fit seamlessly into that society and, once there, to work to bring about its downfall.

On the surface, the project made sense. It was easier and safer to raise Russians from birth to spy in Russia than to recruit and turn (and then trust) a natural-born Russian.

A Warwickian spy turned loose in Russia was really a clean slate—a *tabula rasa.* His cover story might be that he was an orphan, or that he had transferred there from somewhere else in the country. He knew nothing of the overall program of which he was but a small part, so he was not such a tremendous risk. He knew no one else, other than his immediate superior, and he knew next to nothing about that superior except very general details of when and where he was to deliver his regular reports. If arrested, he could talk in vague terms of some spy school in America, but as to any specifics, he was ignorant, he was isolated, and his knowledge could not and would not destroy the whole system.

So, while it is admitted that the Warwick system was certainly not cheaper in a strictly economic sense than traditional forms of espionage, it was much less expensive in terms of risk. Turning natural-born Russians against their country, by definition, put the existing spy rings in that country at risk. Years and years of work could be overthrown with one bad bet. On whom would you gamble such expense and value? On someone who had already proved to be a traitor to his own country?

There was a joke that was quite common in Warwick: Are we men or mice? The question was usually asked as if to say,

"Who are we to ask questions?" or "What are we in the grand scheme of things?" The punchline was: Who can tell the difference? The humor in the joke lay in an understanding of international spycraft. M.I.C.E. is an acronym that defines the main ways used in the traditional recruitment of foreign intelligence assets. The components include:

Money
Ideology
Coercion or Compromise
Ego or Excitement

For millennia, whether through ancient palace intrigue, medieval religious chicanery, backwards third-world coups, or intricate and advanced intelligence operations, spy handlers and controllers have used many means to turn assets against their own people. All one has to do is to find a target who has access to the information, or people, or materials that one wants. Then you find out what drives them. Can they be bought with money? (Most can.) Can they be swayed by love of country? (Most can't.) Are they pliable due to some particular ideology they hold that might be considered deviant to their overlords? Perhaps they can be put into some compromising position (honeypots are older than Winnie the Pooh). Or maybe they are just looking for the excitement involved with being a traitor and a spy? Whatever the case, espionage takes and receives all kinds. But... all of this entails great risks to the organization that recruits the spies. One missed call or false turn and the whole system can be in danger of being exposed. Double-agents are as famous as the singular kind.

So why not raise your own spies? That was the thinking that birthed Warwick.

In traditional espionage, any single one of the elements in this M.I.C.E. list could be the motive played upon in the recruitment of a particular human intelligence asset. But in Warwick, the people themselves had been *bred* to become assets. They were raised and trained to spy as a part of their culture and identity, rather than as a reaction to some perceived personal benefit. When money is the motive for a man to spy against his country, then more money can be used to turn him back against his new masters. The same can be said of most of the M.I.C.E motivations, and a traditional asset, once turned, could be caught out, especially by the sophisticated machinery of modern intelligence. In fact, another joke that was told in Warwick had to do with the notion that the trick was not to build a better mousetrap but, rather, to breed smarter mice. Warwick had been set up as a kind of maze for training better mice. In the process, the line between men and assets had become increasingly blurred.

That was the grand scheme and vision of the military and intelligence officials who'd first conceived of the town, and in accord with this design they built Warwick to look and feel and behave exactly as a typical Russian village might. Its citizens were fully American, but they were indistinguishable from any Russian man or woman on the street. They lived in Russian houses, and they slept in Russian beds. When they went to withdraw money from the bank, they walked into Sberbank and drew out crisp rubles, and when they looked at their wrists to tell the time, they saw a Poljot. These were American citizens, but they were Russians, by culture, habit of mind, and force of personality.

The obvious complications of developing such a people on American soil and giving them the tools of espionage as second nature became problematic once the cold war was believed to have ended.

Some intelligence wonks whose opinions mattered believed that Warwick had become a buggy-whip industry. Not that espionage itself was unnecessary, mind you. Whips still had their place. It was simply that those in the places of power began to question whether it was wise to devote whole factories to their production.

Throughout their history, all of these unique humans, raised and trained in Warwick, had been used as tools of war, in one way or another, amidst the great battles of ideology fought between men of opposing nations. They had been humans treated as a set of assets. They were pawns, played in a global chess game of power. But, when the game had suddenly turned, or seemed to have, during the late 1980s and early 1990s, they were not simply decommissioned or re-commissioned. They were sacrificed, as pawns will be, to the interests of those who had formed them in secret. Billionaire capitalists privatized the place and kept it under wraps in waiting for... what? Maybe they hoped and prayed for a return to cold war profiteering. (One could go hungry trying to live off of micro-wars.) Whatever the case, a decision was made to fund in private what was no longer feasible to fund from the public trough.

Warwick, though she was as authentically Russian as possible, and though she had been erected on a foundation of duplicity, was no Potemkin Village. In the fifty years since it had come into existence, life had taken its natural course there, as it had in other places, and as it inevitably will wherever people are gathered in groups.

People in Warwick, for the most part, grew up in loving families, raised children who loved, dated, ice-skated on Nizhny Pond, watched Russian movies at Pushkinsky-Cine, worshipped and wed one another in St. Olaf's Church, and were buried in the cemetery behind it.

Although Warwick was a town built to train spies, it had been obvious from the first that only a certain percentage of its citizens would ever be put into action. Like any people anywhere, there were sorting mechanisms put in place, devised around talent, intelligence, character, and other factors, and only a few select individuals were ultimately found suited to the task of espionage.

There had been two primary "routes" (for lack of a better word) for the lives traversed by the people of Warwick. At age ten, each citizen was tested and re-tested by the powers-that-be in order to determine which of the routes they would ultimately follow.

One route led to deployment, eventually, to Russia to live and work as a spy for America. Thousands of these Warwickians already lived and thrived in Mother Russia, smuggled in by whatever means necessary over the decades from then until now.

The second route was reserved for those citizens who failed the testing for some reason or another—or for those who possessed some other requisite talent or skill that gave value to the town and its mission. This route meant that, for those who did not make it as spies, they would remain to live and work and serve their country in Warwick for the entirety of a lifetime.

There was no getting out.

Being released into the general American population was out of the question, given the possibilities raised by divided loyalties and the particular kind of expert training that was the lifeblood of the community. Besides, Warwickians would never fit in to modern America anyway. They didn't know American food or cigarettes or beer. They would have been utterly lost in a Wal-Mart. They'd not been raised on The Andy Griffith Show or

Happy Days or The Cosby Show or Saved by the Bell or Lost or Glee or any of the other television programs that had defined any particular generation.

They had received as much American culture as any normal Russian would have, but they knew America only by reputation and by propaganda and not in any real and experiential way. They read Pravda and Izvestiya and Novaya Gazeta and had never, or almost never, seen or read a USA Today or New York Times. It is possible that they might be accepted in a small, agrarian community where their more formal way of speaking and their cultural illiteracy might be considered closer to 'normal,' but otherwise, and anywhere else, they would be immediately suspect. And to be honest (if such a thing as honesty is acceptable in any examination of the mechanisms of espionage and other forms of professional lying), most of the citizens of Warwick—those that had lived and loved and died there since its inception—never really wanted anything more out of life. Historically, this is true of the bulk of humanity since, of course, we are now being honest.

In respect to the kind of life lived—the actual makeup of the society and culture—most people throughout history have believed that what they have is good and right, and they believe this because they've been told to. They love their system because they find it sufficient, even if they want more out of it like anyone else. This is a particular trait of the spirit.

But there are also traits of the flesh. Upward mobility and the desire for anything or anywhere else *other than home* is a particularly western phenomenon, most specifically identifiable in Americans of the last couple of centuries. Warwickians, insulated from Madison Avenue and Hollywood, had been spared this most American of characteristics.

A few people had escaped Warwick, as noted, during the "confusion" of 1992, and an occasional intrepid soul had abandoned the cause while living as a spy in his adopted country, disappearing into the maw of Mother Russia for some reason known only to time. However, for the most part, and for most citizens, life in Warwick was a closed loop. One was born there and lived there and died there, with only the occasional glimpse into the wider world being permitted. Such a glimpse was only allowed when it served the purposes of those chess masters who administered the pawns, and when it advanced the designs of the nation. Life in Warwick was pleasant enough, but that was mainly because, even if discontent arose, such a life was the only game in town.

* * * *

Friday

Winter. Late fall by the calendar, but winter in almost every way that counts. The valley, with its dormant flowers and evergreen seedlings, was blanketed in snow, and throughout the surrounding countryside, the very air was crackling with frigidity.

Standing on a high ridge overlooking the valley in the cold of the afternoon, two men, and a pretty Warwick girl of twenty named Natasha, looked down from a tree line about three-hundred yards to the northwest of Warwick, and they had trouble assimilating what they were seeing. Warwick—the whole town and everything in it, and everyone from it that they have ever known—had become a burned-out corpse. Novgorod of America was dead.

The homes and church and school and fields, the memories they had of moving about and within each... all of it had become a long black scar on the terrain of the Catskill Forest Preserve. The streets and buildings of their memories were gone, replaced by the refuse and boulders and charcoal of annihilation. Even the snow had melted entirely from the heat, and the water and mud and debris remained in steaming piles of scattered destruction under the skeletons of charred trees.

What about the people?

Neither of the men—one very young, and the other middle-aged—could seem to imagine any hope that there would be anyone they knew still alive in the ghastly scene before them. The girl brushed away a tear and emitted an almost imperceptible sob.

How could the destruction be so complete?

How could anyone have made it out of there alive?

Where is my brother? Natasha wondered.

None of the three gave voice to those particular words—or any words at all—but the silence among them amplified the questions. They all knew that life as they once had known it, like the town they had grown up in and called home, would never be the same again. The girl grimaced again in pain and bowed down in silent grief. Unspoken emotion, though voiceless, swirled loudly in the air between them like the wind.

The young one called Lang was the first to speak. It should be noted before going further that this was not his real name. It was merely the identity he had assumed as he stood atop the ridge. In the world of espionage in which he'd been raised, a name was as easy to change as a passport. Easier even. There is a place inside a man where he knows who he really is, but when he searches that place he often finds it nameless, and maybe swept clean to the very corners. What, after all, is in a name? It was merely something he calls himself. The man decided to call himself Lang.

"It must have been the drones," Lang said. "Exactly what we figured."

The pilotless, remote-controlled militarized aircraft, five of them, somehow still operative after the EMP attack, had buzzed past the treatment plant like bees early that morning, low to the ground and in formation. Both Lang and the older gentleman at his side, a heavy-set man, 42 years old, who now called himself Peter, had seen them swoop overhead.

They'd heard the buzzing first and took cover in the shed, only to step outside as the drones passed by, to watch their trajectory as they rose smoothly up and over the mountain. Without even speaking, the two men had figured that the appearance of the drones certainly had something to do with the charm school.

After packing and securing all of their gear from the water plant, they'd hustled up the mountain, and, climbing through the snow and trees and brush, they had come to where they now stood. The snow deposited by the blizzard came up to their knees as they stood and looked out over the valley.

Below them, Warwick was a smoking ruin with not one stone left upon another. It looked like something from a war zone and, in fact, that is exactly what it was. Lang thought of the words of Tolstoy, "What a terrible, terrible thing..." The picture brought him in his mind to visions of Borodino, of Moscow as the Russians had left it for Napoleon, or of the 200 days of Stalingrad. Dark black curls of smoke rose here and there from the rubble like souls returning to their maker.

The jagged gash in the earth left behind by the drones' payloads meant two things to Lang. First, that someone somewhere had known enough to shield their weapons of war from the EMP attack. Someone knew it was coming. Second, it meant that somewhere in the hills of Virginia, or Maryland, or perhaps even in Washington D.C., there was a control room—probably underground—that still operated with full power. That someone had launched and perpetrated the attack on Warwick left no doubt as to its conclusion.

Overkill.

This thought process led Lang to consider something that until then he had not contemplated. Someone obviously thought that Warwick was still a threat. Just that morning he'd been convinced that the town had escaped the worst of the damage, having survived the EMP. He'd even briefly considered returning one final time to make a last ditch effort to find Cole, or to maybe convince some more of the residents to flee.

As he stood on the ridge and looked down on Warwick's apocalypse, this valley of Megiddo, he shuddered and was glad that the thought had only been a momentary one. The devastation was total. Not even a mouse could have survived this attack.

It wouldn't do to have them catch us out here in the open, Lang thought. The drones have infrared capability too, and if they were to return, the three of them standing on the rise would be toast in just seconds.

Peter interrupted Lang's thoughts. "It's all gone," he said, without any discernible emotion. "I can't say I'll miss it."

"That was our home, Peter," Lang replied, sadly. "Not to mention the people... the people. We grew up there," he continued. "You're older than me. I'm barely eighteen, but neither one of us has ever been anywhere else. We used to ice skate and play hockey on the pond behind the church there, just up on the ridge." Lang felt like he needed to choke back a tear as memories overwhelmed him. "We used to have Christmas plays right there in the gym. How can you have no feelings for it at all?"

"It was a town of lies, Lang, and you know it," Peter growled. "Warwick sent our parents off to Russia, mine these thirty long years ago, and we'll never see them again. I lived there as an orphan. As an adult I was blessed enough to smuggle a son—my beautiful little Nikolai, and my wife with him—out of Warwick during the confusion." Now Peter's voice lowered to almost a whisper, though his anger still owned his words. "Warwick destroyed my life. If my family had not gotten out, this town would have eaten them too. I've never seen them again or spoken to them since that day twenty years ago."

Peter looked at Lang, his eyes flashing fury, "So don't tell me what to mourn, Lang."

"I'm not telling you what to mourn, Peter, really I'm not. I'm just saying that the town didn't do those things. Warwick was what it was, but for most of our lives it was just a home. I know what Warwick was. This place was a tragedy for everyone, but it was home, Peter. Blame the people who did this, the Americans or the Russians, but the people who lived in that town are not to blame."

They stood for a moment in chilly silence. The cold in the snow began to hurt in their feet, passing through their boots and into their bodies. Lang shook his head, and then his boots, and shifted the straps on his backpack. *Peter will calm down soon enough*, he thought, but the older man had been in a foul mood all day. He heard the man breathing in the space beside him and noticed him clench his jaw and then release.

"Just don't tell me what to mourn," Peter repeated angrily, before turning and retreating the way they had come. Lang took another long look at the ruins of Warwick Village, and then followed Peter back down the hill.

Natasha stood for a moment longer, hoping to catch some glimpse, some vision of movement, there in the hopelessness of the rubble.

CHAPTER 11

5 Days Earlier – Sunday Night

The candle's flame twisted around the wick and hissed its tiny protest, sending up a small trail of smoke that curled around the motion of waves as the burly man stepped into the hallway and peeked through the peephole in the door. The warmth from the fire in the other room dissipated, trailing away from his body in invisible little traces. The blanket over his shoulders did little to insulate against the cold night air. The blizzard had passed, but it had left behind it the cold of winter and the promise of a harsh season ahead.

When Vasily Romanovich Kashporov walked up the stone steps that wound through the elevated gardens, he'd been unsure of what he would find. Life had taken a sideways jolt for everyone in Warwick, but his life, in particular, was spinning off madly into he knew not what.

The last few hours had been eventful ones. First there'd been the prison breakout, and then the show trial in the gym and a bloody execution. The gang of prisoners, led by Vasily's peers, had first taken over the prison and then overrun the whole town of Warwick. Though Vasily had escaped in the first breakout with the rest of the prisoners, he'd not taken any part in the coup. The leaders thought of him as just a useful idiot.

After the mock trial, the leaders chose Vasily to be the keeper of two men they'd locked away in a jail cell as "enemies to the revolution." They'd chosen Vasily specifically because they believed him to be loyal, and if not loyal, then too stupid to be of any harm. But he was neither loyal nor stupid.

He was, however, in danger.

He'd plotted an escape with the two men who, he hated to admit, were now almost certainly dead.

The first of the two men was an old citizen named Lev Volkhov. Lev had been his mentor, as well as a revered elder and teacher in the village. The other man was a friendly traveler he knew only as Clay.

The three of them had attempted their own prison break in order to escape the dangerous power grab that was evident in the town's insurgent revolution.

After Vasily had set them free from their cell, the plan had been for Lev Volkhov and Clay to leave through an external door at the rear of the prison while he, Vasily, gathered Clay's backpack and exited through the prison's hallway system into the courtyard that led to the town.

At least, that was the plan. The second prison break, unhappily, had happened concurrently with the arrival of outsiders—paratroopers sent by someone to support the coup attempt in the town. It seemed like things might have gone horribly wrong for Volkhov and Clay.

Vasily had witnessed the show trial and the brutality of the takeover, and right then and there he'd made a decision. He was impressed by the old man and the traveler, and he'd decided that his best hope for freedom was to throw in his lot with them.

There were politics involved, as there always are. But there were also the sheer instincts for survival, and in that moment, the two had become fused into one force, and from that point the young man moved with a singular purpose.

He knew more about the kind of politics involved, and the way those politics linked to survival, than anyone in the village other than Volkhov. This was because Vasily—although almost no one knew it or suspected it—was probably the foremost expert on the writings of Alexander Solzhenitsyn in all of Warwick. He'd been introduced to the works of Solzhenitsyn during long tutoring sessions at the hands of Lev Volkhov and had taken the Russian author's words to heart. He'd read Solzhenitsyn's *Warning to the West*, detailing the ongoing communist threat against the world, and this work, written by his countryman, he believed sincerely.

This great man, this winner of the Nobel Prize in literature, this sufferer from the Soviet Gulag, had warned America—the stated enemy of his own country—to be wary of Russia. In the *Warning to the West*, Solzhenitsyn, speaking of the forces of social change in America, and of the ongoing threat of Soviet communist hegemony, had said, and Vasily knew it by heart...

"They are trying to weaken you; they are trying to disarm your strong and magnificent country in the face of this fearful threat—one which has never before been seen in the history of the world. Not only in the history of the country, but in the history of the world."

Solzhenitsyn had warned America of everything that the old man Volkhov had said when he'd addressed the crowd gathered for his show trial, in the moments before being summarily convicted by the gang.

It was Solzhenitsyn who'd once said, *"One word of truth outweighs the world."* Vasily had heard the old man speak that truth in the simple word... No.

Vasily had also read *A Day in the Life of Ivan Denisovitch*, as had most of the boys in his school, but he hadn't let it end there as most of the others had. Wanting more of this truth that outweighed the world, he dove deeper. He read more about his supposed country of Russia in *The Gulag Archipelago*, and in the Red Wheel books. He'd read Solzhenitsyn's short stories, like *Matryona's House*, and unlike the other boys in his school, he had cried, only a few years back, when he'd learned of Alexander Solzhenitsyn's death.

This was the secret life that Vasily Kashporov led, one of books and of the mind, and this is why he chose truth and freedom over any of the other options being offered to him by men of every age who wanted and abused power.

Walking away from the prison, he'd heard the gunshots, and he knew that he was now alone, save for the man who was in this house to which he'd been sent.

Lev Volkhov, before he was killed, promised Vasily that his nephew, Pyotr Alexandrovitch Bolkonsky, would 'know everything' and would know what to do next. Volkhov had ordered Vasily to go to Pyotr and not to look back. Vasily respected his old friend enough to do exactly what he'd been told.

He knew the house, and found it easily, and had climbed the steps with trepidation, not knowing whether the gang might have already arrived, or if its inhabitant had already cleared out. There was fear in his heart, cold and brittle like ice, as he raised his hand to knock on the door.

* * * *

Pyotr opened the door and saw the young man standing there with his face pale from the cold and fear. He grabbed Vasily by the shoulders and guided him into the house and then through the hallway and into a tiny room near the back. An earnest fire snapped in a fireplace, sending shadows of the two men leaping onto the walls. Pyotr poured the young man a cup of coffee, black, bitter, and strong, from a pot on a stove, and pointed him to a chair by the fire. They made introductions as the cup was handed from one set of hands to the other, but such things were unnecessary. Everyone in the town always knew everyone else as a matter of course, or seemed to.

Pyotr had a million questions, and he spoke in rapid-fire Russian, but Vasily was too shaken to respond immediately.

"What was the shooting, Vasily?" Pyotr asked. "Who was shot? I heard so much shooting..." He let the implications of his question hang in the air like the cold. "The whole town's been turned upside down since the trial. I cannot believe it! Mikail shot Todd point blank. And right in the head! And in front of everyone! And then these soldiers fall out of the sky. What kind of thing was that? I'm worried sick about Lev. How is Uncle Lev? Have you spoken with him? Is he ok?"

Vasily brought his eyes up to look at Pyotr, and in the look he tried to say what he feared he could not. He waved at the older man to slow him down, and then dropped his head to his chest. He drew in his breath slowly. He knew that the news that he carried was dark and would hurt Pyotr. "Only English, Pyotr. Only English now. Please. I've come from the prison. It's not good. I don't know it, but I do know it... Lev Volkhov and the man called Clay are dead. There would have been no shooting if they had escaped." Vasily looked up again and into Pyotr's confused eyes. "The shooting was too fast and too soon. They cannot have gotten to the fence. They are both dead, I know it."

Pyotr sat forward, his eyes widened as a flash of despair crossed his face. He opened his mouth, but for a moment no words came out. He clenched his jaw, taking a deep breath through his nose. Vasily could see the man's ribcage expand with the breath and then hold there for a moment, as if in pain, before a long, sad exhale, and the older man pushed his head back in resignation or supplication.

"Uncle Lev is... dead?" he asked, in English. The sound of the words was plaintive. His hand reached out and gripped Vasily's shoulder, steadying himself.

"He is, Pyotr. He has to be. There is no other way for me to know, but he has to be. He cannot be alive."

Vasily went through the story of the planned escape, telling Pyotr about Volkhov's words, and how Vasily was to exit the front of the prison with the backpack, get to Pyotr, and then go to some water plant. He told Pyotr about how Volkhov and Clay were going to try to rush the guard at the back entrance and somehow make it through the destroyed fence line and then head to this same water plant.

"It was always 50-50, Pyotr. We all knew that. Either Lev and Clay would get the drop on the guard, or the guard would get the drop on them. And... and... just as they made their exit, the troops parachuted in on top of them and dropped down all around the prison."

There were tears in Pyotr's eyes as he listened, but he nodded his head and did not interrupt until Vasily had shared his whole story. Vasily told him how the soldiers had landed all over that end of town, and he told of the sound of machine gun fire coming from behind the prison. There was the sense of finality in his voice, a certainty gained not through witness, but certainty nevertheless, based on the only reasonable conclusion he could draw.

"That's it then," Pyotr said, choking back tears. "They're dead."

Pyotr stood and walked over to the ikons on the wall and, with tears in his eyes he bowed his head to the holy saints. "Now... Now I've lost everyone," he said to the saints who were flat and long dead and who could not hear him.

Vasily sat and watched him and the twin of his shadow on the wall. Pyotr stood for a moment before exploding in anger and, ripping the sacred iconography from the wall, he smashed each frame individually against the table that held the candles. He hurled the broken frames against the opposite wall. They burst into a hundred separate pieces against the plaster, each one a tiny fractured narrative describing the man's pain and anguish. Vasily flinched, but he understood Pyotr's pain. He could hear the sound of humanity in his weeping, and he commiserated with the language.

Pyotr wept until he collapsed across a nearby table, his sobs coming in rolling, heaving waves, each gasp passing through his body and then out into the universe.

After a time, through some inner strength, Pyotr regained his composure, steadied himself and walked calmly back over to Vasily. He wiped the tears from his face. His eyes were red, and he seemed to have exhausted himself with the outflow of emotion.

"What do we do now, young Vasily?" he asked. "They will come for you." Pyotr, it seems, was fully Russian. His attitude now reflected the millennia of Russian experience, which was to say... *Enough of crying, I'm done with that, now what do we do?*

Vasily's eyebrows arched. Hearing the danger that he knew was around him expressed in the words of another suddenly made it real, and he tried to push it away.

"Why would they come for me? I was out of the prison before it happened. Maybe they won't know I was involved."

"Don't be silly, son. How did Uncle Lev and Clay get out of their cell, Vasily Romanovich? Think! How did they get out of the cluster? Who could have let them out?" As Pyotr spoke, his voice started to rise in anger.

"Well, they can't know it was me. Maybe Lev or Clay got a key from somewhere else, or picked the lock, I don't know." He was searching in his mind for an explanation, anything... even as he knew he would find none suitable.

"Listen, Vasily. Those paratroopers you saw were probably Russian Spetznaz. Special Forces. Uncle told me that the EMP attack would probably come on Tuesday, during the election. The arrival of Special Forces troops in Warwick means that someone felt like there was a risk of something leaking out before the event. Or maybe there is someone here who they do not want to escape. Maybe Mikail contacted them as soon as his gang had taken over the town and told them he'd captured an American spy. Who knows? That's the thing, Vasily, we don't know anything."

Vasily flinched at the name of the gang's leader. Mikail Mikailivitch Brekhunov was the leader of the gang that had, just recently, taken the prison and overthrown the town. He'd been the one who had misjudged Vasily. Volkhov, before he died, had told the young Vasily not to trust anything that Mikail said.

"Well, I said that we don't know anything, because we don't have a clue what's going on, but we do know one thing," Pyotr said. Pyotr had been raised and trained by Lev Volkhov, and knew his old uncle's mind backward and forward. He spoke steadily now, in perfect accentless English. "We know that we must get out of here right now. I know that's what uncle wanted, and that's why he risked himself to get you out of there first. If you go back up there to find out what's going on, they'll probably kill you. If you don't go, they'll come here and kill both of us. The only option is that the two of us leave right now."

Flee? Vasily thought. It made sense, and that is what the outsider Clay had done. That is what Lev Volkhov himself had attempted. It was, of course, the best, or at least the most sensible, option. But the heart of valor has a stubborn fiber. There were too many friends and loved ones still in harm's way for Vasily to flee just yet.

Didn't everyone deserve a warning? Isn't that what Solzhenitsyn had done? Warn people? Isn't that what the Prophets had done? Isn't that what Volkhov himself had done?

Vasily was no prophet. Nor was he a revered teacher. In fact, he was nothing more than a simple youth thought by his townsfolk to be a simpleton. But having recently been imprisoned with Mikail in the belly of the beast, the town's prison where the brutal uprising had begun, he was determined, like Noah before him, to run to his town and tell the townsfolk what was coming, so they would at least have the option to leave.

Vasily shook his head. "No. No. No. We can't just leave all of these people, Pyotr. These are our friends and our neighbors. We've got to try to get some of them out. What about the Malanovskys? What about Irinna? Do you remember Irinna, the pretty girl who works in the bakery? Are we going to just leave them all here on this battlefield? We have to do something to get as many of them out of here as we can." He was speaking as much from compassion as from bravery. It wouldn't even occur to him to leave without taking others, even as he had given no thought to trying to help the two prisoners escape. For him, there was no higher calling than answering the instinct towards one's fellow man. No greater love hath any man than that he lay down his life for his friends. Vasily, having lost his parents while still a very young boy, had no one in this world but his friends, and he was determined to try to save them

"What can we do, Vasily? What can we do if you go up there and get yourself shot? What can we do if we wait here and the

Spetznaz troops come down here and shoot both of us for participating in Lev's breakout?"

"I've got to go back, Pyotr. I have to," Vasily said, shaking his head. The finality in that word hinted at both conviction and destiny. "You prepare yourself to go, and if I'm not back, or if you get spooked, or if you hear gunfire, you just go." He spread his hands as if to answer any objections. He looked Pyotr in the eye and nodded to him. "Lev would have wanted me to at least try, Pyotr."

Pyotr nodded back at Vasily. "Ok. If that's your decision. Do not be deceived though. If it comes to the point that I think you're dead, I'm gone."

Vasily nodded and wondered when such a moment might come.

* * * *

Together they made plans, and then Pyotr took Vasily down into the basement under the house. To be accurate, it wasn't really a basement, but more of a root cellar that Lev and Pyotr had dug out by hand, many years ago.

Pyotr showed him that along the west wall, which had been concreted using trowels and coated with some kind of plaster or whitewash, there was a large, antique bureau that, upon very close examination, seemed to be attached to the wall. Pyotr pulled out the drawers of the bureau—all six of them—and then removed the wooden uprights and separators. As he worked, the dismantling of the bureau revealed an open space behind the wall. The entire piece of furniture was just an elaborate covering to a narrow entrance that led straight down into a tunnel.

Vasily stared, dumbfounded. Pyotr explained that the tunnel had been dug painstakingly over many years, and that it had remained a secret precisely because it had been known to no one. "Do you understand the significance of that statement?" he asked. "Uncle and I were the only ones who knew about it. The dirt was removed a bucket at a time, hauled up the stairs, and dumped into the multitude of steps and raised gardens and landscaping that surround this house. Uncle Lev had the idea, believing gardens were the perfect hiding place for dirt. Make no mistake though, Vasily. We didn't even let our left hands know what our right hands were doing. And we told no one else about this. You need to know that the moment you ask others to come here, the secret will be out and we will have a very short time to act."

Vasily pictured the gardens he'd just walked through as he climbed the stone walkway to the door, their boxed shapes and raised concentric circles now formed over with snow drifts and rounded to make it seem as if the house sat on a hill. He considered the truth in what Pyotr was telling him. Even if he remained intentionally blurry about the details when asking others to leave with them, it would not take long for them to figure out the truth. He nodded.

"The tunnel leads under the west perimeter wire and then comes up in a small copse of trees only meters outside the fence. From there it's a couple of miles straight through the forest to the old water treatment plant," Pyotr explained. He smiled at the young man's amazement.

A cold wind whooshed through the tunnel and hit the two men in the face. It sounded like a mechanical nothing, a low audial hum, an ocean crashing endlessly upon a gasping needy shore.

Vasily and the older man stood in the cold and listened. The waves on the other side sounded like freedom.

* * * *

Standing in the sparsely drawn cellar, Vasily remembered the backpack that he'd brought with him, and he ran back upstairs to retrieve it where he'd dropped it near the chair by the fire.

Grabbing the pack and an extra candle he found on the table, he returned to the tiny subterranean room and placed the pack down on the floor. He told the older man how he'd come into possession of the pack, and that it was supposed to have useful items, but that he did not yet know its contents.

As he kneeled to open the pack, he thought of the man who'd given it to him, the one called Clay, and he remembered the fear behind Clay's eyes when he'd first met him, but how, when he saw him last in the prison cell, ready to escape, those eyes had become peaceful and resolved, as if something important had been settled in the man's soul.

"This was given to me by a man who loved your uncle," Vasily said.

Even as he said the words, they surprised him a little, but he remembered the way that Clay and Volkhov were talking together in the cell when he'd entered as their keeper. Although the two men had not known one another long, Vasily knew that his own words were true... Clay had loved Lev Volkhov as one loves his own flesh and blood. He knelt in the darkness of the cellar and turned the pack on its side, all the while thinking how it was all that was left of the man who had made such an impression on him.

Vasily and Pyotr opened the backpack and carefully examined what was in it, cataloging the items they found, and talking about the things they would still need. Pyotr removed a camera and a radio. If Volkhov was right that an EMP would be coming soon, these items would need to be protected from the pulse. Pyotr put both electronic items into an ammo can and left them on the bureau by the tunnel so that they could take them when it was time to leave.

They looked at the other items, including a knife, a few books, some clothes, a small blue box, a fishing kit, some blankets, and sundry other things. Vasily wondered at these personal effects, just as one does when finding some item that has been used by another life - maybe in another historical era. He felt like an archeologist, or anthropologist, searching through the lost tools of another culture. It felt peculiar, rifling through someone else's property so soon after their owner had died. Vasily remembered something Clay told him in the prison cell before they'd attempted their breakout. He'd said that Vasily was the best spy in a whole town of spies. That was a kindness that had not been offered by many of the townsfolk—his own people. Warwickians had generally treated him like an idiot because he had not impressed them in the ways that they had demanded. It had taken this stranger to see his potential. He smiled and went back to his work.

After a short discussion, they agreed that Pyotr would continue to sort the items and work on their preparedness, while Vasily would return to the gym. The older man said that he would busy himself devising plans for escape and making sure the tunnel was secured and cleared and ready to be used. They could not know how many people might be willing to leave with them. The more that decided to come, the more difficult would be their escape.

In order to prepare for all contingencies, Pyotr said that he would put together some "go bags"—that's what he called them. These consisted, he explained, of packs with some food, water, and other needful supplies in them, ready to take with you in case of emergency.

When he was ready to walk back to the gym, Vasily thanked Pyotr for waiting, and told him again how sorry he was about Lev.

"Perhaps," Vasily said, "I can find out more about what happened."

"Perhaps," was all that Pyotr could say in response.

"I'll be back, Pyotr."

"I hope you will, Vasily."

"I have to do this."

"I know."

They shook hands, and Pyotr promised to pray for Vasily, and with that, they headed back upstairs.

* * * *

Vasily left Pyotr's house, and as he walked, an omnipresent darkness seemed to sit upon him. It was brooding and heavy like the weight of ages. He was terrified and sad and angry all at the same time. He felt his rapid heartbeat in his throat, and he had the beginnings of a headache from the stress. The pain lay just behind the eyes and radiated outward to his temples. He felt as if he might be walking toward his own death, but then that thought was overwhelmed by his anger at what had happened to Lev and Clay, and what the gang had done to his town. He felt a sudden surge of adrenaline and a desire to fight. His emotions shifted with each step he took toward the gymnasium. Now he was curious and hopeful. Now he was angry. Now he was overcome by the terror of facing Mikail and Vladimir and Sergei and those Spetznaz troops and their machine guns.

He kept walking forward, because that is what he had to do, resolving to do what was before him despite his feelings. Heroism is sometimes an accident of circumstance more than it is a product of design.

The night felt surreal and dark, and the frigid wind spiked past his face and whipped at his coat. Lev had trained him to think in English—it helped with his English conversation, and to do away with his natural accent—but now he had to put that away and think in Russian. It would be fatal for him if he slipped up and gave anyone an indication that he spoke English at all, much less perfectly. Like a switch being flipped in his mind, he made the change to Russian, and he purposefully put on his Russian attitude and demeanor, even changing his walk. He became, step-by-step as he walked toward the gym, just stupid, harmless Vasily, the town idiot from Warwick, who nobody suspected because no one had ever bothered to walk in his shoes.

* * * *

It is odd the way a major event, some birth or death or loss or change, can make one see the world through brand new eyes. It is as if the world is a snow globe, and occasionally it gets shaken up so that, while the pieces all remain in the same environment, the whole somehow fits together differently.

As Vasily walked through Warwick toward the gymnasium to face what could be his death, he noticed the intricately carved latticework on the eaves and rakes of the small wooden houses along his route. He felt the gravel crunch in the hard-packed snow under his boots as he listened to the moon's stillness.

In the distance, he could hear shouting and fluttering of action, and through a window he heard a chair scoot. He had walked through this town so many times at night, and the sounds and sights had always washed over him like rainwater on the windshield of a fast moving train, merely forming impressions, without announcing themselves and demanding that he stop and pay attention. Now, as he walked, he felt everything new, as if waking from a dream and realizing that the material world mattered.

Here was the place that he and Arkady, a young boy who'd lived two houses down from him since the time of his birth, threw stones at a goat and the ricochet of their misses landed them in trouble with old man Kovalenko. Down Bunin Street, he saw the jutting façade of the home of the beautiful woman he knew only as Lyudmila, who paid him to gather stones in the forest, and to build a low-rising step for her door. Here was Irinna's house, and there was the place he had first seen her, walking home from the bakery along a little side street toward her door, her arms full of bread that he could smell from across the street.

This town was the only place on earth that he had ever truly known, and as he walked through the snow toward the gymnasium, he was struck by the thought that he barely knew it at all.

Vasily was born to be a spy. Like some others of his age, this reality had always been clouded by the fact that he was born in a time when his personal value was questioned, not only by the people of his town who, as has been mentioned, saw him as having less than average intelligence, but also by the shadowy authorities who designed Warwick for the purpose of waging war with the Soviet Union. When that union dissolved, those authorities simply left the machinery of the charm school in place without giving it a discernible direction. Vasily, therefore, had grown up with a lack of direction, as if his existence mirrored the existence of the town. Not only was he a young man in a country that didn't recognize him, and in a town that didn't know him, but he was also a dreamer whose highest dream was almost certainly unattainable. He'd been, like all those who eventually did become spies and were caught out for one reason or another, abandoned to his fate and disavowed.

So he'd thrown himself into his studies, but quietly, behaving as a child does who is bullied by his peers. He received threats and intimidation on a daily basis from his classmates, and was ridiculed for his small size, and the delicate features he had inherited from his mother. Of those who'd bullied him, none had done so as prominently as the youths in the gang who had just seized power in Warwick.

Mikail Mikailivitch Brekhunov, Vladimir Nikitich Samyonov, and Sergei Dimitrivich Tupolev had, like him, been born to be spies, and like him, they had failed to achieve their ultimate goal of being picked by the Americans to spy in Russia. Though they had all been subjected to the machinery of the charm school's training, they each were found unworthy of further commissioning into service—the latter two and Vasily because their performance on testing had resulted in less than optimal results, and Mikail because he was found too unstable to be acceptable.

They all had learned, in their turn, that they were destined to stay, live, and die in Warwick, and each had reacted in different ways. Mikail and his gang became more aggressive among their peers, lashing out at anyone weaker than themselves. Vasily became a watcher of windows, a dreamer who decided that his only hope in life was to bide his time and wait for something better to come along. While he waited, he'd read books.

Mikail, Vladimir, and Sergei had noticed their younger cohort's reticence to action from the earliest days in school and in the streets of their town. They saw weakness and timidity where there had been only Vasily's hopes, and they saw stupidity where there was his tendency toward silent and internal contemplation. At some point they had decided that he was an easy mark, and they'd treated him as such. He was, they thought, a fool, but they had read the cover of his book all wrong.

Vasily never understood the gang's need for aggression. He'd simply never felt the desire to belittle, or to rage, or even to be noticed. Well, that is not entirely true. He'd acted once before, and that action was the reason he'd been in prison when the coup erupted.

As he rounded the final corner along Tsentralnaya Street and looked up the hill toward the prison where only a few hours ago he'd plotted with the men he was assigned to oversee, he passed the Orthodox Church and looked beyond it to the cemetery. It was in that cemetery—the only one in Warwick—that he'd been sitting and drinking one night, not long ago in the big scheme of things. On that night, a group of younger boys had passed him on their way to somewhere, and one of them had sneered at him and called him stupid, and he'd simply had enough of ridicule to take it from those who were younger. He fought with the boy and had been arrested for drunkenness and brawling, and the arrest had landed him in jail. That series of events had set him upon his present course. His current situation had begun in that one moment of his life in which he'd stood up for himself, and, having had a moment of doing what had been neglected for far too long, he had taken his first step toward what might now be his undoing... or his freedom.

* * * *

The Spetznaz troops were stationed around the gym, securing the perimeter as Vasily came over the sloping walkway. He felt his feet slide gently across the ice and snow, and the sounds seemed to be amplified in the chilly night. One of the soldiers raised a rifle and pointed it in his direction, and he held up his hands and stopped in his tracks for a moment, intending to show them that he was unarmed. From a commotion near the right of a little group of soldiers, he heard a familiar voice rise up, and as the soldiers parted slightly, he saw the images of Mikail and Vladimir appear and begin to walk toward him.

"You there. Vasily Romanovich! Get over here!"

There are moments one sees not from the perspective of an individual, but as if it were a movie, from a distance. If, from that perspective, one had watched and studied Vasily's situation, one might've seen the two figures of the new bosses, Mikail and Vladimir, walk angrily toward the smaller youth in the distance. Their tones were insulting and angry.

"Where have you been?" was not a question but an insinuation.

"What have you done?" was not an inquiry but an invective.

One might have noticed, had one viewed it as a movie, the youth's quiet, and understood it to be fear, and such a reaction would have been understandable. The mixture of bravado and accusation that the two figures were displaying as they were surrounded by guns in the foreground was rife with contempt and pregnant with threat. The youth simply stood there in silence.

There was a deeper reason for his silence, however. He was not simply cowering before the men who had terrorized him all of his life, and he was not merely carefully choosing his words. Instead, he was looking at four guards from the prison, guards he had known from his recent stay in one of its cells. They were blindfolded and lined up along the wall of the gymnasium. The Spetnaz soldiers were pointing their guns at them and waiting for an order to shoot.

Watching from that distance, one would have seen the taller of the figures approach the youth called Vasily and push him to the ground and the shorter man bend slowly down to whisper to him. A Russian soldier walked over at their bidding and took the youth into custody and tied his hands behind his back. He jerked the boy called Vasily to his feet and marched him, tripping and slipping, across a small patch of hard-packed snow toward the wall where the captured guards were lined up, standing blindfolded, shivering with cold and fear.

From the distance, one would have seen the two leaders approach the guards, and the youth near the soldier would have been placed beside the condemned men. One would have seen the taller of the figures, Vladimir, take out a pistol from a holster.

Vladimir moved slowly, methodically, walking down the line of shivering guards, placing a gun to the head of each. One by one, each condemned man, in turn, cried out for his life only to be cut off in mid-sentence by the harsh report of the gun in the crisp night air as it rang out across the town of Warwick, echoing in the valley and circling through the tops of the trees and then reaching up into the mountains before growing fainter as it faded into the nighttime sky.

From a distance, one would have seen the bodies slump to the ground, one by one, until there was only one left standing, and the two figures approached the shivering boy who was left standing in the midst of the bodies. They accosted him together.

The youth stood in silence, and the taller of the figures placed a gun to his temple and the youth felt his knees buckle and the world turned upside down like a snow globe.

That is when the world seemed strange and disjointed, that sublime and terrifying moment when it cracked open just a little beneath the feet of the shivering youth and then suddenly snapped back into place, and the familiar crept back into the sum of the parts.

Vladimir slapped Vasily on the shoulder. "You poor, dumb, boy. Why are you afraid? We know you didn't do it on purpose. You're too stupid to be complicit."

CHAPTER 12

"You should know that if you keep scattering the dirt willy-nilly like that, it'll only take us longer when we have to put it back in."

Vasily was standing waist deep in one of a series of seven holes. In each of the holes stood a pair of youths, and to the side of each hole was a growing heap of earth. This digging of holes was no easy task just before the onset of winter in the State of New York, but the ground was still workable, if only barely so, and if they'd been forced to dig these graves later into the winter, they most likely would have failed at the task.

Vasily's hole was shallower than the others and his heap less high, although it still came up to the level of his eyes and was made taller, in relation to his small frame, as all the heaps were, by the fact that the fresh dug earth was piled upon the several feet of snow that blanketed the open field.

Vasily pushed the point of his shovel into the earth and stepped onto the foot rest with all his weight, giving a little hop and landing on the shovel until he felt the blade sink into the as-yet unfrozen soil. The handle in his hands felt solid as he leaned back and used his leverage to carefully lift the soil out of the hole and up and over his head. He emptied the dirt onto the heap, more gently this time, making sure it didn't slide back into the hole on top of him.

The young man talking to him—his work partner in digging this hole—was named Kolya. He was older than Vasily and had a reputation for being a quirky intellectual. Vasily had never spent much time around him, but standing now in the hole with him he glanced at the intellectual's pudgy round face and angular glasses and noticed his soft fleshy hands, red from the cold in the thinning moonlight, and he wondered silently to himself what Kolya's interest was in being here at this moment. He had, like the rest of the youths who were now digging, volunteered for this duty.

Vladimir had asked for volunteers to follow him behind the prison in the immediate aftermath of the execution of the guards. There is a way that revolutionaries request volunteers, especially after a particularly brutal display of violence, which insures an adequate level of participation from those who otherwise might just be caught up in the riptide of events. Some volunteer out of a desire to curry favor with violent and powerful men, some do so out of fear or panic, and still others pitch-in out of curiosity, or merely from a lack of any other plan for the moment.

Kolya, standing with a large group of boys around the gymnasium and feeling *voluntold* to work, quickly stepped out of the crowd to follow the brutish Vladimir to the open field. Vasily, too, had gone along, not really as a volunteer, but mainly because he felt internally compelled to do so in order to remain, as much as possible, under the radar. Now he found himself with Kolya and the others digging holes in the ground in the crisp night air.

Had they been digging for treasure, there might have been a celebratory feel to it all, everyone joking and cutting up as they checked their maps to make sure that the spot where they were digging was likely to lead them to the gold, but there was no celebration in the air, and there were no maps either, and the frigid night was filled with diligent grunting without a hint of laughter. They were simply youths—most in their late teens, but a few in their early twenties—in the middle of a field laboring away with cold solemnity. The dead didn't mind or protest, and so this somehow seemed the only appropriate response since, from the moment they had been handed shovels, they'd realized their purpose. They were there to dig graves for those who had departed from this night's horrible events.

Kolya had spoken to him in English. Vasily was careful not to look at him or to give any indication that he understood. Best to just let them think I'm an idiot, he thought. He was still shaking a bit from the fear he'd experienced at the hands of Vladimir and Mikail, and that fear now jumped into his chest once more as he looked up with his next shovel full and saw the barrel of a gun at the end of Vladimir's arm.

"He can't understand English, you fool," Vladimir barked at Kolya. "And get back to work. Morning will come before you know it and we have other work to do! Where did you learn to speak like that anyway? Where did you learn this phrase 'willy-nilly'?" When Vladimir spoke the word it sounded like "will-he, nill-he."

"I read... That's how I know that phrase. Maybe I saw it in Shakespeare," Kolya said.

Vladimir looked at Kolya through narrowed eyes.

"What?!" Kolya feigned surprise. "You think no one in our little *hamlet* reads Shakespeare?" He smiled at the corners of his mouth, waiting for some flash of recognition from Vladimir, but if the brute saw anything clever in what Kolya had said, he didn't show it.

Vladimir switched to Russian. "I don't know and I don't care. Perhaps you should spend some time reading Marx. And before that, perhaps you should spend some time digging this grave or maybe I'll decide to have you dig your own."

"How very bourgeois of you," Kolya answered in Russian. "Or is it me being bourgeois? Standing here and talking to you while I am possibly digging my own grave... and you there, *shaking* your *spear* at me!"

Vasily glanced up at him, to see whether Kolya was being insolent or clever. The young intellectual seemed to be doing neither and both. More so, it seemed that he was merely in love with the sound of the words. He waited again for a response from Vladimir, but only got a threatening snap of the gun against the brute's side in response. Then the gun and the brute walked away and made their way down the line of graves, stepping gingerly around the series of body bags laid out near the holes.

Kolya bent his nose down to look at Vasily over his glasses and winked. He gave a faint little whistle and then took his shovel in hand and slowly began to press himself into service. As he did, Vasily looked up at the black bag in front of him and noticed the hastily scribbled name on the surface of the bag, shimmering in white against the black of the bag in the light of the moon and the snow.

Volkhov.

He felt a grip of grief and looked over quickly at his mate to see if the older youth had noticed, only to give a short dumb smile before he went back to his digging. He heard a grunt from the hole next to him and the plop of earth land at the top of that heap, followed by the shushing of the tiny aggregate as it separated and began to roll slowly down the small hill, willy-nilly.

* * * *

There is a feeling of finality, mixed liberally with the morose recognition of the vibrancy and vitality of still being alive, when one is digging a grave for another human. Eyes peer into other eyes and declare firmly to one another that "we are still alive," and answer back to one another without words the old question, "Why is there existence, rather than the lack of it?"

I dig and therefore I am.

Digging graves is an effective antidote to the most foolish of philosophies. Denying existence is for men who've never dug a grave for a friend.

They finished the digging part as the night settled into the a.m., and wearily climbed out of the graves and stood around waiting for whatever was to come next. They assumed the un-digging part would come next—the burying of the dead—but that part would have to wait.

What came next was the figure of Mikail, walking quickly across the snow, calling out to Vladimir who met him halfway along his path. The group could faintly hear what seemed to be an argument emanating from the two men as they approached. Vasily stood near the back of the group, farthest away from the two men, and watched as Mikail waved his hands at Vladimir's head-shaking. Not from any words he could hear, but from the image of the two arguing, Vasily got the word picture of violent reason butting heads with reasonless violence.

As they drew closer, the argument ceased, and Vladimir commanded the youths to follow him. "We have to go to the church to address a disturbance," he said, as if that statement fully briefed the group to his satisfaction.

Vasily began walking in the direction of St. Olaf's, only to feel a hand grab his arm, his sleeve riding up on his shoulder, and when he turned, he found Mikail standing behind him.

"Stay with me a while," said the stocky young man, pleasantly, and in Russian. "They'll be back in a moment. I have no doubt that Vladimir will be persuasive."

He led Vasily to one of the graves and indicated with a wave that they should have a seat on the pile of earth next to it. Vasily sat down, and Mikail sat beside him in an almost friendly way, as if they were old friends just relaxing on a break from their labors.

They watched the group of youths in the distance, trudging across the snow with Vladimir at the head, and Vasily reflexively inhaled the night air, waiting for whatever Mikail had planned for him. There has to be a plan. Mikail wasn't here sitting with him next to an open grave just to chit-chat. Idle conversation was not the bulldog's forte. Since they'd been boys, Vasily had come to expect that, while he could almost never predict what it was, Mikail always had a reason or a plan for whatever he chose to do. So when he finally spoke, Vasily was surprised.

"Did you know that I had a brother?" Mikail said, matter-of-factly, reaching down into the cold dirt with his bare hand and letting the soil sift through his fingers.

Vasily looked at him, his eyes indicating that this was new information, and puzzling at the sudden weariness in Mikail's voice. He waited for him to go on, and in time, he did.

"Yes, comrade," the bulldog said, nodding his head. "You and I, we have something in common... we've both lost loved ones. You, with your father when you were young... and me, with my brother when I was younger still."

Vasily didn't answer. The subject of his own father's death to disease was common knowledge in Warwick, as was the fact that he'd been raised by a single mother until she, too, had died, but he didn't even think about it much anymore, and he certainly didn't speak of it.

Vasily never suspected that Mikail was anything but an only child—raised by a man with a love of drink and a woman without even the most basic of motherly instincts. He'd always thought this to be the root cause of Mikail's aggression. Even as a boy, Mikail was known to lash out at everyone around him, probably because he'd never truly felt love at home, but maybe that was just more of the world's philosophy that would disintegrate in the presence of an open grave. It just seemed to make sense to Vasily that, being treated like a bastard child by his parents, Mikail had inevitably become a bastard.

"Yes. It's true. I had a brother. A twin. Not identical, but a twin nonetheless. My brother was born dead, after me, with the umbilical cord tight around his neck." Mikail took a handful of dirt, and stared closely at it as he let it tip from the side of his hand. It shushed down the incline of the pile.

"I don't think my parents ever forgave me." He sighed. "They treated me as if I strangled him myself..." Mikail grabbed another fistful of dirt before continuing. "... And maybe I did. I don't have the luxury of any memories of the time."

Vasily looked over at Mikail and suddenly realized how small this bulldog was in stature, despite his obvious attempts to build himself up. He was heavier than Vasily, muscular and fit, but about the same height, and both were much smaller than almost every other youth in their circle. He had a tiny red scar at the base of his forehead, just above his left eye.

"My brother's death was the reason my father began to drink," Mikail declared with certainty. "Did you know that at one time my father was one of the most promising candidates here at the charm school?" Mikail lifted his eyebrows as if the thought of it was surprising. The dirt slid from his hands yet again. "Oh yes! Such potential lost to empty bottles. And my mother... well... I'm told she was lovely. Not loving, perhaps, but lovely. But that was back before the bottles began to fly." Mikail scooped up two handfuls of the cold, cold dirt and rubbed them together in his hands.

"Then I came along, and then my brother did not, and somehow my parent's whole world fell apart, and mine did as well. It was a shame, you know? To be born in amongst the pall and aroma of death, and to have life cut down in front of you before it'd even begun. Surely you know something of that."

Mikail fidgeted with his hands, which were now empty of dirt, and contradictorily he now began picking at a string that had come loose on his shirt.

"It's the reason I have to be so tough, you know. Being small, like you, like me, one has to fight all the time. Just to get people to pay attention, you have to throw a fit and raise hell." Mikail punctuated this statement with a fist, clasped tight and brought up before his face.

"But not that damned Vladimir. All he has to do is walk into a room and everyone pays attention. I suppose it has its benefits, all this fussing. It makes you find other ways of bringing focus. Vladimir just won't listen to reason. He just wants to shoot people. It's all he knows, the use of force. But I don't want to shoot people, Vasily. I would rather reason with them."

Mikail kicked some dirt toward the graves, in the direction of the body bag with the name Volkhov. "Lev, there. Take him, for example. Do you think it was necessary that he died? Or this man Clay? Could they not have been reasoned with?"

Vasily looked at the bag in front of him, and then at the bag in the next grave over, and thought of the traveler he'd met in the cell with Volkhov. He remembered the light in the two men's eyes as they had discussed plans for their escape; the clarity they'd had in that moment; a crystalline notion of who they were and what they were about. He'd not often been in the presence of men who seemed to their purpose so clearly. He remembered the way they'd taken him into their conversation and plans, and how they had treated him as an equal... or something close to an equal. And then he felt the grip of regret that they'd not been successful in their escape.

Mikail didn't seem to notice that Vasily's mind was elsewhere. "Todd... now he was another matter altogether. Do you remember how close he'd been getting with the outside guards? That was not a coincidence, Vasily Romanovich. He was dealing black market goods, having them bring drugs in from outside, giving our food and perhaps more to our captors. He was evil, Vasily. Believe me. I didn't shoot him without cause. In reality, it was an act of mercy. You weren't there when I discussed Todd's crimes with Vladimir. He wanted... no..." Mikail paused. "There is no way he would have been so merciful. If I'd left the decision to him, Todd's whole family would be dead right now. Believe me, executing Todd was a merciful act. Sometimes..." Mikail paused for another moment, choosing his words.

"Sometimes you have to manage events and men in a way that serves everyone in the best way possible." His voice trailed off for a moment, and Vasily wondered why he was telling him this. He was just about to ask that question, almost feeling as if the young man was reaching out to him for understanding, when Mikail interrupted his thoughts.

"Where is the backpack, Vasily?"

Vasily swallowed, and tried not to show on his face that he was going pale. He wondered whether, in the limited light, the nervousness in his features could be detected. He remembered something Volkhov once told him in one of their long afternoons together back when the old man was teaching him English. That was when Lev had slowly taken him under his wing, showing him kindness that few others in the town ever seemed to. He'd said, "Never answer an open question with anything but a question when there is danger at hand." Solid advice that seemed to apply to the current situation. He turned his head slightly towards Mikail, attempting a blank, dull expression on his face.

"What backpack?"

"The guards saw you leave with a backpack."

"The guards you just shot?"

"Yes."

"I have no idea what that means, Mikail Mikailivitch. You'd have to ask them."

"But there was a backpack. It belonged to the man called Clay, the man you were responsible for overseeing before he broke out of prison..."

Vasily tried to keep his voice even. I'm just dumb Vasily, he reminded himself. If it can be said that in the world of the blind, the one-eyed man is king, it is perhaps equally true that in a camp where everyone is trained as a spy, the man who seems least capable is often the least suspect. He remembered what Clay told him when he'd said that no one thought Vasily capable of deception, and how that fact gave him an advantage in a world where deception was second nature. He played the only card he had to play. He told a lie and convinced himself to believe it.

"I don't know, Mikail. Perhaps they lied in order to lead you off their trail. There is no backpack that I know of. Those two," he said, indicating to the two nearest body bags, "were more worried about whether I would get them extra blankets than anything else."

"Vasily, sometimes when you find yourself in a hole, the best way to get out is to stop digging."

Vasily looked at him, and Mikail looked back, raising an eyebrow at him as if to suggest, for the second time in the space of a couple of hours, that he might soon find himself lying in a grave like those before him. Vasily made a face that suggested he didn't know what he was expected to say next, and Mikail placed his hand on the young man's shoulder as if to calm him.

"Listen, comrade, you go home and think about it, will you? It's late. I worry that you are out of your depth. There is a rising tide in this place and it will drown you if you let it." Mikail shrugged his shoulders when he said this, almost as if he was powerless in the town. "It's possible that it will drown you even if you don't let it, but go and get some sleep. Perhaps the walk will jog your memory. I have other things to think about right now, and Warwick has seen too much bloodshed for one day. But remember, Vasily, I'm somewhat limited in what I can do for you. I have to play the hands as they're dealt, and, as with Todd, I have to make use of sometimes unpleasant means to serve the greater good. There is a man with a gun named Vladimir who is not as long-suffering as I am. I would hate for him to have to rummage around and find what you cannot."

Vasily got up to leave, brushing the earth off the seat of his pants, and trying to decide if he should protest his innocence for one beat longer or whether he had already lost that opportunity. He decided to simply drop the whole matter and attempt to relate to Mikail as one human being to another. At that moment, his mind rested on a quote from Solzhenitsyn: "If one is forever cautious, can one remain a human being?" Vasily decided that, at this moment, the bravest thing for him to do was not to attempt to make a correct calculation about the likelihood of his being believed or not, but, instead, to simply show compassion to this man whom he had come to fear in his heart.

"I'm sorry about your brother," he said. "No one deserves to have to live with that burden and to be held accountable for such a cost."

Mikail seemed genuinely moved by his statement. "Yes, Vasily. Well... we all have our crosses to bear. Yours will be to carry yours for as long as you are able, while mine will be to raise Cain." He paused. "I hope we are both up to it."

* * * *

Monday, Early Morning

Vasily walked hurriedly, but with purpose, along the side street to the end of the block, and then turned up the hill toward the house of Aleksei Gopchik. It was 4 a.m., and his mind was tired and his energy level was waning quickly. He'd spent the last couple of hours knocking on the doors of the people closest to him, waking them from their slumber, trying his best to convince them to pack a bag and come with him to an escape.

He hoped with all of the hope that he could muster in his breast that he might convince them that the town was unsafe, but that he, dull little Vasily, would be able to lead them to safety. As he should have expected, he'd been frustrated at every turn by the blank and unbelieving stares of his dearest friends.

The pattern had become painfully consistent. First there would be a sleepy shuffling as the inhabitant groggily made his way to the door, as if to confront a rude interloper. The door would open. Yawning incomprehension was followed by either a blatant display of skepticism or, in some cases, downright hostility. How old is the reluctance to heed the midnight warning? How many prophets have heard the same refrains?

"How can you dare to wake me up at this hour?" each one of them asked. "Do you have any idea how late it is?" He'd heard that last line so often that he'd taken to quoting Solzhenitsyn in response, "Blow the dust off the clock. Your watches are behind the times. Throw open the heavy curtains which are so dear to you—you do not even suspect that the day has already dawned outside."

None of his exhortations mattered. The story was always the same—albeit with different words—at each of the places he'd stopped. He was told that Warwick was indeed in turmoil, but that trouble had been coming for far too long. Volkhov's lessons on the dialectic came to mind. On whatever side one was on, they were convinced that it was high time the other side learned a lesson.

Volkhov's speech! From just a few hours before... The wisdom contained there might as well be buried in that body bag along with the old man's corpse.

While the world chose up sides along false lines outside the fences of Warwick and around the world, the microcosm inside the wire matched it all perfectly. Nothing divides humanity, to its own destruction, quite as effectively as a false choice.

There were those who favored running the thugs at the gymnasium out of town on a rail, and others who favored falling into line with their petite revolution and teaching the old guard ("the powers that be!") a lesson they wouldn't soon forget. There was talk of civil and uncivil war, and assumptions that the Spetnaz soldiers, who had parachuted in and who were now protecting the new government at the gym, would go along with whichever side showed up with the largest numbers. The ghosts of St. Petersburg in 1917 were never far from Warwick. Conflicts that had been brewing for a generation in Warwick were finally coming to a head, and his friends were not only unwilling to join in his exodus, they were hoping to get a scalp or two for their troubles.

"But don't you see that this is no way to live?" Vasily had asked them.

They simply shook their heads in stubbornness and sorrow, for they couldn't imagine any other way. "It has been coming to this, and they will get what they deserve," they'd each said in their turn and in their own words. He'd heard that phrase so often, and with the definition of who "they" were changing to fit the exigencies of shifting opinion, that Vasily had simply come to expect its antipathy.

"But we don't have to choose between two tyrants! We can go outside the wire and be free!" He'd sung, like a free bird singing to the masses in their chains.

"You can die just as easily out there as you can in here, Vasily."

"Yes, I might die out there, but if I do, I will die on my own terms. At least I will have sought something higher and better than the false choices given to me by liars, by those who seek the power to coerce others. And look at the way we're living now! The food will not keep coming from outside. This system is unsustainable. It is already interrupted. We don't produce enough stuff in Warwick to feed and clothe ourselves. However our supplies got here before this trouble, they will eventually stop."

"Dull, dull Vasily. Don't be such an alarmist! We don't need conspiracy theories when we have an enemy closer to hand. We'll deal with them first, and then everything will get back to normal." And one by one they had closed the door on him and gone back to bed until morning. As Volkhov had often said, "anything that one does not want to believe can easily be dismissed as a conspiracy theory."

Vasily had become desperate. He'd decided within himself that he would not give up until he found at least one other person to come along with him. He had to do it. There was that conviction, that destiny, again. He had to do it if only to restore his faith in the power of reason. He was sensing that the world had gone mad, and he was growing angrier in response to that madness surrounding him. "How can they not see this?" he wondered. "How can they not understand that Mikail will kill them all before he is done?" And then, he thought, if Mikail does not do it, then time and the crushing weight of facts will finish them off in due time. This is the way it always is—one might choose to live in delusion, but reality is stubbornly persistent, and will assert itself at the most inopportune times.

After all of that, he now walked up the hill to Alyoshka's house in the hopes that, at long last, he might find a reasonable man.

As he approached the house, he heard a voice behind him. "Why so grave, mate?" Vasily stopped in the street and turned around to find Kolya walking a few feet behind along the darkened path. "Don't worry," Kolya said, "it's only me, your most holy digging friend. And, I might add, that it was very unfriendly of you to leave me to bury that old man by myself. When we returned to the site, everyone else had a partner but poor Kolya. He had to do all the work himself."

Vasily hesitated, not knowing what to say. So he said what one always does in such cases. "I'm sorry, Kolya. I didn't mean to. It was beyond my control."

"That's ok. I figured as much. When I saw that bulldog pull you to the side, I figured you would not have an easy time of it. In fact, I halfway expected we'd have to dig another hole when we returned from our little adventure with Vladimir."

"Yes," Vasily said, rubbing his hands together for warmth. "What was that about, anyway?"

"Oh, just some punk kids fighting over something the grandfathers of their grandfathers once said. Shockingly inconsiderate the ancestors of our ancestors were, leaving us with so much unfinished business. You may not have heard, but our little town is headed for a civil war."

Vasily relaxed. Something in Kolya's jovial indifference made him feel that he was safe talking to him. He laughed a little to himself. If the man were not indifferent, I wouldn't trust him. In a land seething with dialectically opposed agendas, the safest man turns out to be the man without one.

"Yes, I've heard. In fact, I am trying to get people to opt out."

"What do you mean? Not fight? But how can they avoid such a fight when the grandfathers of their grandfathers once said thus and so?" Kolya took off his glasses and winked at Vasily. "But, seriously. What do you mean?"

"I have a way out. I mean literally, an escape route. I am leaving today with a friend, and I'm trying to persuade people to follow... a thankless and fruitless task. Perhaps it's the hour, or maybe I'm not as persuasive as I would like to be, but so far I have been thoroughly unconvincing."

Kolya cocked his head to look at Vasily in that way one does to see if someone is pulling his leg. "You say 'literally' and, unhappily that word is often used today when 'figuratively' is actually intended. An escape route? Do you mean to say that you have a real live escape route, one that leads outside of these fences? Or... are you being metaphorical? I don't see you as a politician, Vasily, or at least not as a very good one. I may be the only one in this town that likes you."

Vasily smiled. "That is not only what I mean to say. It is what I am saying," he replied, then watched as the young man straightened his head and carefully cleaned his glasses and then slowly put them back onto his face. He smiled through his rounded features, and Vasily suddenly became aware of him rubbing the blisters on his hands. He dropped his hand to his side.

The world spun on as sleepers slept in their beds, but in the street in front of Alyoshka's house, there was suddenly an undeniable awareness by two men who in that singular moment were fully awake. Vasily had found his twin, his brother at arms. Kolya looked down and glanced at the earth still caked to his boots and shook it off, sending its tiny granules shushing across the lane's hard-packed snow.

"Can I bring my sister?"

* * * *

The spark of the match punctuated the still black night, and a flame shot up and along the stick and illuminated Pyotr's fingers as he placed the tip of the flame against the wick of the candle. He opened the door and breathed a sigh of relief as he quickly ushered Vasily into the hallway and then closed the door and the curtains behind them.

"I had almost decided you were dead."

"I might still be," Vasily said. "But it seems that at the moment we're free to go about our business."

"Good, and what did you find out?"

"The town is in turmoil. It's madness. We may have a civil war on our hands when we wake up to have our breakfast. People are choosing up sides." Vasily exhaled deeply and shook his head at the waste and futility of it all.

"Four guards were executed and... your uncle... " Vasily caught himself. There was no need to relay such news without compassion. "I'm sorry, Pyotr. He's dead. It's sure now. I just left off talking to the man who helped me dig his grave."

"Wait, they had you digging graves?" Pyotr asked, narrowing his eyes and leaning his head to one side.

"Yes," Vasily nodded, "Mikail is out of control, and Vladimir may even be worse. They're now the little Lenin and Stalin of Warwick. They commandeered a group of us and made us bury the murdered men. They threatened my life several times. It's just entirely unsafe to stay around here much longer."

Vasily rubbed his hands together to warm them, and in doing so he recalled the weight of the shovel and the full night knocking on doors. "I've spent the last several hours trying to find someone, anyone, to come along with us," he stopped, shaking his head. "The young man who lives on Gagarin Avenue named Kolya is the only one who agreed. He and his sister, Natasha, are going to come over at dawn and help us pack so we can leave."

"Fine. Best to travel with a small group anyway, and we'll have work to do before we can set out. Did anyone ask about me?"

"No, not yet. They did wonder about the backpack, and I'm certain they'll eventually figure out where I'm staying since I didn't sleep overnight in the gym. They know that you're Lev's nephew, or at least they should, and they just haven't thought about it all yet. It'll all come together for them at some point. I also visited enough houses since I left to fill a small phone book so, while I didn't mention any specific names, it's only a matter of time, as you said, before we're found out." Vasily exhaled deeply, looking at Pyotr to see how he was receiving the news. Pyotr looked back, calmly, and did not interrupt.

"Everyone I told was disinterested in our plans, Pyotr. They didn't care to leave. They all prefer to join this senseless conflict that's in the air..." Vasily dropped his hands, as if in defeat, "...rather than take a moment—just a moment—to face the bare facts of their unsustainable existence. Still, I talked to a lot of people on both sides, and once those people begin to talk to one another, our plan will become public knowledge."

"Yes," Pyotr said, nodding, "most likely. When they do, they will certainly come here, but we will be long gone by then, Vasily. I have most of our provisions already packed. If things go as Volkhov said they should, the EMP could hit tomorrow."

Vasily's face dropped. He'd certainly felt the urgency to escape, and to save as many of his friends and neighbors as possible, but he'd forgotten about the electromagnetic pulse that Volkhov predicted would likely come on America's election day. Was that tomorrow? Tuesday? He flashed back to the lessons sitting in Volkhov's study, the time he'd spent with the old man in prison just before death. The imminence of the catastrophe that was about to strike braced him.

Volkhov had explained that an electromagnetic pulse (usually abbreviated as an EMP) is a destructive burst of electromagnetic radiation. An EMP could happen willfully and purposefully from the high-altitude explosion of a nuclear device, or it could come from any number of other, less diabolical sources, including as a blast of solar radiation emitted from the sun. It was hard to tell how Volkhov's predicted EMP might be triggered, since most of the militaries of the world had done extensive research into EMP weapons, and he was unclear as to who the various forces were behind the scenes that might desire such an end.

An EMP of sufficient strength could destroy most sensitive computer parts and equipment, melt down power lines, blow up transformers, and destroy just about anything that ran on electricity that wasn't shielded from such an attack.

The memory of Volkhov's warnings, and the minute and scary details the old man had given about what could happen to any technologically advanced society if an EMP of significant strength were to hit, rushed over Vasily in a cold wave. Absolute Destruction. And the EMP wasn't even the war.

"The EMP is just the trigger," Volkhov had said, "what follows will shock even the wildest imagination." Vasily looked over at the candle on the table, and at the shadow of the man on the wall, and thought of what the implications of an EMP going off in an America already spiraling into chaos might be.

Pyotr looked at Vasily, his face ashen and drawn, and then suddenly realized how harrowing the last several hours must have been for him, and how remarkably brave he'd been in standing up to the experience. He turned and walked Vasily down the hallway and into a small room with a mattress on the floor and a wash basin near a chair. He told him to get some rest and that he would wake him in a few hours. Then he pulled the door shut behind him, before thinking better of it and opening it up again to catch the younger man's eye in the shadows and the dark.

"My uncle knew that you were going to be a great man, Vasily Romanovich."

"That's funny, because I am not even sure of that myself. But there is one thing of which I am certain, Pyotr. It is that I will die before I stop trying to be."

"I'm sure you will, my young friend. I'm sure you will."

And with that, Pyotr smiled and blew out the light.

CHAPTER 13

Solzhenitsyn once wrote that the only substitutes we have for experiences that we have not lived ourselves are found in literature and art. While we may take his point with the consideration it requires, it is reasonable to object that, on this one point at least, the great man was partly wrong.

In dreaming, there are no boundaries of perspective or expectation. The uncontacted native in his hut hidden along the thickly-forested Amazon dreams with the same wild unconsciousness as the Queen in all her splendor, once they each gird their loins and dive into that deep, encompassing darkness. In dreams are found the ferocious beasts of our primitive nature and the angelic wings of our best aspirations. Though dreams are fueled by our waking experiences, in the netherworld of sleep, like death, our minds become universal.

Vasily, worn out from the turbulent day and night before, had fallen into a fitful sleep that quickly dipped into chaos and light. He dreamt of long, slow walks along Elysian streams, and then of plummeting, headlong flights through air as thick as water. He gripped himself and passed into a seamless world of dark foreboding. His unshackled mind flashed to beasts of burden in neon glow being torn by jaws of fury, and this he left unconsidered, as we often do in dreams, and instantaneously he passed through infinite waves of sound until he found a still, small island. There, he swam in the love of women he'd never met and basked in the praise of men who despised him.

In his physiological response, he merely laid on the thin mattress in the dark and his eyes fluttered under their lids while his muscles twitched on their stems. But in the caverns of his mind, he was magical and golden, not a soul tied to a body, but a star burning bright in its firmament. He slept the wondrous sleep of saints who have passed through the gates of hell to find their rest in the bosom of plenty.

If the young man's sleep was a dream, the town of Warwick found itself waking at that very moment to a yawning, terrible nightmare. After Vasily had slept for only a couple of hours, the sun rose over the hidden valley, and with it, the world opened wide underneath him.

With the dawn, the sleeping animosities that had been whispered in the darkness of the previous night burst out in full-throated alarm into the full light of day, and the townspeople of Warwick began to gather in groups of like minds, wherein they convinced themselves to take up arms and begin a struggle. The spark struck, the long line of woven animosities had ignited, and the resulting conflagration had begun.

Civil war in this wick began as it does in all such conflicts, with physical violence initiated almost as an afterthought.   Men, enraged that their rights had been taken, and women, inflamed that their futures were dimmed, lashed out in the only way they knew how.   During the night there had been only rumors of war, but, illustrative of the age-old proverb, people had gone to bed with their anger only to find it more wicked and volatile in the light of the morning.

The sudden blinding clarity of long-held ideologies came into sharp (if deluded) focus as the people shook the cobwebs from their heads and wiped the sleep from their groggy eyes, and as they filed into the streets, their usual morning greetings simply retreated behind threats and assaults, as if the nighttime had spread a virus of war, and as if subtle and as yet undefined hatreds had become the currency of the realm.

While no one could have answered, if they had been pressed to do so exactly what those ideologies and threats and hatreds fully entailed, there was a palpable animosity that swept through the population of Warwick, driven by instinct and history and hate. It suddenly seemed as if lives too dangerous to be free had become too unbearable to live any longer. It was as if a political storm had arrived on the heels of the two very real storms the people had just experienced, and the townspeople had no recourse to shelter.

There was the matter of the overthrow of power. There was the reality of the remembrance of promises not kept. Something simply had to be done. It was conviction. It was destiny. No one could go on living this way, the town was heard to say in a collective and contradictory outburst. "To arms!" the townspeople shouted. And they grabbed their pitchforks and burning torches and rifles and hammers and knives, and marched into the street to vent their spleen on the "others."

* * * *

The first shot in the battle for Warwick roared forth from the barrel of a Spetznaz rifle on a group of young men near the church. It was not some kind of planned thing. A soldier had ordered the young men to disperse while they were standing around and developing their arguments, and they had simply refused, thinking that his order had been a request.

One of the youths, alive with revolutionary fervor, turned to the soldier and told him to go back to wherever he'd come from, and then turned back to the group of his peers in order to revel in their laughter. It was an understandable boast, perhaps, the young man's reply. There had been an air of lawlessness in the town since it had been overrun by the gang from the prison. However, in the un-codified law of unintended consequences, those consequences likely became inevitable in the face of anarchy, distrust, arrogance and fear.

Until this morning, the Spetznaz soldiers had seemed somehow unreal, merely props in a movie that the people had been rehearsing for all of their lives. When the young man told the soldier to get lost, he was merely feeling the vigor of youthful rebellion and was attempting to clear his throat using rebellion's howl. Intentions and motivations aside (because who among us can completely judge those?), the facts, as they are wont to do, reasserted themselves. The gun had been pointed into the crowd and had barked its reprimand, and the offending youth from Warwick's last generation had fallen silent before he had even entered the debate.

The shot rang out across the hamlet, and the sound of it congealed in the air as a confirmation to the various sides that the time had come to fight. And within moments, like the bursting of a dam, the town's fury was unleashed, and the citizens of Warwick did fight.

In moments, the air was punctuated by the sounds of smallish clashes that grew into the ageless clatter of revolt. There was the sound of footsteps in the street and the sounds of anger in the peoples' voices that always follow the first sign of battle's confusion.

Excitement and release of pent-up frustration is always the first cause as well as the first casualty of war. In Warwick it was no different. Anger, like opportunity, came knocking at the door and, after waiting a perfunctory beat, had decided to kick the door in.

We should mention here that in most civil wars, with few exceptions (and most of those are Russian), tangible lines that can be seen and felt are established almost at the outset. The people divide themselves to the north and to the south, or perhaps it is to the east and to the west... or maybe they are bifurcated along racial, religious, or economic lines. This civil war, like most things Russian, was not as simple as that.

Mirroring the growing battle they knew not of, one that was at that very moment just beginning to rage outside the fences of Warwick village and across the whole of America, in this civil war it was much harder to tell the players without a program. Opinions, motives, hostilities, and friendships were more fluid. There was a loose and undefined picture of those who might be considered pro-Russia, and those who could, so long as details were not discussed, be considered anti-Russia. But, even within that false dialectic, there were conflicts and boiling volatility. As Malcolm X said, when you fill your house with barrels of gunpowder, and you play around with things that spark, it is very likely that your house will explode. Warwick was a house filled for generations with gunpowder, and the sparks were now beginning to fly.

* * * *

Vasily had continued in his slumber as the earliest stages of the battle formed in ever-widening circles, but when it did widen, his dreams became more intense. He saw the oceans filled with lava and smelled air filled with sulfuric explosions.

His sleep, confusing the beginnings of actual sensory intake with the unreality of his dreamlike state, filled in the details of the clatter with a wild and fanciful narrative. Had it been possible to enter his dreams and shake him out of his slumber at that moment, one would have found the mind of Vasily Romanovitch searching for a shelter from a hailstorm of meteors. One would have found him climbing through the rubble of destruction, calling out into the darkness for a friend, any friend to whom he could cling.

In his dream, he happened upon a hill piled high with ashes and cinders, and he scrambled up the hill in order to get a look at the surrounding landscape. As his feet slipped through the ashes, and as he fell into pile upon pile, he came to taste the ashes in his mouth, the grit filling into the spaces between his teeth, and his calling out for help became choked and muffled. Then, in that micro-instant before he awoke, with a crashing of noise emanating from the street and resounding through his wall, he suddenly saw a brightly-plumed Phoenix rise up into the sky like a capsule lifted aloft by a great balloon, and it began to spin like a whirling dervish.

Heart racing, and in the gray middling between wakefulness and sleep, he clawed to the summit of the ash heap. He spit out the ashes and felt his eyes burn. In that particular way that the helplessness of dreams inspires, he tried to wake himself fully, to connect his dream to his body. He tried in vain to raise his arms from his side. He tried to force the sound from his lungs.

It was in that moment that his eyes popped open, and he sucked in his breath in a gasping lunge. His body shot upright and out of bed, and he suddenly became aware of the knock at the door.

* * * *

Pyotr had risen at the first sounds of conflict and had begun to busy himself around the house, making coffee in the slanting early light that peered from behind and around the curtains. As he did so, he listened to the growing sounds of mayhem, and he wondered at the state of his world.

He heard people come out of their houses, and he made out the rough substance of their shouting and imagined the violence of their movements. He listened to the scuffling from between the houses near his own and sat quietly as neighbors set upon neighbors, and siblings attacked their parents, as the proverb manifested itself in Warwick that a man's enemies were often those of his own household.

As the coffee reached its boiling point, he quietly slipped into his clothes and looked at the pictures on his mantle. He remembered the day now twenty years past when he'd said goodbye to his family as he secreted them out of the town on a truck that he'd arranged with the help of his uncle. He looked at the stove and listened to the street and wondered whether his family was still alive and whether he would ever see them again.

Pyotr Bolkonsky had always been a quiet man, rarely letting people into his thoughts, but as he sat and listened to the growing chaos from the street, he wondered aloud to the point that he blushed at the immediacy of his thought. "How can these people fall upon their neighbors in this way?" he wondered. "I would give anything for a moment to be with my loved ones." As he thought this, he heard stirring from down the hall, and he walked over to the stove and poured two cups of coffee.

There is a contradiction in the Russian soul, Gogol and Turgenev identified it, where a man both accepts his plight dutifully as payment for his sins, and rejects all of the individual elements that make up that reality as products of chaos and evil. As Pyotr brought his coffee to his lips and poured the burning liquid down his throat, he thought of this contradiction.

* * * *

As is the case in peculiarly Russian civil wars, and as has been mentioned previously, in the earliest moments of the conflict, it had been unclear where the battle lines were bound to be drawn. The war that was raging was not two dimensional, but it jutted into the third dimension, and intersecting axes of conflict could probably only be seen and understood from space... or heaven.

There were bubbles of conflict that developed in the street, only to drift until they burst, spilling their contents into the wider community. Men who had no interest in the fight suddenly found themselves engaged in fisticuffs because they had happened to be wearing red, or blue, or yellow when they left their homes that morning.

Women, who were making their way to the market as they might have on any other day, were accosted in the lane for their opinions, or lack thereof, and were immediately drawn into the heat of battle. One might easily pass a neighbor on the street only to decide at a glance that he was not with you (or that he might become one who is against you), or one might remember that an insult had once been received at the hands of a friend and use the war as cover for revenge. Reason had taken flight with the dawn and had left behind only brute and animal feeling. Actions may speak louder than words, but reaction speaks loudest of all.

The personal combined with the political, and both were soon lost inside the immediate. It was dangerous to walk outside of the house, and in some homes it was dangerous to walk outside of one's room, and truth be told, even in one's room it had grown perilous to climb out from under one's bed. There was simply no telling who stood where in those early moments of societal rage.

The people who raged in this battle, the townsfolk of Warwick, could not have known that in the America outside the wire, the microcosm of their struggle had followed an identical course, and the seeds of it had taken firm root. In both cases, like two twins who are separated at birth only to be reunited later in life to find that they have the same taste in food and the same interests in music, the town of Warwick and the nation generally had become inflamed by the threat of collapse. In both cases, the people had been blinded to this reality by the immediacy of their comforts, and by the seeming reality of their delusions. Now that comforts and reality seemed to be lost to the reign of chaos, everything changed.

It was surprising to find, therefore, that passing through the growing chaos in that earliest light of morning was a specter of nonviolence in the form of a soft young man with a secreted supply of reason and a critical eye. He wove in and out of the pockets of turbulence around him like an aircraft passing through a storm looking for good air. He slid by the commotion at the bakery, and walked straight through a crowd fighting at the bank, bumping shoulders with the combatants as if he were one of them, all the while not catching anyone's attention. He moved toward his destination with skillful avoidance of the crowd, becoming lost in plain sight like a benign and pleasing blip on the radar. And all the while, as he piloted through the crowd, he watched with a watchfulness that was complete, as his sister followed along in his slipstream. The two were going to the house of Pyotr Bolkonsky.

* * * *

Kolya and Natasha Bazhanov ascended the steps of the winding garden, being careful not to attract any unwanted attention. They knocked at the door and were immediately let in by the large burly man in the faded khaki hiking gear. The door shut immediately behind them, and they stood in the hallway and stomped their feet. They took off their thick winter jackets before offering a quick exchange of greetings.

"Hello, Pyotr. It's good to see you again," Kolya said cheerily. "Perhaps you know my sister, Natasha. We were told that this is the place to meet Vasily."

"Yes. And hello to you both. Is the situation out there as dire as it sounds?"

"Yes, well, you know. The fog has descended. Brother against brother, that sort of thing." Kolya waved his hand dismissively, paused, and took in the room and its surroundings.

Vasily stuck his head out of the door down the hall and called, "Kolya, is that you? Good. Hello, Natasha. I am just getting out of bed, give me a moment and I'll be out to see you." He nodded good morning to Pyotr, and went back inside his room to get dressed.

Pyotr spoke. "Natasha. Vasily told me that you were coming along. I see that you and your brother have come dressed for a hike. Excellent. I cannot tell you how ill-prepared some people can be when setting out for a journey. This is good. We've a long road ahead."

"Yes, Pyotr, we're grateful for the opportunity to get out of Warwick at last. My brother here was so excited that he never even went to bed," she smiled.

Pyotr looked over at Kolya, who had now bowed his head as if he were in solemn reflection, and his hand rubbed his pudgy chin, and his brow was down in honor of his thoughts.

"Well, we'll find a place after a while where we can hunker down and get some rest. I don't know what Vasily told you, but there is likely to be an electro-magnetic pulse event tomorrow that will be terrible in its extremity. Given what we already understand to be the social disruptions in the eastern seaboard, it will be a shock to the system that will likely never be overcome. Did you hear my uncle's speech?"

"Yes, sir," Natasha replied respectfully. "We paid close attention. But we weren't sure what could be done about it, with all the guns surrounding this place. Honestly, Kolya and I had essentially decided we would just gather whatever information we could glean and then either hide out in our house or make some kind of desperate suicide run for the fence."

Pyotr nodded his head, and as he looked over to Kolya again, he noticed Kolya looking at the blank spots on the wall where the holy ikons had been.

"Suicide is exactly what it would have been. Uncle Lev told me that Mikail will never let anyone escape as long as he has influence over the Russians."

"As long as he is one of the Russians," Kolya corrected him, without glancing away from the wall. Pyotr looked at him, not certain whether he appreciated the correction, but understanding its point.

"Yes, well, anyway, I have go-bags in the basement—packs prepared for a long journey. We'll go down shortly and prepare for departure. Would you like some coffee to warm you up?" He walked into the kitchen and took down a couple of additional cups. The cabinet doors thudded with a light finality, emphasizing not the warmth of the coffee, but the word departure.

Natasha followed and quickly gestured that she would appreciate some coffee, while Kolya reached up to cover a yawn and then to straighten his glasses. "Yes, I was afraid you would never ask. I don't suppose you would have a Pravda on hand or, better yet, a New York Times?" He looked at Pyotr to see whether this request registered any notice. It didn't.

As Pyotr poured the coffee, Kolya's eyes seemed to still be on a distant thought, and Natasha watched her brother as the thought solidified and was formed into words that then came forth from his mouth.

"I noticed something odd during our walk here, and it only now has occurred to me what it was. I don't know what it means, but it was odd, and I thought I'd tell you." He took the coffee as it was offered, and lifted the cup to his nose, where he smelled it and took in the rich aroma. "The whole town of Warwick is up in arms. They've all come out into the streets—all kinds—and they can all be seen running to and fro; and there are battles and meetings and shouting and all of the things you'd expect in a societal meltdown—"

"Yes, we know, Kolya," Pyotr replied, prompting him to further his thought. "Is this the thought that has finally occurred to you?"

"No. The thought is this... where are the oldlings? What I mean by that is, where are the oldest Warwickians, the people who have been here since the beginning? I saw them all in the gym during the trial. And I've seen several of them since then, but it is not what one would expect. Walking here with Natasha I saw people of every kind and age and economic class, and of every ideology, all out there marching or fighting or fleeing. But the old people are... well... they're just gone." He shrugged and took a sip of his coffee, before adding, "It's strange."

"That is strange," Pyotr replied. "What do you make from it?"

"I don't know. I'll have to think on it. Where could they be?"

He took his coffee to his lips for another sip and let the liquid, like the warmth of his contemplation, flow through his tired body.

* * * *

The four of them descended the stairs to the basement, and Pyotr pointed out the packs lined along the wall. He described the materials he'd placed in each, and they quickly discussed a game plan.

He was going to carry the ample medical supply kit that Lev Volkhov had gathered together over the years through some contact in the outside world, and he would also carry the gun—a Ruger 9mm pistol—that the old man had gotten somehow on the black market prior to the takeover. The rest of the supplies he'd divided among the bags by weight and what he thought the individual hikers could carry.

In just a moment they would climb into the tunnel and traverse it on their hands and knees until they reached a spot about fifty yards in, where he and Lev Volkhov had constructed a small dugout that they could use as a way station until the EMP hit.

"There is no sense coming out to the surface until that event takes place," Pyotr informed the team. "All kinds of strange and wild things might happen once the electromagnetic pulse is unleashed. We've never seen planes fly over Warwick, but who knows what will happen when over three-thousand aircraft, a goodly percentage of them at any one time flying over the eastern seaboard of America, come plummeting to the ground when they lose power all of a sudden." At that, the four of them each stopped and pondered the loss of human lives involved in that scenario, and though none of them had ever been on an airplane, they'd seen them on Russian television, and each could not help but imagine, even for a split-second, what it might be like to be on one of the doomed flights.

"When the EMP hits, if it does, there may be fires, and there will certainly be panic, and one never knows what the outcome will be, so we can't stay here. But there's no need, once we're hidden away in the tunnel, to come out until the air has cleared a little.

"Lev said that there will be massive disruptions, and the power plants will go offline—probably forever—and maybe the nuclear plants, not able to shut down properly or use generators to cool their cores, may melt down as well. It's hard to know.

"Most vehicles, any that still have fuel and are still running after the recent storms, will stop right where they are in that micro-second when the burst hits, and the highways and cities will become death traps. This is what we face when we head out there outside the wire. Form that thought clearly in your mind. Life becomes a challenge, once the end of the world as we know it comes about."

"Fine, Pyotr. We will treat it with the reverence it deserves. But if I may be so bold, can we cross that bridge when we come to it? I have a more immediate concern. I have some reading to do. Will we have light there, in the tunnel, in case we need it? Or will the EMP knock those out, too?" It was Kolya with his questions, again. Pyotr was already coming to realize that the young man's penchant for questioning was something he would have to learn to appreciate in the man.

"I've packed flashlights that we can use. I have no idea how well the flashlights will weather the EMP, or if the pulse will penetrate the tunnel. Just in case, I've packed a few extras with batteries into the ammo can with the radio we got from the man named Clay's backpack. We have to be careful about starting any fires in the tunnel since that would both endanger us from the carbon monoxide and threaten to give our position away should any smoke escape the tunnel. I've brought thick woolen blankets to cover both ends of the tunnel and block out the air so we will stay warmer throughout the night.

"Since we only have four of us, we should be comfortable in the dugout. If Vasily had succeeded in convincing more to come along, I was beginning to worry how we would accommodate many additional people."

Kolya looked at Vasily and winked. "Probably a good thing you weren't a bit more persuasive then."

Natasha chided her brother, quick to pick up on the hurt look on Vasily's face, and eager, as always, to tone down her brother's idea of humor. "Yes, Kolya, but lucky for us that he was persuasive, at least a little."

"What can I say?" Vasily replied. "My life is a two-edged sword. I've spent most of it allowing people to think I am a fool and they've begun to believe it."

"Ahhh, a fellow of infinite jest, caught in his own mousetrap," Kolya replied.

"Perhaps, Kolya" said Pyotr, "but he did make the effort, which is more than any of us did. It's bad form to jab at one's hero. And besides, we are men now, not mice." He smiled at his own rare joke.

"And women," added Natasha. "Women, not mice. Don't forget me."

"Wow, sister," Kolya rolled his eyes, "you always know how to kill a good punchline."

She playfully punched him on the shoulder and they all had a good laugh. "Yes," all three of the males added in a good-humored unison. "We expect that you won't soon let us forget you."

"Oh, and Vasily?" Kolya said.

"Yes?"

"I knew you spoke English. Even before, when we were digging the graves."

"Well, good thing you didn't tell Mikail and his thugs. Why didn't you say something?"

"I like to talk, and I didn't want you interrupting."

"Ahhh!" Vasily said, nodded his head and laughed.

* * * *

With that the four set off on their journey. There was camaraderie among them already as they stood in the cellar on the precipice of adventure. They strapped their bags to their backs and climbed down into the tunnel. They all moved as one in making their way out of the home that had been their only world and into the tunnel that would lead to a world they'd never seen.

Somewhere in the mists of time, in an alternate universe, in another record of the times, there was a memory of a traveler named Clay Richter standing next to a red-haired man on a bridge talking about life and love and loss, in the wake of Hurricane Sandy.

"This storm is going to wake a lot of people up," the red-haired man had said. "There are going to be a lot of people who are homeless now."

That was then. This is now.

CHAPTER 14

Red Bear energy drink was founded by Leonid Timchenko while he was on his way to becoming a billionaire oil magnate in Eastern Europe. Needing something better than coffee to keep him awake during all-night trading and gambling binges, he'd searched the world over looking for the perfect elixir. He'd found it on a busy street in Bangkok, and, before long, he'd purchased the rights and the formula. He had it altered to satisfy European tastes and, within a dozen years, Red Bear energy drink was within reach of almost everyone who could afford one anywhere in the world.

To build the brand and to capitalize on the net number of eyes that might be tempted by his advertising for the product, Timchenko had invested millions and millions of dollars in sponsorships, supporting sporting events and concert tours, and other similar venues. He had a preference for anything that seemed dangerous, crazy, or suicidal. For this reason, one might find the angry Red Bear that graced his packaging on the hoods of racing cars at Daytona and Baja trucks in San Felipe, or on the gas tanks of motorcycles as they flew over school buses and water fountains in Las Vegas. One might even find the Red Bear on the wings of solar-powered aircraft that flew experimental technologies and touched the edges of space.

One of Leonid Timchenko's sponsorships was about to pay off in a way that the rest of the world wouldn't even comprehend. Three years earlier, he'd invested millions of dollars in the crazy attempt, by a daredevil named Klaus von Baron, to parachute to earth from space.

The plan was to launch from Roswell International Air Center in New Mexico (just a few miles from the place where the aliens had landed... or didn't) a space capsule that was to be hauled over twenty-four miles into the stratosphere by a huge metallic balloon designed to carry Klaus von Baron into space. From his platform on his tiny capsule, in a spacesuit designed to perfection by a million of Leonid Timchenko's dollars, Klaus von Baron would jump into the history books, plummeting faster than the speed of sound before opening his parachute and landing once again in the desert floor that had been the source of haunting, beautiful myth since long before D.H, Lawrence had written about it or Georgia O'Keefe had painted it or Billy the Kid had ridden through it or Coronado had "discovered" it.

From space the area looks like a giant fall leaf, or maybe the soft tissue of a brain, with its landforms folded on top of each other in a veiny, vascular web. Timchenko liked the idea of his brand, his bear, floating in the sky to land on its pink, dusty surface, after having sped ferociously through space. He liked the juxtaposition that this symbolized for his drink—the hard, fast rush coupled with the sweet soft landing.

From the outset, the magnificent attempt had been fraught with troubles and setbacks. In fact, if one were the suspicious or conspiratorial kind, the concerns that led to the many delays of the Red Bear Starjump might even seem planned or contrived. In 2011, von Baron and Timchenko were sued by a man in Massachusetts who claimed that he'd come up with the space jump idea first, arguing that the two foreigners had stolen his idea. That case was settled out of court, but it did delay the jump by almost a year. On another occasion, von Baron pushed the date back himself after having a concern over data that was the result, his team had found, of a misplaced zero in a set of velocity projections. In early October of 2012, a planned jump was aborted because of a forecast of severe weather at the launch site, only to find on that day a sunny lightness to the air.

All of these delays had been very public, and when Timchenko and von Baron filled out their permits and papers to re-attempt their jump in early November, there were many people in and out of government who had come to feel sorry for the pair. It was beginning to seem that someone was working to sabotage their plans, and then, in the last days of October, they came to wonder if that someone was God himself. This is because, only a week before the newly re-scheduled jump, Hurricane Sandy, and then the arctic nor'easter, had struck the northeast of America.

Those twin storms, and the havoc and social unrest that followed soon after them, made it seem like the Red Bear Starjump was going to be doomed forever. But, luckily for our intrepid daredevil and his financier, someone somewhere in the halls of power decided that perhaps having the whole world watch Klaus von Baron LIVE streaming on the Internet, as he jumped into the record books from space, would be just what a divided and beleaguered country needed. It may not be bread, the feeling went, but it was a circus, and what the country needed in the moment was release. So the jump was set.

Since the election had been delayed in most of the northeastern United States, and since many folks in those areas were suffering without power anyway, as a distraction, the Red Bear Starjump was rescheduled for the Tuesday of Election Day. America needed some good news, some unifying event that would encapsulate why these world changing feats and challenges were uniquely representative of the things that Americans stood for. Sure, the daredevil was a German who was being financed by a Russian billionaire, but the science! The science was purely American, and therefore it passed for religion. It would provide a balm in Gilead, so to speak, made with physical daring of the elements rather than grinding chemistry of nature's bounty. But the point would be the same. It would give the country salve to ease its wounds.

Well, maybe that is a bit overdone, but it wasn't altogether false either. And in any event, there was one thing that was undeniable and unstoppable. The feat was going to be accomplished over America and live via YouTube.

* * * *

Far from being diminished by the initial burst of fury spent, the escalation of the battle in Warwick came in the intervening hours to fill the forest like wildfire.

The thin veil of law and civility that had governed relations between neighbors, bringing them along in the past so that they settled disagreements with compromise, was torn in two with a lawless spree. Not all of the crime was political, of course. The glass encasements of Kopinsky's Jewelry were smashed as opportunists sought to profit from the madness. The longsuffering priest of St. Olaf's church stood in the doorway and watched his chapel stripped of its treasures.

Men who had come to despise their wives gave them beatings without threat of reprisal, and women who were jealous of their neighbors' good fortunes stood in the street and applauded the arson of their rivals' homes. A cruelty that had been unimaginable only hours before suddenly announced that it had been silently brewing for ages.

In the battle lines that formed, there were rich against poor, and weak against strong, and young against old (but not the very old, for some odd reason that almost no one had recognized). In the forming and reforming of alliances, the battles ultimately descended into simply whoever happened to be in the proximity of reach against anyone who had anger and hatred to burn. There was no rhyme or reason to the ordering of the conflict.

Instead, there was simply breakdown and confusion, and double-crossing and intrigue. In such a situation, even the cooler minds had begun to flail in imagined wrongs that deserved redress. In this way, the Battle of Warwick was perhaps no exception to any battle that had ever been fought in a civil war in a community of humankind. It was like a nightmare born of chaos, sired by rumors and fueled by neglect.

If you had asked any one of the townsfolk what they were fighting for (or against) it would have been impossible to find a consensus. The answers would have been myriad. Country, pride, family, flag, brotherhood, freedom, jobs, religion, economy... anything. But in the innermost heart of that wide-ranging chaos, there was perhaps only one true note. Survival. Life itself descended into every man for himself and every woman for her interest. Bertrand Russell once wrote that war does not determine who has won or who has lost, but merely who is left, and this became the overriding ethic of the day's developments.

The point had shifted from taking back the town or impressing upon others a central tenet or ideology, to one in which everyone simply wanted to live through it. Make it right, or make it good, became... just make it.

The fact that the expediencies of war quickly descended into brutality and disorder was not entirely, of course, due to a lack of effort on the part of the gang led by Mikail and Vladimir and Sergei. The triumvirate of power had spent the long previous night trying to put down the initial signs of uprising with the belief that, through a decisive show of force, they could convince their fellow townspeople to abandon their thoughts of war and reprisal and settle into their newly-established places under the leadership they hoped to provide. They believed that the control they exerted over the Spetznaz troops was a definitive advantage that they could use to put an end to the matter before it had even begun. However, here is where the differences in approach between Mikail and Vladimir came into play in perhaps its most crucial twist.

The brutish Vladimir never had any sense of the nuances or subtleties of leadership that Mikail had tirelessly attempted to show him. He'd always believed and ceaselessly relied upon the unerring superiority of physical force as a means of proving his point, and, as a result, there had been perhaps a natural split between the two and between those who were inclined to see the points that the two were each attempting to make in their own way.

Vladimir had influenced a certain contingent of the Spetznaz, even through their very brief association, to shoot first and ask questions later, while Mikail had likewise argued for a more long-term, circumspect, and perhaps more patient approach in which the influence of power could be used without actually having to resort to its display. This had resulted in the Spetznaz being divided between those who were ready to fight the townsfolk immediately in order to secure the perimeter of the battlefield, and those who were more content to simply watch and wait until the action seemed to reach its own conclusion.

The end result was that, as the townsfolk of Warwick descended into chaotic strife, and as the battles became less organized at every turn, it became less and less clear throughout the day for whom (or what) the governing authority, the group with the majority of guns, was fighting for.

Even less clear, as the townspeople grew increasingly agitated that their superior force might win the day, was the outcome that would result from the fact that the power of the government had been turned upon the people at large. To be clear, there were Spetznaz operatives who entered the battle and, as a result, there were people lying in the street bloodied and bullet-riddled. But this reality caused greater, not lesser, agitation among the people, and in those moments when the citizens forgot their differences for a moment and set their sights on conquering the soldiers, it became a question of how likely a soldier or two with a limited magazine clip could defend against an army of shovels and hammers and farm implements in the hands of people who were willing to charge into the face of danger and use them.

In short, the battle plan, if there had ever been a coherent one, was lost, as all battle plans eventually are, to the madness of conflict. The soldiers came to embrace the same survival instinct that the population did, and some simply decided that the best way to survive would be to lay down their weapons and refuse to enter a conflict that was, in the final analysis, against people not unlike themselves.

This reality, too, mirrored what was happening in many other corners of America.

The unraveling of what might loosely be called "the government" came to show, like the loosening of the bonds of civility that kept neighbor in careful compromise with neighbor in the first place, that the glue that holds society together proved itself to be thin indeed.

At some point during the day, Mikail and Vladimir and the others realized that their dreams of revolution were spiraling out of control because those dreams had not been shared in the hearts of a conclusive majority of their fellows. The fact that this is an age-old story in the history of the world made it no less true on that day in Warwick.

* * * *

It was Kolya who suggested that they change to "English names." The four had arrived successfully at the mid-point of the tunnel after having crawled into the dugout through the tunnel from the house. They'd spent a considerable amount of time covering their tracks inside the house, even going so far as to reassemble the bureau entrance and pull the drawers in after them so that the tunnel could not be easily seen from the cellar.

Then they'd prepared the dugout for comfort and settled in for a brief stay while they waited for the day's events, and those of the following day, to unfold.

They each unpacked their packs and took out blankets and a little bit of food and lights and such. Vasily carried the backpack that belonged to the traveler named Clay, and for the first time he actually spent some time examining the contents. He found the items that he'd seen already - the fishing kit and the knife and other items - but in the thin light available to them now, he began to thumb through the books that were in the backpack, and once he did so, Kolya became very excited.

"Oh my, this is Whitman and Hemingway! I've been unable to get hold of these books for so long," Kolya said, smiling broadly. "Everything good in Warwick, I was led to believe, came only through the black market, and I was told that I might be able to get things there that we couldn't get in the stores. But, I never could figure out exactly to whom I should talk about this. I suppose that is one of the huge negatives to being considered a bookworm. People are suspicious of you if they think you might know more than they do. Believe me when I say that one of the reasons that I sought out such back alley subterfuge was that I wanted to find out who could get me more books from the outside. Ahh... these... these are two books that I dearly wanted." Kolya's eyes shone like diamonds as he asked Vasily if he could hold them, and when the books were passed to him he lovingly caressed them as one does a talisman. He ran his fingers across the slightly embossed lettering on the Whitman book's covering, thumbing randomly through the Hemingway, and reading passages aloud to the others. The others sat and watched him as he turned his head away for a moment, and they noticed his faint shadow on the wall reach up and wipe a tear away from its eye.

Kolya reached inside the pack and drew out a thin volume with the title *The Poems of CL Richter*, and he asked what it was. Pyotr harrumphed that it was a load of self-indulgent garbage. He didn't know who C.L. Richter was, but the words, according to Pyotr's judgment, read like the elementary school musings of a spurned lover. Briefly looking through the volume, Kolya had come, more or less to agree, but with certain exceptions.

"Well, it is certainly not Shakespeare," he concluded. "Still, it has its own little moments of beauty and truth. After all, those are the primary things we should seek in poetry. If it is true, then it can be beautiful." He paused, thumbing through the book. "Like here... I like this one," he said, and he read it aloud to them.

How, and Why, and Where I Love You.

Thick, like the sweetness of honey,
Like the Tupelo dream that we shared as we danced in the moonlight,
And thin, like the promise of money,

*Like the watery bond that we shared as we swam in that tune.
White,*

Pure, like the color of holy,

*Like the color of heaven we saw in our angel's sweet blue
eyes.*

And black, like the heart of the lowly,

*Like the dark of the leaven that rises when we tell our true
lies.*

Here, like the dreams that you left me,

*Like the night when they visit and drape me in velvety
slumber*

And there, like the beams of thy theft be,

*Like their flight, when the morning comes on, bringing cares
without number.*

Kolya began to go on about how the poem generally lacked a certain central structure that was hinted at in that title, but, he said, it had never been fully developed, and he told the other three how the poem was merely a kind of list of emotions that the fellow had felt in his obvious loss, so there was truth there, and how the poem had a sad sweetness to it, and how it was like the honey in the first line. It needed, Kolya said, only to be tasted, it would not suffice for an entire meal—and it was then when Natasha had begged him please... please... to just stop. He was killing her with his endless analysis. Sisters and brothers don't always agree on the merits of art, but the one thing they have no trouble agreeing upon is the need to silence one another.

Kolya had stopped, and then he noticed a poem folded into the first page of the volume, a poem by the Harlem poet Langston Hughes. That was when he suddenly looked at the others and decided that they should all assume new names.

"Look," he said. "We're about to enter a world that does not know us and does not accept us, even though we are as much a part of it as anyone else. There are certainly likely to be those who will be unfriendly. We would do well to make ourselves fit as closely as possible. We've already enough going against us. Though Lev taught many of us how to speak perfect, accentless English, he taught us all too well. We are not good at the vernacular, and slang... we know almost nothing of it. We were not raised to live in America. We were raised to live in Russia. If anyone were reading us... say... in a book... they would say, why do the characters speak so awkwardly? And by awkwardly, we would know that they actually mean *correctly.*"

Pyotr nodded. "I agree completely. That's why Lev told us to flee to Amish country. He said we would not stick out there so obviously. Anyone who hears us there will think that we speak painfully awkward, though precise, English."

Vasily, too, decided that he approved of the idea and said that he really liked the ring of the name from the poem that was folded into the volume. He decided he would call himself Lang. Kolya, for his part, decided to call himself Cole, partly because, he said, he had always liked the jazz musician named John Coltrane. "He played a Russian lullaby that was simply spectacular," he said, as if that settled the matter for him.

Pyotr liked the suggestion overall, but wasn't willing to take it much further than he ought, so he decided simply to be known as Peter, the English version of his Russian name. And Natasha—was it the unwillingness to give in to her sibling?—had refused the entire matter.

"Well, you guys can do what you will," she said. "As for me, I will live with the name my mother gave me." And with that, and a firm nod of her head, the matter was settled for her, too.

* * * *

Following this, the newly titled Lang began to dig through the backpack some more and found a small blue box inside. He asked Peter what was in it.

"I don't know," Peter said. "It rattles when you shake it. That is all that I know of that box."

"What?! What?!" Cole asked. "You didn't open it to find out?"

"No. It belonged to a man who has just died," he said. "I believe in letting things be. In showing some respect for the departed."

This was too much for Cole. "But aren't you even a little bit curious?"

"No," Peter said. And the sound in his voice suggested that he was unwilling to budge on the matter.

"What if it's important? What if it has something in it that will aid our survival?"

Peter looked at Cole, unblinking. "Then we will still have it, won't we? If we end up in dire need of something that is in a box and rattles, we'll open it then."

Lang and Cole looked at each other, and then at Natasha, who gave them no sign of help, and then they looked back at each other as younger men do in the presence of their seniors. They decided to let the matter drop. They placed the box and the books and the other items back in the backpack, and then placed the pack along the wall.

They were satisfied that they had seen everything the pack had to offer, but God from His omniscient seat in the heavens knew that they had not. In a small, zippered pocket near the strap of one of the handles was a weathered, crumbling business card that had been given to the traveler who had carried the pack into their community. It was perhaps best that they did not see it. If they had, they might have considered it trash and thrown it on the floor of the dugout to be lost forever. But they did not see it and so they did not throw it away. Instead, they simply sat and talked quietly while they waited for sleep to overtake them. That was a blessing, like most blessings are, in the way it happened without their effort or notice. The card, like the rattling in the box, would indeed be there still if, as Cole had innocently said, it was ever needed to aid their survival.

* * * *

In his sleep, Lang dreamt of the town of Warwick. He dreamt of the people that he left there, of the way they'd passed through thick and thin together, how they'd come through holy and perverse. His dreams were in color and then black and white. He saw the others faintly through the moonlight, on the far side of the shore, heard the clamor of their uprising, and mourned for the loss that he felt in leaving.

One face in particular haunted him in his dream. The face of the sweet girl from the bakery named Irinna. He'd always loved her in secret, and he'd hoped that she might one day love him, too. He'd stood and watched her pass through the town as she made her deliveries for the baker. He'd watched her gently sweep away a wisp of hair from her lovely brow, leaving just a gentle trace of flour at times, which she would then wipe away with her sleeve and smile in embarrassment. He'd hoped that someday he might convince her to go on a date with him, but he'd never had the courage to ask

Her house was the one he'd gone to first when he was asking people to come along on their journey, and for a brief moment he'd hoped she would come. She'd seemed curious and receptive, asking questions about where they would go, how they would get there, when they would leave. He'd laid the plans out in hopes that she'd follow, but in the end she'd shaken her head and declined. She didn't give a reason, simply saying that she wished him well, but that she just couldn't go. He'd left in sorrow, and as he slept that sorrow returned.

Had he been able to extract himself from that dream at that moment and spirit away to the town of Warwick, and if he could have hovered there to view the village where the chaos had overtaken even the premise of any workable resolution, he wouldn't have been so inclined to feel that way. For as the town fell into complete and utter disrepair, the lovely Irinna was indeed inside her house making her own plans for escape. She was readying her belongings. She watched out the window to see whether there was any hope that the Spetznaz soldiers would bring the town back into some kind of order, or whether a coalition of the people would rise up and turn the tide in a decisive way.

As she watched, it became clear—it became clear to everyone, even the gang from the prison that had begun the trouble—that the cause was lost, and without it, so was the town. She sat quietly and waited until she heard a predetermined knock at the door that her escape route had arrived.

As the chaos descended and the town crumbled, she heard the knock. Rushing to the door in breathless anticipation, she found standing there a man whom she had come to love dearly. The match was made secretly as she made her bread deliveries in and around Warwick. She'd passed his house many times, and one time she stopped for a moment to chat, and then eventually stayed too long and then eventually wanted to stay even longer. And now she was ready to leave with her love.

She rushed to the door to find him standing there, just outside the window in the door. She looked up and saw him motioning silently through the glass to her. And with that, she grabbed her belongings and opened the door and took the hand of the stocky bulldog named Mikail Brekhunov.

* * * *

Mikail had a few of the loyal Spetznaz soldiers with him, and the small group had decided that the cause was indeed lost in Warwick, and they were going to make a break for it and try to leave before some form of authority was restored and recriminations started.

They talked as they carefully made their way in a circuitous route back to the gym to gather up Sergei and Vladimir and the remnant of their loyal forces. In passing, Irinna mentioned to him, since they were now discussing escape, that the young, dull boy... Vasily... had come to her house last night and had asked her to escape with him. Apparently, even the town dunce had a way out.

This surprised Mikail, and not just a little. The red scar on his forehead began to throb and his mouth twitched as he mulled the thought in his mind. As they drew close to the gymnasium, his rage began to build, and, although they had not reached a place of safety, he grabbed Irinna harshly by the hand and spun her around to face him, his rage to the point of boiling over.

"How were they getting out?" he demanded angrily.

"I have no idea, Mikail. He gave no details. He just said that they were going to be leaving and that he wanted me to go with him."

"Oh he did, did he? Who was going with him?!" He spat the words. "Damned fool!" It was unclear from the way that he said this exactly to whom he was referring. "Dumb, little Vasily! He wanted to take the most beautiful girl in Warwick with him?! He had a way out! Maybe young Vasily wasn't so dumb after all!" He said this not in a way of kindness or to flatter Irinna, or even Vasily. He said it in anger. The soldiers escorting the pair were growing wary of being out in the open with the town in rebellion, and they attempted to move the two arguing lovers along with them in order to get them as quickly as possible into the safety of the gym.

"I kept that little idiot alive when Vladimir wanted to kill him! I gave him life! And this is what he gives me!"

"Mikail, there was nothing! He seemed to be going house to house. There was nothing between us!" As she said this, the soldiers grabbed the two and forcibly moved them toward the gym, toward cover.

The soldiers were moving in formation, sweeping their guns in wide arcs, and as they did so, the chaos of the town opened up around them and the people formed in crowds and looked on, urging an offensive.

A sharp crack split the air, and the soldiers dropped to the ground instinctively. Mikail spun around and dropped to the ground with them, looking at the crowd to see if he could determine who had fired on them.

Just at that moment, the lovely Irinna stood still in the street. She reached her hand up to brush away the wisp of hair from her face and, as she did so she left a small trail of blood smearing across her fast-draining features. Looking up, Mikail reached for Irinna's hand to pull her down with him, and only then did he see the blood running down her face, down her dress, circling the curves of the one he loved so. Her legs collapsed and she fell to the ground, falling into Mikail's arms as he attempted to understand what had happened.

Mikail crouched over her, and the soldiers grabbed at them both and began to drag them, and then, seeing that the girl was dying, the soldiers dropped her and began forcibly to drag the unwounded Mikail towards the gymnasium, toward safety. Finally they broke out into a sprint as Mikail stumbled along in their midst. He gave a final look over his shoulder, over the shoulder of a soldier, and saw his lovely Irinna lying in the snow, bleeding into it. He turned his face toward the gym and picked up his pace with the soldiers, until they came into the warm embrace of their shelter.

In that look and in that moment, Mikail focused his mind on what was ahead of him. For now, perhaps for the first time in a lifetime of calculation, he found himself feeling an entirely new emotion. It was a feeling that he suddenly confronted but did not have any real way to account for in the way that he always calculated everything. It was feeling of overwhelming and ancient reckoning, a feeling of un-appraisable anguish.

Mikail now had a reason to hate.

CHAPTER 15

Tuesday Afternoon – Election Day

It was nearing noon as Klaus von Baron stepped out onto the platform of his multi-million dollar Red Bear Starjump capsule and looked downward, 128,000 feet, toward the blue, grey circle of the earth. In its curvilinear contrast to the deep, black expanse of space, the planet splayed beneath his feet, looking mysterious and malleable, like a floating lump of clay waiting to be formed if only he could get his hands around it.

"Checklist, item seventeen," Klaus heard through his headset from Starjump Mission Control in Roswell. "Engage capsule release timer. Near your left hand, Red Bear, down below the seat reconnect and next to the O2 injection port. Flip up the guard and throw the red switch."

The command sounded like a faraway dream reaching into his conscience, the only other sound being the measured rhythm of his own thick breathing. Klaus looked down, as did the millions of people worldwide watching over his shoulder, over the internet, and took in the awesome scene, feeling his smallness against the massive earth.

With the bulky suit restricting his movement, he moved clumsily in response to the instruction. He thought about the millions of dollars that had gone into manufacturing the suit knowing that, in just a moment, he would be plummeting at greater than the speed of sound, the first human to break the sound barrier outside of a vehicle, without a capsule or ship, in a tumbling, rotating freefall. The suit would be the only thing between him and death. In fact, without it, right now he would already be dead.

Klaus was already twice as high as the "Armstrong Limit," which is the height at which the barometric pressure is so low that water will boil at room temperature. No human can live above the Armstrong Limit in an unpressurized atmosphere. The suit was his life, and it represented all such systems of human dependency. When man throws his life into the dead hands of the machine and counts on the inanimate to operate as it should, he becomes acutely aware of the tenuous miracle of creation. If the suit developed a rip or tear now, his blood would boil and the capsule would be his airy tomb. In that case (if he failed to complete checklist item seventeen), the Starjump capsule would float along, losing atmosphere, until it fell randomly somewhere, probably into an ocean.

If the suit failed at any time during the fall, traveling at 800 M.P.H. or around Mach 1.2, depending on the altitude, Klaus would either flash freeze, or he would pass out and be dead in seconds. Whether his chute opened or not at that point would be immaterial, because it would just be an instrument for delivering his body back to earth for burial.

Klaus knew that his jump was an historic one. He knew it was being played LIVE on YouTube. He knew that once he stepped off the platform and threw his body into space he would have a limited time to stabilize his fall and straighten out his body before he reached the point of no return where he would either have to pull the cord to his parachute and slow his all too rapid descent or push along in the slip of atmosphere until his body passed the wave field that would produce a sonic boom. He knew that only bullets and missiles and spaceships and meteors had ever achieved what he would now be doing with his own flesh and blood inside the mix of chemical-laced fabrics that contained the technology that would keep him alive like an umbilical cord inside a womb. He knew that over eight million people were watching him go through his egress checks as he slid to the edge of the capsule. Beyond that, he knew very little.

He did not know, for example, that when he engaged the capsule release timer that he was not actually activating the capsule's controlled descent functions. He did not know that, in fact, when he flipped the switch he would set in motion the genesis event that would signal the end of the world as everyone knew it, and the beginning of a whole new era. He did not know that, by innocently throwing the red switch as he'd been commanded to do through the signal in his helmet from mission control, he would sign the death warrant of over 300 million people in the United States alone, and that of over six billion people worldwide. He could not have known that flipping a toggle switch would rip a tear in the pressurized space suit called "the grid," an artificial system that was absolutely necessary to keep humans alive in the beginning of the 21st Century.

No, Klaus von Baron was innocent when he flipped the switch that started the timer that in four minutes would silently launch a small ultralight craft, no larger than a breadbox, that carried a miniaturized "super-EMP" warhead, that would glide completely undetected through space to its designated vectors. There, when it detonated, it would change the world forever.

Klaus was innocent. At least... he was as innocent as anyone can be who gives his life and the lives of his fellow humans over to be governed and maintained by the machines.

* * * *

"Checklist, item seventeen. Check."

It will take Klaus about eight minutes to complete his historic jump into the record books, and eight minutes hence, when he stands up and raises his hands in victory on the desert of a pink, dusty New Mexico badlands, he still will not know that he has landed on a completely different world than the one he left only that morning, the one he saw from his perch twenty-four miles up in space.

He does not know, and he will not know, that the moment of his greatest triumph is the moment of humankind's end... at least, an end to the world the way almost everyone alive has ever known it.

Perhaps it is not too much to say that Klaus von Baron's jump was one small leap for man, but one giant leap backwards for mankind.

* * * *

In Warwick, the very un-Civil War raged on. While neighbor continued to fight neighbor and ancient rivalries flared back up into contemporary reasons to kill and harm and maim, a search was on.

Sergei Dimitrivich, Vladimir Nikitch, a handful of their Youth Revolutionary Forces, and six Spetznaz soldiers were going door to door in the town looking for Vasily Romanovich Kashparov and whatever other traitors to the Revolution could be found. Truth be told, they wanted Vasily mainly so they could find out what he knew about an escape route out of Warwick.

Frankly, the Spetznaz and their Communist bosses who had sent them to Warwick in the first place could not care less about Vasily Kashparov. They wanted the oldlings, and they wanted *all* of them. To the Russian Special Forces operatives, capturing the oldlings was the entire reason that they were going through any of this. That was why they had parachuted into Warwick before the planned attacks on the U.S. and the West. Mikail, the Youth Forces, all of them, were just tools—useful idiots—mechanisms used to bring about a necessary end.

Their orders from their commanders in the GRU had been clear. Support and stabilize the town so that the oldlings of Warwick—the ones who had been there since the very beginning—could be intensively interrogated.

The new leaders of the New Soviet Union, after they were done brushing America and the West off the map for eternity, wanted to be able to track down every American Spy in Russia, and Warwick had been the main supplier of authentic Russian American spies since the 1960's. Every one of those agents of capitalist America would need to be rooted out, and, within the aged minds and feeble memories of Warwick's oldlings, those names would be stored like they were in a computer databank. Eighty of those oldlings were already being questioned in the locker rooms under the Warwick Gym. There were more out there, at least there ought to be.

Lacking any better options, the Spetznaz troops had thrown their weight behind Mikail in the battle for Warwick. That decision wasn't turning out well, and they were beginning to have doubts about his ability to deliver on his promises, but for now their primary function took priority over their personal feelings. In addition to the large contingent of troops "manning the walls" so to speak—guarding the village to keep the people in and the rest of the world out—there were specialists involved in the interrogations in the basement of the gymnasium. There were also soldiers still involved in trying to police the town and stop the fighting. These were the units traveling with Vladimir, trying to root out all resistance and end talk of revolution or escape.

To the Russians, if this Vasily Kashparov knew a way out of the Charm School, then he would also know if any of the oldlings had already escaped, or if any more were hidden in the town's many root cellars and basements. They wanted to find Vasily merely so they could find any oldlings hiding from this new Inquisition.

The search for Vasily, like the revolution itself, was not going well. Two of the Youth Forces, untrained and lacking in military skills and tactics, had already been killed executing the searches. That fact had angered Vladimir to no end. The young man, already a brutal sadist, became doubly efficient and intensive in his application of whatever means he deemed necessary to extract information from the people of Warwick.

A proper search, meant an everywhere search, and that meant a systematic, door-to-door examination, even while a pitched and rolling battle was taking place in the town. Warwick was not a normal, modern village. The people were Russian, and mostly agrarian. They liked to dig, and almost every house had storm cellars and basements and even vegetable larders formed of concrete, or crafted from old freezers buried in the backyards. There were a lot of places to hide and therefore, a lot of places to search, to coax the earth to give up her secrets.

Vladimir's brutality had grated on the Spetznaz soldiers, who, though they were certainly not humanitarians or choir boys in their own right, recognized that if this young Stalin ever intended to lead people, there might need to be some people left to lead. His tactics were more akin to an extermination than a systematic search of the village. They noticed, but did not question (yet) his brutish methods, mostly because they needed him to guide them through the town and its maze-like structures.

Coldly, and violently, the team went from house to house on their mission.

* * * *

In the Warwick Gymnasium, Mikail was doing his best to hold together both his crumbling coalition and his relationship with the Spetznaz soldiers who nominally had the most firepower in the town. The civil war was turning against Mikail, mainly because the splintered and fragmented opposition was starting to coalesce into a loose affiliation of those whose only unifying tenet was their opposition to Mikail and the Communists.

The tide had turned sometime during the mid-afternoon. Mikail couldn't precisely pin down the moment his short reign in Warwick had come to an end, but he increasingly recognized the signs. Hitler had experienced such a turning point, as had Robespierre and other failed revolutionaries. In fact, almost all agitators who advocate for a takeover of power, unless their cause is backed by consent of the people or sufficient force to ignore such consent – almost all such would-be dictators in their turn come to the realization that all is lost. As a student of history, Mikail knew that there was only one avenue possible once his grip on power released, and that was... recriminations.

Recriminations. That's a very nice word for "payback," and such a fancy word does little to describe the awful meting out of revenge that can follow tyrants like a shadow follows a man on a sunny afternoon. Mikail knew his moment in that sun had passed as he felt the fiery orb setting over his small, troubled town.

There was a look in the eye of the Youth Revolutionary Forces, and that look began to evolve and spread, and soon a unit of Spetznaz forces approached with the inevitable official announcement that Mikail was very earnestly encouraged to meet with representatives of the coalition forces in the village. He knew this meant he would be asked to arrange his own surrender for trial.

This was how it had to be. It was destiny. History tends to impress this fact on the mind for those who care to venture into books to learn of the spiritual physics of such things. Mikail had done so, and he knew the implications.

So Mikail met with the "peace" commission, and terms were arranged and agreed to, although he did not go completely quietly into the approaching, dark night. He had a word for them as they departed.

"The only thing you all have in common is your hatred of me!" Mikail shouted at the backs of the opposition commission as they turned to leave the gymnasium. They turned to look at him in contemptuous regard. He laughed out loud. "What will you have when I am gone?" he asked. "You will have civil war and strife until you are all dead!" He said this in the way that prophecies are often uttered, though perhaps even he didn't realize that what he said was so prophetic. It was more of a statement of fact mixed with the slightest hint of wishful thinking.

"That is what we have now," Konstantin Kopinsky, the jeweler's son, shouted back. His anger was emphasized by the sound of the gymnasium door slamming itself shut, effectively ending Mikail's reign over Warwick. Mikail was given twenty-four hours to cede control of the government and all of his forces to the coalition, at which time he would be arrested and taken to the prison, where he was certain he would be locked away for the rest of his natural life.

That was the deal that he agreed to, though he had no intention of hanging around Warwick long enough to honor it. He would not allow himself to be the subject of his own revolutionary dogma. He would not suffer the indignities of his own interminable crimes. He would not allow his indiscretions to result in the crowd's recriminations.

* * * *

On Tuesday morning, Peter announced to the other three in the tunnel that they needed to put a watch (or more accurately, a "listen") back at the tunnel entrance, inside the tunnel but below the bureau in Peter's basement. They would want to know, he said, if anyone came snooping around the basement and, by listening from the post below the bureau, a person could faintly hear the racket going on outside, in the town. Cole was the first to volunteer, saying he liked the opportunity to read the scene by the details coming from the imagination he applied to the noise.

The battle had raged through the night, and by the morning of Election Day in America, some of the fury and rage in Warwick had spent itself, but not all of it. Upon his return to the dugout, the pudgy intellectual gave a full report. "There is still sporadic fighting. It's hard to hear from the tunnel, and we only get an idea of what is going on in that one area of town, but the tempest certainly isn't as loud as it was last night," Cole said. He took off his glasses and began to clean them. "I wouldn't say it was all much ado about nothing, but I suppose all's well that ends well."

"Oh, you and your Shakespeare!" Natasha said. She shook her head, but you could see that there was the slightest hint of a smile on her face. She looked over to Lang and added, "I've had to put up with this my whole life!"

Kolya put his glasses back on to his face. "As you like it, dear sister." He then turned to Lang and said, "my dearest blood-kin here is a shrew that needeth to be tamed." He winked.

Peter glared at Cole, not entirely appreciating his humor in such a critical moment, but then his face softened and he smiled. "Well, I'll not try to keep up with you measure for measure, so we'll end the Shakespeare titles game and maybe you can give us the rest of your report?"

Cole smiled. "Well, it didn't sound like anyone has been in the basement. The bureau is still there and secured, and the whole time I listened, I didn't hear a thing, except for the occasional bark of a pistol or a shout from someone off in the distance."

Peter nodded his head, but remained silent while Lang shifted his weight, giving an indication that he was uncomfortable just sitting around in the dugout.

"Why don't we go find this water plant, Peter? We can't just stay down here for days. Anyway, we can hide out there until things become less... cloudy."

"I figured we'd just stay here until maybe Friday. It is safe and warm, and besides, we have such nice toilet facilities in here!" Peter pointed his thumb in the direction of the underground "outhouse." In the dugout, which was at the midway point in the tunnel, Peter and Lev had dug a tiny (and short) little indentation into the dirt, which turned to the left so that the person using it could have a little privacy. The facility consisted of a hole dug three feet deep with a wooden box atop it. The box had a hole cut into it. There was a bucket full of sawdust next to the toilet so that after it was used, the waste could be covered with a thin layer of wood shavings. This kept the scent down. Lev Volkhov and Peter had used the toilet while building the tunnel, so that they didn't have to go all the way back up to the house each time they needed to eliminate.

"The toilet is fine, Peter. A fine invention it is," Lang said, smiling. "But I'm getting a bit batty just sitting around. Cole can read the same books over and over again, and I think he's memorized The Poems of C.L. Richter, but since I didn't find any Solzhenitsyn in Clay's backpack, I need some fresh air and some trees over my head. I'm just getting tunnel fever."

Cole shook his head and tried to change the subject, to divert his younger friend from his growing agitation. "Actually, I've come to really appreciate the poems of Mr. Richter, whosoever he is. They have a sort of charm that is lacking in a lot of poetry."

"Self-indulgent nonsense," Peter sniffed, kicking a clod of dirt across the dugout floor.

"Be that as it may, Peter," Cole responded, "the poems are true, and sweet. They come from that place inside of us where everyone touches the poetic imagination. I think that, in a dark world that is crumbling on its rotted foundation," he pointed upwards with his index finger, "sweet and true is nice to have around."

Peter took a deep breath and thought for a moment in silence. It seemed that he had been unofficially elected as leader, and the other three younger members of the group seemed to want his approval even as they sought, as youth always does, to act as if their world didn't hinge on receiving it. He nodded to Cole, as if in resignation, but he thought to himself how perhaps the book's pages could be better used as an accessory kept near the tunnel's toilet. He smiled at his own wicked humor.

"I suppose we can go check out the water plant, but if we go, everything needs to go with us. We'll just stay there. We'll have to find a way to obscure our footprints from the snow, and we'll have to move quickly and silently. We'll surface only meters outside the fence, and if there are patrols in Warwick, then they would see us. We'll need to be ready to run for it."

"This will be the most dangerous thing we've done yet," Lang said, nodding his head.

"Well, I disagree with that, Lang," Peter said. Cole nodded, agreeing with Peter. "Your trip from here back to the gym and then through the town door to door was extremely dangerous, and perhaps not a little stupid," Cole gently agreed, and the three let Lang bask in that recognition for a moment.

Natasha smiled. "I'm glad you did it, Lang. I'd hate to be back there in Warwick, trying to hide from the mob or from Mikail's goons."

"Well, we aren't out of Warwick yet," Peter said. "Perhaps it is good that we leave now. We'll get some distance between us and that stinking pit of a town."

* * * *

An unabridged retelling of the historic mad dash from the tunnel's exit to the water plant might be in order someday, if the story ever gets told in its entirety. The escape was historic, because, as far as any of them knew, no one had successfully escaped Warwick and gotten away since the great confusion in '92. It was mad because the four individuals who made the escape had no idea what awaited them on the outside. They did not know if anyone, perhaps even the Americans, still patrolled the forest. They did not know if the Russian Spetznaz had snipers or soldiers watching the perimeter to prevent escapes. They did not know if they would run into mayhem or violence in the forest from people escaping the cities, and they did not know if the water plant was occupied—if perhaps gangs of refugees were using the treatment facility as a hideout or headquarters. In short, they knew nothing, and that is what made their historic escape an act of madness. It was a rush into the unknown.

But they made it, and, in reality, the whole escapade went off without a hitch. They poked their heads up into the clear cold air outside the fences of Warwick, and they saw neither soldiers nor gangs. The first sprint into the deeper forest was accomplished purely on adrenaline, a pounding heart terror that embraced and squeezed the mind. After the four of them were clear of the open and lightly treed area, they moved slower and more circumspectly. They used branches to try to obscure their direction, and several times they doubled back in order to hide their intended path.

They didn't know how successful they'd been, and wouldn't know for some time, but they did make it to the water plant, and, once there, they did a thorough reconnaissance of the plant before digging in for a stay that they figured to last four or five days.

"I say we stay until Friday," Peter said. "By Friday, we'll know more about if the EMP has actually taken place, and what its ramifications are."

"You're the leader, Peter," Cole said, as he walked around the sheet-metal covered work shed that they'd chosen as their temporary home.

"Yes, Peter," Natasha said, nodding. "We're with you, so you tell us what to do, and we'll do it."

"Ok, then," Peter said, "we'll need to gather up some wood for a fire. This place is ventilated up near the roof, and it'll be cold at night, but we can use several different tricks to stay warm. The

EMP, if it is coming, hasn't happened yet, so our main threats, if they come, will come from Warwick. After the EMP, it won't get any worse immediately, so we shouldn't have to worry about strangers hiking through the woods quite yet."

"Well, Peter," Cole said, scratching his head, "if what you are saying is accurate, and I have no reason to believe that it isn't, then why don't we head out on our walk now? Wouldn't that give us a few more days lead time before things get bad?"

"Not really, Cole," Peter said. "The EMP is supposed to happen today. That means all sorts of things can happen, including planes dropping out of the sky, explosions from power lines and transformers, fires, and all sorts of things that remain unknown to us. In addition, the violence could break out almost immediately when the EMP hits—not here, but out there—and it will grow over several days. We're hoping that the biggest brunt of the effects— after people realize that they are in big, big trouble—will happen in the first three days. After that, it won't be much better, but at least we will be able to watch where we are, where we are going, and what is ahead of us. If we go now, we could find ourselves in the middle of trouble in unknown territory when the match strikes the fuse. I just think we should wait and then make our way once we have more information."

"Like we said, Peter, you're in charge," Cole responded with a smile. In his smile, he hinted at the smallest bit of doubt.

* * * *

Peter opened up his pack and pulled out one of the radios he brought from the house. He left Clay's radio in the ammo can, just in case, but he wanted to listen awhile, to hear what life was like outside, and gather whatever intelligence they could while they still had the opportunity.

Lang, Natasha, and Cole crowded around Peter as he tuned the radio, and before long he found a station that was on the air. The newswoman went through a litany of stories about the recent "troubles." There were reports of riots and looting in the cities, places like Boston, and Philadelphia, but most of it was less dire than the Warwickians had heard from inside the village. Lang reminded them that one of the last things Lev Volkhov had told him was that they shouldn't believe anything they hear, especially from the "authorities." Governments will lie about the extent of unrest and violence, if only to keep that violence from spreading to as-yet unaffected areas.

It seemed from the news broadcast that the authorities were trying to make the recent troubles and turmoil out to be purely economic. As of this morning, the reports said, the stock market had crashed in a magnitude unseen in history. Despite what seemed to be obvious attempts to minimize the extent of the disruptions, the reporter mentioned riots and street disturbances in most of the big cities of America, civic unrest and citizen complaints about delays in food relief efforts, and they were now speaking openly of an event they were calling "The Crash." The fact that many of the riots had preceded the stock market collapse seemed all but forgotten, and the fact that Election Day was postponed in the northeast was not even mentioned. You would think that something so monumental might be in the news on that first Tuesday in November. But if you thought that, you would be wrong.

* * * *

If a mission to Mars had landed on that undiscovered planet and the astronauts had descended onto its barren rocky surface only to find that their radios were tuned to a broadcast from Olympus Mons, the effect wouldn't have been any stranger than it was on the four Warwickians who sat and listened to the details of a news broadcast from a place they had only known through reputation. They crowded around the small radio there in the water plant and listened to a report about some crazy German who was about to jump out of a capsule that hung from a parachute on the edge of space. Apparently, with all that was happening in the world, somebody, somewhere, someone of great importance, had decided that a man perhaps jumping to his death for notoriety was newsworthy, while the society crumbling around them was not.

The reporter breathlessly turned away from the description of the day's and week's events, of the tales of hunger and societal breakdown, of the scrambling of the governmental elites to contain the situation, to speak of a daredevil, a Mr. Klaus von Baron, who at that very moment was stepping onto a platform and seeing the wide world float through space beneath his feet. The reporter described it all. Millions of people were watching the event all over the world on YouTube, the newswoman reported. After completing what the reporter called "his egress checks," Klaus von Baron stepped off the platform and threw himself toward the ground, and the reporting paused as he began his awesome free-fall.

There were gasps and oohs and aahs coming from the newsroom as the newswoman described the event. "Klaus von Baron has begun to spin slightly. From the deck of his capsule we can see that he is disappearing into the haze of atmosphere and distance. There is, of course, a fear that he might go into an uncontrollable flat spin that could cause him to pass out." The reporter relayed these facts as though the audience perfectly understood the machinations of velocity and turbulence, but it was necessary to say them anyway, just as a record for the times. The audience was informed that von Baron had a special parachute that would automatically activate if the g-forces came to be too much and he lost consciousness.

The four sat and listened. The reporter was openly speculating about whether or not von Baron was going to break the sound barrier, when the four Warwickians, listening around the radio, heard a loud pop, and the radio went dead.

Simultaneously they heard an intense, buzzing hum, and from the doorway of the water plant they saw an old transformer atop a power pole, one that was no longer even operating, blow completely off the pole. As it did so, they heard a frightening explosion from the power junction box about twenty feet inside the building. It suddenly burst into flames.

Peter knew immediately what had happened. Somewhere, up in the atmosphere, and probably not too far away, a "super-EMP" warhead had detonated sending a wave of supercharged electrons piling up on one another until they had burst outward, like when the sound barrier is shattered. The resulting massive wave of electromagnetic energy had spread throughout the atmosphere and imploded the grid of electric energy, and with it the comforts and hopes and aspirations of the world's long climb to what modern man recognized as *civilization*.

At the moment, Peter was one of the few people in the entire world to know that everything had changed. For everyone. Forever.

CHAPTER 16

Tuesday Afternoon – Election Day

The etiology of disaster's onset and the projection of its effects are never easy things to pin down, but history does provide examples for our consideration. On March 4, 1918, in a small town in Kansas, a cook at an army training camp called in sick. Within a week, over 500 men in the camp had contracted the illness, and the virus had spread all the way to Queens, New York. Within a year, approximately fifty million people worldwide had died of what came to be known as the Spanish Flu. Up to 30% of the world's population contracted the disease. Coupled with the concurrent devastation visited upon the world in the four short years of World War One, wherein sixteen million people died and another twenty million were seriously wounded, you can see how quickly things changed in the four short years between 1914 and 1918. The lesson for us is that history can turn on a dime. All the sophisticated machinery of modern civilization is no match for the wild rampage of nature and the brutality of human ingenuity.

While this may seem like an extreme example—as if a wartime virus is worse than the collapse of the electrical grid upon which modern society is built—consider the fact that when the lights go out, there is no medical equipment for use in treating disease. There is no transportation to get food or people or supplies from one place to another. There is no telephone to call the police when the criminals show up at your door. There is no Internet, no security alarms, no heating or air-conditioning to tame the elements. In a grid-down situation, and especially if that situation is caused by a massive electromagnetic pulse, there is no gasoline, and there are no automobiles to need that gasoline. There is no refrigeration to cool food in the concrete jungles that house most of the world's population. When this disaster occurs, there will only be darkness, and stillness, and whatever you hold in your hands, head, and heart to face down the long night.

The EMP strike over Ohio on Election Day in America was the crime of this and perhaps any century, and it would lead— eventually—to over 300 million deaths just in the United States, and many billions of deaths all over the world, but no one knew that yet.

At the very beginning, it was like the call coming in to the kitchen staff saying that a cook won't be in that day. It was like a woman who was involved in a car wreck and broke her neck, but she didn't know it yet. An hour later, she was talking to a cop, and she turned her head to point out to him exactly where the collision occurred, and the cop heard the snap, and her head fell to the side, and the body fell limp to the ground.

There is a delay between the moment when a trigger is pulled, and the moment when a target is struck. That interim—that delay, however long it lasts—is when the world continues to move and decide based on the old reality and on facts that are now immaterial. It is in that interim that decisions are often made that will eventually determine who lives and who dies.

No one had yet figured out what had happened, although people knew from the fires and the smoke and the already eerie noise of the gnashing of teeth in the stillness, that something had gone terribly wrong. But no one yet had recognized its permanency.

Still, in that moment, a few kept their heads.

* * * *

Veronica D'Arcy was sitting in her kitchen in her warm house in Harlem, writing in her journal, when the lights went out.

She'd been thinking a great deal lately of her late husband John, a gem of a man, gone too soon due to a heroic attempt to save a woman who'd fallen on the tracks from a subway platform years ago. The woman was saved, but her husband had not survived, leaving Veronica to raise their son by herself.

In the way that thoughts sometimes seem to tumble or intermingle like towels in a dryer, or how one thought brings us inexorably to another, Veronica's thoughts about her husband, and heroism, and the life of responsibility, led her to recall the man named Clay Richter who'd recently stayed at her house for a night. Apparently, Clay had lost his whole family in an automobile accident. The simple, sweet man had touched her life through an act of kindness towards her son, and now, as she sat thinking about Clay and his escape from the city and his search for liberty and peace, she began thinking about family and the loss of it and the need to protect her own.

Her son, Stephen, was in their living room working on a laptop. He was staying home from school for yet another day, as all New York students were. The compounded troubles from several successive natural and unnatural disasters were taking a toll on the city. First there was the hurricane, then the blizzard, and now there was increasing civil disorder resulting from the canceling of the national elections.

Veronica herself hadn't been able to return to work since Sandy hit. She was a landscape designer at the Brooklyn Bridge Park, and with everything going on post-hurricane, there'd been no need for her to go to work. She'd been told to stay home, and now she and Stephen had been inside for days on end. She thought about it and then counted on her fingers. It was exactly a week ago Tuesday that Clay Richter had helped her son and had stayed the night in the guest room. It seemed longer to her.

She'd grown up in the house of a man who believed in preparation, like his father before him had, a vestigial leftover from colonial-days thinking in Trinidad, when life was uncertain and one had to always be ready to take whatever steps were necessary to maintain it. An aware mind and a preparedness mentality were some of the values that had attracted her to John, who was a survivalist in his own right.

She and Stephen had been protected from the civil unrest raging outside by her foresight in planning for emergencies. They had a generator, and they had always stockpiled food, and had acquired over the years, through self-education, the means to protect themselves from the kind of madness that had increasingly gripped the city. Still, she was getting antsy to get out of the house, and Stephen, too, was looking for diversion.

He was in the living room when the lights flashed and blinked out and the power died. He'd been watching on the laptop at that moment as a daredevil jumped out of a weather balloon and plunged over twenty-four miles toward the earth.

I wonder if he lived, is what Stephen thought as the computer and the room went dark. Strange, he thought. I wonder why the computer didn't keep running on battery power?

The click of the lights and whirr of the winding-down machinery had been the first signs that there was trouble. Then Veronica heard an explosion down the street, followed by numerous collisions and grindings and blasts. Thinking about the laptop, and why the thing had just instantly shut down, Stephen had been the first to ask why the sounds of cars in the streets had stopped if only the electricity had shut down. Just as Veronica was about to answer, they heard a whistling grow above their heads.

Veronica ran to the door with Stephen just a foot behind her, and they stuck their heads out the door and saw in the space above their street an airplane crossing through the blue sky. It was spooky the way the craft simply hung in the air without the sound of engines whining as it made its descent. It was all Doppler Effect of gravity and the atmosphere pushing against the hunk of metal in the sky. The plane turned in a slow, lazy arc and settled into a pocket of air, which made the whooshing noise they'd heard as wind rushed around its wings.

The crashing noise could not have been more than half a mile away. Veronica could have sworn that she felt the ground rumble under her feet before they heard the awful explosive clatter of the plane crashing into the city. Her thoughtful eyes scanned down to the street and noticed the cars clogging up the main artery of the street down the block, and the people running toward the sound of the crash. Images and fragmented memories of 9/11 flashed through her head. Veronica pushed her son back into the house, and the young man looked at her his eyes full of fright, and he asked her what was happening.

Veronica answered with a single sentence. "Stephen, you see de animal, but you don't see de beast." And with that, she sprang into action.

The mother directed her son to go down to the basement and grab two black bags she'd packed with survival gear for a journey. Without hesitation, she ran into their rooms and pulled out warm clothing, changing her own clothes at the same time, all in a flash.

Coming up from the basement with the bags, Stephen asked what was in them. "Don't ask questions, child," Veronica said. "Act." She directed Stephen to change into the clothes that she'd just pulled out for him—hiking gear in layers and warm boots—as she went into the kitchen to gather food and water. Within fifteen minutes, they'd left their house and were setting out on foot through the city... toward Brooklyn.

* * * *

At the foot of the Brooklyn Bridge was an almost unknown cold war era nuclear fallout bunker. Veronica had come across it while working at the Brooklyn Bridge Park because it was adjacent to a storage facility where she kept all of her tools. She remembered reading about the discovery of the bunker in 2006, when city workers had stumbled upon it during the course of routine inspections. It had been long forgotten, and as soon as it was discovered, it was forgotten again, but Veronica had not forgotten about the bunker at all. She'd previously wheedled her way into getting a key to the bunker from a city clerk who was easily confused by the numbers on a blueprint. Now, the two of them, mother and son, wound their way through the city toward the stone enclosure in the hopes that they would find it still functional.

Having a goal and a plan has a huge impact on the mental state when things fall apart. As they walked, she saw people moving in circles, running heedlessly, or sometimes just standing and gaping with their mouths open and their eyes blank in horror, confusion, or indecision.

The city had been wreaked by havoc in the past week, and now havoc had turned into a conflagration. Fires and destruction were everywhere around them, and Veronica and Stephen took advantage of the mayhem to move silently and purposefully through the city. They moved along the side streets, dipping into Central Park, and then back along the thoroughfares that would lead them downtown, making their way so that they avoided as many people as possible. Before leaving the house, Veronica had slipped a small pistol into her waistband, a gift from her husband on the Christmas before he died, and she hoped that she would not have to use it.

As Stephen followed her, he tried to ask her questions about why they were leaving so quickly, and where they were going, but Veronica simply kept his mind occupied by telling him stories of his father.

"You know, your grandfather was a man who was admired by everyone who knew him. He was an engineer, and he built buildings in Trinidad that were not as tall as these you see here..." she motioned to a building that was ablaze in the distance, its giant face perforated by the wings of a second aircraft that had fallen from the sky only moments before, "...but they were impressive nonetheless." She focused on blocking out the horror, and directed her mind towards that which she had to do to eliminate panic in herself and her son. There was no shaking in her voice, only calm and certainty.

"When he met your father, he asked him what he'd do if he ever found himself in trouble. You know – what he'd do if things fell apart. He was a cantankerous man, your grandfather, and I was his baby, and he wanted to say a little something that might scare John a little, to see what he was made of. Well, if that is what he wanted to do, he failed. Your father answered with an old Trini proverb that immediately won over your grandfather. Your father said, 'When yuh neighbor's house on fire, throw water on yours.'

"Do you understand, Stephen?" She looked over at her son as they hustled through the city, reading his thoughts as they passed people who seemed to be crying out for help.

"There are times when we need to be good citizens and help others out. But in moments when it is life and death, we should take care of our own. Do you see what I'm saying?" She paused and saw in his eyes that he was doing the best he could to follow. "There is something terribly wrong here, son. I'm not sure what it is, but I have an idea. Now is not the time to question and fret. Just move your feet and keep your head down. We have to make our way to safety."

Stephen nodded and tried to keep pace as they wound their way through the city. They passed through the crowds and around the puddling of slushy ice water that was beginning to pour into the streets from the numerous fires that sprang up around them. They headed as straight as they could manage past the infernal turbulence that was the city, toward the safety of the bunker in the bridge.

By evening, they had reached it.

* * * *

From a distance, one could hear the faraway strums of the guitars slowing growing. The distinctive clattering echo of the twang-twicka-twang was matched by the chunky percussion. As the man on the bicycle came closer to the small group of people gathered by the entrance of a parking lot on the Lincoln Highway in Trenton, New Jersey, the group looked up and heard the wailing urgency of the opening lines of a U2 song.

Although they had only moments before been wondering aloud when this waking nightmare would end, when the government would get its act together and deliver food, where the police were in all of this, they happily stopped their grousing for a moment and watched as the bearded, red-haired specter rode up into their midst, and asked if they knew where he could buy some balloons.

"Balloons?!" asked one of the loudest complainers in the group, incredulously. "Have you flipped your gourd, bro? What in the world do you want balloons for? You should be worrying about finding a new coat to replace that nasty thing you're wearing. And food... you should be worrying about food. And safety. You do know that we're in the middle of a national emergency, right?"

Looking at the man, they thought they'd sized him up. Perhaps he was a lunatic, flittering along the highway on a bicycle in the snow, heading who knows where. Maybe he didn't even know, they thought. The red bearded man just smiled and did nothing to dispel this notion.

"Oh, it's ok," he said. "I'm not worried about safety. I know how to make myself invisible. But I need some balloons. I'm going to build a rocket ship and float on out of here." He reached down and turned down his boom box just as U2 was singing about a place where the streets have no name, as if in answer to where he was going. He changed the subject off of himself. "How bad is it out here, anyway?"

They stood together for a moment and talked about the conditions around them, how the grocery stores had been stripped bare since the blizzard, and how the streets had become dangerous in the last few days, and not only at night. One trucker who'd just driven up from Mississippi before the storm told him how he'd run out of gas and his rig had been stranded for a week.

"Yes, well that's a shame," the red-haired man said. "It surely is. You know...," the red bearded man nodded, as if they should know, "...when Thomas Edison invented the light bulb, he worked by candlelight until it was done." The red-haired man looked at the crowd of faces around him to see if anyone understood his meaning, but he was met with only blank stares until someone in the gathered group told them all to hush. A woman waved her hand to silence the crowd. She was picking up some news on her radio. The news had interrupted their broadcast to go to live coverage of a man who was going to jump from outer space and parachute back to earth.

"What kind of thing is that to do while the world is going to hell?" someone asked.

"Shhh... quiet!" someone said. "I want to hear this!"

The crowd sat and listened as the radio announcer relayed the sequence of events and watched as a few remaining cars went weaving through the broken down traffic along the highway. The daredevil was plunging towards the ground, and they were all listening in stony silence when there was a loud explosion from a transformer down the street, and the cars and the radio and the red-haired man's boombox stopped simultaneously, leaving the crowd waiting for a finish to the song that never came.

A groan went up among them. "Oh, what now?!" But the red-haired man did not ask this question. He seemed to know what was coming next, or maybe he just did not care, which to the observer looked like the same thing. He unstrapped the bungees that held his boombox to the handlebars of his bicycle and tossed the hunk of now useless plastic onto a pile of trash stacked near the road and mounted his bicycle and wished the crowd well.

He pushed off from the curb and headed up the highway with his bicycle, leaving the crowd open-mouthed as they watched him slowly pedal through the stalled cars and the snow and pedestrians, weaving slowly in and out until his image grew increasingly smaller in the distance.

And then, true to his word, he disappeared.

* * * *

Mikail's guards were now his captors. He had not been "officially" arrested yet. The cease-fire agreement supposedly allowed him twenty-four hours, until midday on Wednesday, to cede control of Warwick and to surrender to the coalition force that now had supremacy in the village. The coalition had neither great leadership nor any concrete plans for how to move forward or deal with the burgeoning crisis. What they had were the Russian Special Forces soldiers, and for now that would be enough.

In Warwick, there was a broad array of emotions; anger, regret, horror, sadness, even hope. This stew of feelings led the people to be weary from the day's sudden and terrible events, and to hunger for a moment of rest. The coalition held, and the Spetznaz were able, for a time, to maintain an uneasy peace. People stopped battling one another and began to pick through the shattered homes and damaged storefronts. Bodies were being washed and prepared for burial, crimes were being catalogued, and some arrests were being made. There were apologies, accusations, and the promise of recriminations. The prison in Warwick once again held the unhappy losers in a long, grand, and sad social experiment.

"You will be held responsible for the actions of Vladimir and his team," a coalition 'advisor' warned Mikail, as if his control over Vladimir had been anything more than nominal to begin with.

"I cannot be held responsible for the actions of people who have long since gone off on their own and who fail to obey me," Mikail responded. He was being untruthful. While Vladimir certainly had a mind of his own, the young man was not entirely "off on his own." Whatever were his private motivations, he was still ostensibly working for Mikail as his team made their way through town, searching for Vasily and the way out.

Just before noon, someone turned on the radio, and the guarded—along with the guards—listened to the world melt down in real time. After a quick rundown of the condition of America, including woefully rapid and undetailed reports of riots, economic collapse, stores being stripped to the very shelf lining, fuel shortages, nuclear plant shut downs, and impotent government responses, the news cut to the story of a German man jumping from a balloon in space.

Mikail was only half-listening to the broadcast, but he snapped to full attention when the radio buzzed and then zapped and then fell silent while simultaneously the lighting failed and the rumble of the generators gave way to a preternatural silence. A smile crossed Mikail's face just as another messenger came through the door of the gymnasium with a message from Vladimir.

* * * *

A strange-looking vehicle, something like an ill-considered hybrid between an RV and a highly hardened off-road vehicle, made its way through the winding mountain roads of northern West Virginia. From a distance, the vehicle looked like some kind of transformer vehicle created by Hollywood for a blockbuster summer movie. It was chaperoned by a contingent of black, military looking vehicles, Humvees, APCs, and SUVs. The lead vehicle was a large and heavily armored truck with what looked like a cattle mover or snowplow attached to the front of it. When necessary, this lead truck would push stranded and inoperative vehicles off the road.

"The warhead would have been delivered by a very small rocket," the driver of the hardened RV said. "The amount of energy used to propel the craft containing the warhead would have been insignificant because the launch platform, the capsule, was brushing the stratosphere, and that means that it almost certainly did not trigger any warnings from NORAD or any of the other early warning systems. It was not a ground based launch. It wasn't even a high-altitude launch from a Russian bomber...I mean most bombers have a service ceiling of around 50,000 feet, and we're talking close to 130,000 feet here. And it wasn't one of these mostly theoretical weapons that might be deployed from a high earth orbit satellite. No. No, this capsule was in the middle area, where no one was looking for it. It was perfect."

The passenger of the RV stared forward out of the windscreen and nodded his head, but he didn't interrupt with the questions that filled his mind as the driver spoke. The driver wasn't finished talking, so the passenger just nodded his head as the man continued.

"The EMP probably will not have knocked out absolutely everything, and it was most likely 'local' to maybe a little more than a third of the U.S. It was just a first blow, opening the door for further strikes that will finish the job throughout the rest of the country. I am speculating, of course, but from our figures and the readings we gathered back at the base, I'd say the warhead was detonated high over eastern Ohio. We'd be totally guessing if we tried to declare a yield, but I'd say that more than 95% of the electronics, computer, and technological infrastructure on the eastern seaboard – from Maine to most of Florida, and from the

Atlantic to as far as Nebraska, will have been fried. There are probably fires burning out of control in every major city in that area, and the fires will get worse as time goes on because there'll be no water to dowse them. The trucks that put out fires won't work, and the communications that control emergency response is now gone, and probably forever. The damage done will make the work of Mrs. O'Leary's cow look like child's play.

"The few vehicles that are operating, those that are older and therefore not susceptible to EMP, along with those that were accidentally or purposefully shielded—like these vehicles for example—will stop operating when they're either unable to move about due to the blockages and mayhem on the roads, or as soon as they run out of stored fuel." The driver looked over at the passenger and nodded his head, then leaned forward and looked upward through the windshield. "I reckon almost 3,000 planes have crashed, if that gives you any inkling of what's happened so far today." He looked back down at the dashboard and then at his watch. "Everything has changed," he said, "and it all happened in a moment. In a split second of time."

The passenger looked out at the country road, and, as he did, the old John Denver song about a country road in West Virginia came over the sound system in the RV. His mind flashed to a time not that long ago. Denver had died in the crash of a single person experimental aircraft. Sometimes the irony—or maybe it was the poetic symmetry—is particularly rich.

The man in the passenger seat thought of all those planes falling out of the sky, and realized that none of them were natural. He looked towards the driver, just as the man ended his dissertation on the EMP weapon that had just detonated over the eastern United States. All the while, the voice of John Denver sang on.

The passenger strummed his fingers on the armrest and thought about all those billions of miles of wire that had been strung across the landscape and buried under ground, and thought about how humankind had now hung itself with its own rope. Time had proven, as it inevitably must, that man had strayed too far from the dirt, which is his natural home. Like Icarus, he'd flown too close to the sun, and now he'd had his wings clipped. The forces of spiritual physics, and gravity, and inertia were likely to bring everything back to earth eventually, and it looked like that homecoming was now in the offing. John Denver was singing that he should have been home yesterday.

"So... how did you know? I mean, how did you absolutely know without a doubt that the EMP would actually be deployed, and when it would happen?"

The driver looked over to the passenger and smiled beneath his thick mustache, and his eyes betrayed just the hint of a twinkle that accompanied the smile. "Did your grandmother ever just know it was going to rain? And when she told you to come in before the rain started, did you know to listen to her?"

CHAPTER 17

Tuesday - Afternoon

Vladimir and his team quickly returned to the gymnasium after it happened, interrupting their violent, but fruitless search of Warwick. Vladimir was the first to know something was wrong by picking up on a series of static crackles in the street as they were doing their door-to-door searches. He didn't know what had happened, but for once the brutish fellow showed instincts that were adorned with something other than mindless force. He'd already sent a messenger to Mikail to tell him that his wild-goose-chase was going poorly and to ask for any further instructions, and now, sensing that something important had happened, he decided that he'd better return to the gymnasium himself in order to see what the power surge had been about.

He was flush from the thrill of the search, energized by the violent power he'd held in his hand, but frustrated that he'd not yet found his target. If truth be told, just at that moment, he was also a bit worried that his power—that one thing he craved so much—would be questioned because of his failure to locate Vasily and the rumored escape route out of town.

As he stepped inside the gymnasium, the doors creaked on their hinges, and he noticed the room had been darkened. He looked down on the swath of light thrown across the hardwood floors. He watched as his shadow preceded him into the space. It took a few seconds for his eyes to adjust, and he grimaced as he looked up at the blank round bulbs in the ceiling above his head.

Mikail and his guards were congregated in the center of the gym as Vladimir approached and began to share his report. Mikail and his people, who were discussing where next to search for Vasily, paused as Vladimir brought them up to speed on his failed hunt.

The group of men stood and talked around a table laden with a rudimentary mockup of Warwick, tracing with their fingers several possible alternatives. There was a quiet, scientific exactitude to their conversation, and just as they were beginning to argue about whether two crossing streets had been properly searched, and just as Vladimir was trying to assure them that they had, the doors to the gym burst open and events accelerated.

Thinking that he had more than half of his twenty-four hours left, and planning to use all of them before surrendering, Mikail was quite surprised when the Spetznaz leadership, along with the coalition spokesman, rushed into the gym and arrested everyone among the revolutionary leadership on the spot. "Gentlemen, surrender your arms," said Yuri Belov, newly elected spokesman for the townspeople. In Russian, the words sounded like an overly harsh insult.

Mikail and Vladimir looked at the array of Special Forces, their guns pointed down toward the ground but their muscles tensed, ready to respond if coercion was needed. Mikail realized that it would be hopeless to resist. He glanced at Vladimir, fearful for a moment that, knowing no other language than power, he might attempt to fight his way out. He raised his hands to waive off this possibility and spread them calmly, as if in supplication. A Spetznaz solider approached and placed handcuffs around his upturned wrists.

The dismantling of Mikail's team proceeded quickly, in a manner common throughout history to that of all failed revolutionary movements. Those few at the top were held accountable for the actions of the many beneath. Low-level gunmen and soldiers of the Youth Revolutionary Forces were only arrested if they were guilty of some particularly heinous crime. For the most part, the foot soldiers just switched sides. Most of them, in fact, were re-tasked as gophers and servants to the Spetznaz teams and their new coalition overlords.

If it seemed from this ceremonial display that the Spetznaz were now in the control of the people, a quick inspection of the entire gym would have put that notion to rest. At that very moment, the Russian officers in the basement kept up their work interrogating the oldlings, working with battery-powered lights that had been protected from the EMP. They worked their interrogations as if no change in regime had taken place at all, because for them, it had not. They cared not who was nominally in charge, since the interrogation of the old spies, the collection of intelligence, had been the only reason for all of this anyway. Frontmen come and go... presidents, prime-ministers, magistrates, even revolutionaries, and they are deceived if they think that their power is anything other than illusory. The Russian agents were preparing their case, laying the predicate for what would eventually come. The broader war could not commence until the Russians knew the names and whereabouts of every Warwickian in Russia. In the Russian homeland, a thorough search through houses, a turning over of stones, and the intensive location of traitors who would be held accountable for their actions would take place one day based on their findings.

Recriminations.

Occasionally, or maybe intermittently, like the pause between swipes of a wiper blade across a windshield in a rainstorm, a body would be hauled up from the locker rooms. It looked like that moment of clarity between the blades, if only one could see it between the drops of rain that otherwise pummeled one's vision and spread out on the protective glass leaving only an impression of reality. Two soldiers were walking upward on the stairs, struggling, lifting a body bag which they would then carry to the doors of the gymnasium, swaying from side to the side with the dead weight of a new corpse, hauling the contents to be buried in the field behind the gymnasium.

Meanwhile, administrations changed, and new leaders carried on with their elaborate charade.

* * * *

Mikail, Vladimir, Sergei, and the rest of the revolutionary leadership were marched at gunpoint back up the hill to the prison they'd escaped less than a week earlier. It was a long and humiliating walk for Mikail, but he was not distraught. He was surprisingly reflective and focused.

He'd been angry before, and he still held on to the hatred he now felt for the people who had taken his love, Irinna. He'd also grown angry at Vladimir's recklessness. He fumed at being played by that idiot Vasily.

Mistakes. Catalogued. Never to be made again.

His anger now gave him purpose and a larger view of what had happened and what was now occurring around him. He looked at the Spetznaz soldier walking in front of him, gun pointed toward the ground, and he thought how only a few hours ago he might have successfully ordered that soldier to fire into the crowd that was now lining the street.

The crowd. Boos and hisses could be heard coming from the mass of Warwickians gathered for the procession.

Mikail felt the red scar on his forehead throb, and he reached up with his handcuffed hands and brushed the hair on the back of his arm across the slope of his brow. He felt his temples pound, and glanced up into the sun. It was hard to imagine that only a week had passed since the Hurricane had ripped through the area. He'd gotten an education in that week. He readily admitted that.

Tuesday morning, a week ago, he'd been a prisoner trying to win over converts in his cell to help his cause. He'd used the time during the storm to convince even Todd, the guard of his cell block, to play along with his plans. The nor'easter had gone through just a few days later, and then there was the breakout and the coup. Now the EMP had been released right on schedule and everything should have fallen into place perfectly. However, rather than be on top and running this part of the operation for the new Russian government, he'd been abandoned by the troops sent to guarantee his authority and position.

Mikail thought about that for a moment as he walked, whether there was anything that could have been done to avoid this. He wondered whether he'd been too bold, too delicate, too reasonable, too extreme. Then he pushed these thoughts from his mind, and was about to turn them toward what came next, when a woman stepped from the crowd and placed herself squarely in his path. He barely had time to notice her and to look up into her eyes when she spat in his face. The crowd roared their approval as a soldier gently guided the woman back into line with the crowd.

In a way, Mikail's rapid removal from power had been the fourth storm to hit Warwick, once the natural and human disasters were accounted for. If someone had asked him, he would have said that only one of them—the EMP—had been expected. Each of the others had occurred, in its turn, as an opportunity, and he'd merely taken advantage of the situation, using what seemed to be acts of God to hasten plans he'd been making with his secretive contacts in Russia for several years. Now he realized that this storm had caught up with him, and he began to wonder whether there might be some opportunity to be discovered even here. One thing felt certain: as a student of political movements, and a firm believer in the inevitability of his ultimate cause, he was sure that there'd be a fifth storm. He just didn't know when or where it would strike. He determined within himself to be ready when it did.

The glint of gunmetal contrasted against the white of the snow, and Mikail's brown boots made an indentation in the slushy, worn path just beginning to melt in the heat of the sun as he trudged up the hill. He noticed the heavier footprint of Vladimir, who was being marched along a few paces in front of him, and wondered what was going through his comrade's mind, before he returned again to his own thoughts.

The coalition was going to seek his execution, this he knew. And if he was right about them and their need for blood in exchange for blood, the recriminations would start soon. Still, he had no fear. The newfound clarity in his thinking gave him a sort of certainty that his position and purpose in this world had not passed. Failure and humiliation can be crippling to most people, but Mikail wouldn't trade what he'd gained from this experience for anything in the world. He was actually thankful that his efforts had failed, because success would have only left him naïve and foolish and weak. He knew now that when the time came someday for him to take power again – because even in that moment, he was determined that such a day would come – he would have valuable insight and experience that would suit him to the task. He rolled his shoulders in their sockets, feeling a hump form along his back, and he stretched and looked toward the ground and the melting snow and thought of the coming spring.

* * * *

As they passed through the fences and slid back up the icy walks towards the prison, Mikail sought to put together all of the different and disparate pieces of information he'd gathered while he was in charge.

There was a way out, and it looked like Vasily, of all people, had been the one to find that way out. But Vasily would not have been working alone. Someone was helping that stupid boy. It simply had to be. But who could it be?

As the prisoners were escorted into the facility, the wide double doors swung outward into the courtyard, casting a shadow on the open snow, like two giant jaws opening to devour a prey. The prisoners stepped shamefacedly into the same corridor that they had emerged from only days before in cocky self-assurance. Mikail, Vladimir, and Sergei walked into the darkened corridor and focused their eyes to the compact blackness. They were led down the maze of hallways toward the pod of cells that would be their new home, the locks tumbling and the pins clicking with each successive door they stepped through, until they were pushed into their chamber. The thick prison doors swung open and closed with the expected thuds and clanks. All of these familiar sounds served to focus Mikail's attention on the problem at hand.

He was thinking through the situation more linearly now, and walking into the prison had a way of clearing his mind. Thoughts he should have had, and memories forgotten in the clash and fog of war, were now occurring to him in crystalline clarity. As they were left alone in their prison cell, he turned to regard his larger comrades and noticed for the first time that his friends were white with agitation.

"Vladimir Nikitich, did you check through the family ties as you searched the village?" Mikail asked his aide, as the three shuffled into the corners of the cell.

"Vasily had no family, Mikail Mikailivitch."

The young men stood in the dark of the cell. It was the same cell that had once housed the stranger named Clay, and old Lev Volkhov. The surroundings and the ghosts of the place caused Mikail's mind to clarify even further. As the lock snapped on a door down the hall, he turned to Sergei and smiled, and then turned to Vladimir again with the smile still spread out on his face. "Not Vasily. Remember, there were two men housed in this cell. Vasily left here with two things, one from each of his cellmates."

Mikail moved very close to Vladimir, so he could see the large man's reaction, and as he spoke again he moved even closer. The cell was in almost complete darkness, and only a faint light came in through the glass window, criss-crossed with chicken wire. His voice was very low, and it was tinged with a certainty that it had not had for a few days. "Our little friend had a backpack that he received from the traveler named Clay."

"This we know, Mikail," Vladimir answered, "but we were unable to find Vasily or the backpack." There was a slight tremor of fear in Vladimir's voice as he said this, and that almost indiscernible hitch spoke loudly and clearly to Mikail. Mikail knew that it was his proximity, and his certainty, that was frightening his friend, a man who previously had shown no fear at all. He paused, to let that fear take its full effect.

"The other thing he had, comrade Vladimir Nikitich," Mikail said, as he slid another half step toward Vladimir, "the other thing he carried with him when he left this very cell, was a plan. You see, old man Volkhov had a nephew. I'd not thought of it until just now, and perhaps it is too late, but I think that it is not. Volkhov's nephew lives in a very peculiar house, in a very peculiar spot in the town."

"How is that, Mikail?" Again, the tremor in the voice. Vladimir shuffled his foot on the floor, as if looking for someplace to go, but there was nowhere else to go.

"His nephew is Pyotr Bolkonsky," Mikail said softly, "and Pyotr Bolkonsky lives on the very edge of town. In fact, his house is probably closer to the perimeter fence than just about any other house in Warwick."

"I know that house, Mikail. It is the one with all of the raised gardens and strange landscaping. But we searched it and found nothing."

Mikail's right fist caught Vladimir in an uppercut to the solar plexus that doubled the larger man over just as Mikail's knee came up and hit Vladimir directly in the face, breaking his nose. Vladimir fell to the ground and Mikail stomped him brutally until he was unconscious and bleeding.

The violence happened so fast, and was so unexpected, that Sergei shrunk silently into the darkness until his back hit the far wall of the cell. He saw only shadows, and heard only the grunts that came from Vladimir until he saw that the bigger man was out cold on the ground. Even after what he had seen in the last few days, Sergei was shocked at the brutality of the beating.

When it was over, Mikail stood over Vladimir like a bulldog over a bone and spoke to the unconscious man in flat, low tones. "You are correct, Vladimir. You found nothing. And no one. I had not wondered, until just now, where all the dirt came for those peculiar gardens and all of that strange landscaping. But now I have wondered, and I think I might know how our comrades, Vasily and Pyotr Bolkonsky, have escaped Warwick."

* * * *

"I left my glasses in the tunnel," Cole told Peter privately. "I don't know how I did it, but I did. I took them off before we left, perhaps when I was using the privy. I didn't even think about them with all the excitement of leaving the tunnel. It was dark. I couldn't see anyway. What can I say, Peter? I'm sorry."

"Well, you cannot go back for them, Cole."

"I must. I'm not heading out into this broken world as a blind man."

"Are we to risk everyone's lives, even your own sister's life, because you forgot your glasses? Don't be a fool!"

"Well, I feel somewhat like Gloucester without them." He looked at Peter, to see if the older man understood his reference. Sometimes a man makes references to prove to others how clever he is, and other times he makes them because they give his life meaning. For Cole, it was almost always the latter. Before he could decide whether Peter's frown indicated understanding or not, he continued, as a way of explaining. "I'll be helpless without them, and every one of you will be at risk if I cannot see, so don't sit there like a king, leering at me." Nothing. Maybe a half-smile. "I have to go back. And besides, we need to know what's going on back there, anyway," Cole said.

Peter shook his head. "It's too big of a risk. I can't let you go."

"Listen, Peter, if Lang had not come back through town in his heroic attempt to save people, I wouldn't be here anyway. And you wouldn't be worrying about me, would you? I'm not going back into town, friend. I'm just going to the tunnel. I can be back in a few hours' time."

Peter wanted to argue with him, but the older man knew that Cole had made up his mind. He tried to recruit Natasha and Lang to help him dissuade Cole from the trip back to the tunnel, but they'd both, surprisingly, been on the younger man's side.

"He'll need his vision if he's going to survive long out there, Peter," Natasha said. "Who knows when, or if, such glasses will ever be available again in our lifetimes? We will need every tool we can muster if we're to make it to safety."

Cole looked at Peter and saw the seriousness in his face. "Please, Peter."

Peter sighed in resignation. "Ok," he said. "But if one person is going back, then we all go back."

Cole protested. "No. I'll go alone. It is my responsibility and I will manage it." He was respectful, but he persisted. "I can see fine during the bright daylight, and it would be silly and foolish for all of us to put our lives in danger just because I was stupid enough to forget my glasses. It was my mistake, and I need to fix it."

"But if we all go, Cole, then we can protect each other and cover for one another if something happens."

"If something happens, Peter, then that means that things have gone horribly wrong, and we will have the whole group at risk." Cole knew enough to appeal to Peter's leadership feelings and his responsibilities. "I know you would admit that, in a worst case scenario, you would rather lose one unimportant member rather than the whole group. Be reasonable. You have Natasha and Lang to think about. I need to go alone."

Lang chimed in with his agreement. He also believed that it was a bad plan to travel back as a group. They were more likely to be seen with four of them trying to make it back into the tunnel, he suggested. Peter considered the case and saw the reasonableness of this conclusion.

"I see your logic, Cole, but please do not say that you are unimportant. I don't think that you are unimportant to your sister, and you are certainly not unimportant to me or Lang. I'll allow it, but you should at least wait until tomorrow. It's late in the day now, and it'll be getting dark soon."

"Ok, Peter," Cole said, smiling.

"And if you don't make it back, I'll be very upset with you— and with myself for giving in to you."

"You'll see me again, Peter. Never you worry. In the end, you'll see that this is much ado about nothing."

"Yes, well, let's hope. So far it seems more like a comedy of errors, with very little to laugh about."

Cole smiled at this, and gave his friend a thankful squeeze on the shoulder. He looked at him and suddenly felt overwhelmed with the warmth of emotion.

In short order, it was arranged, and on mid-morning the next day, Cole started off on his retreat back to the tunnel.

* * * *

Wednesday - Morning

Mikail stood by the door in the darkness and waited, staring single-mindedly out of the glass window. He'd not said many words to Sergei through the night, and when Vladimir finally came to and began to stir, there'd been an unspoken agreement that the issue had finally been settled once and for all. It is common with violent men like Vladimir that, like chickens or dogs or wolves, once they are put in their place, they become loyal followers pretty quickly. It is the bully that is the pose in such men. The truth of the bully lies in their cowardice.

As the silence built up, piling upon itself in the cool of the early morning, Mikail's certainty and resolve grew. He turned to his comrades and barked out orders.

"When I make my move, you'll know what to do," he said, brusquely and without emotion.

"Yes, Mikail," the other two men replied as one.

Although he was not there when the traveler named Clay, Lev Volkhov, and Vasily had broken out of this same cell, he imagined that their planning had gone much differently--and their plan had failed. He was assured in his own mind that his plan would not fail.

"I will expect you to move quickly. I will not..." he paused, to let the implication of that word sink in, "...tolerate failure."

The two larger men looked at him and nodded their understanding.

About thirty minutes later, there was a rattling of keys and the door slowly opened. A young man, one of Mikail's recent Youth Revolutionary Forces, stepped into the room with a tray of food. Before he could even say a word, Mikail pounced, raising his hands quickly to knock the food trays upwards, throwing hot soup into the youth's startled face. There was only a short squawk from the young man as Mikail took his pistol from its holster and clubbed the boy unconscious with it. He fell like a noodle to the floor.

Mikail walked calmly out into the day room, ignoring the two armed Spetznaz soldiers who were lounging somewhat carelessly near the front door of the cluster. They saw him, but his calm demeanor and the purpose in his gait threw them off for a few beats. In that interval, Mikail grabbed a cushion from the sofa and, turning quickly and gracefully, he shot the first soldier through the cushion and in the face. The second soldier began to lift his machine pistol but it was too late, and Mikail's second shot burst through the soft padding and hit the man in the temple. Both soldiers, professional and experienced special force operators, hit the ground without firing a shot.

By the time Vladimir and Sergei came peeking out of the cell, Mikail was already taking the uniform off the smaller of the two Spetznaz men.

"Vladimir, this other one, he's big like you. Put on his uniform. We're going to escort Sergei out of the prison like he's one of our prisoners."

"But... what if we're stopped, Mikail?" Vladimir asked, as he began to undress the larger man.

"We won't be. Not if we walk with purpose. But if we are, we've got to fight our way to Pyotr Bolkonsky's house. That is our destination and we have to make it there no matter what." He looked at the two larger men to make sure they understood. Then he could not help the boast that was welling up in his heart as he saw in their eyes a new servile feeling growing in theirs.

"I don't think we'll be stopped. I just disarmed three armed men by myself, and two of them were highly trained specialists. I assume that you fellows can keep up with me, can hold your own in a fight, if the need arises."

God in heaven, looking down, would have seen three school boys on the playground, two larger bullies, all muscle and violence, and another, smaller young man full of ruthless intelligence. The pendulum had swung back and forth during the course of these men's lives, and the weight of fists and sinew of muscle had never been far behind those shifts as they'd bullied their way across the streets of Warwick.

Now as they stood and made their plans to escape, Mikail turned away from his threatening physicality which had surprised his larger friends in the night, and now he turned to attack their pride in the way that only he, among the three of them, had ever been able to do. He called on their masculine brutality because he knew that they might need it for a fight, and he served as brain to their brawn, and focus for their force.

Mikail looked at the two of them, all potential and potency without direction. He spoke with an urgency that allowed no contradiction.

"We *have* to get to Pyotr Bolkonsky's house."

And with that, he turned the dialectical force of common sense inside out and gave the point to ideology when used in the hands of capable leaders. He wielded his intelligence like a pen to the awful sword of their brutality.

Words... speak louder... than action.

Mikail placed the handcuffs on Sergei, loosely, so he could slip free if need be, and the three of them stepped out into the corridor.

* * * *

Friday - Morning

Now Peter was in a very bad mood. Two days had passed, and Cole had not returned. They had every reason to believe that he'd been captured, and, if he'd been captured, then he'd probably been either shot or taken back into the village by the guards.

The two days living in the metal shed at the water plant hoping for Cole's return had passed like weeks.

The three friends had no news from the outside world except the gossip heard on the shortwave radio the night before, and now, on Friday morning, the day of their planned departure, they faced the fact that Cole might be lost to them.

Natasha was distraught, as might be expected, but she was stoic nonetheless, and only occasionally broke down in whimpers, or felt the hot track of a tear as it escaped from her eye and dampened her cheek. Silly sibling rivalries aside, she loved her brother very much, and she still hoped that, by some miracle, he was still okay.

While they waited, they worked. They'd practiced making fires and sharpening knives and building shelters, and over the past forty-eight hours, Peter had spoken to them of tactics to be used while traveling. Between anxious moments when he'd looked out the door of the shed and back into the woods towards Warwick, he'd shown them hand signals they could use to communicate with one another without words. He'd talked to them over and over again about the horrors they would likely run across, and how they must stick together and constantly be focused on their survival.

Peter showed them the most basic rudiments of orienteering and shared some of his knowledge of tracking and woodland survival, and during most of this time he had maintained an attitude of patient instruction. But now Peter was no longer patient. He was growing angry and resentful at being so helpless to assist Cole. On this Friday morning, he seethed in silence.

The night before, after they finished their training and practice, Peter risked pulling the second radio from the ammo can in order to see if they could receive some information from the outside world.

They put the batteries in the radio, and for a long time they were unable to find any stations at all that were broadcasting. As the night wore on, and as Cole still did not appear in the shed, the buzzing of nothingness coming through the radio only amplified their feelings of sadness and fear.

Just before midnight, as Peter was about to give up on the radio altogether, he brushed past a very weak broadcast on the shortwave band. It was nothing more at first than a weak modulation as he swept across the dial, but as he tuned it finer, he got a slight signal, and as they leaned in and listened closer, they made out a man's voice in amongst the electronic hum and static. They all sat up with excitement as they heard the voice speaking through the atmospheric interference.

The voice said that it was broadcasting from Montana. They could barely make it out, but the male voice relayed information that he said was derived from Ham radio reports from around the country and the world. The reports, the voice said, were spotty. Only radio operators from as yet unaffected areas, or those who had thought to shield their equipment, were still broadcasting.

Anger could be detected in the solitary voice, as the man reported that before and after the EMP attack, U.S. military units had moved unilaterally and without provocation against "innocent" militia and patriot groups. The voice speculated that the whole worldwide collapse had the distinct feel of a concerted and well-developed plan. "I am certain," the voice said, "that this catastrophe could not have proceeded without the approval and planning of a central elite somewhere. It was too organized, over too great a distance, involving too many, to be simply the actions of a rogue few."

Ham radio broadcasters reported that, subsequent to the first EMP over the east coast, several more high-altitude nuclear devices were detonated over the Western United States. America, the voice said, had retaliated against Russia, China, and North Korea with EMP strikes, but there had yet to be any reported low-level nuclear explosions, in the U.S. or anywhere else. So far, and for some reason, it seemed that the exchange had remained limited—directed at electrical and technological infrastructure. "It seems that governments have decided to cut off the head of the beast first," the voice said. "Who knows how long that will last? You know... before they go to work on the body."

As the voice on the radio faded and eventually the signal was lost, Lang remembered what Volkhov had said to him. He'd predicted that actual physically destructive nuke detonations over cities wouldn't happen for two weeks.

Two weeks, the old man had said. That's how long you'll have. Then the law of human ingenuity will kick in. Despite key-codes and fail-safes and guarantees, it will only take two weeks before some brilliant minds on every side figure out a workaround. And they will figure out a workaround, you can bet on that. They want war, and there will be war.

That had been the night before. It had seemed a happy, if disconcerting, diversion as they waited for Cole to return from his trip to the tunnel. The news was not "happy," but the fact that there was news was a good happenstance.

Now, early on this Friday morning, Peter stared angrily outwards from the door of the metal shed, and wondered how much longer they could wait. He was realistic. He understood that Cole had probably run into trouble with someone from the village. Perhaps he'd been seen by a guard at the fence line and been captured for interrogation. Whatever the case, Peter had told Cole that they would have to leave on Friday morning, with or without him, and Cole had agreed to that as a factor in his decision-making.

Peter cursed himself for letting Cole return in the first place, realizing that the younger man had probably traded his life for his need to see clearly. If youth could but see in the first place, Peter thought, but curses aside, he knew he could only wait a minute or two longer before they would have to abandon Cole and head off on their own.

* * * *

At first, it sounded like a growl rising up from the throat, tiny and imperceptible, but with a slight menace even in its faintest whispering. The low hum magnified and grew louder and louder still, until it became obvious that something was coming and was nearby, and their initial reaction was to find somewhere to hide inside the shed. Lang, Natasha, and Peter heard the growl like one hears a hostile dog. The sound was muted, but angry with promise. They approached cautiously to see whether the source was aiming for them. They all stepped forward to the edge of the shed's door, and there, in the space of the light that streamed in through the door, they saw the drones buzz by in formation, five of them flying low and near the ground, seemingly cognizant, as if guided by some inner intelligence. They noticed the drones' silent shadows trailing along on the ground, rising up over the mountain, flitting through the trees, along the brush that peaked its head out of the snow, along the snow itself, as the shadows climbed, like the drones that cast them, up to the top of the mountain in the distance, and then disappeared in the horizon and the blue of the sky.

They were headed, it seemed, towards Warwick.

* * * *

Friday - Night

On a low rise, just outside of Mt. Vernon, Virginia, an odd looking RV, flanked by black militarized vehicles, sat parked with the windshield pointed towards the northeast. It was fully dark and there was no moon to be seen, and the area in view of the RV, usually twinkling brightly with city lights and traffic, was mostly darkened. Mostly. Fires glowed all around the D.C. metropolitan area, and the white and red armies of vehicle lights that usually spread out like ribbons along the highways and byways of the darkened urban area did not march up and down as they had for more than a century.

There was only one area that was lit up as if nothing world-changing had happened, and it was to this area of illumination that the driver of the RV, a man named Clive Darling, pointed as he turned off the radio and flipped a switch on the dash that killed the array of blue and red and orange lights coming from the console. The darkness of the night invaded the RV and gave emphasis to the little lighted city in the distance.

"Andrews Air Force Base," Clive said in his Savannah drawl. Something in the way he said it made the words sound like the most important thing that anyone had ever spoken.

The two men seated in the RV were surrounded by what amounted to a Faraday cage. The wire box that encompassed the driver and passenger area of the RV was grounded to the frame and, using proprietary wiring and chips and breakers, the RV was virtually completely shielded from any possible electromagnetic pulse.

In the distance, as the two men looked out over the little lighted island in the inky sea of darkness, an aircraft with blinking lights pushed back from a hanger and was being taxied to one end of the runway by a large tow truck with lights burning so brightly that it looked like a spotlight falling down from the sky.

"Somebody important is making a break for it," the driver said, his words smooth and melodic. "Some group of *influential people.*" Somehow the way he spoke the words, he spit out the syllables so that the "flu" sound made the word sound like a virus. "People on that plane are partially responsible for all of this," he said, indicating the darkness all around them. "And now, they are getting out of Dodge. Does that seem right to you?"

The airplane was released from the tow and started forward down the runway, picking up speed as it lumbered, until it evened off in a smooth flow of motion, and the front wheels left the ground as the pilot pointed the nose of the craft skyward.

"I don't know what you're asking me, Clive" the passenger answered, "but I suppose that the powers that be will always cover themselves. That seems to be the way it goes. It's always the regular people that suffer at times like this."

"Well," the driver said, "not always." He then reached up on the dashboard and flipped another switch that instigated a deep and roaring whush, heard instantly, coming from the back of the RV. The whush turned into an unearthly electric hum and grew until the vehicle itself vibrated and shook as if it were in an earthquake.

The plane left the ground and banked hard to the right, turning out over the Chesapeake Bay until its lights, the only lights in the sky save those from the heavens, began to rise into the night's deep black. Just as the RV seemed like it might vibrate itself into pieces, the driver flipped up a switch cover and punched a red button. At that moment, the heavily electric hum turned into a sound not unlike a large wave hitting a beach, and there was the feeling of a flash as the lights on the base blinked out.

And as they did, so did the lights on the aircraft.

Moments later, there was a fireball over the horizon. The night sky briefly lit up like a strange reverse snowglobe, or a sunrise, or a rainbow, bursting brightly in a flash of light that rose up against the dark as the plane plummeted into the bay. The brief burst of light in the sky quickly disappeared as the plane's cabin broke apart and the pieces and jet fuel and the cargo and the people slowly sunk under the murky depths of the water.

"Insufficient shielding." Clive Darling pronounced with certainty. His drawl was even heavier now. "We warned them about it for years, but they didn't want to listen. They just wanted to play politics, thought somehow they could reason with an EMP." Clive reached down and turned the lights back on inside the cabin of the RV, and reached into his shirt pocket and took out a small note pad. He opened the pad and quickly made a few marks in it while the passenger beside him sat and looked out over the nighttime sky.

"What can you do, you know? You can't reason with a man who has his reasons..."

In the distance, the fires around Washington, D.C. burned out of control as the driver of the RV flipped a few rocker switches on the dash, then started up the vehicle in earnest. The sound of John Denver's voice once again came over the speakers, singing a song about how sunshine on a man's shoulders can make him happy, how sunshine looks lovely on the water... The passenger looked out over the scene before him and thought that those words were true.

Clive Darling thought so, too. He softly began humming those words to himself as they pulled away into the enveloping night.

KNOT THREE

EXODUS

CHAPTER 18

At the bottom of the hill they turned west for a moment and then followed along the banks of a stream until they found a fallen tree that formed a natural bridge—large and solid enough to carry their weight as they traversed the stream's width. With Peter in the lead, they hiked through the Forest Preserve, heading generally in a southwesterly direction, making their way by the angle of the sun in the fall sky. The walking was rough because the snow was high, but they settled into a rhythm that kept them pushing forward with firm conviction.

They did their best to stay cloaked under a cover of trees because they had no way of knowing whether they might be spotted by the swarm of drones that had, just hours before, swept in and laid waste to the town behind them. They were survivors and, from the stain left on the earth back in their village, it was clear to them that whoever had ordered the drone strike did not intend for there to be *any* survivors. Although manageable, the cold was persistent with its stinging rebuke, and it forced them to keep moving to stay warm.

They walked, occupying themselves with thoughts of how their lives had come to this, and what might lie before them. Everything was going to change now. These three were free human beings, perhaps for the first time in their lives, but that very thought carried a terror all its own. History is replete with examples of brave men and women who found peace in the depths of a prison. Names like John Bunyan, Mandela, Ghandi, Bobby Sands, or Vaclav Havel come to mind. However, the Israelites followed Moses out of Egypt only to turn to newer and more willful forms of enslavement. Often, once the bonds of the physical have been lifted, the spirit and the mind still remain in chains.

Unfettered now by entangling alliances, oaths, and contracts signed by strangers on their behalf before they were even born, the three traveled onward, not knowing yet how they would respond to trials they'd meet along their way. Emerson wrote that when you travel, your giant travels with you. Now Peter, Lang, and Natasha quietly pondered whether they were prepared, whether they would survive, whether they could shoulder the giants of their past while trudging through the snow toward...

What?

There was no answer to that question. At least for now.

Peter's plan had been roughly sketched long ago through talks with Lev Volkhov, the wise old leader who'd foreseen the trouble they now faced. Generally, they intended to head toward Amish country in Pennsylvania. The reasons for this were not entirely clear to the younger Lang and Natasha, but those reasons were actually quite simple in their conceptualization. Volkhov believed that, were a systemic collapse or disaster to come, refugees from Warwick would fare better in Amish country than anywhere else. It was that simple.

The Warwickians' small town and provincial ways, as well as their ignorance of the means and patterns of modern life among the "English" (which is the term used by the Amish for all outsiders—since we are speaking of them) would be a two-edged sword in this journey. First, simple ways and an unorthodox manner would make Peter, Lang, and Natasha more vulnerable to the conditions in the wider American landscape. Second, they would explain away any idiosyncrasies of behavior once the refugees could become enmeshed among another group that had been born and raised in an insular society. Both considerations argued for their plan. No matter which way the sword cut, it suggested they should go to Amish country, because if they could get to the Amish they would have a better chance to survive. Or at least that was the hope. Peter considered these things as he looked up and along the ridgeline in the distance and braced his chin against the cold of the coming climb.

Had the three travelers been born In Los Angeles or Des Moines, or almost anywhere else in America other than their insulated Russian hamlet, they might have wondered about the logic of the plan. Why go to the Amish during a time of war? Aren't they pacifists? Won't they be the first to meet their end? This seems like a reasonable objection. However, there is a supposition behind that thought that had to be addressed. History tells a story of the pacifist Amish that contradicts the implications of the argument. The bare essential of that history is that, pacifist or not, the Amish—as a people group with a government, laws, and practices—have been around for more than five hundred years. Most of those years have been lived out in the most violent places and times in the history of civilization. Napoleon and his armies had come and gone, as had the Russian Empire, the Japanese Empire, and most of the British Empire, but the Amish still abide. Whether one attributed this fact to the protections offered by their religious faith, or the fact that, as a community, they took care of their own, or to a latent human conscience that respected their passivity and way of life, the fact remains that they were survivors. Their pacifism and faith protected them like the Alps protected Swiss neutrality. Being a student of history Volkhov understood this

The old sage had not known how the war would unfold, but he did know that it would be brutal and ugly for the physically pampered and mentally weak Americans, who were notoriously unprepared for what war could be like if it occurred on their own soil. Volkhov would often point out that the total number of American deaths by war during the American Civil War was 150% of those experienced during World War II, this despite the fact that the total deaths by combat in that earlier war were only 75% of those in the latter. The same relationship was evident in a comparison of, say, the American Revolutionary War and the Korean War, with the corresponding numbers being 70% and 24%. This is not even to mention how untrained and ill-educated Americans are when it comes to the basest necessities of survival and for facing hardship if such a conflict were to break out in the homeland.

The point in war, Volkhov was fond of saying, *is to stay alive,* and too many Americans miss that point when war occurs in the streets of their own towns. As he climbed, Peter looked over his shoulder at his younger colleagues, who were at that moment lost in deep thoughts of their own but struggling gamely onward through the snow, and he decided that, if he had anything to do with it, they would not fail.

* * * *

While packing their go-bags for the exodus, Peter had noted that, though their provisions were in good condition, he couldn't say the same for himself. He'd leaned down a little too quickly to lift up a box, and then stood a little too awkwardly to set the box on the table, and felt a sharp pain in his back, the signs of aging that had plagued him more and more over the last several years. Throughout his life he'd participated in extensive military and espionage training, and he'd even been an instructor in the charm school's *SERE* course for two years, but that was when he'd been quite a bit younger and in a lot better shape. Search, Evasion, Resistance, and Escape training and experience would help, he thought, but he was out of practice and (if truth be told) out of shape. Like many people his age, he'd become soft and addicted to his creature comforts. For his younger colleagues, they had youth, but that youth was burdened with inexperience. *If age but could, if youth but knew.* He tightened his jaw and thought to himself that they would have to combine their wits and abilities if they were to make it out of this alive.

* * * *

Peter knew that it was not a great plan. It might not even be a *good* one, but it was all they had. What they knew with certainty was that they could not make it through the winter on their own. If they'd stayed in Warwick, they would be dead already, and if they were caught by either side in the war that seemed to be around and upon them, things would not go well for them. If any of them were tortured or even closely questioned by either side, they would inevitably be found out, and all the protestations in the world wouldn't help. The body of truth lies dead in the ditch in almost any war, a casualty of necessity and fear. Simply by virtue of their being Russian, they would be suspected and hated by anyone who caught them. *What happened next would not be pretty,* Peter thought. *Especially for Natasha.*

It is an interesting irony that in those cultures and times when women have been less equal, they have been more honored, treasured, and protected from war. *Perhaps I am old-fashioned,* Peter thought, grabbing a limb to steady himself as he stepped over a fallen log, *but I know this to be true.* Despite what many modern folks have come to believe, history reveals that when the artificial veil of civility is rent, and when the ghostly wisps and remnants of chivalry and ancient patriarchy are eradicated altogether and thrown to the ground during times of general upheaval... well, let us just say that throughout antiquity, and in every place and every time, women have fared the worst in times of war. Men are usually granted the dignity of *just* being killed, Peter thought.

He scratched his beard and glanced up into the sun. The more liberated the culture, the more horrible has been the treatment of women during and after that culture crumbles. Well, Natasha would have to be protected and watched over, he thought. *She has no family left... that I know of.* He looked around and watched the young woman walking behind him, and saw the lines of concern etched on her face. He determined that, even if she didn't want it, he would stand in the breach and protect her.

All three of the travelers had some training. All three had gone through mandatory classes on spy craft, weapons, and tactics. However, they would now learn that there is a universe of difference between theory and the real world. Peter just hoped that the learning curve would not be too steep, and that the course in harsh reality wouldn't kill them.

* * * *

The air was crisp and cold and the sky was the bluest of blue—the kind of blue that seems impossible except by contrast. Every now and then a sharp breeze would blow and snow would fall from overhead branches where it lay trapped by pine needles and oak leaves. The snow, blown from the deposits in the trees, would swirl around them and make them uncomfortable, and, on a few occasions, it would crash down upon them, falling into their collars and sliding down their necks, melting from the heat of their bodies and trickling icy cold sludge down their backs in lacy jags, adding impetus to their chill. The cold on their backs mixing with the cold in their feet sent jolts through their systems to keep them moving ahead.

Coming over one low rise, they saw a small camp in the distance. They were far enough away and downwind so they hunkered down and watched the camp awhile from afar, wondering silently what they should do. The encampment seemed to consist of a few families, huddled around a roaring fire, their three large camping tents arranged in a triangle around the fire with the door flaps opening inward, toward the blaze.

Two of the campers, a man and a woman, were arguing loudly, and hints of words and voices tumbled through the icy air toward the hikers. They seemed to be married, the man and the woman, but it wasn't entirely clear from the snippets of sound that reached the trio hiding along the ridge what the point of their argument was. Perhaps she was insisting on equality in the camping chores, or maybe he was blaming her for their current horrendous state. Whatever was their contention, it was clear that they blamed each other—as if either could have held back the uncertainty that now approached them. Pulling together in times of utter peril is a sign that the peril is understood and embraced. These people had no idea what they were in for, but they had camping gear, survival food, and with it, anger mixed with unhappiness. They thought they had prepared for occasions such as this, but now, as they argued in the cold, they found that they were woefully mistaken.

Peter turned to Natasha and Lang and put his finger to his lips, before whispering to them. "Obviously, these are some people who decided to 'bug out.' That's the term used by *preppers* or survivalists who are of the opinion that they can rush out into the woods when things collapse and they'll be okay. Volkhov purchased dozens of books that spoke of, or even encouraged, this phenomenon. He said that many Americans anticipated a major collapse of their society, but they were deceived in their ideas about how best to deal with it. Millions of people made rudimentary plans to escape the cities and towns by heading into the wilderness, but most of them have little or no training, let alone knowledge of what it would be like to live out here. They didn't consider that there were millions of people, just like them, thinking the same thing. This will make things tougher for us."

Peter looked down on the campers, shaking his head. "Most of these people are untrained and unpracticed, and their fantasies of wilderness survival will become nightmares within days. It won't end well for them. But, some of the people we might run into are militia types and hard-core survivalists. These families here do not look wise or well trained at all. The other kinds—the woodsmen and real survivalists—they will have sentries and possibly scouts. We wouldn't have been able to walk up on this ridge like this without alerting them. They'll be better trained. Some groups might be benevolent, but others will be violent or criminally-minded. Many will be looking for trouble, for a fight. We're better off avoiding all of them."

Natasha chewed on the end of her glove, her eyes searching the scene in front of them. "Maybe they can help us?" she said, her voice betraying hope as well as innocence.

"No, Natasha, we mustn't think that way," Lang said, whispering softly. "One mistake and we could be done for. One individual or group that suspects us or is wary of us, or perhaps is just looking to steal and loot their way to survival, and we could all be killed. You heard the radio back at the plant before the EMP. Our world has changed, but *their* world," he indicated with his hand the group in the clearing below and beyond that the wider countryside, "*their* world has changed even more. We have to be smart, like Peter says."

Lang reached over and touched Natasha lightly on her arm, and let his hand rest there a minute until she looked at him with understanding. He sympathized with her fears and even her natural tendency to trust and hope for the best, but that type of naiveté would have to be one of the first casualties of this conflict. "I agree with Peter. We need to avoid people at all costs. I'm already worried because we're walking out in the snow, leaving a trail behind us. There's nothing we can do about that, except try to track close to the trees and rocks. When we can get up on those rocks or exposed land, we do so. We stay midway up the hills and the mountains. Not in the valley, where we can be seen from above, and not on the peaks where we can be seen from below, but halfway up, as much as we are able, all of the time.

"But we don't want to invite trouble by interacting with people," Lang emphasized, looking Natasha in the eyes. "What if they know that the Russians are the ones that attacked? What if one of us slips up and speaks Russian?" He paused and let the questions answer themselves. "Even if we've had nothing to do with the attacks, we would be guilty in their eyes. No. Peter is right. Let's just avoid people and look for a route that avoids contact as much as possible."

"But we're Americans," Natasha whimpered.

"No, we're not, Natasha. At least not to these people. We have no country," Lang replied.

"Lang's right," Peter said, "we need to go over this rise and stay hidden from them or anyone else like them." He looked into the bright blue sky and judged the time. "We'll keep our eyes open and stop every fifty yards or so to look out and around us. Each of us should be watching and aware of our surroundings all of the time. Listen and look. Remember all of the training we did back in the shed at the water plant. Remember what you learned when you were in school. Keep moving and constantly be aware. We'll stop regularly and check our surroundings so that we don't walk into a trap."

Natasha looked back down over the impromptu camp and she wondered what would happen to these people. Whatever it was, she feared that it wouldn't be good. The campers seemed to be heedless of any real danger. They acted as if they were just on a day trip; as if things were going to get better in a few days; as if they could all go home soon. Perhaps if they'd seen their homes, families, and friends wiped off the map by a handful of drones, as the Warwickians had, or if they knew that there was no home to go back to, they'd have a little different perspective. As it was, the children ran and sang and shouted and threw snowballs, and the parents just sat looking dead-eyed into the fire - all except, that is, for the one couple that screamed and shouted at one another, each unsatisfied with their situation and blaming the other, each hoping that the other would somehow make it all better.

* * * *

The walk proceeded, and the trio made good time, keeping to their plan. Not too long after they passed the last group of campers, they spied another man walking along the crest of a ridge. He was silhouetted against the sky and was scampering over the rocks heading who knows where. They watched as the man leapt over something in his path and came down on a branch at the top of the ridge that sent a crackling echo down the mountain. He sank down in the snow as the branch gave way beneath his feet.

They stopped, well hidden in the trees, as they watched the man disappear over the ridge. Peter pulled out his map and partially unfolded it across his knee as he knelt in the snow. He compared the map to the compass, and he nodded his head in the direction that they should go.

"We need to head towards Carbondale. That ought to let us avoid the worst of the towns and highways, although we'll inevitably have to deal with some of it. On the track we're following, hopefully we'll cross Highway 17 sometime this evening. We need to be across that highway and have it far behind us by dark fall. We don't want to stop or camp anywhere near roads or people." Peter traced the intended route with his finger on the map so his two companions could follow.

On their way again, they benefited by not having to cross fence lines or private property. Being in the Forest Preserve had its advantages. As they walked, they noticed in the distance the occasional plume of smoke, heard the random blast of gunfire, but they stayed well clear of any sign of humans, and, in time, they found themselves walking with a single-mindedness that comes from being alone in the wide open spaces.

CHAPTER 19

Mistakes are part of the learning curve, and often they are fatal. Sometimes, for some unknown reason, they could very well have been fatal, but are not. Rounding the corner of a stand of trees almost too thick to walk through, Lang saw him first. Looking up to watch a flock of birds shoot out into the wide blue sky, Lang caught a glimpse of a black coat behind the thick brown branches.

Seated in the trees, with a scoped deer rifle pointed directly at the three refugees from Warwick, a young man sat accompanied by a woman who was huddled next to him in the cold. The two, perilously balanced in the crook of a branch, cowered behind a second limb.

Lang could see that the gunman's hands shook as he pointed the gun first at Lang, then at Peter, then back at Lang again. Despite his superior position, the man was afraid and his fear caused his hands—and therefore the gun—to shake uncontrollably. Peter and Natasha did not see the man at first, as they fought through the branches, and Lang had to alert them, tapping Peter on the arm and indicating toward the gunman in the trees.

"Okay, okay, okay..." Lang said loudly, but calmly, bringing his hands up to show that he was unarmed. As he did this, Peter, and then Natasha, looked up and saw the man with the gun, and the woman behind him. Natasha instinctively dropped to the ground as if she were on fire. She brought her hands up as best she could into the air, though her face remained buried in the snow.

The quick motion spooked the gunman, and with a terrified squeal more than a shout he hollered for the trio to "freeze!" which they all did instantly. Natasha steeled her nerves and pulled her face out of the snow, straining to look up into the gunman's eyes. Peter raised his hands slowly, and Lang tried to clear his thoughts and take in a fuller picture of what was going on.

The man is not going to shoot, Lang thought. *Not on purpose, and not unless he is provoked.* The young man with the gun was scared, and Lang determined that he wasn't a killer.

Judging from the look in his eye and the uncertainty with which he held them through the scope, he wasn't going to murder them in cold blood. *He might kill one of us on accident, though.*

"Easy there," Lang said, firmly. "Easy with the gun. We're unarmed. Just take your finger off the trigger for a second, and let's talk. We don't want anyone getting hurt because a muscle twitches in all this excitement."

It was not true that they were *completely* unarmed. Peter still had the Ruger 9mm pistol in the pocket of his coat, but the man with the rifle didn't know that.

The man obediently took his finger off the trigger, actually moving his head from behind the scope and looking at the trigger guard to see if his gloved finger was clear. He wasn't planning on shooting anyone; this Lang knew, and the knowledge allowed him to relax his body slightly.

"Easy there, and thank you for not shooting us." Lang didn't move, and made no motion as if he were going to approach. *No need to be foolish.* However certain he was that the man was harmless, at least in his intentions, Lang wasn't taking anything for granted.

Lang concentrated and put on the best New England accent he could muster, though it wasn't great. "Okay, pal. We're just moving through, here. We're just trying to get home, and we're unarmed and we're not going to hurt anybody. We're not even going to approach you. Do you understand me?"

Peter looked at Lang and communicated wordlessly that it would be a simple thing to rush the man, to pull him down from the branch and disarm him, but Lang slowly closed his eyes, silently saying "No." The two men agreed without saying a word.

The gunman nodded, and the woman next to him huddled closer behind him, as if she were a little less sure of the group's lack of harmful intent. "Just keep moving!" he shouted. "Don't make me *shoot* anyone!" He tried to make the words sound ominous and threatening, but Lang could hear the desperate uncertainty in his voice.

"We don't want you to shoot anyone either, bro," Lang said, calmly. "We're just going to walk on. You're welcome to come with us, if you want. We're heading towards Pennsylvania."

"Yeah?" the man said, with a voice that suddenly betrayed a hint of a sneer. "Well, you can *have* that!" He looked at them as if they would understand, but they didn't. "I wouldn't go anywhere near the highway if I were you. It's a bloodbath over there." This seemed to be all he was willing to give them as far as explanation, as if his reasons were too painful to discuss. He rattled his gun again. "You guys keep walking or I'll shoot, I swear!" There was a little more certainty this time, seen in the steadying of the gun.

"Okay, man," Lang said, nodding his head as he reached down to help Natasha lift herself out of the snow. He pulled on her with one hand and she was able to rise up. She dusted the snow off her coat and shook her legs as she did. Lang kept his other hand up, and he whispered to Natasha to quit dusting herself and raise her hands. She did so and then the trio backed slowly away. As soon as they were thirty feet or so past the shooter, they began moving faster, and soon they were over the next rise.

"How did you know he was harmless?" Natasha asked, after they had walked for a moment.

"He didn't know what he was doing with that gun. Probably never shot it before. I'm not even sure it was loaded. He just wanted to scare us off. He was scared out of his mind. Probably peed himself."

"I almost did too," Natasha said. "I'm glad he just wanted to frighten us, but I don't understand people. I've never been so afraid in my life... except... maybe when Mikail shot Todd Karagin." Her hands shook as she wiped the melted snow from her face.

"Let's try not to make that mistake again," Peter said, exhaling deeply. He peered ahead into their path with a little more intention.

"You're right, Peter," Lang replied. "But we may not always have warning—and we may not always meet people who don't know which end of the rifle to hold. It'll get tougher when we cross 17 and get into farm country."

"Don't scare me any more than I am already, Lang," Natasha said in protest.

If one listened closely, in that protest could be heard the faintest beginnings of strength.

* * * *

After several more uneventful hours of walking, Peter called them to a stop with a motion of his hand, and they gathered near a rocky outcropping, and took some time once again to look at the map and compare it with the compass.

"We look to be right in this area," Peter said, circling a section on the map with his finger. "We'll be to Highway 17 in two to three hours if all goes well and the conditions hold up." He turned and looked towards the sun, which was already past its apex, and he held his open hand with the top of his index finger just under the sun facing westward, and then moved his hand downwards four fingers width. He did this several times, then, adding a finger and a half for the hilly terrain, he turned to the others and told them that it seemed to him to be after 1 p.m. "Maybe 1:30," he added.

"Well," Lang said, "I guess we're making good time?"

"Good enough," Peter answered. "When we get near the highway—anywhere within a mile or so—we're going to want to go very slowly and use all of our senses. Like the gunman in the trees said, the highway might be really rough, and we don't want to get caught up in anything."

The three pulled off their packs, and Peter let out a deep sigh when he dropped his to the ground. Of the three, he carried the heaviest load since his pack had the ammo can with the electronic equipment in it. In his mind he lamented his poor physical shape and was kicking himself for not getting more exercise. He felt the cramping in his muscles and reckoned that he would be sore and miserable for at least the first week of their journey.

They opened the ammo can and pulled out the radio. Peter put in the batteries and tried to tune in anything... anything at all... but all he heard was a vacant and incessant buzzing, the vacuous chorus from all the ambient electricity in the universe.

The three pulled out some of their food, and ate quickly, and Peter ate while standing guard. They all took deep breaths while stomping occasionally to ward off the cold. The three travelers were grateful for the rest, but the cold and the light in the sky gave them reasons to keep moving.

By around 4:30 p.m., they were within a half-mile of the highway and they occasionally heard the random blast or sharp staccato of gunfire. Their current location, because of the thickness of the forest, didn't seem to be a regular path of ingress or egress to the highway, though they had crossed a few places where it had become obvious that masses of people had diverted from the highway as they set off into the forest. Peter told them that he wanted them to stay away from any areas that had become cattle paths for escaping humans.

They moved slower now and with purpose, and, though they were still in the trees, the land was flatter here. There were fewer places for natural cover. They crept along slowly, spread out five to ten yards apart, and each covered and watched a given area. They moved in short hops as they made forward progress slowly.

By 5:30 p.m., they were within fifty yards of the highway and the gunfire had slackened, but only a bit, and now they heard the almost indescribable din of human traffic and misery. The sound was like a wailing that came in around the window on a cold winter's night, a dull cacophony of random shouts and the background sound of feet shuffling and dragging, and the cries of pain and suffering. All in all it sounded like one imagines hell to sound, but maybe not down in the very deepest dungeons. Maybe up at the front, near the check-in desk, where they keep things nicer for the tourists.

It was entering early evening, and the shadows had grown long, and darkness—not full darkness, but the gloaming—would be upon them soon. They still had not seen any people, but in the distance, over the horizon to the south, they could see smoke rising, and they still heard sporadic gunfire, and they were frightened, though none of them spoke of this fear aloud. Instead, they clenched their jaws and waited for the night.

* * * *

They approached the highway access road through the trees, and, crawling slowly through the snow, they peered out over the war zone that Highway 17 had become. There were cars on fire, smoke filled the air, and a gauzy fog hung ominously in the ether. Masses of people moved by like soldiers in full retreat, solemn in their drudgery. Occasionally, fights broke out in little pockets of disturbance, like dust devils swirling across the desert floor in a sweltering heat – only it was cold, and the sound reached them through the icy air like sharp reports or echoes.

The trio looked on helplessly as armed gangs opened fire on groups of the marching people. They watched as mothers, pulling carts with their children and belongings in them, were pushed to the ground by human animals so that unspeakable acts could be committed.   They saw men beaten without provocation or limitation. Gunfire erupted so often, and with such alacrity, that in every way imaginable the three Warwickians could only describe what they were viewing from their vantage point as a massive, running gun battle the likes of which they'd only heard from the safety of their houses when the civil war had broken out in Warwick.   Only Natasha had been out in the street during that battle; she swallowed and felt a bitter empathy for the people below.

To the right, northward up the highway but still in their view, a group of men rocked a van loaded with people, and the van eventually overturned, and the men hopped up on it and stomped at the windows until the glass shattered on the occupants inside. They reached their arms into the van and ripped the doors open, pulling the occupants out violently. A few of their victims inside the vehicle escaped and ran up the highway, slipping in the snow, trying to disappear among the crowds. Others, thrown to the ground, lay haplessly while the vandals stomped them and struck them with sticks, rods, or anything else that was at hand. The gang then rifled through the van, stealing whatever they could, before moving on to the next car and repeating the scene.

A high-powered rifle shot rang out from somewhere and one of the gang members fell to the ground, then another shot rang and another thug fell. The crack of the rifles echoed through the clearing like a gong. The surviving gang members took off running northward, leaving their dead comrades behind.

In the distance, there arose a mechanical growl of grinding machinery rolling over the boisterous frenzy, and the three turned their heads to see what could be making such a noise. Eventually they saw it. A line of military vehicles, evidently spared or shielded from the worst of the EMP, crawled clumsily up the highway from the south, and most of the vehicles had guns mounted on the top of them. Soldiers, probably National Guardsmen, perched on top of the vehicles, operating the guns. Quite often though, the gunners disappeared because they ducked down whenever gunfire erupted from some unseen attackers.

The convoy moved slowly but did not stop for anything, and groups of people ran alongside, pawing at the metal of the vehicles. Occasionally someone would try to climb up the outside of the armor, whereupon a shot would ring out from a trailing vehicle and, like a flea picked cleanly off the dog, the climber would slink to the ground and be trampled underfoot by the crowd.

The vehicles slowed a few times, and when they did, the crowds would clench around them, forcing the convoy to push forward again, clearing abandoned and crippled cars in their path by pushing them to the side as they advanced. This give-and-take uncertainty caused the mass of crowd and metal to be intermingled, and sometimes when the convoy picked up steam it would lurch quickly and run over something, *or someone*, lying in the road.

Heedless, or perhaps spellbound and in shock, other refugees along the highway kept up their march, heads bowed and gathered tightly in packs, their children huddled in the midst of them. These people didn't even look up to notice the bodies of the dead and the dying. Screams broke through the cold air like glass breaking, but the packs of humans huddled even more closely together, shuffling like zombies into the coming night.

The trio sat under the cover of trees and watched the scene in its horrifying extremity. Lang looked down and wondered how they would ever get across the highway. It is odd where minds go for answers in such moments. Lang unsnapped his backpack and lowered it slowly to the ground. He wondered for a moment if there was anything in Clay's bag that would provide them a solution, or perhaps comfort, in the present situation. *Maybe Walt Whitman, or Hemingway, or C.L. Richter had some advice for crossing through a war zone highway... for passing through death,* he thought.

Probably not...

From Walt Whitman:

Allons! through struggles and wars!
The goal that was named cannot be countermanded.

Have the past struggles succeeded?
What has succeeded? yourself? your nation? Nature?
Now understand me well- it is provided in the essence of things that
from any fruition of success, no matter what, shall come forth
something to make a greater struggle necessary.

My call is the call of battle, I nourish active rebellion,
He going with me must go well arm'd,
He going with me goes often with spare diet, poverty, angry
enemies,
desertions.

Allons! the road is before us!
It is safe- I have tried it- my own feet have tried it well- be not
detain'd!

CHAPTER 20

Prophecy is a funny thing, but not for the reasons one usually assumes. Of course, there is the humorous aspect of it in the common mind, with its messengers in sackcloth, pulling the twigs out of their beards as they stand before the people like mad messengers of doom. That is funny as far as it goes. And it is funny that no prophet is received in his own homeland. It would seem that the people should be more likely to accept the word of someone they know rather than someone they don't, perhaps especially so if they knew the courage required to stand up and warn one's neighbors. However, this is distinctly *not true* with prophets. The people would rather they go warn somebody else and leave them be with their pesky opinions.

No. All of that is true, but none of it is the reason that prophecy is funny. Rather, it is funny because prophecy often tells us one thing, but we distinctly hear something else. It is as if God in heaven decided to give us a message, and chose to do it through one of our fellows. Somewhere along the line, the message is garbled, like in those games we played as children where we sat in a circle and passed some sentence around, so that the last person heard something totally different from the original intended message.

Couldn't God, if he were inclined to give us a message, find a more suitable way than to pass it through gossip? Couldn't the people be saved from their vices if they were simply inclined to listen a little better, perhaps to see with their own eyes?

Of course not. Because prophecy, by definition, is pointing to something that hasn't happened yet. And we, in our moment, only see what affects us in our immediate space. Everything that hasn't happened yet *to us* is speculative in our eyes.

That was the case with Lang as he sat as still as he possibly could, pressing his head against the stone wall, feeling its cold against his temple. His memory suddenly flashed to a prophecy given by his hero, the great writer Alexander Solzhenitsyn. *"The next war..."* Solzhenitsyn said, *"...may well bury Western civilization forever."* That should have suggested to him the larger picture of the wider world. It should have made him remember the long talks with Volkhov in which the old man had told him of impending worldwide calamity.

Instead, as he sat nursing his bullet wound, trying not to cry out in pain, all he could think about was how "western civilization" had come, in his own mind at that moment, to equate with him— *just him.* That somehow he was the entire focus and culmination of history. Being wounded, and living through it, had a way of drawing a man inward, and as he sucked in his breath and felt the tug as Peter stanched the blood, he wondered whether the war that was around him would bury him like it seemed to be burying western civilization.

* * * *

The crossing of Highway 17 hadn't gone smoothly. They'd decided from their vantage point at the tree line overlooking the road that they would move as silently as possible up the highway access road, camouflaged within the thick stands of trees that pushed up against the clearing. They were looking for a better place to cross. Peter explained that they wanted to make their move sometime after dark, and they looked for a place where the clearing between the trees narrowed and the crowd thinned somewhat.

They found one, a place where the road was somewhat more destitute of refugees and obstructions. They walked a mile up the highway, toward the north, and as they walked they noticed that most of the traffic had stopped for the night. The road there turned straight westward and took a short dip to the south, and they found a little bend in the highway that they determined would be the best place for them to attempt a crossing.

As darkness descended like a curtain on the area, the three halted their plodding through the trees, hid among the bushes, and surveyed the scene before them.

The refugees on the highway huddled in small groups and started large bonfires from anything they could find that would burn in order to stay warm. While there was scattered violence here and there, the people down below them seemed to be intent on hunkering down for the cold night on the highway and its easement for some reason devoid of any appreciable logic. Misery loves company, but less often is it recognized that company, especially the wrong kind, often *invites* misery. As the three looked down on the scene, they saw that there was less company here perhaps, and therefore less attendant misery, so they determined that it was here that they would take their shot.

Peter spotted a place where there was at least a football field's distance between campfires, and he pointed out quietly to Lang and Natasha that there were no campfires burning in the woods in the distance across the wide expanse of roadway and greenbelt. "This is where we cross," he said, as they looked down on the stygian scene.

The plan was to sprint the distance in irregular intervals so that they would not *all* get caught out in the open at the same time. Looking out across the distance, they determined the shortest route and marked a reference point to run towards, and they decided that Peter would go first. He would carry both his own bag and Natasha's. "If something happens to me, God forbid, if I stumble or fall, I'll throw the bags as far from my body toward the opposite side as I can, and you must try to gather them in on a sprint as you make your own way across." Lang thought of stories that Volkhov had told him of the storming of the beaches at Normandy. The soldiers, when taking heavy fire from the enemy, had tossed their guns up the beach so that, if the worst happened, the soldiers who actually made it farther up the sand would have more firepower ahead of them in their fight.

"Don't look back, or to the side. Just put your head down and fly," Peter said as he touched them each on the shoulder. With that, he gathered his breath in and turned to run.

Lang and Natasha watched his burly figure push out across the snow and then gather speed when he reached the road, keeping low to the ground. In a normal circumstance, Peter's movements would have appeared clumsy and bulky as he sprinted like a bear across the clearing with the two bags heaving on his back. Perhaps from the perspective of anyone who might have seen him, he did appear to be a bear, but in any event, he made it safely across without even raising a protest from the distance, and he disappeared into the woods beyond. Lang was shocked. *Maybe this is going to be easier than we thought*, he tried to encourage himself.

Once on the other side, Peter made his way into the trees and found a safe place to stow the bags, and, returning to the tree line, he stood poised to watch the others cross, to be ready in case they needed help.

Natasha crossed next, and she did well enough, though one of the parties surrounding a campfire spotted her and a shout of "Hey! Over there!" rang out through the night. Peter was on alert to see if she was going to be chased or followed, but she wasn't, so before long, panting and out of breath, she joined Peter in the trees on the south side of the highway.

There was a stirring in one of the camps, so Lang waited several more minutes. When no one came out searching, or ventured over near the wire where the two had crossed back into the woods, he decided it was safe to make his own venture across the Rubicon. He thought of old black and white films of East Germans sprinting for freedom before a shot would ring out, and their bodies would tumble headlong into the razor wire. *That ought to keep me running*, he thought, and he reached down with a stick and cleared the snow from the soles of his boots.

Lang made his start, and, almost from the beginning, Peter could see that the attempt was not going to go well. Lang tripped at the starting gate and fell, sprawling into the snow on the upwards low climb to the main highway, and Peter, from his vantage point, noticed that some men to his left, who had reacted to Natasha's dash across the roadway, were gathering and pointing toward the shadow he made on the snow. They began to approach the area at the top of the incline where Lang was struggling to regain his footing. Peter watched as Lang regrouped and began his run in earnest.

The men broke into a jog toward him as he crested the low hill, and Peter saw that they had an angle on him, so that they would almost certainly cut him off before he could make it to safety. He watched as the men converged on Lang's path and anticipated whether he would have to run to his aid.

Feinting to the left, Lang made it past the first defender, before a second man who made it into the middle distance between Lang and the trees cut him off. Angry shouts rang out and someone yelled, "Hey, give me that bag!"

Lang picked up his speed, finding traction now as the adrenaline rush made his body surge forward. Another of the assailants was sprinting toward him trying to stop him in his tracks, but Lang swerved and pivoted in the other direction. He had spent his life fleeing bullies, and now that lifetime of training kicked in. He maneuvered across the field at an angle, determined not to let these untrained hooligans do what the professional bullies he'd faced in Warwick could not.

Sprinting now at full-speed he almost casually and effortlessly detached his backpack's waist band, and, grabbing the padded arm strap in a single fluid motion, he swung it's full weight at his nearing attacker, juking to his right again simultaneously. The bag caught the man flush in the side of the head, and the bully tumbled to the ground, yelping in pain. This action caused a cacophonous cry of protest from the other men who were approaching from the rear, slow and lumbering, unable to get any traction in the ice and snow. Lang bent over, scooped up his bag, and ran toward the trees.

In the flickering night, he suddenly sensed a smooth air of calm as he warmed with the excitement and accomplishment of his escape. He noticed his shadow on the ground, running before him, as cast by the moon over his shoulder. He thought it beautiful and sublime, the motion of its lengthening stride, the way its feet met his own as it sprinted toward safety in front of him.

Just as suddenly as he had come to appreciate the pleasure of his own shadow—his own running—he came to question what became of it. In that expanded microsecond he heard a calamitous noise in the distance, and it sounded like an explosion over his shoulder, and he looked down at his shadow and saw the red splotches on its torso. He spun around in a jerking, involuntary motion like someone had run over him with a car, but he turned his head to watch his shadow until the last moment, and then he slammed to the ground whereupon the shadow disappeared.

Now, he was only Vasily Kashporov lying on the cold hard ground in the snow, with a bullet wound in his shoulder.

* * * *

Lang knew that something had struck him but did not know what it was and he felt no pain. He had to get up, and as he did the thought crossed his mind that he was already free. He didn't know at the time *why* that particular thought crossed his mind, but he did know that he was no longer helpless little Vasily, cowering from bullies. He was now a free man, and had tasted freedom, and he liked it. Solzhenitsyn said, "You only have power over people so long as you don't take everything away from them. But when you've robbed a man of everything, he's no longer in your power—he's free again." Lang had suddenly come face to face with his death, and he determined that he would get up and run, and somehow this made him feel whole again. He liked being free, and he ran like the wind.

Almost instantaneously upon hearing the shot and seeing Lang tumble to the ground, Peter had vaulted out of the trees and, operating on adrenaline of his own, he was sprinting towards Lang like an Olympian with the 9mm pistol readied in his hand. The younger man had regained his feet and was rapidly continuing his progress. Peter met him and grabbed him firmly, hurrying him along, and the two friends made it back into the trees before the men in the distance could decide just what they'd seen.

The assailants stopped, tired and out of shape, and they did not follow their victim into the woods. If they had been asked what stopped their pursuit, they would have sworn up and down that they had just seen a bear run out of the woods to save a man.

* * * *

Most Americans, prior to the events that were now unfolding in their country, would have denied that such random acts of violence and wanton cowardice would have been possible, but that is precisely because most Americans are insulated from reality. Woefully so. They are ignorant of world history and the conditions of life experienced through most of the last millennia by much of the rest of the world. When people have lived their lives carelessly, in the lap of comforts and the bosom of excess purchased for them by the hard work and sacrifice of their ancestors; when they have counted on laws and government alone to keep them safe, they come to believe that the same kindnesses they have experienced at the hands of their neighbors heretofore will be granted them when that world collapses. They believe that humanity will not revert to its animal nature when there is a disintegration of those laws, and when the power and ability of that government to impose and keep those laws is not just diminished, but eliminated. In this, they are wrong.

Man, loosed from the bonds of all law, and religion, and conscience, even if those restraints have been false or damaged to begin with, reverts to the animal nature that animates him. It is inevitable, then, that masses of men, loosed from restraints and deprived of access to the artificial means of provision they have counted on for all their lives, will soon experience unprecedented violence and mayhem. Even if it begins in small places, a little leaven will be enough to leaven the whole lump, and eventually social feelings will collapse along with society. We don't have to like hearing it, but the truth has a way of not caring whether we like it or not.

The world is a violent place when restraints are removed. The already vanishing traditions of human care and kindness, peacefulness, and lawful living have been systematically eradicated by dialecticians who maintain power by championing division and by pitting neighbor against neighbor, race against race, and party against party. The bloody product of this will seem barbarous and horrible to those who have yet to experience it. This is strong medicine. But in times of sickness, it is medicine that is needed.

CHAPTER 21

Peter checked to see if anyone was following them. No one was. Tracking quickly through a low gully and into the deeper woods, after a good five-minute walk, they came upon a stone fence line in the snow separating a field from the surrounding forest. He pulled Lang down into the snow and, by touch and instinct more than sight, he felt for the wound that he knew to be in Lang's left arm or shoulder. He needed to know how serious it was before he made any decisions about what to do next. He found the wound, and it seemed to be a minor one in the larger scheme of things, with a clear entry and exit in the fat of the tissue. Lang was blessed that the bullet had not struck any bone, and the young man was working on adrenaline and seemed to be unconcerned by the fact that he'd just been shot. In fact, he was slightly delirious.

"You've been shot, Lang." Peter said. "But I don't think it is too serious. A scratch, really."

"Wow," Lang replied, his right hand reaching upwards to feel the wound. He drew back his hand with blood on it, and he grimaced slightly, but not from the pain. "I've never been shot before."

"Well, now you're an expert," Peter said, cupping his hand behind the young man's neck. "I think you'll be okay. We'll move on so that we can put some distance between us and that madness, and then I'll see if we can build camp and clean and dress the wound." He looked at Lang and gave him a smile, then a wink.

"Thank you, Peter." Lang looked back at him with sincere appreciation in his eyes.

"No problem, son," Peter said, his smile perhaps grimmer than he had hoped. "Now let's move out."

The way was dark and they moved very slowly, mostly by feel. Natasha switched bags with Lang so she could carry the heavier of the loads and take some of the weight off his shoulders as he slowly began to come back into his body. There was just enough moonlight to allow them to see from tree to tree and make their way, as if by Braille, through the low valley. The branches clung like webs to the nighttime sky, and the brush caught their clothes as they swept past.

These valleys, cut by receding glacial ice, ran primarily from northeast to southwest, which was good for the Warwickians as they made their escape. It meant that they could move steadily through the darkness without having to do a lot of climbing and descending.

Peter intended to walk for a good thirty minutes, but their pace, though steady, was so slow that it was nearly two hours before he felt that they had put enough distance between themselves and the road. They walked a little further, and then the trio came upon a low stone building, very small—maybe eight feet by eight feet. Peter identified it as an old well house.

The building had a wooden door that had mostly rotted away, and around the top of the building, where there had once been a few small windows, were now jagged slices of glass, long ago smashed and broken by who knows what or whom. It took the three of them a good fifteen minutes to drag out all of the trash that had accumulated in the building over the years, but before long, they had it cleaned out enough to use for the night. The floor of the well house was cement, and in the center of the building was only a protruding water pipe, maybe six inches in diameter, which someone had covered with a large rock.

Peter built a very small fire inside the building and explained that he would only let it burn as long as necessary. Fire is a beacon, but sometimes it is necessary, so he intended to obscure it from view as best as he could. He needed to produce coals that they could use to cook their food and heat water for cleaning Lang's wounds, and then he would let the fire burn just long enough to heat the stones of the building itself, for heat in the night, before the fire would be extinguished.

The big man prepared and started the small fire and showed Natasha how to feed wood into it without letting the flame get too big, and then he took the gun and told Lang he would patrol the perimeter and keep watch until they had enough glowing red coals to do what they needed to do. He stepped out into the night to have a look around.

Lang and Natasha sat for a moment, and she tended the fire and watched him in silence.

"Are you holding up?" he asked, seeing her sink deeper into thought.

"Yes," Natasha sighed. "I'm fine. I'm just worried about you... and thinking about Kolya."

"I know," Lang said. "I am sorry Cole didn't make it back in time."

She looked up in distress at the mention of that name, with a silent insistence that he call her brother by his given name.

"Natasha, I'm going to keep calling him Cole because I believe him still to be alive. I'm sure he's okay. He's a resourceful fellow."

"Oh, there is no need to lie, Lang. We both know that he would not have disappeared unless something bad had happened to him. He probably fell into some criminals' hands and now he's—"

"Stop. Don't think that way. He's fine." Lang looked at her and wished that he could be more certain of that fact, but the remembrance of the bombed-out remains of Warwick flashed through his mind. The simple truth was that nothing was fine. He shifted his back against the wall and suddenly felt a pain shoot down through his arm and realized that, even on that account, there was nothing about the situation that was fine.

"Here. Let me take a look at you," Natasha said, and she pulled Lang's shirt back slightly, hearing the cold sucking sound of the coagulated blood ripping slightly from his skin as she bent over his wound.

"Ow, Ow. Ow!" Lang said, before he gritted his teeth and leaned back again into the wall, suddenly becoming aware of the warmth in her hands.

"Is it bad?"

"It's fine. It'll be okay."

"Now who's lying?" Lang replied, attempting a small grin as a kind of gallows humor. Natasha grinned back, and somehow this made the pain in his arm begin to lessen.

They sat and talked as Natasha tended to the fire, and they both tried to encourage each other for what seemed like an hour. They spoke of the strangeness of their journey and the tiredness of their hopes. They talked of how their lives had seemed somehow... shortened... having been ripped out from under them by the flash of recent events. "It seems like yesterday that Kolya and I were getting ready for the Fall Festival," Natasha said.

"It seems like a minute ago that you were telling him to stop with his damned Shakespeare," Lang smiled. "I wonder what he would have to say about this fine mess?"

In that vein, they went on speaking and reminiscing, echoing the same kind of conversation that was taking place around millions of campfires at that very moment, spread across the landscape of America and, beyond that, the globe.

Indeed, had one been lodged in the middle distance between heaven and earth at that moment; or maybe parachuting down from the outer reaches of space in a tumbling freefall that had not yet leveled out; had one not gained a controlling vantage point in that middle distance; if one had looked upward and then downward in that tumbling spiral in the darkness of space, it would have been difficult to tell which were the fires burning on the ground around the millions of campfires like this one, and which ones were raging in the hearts of a million stars.

* * * *

Before long, Peter returned from his patrol, and, seeing that the fire was prepared and ready, he used a piece of scrap corrugated tin from the refuse pile to scoop hot coals into two shallow holes dug just outside the building. Each of the holes was about five inches deep and just big enough around to receive the stainless steel pans from the mess kit in his pack.

He built up the fire in the building by adding more of the old two-by-fours and scraps of wood from the refuse pile, and then he closed the dilapidated door to obscure the fire, as much as possible, from anyone who might be lurking in the shadows of the woods. They would let the inside fire burn for an hour, and then they would sweep it out and douse it with the snow. The old stones of the building would then emit their warmth throughout the night as the three friends slept like buns in an old stone oven. At least, that was the theory.

Lang and Natasha watched as Peter filled one of the pots with snow to melt for boiling, and in the other, he placed some food from the backpacks to warm. He watched diligently over both pots and continued to add snow to the water pan as it melted down. Lang noticed that it took a lot of snow to create an appreciable amount of water. Once that pan was full and boiling, he placed two ripped cloths from his pack into the water and let them boil for several minutes, and while they boiled, he examined Lang's wound.

"It looks like you were hit with a .22 or a .38. Something small. There is no bullet in the wound, and it's still bleeding, but not too profusely. As the bullet passed through, it ripped the skin and flesh, but it doesn't look like it pierced the muscle too deeply." He was silent for a moment as he worked, then he turned to Natasha, who seemed to be terribly worried and afraid. "No arteries were hit, and the bleeding is steady, but not heavy. More of a seepage than a flow." She nodded her head but kept her hand covering her mouth, as if she might need it there to stifle a cry or sob. "Natasha, dear, could you bring me that bottle of vodka from my pack?"

"Sure," she replied and hustled off to get it, happy again to be of some use. She made a point as she went through the pack to catalog in her mind all of the things she was seeing. She wanted to be able to do this if ever the situation, God forbid, were to arise again.

Returning with the clear bottle of alcohol, she asked, "Are you going to sterilize the wound with it, or give it to him as an anesthetic?"

"Neither, Natasha," he said as he twisted open the bottle and chugged a significant amount. He wiped his mouth with his sleeve, smiled, and then took another long swig before twisting the top back onto the bottle. "I'd give him some as an anesthetic if I were doing major surgery or amputating the limb, just to get him to lie as still as possible, but we're trying to get the bleeding stopped, and alcohol can thin the blood, making it harder to accomplish that. The vodka was for me, to steady my hands and give me strength, because Lang," he said, now looking Lang straight in the eye but with an encouraging smile on his face, "this is going to hurt you *way* more than it's going to hurt me."

Peter extracted one of the cloths from the water with the knife from Lang's pack, and, when it had cooled only a little, he balled up the cloth and applied heavy and direct pressure with the sterilized rag on the wound for five full minutes. This was a bigger chore than one might think, and Lang grimaced from the pain but found the pressure to be soothing in a way that seemed contradictory to him.

After the five minutes was up, Peter released the pressure and gave the wound another five minutes to seep a little so that he didn't rob the whole arm of necessary blood and oxygen. He then reapplied the pressure with the second rag and returned the first one to the boiling water. The five minutes of pressure seemed like a short time to Natasha, but on the spot and under stress, it seemed like a lifetime to Peter and Lang. She was surprised when Peter removed the pressure this time, and the bleeding had slowed to just a faint trickle.

Natasha viewed the whole scene with amazement, and she was impressed with both Peter's skill, and Lang's bravery and calm during the procedure. She watched as the older man went through his pack, pulled out the first aid kit, and withdrew some tweezers and a scalpel and scissors. He sterilized the medical tools from the first aid kit in the boiling water, and when he was ready, he turned to Natasha and said, "Lang did well with the last step, daughter, but we'll see how *manly* he is now!"

Lang grimaced at that, turned the wince into a weak smile, then closed his eyes, and rolled his head back until the back of it pressed against the stone building.

Peter had Natasha hold the flashlight from Lang's bag, and then he carefully and cautiously removed the dead skin and dying flesh with the scalpel and scissors until he was reasonably certain that the wound was clean and ready to bind up. He then packed the wound with sterile gauze bandages, wrapped it loosely with more gauze from a roll, and then secured it all with medical tape. "You want to keep it fairly loose," he said. "We definitely don't want to cut off the blood supply. A wound needs oxygen, blood flow, and as sterile an environment as possible without infection in order to heal."

"Shouldn't we sew it closed or cauterize it?" Natasha asked.

"No. That's almost never a good idea when in the field, at least in my limited and unprofessional opinion. I would only cauterize it if we were on the run and either Lang, or the limb, was probably not going to make it otherwise. That process is really only for sealing veins or arteries when you don't have time to actually work carefully on the wound. And when you sew it closed, you sew in infection and any dead tissue that we probably missed. Since it doesn't have a way to exit, the wound can then get infected. Better to leave it open and let the body heal itself. There'll probably be fluid and pus discharge, and we want that. That's the body's way of cleansing and healing the wound. We'll just keep an eye on it and change the dressing when we can. And listen,

Natasha," Peter saw her trying to catalogue all the steps in her mind, and wanted to help her understand, "there are as many opinions about ditch medical care as there are people who have to do it. Always keep your eyes and ears open. Learn and listen. I'm not a doctor or even a paramedic. I've had a few lessons through the years, and I'm just doing what I know. You can always learn to do things better."

Natasha nodded her head. "What about antibiotics?" she asked.

"Uncle Lev had some Cephalexin and Doxycycline in that first aid kit. Grab the Cephalexin and bring me the equivalent of 500 milligrams. If they are 250 milligram pills, then bring me two."

"They are 500 milligram capsules, Peter," Natasha said, bringing the whole bottle to him.

"Just give me one then. We'll give him two a day for a week and hopefully that will knock out any infection."

Peter gave the pill to Lang with some water from a water bottle to wash it down. "That's one of the good things about Warwick—" he paused, not really wanting to say anything good about the town. "Anyway, that was *one* good thing. We didn't have to have prescriptions from a doctor to get first aid medications that are non-addictive. In America, they have to outlaw anyone treating themselves because the medical system and pharmaceutical businesses *were* a lynchpin in the whole economic system. That little bit of corruption was just another finger in the dike of western civilization. The socialists looked at the system and said, 'See! We're keeping the economy afloat!' but look around now and see what their logic has given us. You can float a house on a balloon, but it will pop, and when it does... ahhh, such is the ruin of that house!"

Peter looked at them, to see if they were following his argument. Both of his younger companions seemed more concerned about Lang's pain and discomfort than his argument. They were unaware that he was trying, precisely, to draw their minds *away* from the injury by diverting their attention elsewhere. "Ahh, children," he smiled. "I didn't tell you I was also a Doctor of Philosophy, did I?" He looked at them and pulled a long face, clowning like a parent does with a child who has scraped a knee, until the two youths finally gave in to his merrymaking.

Lang, who had been stoic and brave throughout his treatment, was the first to smile, even though the process of removing the dead and damaged flesh was to the very limit of what he thought he could handle. He thought about what it would be like to be in one of the gulags during a Siberian winter. It's strange what the mind locks onto in such moments. He looked at Peter and told him with his eyes that this experience had not been bad at all.

When Peter was done, Lang thanked him for the work. Peter looked at him and said, "Tonight is probably going to be tough for you, little son. You probably won't sleep because the wound will swell a lot and throb. The shock of the run and the adrenaline from your close escape will wear off, and then the pain will set in. Tomorrow it will hurt a lot, but less so than tonight. If, by tomorrow night, the bleeding has stopped and it looks like healing has begun," he paused, and winked, "I'll get you loaded on the vodka so you can have some relief from the pain and get some sleep."

"Well, I don't think I'll need that!" Lang said, laughing.

"That's what you say now. But tomorrow will be a different story. And if not, then... more for me." With that, Peter took another swig from the bottle before stowing it away in his bag.

CHAPTER 22

When she awoke in the morning, Veronica D'Arcy sat bolt upright from her sleeping bag on the hard, flat floor and felt around in the dark for her son.

"Stephen!"

Her voice echoed through the smallish chamber and disappeared into a darkened door leading down a narrow concrete corridor. She peered into the darkness, feeling her son's empty sleeping bag beside her, and called out again, this time with rising emphasis.

"Boy?!"

"Mom?"

The answer came back, a little muffled, from deep in the dark. As Veronica's eyes came into focus, she saw the faint light of a candle playing in shadows at the end of the small, cramped passageway, and that light suddenly turned the corner, throwing a dull orange glow on the walls of either side of the hallway as her son stepped out into the corridor. She saw the glow of the candle illuminate her son's face, his hands leaning the candle forward slightly so the wax would drip on the floor. The flame wicked up in sharp little whiskers, and she could see his wide smile in its effulgence. She watched as he proceeded toward her down the hall and into the chamber. She let her breath out in one long sigh, then remembered where they were and how they'd arrived there.

"Mom? Did you know that there are boxes of stored food back there, and water? There's even a box of contamination gear. And some bikes! There are probably ten or so. I thought you told me this place was abandoned."

"It is. This was a nuclear bunker once upon a time, boy. It was discovered years ago, but that stuff should have been taken out. It's got to be fifty years old by now."

"No. That's what I'm telling you... It's dated 2011. Those boxes are new."

Veronica looked at him, to see if he was pulling her leg. He was a sweet boy, but he had his father's penchant for practical jokes. She looked into his eyes to see if this was one of them. They were the eyes of her John—strong and sparkling—always with a little mirth, but now they just looked hurt, disappointed that she would doubt him. In this moment of all moments, he wanted her to know that he understood the gravity of their situation and why they had dropped everything when the lights went out; why they had fled through the city to this bunker and slipped in under the cover of darkness. He did not, of course, *fully* understand. But he wanted her to know that he was trying.

"Mom, I'm telling you, this place has been prepared for something *now*. There are supplies back there that someone just brought in. It looks like someone means to use this place."

Veronica reached in her bag and felt for her flashlight. It wasn't that she didn't trust her son, but she was interested to see for herself. If someone had prepared the place, that meant that they might be on the way, and that fact could change her plan, even as she'd made that plan up on the fly. As she searched her bag, she gently checked her pistol, running her finger over the safety to make sure that she had firmly locked it in place.

"Well, let's have a look then, Stephen," she said, getting up creakily from the floor, her joints aching slightly from sleeping on the cold, hard concrete through the night. She switched on the flashlight and Stephen led her down the hall, the mix of candlelight and flashbulb throwing varying shadows on the walls as they bent over and crept down the hallway to the end of the corridor.

They entered a small stone storeroom and Veronica was amazed to find it exactly as Stephen had described it. There were boxes of recently stored food and water, ammunition, nuclear fallout gear, bicycles, and some medical kits, along with a couple of lead-lined containers with batteries and walkie-talkies. The find both thrilled and alarmed Veronica, as it presented a tempting cache of items they could use for their survival, but also suggested that they might not be alone for very long. She would have to make a decision. Should they hunker down and hope for the best, or should they grab what they could and make a run for it? Where would they go? What would happen if they left too soon, or too late? These were the questions that swirled through her mind and mixed with the need to tell Stephen, who was smiling and eager beside her, something—anything—to let him know what she suspected might be coming.

"Okay, boy, now we have to think about what we will do."
She looked at the beautiful face that, for the last several years, had
slowly been approaching the height of her own, perched upon an
awkward teenaged body filling out with sinewy muscularity. She
took his face in her hands and kissed his forehead. "We have to
decide in the face of uncertainty what we are going to do so we can
face this world down... wash our feet before we get in de dance."
Stephen's face looked back, not comprehending, but ready to
follow where she led. Then he smiled.

"Cool, mom. But first, can we have a little breakfast?"

Veronica laughed at her son's bright humor. *There's that
playfulness, even in the face of this calamity,* she thought. She
pulled a small box marked "Energy Bars" off the top of the pile,
and pulled out a small penknife from her pocket and opened the
tape. They'd just begun to sift through the box and catalogue its
contents when they heard a scuffling down the hall.

At first, it sounded like the sound of their hands in the box,
crinkling and sifting, echoing across the concrete. Veronica even
thought that it *was* their hands for a moment, so she grabbed
Stephen's in hers and forced them to be still for a moment so she
could listen closely. There. It was distinct now. There was a
shuffling of boots across concrete, the noise muffled by the thick
steel doors. There was the sound of an argument, bodies pushing
and pulling against each other, and then, as certainly the sound
began, it ended.

They stood in silence. Veronica wished she'd taken her gun
from her bag and placed it in her waistband. She turned to go back
to the front of the bunker and retrieve it when she heard a barbaric
yawp, a bloodcurdling cry from outside the entryway, and what
sounded like several bodies came crashing against the outside of
the door.

Someone was trying to get in.

* * * *

Saturday

Despite what Peter told him, Lang fell asleep easily, passing out from sheer mental and physical exhaustion. He slept through the night, even though the ground made his sleep restless and unsatisfying. The building was warmer than he had supposed it would be, and, for most of the night, the warmth from the earlier fire radiated from the stone floor and walls, and he appreciated that warmth. He even dreamed... in a fit of restless half-waking as the morning neared.

When he was fully awake, he realized that Peter had not come to bed, but had stood watch all through the night. Lang noted that the older man was doing everything he could possibly do to keep him and Natasha safe. He wondered whether, in Peter's mind, because he'd been denied the presence and care of a real family of his own for most of his adult life, he'd adopted the two Warwickian youth as his children. He had now called Natasha "daughter" once and Lang "son" twice. He'd called them his "children." This had happened naturally, but with a hint of reserve, as though Peter hadn't thought about it when he'd done it, but didn't want it to be commented upon now that it was done. This didn't bother Lang at all.

It was evident that Peter had embraced their situation, and Lang noticed how the older man now seemed comfortable in his skin, as though his natural skills and human feelings at last had an outlet. After the initial blunt and angry outburst while they were looking out at the wreckage of Warwick from that hill in the distance, Peter had settled into this newfound father figure role admirably. He'd treated both Lang and Natasha tenderly, and he seemed to relish the responsibility he felt for both of them. This gave Lang a twinge of emotion he had not expected to feel toward the man, as he came to feel something that echoed his own long lost sorrow at never having had a father.

When Peter came by to check on the two that morning, he didn't seem to be tired at all. He claimed to have fallen asleep for several hours leaning against a tree in the darkness, but both Natasha and Lang knew that this was not true. Peter had taken the gun and watched over them all night like a parent watches over his children when he feels they are in harm's way. Somehow, Lang thought, looking at Natasha and seeing that she shared the sentiment without having to speak it, they had to find a way to get Peter some sleep.

Together they built another fire in the building, and again Peter filled the two holes with hot coals. This time he boiled water in both pans and then he went through the process of checking and re-dressing Lang's wound. When he pulled the gauze out of the wound, Lang yelled out, and Peter calmed him and told him that the pain was a good sign. He gave Lang a small piece of leather, the sheath of the knife that Clay had once gotten from Veronica, to bite down on.

"That means the wound is healing and the gauze has dried into the wound," Peter said. "Even though it hurts, ripping the wound open is actually good for it."

Lang bit down and looked at Peter through bleary eyes. The older man spread his hands as if to indicate that he could not quite explain exactly *how* it was good, but Lang would just have to trust him. Lang leaned his head back against the now cold stone and blinked that he did.

After Peter was finished caring for the bullet wound, they boiled enough water to fill all of their water bottles, and Peter said that this was the best they could do in the moment as far as water purification.

"Does boiling the water guarantee that the water will be pure and free from any dangerous bacteria?" Natasha had asked.

"Nothing ever guarantees anything," was all Peter had said to that.

After packing up their gear, by around 8 a.m., they were ready to continue their walk. Checking the map and the compass, Peter plotted a course for them, and they set out through the snow, feeling the weight and mileage in their legs from the previous day's trek.

They continued their southwesterly advance, and they were surprised and pleased to discover that, for most of the day, they moved through empty forestland and not suburban tracts or areas thick with farms and their fences. They made good time, and kept up their cautious movement, advancing steadily until the day began to morph into evening.

* * * *

As the darkness began to fall, they saw from a low hill a space in the distance where the forest seemed to end, and they noticed the long black shadows of some type of structures that rose above the trees. They couldn't quite make them out at first, but in a moment they could see them, distinct in their regularly placed intervals and structurally different from the chaotic mass of limbs and branches reaching like tentacles into the nighttime sky. In the gloaming they looked like dinosaurs against the darkening heavens, sitting up on a ridge where their skeletons towered over the valley.

As they grew closer, the structures disappeared into the mishmash of branches and darkness immediately over their heads, and they began to hear the now familiar sounds of people and gunfire, first in the distance, and eventually in the foreground. They slowed their approach and wove through the trees, staying hidden among the trunks and the brush until they eventually stepped to the edge of a clearing and saw spread out before them what looked, for everything in the world, like a battlefield.

The clearing was now deserted. However, this desertion had only happened recently, because the fires of a large encampment—one that would have served a large group of families—were spread here and there throughout the long, clear-cut strip, and the fires still burned.

As they surveyed the damage and looked around for any signs of movement they heard a crackling overhead and one of the wooden dinosaur looking structures, burning at its base from a fire set near a group of tents around the foundation, came suddenly to groan and creak and then to give way. It crashed to the ground in a huge, roaring din, its tail, connecting it to the other structures, tightening from the weight of the fallen beast before the tension was too much. The fall of the dinosaur and the tension in its tail caused it to snap and whip back upwards, sending a high-pitched ricochet through the valley that made the hikers flinch and step back as the noise whistled down the valley.

* * * *

The trees and forest ended abruptly in a straight, ruled line and there was a long clearing, and when the three travelers examined the scene they noted that the strip was actually a long beltway that ran from northwest to southeast. Down this long, cleared strip ran power lines, held aloft by enormous wooden towers. The streak of land cut through the forest like a landing strip, and the scene looked, if they hadn't known better, as if planes had merely skimmed in low to the ground and strafed the dozens of encampments along the strip with gunfire. Obviously, the refugees had been using the stretch of clearing as a highway to move from wherever they were to wherever they were going, and, not unlike Highway 17, which was still clear in their minds, this well-traveled route of escape had become a death trap for those who had thought to take the easy way out. In fact, if anything, this strip was the worse for having had one day more for the crowds to indulge in their mayhem.

Peter made sure the trio stayed low, and they moved quickly and with purpose, and they kept their eyes peeled to their surroundings as they surveyed the remains of the battle that had taken place, seemingly just moments before, in the field.

From the destruction, debris, and corpses lying around in the snow, Peter determined that this had been a makeshift refugee camp. He deduced that maybe thirty families had been staying in the clearing until only moments ago. The battle was not long in the past—perhaps an hour or so—but not longer.

The older man knelt down, and his eyes took in the gruesome scene. He looked out into the woods to the south, and he pointed so that Lang and Natasha could follow what he was about to say.

"It looks like they came from that way, through the woods. Some kind of looter raiding party. A gang of thugs, or... maybe they were middle-class teachers, grocers, and lawyers? Who's to know? I'd say it was ten or twelve of them. The attackers came out from the woods. It was not long ago, this very evening, because the fires were burning. We heard that noise earlier. It's likely that the refugees had no night vision from staring into the fire. Some of the tents and supplies spilled over into the fires in the confusion. The raiding party probably staked out the place from those trees." He pointed back to the south, along a thicket of brush.

"They waited until they felt it was the right time, and then they hit hard and fast. It looks like about two-thirds of the people in this camp didn't even stand a chance, cut down before they could stand up and figure out what was going on. No chance at all to get to any kind of cover." Peter turned and swiveled on his heels as if he were watching the attack in real-time as it played out before him.

"The looters took what they wanted, then they went that way." He pointed to the northwest, following with his finger up the greenbelt.

Peter didn't want to spend too much time in the refugee camp, but he felt it prudent to do a quick and cursory search for supplies and weapons, anything the looters had missed. They moved quickly. Wrapped up inside a fallen tent, they found a .22 Marlin squirrel rifle and about ten boxes of ammunition. Lang was the first to find it, and he silently held it up for Peter to appreciate.

Natasha protested at first, when Peter and Lang took the rifle and packed away the ammunition in Lang's backpack, but Peter explained to her that the people who owned this stuff... they were all gone. And the gun, if left here, would be taken by someone else coming by, either by good people with benevolent intentions, or by wicked people with evil intentions. "The only way that we can ensure that it falls into the right hands," he spread his own hands, as if the answer were obvious, "is to take it ourselves. Use it for right purposes."

Despite the clear logic in that argument, Natasha felt conflicted. "You need to know right now," Peter told her, in a firm way, but with concern and kindness, "that much of what we're going to need to survive is going to be found and salvaged from this point forward. We don't have the luxury of hunting down the next of kin, or taking found goods to the sheriff's office or authorities. There are no stores or businesses now, not from what we've already experienced. From what you've seen with your own eyes, Natasha, *there aren't any authorities.*"

Natasha nodded her head, and Peter told her he was glad she understood and that he hoped that she would have the stomach for everything that was ahead of them. "Even if you don't, however, you have to be honest about what we're facing. This is not a movie at the Pushkinsky-Cine, little daughter. This is our *life* now."

She nodded again, and told him that she knew what was required, but that she just didn't want to lose her humanity.

"I am helping you to *save* that humanity, dear girl," Peter said. He let that sink in for a beat. "We are not in the land of the living anymore."

Peter frowned and she grimaced. Lang bent to pick up his pack. The three of them stood in the clearing for a moment, and the ancient differences between men and women swirled around them as they weighed their thoughts. Unlike the couple from the day before, they silently agreed to let those differences help them rather than tear them apart, and eventually the three of them turned to trudge back toward the tree line, to make their way out of the clearing.

Just as they were turning to take their leave, however, Natasha told them to stop. The men almost responded in anger. Peter drew in his breath to rebuke Natasha and tell her to get past her doubts. He looked at her as if to warn her that they had to get moving and was just about to speak in his impatience.

It was only then that he heard what she was hearing. Natasha raised her hand as if to quiet him, and he held his breath and his eyes followed in the direction of her pointing.

A moan came from one of the collapsed tents. They rushed to it and lifted its canvas and dug into its crevices to find the door. Once they had found it, they gently lifted the tent away until they found her.

She was beaten and bruised, and terribly afraid, but she was alive. She was still in the land of the living.

CHAPTER 23

Dostoevsky said that "the best definition of man is: a being that goes on two legs and is ungrateful."

Lang could not help feeling that this was true of himself at that instant, as he realized that the woman in the tent was alive and that her injury was minor and survivable. He did not mean to think of rushing away and abandoning her. Such an act certainly would never have occurred to his conscious mind willingly, but it occurred nonetheless. Somewhere in his unconscious mind, his reckoning of the stench of death and fire in the clearing mixed with his guilt at the thought of leaving, his conscience burned brightly like the flames of perdition. He smelled it like charred goose feathers in his nostrils, and he melted in those flames. Had he so soon forgotten his own relatively recent deliverance from bondage? From injury? Was he that ungrateful? He considered himself a man of human compassion and was he so soon to be devoid of that feeling? His face flushed.

Lang had never really read the Bible much, but he was aware of many of its teachings, and one of the ones he liked most was the notion that a man could show no greater love than to lay down his life for others. He caught himself in his quick brush with self-centeredness and reached down a hand to help the woman off the ground. Maybe only a man who is aware of his weaknesses and failings can properly love in that way.

* * * *

Elsie was her name and she was barely conscious. It took some doing to carry her into the woods and into some similitude of safety. Lang had a wounded arm, and they dared not drop their packs or weapons, so the going was slow, but they eventually accomplished the task. Once they were in cover among the trees, Peter went to work again with the first aid kit. Before long, he had her forehead wound cleaned up without too much trouble. It was harder to get her to take the two aspirin that Peter gave her for her headache than it had been to carry her into the woods. She didn't want the pills, but it helped Peter that the woman was in shock and that she didn't put up too much of a fight.

Before long, and with some water and attention, Elsie was able to give her name and ask where she was. Slowly, she began to piece together her new reality. Peter noticed right away that this lady was made of stern stuff.

Elsie knew that her husband was dead. She'd seen as much before she lost consciousness. Even though she'd been struck in the head with a rifle butt at the onset of the attack, she didn't lose consciousness immediately, she told them. Her husband, before being shot to death, and in the midst of the confusion from the raid, was able to hide his injured wife in their tent. She was peeking through the tent flap with her hand over her own mouth to stifle her cries and her overwhelming need to scream, and she'd started to lose consciousness when she saw one of the men shoot her husband in the head. That's when she passed out. Now, here she was awake, only to find out that her nightmare was very real.

As she told her story, Natasha sat down beside the woman and placed an arm around her waist. She could tell that Elsie wasn't sure what the intentions of these three people were, and she wanted the woman to know that she was in good company now. With the telling of her story done, through sobs and tears, Elsie collapsed into Natasha's arms and the men fell silent with nothing to say that might even begin to help.

Peter and Lang had their guns at the ready, torn between allowing this woman space to grieve for a short moment, and the need to get moving before more trouble came through the woods or up the greenbelt.

Elsie's sobs faded, and now she seemed to draw strength from somewhere unknown. She placed hands on her knees and tried to push herself up, falling woozily back into Natasha's arms as Peter reached out to lend a hand.

"We have to bury my husband."

Lang and Peter exhaled in unison, and Peter's jaw tightened as he drew in another breath. He consciously scanned the horizon in every direction for the trouble that he knew was surely coming. The two men stepped to the side to confer, leaving Natasha to comfort Elsie.

Peter and Lang stared into one another's eyes for a moment, recognizing the difficulty of the situation. Neither man said a word for one, two, three seconds... then Lang's eyes softened. He shrugged and nodded, and Peter's jaw tightened again, but this time the older man closed his eyes and nodded his head in agreement.

"Ma'am," Peter said as gently as he could manage, kneeling down in front of her so his voice would be soft and low. "I am sorry about your husband. I know that doesn't help you, hearing me say that, but it's the truth. The three of us have lost more friends in the past couple of days than you can possibly imagine. None of us is immune to loss... but," he paused and searched for the best words to say what he had to say, "there are some things... I need..." He paused again and took a deep breath.

"Ma'am, we're in the middle of cataclysmic meltdown. The whole country and, really, the whole world as far as we know – it's never going to be the same. I can't explain entirely, but let's just say that I have an uncle, he was a friend to all of us. His name was Lev. He was... well... let's say that he was a highly-placed official. He wasn't really, but that'll help you believe what I have to say. Lev told us that there are probably going to be 300 million people dead or dying in the next year, and... well... frankly..." he hesitated for a moment, looking at her to see if she was willing to believe him, "...we can't bury 300 million people.

"All of them are real people, and they all have loved ones, but we just can't do it. Nobody can."

Elsie looked into Peter's eyes without anger or hatred or even confusion. He saw that she believed him, even with his roundabout way of telling her the truth. But then something else flashed in her eyes.

"I'm not asking you to bury 300 million people," she said. "I'm merely asking you to bury my husband."

* * * *

The attempted burial was difficult to an extreme. The hard ground, frozen solid in the north in winter, meant that in the old days, bodies were simply placed in a back, unheated room to wait for spring. Burials happened after the thaw when the ground softened and shovels could break it more easily. However, you try telling that to a woman who just saw her husband murdered before her eyes. Tell her that you can't bury the body because the ground is frozen.

Peter looked into her eyes and determined that she was an intelligent woman, and reason would return to her in good time. Nevertheless, for right now, Elsie needed a token that would let her turn her back on her dead husband and walk toward the rest of her life. She needed to have closure, and so Peter needed to find some way to bury the man that would give her that token... but it needed to happen quickly, and they had nothing even approximating the proper tools.

Peter had a mini camp shovel in his pack, and Lang had the knife and a stick. They quickly located and dragged Elsie's husband into the woods. She'd pointed out the area where he had gone down and described what he was wearing, and they had rushed quickly out into the clearing to retrieve him; so quickly in fact, that they had pulled off his shoes while they were dragging him.

Glenn was his name. Peter seemed to be intent on noting that as they collected his body. Lang just noted aloud that he was tired of digging graves.

They set themselves to digging. They couldn't go very deep. To do so would just be impossible with the tools at hand. They scratched down a few inches under the snow, and when they could go no further, when all of their efforts resulted in nothing at all, they dragged Glenn's body into the indentation and searched around for twenty minutes to find enough rocks so that they could pile them on the body. They ended up with an above ground burial. The rocks would serve—as much as possible—to keep the animals away from the corpse. Elsie would just have to understand, because, well, it was winter and the ground was now frozen. They had no tools. What else can you say?

They gathered around the grave with Elsie, and no one said anything. What do you say in such moments, standing at a stranger's grave with a woman you don't know who has just lost her husband? Peter thought of his wife and children. Lang thought of his town and felt the pain shooting through his arm. Natasha thought about her brother.

After a few minutes, Elsie just nodded and walked away. Peter and Lang once again caught one another's eyes as they turned their backs on Glenn and the specter of needless, wanton death. Natasha lingered for just a moment and looked into the night's sky.

She saw in a patch of blue-black darkness a line of geese flying overhead through the stillness. She would have sworn that the geese's *Ya-honk* was an accusation, but for the life of her, at that moment, she could not have explained just why.

* * * *

They picked up their trek to the southwest, and Natasha walked along near Elsie, asking her questions as they passed through the snow. Elsie stayed behind Natasha, and the men were on each flank, stationed ten yards to each side of the women. When the way narrowed, Peter would go first, Lang would bring up the rear, and they had learned to be more diligent and aware, as they were a larger group now and it was more likely that someone might spot them from a distance. Twice they properly spied out other travelers and were able to hunker down and wait in cover until the walkers passed by. On one of those occasions, five men carrying guns walked through in single file and at close ranks, oblivious to their surroundings, within yards of our four travelers who silently hid in the brush—Peter and Lang with their own guns at the ready.

Back on the march, they occasionally talked to one another, but only barely above a whisper, while their eyes still scanned the surroundings.

"We were married for 24 years," Elsie told Natasha. "I can't say it was perfect, but what marriage is? It was better than anyone else's that we knew, for most of those years, anyway. I loved Glenn, and I know that he loved me and our children." Her voice trailed off as she thought about her children. They walked on in silence a few steps, then she continued.

"Two girls and a boy... two women and a man now... they've all moved away. We were all raised to believe that children leaving and going out into the world is the way it's supposed to be, you know? I don't believe that anymore, but that's the way it was and we didn't know any better. Anyway, they went to college first, and then to distant jobs. The two girls are in New York City, and our boy, Glenn, Jr., he's in Idaho. Boise, we think." Natasha looked at her, as if to ask the question, and Elsie answered before she could. "We don't get to talk to him much. He was *different*."

"What do you mean 'different'?" Natasha asked.

"He talked about all this... *stuff*," Elsie said, indicating all around them with her hand. "You know, the stuff that's going on right now. He was a survival nut. I guess you'd call him that. We called him that anyway. You know, in trying to reason with him. But he wouldn't be reasoned with. He was always going on about something. Anti-government is what I thought, though he always denied it. He was always predicting the end of the world, even though he denied that too. I guess, thinking back on it now, I heard what I wanted to hear - anything that would allow me to reject the things he *actually* said. What he did say was that some bad things were going to happen, and that we should change our lifestyles and be more preparedness minded. I didn't understand it all, but... well..." She let the implications of that hang in the air, still unwilling, entirely, to believe it.

"I'm sorry that you didn't get along," Natasha said.

"We just took everything he said as a rejection of us *personally*, as people, as parents, as Americans, whatever. When someone tells you that your way of living is unsustainable or foolish, it makes you mad as hell, you know? Not in a way that is measurable though, it's more like a burning in you that really gets to you. It makes you want to lash out and defend yourself, your worldview... your... I don't know how to say it. Anyway, I know now. I figured this out when I watched your men here bury Glenn. All that anger I felt was not at anything Glenn Jr. ever said. I was angry that what he said made my conscience burn."

Elsie was quiet awhile, thinking as she walked along, and Natasha did not interrupt her thoughts.

"The things I said about my own son, the things I did behind his back, well, they were shameful. I wanted to have a relationship with him, but it was like having this accuser around, looking me in the eye all the time. Even when Junior wasn't around, I felt him accusing me."

Natasha walked, and listened. She reached her hand out to steady Elsie as she became aware that the older woman was breathing hard.

"I mean, he wouldn't do it directly... not directly. He just said these *things*. And he believed them. I mean, he'd let other people take them or leave them, but he was so damned sure of himself. He never said, 'you are a bad person' or 'you shouldn't do this or that,' or anything like that. But when he talked about the world and the problems in it, then I felt like he was talking about *me*. I took that personally, wouldn't you? I felt it was a personal attack.

"Of course I know that it was not meant to be personal. I mean, I know that now. I'm his mother, for goodness sake. But it hurt our relationship. Things were always tense. Truth be told, I guess I got somewhat personal myself on occasion. I would have preferred that he had fallen into line, tossed out his beliefs and just embraced what all the rest of us believed. That was wrong of me. I see that. And it would have been wrong even if it had turned out that he was wrong and everyone else was right." Elsie's voice trailed off and her thoughts went elsewhere for a moment.

"I would give anything to have him here with us while we are going through all of this."

"Did you say he was in Boise?"

"Yes. He moved up there a few years ago. I hear that there are many survivalist-minded types up there. I called them worse things before all this happened, but I won't do that now. He tried to get us to come and check out his place, but we wouldn't do it. We thought he was crazy."

"Well, just because he was right about the world, doesn't mean he wasn't crazy!" Natasha said, trying to lighten Elsie's mood.

"He wasn't crazy," Elsie replied flatly.

* * * *

"We left Binghamton the day after the power went out. They told me it was an 'EMP', but I still don't really know what that means. The stores were soon out of food. It only took four hours and they were stripped bare. My son used to rail on about that. I remember it now because I hated hearing it.

"He would say, 'People are crazy if they really believe that the food in the system will last three days after a big enough collapse!' I just wanted him to shut up about it. But he was right. We went into some stores and there were fistfights over the stupidest things. On one aisle, the only things hanging on the wall were some of those gel soles things... you know... the gel-filled pads you cut and put into your shoes to make them more comfortable? Anyway, people were actually fighting over those. Actually fist-fighting over them. Violence! Over some stupid gel soles." Elsie shook her head and Natasha smiled, hearing the incredulity in the woman's humor.

"We just got out of there. All you were going to get in the stores was *killed*."

"That's almost unbelievable. I mean, if we hadn't already seen the things we've seen, I'd call you a liar." Natasha said.

"There's no lying about it. We had almost no food in the house. Not anything to speak of. We usually ate out before this happened." Elsie shook her head. "We made it a few days, but things were getting really thin, and we heard about gangs and looters going door to door. A couple down the street got shot to death right on their doorstep. That's when we decided we needed to get out."

"Where were you planning to go?"

"There was no real plan. Some of the neighbors got everyone on our block together—whoever would come—and we had a meeting and just decided to get out of the city. That's all we could think of at the time. Just get *out*. You know? Get a tent and get out into the country and just forage. It sounded easy. It wasn't. But I suppose you all have gone through the same things?"

"I guess you could say it was something like that," Natasha answered.

"One of the men on our street had a bunch of survival food, and a little hand-pump water purifier, so we figured we'd just walk into the woods until we found some place better than where we were. Isn't that the story of all refugees for all time?"

"I suppose it is."

"So tell me about you all. Who's who?"

Natasha thought for a moment, not knowing what she should say. "Our story is not unlike yours. We're from a town called Warwick."

"Oh, Warwick... I've heard of it," Elsie replied.

"My brother was with me," Natasha said quickly, hoping to cut off any questions in case Elsie knew someone in the other Warwick, or in case she might ask details that would not match up if cross-checked. "He left his glasses at one of our camps and went back for them. We haven't seen him since. I'm very worried."

"Oh, honey! I'm sorry. I'm so sorry. I'm sure he's okay."

"I don't know."

"You probably all should have stuck together, you know. But he'll catch up with you, I'm sure of it."

"I hope you're right," Natasha said, but she didn't believe for a moment that Elsie was right. After the experiences of the last few days, Natasha rejected the kind of Pollyanna thinking that was common to so many modern Americans. Peter had warned them to beware of it. This one thing was a tiny microcosm of what had caused the dependency, lethargy, and deception in the first place: the tendency to believe that everything would somehow work out okay.

Elsie smiled at her, trying to be comforting. "The sun will come out tomorrow, and he'll be here. You can bet your bottom dollar on that. He's probably just a day behind us. That's all," Elsie said.

This woman, Natasha thought, however good her motives might be, didn't have a single fact on which to base her assessment. She didn't know what had happened to Cole, and an honest judgment, based on the facts on the ground as they had all seen them, did not offer much hope for Cole at all. But discourse in America was about emotions and feelings, and never truth and facts. Natasha had to get used to this reality, because it was a tricky one that could trap you if you weren't careful.

People had the idea that if they were just *positive minded* then nothing bad could happen to them. Or, they thought that if they lied to themselves and one another, then the truth would be easier to swallow later on. Natasha was not going to fall for that, but she appreciated the heart behind the deception.

Herein she could see the clash of worldviews that had multiplied and expanded to bring about this catastrophe, and would continue to cause dissolution if it continued going forward. Beyond the wars and fighting and destruction, there would need to be a reassertion of the age-old desire for truth and honesty. The mind of reason would need to triumph over the long reign of emotionalism and lies. What was it that Lang was always saying? It was a Solzhenitsyn quote that he'd repeated several times since they'd fled Warwick...

"One word of truth shall outweigh the world."

Natasha hoped that somehow, from among the rubble, the truth, and a love of it, would one day rise, stand back up on its feet, and stare the world down again.

CHAPTER 24

Life can turn on a dime. Sometimes, things are going along as expected and then a vicious pirouette occurs. It's as if we are chasing a beast through the forest and we think we have it right where we want it, and then it turns. It pivots and bares its fangs. In a flash, tables are turned, momentum is lost, victors become vanquished, and lives are lost. In those moments, all we can do is hold on and watch the thing happen.

Sunday

The day was crisp and clean, and except for the snow that was still thick on the ground, it might have been spring. It was that bright and airy. The snow crunched under boots, and the reflection off the snow made the eyes of the four cautious hikers squint into the brightness. After a few hours of good, hard walking, Lang called to Peter and told him that he needed to take a pause. Nature, he explained, was calling. He needed to urinate.

Peter smiled, and in that smile, he let down his guard. He also let down his pack, and so did Natasha. The hikers came to rest on the side of a low mountain.

Moments like these can be critical. They can define ultimate success or failure. Perhaps this is unfair, but it is undeniable. These moments represent that one small turn of the screw, or that one nail left undone, that can bring the whole structure down. They are the gaps in eternal vigilance, when people are in moments of peril, and when they ought to remain in a heightened state of awareness – but instead, there is a beat of relaxing just a little too much, or a tendency to make false assumptions about the situation, or to discount the proximity of danger. It is in such moments that mistakes are made. It happens in war and in peace, and it often costs lives.

And it is easy for others to judge, when they've not lived through the same circumstances in real life. Often, those who have lived through them, will later harshly judge themselves. How many times have we read a book or watched a movie and we've said, 'I wouldn't have done thus and such,' as if perfection is something that is easily maintained when the entire world is plummeting into hell. Armchair quarterbacks always survive when they have the benefit of distance and, maybe temporary, safety.

Peter had already made a few mistakes, but he was not immune to making them again. Nobody is perfect; but imperfection, depending on the situation, can bring about a wide range of consequences – from the inconsiderable to the severe. Peter had only taken a moment, just a small little window, to relax and talk with his travel companions, utilizing Lang's break for a break of his own, but that was all that was required.

Lang walked into a nearby thicket to do his business. He looked into the sky and watched a hawk swoop by, and he felt the relief ease from his bladder. Done, he was beginning to zip his hiking pants when he heard the shouts. It was a loud, unfriendly commotion.

Spinning around, Lang left his pack in the bushes and cocked his body forward slightly, pulling his head down between his shoulders as he edged back toward the group. He stayed low along the tip of the thicket to remain out of sight for as long as possible. From a distance, he could see that three men—obviously hostile— were confronting his friends, and one of them had what looked to Lang like an AK-47 rifle pointed at Peter. The other men held long knives in front of them, pointing them at the women in a threatening manner.

The three hostiles were dressed like accountants, or maybe like frozen accountants who'd been lost in the woods for a good while. That detail was shocking to see. Almost unbelievable. Except for a lack of ties (one of which was tied around an arm of one of the men holding a knife, as if it were a tourniquet), the men looked as though they might have been executives out to lunch at an Applebee's who had together decided to hike into the forest and rob someone at gunpoint. They weren't dressed for the elements at all, but they had weapons. The incongruity was alarming. They were using the weapons to threaten, waving them like spreadsheets in a boardroom melee.

Lang approached from behind the men, and Peter saw him, and Lang saw that he saw, but the older man gave him no sign that he could interpret as an instruction, so the young man crept just a little bit closer. Almost imperceptibly, Peter indicated with a slight motion of the hand that he wanted Lang to *stop* just as the man with the AK-47, shivering with cold and fear, began shouting that he wanted Peter and Natasha to throw over their backpacks.

Lang stood still, unsure whether Peter wanted him to just stand quietly, or move to cover. In such moments, you have to decide one way or another. So Lang decided on the latter, and, as he moved toward a nearby tree, his foot snapped a fallen branch that lay buried under the snow. The crack of the wood alerted the three bandits to his presence, and instantly bodies moved into motion and events seemed to slow down for everyone involved.

The man with the AK-47 wheeled around to see who was behind him, and Peter, reacting with shocking speed and agility, crashed into the man and they tumbled over into the snow. Peter snapped the weapon from the man's hands with little trouble at all as Lang rushed to help. In that moment, the two knife-wielding bandits took advantage of the scuffle to snap up the two backpacks, and, before anyone could shout or protest, they had bounded awkwardly into the forest. They left without looking back for their colleague, sprinting into the woods, slipping and sliding on their flat leather dress shoes, winding in and out of the trees... and they made their escape.

Lang never even thought about giving chase. The man who had held the AK-47 jumped up to his feet. He looked at Peter with a murderous gleam in his eye and demanded that Peter give him his gun back. Demanded it. If it had happened more slowly, Peter would have stopped to laugh at him. Here was a thief that had, seconds before, been threatening to kill him over a couple of backpacks, and now he was brazenly demanding that the weapon used in his crime be returned to him, as if some cosmic injustice had occurred. The man's sense of entitlement was both shocking and bizarre – but it represented the thinking of his type of people. In that instant, the man realized that life, indeed, could turn on a dime.

Peter didn't have time to react with amazement. The man rushed at him, apparently in the expectation that Peter wouldn't know how to work the gun. In this estimation, he was wrong. Peter gracefully stepped backward a half step as the man flailed toward him, causing the charging man to miss him. Peter pivoted, just a small twist on his rear leg, and swung his body around so that the direction the barrel pointed was not towards Lang, or Natasha, or Elsie, but instead the gun was pointed off in the direction the two other men had run. When the attacker recovered from his missed lunge, he spun back around and rushed at Peter, again. And, as simply and effortlessly as one might drop a dime, Peter shot him point-blank in the chest.

The bullet hit the man in the center of his mass. The sound of the blast ricocheted off the snow, climbed up into the mountain, and spun around in the cool, crisp air. The man fell backward, into the snow, and he died. His sense of entitlement died with him.

* * * *

Peter didn't spend any time at all frozen in place, or grieving over what he'd done. He simply checked to make sure that Elsie, Natasha, and Lang were alright. He looked up for a moment, as if deciding if he should chase the other two bandits into the woods to retrieve the backpacks, but he decided against it. At his age and in his condition, he probably would not catch them, and he'd definitely leave his three friends in danger. If the bandits were working with anyone else, it would not be wise to split his group. In any event, the time lost wouldn't benefit anyone. The two packs were simply gone. He shook his head as if to apologize.

Peter quickly made a mental rundown of the situation. They'd gained a battle rifle, but at immense cost. He was not sure that he would have made that trade. He worried about the loss of medicines and food, but what was done was done. And they still had Lang's pack.

Lang's pack!

"Lang! Where is your backpack, son?"

"Oh! Uh... I left it in the trees when I heard the ruckus. I'll run back and get it."

"No. Wait, Lang," Peter said, firmly. "We'll go together."

Walking over to retrieve the pack, Peter checked the weapon, pulled out the clip and felt the heft so he could determine its capacity and estimate how many rounds were likely in it. His mind continued cataloging, prioritizing, and planning. Killing the bandit in self-defense was something he'd had to do, and this was not the time to fret over things that could not be undone.

With the pack retrieved, they walked back to the body of the dead accountant, and Peter knelt and began frisking the corpse. In his pockets, he found a cell phone (dead), car keys (useless), a pen (useful), and a tube of Chapstick (useful). Actually, he thought, the phone and the keys were useful for other things, too, so stuck them into the side pockets of his pants. As he did so, he made a mental note that the man had all of these things with him that were, for someone like him, now useless, but he did not have a lighter or a knife. *What kind of man doesn't carry the simple things that he should have with him at all times?* Peter shook his head. *But what kind of man lets such a man sneak up on him in broad daylight?*

The dead man had no wallet, or, at least he had no wallet on him. As he finished the quick frisk, Peter looked up at Lang when he noticed the wedding ring on the man's finger. *Gold.* He slipped it off with some difficulty, and, catching Elsie's wince, he looked at her without shame on his face. "This will pay for what his friends stole." He adopted a tone that was not angry or scolding, but was instructional and encouraging. He hoped that she was the kind of person who could take patient instruction.

"Sentimental notions like leaving gold on the ground while thieves run through the forest with our property, those have no place among us anymore. We certainly need to keep our humanity, but humanity has been accompanied with a large dosage of sentimental stupidity of late." He waved his hand as if in accusation at the world. "All *this*... this collapse... it is all a part of the result of that kind of madness. We didn't steal from this man. We didn't provoke him, or cause him to do evil things. He *made* me kill him. He would have kept coming at me until I did, which amplifies his guilt."

Peter studied her face to see how she was taking his words.

"We need to be able to replace our gear at some point, and we'll need to buy it from someone, since we will not use our guns to steal. This is merely recompense for the trouble he has caused us."

He looked around again at the faces of the others, scanning for understanding. All three of his friends nodded at him. He might have seen, though he probably did not, that they were even grateful. As they searched their hearts, they found a willingness to let the strongest among them carry not only the heaviest burden, but also the weightiest questions. Peter showed, by his demeanor, that he, too, was grateful. With a sideways smile he indicated that he realized that part of the reason they now found themselves in this predicament, having their food and medicine sprinting away from them in the hands of interlopers, was that he'd allowed himself a moment of all-too human frailty and had relaxed his watch. He tried to reassure them with his eyes that he felt his burden and accepted it, and that he would not let it happen again.

With that, the four turned on their heels, turned back up the mountain, and headed toward the southwest, continuing their climb.

* * * *

An hour after the incident, they stopped for rest and decided to eat some food. They only had Lang's backpack now, and Natasha carried it so that Peter could wield the rifle more easily. Lang's arm was beginning to hurt him, and Elsie was wheezing from the long, slow climb up the mountain.

Peter hiked out a few hundred feet into the woods and picked a good place to hide himself so that he could stand guard while the others rested and ate. The other three did not sit clumped together in a group despite the fact that Peter stood guard over them. They kept themselves spread out by several yards, just far enough apart so that they could still talk and interact while minimizing the likelihood that a sniper or attacker, should there be one out there somewhere, could get to them all at once. They opened up the bag and pulled out some foil packs of tuna, and Natasha went through the process of starting a small fire to warm them and to boil and purify more water.

After a half hour, Lang went and took the rifle and replaced Peter so that Peter could eat and rest awhile. Before the two men parted, Lang stopped Peter and indicated that they should both squat down so that they could maintain cover while they spoke. Lang winced a little when he knelt down, and Peter noticed it.

"How are you doing, Lang?"

"I'm alright. Just a little sore and tired." He wiped a sleeve across his face. "I'll make it."

"We're going to have to stop at some point and take a look at that wound."

"I know, but listen, that's not why I want to speak to you."

"Oh? Is something wrong?" Peter asked.

"Peter..." Lang started. He paused and thought for a second as he looked around, his head on a swivel, remaining vigilant even while they spoke. Peter did the same, but at this point, their eyes met. "Peter, I know you blame yourself for what happened back there – us falling into the hands of those bandits. I know you do—"

Peter tried to interrupt him, but Lang stopped him with a raised hand.

"Listen to me, Peter, and I'll say what I want to say. We need to keep this short. I don't expect a reply or an argument."

Lang was only eighteen, but he had matured more in the last few days than in all of the previous years of his life combined. Peter recognized this, nodded, and looked downwards for a second.

"I know you blame yourself for that, and, well, we *do* need to be more vigilant if we want to survive. I get all of that. Nevertheless, no man can keep us perfectly safe in this new world. No man. There are four of us, and in these woods, and now this country - there are simply too many people to expect we won't run across someone. Starving people, angry people, criminal people, lonely people," he paused again, giving his statement some weight. "The best team of Special Forces soldiers in the world couldn't guarantee that they won't stumble into a firefight or an ambush. No amount of being alert is going to guarantee that. Nor can anyone guarantee that we won't die out here. In fact, just the opposite is true. We will *all* die some time. We can't cover this team the way it should be covered, and we don't know the terrain. The hostile forces out there outnumber us by the millions. Let's not fall prey to this notion that just because we have guns and a little training there will be no mistakes, or that we can't be surprised and overwhelmed."

Peter looked up at him, nodding, but did not speak, so Lang continued.

"I just want you to know that none of us expects you to be God. You're not qualified for that job. We need to learn from our mistakes and get better, but only a fool would think that anyone could do much better than you've done. After all, and I mean this with the utmost in love and respect, Peter, but, after all, you are a middle-aged man who has been out of practice for a decade or more. And you're shepherding three people who have little more than desk training and theory. Natasha and I? Our training was in spy craft and deception, not in wilderness survival or unit defense tactics. So don't be too hard on yourself, okay?"

Peter looked at him and closed his eyes for a moment. He was very thankful to hear Lang's words, like a man given permission to be human, with all his frailties intact. He reached out, grabbed Lang's hand, and allowed the young man to lift him as he stood and shook out his creaky bones. "Okay, my son." He smiled into the eyes of his young friend. He lightly patted Lang on his good shoulder, then walked back toward the camp and left Lang to watch and guard.

* * * *

While he lay down to sleep for a short nap, Natasha and Elsie talked more about their situation, what they hoped to find if they succeeded in reaching Amish country, telling the small tales of life that had led them to this point, branching off into the wilderness of conversation as old friends might. Each of them encouraged the other to stay strong, to be more vigilant, and to persevere.

"Peter saved us yet again," Natasha whispered, smiling at the man sleeping huddled in the snow with his head propped up by a smooth rock.

"I get the feeling that he is very fond of you and Lang, and that he's glad to be able to protect you and to take care for you," Elsie replied.

"He's a good man," Natasha said. She looked on him fondly, and wondered how she'd never noticed his gentle side before.

"I see that."

"He's lost his family, and we're all he really has."

"Oh!" Elsie started, "were they—?"

"No. No. I'm sorry," Natasha said. "They left long ago. He hasn't seen them in twenty years."

"Divorce, then?"

"No. Oh... Listen... Elsie, I'm sorry," Natasha said, suddenly remembering that, even though they had already passed through a great deal together in a short time, it was not her place to share Peter's story if he didn't want it known. "I probably shouldn't be talking about him. I shouldn't have said anything. It's his business to tell you about himself as he sees fit. I just..." she stammered, embarrassed for having taken the conversation into more private concerns, "...I just wanted you to know that he is a very good man."

"I do know. I see that," Elsie said, smiling. "So, my dear, let's just leave it at that." She looked at Natasha and gave her the kind of loving smile that a mother gives a daughter. Natasha noticed it, and she was happy to have seen it.

Just as the two women finished their conversation, they heard the sharp crack of a small-caliber rifle being fired. Peter jumped to his feet, just in time to see Lang sauntering into camp swinging a white rabbit that he'd shot with the .22 Marlin. Without saying a word, Lang tossed the rabbit so that it landed within a few feet of the fire, and, keeping his head on a swivel and his eyes alive, he turned softly and walked back to his station to stand guard.

CHAPTER 25

Peter figured that they were within thirty minutes of reaching the outskirts of Carbondale when, while coming over a low-rising hill, they happened upon three men sitting around a fire. Peter saw them first, and the three men saw Peter's gun almost immediately.

Two of the men leapt up from the log they were sitting on and sprinted away as though they were acting out of pure instinct. The third, reacting more slowly, sat frozen in place for a moment. He watched the four hikers approach him, and he finally rose to his feet and began backing away while keeping his eyes on them. Peter lowered the weapon, raised up a hand and tried to indicate with his eyes and his actions that he meant no harm.

The man looked uncertain, as if he were about to run after his mates, when Lang said calmly, "Listen, sir, we mean you no harm. You can go peacefully, or call your friends and have them return to your fire. We're just traveling through. We didn't see you from further away, due to the hill, or we would have avoided you. We have no desire to hurt anyone. And we're not bandits. We're simply passing on."

"Umm..." the man sputtered, his eyes racing from point to point as his mind flipped through his options and the probabilities attached to each. "Yes. Well, okay then. I'll just... I'll just go get them. They won't have gone far. I'll be right back."

The man began to walk nervously away through the trees, almost as if he expected Peter to shoot him in the back at any moment. After a few seconds of this trepidation walking, he broke out into a run as though the anxiety was simply too much.

"Do you think he'll come back? Elsie asked.

"I don't know," Peter replied. He looked at Elsie, then at Natasha and Lang and shrugged his shoulders, as if to say, "This is what life is like now."

"What can you do?" Peter said. "Everyone is spooked. And they should be. These people seem harmless enough, but keep your eyes on them and watch their every movement. Watch how they interact with one another. Be looking for clues that perhaps they are not as harmless as they look."

Before long, the three men came walking back sheepishly through the woods. They did not look malevolent, but they were very nervous, like cattle, hungry but cautious.

Lang spoke first. "We apologize for interrupting you. As I am sure your friend here has told you, we're just traveling through. We mean no harm at all. We've seen our share of death and violence, and we understand your concerns. We've lost our homes, and we're traveling into Pennsylvania to meet up with some friends."

One of the men, the one who had been too slow to escape at first, shuffled his feet in the snow and then looked up at Peter, and then at Lang. He nodded his head to the two women with them, as if by way of formal greeting.

"Well, if you are traveling into Pennsylvania, you'll be glad to know that you've been there for some time. We came from Carbondale, just over that hill. You can see it from up-top there." He pointed along a ridgeline to the southwest and squinted into the sun.

Lang nodded at the man, thanking him. "We don't intend to go there—not into town—but if you have any news you'd be willing to share, we'd appreciate it. At some point we're going to have to find some supplies or—at the very least—some way to find out what's in front of us." He left a kind of open-ended invitation hanging in the air for the men to tell them anything they found to be appropriate.

"I'll tell you," the man said, with a bitterness that verged on anger barely disguised in his voice. His visceral passion was surprising to the four hikers. "You don't want to go anywhere *near* Carbondale. In fact, we're still too close to it for my own comfort." He looked sideways at his colleagues, and Peter judged that their proximity to the city had been a matter of some debate as they'd sat around their campfire. "And as for supplies, I think you're gonna be out of luck, man."

"What's going on in Carbondale?"

The three men exchanged looks that betrayed a shared experience, and in their looks, Peter saw what he could only call fear. The air between them dripped with anxiety and concern.

"The town's been taken over by the National Guard." One of the men snorted at the mention of that name. "*Supposedly*," the man said, making quotes around the word with his fingers, "they did it to help feed and shelter refugees pouring into the area from New York and the surrounding area. A couple of weeks ago, the town had about 9,000 people living in it. It was nice. We grew up there," the man said, making a little waving motion with his fingers, pointing back and forth between his mates. "Industrial town, but nice. Anyway, it was a little outlying suburb of Scranton. But..." the man's voice halted a bit, and he closed his eyes for a few seconds before he started talking again. "Scranton is gone. It's just *gone*. Burned to the ground. And now there are over 100,000 people in what can only be called an internment camp. A death camp. Something like out of the war." He didn't say which war, but, judging by their age, Peter guessed that he probably meant the one their grandfathers had likely fought in, the Second World War. "There are thousands more arriving by day and by night. It's a hellhole."

"What do you mean? How so?" Lang asked. He reached up and soothed his aching shoulder as he did, feeling the heat of the wound radiate along his arm.

Another man picked up the conversation and answered. There was anger in his voice as well. "The place has turned into nothing more than a prison camp. The National Guard unit running the place was up from Missouri to help in the emergency following Hurricane Sandy and the Nor'easter. They were working in New York, I believe. When all the power went out and the authority structure broke down—whatever that was that knocked out all the lights—they just took control. Rolled through here and began knocking people around. They supply the camp by doing raids in the surrounding area. They rob farms, loot whatever stores are left, kill people in their homes." The man relayed this information as though he himself couldn't quite believe it, emphasizing at the end of each phrase a kind of incredulity, as though there had been something sacred in the very mention of such places.

"It's hard to know how it all got started. People were standing around outside the main grocery in my neighborhood bumming cigarettes and sharing news, when these trucks just rolled into town. From a distance, we thought it was the power company. Hell, everybody cheered! But no one is cheering anymore."

One of his mates kicked a rock and looked off in the distance, over the ridge, toward the city. "Ain't that the truth," he muttered, under his breath, to no one in particular.

"There was a group of homesteaders... whaddya call'em? *Survivalists?* They lived in this little community back in the woods a bit. The Guard just wiped that place out. We saw that with our own eyes as we were hiking out this way. They came in and commandeered all the supplies, fuel, goods... even the people. In the first few days, they interrogated people, treating them like *prisoners.* They asked and prodded and even tortured people until they found out where these end of the world types were, you know, the people who had stored up food and supplies. Then the guardsman sent out the word that people who did that were *'hoarders.'* That's what they called them. Then they outlawed hoarding and announced the death penalty as a punishment. I'm telling you," the man shook his head, "I wouldn't have believed it if I hadn't seen it myself."

Peter took in what they said and didn't ask questions. He was calculating how to adjust the trajectory of their hike in relation to this news. One of the men, the first one who'd spoken, now chimed in again, pointing to Peter's weapon and the one Lang had slung over his good shoulder.

"Those guns. You better be careful with those. The Guard has been shooting on site anyone caught with guns and ammo. They don't even ask questions. They simply fire and then relieve you of your burden. And they have snipers posted at outposts all around the town." He nodded at Peter as he said this, as if to promise him that what he was saying was true. "They shoot first and ask questions later, buddy. And they rob and steal at will, and they are deadly efficient at it."

"Lord, have mercy on us!" Elsie said, almost involuntarily. Her gloved hand covered her mouth and her eyes betrayed her fear.

"Well, you better hope that the Lord does, because the people running Carbondale will not."

Lang scratched his chin. He, too, was considering this new information. He'd learned from Volkhov to dig deeper, and so he did. "And they *all* went along with it? The whole National Guard unit?"

"Oh, no," the second man replied. "That's just it. There was... there *is*... a battle going on over that very thing. That's one of the problems right now. It's hard to tell who's who. There was a large portion of the Missouri Guard unit that wouldn't go along with the plan, and they've kind of formed themselves into, I don't know... what would you call it?" He looked at his friends and they shrugged. "...A resistance unit?" His friends shrugged again. "They call themselves the FMA, the Free Missouri Army. Man," he said, shaking his head, "you can't make this stuff up. Only a few weeks ago I was buying milk on the way home for my wife, and now we have armies battling in our streets. A lot of former cops and ex-military – those are the ones that don't seem to be going along with the Guard's tyranny." He looked at one of his friends. "Well, dang it, it *is* tyranny," he said, obviously continuing some argument the two had been having. "You can call it *temporary measures* if you want, but it ain't temporary for those folks lying in the ground."

Turning his back to his friend, he continued. "Anyway... so, there is a group that has set themselves up as an alternative, and they do seem to be more reasonable. If nothing else, they have local folks involved. And this FMA is the only hope that a lot of rural people have around here not being forced into the camps. So right now, we're all in the middle of a little 'civil war', and it really just comes down to who you run into."

Peter sighed deeply and looked at Lang. The two men raised their eyebrows at each other, and each waited for the other to speak.

Peter spoke first, and he spoke to his group.

"I suppose we should head straight west. We'll have to find some way to cross Interstate 81, and that might be worse than Highway 17 was, but if we make it we can turn south. It'll be a longer walk that way, but we'll avoid a lot more trouble, and it seems to me like the farther we get away from Carbondale, the better."

Lang nodded his head, and then turned back to the three men.

"You said we can see Carbondale from the top of that hill? Is it safe to take a look?"

"Probably," one of the men said. "As I said, there are snipers here and there, or at least we have heard that there are. Hell, most of what we've just told you is hearsay, except for what we've seen with our own eyes, but what we did see was bad enough. So you prolly want to lie down and keep low and don't stay on the ridge very long."

"I'd like to check it out, if that's alright with you, Peter?"

"Yes. I think I'd like to see it too, but, you go ahead. I'll stay here with the ladies." He looked at the three men and smiled, before adding, "No offense of course."

"None taken."

* * * *

Lang walked up the hill, and as he walked, he noticed that the pain in his shoulder had increased. Perhaps it was the standing around. The constant walking gave him focus and took his mind off the pain, but the time spent standing and talking caused him to feel every movement of the wound. He could feel the ache throb through him like a knife. It pulsed with his heartbeat, and the pain spiked if he breathed too deeply.

As he reached the top of the hill, he dropped down on all fours in the snow and crawled the last bit until he crested the plateau. Looking down on the city, he inhaled sharply at the sight and felt the pain shoot through him, even down into his lower back.

Spread out before him was a landscape only seen, in our age, in the movies. There was an encampment consisting of thousands of large tents pooled in the middle of a low-slung valley. Sitting up on the hill was the highway that wound around a mountain and ran through the heart of what used to be Carbondale. The camp was bordered on all sides by trenches dug into the earth - scratched in, really - with razor-sharp wire strung along the borders and watchtowers being constructed at the four-corners by people being herded through their labors by men with guns. Along the outside of the fence, men and women were digging the trench deeper, and the occasional guardsman placed around the perimeter shouted orders to hasten the work.

The town was a direct likeness of a World War II era Nazi prison camp. There were tents stretching almost as far as the eye could see, and prisoners, most of them in clothes better meant for the city, were trudging through the gates and wandering aimlessly along the inner areas of the fence, as if they were plotting an escape, or hoping that the fences would hold fast against whatever terrors had attended their way to the camp.

Off to the east, placed, it seemed, so that the newly arriving refugees had to trudge through it on their way to the camp, was a fresh cemetery, a burial ground for the thousands of dead. Diggers worked feverishly in the snow.

Lang pierced his lips, blinked his eyes, and surveyed the scene. He thought about the two graves he'd already had to dig in the snow, and he knew that the ground was getting harder day by day. That wasn't the only reason he felt sympathy for the people down below, of course, but it was one reason. He knew how hard their work was and how much harder it would become.

Pretty soon, he thought to himself, those people are going to have to find something else to do with the bodies.

CHAPTER 26

"Hey, wait! Let me turn it up. That's my jam!"

Calvin Rhodes ran across the painted concrete floor and slid the last four feet, the brand new leather soles of his Tony Lama boots sliding, almost frictionless, to a stop at the edge of the floor-length toolbox. He reached up, cranked the handle on the radio/CD player, and then swiveled on the pointed toes of his boots, grabbing a ratchet from an open drawer in the process and using it as a microphone while he broke into a rap that betrayed a hint of accent from his Chinese heritage.

"*Yo, microphone check... one, two. What is this? The five foot assassin with the ruffneck bizness.*"

His companion, the older man leaning over the engine of an old Ford pickup, looked up and wiped the grease from his hands on his jeans. He laughed as Calvin did a little dance across the floor, throwing his knee out to the side and then pulling his hips into alignment, waving his free hand above his head and giving a little hop. He looked like a bony windmill-like contraption, or one of those air puppets that you might have seen, not long ago, in front of party stores.

"Cal, you're a clown. That song is older than you are! You got moves, though, I'll give you that." The old man changed his smile into a look of mock seriousness. "Okay, young man, we have to get busy. I'm fixin' to see if I can get this thing started."

Calvin stopped his dance and came over to the front of the truck, leaning in studiously to let the man tell him what he was doing.

"Now, this thing runs pretty simply. It's four on the floor, and as long as you keep some coolant in the radiator and check your oil as you go, it should get you where you're going. It's not gonna win you any speed contests, and the only lights I have workin' are the headlights, but if you'll look here..." the man pointed down to the front of the motor and then traced with his finger towards the back of the engine compartment, "...I've been able to replace all the belts and spark plugs... put in new filters." He paused. "And the tires are good. She should be fine."

Calvin looked into the engine. He was like most young American men his age and had almost no idea what he was looking at or what the mechanic was talking about. He'd been brought up in a time when cars ran on computers, as if by magic, and he wanted to ask questions so he could know what to do if the engine stopped, but he didn't even know where to begin. The man saw the doubt in his eyes.

Calvin looked at the man a little sheepishly. "I know that once upon a time men were both drivers and mechanics. But *my* generation..." Calvin was searching for the words when the old man helped him.

"Well, you've done the first poorly, and the second not at all."

Calvin shook his head. "Yeah... They just became so complicated. I mean, if you can't do it on a video game..." he paused and the old man thought, *well, that won't be a problem anymore...*

"I've just never even tried to work on them."

"Relax, Cal. Compared to those new machines, this ol' dog is a bicycle." He fiddled with a connection on the distributor cap until he was satisfied and then closed the hood.

"This here is the Ranger model of the 1965 Ford F-100. It was a new thing in its day, and they only made a handful of 'em. This special model had bucket seats, which was pretty unique for a pickup truck back in them days." The old man walked around the front of the pickup toward the toolbox, cleaning a socket wrench with a rag as he walked. "It had carpeting, which has since been worn out, and a curtain that covered the gas tank behind the seats." He sorted through the open drawer, found the tool he was looking for, and then turned to Calvin. "She has a couple hunnerd thousand miles on her, but it didn't get there by not being solid. Long as you keep gas in the tank and don't get in a hurry, and don't git y'self killed along the way, it'll get you to Pennsylvania."

Calvin shrugged and smiled at the older man. "I have no doubt. I just hope I can find gas between here and there."

"Well, that's just the thing. Your man and me, we're gonna set you up with a couple of stops along the way that'll take care of your needs in that regard. This thing has been outfitted with a twenty-gallon tank, and I'm going to put as many gas cans as I can muster in the bed, covered by a tarp. That'll get you as far as, maybe, Memphis." He pointed to the running boards along the pickup's short bed. "Now, those things there might get you into trouble. If you run into anyone on the road, don't let 'em get close enough to jump in the back using those things. I've turned the rotors and replaced all the pads so the brakes shouldn't give you any trouble, but you'll have to be awful certain that you don't get into any wrecks or stop too soon. If you do...," he brought his hands up into fists and splayed his fingers and then his hands out in a slow-motion pantomime... "Poof."

"I got ya."

"Now look here, Calvin. You're not gonna wanna to stop for nothin', right? There are bad folks out there and they ain't as nice as you are. You gotta get this package to your man's folks up in P.A." The way he said that made Calvin smile... *peeyay*. "There are people that'll try to stop you just for something to divert themselves. Once you hit that road, you put your ears back and go. You hear what I'm tellin' you?" Calvin nodded. He understood that it was an important mission that he'd been entrusted with, and he was glad to do it.

"Believe me, this truck is gonna be the fanciest thing on the road. Everything else out there... all those automobiles that were dependent on a centralized electric nervous system... they've recently met with their death—powered *down* for the last time. However, the ol' dog here, she's in her prime. Even with the springs pokin' up through the seat cushions, you're gonna be ridin' on a gold mine. That's the reason I've kept her around for all these years." He ran his hand along the rusted fender as lovingly as a mother might stroke the hair of her child. "That, and the fact that my granddaddy drove it, and he didn't leave my dad much besides it. Then my dad left it to me." He paused, his mind gone elsewhere, and then came back to himself. "So anyhow, son, now I'm leaving it to you. You take care of her and she'll take care of you." The older man placed his hand on the young orphan's shoulder, this boy whom he'd come to know and love as if he were his own son.

Calvin gulped. He didn't much like displays of emotion, even if it was coming from the man who'd largely raised him. He was about to blush, and he could feel it, when he became aware of the sound of a screen door slamming over near the main house and the crunch of footsteps walking on the gravel across the yard toward the garage. He heard the radio wind down to the chorus, as a Tribe Called Quest rapped about how they were buggin' out. He saw the pretty, young face of the girl he'd come to think of as his sister as it rounded the corner into the open doorway. She stood silhouetted in the frame of light, cleared her throat, and told him that Jonathan Wall was standing in the kitchen and wanted to talk to him.

* * * *

Stephen sat in the dark and listened to his mother breathing. Ever since they'd heard someone try to break into their bunker early that morning, his mother had been a bundle of nerves, but he'd finally convinced her to lie down and take a nap while he continued to prepare things for their escape.

They would take a couple of bikes, some sets of the hazmat gear, and as much food and water as they could haul with them. They'd carry whatever they could load onto their backs and onto the bikes and still be able to ride safely and swiftly. The plan was to take their gear and flee southward, out of the city. They both admitted that it was a crazy gambit, but what else could they do?

While inspecting the place, Stephen's mother had discovered that the bunker had an open airway at the back of the storeroom, a small pipe that lead somewhere that they couldn't figure. That fact made their plan to shelter there as bad as being outside, because, who knew if that airway was filtered, or—even if it was—if the filtration system even worked?

"We need to get as far away from here as we can get," she'd said. "This place won't do us any good against what I fear is coming. And worse, if someone with a little more sense or a better tool than a shoulder tries to break down the door, we're sitting ducks."

"I understand," Stephen had said, "but why isn't this place built better? Why would somebody go to the trouble of building a bunker that doesn't protect you from the very thing it's supposed to?"

"Peace of mind, Stephen. Or marketing. Back during the cold war, there were people getting rich building facilities that they sold to people based on their fears. They'd weave a swell story, tell the people how only *they* could fix a problem, and then they'd come in and throw up some half-designed thing that would seem to the uninformed to suit their needs. Most people just want to *think* they are safe. That's always true, Stephen. It doesn't really matter whether they are actually safe or not. The same applies to a lot of the survival industry. Companies sell cheaply made goods that wouldn't do what they were advertised to do even if the sellers *had* intended them to. A lot of them simply push products to make a buck. Castles in the air." Veronica paused. She knew her rants sometimes disturbed the boy, so she got back to the point. "Of course, we don't know if that happened here or not. Maybe that airway has a fallout filter on it and is perfectly fine. That's just the point, boy, we don't know. The airflow seems to be a bit too free for me to feel safe about it. Maybe it was just a design flaw, or a contingency plan, or something that, in all those years of lying dormant, got uncovered. Either way, this place is useless to us now because we can't trus' it. We'll have to leave."

Now they were just waiting for nightfall before venturing out, and his mother had finally drifted into a fitful sleep. Stephen had unpacked and repacked their bags, putting in the things his mother had laid out for him. He hummed to himself quietly while doing so, drumming his fingers on the tops of the boxes in the storeroom. He thought of his iPod and his CDs and his video games and wished he had a guitar and had learned to play it.

He listened to his mother breathing, and wondered how long it would be before he could live, once again, in a world of music like she lived in a world of art.

* * * *

The campfire crackled when the log split open and tiny embers flew up into the air, rising on a small puff of wind and lifting toward heaven before burning themselves out and disappearing into small bits of ash.

Four men sat looking into the fire and calculating how much food they had left and how far it would take them. Three of the men had set out on their journey together, and they had a bond that seemed solidified by some past history, perhaps the commission of a crime, while the fourth had joined them by happenstance. It was clear from the tenor of the conversation that, despite their journey thus far, the fourth remained the odd man out.

"Mike, we need to pick up our pace if we are going to get out of these mountains before our food runs out," Val said. Val was a hulking brute of a man, and gave off an air of one who ought not to be trifled with.

"Relax, Val. I know what I'm doing, and listen, try to use contractions more. For example, instead of 'if *we* are going to get out of these mountains,' you'd say, "if *we're* going to get out of these mountains.' Americans use more contractions and speak more lazily and fluidly. You sound like a robot." Mike looked at Val and didn't quite smile. His eyes smiled, but did so with a hint of authority and superiority. He continued.

"We don't have much farther to go before we'll be in an area where we can find shelter, and we have enough food to last a couple more days." Mike was short and stocky. He was clearly the brains of the group of three men who'd initially headed out into the wilderness together. The third man, Steve, seemed to be mere window dressing. But not like in a clothing store. More like a mannequin you'd find on display in a hardware store or in outdoor gear store. The strong silent type, with a heavy emphasis on *silent.*

"Steve, would you like a little more stew? I think we have enough for everyone to have another bite."

Steve nodded and held out his cup.

"Ken?" Val asked, offering him the spoon.

"Oh, for heaven's sake! It's Kent!" Kent was the fourth man. The outsider. He made a point of spitting the last letter off his teeth. "Kent. The 'T' is *not* silent. If we're going to call each other by new names, the least you could do is *try* and get the name right," the round-faced man said, his eyes burning with fire. It was clear that he didn't like Val, and from the way the brute arched his back at the tone of Kent's voice, one could tell that the feeling was mutual. Val turned to face Kent, squaring his shoulders as the smaller man sat forward on the log and seemed about to rise.

Mike smoothed their ruffled feathers. "Gentlemen! Give it a rest. We have a while still to travel, yet. Perhaps you can learn to get along better so that Steve and I," he made a nod to the silent man to his left, "don't have to douse the both of you."

"I can't help it, Mike. He burns me." Val made a motion toward the smaller man as if he would slap him with the back of his hand if he didn't have better self-control, and it wasn't clear that he really did.   The round-faced man didn't flinch, and his eyes betrayed no fear. He simply sat and looked back at Val and spread his hands.   He made them into fists and did a little punching motion into the air, and then, turning away, he looked with boredom into the fire. Reflexively, he reached up and removed his glasses and began to clean them.

* * * *

Calvin Rhodes was born in Austin, Texas, in 1994, where his parents lived as they attended the University of Texas on student visas. His father, a Chinese pharmaceutical engineer, had come to the states to complete a graduate degree program, sponsored by the Chinese government in an ongoing effort to reform China's national healthcare system. His mother, a musician, died giving birth to Calvin, and thus his father had to raise him alone.

When it came to being a single father and trying to maintain his course work at the university, Cal's father was lost from the very start. In fact, he'd have simply withdrawn from the university and returned home to China to enlist his family's help with the child, if it weren't for the mildly aggressive way his embassy office had handled the news of his wife's passing. Gently, but firmly, and with no room left for doubt, the consular attaché told him that he was to continue his studies. A small stipend was provided so that he could secure childcare, but nothing else was offered by way of help – certainly not understanding.

Cal's father had done the best that he could. One of the things he'd done while he was looking for answers and for strength to face his struggles, was turn to the search for spirituality. He'd never been a particularly religious man, and he'd always made his way in the Chinese system by offering the kind of public acceptance of science as the supreme answer for everything that was expected of him.   While he secretly admitted to an appreciation for traditional Chinese medical practices, and he had a deep and abiding faith in certain ancient Chinese cultural mores, he'd been successful in his career, to the point that some in the Chinese politburo were eying him for regional directorships. His success therefore, was precisely a result of his being seen as a man of industry and science and not of mythology. He'd been exactly the type of man the country needed as China moved toward more

Western-style medical standards. At a minimum, he was good at managing business, a useful thing in a time when the pharmaceutical business in his country was on the ascent.

Still, there was the matter of the boy. Calvin was a fussy baby. From his very earliest days, he behaved as though he took it as a personal affront that his mother wasn't there for him. This was understandable, but it didn't make matters any better for the harried young father trying to raise him. The fact that Cal's father had proved to be only a middling student made things even worse. In order to advance, he'd been forced to spend many hours reading and rereading texts that other students simply seemed to grasp at first glance.

Perhaps the turning point for Calvin's father was the day he'd received, in the mail, from his family back home, a small book by a moral philosopher named Li Hongzhi. This philosopher had recently become famous in China for developing a movement founded on traditional Chinese physical exercises combined with the practice of certain moral beliefs. Chief among these beliefs were truthfulness, compassion, and forbearance. The book had changed Calvin's father forever.

The pharmaceutical engineer became a member of the outlaw movement that eventually became known as Falun Gong.

Drawing strength from his new-found religion—if it could rightly be called a religion—Calvin's father threw himself into his tasks. He took to his studies with a new vigor and seemed to grow in his role as a father in a way that surprised even his family back in China, as well as the few friends he'd made on campus. He became, in short, a zealot, and that zealotry infused him with energy.

All of this is by way of explaining why, on a day he'd taken to get out of the city and tour the beautiful hill country he'd heard so much about, he was doing his exercises in a small park next to the *Vereins Kirch* in Fredericksburg, Texas, and not caring a whit for the stares that he got from the people in that small Central Texas tourist town.

People were not used to seeing a Chinese man with a toddler at his side standing in the middle of an artsy Texas village next to an old Colonial-era Lutheran Church moving his body as if he were pushing the wind. The folks walking by stole their furtive glances and tried not to stop and stare. They were polite in their peering insouciance, but if one had stood to the side and watched, it would have been clear that their reaction was unimportant to Calvin's father. He was impervious to even their walking amazement.

One young man in his later teens, standing in the park, did not steal furtive glances or peer through the side of his eyes at the Chinese man's antics. That man noticed both the crowd and the man's practiced disregard of them. He knew what it was like to be watched sideways and marginalized, and he figured that if you were going to look at a man, you should just go on and look at him.

His name was Jonathan Wall.

In the future, Jonathan Wall and Calvin's father would become very close friends - and Mr. Wall would become even closer to Calvin.

CHAPTER 27

"Stephen, we have a serious problem."

Veronica looked at her son with her fists on her hips, frowning—not at him particularly—but at the problem.

"We have to ride south through Brooklyn, and that will be difficult enough, boy, but then we have to cross the Verrazano Bridge, and that could be next to impossible. The bridge will almost certainly be blocked by bandits; people who will want to take our bikes; people who will steal our food if we will let them; people who might want to take our lives."

"You think it will be that bad, mom?" Stephen asked. He concentrated on making sure that his face showed bravery and masked his fear.

Veronica noticed Stephen's efforts and she was pleased. *Half of any hard victory consists of overcoming the fears that might keep us from the battle in the first place,* she thought.

"I think it will be worse than I think it will be," she said, smiling.

"What's the plan?"

"Getting over the bridge is the first thing. We'll take our battles one at a time. We need to be prepared to ride fast and yet carefully. Watch for trash on the roadways, son, nails in particular. A flat tire on your bike makes it as useless as not having one. I found spare tubes in the storeroom, but there will be no time or place to stop and change them. We need to avoid anything that will keep us from getting out of here quickly."

Stephen looked at his mother, wanting to mention a thought that had occurred to him While she was sleeping, he'd been silently drumming because drumming always seemed to help him think clearly. As his hands worked the rhythm in his head, his mind flashed back to a day when he'd been riding the subway. Beating the heels of his hands like a madman on the tops of his knees, keeping time to a song playing in his ears, he'd looked up and noticed that people had slid away from him on the seats, leaving him alone at the end of the train.

"What if we put on the fallout gear now?" he said, smiling. "It will freak people out. They'll think we're scientists or something, or maybe from the government, or that we're sick. Maybe they'll leave us alone."

"Boy," Veronica said, placing her long thin fingers on his cheek and giving his nose a little tweak, "I knew some sense had crept into you. Yes. What a great thought! And the suits will keep us warm... and... and.... they'll be one less thing we have to carry. That's an excellent idea!"

Within half an hour, they had packed, dressed in the hazmat suits, and were ready to go. They opened the bunker door, and, checking the area carefully, they proceeded out into the night.

* * * *

Calvin Rhodes climbed into the cab of the truck and put the key in the ignition. He turned it forward a bit and heard the slow, whining grind of the starter kick in, pumped the gas pedal slightly and felt the motor rumble to life.

Pulling out of the circular driveway, he waved to the small crowd of people standing at the foot of the porch, and then proceeded slowly along the gravel driveway, hearing the crunch of the tires underneath him, until he came to a stop where the driveway met the county highway. He looked both ways, although that wasn't really necessary. His was the only vehicle moving on the road. He pushed the knob forward, finding his gear, and gave the truck some gas. Cautiously, he drove the first ten feet of a journey that he hoped would take him halfway across the country. Gently shifting gears, he settled his butt into the seat.

The first hundred miles were mostly uneventful. He stuck to the back roads, cruising through the rural scenery of the rolling hill country, passing family farms and churches and schools and small towns, or the burned out buildings that had once stood for them.

Mostly, there was an eerie quiet, although in some yards kids were still at play as their parents watched warily from the windows. In many places, the storefronts along streets were smashed, and the shelves were emptied, leaning over like dominoes one against another, tossed by looters or panicked citizens or both.

Coming to a stop at a rural junction, Calvin saw two corpses splayed out over the hood of a broken down car. Pockets were turned inside out, and the doors of the car stood wide open and the trunk was pulled up. The scene left little to the imagination, and it played before Calvin's eyes in seconds in blue-black flickers, and ended just as he saw it now, in tragedy.

He slowed just enough to hope for peace upon the souls of the families of the dead, and to be grateful that he wasn't the one lying there, perforated with bullets, stretched out like a deer across the hood of a car.

The advantage to being in the country during this moment was the benefit of not having as many people to dodge. The people in this neck of the woods were probably hurting and hungry, but they weren't competing with millions of others for the rare materials of sustenance and survival. Statistically speaking, that was a very large advantage indeed. Calvin would drive along highway 79 almost as far as Memphis in order to avoid the Interstate highways, and he would pass, almost exclusively, through a few widely separated small towns—towns such as Hearne and Henderson and Carthage.

As he drove through the Piney Woods of Texas, he thought about all the places he'd seen and known and loved in the state. It was difficult for people who weren't from there to understand it - how Texas had plains, mountains, mighty rivers, and woods and forests, as well as deserts, and oceans... and skies. Plenty of skies. Of course, the state also had its large cities and its little towns, and that was what made it special for him—as a native Texan who was also an outsider of sorts. Texas didn't necessarily have the best *in anything*, but it had the best *of everything*. It was self-contained in a way that other places weren't. As the people often said, *Texas is a whole other country*. As he drove through the silent night, he looked up at the stars and saw that they were big and bright, and already he missed being deep in the state's heart.

* * * *

Outside of Shreveport, Calvin took gunfire. There was simply no other way around it. Shreveport, that is. The Louisiana city was a vexation that could not be avoided. Literally. He *had* to go through the town in order to reach the bridge that would take him over the Red River. The river, usually an afterthought, its muddy waters rolling lazily along as if the world and its affairs were none of its concern, had become a barrier that he needed to breach. Bridges, by nature, were bottlenecks, and danger always loves a bottleneck.

Calvin timed his approach so that he'd come to the crossing in the middle of the night. Winding his way south around the city, he came up to the bridge on 70th Street, running adjacent to the old skeletal structures of Hamel's Amusement Park, which had closed down more than a decade ago when a tornado bent its Ferris Wheel in half.

He'd been thinking of the Ferris Wheel and comparing it in his mind to the recently destroyed one on Coney Island—the one from Hurricane Sandy— that he'd seen on the television and the Internet just before those forms of media had gone black forever. He was driving alongside the amusement park looking out over the rusty machinery, the steel and wood standing alone in its abandoned memories, remembering how the recent world had simply stopped in the wake of Hurricane Sandy when, out of the blue—or the black, actually—he heard a ping. Then another.

The shots ricocheted off the fender of his pickup, and he swiveled his head to see where they were coming from. He almost ran off the bridge just as he entered its mouth.

Somewhere back at the amusement park, he thought. Not amusing at all.

He hit the gas, tore across the river, and looked up into his rear-view mirror to watch the rusted old skyline disappear into the night.

* * * *

"Why do you keep taking off your boots? Are you trying to slow us down?"

It was Val. He was standing over the round-faced man and sneering at him. The bespectacled young man, currently called Kent, peered into his boot and seemed to be searching for something that wasn't there. He was a little drunk. They'd taken turns watching through the night, and Kent had spent most of his turn sneaking drinks of vodka from a flask he'd kept secretly in his pocket. In his mind, his life had turned to dung and the vodka made it almost, but not quite, bearable.

"Leave him alone, Val. Just don't start it up again." It was Steve. The silent one. Like his comrade Mike, he was getting tired of the constant bickering back and forth between Val and Kent, and he'd come to conclude that Val was mostly to blame. Val was like a rooster who, with nothing worthwhile at which to peck, pecked at anything near him that he deemed to be weaker than himself.

"Yes. Listen to our amigo, Esteban, here." Kent felt himself slurring his words. When he said 'Estaban,' it sounded to him like 'Esh-tra-gon.'

"Time's out of joint..." (He was speaking so slowly!) "...no need to get your nose out of joint, too." The words came out like molasses, awkwardly, and ran together in his ears like they did not in his head.

The brutish Val looked at him and thought that someone getting his nose pushed out of joint was exactly what was needed. They were waiting for Mike to come back from a little hike up ahead to scout out their direction, and passing the time with Val was, as usual, not turning out to be rewarding for Kent, so he excused himself to walk over to a small group of bushes to let the vodka finish its pass through him.

"Stupid idiot," he muttered to himself as he half stumbled and half climbed up a small rise toward the bushes. "Of course, I'm trying to slow you down, you moron...," he slurred to himself.

Walking over the rise, he stood at a small hedge line and was just about to unzip his pants when sobriety snuck up on him and a shot of adrenaline flew through his system like lightening. There, at the bottom of the hedges, in a small clump of trees, was a man dressed like an accountant. Blood, turned black and inky like impenetrable night, lay frozen in a pool around him.

* * * *

The man held up his hand for his friends to shut up. They were gathered in a group at the foot of the bridge where they'd been sitting for several days - doing business. Stalled cars and buses formed a zigzag maze purposefully designed to block access to the bridge from all vehicles, and to force pedestrians to walk across the bridge - but only after paying a toll.

The friends had learned that it was easier to allow the food to come to them by standing across its mouth with knives, boards, and chains, than it was to go out in search of supplies for themselves. Looting was turning out to be dangerous business in the city. The rumor was rampant that some looters had even been cooked and eaten. Charging tolls was much safer. They'd placed a sign on the off-ramp side of the bridge that told the people who were escaping out of the city that they needed to pay to cross—a fee for the right to exit hell. The gang told the citizens that the toll was something like an indulgence, and the gatekeepers, the popes and priests of the new world disorder, administered punishments upon anyone who tried to exit purgatory without paying. The sign made it clear what forms of payment were acceptable...

Weapons. Food. Money.

It was unclear what they planned to do with the money.

"Hey. Shhh. Shhh. Shhhhhh."
They watched as a couple of yellow suits on what appeared to be bicycles came drifting down the decline. The bikes were taking their time, weaving slowly in and out of traffic and the suits riding the bikes turning their hooded heads first to this side and then to that side. The yellow suit in the lead seeming to point out little features on the ground to the suit in the back as they crept lazily, silently, eerily, through the deadened line of vehicles.

"What the...?" A man with a two by four with a few rusty nails protruding from the end was the one who couldn't quite find the last word he was searching for. He stood with the others, because all of them were standing now. As a group, they watched the yellow suits calmly apply the brakes on their bikes.

From a distance, maybe from the top of the bridge, one would have seen the tallest of the yellow suits dismount from the bike and calmly unstrap a pack tied to the back of the bicycle. The suit walked to the foot of the bridge, approached the circle of men, setting the bag slowly on the ground. From the height of the bridge, the yellow suit, looking something like an astronaut or a technician trying to control a viral outbreak, bent down, opened the bag, and began fishing around for something inside it. The other suit waited with the bikes. The men stood and stared with their weapons in anticipation...

In a movie, the music would have built to a crescendo, but this was not a movie. It was real life. When the yellow suit stood up with something strange in its hands, the men screamed, broke, and ran. They scattered in all directions, running for cover like men chased by bees, or devils... or death. They never looked back.

With her head down, looking at the package in her hands, Veronica had missed the sight of the armed men fleeing in panic. Now, finding herself alone, she reached up and undid the helmet of her fallout suit and removed it, feeling the cold air slip across her face. She opened the box of graham crackers she held in her hands and carefully tore open the interior packaging. Removing a cracker, she took a bite. She slipped the cardboard flap back in its slot and dropped the box back in the bag, and, throwing the bag across her shoulders, she walked back to Stephen.

"What was that about, Mom?"

"I guess they weren't hungry," Veronica said. "Besides, they weren't going to stop us with a silly board with nails in it!"

She put her helmet back on and mounted her bike, and she and Stephen rode down into the highway leading into Staten Island.

CHAPTER 28

The man struggled gamely, but he was stuck fast. He'd fallen through the boards of the dilapidated bridge, and the wood had given way just enough to bite into his leg but not enough to allow it to wriggle free. He didn't have the leverage or the angle to pull his leg out. He was looking at the leg as if deep in thought, perhaps determining whether he had other choices. He ran his hand along the back of his neck and then over a few day's growth of beard.

Hidden in the trees, Lang could see that the man's ankle had become wedged in the supporting cross braces of the old footbridge, and that he was unable to reach down through the broken boards to free himself no matter what he tried.

Peter watched along with the others as the man struggled, and he noted aloud that the man had better find a way to get loose. "If he doesn't manage to free himself, he's surely going to die..." Peter paused. "...if not from the injury or starvation, then from some group of troublesome passersby looking for gear, guns, or just trouble. They'll eventually come upon him."

"We need to help him," Lang told Peter, looking at the older man with a face that betrayed both fear and compassion.

"I don't know, Lang," Peter said. He stared, unblinking at the man on the bridge. He could not help but see both the metaphor... the bridge itself... and the danger. "Helping him could put us all at risk. We could be found ou—"

"Oh, for heaven's sake, Peter!" Natasha snapped, interrupting him. "What if that was you stuck there on that bridge?"

"Well," Peter said, "sure, I would want someone to help me, but I'd also not expect it. I'd understand if they couldn't do it without great risk to themselves. No one *deserves* the heroic, Natasha."

"Still, I'd like to go and check on him, Peter," Lang said.

"You can't go, Lang." The old man looked at the youth, his skin pale and beginning to look almost transparent. "You can't even lift up your arm! How are you going to help this man get free with one arm?" Peter paused, staring at Lang. Then he looked down for a beat before adding, "No... If anyone is going, I'm going."

"Peter, be reasonable," Lang said. "Who's going to protect Natasha and Elsie if you get shot out there? It has to be me. I'll go."

The two men continued their argument, and as they did, Natasha's eyes grew wide, and she knelt down as if she needed to inspect her boot. She looked up, then left and then right, and before either Lang or Peter could say anything to stop her, she was sprinting full speed towards the bridge. She stayed low to the ground, maintaining maximum cover as she ran.

Her actions caused the others to stop in their tracks, and then spring into action. Without a word, Peter raised the rifle and balanced the barrel on the small branch just to his left. He adjusted the iron sights, allowed a bit for windage and the expected drop, and began to steady his breath, willing himself to slow his heartbeat.

If this man makes a wrong move, Peter thought, *I'll drop him.*

Without taking his eye away from the sights, Peter whispered to Lang, who was mentally already on his way, leaning in anticipation, to take the .22 Marlin and run to the low hill to the northeast.

"Stay under cover," Peter raised his voice. "That gun is good, as-is, from seventy-five to one hundred meters. Keep your eyes on the woods and watch the dirt road as it comes around that bend. If anyone, anyone at all approaches..." He let the implications hang in the air and whispered quietly under his breath, to himself as much as to Lang, "Don't miss."

* * * *

Natasha reached the old, decrepit bridge, and the man finally saw her. He slowly lowered his right hand, moving as if he were testing her, determining whether she was going to ask him to stop - and she saw that he had a Glock pistol strapped to his good leg.

"Wait!" Natasha shouted, with authority. "Don't do it! If you move, and your hand gets near that gun, your head will explode. Trust me. You are in the sights of someone who is very, very good.

Just... please... don't be stupid. I'm here to help you, and I'm unarmed."

She turned around slowly with her hands up, and lifted her coat so that he could see she did not have a gun of her own.

The man stared at Natasha for a second. Without blinking, without giving any indication on his face of his thinking one way or the other about anything, his hand opened up very slowly, and swiveled at the wrist to show whoever she was talking about... whoever was pointing a gun at him... that he had no intention of doing anything stupid. Methodically, he put both hands flat down on the wood surface of the bridge, and then paused, just staring at Natasha without a word.

"That's good. I see that you are clever," Natasha said, moving again toward the man. "I'm going to climb under the bridge and see if I can get your ankle free. If I were you, even if it hurts horribly and you want to scream out, I wouldn't move very much, or make any noise."

The man didn't respond at all. He just answered with his eyes, a slow blink that declared openly and plainly that he understood what this woman and her people expected of him. That he'd been given a kind of trust.

With that, Natasha hurried down the embankment, and, near the edge of the tiny stream, she climbed upward into the ancient trusses and supports that held the weight of the old bridge.

* * * *

Ten minutes later, they were sitting in the cover of trees. Peter worked on the quiet man's ankle, examining it to determine if it was broken or if there was any serious injury. Just a moment ago, Natasha and the quiet man had come hobbling in together. Drawing close to Peter's location, Natasha ran ahead to get the medical bag, before remembering that they no longer had it. Happily, there was no need for it; the man's ankle wasn't in any serious danger.

"It'll be sore awhile, and if we were in the old world I'd tell you to stay off of it and take it easy, but obviously you can't do that now." Peter looked at the others and wondered if they remembered what it was like to be back in that other life, then he looked back to the man to see if he gave any indication of his thinking, but he did not.

Peter turned to Lang, "I don't even know if he speaks English or if he understands me. Perhaps he's a mute." He raised his voice to the man, speaking slowly, "Do you understand?"

"He speaks English," Lang said with a slight smirk on his face. "And he understands you. At least, he understood Natasha well enough, back at that bridge."

"People communicate in many ways," Peter said, "sometimes body language conveys as much understanding as words."

Natasha nodded her agreement to Lang's opinion. "He understood the words I said. Apparently, he's just the quiet type."

The quiet man—about twenty years old, handsome and well built, with blue eyes and sandy-colored hair—looked slowly over to Lang and smiled without saying a word.

"Well, there's not much I can say for his gifts of conversation," Peter said. He helped the man re-lace his boot and then stand to his feet. The man gave a little hop as he did so. The ankle was tentative, at best, but he applied weight to it and then stood up straight, as if to indicate that the injury was not going to be a problem for him.

The man was dressed in what had once been an army green coat and BDU pants, but the man had engaged in some makeshift winter camouflage attempts, and the coat and pants had been hastily spray painted with splotches of white paint, and here and there outlines of green pine branches appeared among the white patches.

His gun, a bolt-action sniper rifle with a pricey scope attached to it, he'd camouflaged with white and green as well. His backpack matched the rest of him.

Peter nodded to the man, and then to the weapons each of them carried, as if he was bringing attention to the fact that he was not going to cause anyone trouble, and he didn't want any in return.

"Well, sir," Peter said, "I don't know who you are, where you came from, or what you're doing out here." He glanced at the man. "We don't know whose side you're on, or if you are a good guy or a bad guy, but—"

"It's okay," the man said quietly. It was the first words he'd spoken. "It's really... it is best..." The four others stared at him, and he shook his head that he meant it. He wanted the older man to understand that he appreciated the hospitality, but he understood that the group now had to be on their way.

"We should just part and wish each other well," the man said.

Then, the awkward moment was over, and the man just stared at Peter without any hint of a response on his face.

"Well, sir, you're free to travel with us," Peter told him, in case that might influence his decision. "We're short-handed and under-trained, but we could use the extra gun and skills. Up to a point. It's up to you."

The man shook his head no, and he picked up the rifle and tossed it over his shoulder by the strap before doing the same with his bag over the other shoulder. He turned to walk away, limping only slightly on his injured ankle. Just as he was about to disappear into the thick brush of the woods, he turned and looked at all four of the travelers, one at a time.

"Ace," he said, matter-of-factly and without any apparent emotion. "That's my name," he said. "And thank you all." He acted as if that was all that needed to be said. Ace then turned back toward the woods, and with a few confident steps, he was gone.

Lang looked at Natasha and Elsie and noticed that they sat there staring for a few extra beats, watching as Ace disappeared into the woods. Ace was a good-looking man, no denying it, Lang thought. He didn't blame the ladies for being a bit taken with him. A smile broke across his face. He shook his head, and they all stared at each other for a moment, searching to see if everyone was having the same thoughts about the strange encounter with this man, and then they all broke into laughter.

* * * *

They came upon the abandoned cabin just as darkness began to fall. Some kind of violence had occurred there, though there were no corpses evident lying around the place. They could tell there had been violence by the pockmarking of bullet holes in the walls, and the telltale signs that looters or bandits, or maybe just regular folks had ransacked the place. The door hung loosely on the hinges, and the glass from most of the windows was lying shattered on the ground instead of safely in its frames.

We know the events that we experience, and we have some knowledge of the legends that we are told, but the mind reels at the stories a place like this could tell when the world as we know it has ended. This lonely cabin in the woods had seen numerous such tales play out as individuals, groups, and bandits, and maybe even armies had crisscrossed these woods in search of someplace "safe." The story of our four travelers was just now intersecting with this cabin, but dozens of other stories, all of them just as important to the characters living through them, had unfolded here. From the looks of the place, not all of them had ended well.

"Buildings make me nervous," Peter said. "We don't have enough people to secure a building, for one thing." He paused, as if there were no reason number two. "It is shelter, sure, but it's not much more than that." He looked around at the place and considered the things that to him were painfully apparent, if one only cared to look. "If we stay too long, more people will be coming along."

"Lang has to rest, Peter," Natasha said. Elsie nodded her head in agreement and added, "And his wound needs treatment. He's growing weaker, and the pain is obvious on his face." Natasha touched Peter on the arm, and gave him a little smile, "We need to stop."

They went through the building thoroughly, checking every place where someone might be hiding, but they found no one. Then they began to prepare an area to treat Lang's wound. Peter briefed the women on what they would need to do, which didn't take long seeing that their meds and first aid case had been stolen.

He patted Lang lightly on the back, then told Natasha, who'd been standing lookout at the door, that he needed go up front and secure the premises.

"You guide Elsie through the steps that I taught you. Do it thoroughly, and call me if you need anything."

Elsie helped Lang remove his shirt, and it became clear, very quickly, that things were not right. The skin was pale and the area on the arm surrounding the wound was angry, red, and warm to the touch. The gunshot wound was infected, and it was much worse than they'd suspected.

The darkness was starting to invade the cabin. Natasha called to Peter who came down the hall, and, as he did, she stepped out into the hallway to meet him. Peter knew that if there were anything at all that they could do to help Lang, they'd have to do it quickly, before the cabin became shrouded in darkness. *He might not survive another day if we don't do something now,* Peter thought, *the world itself might become shrouded in darkness.*

Something must be done. But what?

* * * *

Clive Darling guided the rigged-up RV he called *Bernice* up a small incline until he could just see Carbondale over the bulge of the dashboard. The black, armored chase vehicles that accompanied him split up as he brought Bernice to a stop. Some moved to his left and others to his right. They moved in a line, the vehicles, until they came to a stop, like sentries out on a search, an ancient tribal ritual played out in modern sleek machinery. Doors and hatches on the vehicles opened up with precision, and soldiers poured forth from them, and in seconds the team had set up a secure perimeter, which included snipers and patrols.

Clive turned to his passenger and explained that he'd learned that the maniac running the Carbondale "resettlement" center had secured generators and a power plant. Clive explained that the officer running the prison camp was planning on electrifying the fences and illuminating the control tents where interrogations were said to be taking place around the clock.

The listener listened. He watched the man speak with confidence about how a life ought to be lived. He heard in that voice, the voice of the man named Clive, the intonations and ideas of a brother.

As Clive spoke, the listener saw a man who knew what he was about. Clive's mannerisms showed the listener that the man with the Savannah drawl really believed the words that he said, and that he was not full of guile. This made the listener think of his own journey, his own modern ride, his own tribal ties.

"They don't need electrical power to terrorize the public," Clive said to the passenger, his slow drawl emphasizing the horror in the word... *Terrorize.*

Clive indicated with his hand the general world; first the world outside and then the world inside, over there in Carbondale.

"They seem to have been doin'," he paused. "...You know... the terrorizing... alright by themselves. But—"

Clive paused and looked at his passenger, the man so odd in his own weird skin, this man who seemed to mold himself around the world, and yet, who in the end molded the world around him. He watched his passenger listening, as they sat in the RV with their soldiers spread out in a perimeter around them. As they waited, the two men just passed time, just sharing like friends would.

The friends noticed when the power blinked on in the Carbondale camp, first with some hesitation, and then more insistently.

The lights pierced the surrounding darkness.

But not everywhere, though. The lights only burned in the tents of arbitrary power.

* * * *

Clive massaged his heavy mustache with his left hand and looked over to his passenger. He indicated to the broader world again, and when he did, his passenger listened.

"There's no way we can insure fairness in this world, and even if we could, I don't think I'd want to. People are not equal, and no one can make them what they are not. However, the use of arbitrary power in the hands of tyranny perturbs me. We Luddites look to impair, obstinately, such terrorism wherever we find it."

Clive looked at his passenger and his passenger looked at him.

"My friend, would you like to do the honors?"

The red-bearded passenger smiled, and his eyes lit up.

Clive lifted up the protective guard on the dashboard, exposing the lighted switch.

* * * *

In the Carbondale Resettlement Camp, the technician had just finished a long day of fixing, and prepping, and wiring, and fueling up the huge generators. He pulled down the three large levers that would connect the machines to the makeshift "grid" in the camp. After running through a series of checks, the technician flipped up a plastic button guard, and then pressed in the red button with his thumb.

The generators fired up in unison, and the technician was pleased to see the lights in the maintenance tent first flicker, and then begin to burn brightly through the plastic windows.

He'd just packed up his tools and was rushing back to the tent to get out of the cold, when he heard the loud rumble accompanied with the otherworldly buzz.

It seemed that there was a split-second of silence before the entire control panel and junction box on the front of each of the generators blew up, showering pieces of metal and wire around the camp like rain.

The technician ran quickly along the packed white snow as the electrical sparks shot out in in white arcs above his head...

From a distance it might have looked like an umbrella, or a fireworks show.

On the other hand, maybe it looked like a mushroom cloud.

It was hard to tell. The artificial light was so brief. And so rare.

* * * *

The red-bearded man smiled when the lights went dark again in the camp.

"I sing the body electric. I celebrate the me... yet... to come!"

He looked at Clive, who smiled at him under his thick mustache. "It's almost like bein' the Good Lord there for a few seconds," he said with a wink, his eyes wide, like a child's.

He sat there, Clive did, and looked over the dash to the darkened prison camp that was Carbondale, Pennsylvania.

"Insufficient shielding," Clive Darling said, matter-of-factly. "We tried to warn 'em."

CHAPTER 29

Natasha did her best not to show concern on her face, and she smiled stiffly, but she was worried. They were in the middle of nowhere with no antibiotics, no herbal remedies, not even any natural antibiotics like garlic, echinacea, or even honey. She'd instructed Elsie to start a fire in the fireplace to boil some water, while she went to find Peter to determine what she might do next to prepare, aid, and support whatever treatment Lang might need.

She found Peter moving stealthily towards the tree line behind the cabin, catching up with him with a low shout. "The wound is infected, Peter," she said, "and I don't think just cleaning it and repacking it is going to do anything but cause him excruciating pain. You're going to have to come and help."

Peter grimaced. The last gray-blue of dusk was highlighting the trees, and a cold wind began to whip through them, making the shadows move across the snowy ground. He was concerned about Lang, and he saw fear and nervousness etched across Natasha's face.

"Absolutely..."

Peter's mind was torn. He was also concerned with security. Lang was his friend, and was like a son to him, but with the four of them all inside the house, they'd be blind, and exposed. He wasn't happy about that. Security was really everything right now. *If only the women could deal with Lang...*

He didn't know what he might do with the wound that the women could not either. He wasn't sure there was anything to be done at all.

Still, he had to do something to help Lang or the boy wouldn't last long. Sepsis was a concern, and there wasn't anything he could think of at that moment that frightened him more than that. If the infection got into the blood stream... well... he'd just have to see if there was anything he could do.

* * * *

Walking back into the cabin, Peter struggled in his thoughts. Absent a medical solution—and he had to admit that his own library of knowledge and experience had already been taxed to its limit—there wasn't much left he could do.

The rudiments of an extravagant *placebo* plan had run through his mind when he first noticed that Lang was getting worse. Convincing someone that a medicine or a procedure is effectual—when in reality it was not—can be very powerful, not just in convincing the injured or sick person that they are getting better, but often enough the positive effects of a placebo extend to actual physiological healing.   The body, convinced that something powerful or helpful is going on, will often ramp up its own defenses to match or meet the expected results. In this way, patients have had their pain alleviated during surgery and recovery, and there were even cases of people healed of cancers and other real diseases with the use of placebos alone. In his own mind, Peter called his plan 'The Sugar Pill Plot.'

Placebos were often just sugar pills, made to look like the real thing. In tests, doctors or scientists gave sugar pills to some subjects while others received real medications. Often, those who received the sugar pills responded to the treatment as positively as those who had received the real medicine.

The mind is a powerful thing. Peter knew that, and, without any other solution, he was contemplating a very involved ruse as a last ditch way to try to help Lang.

He felt in his pocket and noticed that he still had the cell phone from the man he'd been forced to shoot. Peter knew that cell phones were loaded with trace amounts of gold and silver, and that both gold and silver have been used for millennia as antibiotics and antivirals. He also knew that he didn't have the proper tools, chemicals, or equipment to extract the gold and silver from the phone... *but*, he thought to himself, and this was the thing, *Lang doesn't know that.*

The first thing Peter did was to gather Natasha and Elsie together. He told them that the three of them needed to black out the windows. They were going to have fire and light in the cabin, and they wanted as little evidence of that to be evident from outside the cabin as possible. The smoke from the fireplace was bad enough. Peter thought that he should have asked them not to light a fire in the first place; however, since they'd already started the fire, he would use it to sterilize the knife and prepare his placebo ruse.

Using the flashlight for light, Peter proceeded to cut large squares of carpet from the floor of the cabin and instructed Natasha and Elsie to find nails, staples, or any other materials that might be useful for hanging the squares. He told them that they could fasten them over the windows by pounding bent and rusted nails through the carpet and into the window frames using a brick and a rock they'd found behind the cabin. It took 45 minutes for the water to boil sufficiently for Peter to get to work.

He started by taking the phone apart. He made a big show of the disassembly process. In his mind he noted that he was not only *disassembling*, but he was also *dissembling*, which meant lying. It was good that the trick was a secret, because he didn't know how poorly his word play might be received at such a time.

He removed the chip, the processor, wires, and connector from the phone, all the while announcing loudly and confidently everything that he was doing. He convinced himself of the lie, so that his patient might more readily believe him. He gave a short dissertation on the antibiotic, antiviral, and anti-bacterial benefits of silver and gold in solution. *All that part was true*, he thought. He worked like a magician, using sleight of hand and showmanship to make the whole display believable. Nobody doubted him. He noted that he was manipulating the trust of his friends, *but*– He forced the thought to leave him. He didn't have time for self-recrimination.

"Natasha? Elsie? Have you finished blacking out the cabin?" Peter called out from down the hallway.

"Yes, Peter. It's all done," Natasha replied.

"Okay, while I finish this, I want you two to do a top to bottom search of this place. Examine every cabinet, drawer, cubbyhole, shelf... *everywhere*... anything you find, call it out loudly, OK? You holler out what it is to me, and I'll tell you if we can use it. There's probably not much to be found. The place looks like it's been stripped bare, but you never know."

He stepped back into the room and then stuck his head into the hallway again, as an afterthought, choosing to err on the side of caution. "Stay away from any windows," he warned. "Even brushing up against one can cause a disturbance that might be seen from outside."

The two women called out agreement and began their search. Peter used the momentary diversion to pour out the solution he'd been concocting. He filled an empty coffee cup with water from one of his water bottles, then added a tiny pinch off of the ChapStick to the water. His plan was to heat the water in the cup by the fire so that it would melt the tiny amount of ChapStick. The oily substance would add a peculiar taste that Peter hoped would amplify the placebo effect on Lang's mind.

* * * *

"An old aluminum soda can!" Elsie shouted from one of the bedrooms.

"Keep it!" Peter responded.

"An empty bourbon bottle!" Natasha yelled, even though she was just fifteen feet away in the little kitchen nook, searching through the cabinets.

"Keep it!" Peter yelled back, laughing.

"A knitting needle!" Elsie hollered.

"Keep it!" Peter and Lang shouted back, in unison. Lang was now laughing through the pain, and the diversion was good for him.

"This place is a veritable treasure trove of valuable artifacts," he said. He was surprised that there were so many useful things still available in the cabin—items most people would probably think were useless.

Peter took the hot coffee cup away from the fire and allowed it to cool for thirty seconds or so. Then he handed it to Lang and told him to drink it all down.

"Swallow it to the dregs, son. That concoction will make you right as rain."

Lang did what he was told and scowled a bit from the strange oiliness in the water.

"A quarter bag of sugar!" Natasha yelled.

"Keep it!" Lang shouted, chuckling at the game.

"Woah! Wait!" Peter said. "Did you say *sugar*, Natasha?"

"Yes, Peter. Refined sugar. Kind of clumpy, but still white."

"Oh my goodness," Peter said, and excitement lit up his features. "Bring it here, daughter. You may just be a lifesaver!"

Natasha walked over by the fire with the bag of sugar. "Why?" she asked. "What good is sugar? Are we going to eat it?"

"Well, young lady, refined and bleached sugar has a multitude of excellent uses, but eating it is *not* one of them. In fact, one of the poorest uses of refined sugar is as a food substance. It has killed more humans than Stalin and Mao combined." He paused, winking at Lang, as if to say... *it's true...* then he continued. "But it is good for many medicinal reasons, not the least of which is the fact that sugar and honey have been used as an antibacterial agent for millennia." The older man began to elucidate on the healing properties of sugar but, at that moment, Natasha and Lang were not entirely paying attention. They were looking at one another.

When Natasha had entered the room with the bag of sugar, she'd glanced sideways at Lang. They caught one another's attention and held the look for what was a tiny moment that seemed like much longer to each of them. The glance was a tiny visual embrace, but then they released it and smiled to one another, as if to say... *There he goes again.*

* * * *

Monday

No one got much sleep. Treating Lang's infected wound stretched into the wee hours of the morning, and it had been a soul-wrenching mind siege, every single minute of it.

Before Natasha found the sugar, Peter hadn't had much hope left at all. The placebo trick wasn't real or tangible, but, at the time, it was the only real hope he had of halting or reversing Lang's infection.

The boy had been valiant. He had not even complained, not once, though Peter knew that he was in severe pain. In the older man's mind, finding the sugar had been a miracle. He'd exhausted his knowledge and experience, and, without just such a miracle, a stupid mind game was all that he had remaining in his bag of tricks.

Peter wasn't sure how far to take the whole miracle thing. *Even if we had the strongest antibiotics, nothing can* guarantee *success*, Peter thought. He grimaced, thinking that such was always the case. There were never any guarantees. Perfectly healthy people were dying by the thousands and tens of thousands every day.

He recalled the story of a group of people who had rescued a young, injured seal. They worked hard and nursed the seal back to health, and on a glorious day under a bright, blue sky they released the seal back into the wild with great fanfare, only to have the seal eaten by a huge shark within seconds of being set free. Life is tenuous. Peter knew that. Even when everything goes right, it is tenuous. He wasn't deceived about the probabilities of any of them living through the next year. *My dear uncle*, he thought...

Peter recalled his uncle Volkhov, and smiled when he considered what Lev would have thought of this young man who was being so brave. He wondered, grimly, whether his uncle would turn out to be right – if he'd been correct when he'd predicted that more than 90% of the population would die within a year.

Locating the sugar changed everything. Sugar, indeed, was one of the most effective natural treatments for infection known to man. This was no tall tale or attempt at alchemic voodoo. The problem is that, in order to apply the sugar remedy properly, the wound had to be opened, debrided and prepared. That meant that, due to the pain and sensitivity caused by the infection, Peter had been forced to subject Lang to a torturous several hours of the most excruciating pain that either one of them could have ever imagined.

Using the knife from Lang's pack, sterilized and wielded somewhat clumsily by a man who was knowledgeable and wise, if not practiced and efficient, Peter had removed all of the dead and infected flesh, some of it already turning gangrenous and rotting into the wound. The process was slow and exceedingly painful.

The debridement, which entailed the physical removal of all dead and infected material from the wound, was difficult, and Lang had to suffer through it without any anesthesia. They didn't even have the vodka. That had been in Peter's backpack when it was stolen. All they had now was the leather sheath, and Lang had endured the torture admirably.

After cleaning and debriding the bullet hole (on both sides), a waiting period ensued while the wound bled a bit, and then they waited until that blood seepage stopped and coagulation had begun. Peter then packed the wound with the processed white sugar, which would act much as it does when it is used as a preservative on meat, blending with the blood and juices to create a thick "syrup" that then caused osmotic shock to the cells in the wound.

Peter explained this all to Natasha as he performed the treatment.

Elsie also sat and listened, taking notes in case she ever needed to remember how to do this. Taking notes also helped Elsie keep her mind off of the pain that Lang was evidently suffering.

Peter spoke on. "Osmotic shock means that the cells will give up their moisture and basically become dehydrated. This will rob the infection and bacteria of oxygen and water needed to spread and grow." He raised his hands, as if making a choking motion.

"Sugar has been used to treat serious battle wounds for centuries, and, even in the 21st century, some doctors and experts had come to believe that it should be the primary means of treating bullet wounds and subsequent infections."

Peter and his lectures, Natasha thought for a split second. She looked at Lang but he did not meet her gaze. He seemed to be too weak to show her any interest.

* * * *

Hours later, Lang rested comfortably, and the women were off talking in one of the other rooms of the cabin.

Peter ruminated on one of those odd little coincidences in life. Really, and truly, they have no real reason to exist. And yet they do, those moments of perfect harmony and beauty.

At that very moment, Peter was standing guard over his flock like a mother goose, or a father goose. He was thinking about the usefulness of the sugar. And he was thinking how that such knowledge—so much of it—is lost on the new generations. Then again, he also realized that he did not know as much as his Uncle Lev. *So many people*, Peter thought, *do not know or value what they have right there in front of them. If only they had eyes to see.*

Now, he was packing and repacking the backpack, while mentally sorting through the small little disturbances in his system. He needed to maintain a tightly catalogued system to know what they had and what they lacked.

And he came across a small blue box.

The box was in the backpack that had belonged to the man named Clay.

He looked at the box, held it up and wondered what was in it. He'd said he would open it if ever there was a moment when the contents might be used to help them survive or to save a life. He'd not thought of the box when he'd almost given up on treating Lang with anything other than a parlor trick.

Peter did wonder if anything in the box could speak to the issue, but, just in the nick of too late, the sugar had come to the rescue, and now he felt like the sanctity of the box must remain intact. He could not have explained *why,* if you'd asked him to, but he trusted his gut. He placed the box back in the bag, sat, and thought.

Altogether, for Peter, it was a moment of perfect beauty, the placing of the sugar in the wound, and then the box in the bag. Like in some, perhaps even many, of our best moments, there was a connection, something tangible but also spiritual. He felt that there was direction in the confluence of events that was unknown because unknowable. There was something in *not* looking in the blue box, because that box had a purpose, and that purpose was *not yet.* If Natasha had not found the sugar, and then Peter had been searching the backpack, he'd surely have opened the box. But Natasha had found the sugar, and it was perfect. It was what was needful at the moment.

Sure. He'd be disappointed if, upon opening the box someday, it turned out that the box was full of childhood teeth, or Chiclet gum, or beads from some bracelet or necklace from long ago. That would be a downer, for certain, because Peter believed that whatever was in that box was important. It was for saving lives. It had to be, and it was for the sustenance of that crucial belief that he once again refused to open the blue box. This once... this one shining moment... Peter trusted his gut.

* * * *

As the darkness gave way to gray, and then the gray in its turn succumbed to the brightness of the new morning, three of the travelers slept a little longer than they should have, and the fourth, Peter, hadn't slept at all. He'd tried to maintain watch but had drifted in and out of deeper and deeper thought. Anything to keep his mind off of Lang.

For this reason, none of them were ready when the attack came.

It all started peacefully enough. Peter, eyes open, was slipping in and out of brain sleep as he leaned against a tree. He'd been looking down at the cabin from a small ridge to the southwest of the structure when some men rode up on horseback and said hello.

He never saw them or heard them coming.

CHAPTER 30

Life often goes along in a stream. The details float by like a leaf on a river. The current is pushing and pulling the leaf, but we do not see it because we are standing on the banks of the river, attending to our lives. There are moments when the leaf is caught up in little eddies. Events pile up. They gather like twigs—like flotsam and jetsam—caught up in the stream of life. Time blocks and unblocks in little bursts at such places. Information pours through like water. The details crystallize. Various pressures and turbulences in the river, pouring into the sea of life, push and pull, but we do not see it. We do not see the leaf *or* the pushing and pulling.

Because we are standing on the banks, attending to our lives.

The leaf cannot be blamed for our missing it. Nor, from its perspective, should it care that we missed it. For its part, it is merely floating down the river on its back, caught up in swirling little curlicues of water, looking up at the stars. Perhaps, in the end, it is a matter of perspective after all. Perhaps if the leaf were to notice us, standing there on the shore, *we* would seem like mere details. Perhaps the leaf would think that *we* are just details among many other details, standing there along the banks, trying to be seen or to avoid being seen.

But sometimes even that is not the case.

Sometimes we are the leaf.

We get caught up in ourselves, in our own bodies, or in the stream. We are running, or driving, or riding, but almost always we are in motion. The details, the narrative flow of our lives, the events, they simply stream along past us. Drawing from the past, pushing toward an unknown future.

Perhaps we can be blamed for what we miss, we who are in perpetual movement. Perhaps not. We feel the miles roll by underneath us on the highway and feel them to be, like the stars overhead, endless, when they are not. We drift along on those details, noticing them as if they were standing on the river waving to us as we stream along. But we do not really notice them—the details—not really. Because we are on automatic pilot, just lazily floating down the river.

This happens even in catastrophes. We miss the signs.

* * * *

It was almost midnight, and Veronica and Stephen had covered an incredible amount of ground on their bikes in two straight days of riding.

They'd ridden across Staten Island, and then into New Jersey, and on into Pennsylvania. If you had asked Veronica to tell you her plan—what she hoped to do—she would simply have pointed to the ground and said: "Get as far away from *here* as possible."

After crossing the Verrazano Bridge, they'd passed through the destruction of the storm called Sandy on Staten Island. There were still boats in people's yards, some sitting on roofs of houses, and rubble and debris were everywhere. The Island was all covered with snow now. Here and there, the rubble peeked up through the piles of snow, as if to remind the people that it—the rubble—was still there.

Veronica and Stephen rode along through the broken city and past the destruction, past the piles of snow. Here and there they dodged rats that skittered across their pathway. Their hazmat gear barely raised an eyebrow as they rode along the coastline, and they rode on through the frozen fog likes ghosts, their yellow suits shimmering with a light glistening of moist sea air.

They rode past the piles of broken boards, the twisted pieces of siding, the musty old couches, all frozen under snow piled high along the rubble's edges in heaping white mounds. They passed by in silence.

They passed into New Jersey and into the suburbs and crossed bridges and hills and streams. They pushed forward like pilgrims, seeking a celestial city, or at the very least, a better country.

* * * *

Closer to the cities, the people were fleeing. The crowds were fleeing. They were on the bridges and the byways. They pushed like cattle through a chute where the roads narrowed around the debris of cars and trucks strewn through the streets. Vehicles and obstacles caused the waters of humanity to bulge around them like boulders in a stream, and, at the overpasses, the humans would stack up and bubble and roil until the waters made their way to the narrowed passage where they would gain speed and pick up momentum before shooting out of the other side. The people streamed along as if they were being drawn out of the cities and into the countryside by gravity or some other force of physics. They all walked with purpose, heading... *Where?*

* * * *

Veronica and Stephen had passed through the crowd as if in a protective bubble. Their hazmat suits worked like talismans. The crowds opened up around them as if they had the plague, as if they were aliens just landed on earth, and no one wanted to get too close.

Veronica and Stephen traveled as if under a star.

As darkness began to fall, the crowds thinned. Then, eventually, they disappeared altogether.

It was almost midnight.

Veronica and Stephen cruised along the back country roads that spread across the Pennsylvania countryside like a capillary system, drawing the goods from the richest farms in the world to market.

Every once in a while, they would get off the bikes and walk them for a spell. Or, they would stand and rest for a few moments and look at their surroundings in excitement and wonder.

"These roads once all led to Hershey," Veronica said. She pointed off in the distance to a skyline that was darkened except for what was illuminated by the moon.

Stephen smacked his lips. "Man! If *I* only had a Reese's cup right about now!" He poked her in the ribs.

"Naughty boy. One day, I will show you your Gramam's recipe for chocolate. It is twice as good!"

Stephen just laughed and they stood with their bikes and looked down the fence lines at the farms along the road.

"These farms are among the most productive in the world, and the most beautiful." She indicated with her hand to the farms. "And see how the fields spread thick with snow in wide, white blankets?" She pointed with her hand to the thick white swatches of color in front of them. "They look like that most winters. The snow lies there and replenishes the earth. And in spring they turn the pig manure under. Ewww!" She waved her hand in front of her nose. "Then the whole county stinks, but it's not so bad when they use horse or cow dung."

"How do you know all this, mom?"

"I learned how to read, boy. You should too." She looked at him sideways. "You with your video games." They shared a look and remembered where they were, and what the world was like now.

It wasn't really hard to do, the remembering, standing there, as they were, in the midst of the wide blue world, the ancient winter of Pennsylvania farmland rising up around them in a glow, their bright yellow suits shimmering with moisture in the moonlight.

* * * *

"Dude, I saw this interview with Manson once. He said the difference between him and the regular people out there is that—" The tattooed teenager paused and leaned forward. "Give me a loosie." The other young man handed him a cigarette. He lit his match and fired up the end, and then he indicated to the world with the cigarette. "If the regular guy out there, if he stepped off a bus in Des Moines at 10 p.m. and called his Aunt Gertrude and she wasn't home...," The tattooed young fellow blew out smoke in tiny little circles, and coughed. "...and Aunt Gertrude was his only ride, and if he was flat broke, the average guy wouldn't know what to do with himself. Whereas he—Manson—would dip into an alley and grab a tire iron and he'd be in business."

Snort. Hmph! The second young man, who was listening to the tattooed young fellow rattle, gave only this harrumphing series of audible gesticulations as retort, and this conversation continued thusly for a while.

The two teens were sitting by the roadside, crouched low to the ground in a ditch. They were part of a militia patrol unit sent forward to scope out the road. Actually, they were scouts for a group of bandits, but they liked to think of themselves as a militia. They'd copped some uniforms, and several of the older bandits had some military experience, so they'd received a little training, but not much. They called themselves the *Pennsylvania Anarchists Corps*, the PAC, or usually, "The PACK."

This unit, made up almost entirely of new recruits, orphans, and people forced into duty by the leaders, had been sent forward to make sure the road was safe, but right now the boys were sitting along a ditch. Actually, to be accurate, they were sitting *in* the ditch and telling stories to one another—trying to impress each other with their toughness, their readiness to do whatever it takes—the way teenaged boys will.

They didn't notice at first when the two yellow suits rode up on bikes.

* * * *

Sometimes life can go by like a stream of details in a narrative. Page after page, the stream of time pushes through, gathering force. The details can be like brushwork on a painting, the buildup of the paint. Or like the fingers at the keyboard, the wastebasket full of crumpled ideas. The drink of scotch, the scratch of a head, the scratching out of ideas on pads of paper. The pushing in of soil around the roots. The coming of spring. All this is done in the pursuit of art. Beauty, and Art. Which are to enliven and protect life. Because the point of all this is to enliven and protect life. To live, that is, in the here and the now. To live thoroughly and authentically. To live in nature. To walk out under the stars like Whitman and look up in the silence and take it all in.

Veronica was thinking these things as they pedaled along.

It is really very simple, Veronica thought. *The point is to live-and to keep living.*
Hear that, she told herself.

The point is... *to live.*

* * * *

Veronica and Stephen had no idea what they were riding into because all they could see was white and even more white. Patches of field spread out across their view in the moonlight, enhancing the panorama with its breathless series of farms and fields. It looked like an Amish quilt. The fields of white were intercut with black segmenting lines that ran their way around the edges of the farms.   Veronica and Stephen were simply riding along enjoying the cool night air, weaving down another mile of long, thin ribbon.

At first Veronica didn't even see him.   The man simply stepped out into the roadway and held up his hand.   It was probably his rifle she saw first.   Slung over his shoulder the way it was, it hung across his body, intersecting his torso, pointing up at right angles to the nighttime sky. She had just begun to focus on the rifle when she felt herself motioning to Stephen to stop. She began to search for the pistol she had strapped to her bike.

That's when a gang of bandits descended on them from all sides.

* * * *

Calvin Rhodes also cruised along the stream of time. He also drove on his ribbon of highway, stringing up and down the rolling hills and stretching plains and backwood hollers and the ancient farmland of This Great Country (That's the way he'd always heard it said where he'd grown up. *This Great Country.*)

The countryside he'd passed through was some of the richest farmland in the world.   He passed mile after mile through the Piney Woods, then through the Ozarks, and through West Virginia coal mining country, into Pennsylvania. He drove into that state's coal country and then dropped southwards along the state's border, and into what is perhaps the best farmland of all.

But before that—along the way—along the seemingly interminable stretch of highway that is Tennessee, he'd stopped at one of his checkpoints.

"I knew yer daddy. He was a good man."

That was all the man had said to him. Then the man leaned into the window and shook Calvin's hand. He told Calvin that now he ought to have enough gas to get him to his next stopover.

"Tell Mr. Wall, when you see him, that Lem said hello."

Calvin nodded solemnly, and the old man put his foot on the kickboard and made a motion with his arms like he was slinging the truck outward into space, throwing his arms out, as if to say '*on your way!*'

Everyone, it seemed, knew Jonathan Wall. Everyone who was helpful at a time like this had read Mr. Wall's books.

Calvin pulled out along the winding road and out to the county highway, and the adventure continued.

He thought about home as he drove along. He thought about that word. *Home.* He thought about Texas. Then he thought about his dad. He'd always had a kind of fluid identity. Maybe his dad had passed that on to him. *Most men are*, he thought, *fluid beings. They either bend with the times, or they are of the sort that shape them.* His mind had wandered, and he wondered whether he was a *"home is where you hang your hat"* kind of guy. Then he thought again about the man who'd sent him on this journey, Mr. Wall. Jonathan Wall was a man who shaped the times. His name described him more than anything else did. Everyone of any import in this new world knew Jonathan Wall because Mr. Wall was the man who'd said that all of this would happen. He was the man who, in his books, told people to expect it and to prepare.

The rolling hills and the beautiful trees and the quiet of the nighttime sky whizzed by, and they all could have been waves on the ocean for all Calvin noticed them. He was riding on a train of thought down a track.

He watched the road ahead of him the way a person who is getting sleepy watches the road. In a daze. That is perfectly understandable. It is in the nature of things.

Because it was midnight, and Calvin *was*, in fact, getting sleepy.

CHAPTER 31

The lamps from Calvin's old Ford pickup threw a distinct pair of spotlights onto the roadway. They were not centered on the stripe, aiming at some unified middle distance. They simply pointed straight forward out onto the roadway just in front of him, but only *just* in front. Headlights are one of the things that did, indeed, improve over time.

The Ford's lights only revealed the world in stages. They lit up each successive field of vision only a slight... bit... further... ahead. Having driven mostly by instinct for an hour, flying mostly blind, Calvin was blurrily staring out into the dark of the night. He was looking into the space that the lamps lit least. They shone out as if they were spotlights on a stage. They pointed downward from the balcony onto the stage of his life, which, right now, was the roadway. Seated in that balcony, he was only a spectator.

In the two globules of light, spread out and amplified by the white of the snow, framing the shot, were two yellow suits fighting for their lives.

They were fighting as if they wanted *to live*.

* * * *

Calvin saw them but he did not know, at first, what to make of them. It was a surreal vision. They were off in the further distance, just on the wings of the stage. The scene, gathering light, only came slowly into view. There were two groups of men. Boys, really. Fighting with the suits, trying to get them into several trailers or wagons parked along the road. The yellow suits were struggling to escape from their captors. The taller of the suits was reaching backwards, toward something lying in the road.

* * * *

Calvin can almost make it out. He can almost *see* what the thing is laying in the road. It is coming into his headlights. And then he is upon it. The miles and the yards and the feet... and the inches. They all flew by him. He came to a dead, forward, thrusting standstill.

He heard the gas cans slosh behind him as the pickup rattled to a shuddering halt. *Sheesh!* He ducked his head down and held his breath, cringing. He'd heard of static electricity building up in gas cans that are not grounded, then blowing up like a bomb. He sniffed the air for any smell of leaked gas as he got out of the car and ran around to the front. He smelled no leaks and bent down to inspect the items in the road. Two bikes, with some bags strapped to them. Stepping out, he gathered both bikes and threw them into the back of his truck bed, moving deftly and staying low around the truck. He didn't know exactly why he was doing it, but it felt right, and he didn't argue with himself. He worked quickly and instinctively, without a plan other than to help. He swung around the door and jumped into the cab and realized that he had not turned off his lights on approach.

* * * *

Some of the men who'd been fighting with the yellow suits, the ones in motley military uniforms, were now coming towards him. They were shouting at him and waving their arms. Calvin could not make out what they were shouting but he did not need to.

He inched the vehicle forward, as if he were pulling up to ask directions. As if he were just some guy out on a Sunday drive and he'd taken a wrong turn. He came upon the first of the men, and he punched the truck forward. He pushed at the horn but with no effect. He was just ad-libbing now, an actor on the stage who didn't know his lines. He just did what felt right.

He swerved this way and that as the thugs tried to run along beside him and reach into the cab. He swerved into the snow embankments on the sides of the road, spinning the wheel and the truck to shake the men off, and he just kept driving. The men in the uniforms up ahead, the ones fighting with the yellow suits, stopped and gawked at the spectacle. Everyone stopped for a moment as Calvin broke free and drove like a maniac toward the yellow suits and toward the uniforms.

* * * *

There was a moment when, in the headlights of the pickup, Calvin saw in the eyes of the uniformed bandits that they thought they might intimidate him. They raised their guns and pointed them directly at his head. They stood in the roadway as if they thought that would stop him. They thought that it would stop *anyone*. They can't be blamed much. It is in the nature of things. The guards were simply not accustomed to dealing with people who did not understand the underlying force implied in such situations. They lived, unconsciously, by the Maoist doctrine that truth was found in the barrel of a gun, and they were not accustomed to coming across people who were not familiar with such a philosophy. The guards weren't normally challenged in such a manner. But it didn't take them long to figure out that they didn't like it.

They stood in the roadway with their guns pointed at Calvin's head, and they wondered whether the driver of the approaching pickup knew just *who they were*. Did he know exactly *who he was dealing with?*

The answer to that question, had they bothered to actually ask it, would have been "Yes."

But that wasn't the problem.

The problem was not that Calvin did not know who the men in the road were, or that he did not see their guns, or that he did not assess the danger. Rather, it was exactly the opposite. The problem was that the soldiers in the road, pointing at him with their guns, thinking that threats were all that needed to be said on the matter, did not know Calvin Rhodes.

The light of the headlamps bore down upon the guards and they scattered like cockroaches before it. One of the rear guards held his ground though. As the guard sighted down his gun to shoot though the windshield, Calvin leaned slightly to his left, and then turned his head towards the side glass. He prayed.

As the bullet ripped through the windshield, and the cab, and then the back glass, missing Calvin's head by inches, he slammed on the brakes and the truck slipped sideways and struck the gunman with the passenger-side rear fender back by the bed. Calvin thought, *that guy ain't gonna make it,* and then he accelerated again, streaming by the other bandits, heading towards the yellow suits.

Calvin came upon the yellow suits as if in slow motion, and they looked like aliens, these people, in their hoods and breathing apparatus. They leaned toward his pickup, in the ball of light created by the ancient headlamps, and held up hands as if in supplication. Their bright yellow suits were set in contrast with the red of the truck, the green of the tarp, the white of the snow.

Calvin leaned over to look into the framing of his pickup truck's window. The taller suit leaned in to stare at him as he passed. *A face in a window.* The truck paused.

Time itself paused. It was a woman's face, looking out the plastic window of the hazmat helmet. Her breath momentarily, just for a micro-second, fogged up the shield of her helmet as he passed by, but then it cleared. Her startled visage was luminous in the nighttime glow. Not even for a moment did she look frightened. But she looked at Calvin, and he noticed it. And she mouthed the words...

Help Us.

* * * *

Get In! He mouthed the words back at her. He pointed to the back of the pickup. The two yellow suits put their weight on the running boards and pushed their way up onto the bed, even as Calvin peeled out along the highway. He punched the gas and shifted gears, and they were almost fifty yards away before the bullets began to rain down on them. The shots, thankfully, were not very accurate. He was half a mile away before the sounds of gunfire faded into the night and were masked by the crunching of the tires on the road and the cold wind knifing through the bullet hole in the windscreen.

He'd learned from his recent mistakes, and, after the two yellow suits had piled into the bed of the truck, he'd flipped the headlights off. It's hard to hit what you cannot see, his father had told him. But now he was driving blindly through the night, and he tried his best to use the glow of the stars in the nighttime sky to drive by, watching intently for the faint reflection from the road that disappeared near its edges.

He drove unconsciously, and couldn't have told you if you'd asked just how long his mind was frozen in the shock of the moment.

Kerthump.

Calvin heard it, but it didn't really register. Then it came again and again.

Kerthumkerthumpkerthump... kerthump!

He struggled to hold the wheel on the road, and as he gripped the wheel in a white-knuckled embrace, he became aware of the knocking on the window behind his head. The car rumbled and shook. The drive shaft shook too as he fought to keep control. He glanced at the gauges. He'd been doing sixty-something in the dark. Maybe more. Adrenaline exploded through his mind and body. The truck slowed to almost nothing, and the sound of muffled screams through the busted window behind his head. It was timed with the pounding of a fist on the cab top.

* * * *

Calvin had driven into a ditch. He was riding on four flats tires. *Blowouts,* he thought, *On all four, and all at once!* He'd been blessed that the truck hadn't overturned... blessed to be alive.

He sniffed the air and jumped out of the cab. Again, no fumes. Calvin gave a little hop to look over the truck bed, where he saw a tangle of tarp and bikes and cans... and yellow hazmat suits. He looked in at the wriggling bodies inside the suits. The tallest of the them eventually righted itself and reached up to unbuckle its hood. It was the woman. The face in the window. The shorter suit was a boy, obviously her son. The resemblance was clear. They were beautiful, the two of them. Calvin smiled.

"Sorry about the ride."

"What?! Are you trying to kill us der, boy?"

Calvin looked at the woman, and then she smiled at him. It was all the thanks he needed, her smile. There was something poetic in it, the same quality that made people stand in front of the Mona Lisa and stare.

* * * *

Stephen looked at his mother. He'd noticed that her accent was coming out with the stress of the travel. He looked at the guy who had just saved them, and they both broke into a grin. Stephen jabbed his mom in the ribs. "Kill us *der...* Mom? *Der?* Really?"

Stephen smiled at Calvin again and nodded his head to the older youth. He did it in a way that said *Hey, nice rescue and stuff.* Calvin looked at the two of them, these yellow suits, whom he'd just rescued from a gunfight in a snowfield... and he screwed up his face. It should have been an awkward moment, but it wasn't.

He looked at them with his most inquisitive look... and asked, "Hey... got anything to eat?"

* * * *

"You looked like those guys on Breaking Bad," Calvin said. There he was again, referring to a television show. The two of them just laughed.

"Yeah, I guess we did," Stephen answered. "Good thing, too. I was about to go all Heisenberg on them." Calvin and Stephen laughed again. They were sitting with their backs against the truck while Veronica scouted out an area to see if she could find some little nook or cranny where they might hide throughout the night.

"We'll attend to the vehicle in the morning," she said. And then she'd gone to scout.

She'd only been gone fifteen minutes, and the two teens were already talking like old friends, remembering what that *other* world was like, as if it weren't really gone.

"Dude... did you see that one show that was going to come out on F/X?" Stephen paused. That was one way to tell that the boys were beginning to reckon with the new world. They'd begun to talk about the old life in tenses that showed they'd once thought for a moment that it might return, but now they no longer did.

"Yeah ... that show that was gonna be about Russian spies in America? What was it gonna to be called?"

"Oh yeahyeahyeah. That one from the Cold War, with Reagan and Michael Jackson and stuff. Ummm, *The Americans?*" Stephen said, nodding his head. "I saw the preview. It looked like it was going to be good."

"Dude, that chick on that show was hot," Calvin said, looking at Stephen and smiling. "She looked like she could kick some butt."

"Yeah," Stephen said. He smiled and thought of a girl in a bodega in that other world. "I'd betray my country for a chick like that."

"Yeah... a chick like that, or..." Calvin made a little mock motion of sniffing the air, "some French fries."

Veronica could hear their guffaws from several hundred yards away as she walked toward them in silence through the night.

* * * *

Veronica stayed up through the night, watching. She had her pistol and she hoped she'd never be forced to use it. They'd walked a good quarter-mile into the forest before bedding down for the night. Stephen and Calvin slept in fits and starts. Before morning broke, she roused them, and they put on their clothes while she put out some food for them. She hummed a song under her breath, and occasionally she'd break out into a small bit of lyric. She sang the line in its lilting, sing-song herkyjerkyness. She swung her head to the side when she did it, her long ropy braids whipping over her shoulder. Then she stopped, and caught herself. She'd thought she was humming under her breath, but she'd actually sung out loud. She stopped, and the boys looked at her. She was caught like a deer in the headlights.

"What's that song, Mrs. D?" Calvin was already fitting in the way that kids like Calvin do, seamlessly. He was already calling her "Mrs. D." He looked at her, expectantly.

"Oh, just a song that I was listening to before," Veronica said. As she did so, she waved out into the nothingness, as if to say *all this.* Stephen rolled his eyes. "Oh, again, with the Clay stuff." Veronica cut him a sharp glance. It was clear that whatever "the Clay stuff" was had been a topic of some conversation between them. Calvin looked at them both, wondering what he'd stepped into.

"There was this guy that came by our house during the storm." Stephen indicated with his hand somewhere *back* there. "He was cool. He and my mom connected. They listened to this group called the Mountain Goats, and...," He rolled his eyes at his mom.

"What? It's a good song," Veronica said.

"I agree," Calvin said. Stephen looked at him sideways like a sibling who realizes he has competition. Stephen made a mock look of pain.

"No, really. They're cool," Calvin said. "I mean, I haven't heard the *new* new stuff, but they are always good." Stephen stepped back as if to say *You're killing me.*

Veronica laughed at their antics. "The thing that *really* bothers Stephen about the Clay *situation,"* Veronica said, nodding her head to Stephen as if they'd had this conversation before, "I may have overstepped my bounds when the man stayed with us. I took some poems of his and had them bound without his permission. Stephen thought that what I did was a horrible breach of privacy. But I couldn't help myself." She looked at Stephen and he looked at Calvin. "Well, some of them were..." she searched through the air to find the word, "...lovely."

They were walking low along a hedge at the edge of a paddock, keeping their eyes peeled across the pristine field of white. The boys could tell that she was bound to go on and so they let her.

"There was this one poem that described a Van Gogh painting. And I *love* Van Gogh. It was partly him who inspired me to paint! Anyway, the poem described the lush fields and broken doors on their hinges, and the sea, and the sea of faces that are found in his paintings. But it was more than just about the color. It was also about the loneliness of being Van Gogh, in his brilliance, and his madness. We almost never knew him, you know? It was only through the support and the promotion of his brother that he became well-known. Otherwise, he was an outcast. In Gauguin, he had a friend who seemed to understand him, but Gauguin was always *promising* to come and see him. He rarely did."

Veronica and the boys walked circumspectly as they talked. She indicated to the wider world with her hand, the white of the field, the hint of blue invading the gray of the morning sky. "Anyway," she said, "it was a lovely poem."

With that, Calvin, Stephen, and Veronica found themselves standing at the back bumper of the rusted red pickup truck in the brown-white slush of the accident. "It was a nail strip," Veronica told them. "I found it last night when I was out on patrol. Whoever put it there will be around soon enough to check it. We have to work quickly."

Standing in the thin blue light of morning, their breath rose up before them. It rose in little puffs against the coldness of the air.

From the Poems of C.L. Richter

A question

And what is to stop a *Van Gogh* –
*Weary from too many Arlesienne nights lost in a haze of whores
and absinthe,*
Mad from waiting for a Gauguin, who never comes, to come –

*From getting up from his makeshift bed, loose-joined planks
creaking under the weight of his rising shift, tangled sheets
clamoring, twisting underneath him, stretching out their
gnarled arms to hold down his gaunt form,*
*From dressing in his threadbare clothes, simple sepia-toned,
basket-woven fabrics, dried on a hook, stiffened, still-
containing smells of flesh, earth and sea-breeze,*
*From running his thin, rangy hands across his haggard face, five
days growth of shocking redorange beard skeining through
his fingertips, rioting against the calm in the browns of his
shirt, the blues of the walls, his own fleshy tones,*
*From binding up his canvases, hands stippled with spikes of pure
color, soft as leather, strong like wire, and lacing the
binding under his arm, his ragged hat cocked slightly on
his head, pulled over one ear, shading light over one eye,*
*From walking out of his cottage, down the pebbled pathway,
redbrown door swinging slightly ajar, quivering uncertainly
in the thin morning light,*
*From walking along a broken trail and, at its end, across a golden
field,*
*autumn grass bending in a breezy sway, nodding toward a
still further field where sunflowers rise like soldiers, their
sharp sentry eyes scanning the surrounding hills, warily
watching a row of greenbrown olive trees congregating at
the edge of the plowline, their smaller hedges rising up
like smoke in wispy branches,*
*From traversing the field in sharp diagonal lines that lengthen out
and flatten as the hills give way to coastline and miles of
organic biomass teeming in a salty, towing surf, heard
before it can be seen, smelled before it can be heard,*

From finding a small yellowblue dinghy tied along the greengrey waterline and fashioning a makeshift sail out of stitched-together canvases, hoisted up the boom and creaking against the rigging as they unfurl and expand to reveal radiant flowers, swirling firmament, and boldly textured faces in the shimmering sunlight,

And from loosening the mooring, leaning his weight into the pull of the halyards, and setting off towards the distant horizon, where line and form are one?

CHAPTER 32

The shot and the echo of the shot rang out across the little clearing and bounced up into the trees and then the sky.

Peter turned and saw the man on horseback, his arm raised, holding a rifle at a right angle to his body. His brain at first refused to believe the information being transported to it by his sleepy eyes. A warning shot. The man brought down the rifle and aimed straight at Peter. He wouldn't warn again. His uniform was that of the Missouri National Guard.

Peter understood enough of what was occurring to know that he should not raise his own rifle. He put his hands in the air, and from around him appeared other soldiers who swooped down on him like hawks. They disarmed him and pulled his hands behind his back.

The man on the horse, the one with the rifle, was lecturing him about the new laws. Specifically, the man was telling him that it was a death penalty offense to be carrying a weapon of any kind. The officer droned on for a moment, the horse turning from side to side, as Peter was led to a tree at the edge of the clearing. It took the entirety of this time for Peter to become cogent enough to understand that he was not in a dream.

The man ordered the other soldiers to tie Peter to the tree, and they did so without any hesitation. It was at this point when reality zoomed back into focus, the brain sleep cleared, the adrenaline began pumping, and Peter realized that he was seconds away from being killed.

* * * *

When the firing started from down the hill, the man on horseback, the leader of this Missouri National Guard unit, was sighting down his rifle and just about to pull the trigger in order to execute Peter for the crime of illegally bearing arms. He hesitated though, just as he was about to squeeze off the fatal round, when he heard shots ring out from just down the hill, near the cabin. His eyes shifted towards the sound of the shots and he spotted the interruption just in time to see the second soldier, who was just then attempting ingress into the cabin, fall mortally wounded.

During that millisecond when his eyes cut to the cabin, his rifle swayed. It was a tiny motion. Most people would have never noticed it. Perhaps the sway was involuntary, but it was enough. Bringing his attention back to his task, he had to take just a tiny second longer to steady his aim, sitting on the horse, and at that moment, almost the instant he found his target again, his head burst into a spray of blood, brains, and bone.

The body toppled off the horse, and as the dead officer's blood began to pump into the snowy ground, his body writhed. Two more of his men dropped in succession—felled by bullets fired from somewhere in the distance.

The shots that killed the soldiers could only be faintly identified as sharp cracks piercing the crisp morning air. The sound echoed for a moment and then was gone. The remaining soldiers began to drop to the ground in panic, and they attempted to crawl back over the low rise, but before they could find cover, two more of them were shot dead from afar.

It was a turkey shoot.

* * * *

Lang awoke to the sound of gunfire. Really close gunfire. He remembered waking up this way that last morning in Warwick, and he instinctively rolled over and felt the pain shoot up his wounded arm. It was a different pain, and his brain registered the difference. He was feeling better, he could tell. The sugar cure was working, and even without any food last night or breakfast this morning, he felt like life was returning into him. He'd gone to sleep not knowing if he would ever wake up again, but now he was awake, and the gunfire gave impetus to his feelings of being free and alive. However, now there was shooting going on, and he needed to find out what it was all about.

He low-crawled into the hallway and saw a dead soldier slumped over the broken wood of the door, and could see another dead soldier only a few feet outside the entryway, splayed backwards and bleeding from his mouth and nose.

Lang heard shuffling and felt a strong tug on the back of his jacket. He looked up to see Natasha and Elsie pulling him. He lurched to help them, and they dragged him out from the sight lines of the doorway and into the front bedroom. He looked around at the room. It was the one that Natasha had first rolled into when the men tried to invade the cabin. He rolled up on his shoulder and, just as he did, more gunfire shattered the morning. Bullets pierced through the walls like they didn't even exist, and Lang noticed as little holes of light appeared in the walls and streams of sunshine flowed through the little holes and splashed across the floor in tight lines. *A wooden building is not a great place to be in a battle,* he thought.

"Nope. Not this room!" Natasha shouted, and now Lang was being dragged again, like a mannequin, past the hallway and into the kitchen. Natasha had noticed when they'd first entered the cabin that the exterior walls of the kitchen were made of heavy field stone. If she remembered correctly, the stone went at least four feet up the surface. Natasha, Elsie, and Lang stumbled in their low crawls into the kitchen area as the cabin began to rock with the gunfire that relentlessly pierced the structure.

* * * *

Kent was sick. He could feel his stomach spasm, and the stew and vodka tumbled around in his gut and would not settle. It was not the food and drink from the previous night that had made Kent sick - at least it was not *primarily* the food and drink. He was sick of everything. Mostly he was sick of Val.

"Damn, are you drunk, again, pudgy boy?"

It was Val, talking over his shoulder. The large, brutish man had become for Kent a symbol of everything that made him sick, of everything that was making the whole world sick.

"I drank but one cup last night," Kent muttered under his breath. The alcohol sloshed in his stomach. He knew that probably wasn't true.

The four were struggling up a sharp incline, and Mike had ordered Kent to carry the new backpack—the one they'd just taken from the man that Val had recently killed.

The four travelers had stumbled upon the man sobbing in the woods. He was wearing what might have once been a business suit, and he didn't hear the approaching party until it was too late. In fright, he'd spun around, and as he did so, he lifted a hunting knife, and before he could even rightly wield it or threaten anyone with the instrument, Val had kicked it clean out of the man's hand.

What had happened next was the reason that Kent was sick.

The man had immediately dropped to the ground and had begun pleading for his life. His story spilled from him like water over a dam. The story went by so fast that it was hard to make out, but Kent had gotten the gist of it.

The man and two of his friends had been traveling on behalf of the Governor of Pennsylvania when all the cars had simultaneously stopped on the highway (the EMP, Kent noted.) The three men tried to escape the horrors of the highway by making their way through the woods, but, in the last few days, both of his friends had been killed.

While the man whimpered and sobbed through his story, Val was busy rifling through the man's backpack and noticed that it was full of survival gear, ammunition, and food and even an ammo can with a radio and other electrical devices.

"Where'd you get all the swell survival gear, huh?" Val asked with an accusation in his voice. "I'm pretty sure that Governor's aids don't carry this kind of gear on business trips."

"Uhh... ahhh... well, we just came upon it," the man answered. Guilt and shame were evident on the man's face, and this, more than anything, enraged the brutish Val.

Val stopped his rummaging and walked over to the man and kicked him straight in the face as hard as he possibly could. Kent noted to himself that it was remarkable what a boot can do to a human face. Remarkable and grotesque. The man, bloody face buried in the snow, began sobbing again, and now he'd locked down completely. Emotionally and mentally the man was just spent. He didn't respond to any of Val's questions, and this struck Val as a lack of the proper respect he thought he was due. Mike, Steve, and Kent had all tried to stop him, but Val began to stomp the man, and in short order, he'd succeeded in leaving behind a bloody corpse.

This is why Kent was sick to his stomach.

* * * *

Elsie's mind was churning, and her eyes flicked from left to right as she tried to calculate and understand everything that was happening.

She shouted it. "Peter!"

"He's up on the ridge!" Lang said over the thwacks and zings of bullets coming through the building.

"I've got to get to him," Elsie whispered.

"You can't go out there, Elsie," Natasha said. "They'll cut you down."

"I can go out the back. The firing is starting to slow down, and it has all come from the front. I'll run out and keep low and get into the trees and then work my way up to the ridge." She looked at them. "I have to." She had the beginnings of a tear in her eye. "He's up there all alone."

"Peter can take care of himself," Lang said, a little too sharply.

"He's not up there taking care of himself, young man." Elsie shot back. "He's up there taking care of *us*."

"If you go," Natasha said, as debris from the walls rained down around them, "take Lang's backpack... in case you get lost, or we don't make it."

"You'll make it, Natasha. Both of you will. I just know it!"

Natasha smiled amid the horrors. *Nothing like a Pollyanna to give you hope when the world is collapsing on your head.*

Elsie saw Natasha's smile and returned it. Then she broke for the back door, picking up Lang's pack and throwing it over her shoulder on her way out.

Lang grabbed the .22 and Natasha lifted the pistol. Both weapons were woefully inappropriate for such a gunfight. Still, both of them began to tug at the carpets that covered the windows so that they could lay down some covering fire for Elsie. They did this because both Natasha and Lang were thinking about Elsie and Peter and not about themselves.

* * * *

Kent had finally made it up to the top of the grade when he felt his gorge rise, and in a second he was doubled over, vomiting onto the snow and rocks.

"Great," Val sneered. "What a winner you turned out to be. Just look at you. I'm sick of your weakness!"

Kent wiped his mouth with his sleeve and dropped the pack. He took a step towards Val, "Then why don't you try to stomp me to death, you sadistic bastard!"

Val seemed willing to do just that, but Steve and Mike jumped between the two before any more violence could commence. After the two men had been pulled apart, Mike stepped into Val's space and put his face only inches from the brutish man's nose. He'd done this once before, back in a prison cell in Warwick. Val was a full foot taller, but Mike's presence had a weight and gravity all of its own.

"One more argument," Mike said. He cleared his throat. "One more threat. One more unauthorized stomping. One more unauthorized *anything* from you Vladimir, and I'll kill you myself. Do you understand me, Comrade?"

The man who now called himself Val dropped his eyes and took a step back. "I understand, Comrade Mikail Mikailivitch."

Mike looked over to Kent and pointed to the fallen backpack. "Pick it up."

Kent did.

* * * *

The four men fell back into line, and as they hiked in a southwesterly direction, they saw the valley open up below them, and Kent was glad that at least for a little while they'd be walking downhill.

He took up the rear, right behind Val, and as the group marched forward through the snow, Kent whispered so that just Val could hear him.

"I called you a sadistic bastard because you are literally a sadist and the fatherless son of a whore. So there's that, Vladimir. And, also this. Before this is over, I am going to kill you."

Death and violence have a tendency to multiply when the shackles of civility are thrown off. Men who are violent and rapacious killers can be identified more readily, and men who might otherwise be peaceful and passive are sometimes not able to resist the desire to rid the world of soulless predators. There are such men even among the poets.

* * * *

Elsie sprinted towards the trees and bullets zipped around her. Snow popped up into the air where the shots plowed into the ground. She could hear that gunfire was being returned from the cabin, and she could see the impacts popping at her feet. Then the shots that were loosely aimed in her direction stopped, but she did not.

Rounding the edge of the hill, she was surprised to meet up with Peter who was on his way down toward the rear of the cabin. He had the AK-47 at the ready, and he grabbed Elsie by the arm and pulled her over to a stand of trees, and they crawled into the brush near the base of the stand.

"How'd you get out of there?" Peter asked.

"Natasha and Lang covered me," Elsie answered, breathlessly.

"Why didn't they escape with you?"

"Lang is better, but he is in no condition to travel. Natasha would never leave him. I would have stayed too, but I thought... I ought to find out what happened to you. We—" she indicated to the cabin with her hand. She tried to brush a wisp of hair away. She tried to do it with the gentleness of her fingertips, but they were clammy with dried blood, so instead she raised the sweaty backside of her arm to her forehead and wiped away the strand. "We... we thought you might be dead," Elsie said, her eyes dropped to look at her knees in the snow.

"I'm not dead, but I almost was. I was captured on the ridge up there by the Missouri Guard. They were going to execute me."

Elsie sucked in her breath. "I'm sorry." Peter shook it off as if to *say no need.* "How'd you get off that ridge, Peter?" Elsie asked.

Peter looked at her and shrugged. The knowledge that he would certainly have been dead by now was fully upon him as he stared at Elsie. He smiled a crooked smile and said one word...

"Ace."

* * * *

The sounds of gunfire from the battle grew louder as Mike, Steve, Val, and Kent moved to the southwest. They came to a ridge, approaching from the northeast, and they crawled up to the top of it to see if they could make out what the fuss was all about.

What they saw shocked them. At the top of the ridge were a number of dead bodies. All of the corpses were in uniform, and Mike, crawling to one of the men who had been shot in the back of the head, saw the insignia for the Missouri National Guard on the uniform.

Looking down from the ridge, they could see that a gunfight had erupted around a small cabin. Forces in the woods opposite the front door of the cabin were pouring fire into the structure, while every once in a while random and impotent shots would ring out, fired from the windows of the cabin itself.

Staying as low as possible, Mike, Steve, and Val moved quickly, checking the bodies of the dead soldiers for weapons, ammunition, or other valuables. Even on the ridge above the valley of death, there is salvage to be had. Kent, meanwhile, had come across another body—this one looked to be the corpse of an officer—and he discreetly secured a pistol he found on the ground near the body. He was an intellectual and not a fighter, and prior to the end of the world, he'd have never considered hurting anyone. Sometimes, however, a gun can come in handy, and Kent figured that such a time had now presented itself.

Mike never saw Kent take the gun. He was now busy spying out the battle taking place below him. He heard a sharp crack from the distance ring out. He could not make out from where the shot was coming, but he saw one of the soldiers from among the contingent assailing the cabin fall dead.

Another crack from the distance, and another soldier fell. Mike's eyes began to scan the hills in the distance to the east. He knew from his training what was happening...

Sniper.

CHAPTER 33

Veronica said, "Okay, now this is what we're going to do, boys." They looked at her expectantly. "My dad was a resourceful guy. Back when he was doing work on the faraway settlements in Trinidad, he saw these Indian guys packing straw into their tires, because there was no compressed air to be had."

"Yes!" Calvin said, excitedly. Veronica and Stephen looked at him with startled looks on their faces. It was something in the way he said that *Yes!* He made it sound like he had more important things to say on the manner. So they let him speak.

"My dad, he was a pharmaceutical engineer back in China. Back before the crackdown. During it, really." He paused and looked at them.

It should have been strange. Just last night he'd rescued these two strangers from a gun battle, and now he was telling them things... *things about his dad.* It should have been strange, but it wasn't.

He continued. "Yeah, so my dad, he told me this story about how the Chinese government sent him to the outback, you know, down in Australia. They wanted him to find this one plant or something, to make an assessment of its chemical potential on the spot." He paused. "They were testing him." Calvin felt a little flush rise in his cheeks, just a hint of anger. He looked at the two of them, and then remembered where he was, and what he was doing. He blushed in full.

"But anyway, he told me some natives did just that. They simply rolled the car over on its top and filled all four tires with straw, all at once. My dad said those guys were like a Daytona pit crew, just all wild and crazy. Detailed *and* quick *and* efficient. They packed the grass and straw together, wetting it down. If they had water handy, they'd mix it with thick mud, like cob. They'd bend it into the curves of the tire and then pound it in with rocks." He rubbed his face with his hand. "If they didn't have water, they just packed the grass and straw really tight... just pound it as tight as they could get it with the stones.

Veronica and Stephen smiled at the image.

"Strong at the broken places..." Veronica whispered, under her breath.

"Ma'am?" Calvin stuttered.

"Oh, 'strong at the broken places.' It's something Hemingway wrote. I was thinking how the straw in a way becomes strong, inside the tire, by bending, by bonding with the others, by utilizing both its tensile and flexile strength." Her voice trailed off at the end of the sentence. She'd seen the hurt in Calvin's eyes when he talked about his father. She'd also heard the anger in his voice, although she did not know where that anger came from. Veronica knew, without his having to say it, that Calvin had lost his father. She wanted to say something to help him, but she realized that, in this time, there was not much room for such niceties. Still, she wanted to him know. She wanted to say the words... *We know. We've lost someone, too...*

* * * *

"And I was also thinking of you, young man!"

Veronica turned to Calvin, who looked startled. "You've lost your father. Anyone who has eyes to see can see that. My son has lost his father, too." She paused, and looked at Stephen. "And I have lost a husband. But, we become strong at the broken places. Even here." She placed her hand to her heart, her hand in a fist. She tapped her heart two times. Calvin looked at her, and he wanted to say something, *anything,* to let her know that he understood.

"And here you are, young man. You have been given to us a second time. First, with the truck and now, well, with the truck again." She indicated with her hand to the tires. "You know how to do this good work, because your father passed that knowledge down to you." She looked at him as if to say that Stephen would be his brother now. As if they would look out for each other, and she would play mother hen. "So... Do you see?"

She pointed to the tires, ground down to the nubbins. She pointed to a toolbox and a jack that she'd pulled out for them. She pointed to the ruts in the ground and the tires buried in them. "Strong in the broken places." She clapped her hands together. "Let's go. Let's get this done!" The boys grinned. They were laughing to see her happy. She had the kind of smile that made a person happy just to see it.

"Calvin, you organize. Stephen, help him and keep him honest. Do one tire at a time, and do it right the first time. Do you hear me? The first time! Lay it in thick. And tight. Pound it in with a rock... I am going to walk out on the road and keep a watch out. If you hear a shot, any kind of gunfire, hide in the forest and wait for me. Do you hear me?" The boys nodded. And with that, she was gone.

* * * *

Calvin unfastened the green tarp, and then pulled it down from the bed of the truck. He laid it out on top of a small, raised area of grass that stuck up above the snow. The truck, sliding off of the roadway, had dug deep and muddy ruts into the snow, and now the brown ruts were stark against the frozen white. He and Stephen shoveled wet mud onto the tarp until they had a good coating covering the center of the green, maybe three inches thick. Then they walked over to the fence line and anywhere else where the grass grew up through the snow, and they gathered armloads of organic material... grass, straw, weeds, and hay... anything.

Then they did the mud dance.

They stomped on the mixture for five to ten minutes at a time, then Calvin would pull one end of the tarp and then the other to flip over the thick, heavy "dough" that they were making, then they'd stomp it again. As they stomped, they talked and laughed like brothers. They made up a rap called the mud rap, and each one added a verse each time as they stomped heartily in the cold morning.

When the straw and mud were thoroughly mixed, they dumped the whole pile near one of the rear tires of the truck, and then began the whole process again.

This process went on for over an hour, and at the end of that time, they had enough mud/cob mixture to fill the tires.

Next, they jacked up the truck and removed the tires one at a time. Calvin showed them how to use the tire iron as a lever to remove the rubber from the bead without pulling off the whole tire. Then they stuffed. They stuffed and stuffed. And they pounded. Pounded and pounded.

When they could not get another ounce of cob into the tires, they finished, remounted the tire, and went to the next one.

"When we drive down the road, the cob will heat up and expand and fill what's left of the cavity," Calvin said.

"Are you sure?" Stephen asked.

"No!"

"You aren't sure?"

"Nope! I've never done this before! I just told you that my father saw it done. It's supposed to work, though."

* * * *

"Dude, your mom's kind of intense," said Calvin as they were pounding the cob down into the last tire with a rock that they'd found in the woods. The truck had slid down an embankment and down a smallish hill. They both knew it would take all the strength they could muster to get it up the hill, back onto the road, even under ideal conditions. They were working to better their odds.

"Yeah, she is." Stephen looked into the distance, as if he were thinking of another time.

"What happened to your dad?"

"Oh, he was killed in a subway accident. Years ago. He gave up his life saving this woman he didn't know. Jumped down on the tracks and lifted her up and..." He split his hands apart, helpless to find the words.

"Yeah, people called my dad a hero, too. He died to *keep* from hurting someone else." Stephen looked at him blankly. Calvin continued, "It's not really the same thing, but it is. Kind of."

"Yeah, bro. I hear you."

So, the conversation went on this way. The boys talked and worked. Occasionally, Veronica would come back to check on them, and she would encourage them through the process. She would always mix her little pep talks with object lessons. The boys would listen intently, and, as the sun crept across the morning sky and started to blend into afternoon, they completed their work.

* * * *

The line of military-style vehicles pulled up in a straight edge on a long road that ran through the heart of Pennsylvania farm country. The lead vehicle, an odd looking RV that seemed to have some kind of plated armor that made it, from a distance, look like a spaceship or a dinosaur, pulled into a small rounded driveway. The drivers were driving with purpose toward a destination known, apparently, only to themselves.

They pulled into the small driveway and stopped at a checkpoint on the private driveway. The men driving the military vehicles showed some kind of credentials, and then there was a conference, and then the vehicles proceeded down the drive and dipped along a long winding road that led up to a farmhouse. They pulled in with practiced precision and lined up in beautifully stacked rows. The vehicles were orderly in their performance and worked together as one in a mechanical ballet.

The last few vehicles did not enter the driveway. They didn't stop at the checkpoint and they didn't follow the others up to the farmhouse. These few continued down the farm road, heading somewhere else.

* * * *

The RV called 'Bernice' was parked behind the farmhouse, and inside the odd-shaped RV sat two men. One of the men looked like a cowboy, and the other looked like a leprechaun. A wee bit, anyway. They got out of the lead vehicle, the cowboy and the leprechaun, and they walked up to the doorway of the farmhouse. From a distance one could make out through the late afternoon haze the cowboy tipping his hat to the person who opened the door. The cowboy tipped his hat, and the leprechaun bowed at the waist. The leprechaun then did a little dipsy-doodle shuffle of his feet as he walked in behind the cowboy, and the door was shut behind them.

* * * *

Red Beard looked at Clive. Red Beard's real name was Pat, but by now we all know him as Red Beard. That's what Clive called him, too. The two men found themselves seated in an old-fashioned drawing room. In the corner of the room was a small, simple table with a kerosene lamp. The light was evening out in fine shadows across the floor. Red Beard leaned back in his chair and said, "Let me tell you a story..."

Clive looked at Red Beard. "Tell it."

Red Beard looked at Clive again. "Well, I think I will..." He gathered himself in order to give the story the weight it deserved.

"There was once this man who started a business. It was a small business. The man struggled. He scrimped and saved. He beat the bushes to find new customers and worked the ice cream socials at the local church. He joined the PTA." Red Beard paused.

Clive put his hand out, as if to stop him. "But did the tax man get his share? That's all I care to know." Clive flashed his best Sam Elliot smile. Red Beard spread his hands out before him.

"Of course. Indeed."

Red Beard continued. "So, his business was coming down to a crisis. It was one of those situations where sometimes you get the bear," he paused, "and sometimes the bear gets you... but, in this case, the bear was just about to have the final say."

Clive put his hand out to stop him again. "You know if you change *bear* to *beer* in that story, it still reads the same...?" He chuckled to himself and Red Beard paused.

Again, he smiled. "Indeed, it does."

"So, the man finally begins to make it," Red Beard said, "you know? And he hires a sales force. And his tippy-top sales guy – his very, *very* best – turns out to be a loafer."

Red Beard leaned over to whisper to Clive, as if conspiratorially, "I lean and loaf, at my ease..." He indicated with his hand across the ground... "observing a spear of summer grass..." He acted out the drama, and looked at Clive as if the words spoke for themselves. He wanted Clive to *know* that he had an eye for such things. He was a loafer, he seemed to say, but practiced and studious about it.

Clive also looked down at his feet, at their feet. He too imagined how lush and green this farmland was, the imaginary farmland under their feet, how valuable it could be.

"So what happened to yer feller? The loafer?" Clive watched as Red Beard came back into his thoughts. Clive had never left his.

"So, this guy's sales force was incensed. Right? The whole lot of them. As a group. Pissed off. They couldn't put up with such debasement. Naturally, it did not matter to them that the loafer had the best numbers in the office. How did he get them?! *That* was the question. And the loafer didn't help his cause any. He'd spend a couple of hours a day doing his sales calls, and then he'd go across the street to the Y and play cards. He'd gamble all day with his feet on the table. On the table! Can you imagine it?"

"I can!" Clive said.

"So, you can imagine the consternation of the crowd. The business owner hired a consultant. He asked him to solve the problem. The consultant did a month long study of the problem, looking at the business, its productivity, its camaraderie, the social cohesion, morale, and the experience of the layout of the hermeneutical biodegradable whatever, whatever, the whatever... The consultant went through whole shebang, got it?'

"I do have it, sir!" Clive nodded.

"And the consultant came to a final conclusion and put his answer in a one sentence report. *Get rid of the whole office and hire ten more like the loafer.*"

Red Beard indicated with his hand the lush bounty at their feet. He held up his ragged boots, as if he were looking past them into springtime, as if he and Clive were, at that moment, in a green field with cold beers in their hands, steaks on the grill, kids running through the sprinklers on the lawn. He looked down at his feet and saw them as if lightly resting on the long wispy strands of grass on the lawn of a warm spring afternoon in the ancient green of Pennsylvania.

* * * *

Clive indicated with his hand to the ground. "May I?" he said, with a low sweep of his arm.

"By all means," Red Beard answered, and settled back in his chair for the ride.

"That's what we're doing here," Clive indicated with his thumb and forefinger to both the time and the place. "We're firing the lot of 'em. Both the criminals who corrupted capitalism and turned it into a private candy store for cronies, and the democratic socialists who want to steal everything and then run the world their own way. Believe it or not, the fascists are working with the communists. But we're clearing the decks of the lot of 'em – or at least we're taking away their *power*. We didn't start this war, but we saw it comin'. People won't get it because they can't see the whole thing yet. Someday they will, if they live long enough. Maybe they think we're terrorists or something. They'll never understand the Luddites until a new world gets built on the old one. They still think the Russians and Americans are goin' at it, when in reality the powers that be... the industrialists, the banksters, the globalists, and the international socialists are the ones having a go at the people. They didn't expect us to muddle with their business, but we're doin' it anyway.

"We didn't set off the EMP. The commies did, and they did it with the help and aid of the corporatists and the globalists, on the left and on the right. The old-guard Soviets built the micro-nuke in North Korea while our folks twiddled their thumbs and guaranteed the people there wasn't a threat. Nope. We didn't start the fire, but we knew it was coming, and we let it happen because the world needed a re-start."

Clive rubbed his hands together and pointed at the imaginary field of green under their feet. He nodded his head at Red Beard before he continued.

"But we're not gonna let 'em do what they have planned. The invasions will never happen. Their forces aren't going to re-group, because we'll hit them every time they get started. They can't see us, and we're everywhere. We're a Luddite army, worldwide and not on the clock, and this time we've got the best toys. Just the irony alone is worth the expense."

Clive concluded his story, and, when he did, he looked over at Red Beard, and he saw that the man was riveted.

"You can't talk to 'em now, Pat! They all want it back. – the 1% and the 99%. Mind slaves! They want the comforts, and the velvet handcuffs. They want the empire and the tyranny, too! They want the degradation and the mindless and soulless jobs and the promise of a vacation in a tiny camping spot by a poisoned lake, and food genetically modified to last forever and never spoil. They want it all back, Pat, so you can't talk to them now. In ten years... twenty years... maybe then you can explain what has happened to them. Now? They're digging roots for calories and figuring out how to drink their pee. You can't talk to them until the dust settles."

Red Beard smiled. "Do you think that maybe your plan is a bit hypocritical and... just a tad morally ambiguous?"

"Of course."

"Okay then."

"Twain said that *history doesn't repeat itself,* my friend," Clive began. Red Beard held up his hand as if to let Clive know that he would finish the sentence, this time, for him.

"But it rhymes.*"

* * * *

Red Beard listened to Clive go on for a while longer. The glow from the kerosene heater in the corner of the room made his beard glow along with it. Its orange hue was set off by the umbered darkening air of the evening. The light began to fade. They both glowed as they sat in the chairs, waiting there in the drawing room. They shared more conversation and were electric with ideas. And ideals. They glowed in their seats.

They felt like... equals.

Neither of them cast a shadow.

* * * *

Veronica and the boys had pushed and pulled for a half hour, but to no avail. This light was beginning to fade, and she knew they could not be out here another night. "We *can* do this," Veronica encouraged them. "We just have to find the Archimedean point!" She gave a grunt as she said the last word, lifting up on a branch she had wedged under the bumper, trying to find a solid place in the sludge under the truck from which to gain leverage. The truck bumped a little. Calvin and Stephen heaved just as she did the lift again, and the truck bumped once more. "Okay, boys. I might have found the sweet spot. We just need to put more rocks under the wheel over there," she indicated with her hand toward the rear tire, "so we can get more traction..." Stephen placed some small rocks under the tire as she lifted on the branch. "And Calvin keep it in low, and give it a little gas ..." Veronica paused to make sure both boys were ready. She took a breath.

"And... Heave!"

* * * *

Sometimes in life, the narrative steps sideways. It simply takes a step to the left or the right. Whichever way you want to imagine it. Like when you close your left eye and you see a slightly different world than when you close you right eye. Time shifts, in inches. The world becomes different... but only slightly different.

* * * *

Veronica lifted with all her might. She leaned into the branch and lifted from her knees, from her loins, from her heart. Stephen stood at the back bumper with his mother. He shifted his feet in the sludge and tried to find solid footing from which to push. He leaned his shoulder into the bumper and gave it his all. Calvin jerked his body forward slightly in the bucket seat, as if that would help with the momentum, and gave the truck a little gas.

It caught, just slightly. The truck rocked back just a bit, and Veronica lifted again, getting her shoulder under the branch. Calvin heard the whine and felt the blessed pull of forward momentum. Stephen slipped in the sludge once the tires caught, and in Calvin's excitement at applying pressure to the gas pedal, the truck lurched forward and pulled up into the track from the night before.

The truck was on the roadway before Calvin saw the two military vehicles bearing down upon him with frightening speed. He was out of the truck before the men with guns had stopped their vehicles and spread out along the roadside. Stephen and Veronica came up out of the ditch and saw the men standing there and looked at Calvin and he looked at them. The soldiers raised their guns. Calvin stepped into the middle of the road and did a little hop, raising one hand in the air and reaching into his back pocket for something.

A piece of paper.

The guards aimed their guns, and Calvin came out of his little hop, caught himself and stood up taller and held both his hands high in the air. The white paper in one hand, now unfolded, spilled out of his fist like a flag of surrender. He offered it to the guards, and one of them made a little motion toward him, as if to accept it.

"It's OKAY. It's OKAY," Calvin said, with his hands still raised above his head. The men with the guns pointed at him, and then tensed, and then relaxed with Calvin's next words.

"I'm with Jonathan Wall."

The gun barrels dropped toward the ground in unison.

* * * *

The stream of life sometimes gathers its force and pushes into the present with an amazing burst of energy. Like a bomb. Or like something plunging off of a cliff. There was a traveler once who had such an experience. His name was Clay Richter. He went for a walk in the country, and stepped off the edge of the earth. He had a strange encounter with an alien force. Not the outer space kind of alien, but the surreal and perfect kind of alien, a mirrored self in a way, a shadowed self. Clay had that strange encounter with this alien self... this *other*... and it changed him. He'd had this strange encounter at precisely the moment in time when a revolution was sparked. He'd found a friend in the midst of his trial, an equal, a man named Volkhov. That meeting had changed him.

At this very moment, on a small patch of farmland in south central Pennsylvania, the world of Clay was gathering. These were people whom this traveler happened to meet on his journey. Clay Richter was no more, but in one way or another he was a part of the lives of these people who were now being drawn together.

It is not what you'd expect though. They did not know him in great detail. They knew him not *exhaustively*. They knew him as you might know the shoreline if you were floating downstream on a summer day. He'd been one of the many details in their lives, waving from the shore.

For example, as Clive and Red Beard sat in the drawing room waiting, they did not know that they each knew Clay.

Veronica and Stephen, who at that very moment were on their way down the drive of the farm complex, still amazed at this boy, Calvin, who had just saved them *again...* Veronica and Stephen did not know the men waiting in the house, and they could not know that those men knew Clay. And Calvin, of course, did not know Clay. He did, however, share in some ways his memory. And there was something else. Calvin was in Pennsylvania, having been sent on this adventure by Jonathan Wall. The writings of Jonathan Wall had played a large part in setting Clay off on his journey.

All of the people converging on this farmhouse shared Clay, in some ways, but only through memory and circumstance. As a result, when they meet, they will not discuss him, at least not directly. Though they will be poorer for it, they will discuss him, if at all, in terms so vague that they will not be able to make him out. They will tell stories of a friend, with whom they had once shared an apple, or a guy who had a real appreciation for Johnny Cash, or a guy who wrote these beautiful poems. But they will not speak of him. Not truly. They will not call him by his name.

And perhaps that is unimportant, after all, what is in a name? Would these friends of Clay not remember him just as tenderly, just as accurately, if they referred to him as Ned Ludd? Or Mr. Fugitive? The stories would probably all ring just as true for all these people.

No, the reason these people will not know Clay, will not recognize him even when they meet others who know him, is because they do not see him entire. They are like the blind men inspecting the elephant. One touches the belly and thinks he has found a wall, while another touches a leg and thinks he has a tree. Separately, none of them know exactly what they are dealing with.

So it is in the life of a man. There are things his fellows did know about him, but there were many other things they did not know. For example, they did not know, because they could not know, what had happened to the traveler. There was another man heading their way who had that piece of the puzzle. They did not know that Clay had been transformed by his contact with that *other* world, how he had met Volkhov as an equal. Nor did they know, because they could not know, that the traveler named Clay had a backpack that had traveled on without him. They did not know that the backpack, too, was on a journey.

Perhaps they can't be blamed, these friends of Clay, for their not knowing. And as they sit down in the drawing room together, where they will wait for... *What?* Gauguin? Godot? The set of boots and the backpack now trekking across the forest?

No. Now, as they sat in the drawing room and waited, they couldn't be held responsible for not knowing Clay better. They had each reached out to him on their brief sojourn with him, but he was a difficult man to know. You could prod him for answers, but he'd always take his time in getting you the answers. He was patient that way. You could ask him to hurry it up, but he'd just say "No."

CHAPTER 34

Natasha and Lang huddled together in the kitchen as gunfire ripped through the building in waves, like music, or the ocean crashing against the beach in thunderous intervals. They held on to one another like one would hold on to a flotation device or a buoy if one was drowning in the violent ocean crashing around them.

At irregular intervals, Natasha would pop up and fire a round from the 9-millimeter pistol, but she was running out of ammunition. She looked Lang in the eyes with a look of pure affection, and then she jumped to her feet again and fired through the open window, expending the two final rounds that remained in the clip. She slumped back down next to Lang and looked at him again, still smiling.

"You're something else," he said.

"So are you, Lang."

"Well... *we're* something else then." He reached over with his right hand and clasped her hand in his. He gave the hand a light squeeze, and neither of them was anxious to let go.

"Do you suppose Elsie and Peter are alright?" she asked.

"I don't know. Things don't look particularly good for any of us right now."

"No. you're right."

"If they rush the place—" he did not complete the sentence.

"I know."

The two young people looked at one another, and their wordless communication was un-gilded, un-scripted, and unreservedly honest. The things that they did not say to one another were true, and they both meant them with all of their hearts.

Afraid that the opposing force might take the lull in fighting as an invitation to attack, Lang shuffled to his feet, and, balancing the barrel on the window frame, he popped off three quick shots from the .22, just to remind the enemy that someone armed was still in the cabin. It was a weak little protest, and it was met with a more powerful response. A bullet passed by Lang's ear so closely that it nearly took the appendage off. He dropped to the ground so fast that for a second, Natasha thought that he *had* been hit.

"Whoa," Lang said, and laughed nervously. "That was close. They're getting better at this. I think they're timing our return fire."

* * * *

The round-faced man, like many in his tribe, bore many names. He decided on the spot that he preferred another. He was going back to being called Cole.

Cole made his escape while Mike and Steve were busy trying to locate the position of the sniper. Neither one wanted to move in any particular direction until they knew that they wouldn't be moving into the crosshairs of someone with an agenda different than their own.

The three Warwickians, Mikail, Sergei, and Vladimir had retreated back away from the ridge when Mikail indicated to the others that there was a sniper somewhere who was shooting at the National Guardsmen. The bulldog wordlessly ordered Val and Kent to circle around the ridge to the southeast in order to try to see who might be holed up in the cabin. This order gave Cole just the opportunity he'd hoped for.

Cole carried the new backpack as the group split in two. Just as soon as he and Vladimir had cleared Mikail's line of sight, Cole smoothly and fearlessly pulled the pistol from the band of his coat. He placed it to the back of Vladimir's head and pulled the trigger.

That was that. There was no ominous or threatening chit-chat. There were no syncopated rejoinders or catchphrases popping back and forth between the executioner and the executed. Cole was too smart for that stuff. He wasn't giving Vladimir an opportunity to weasel out of what he had coming.

Cole did not struggle within himself with the decision to kill Vladimir. He knew that Vlad was a coiled and poisonous serpent. A snake can and will strike anywhere and anytime. Vlad was a murderer many times over, and, as a cold-blooded psychopath, the man was too dangerous to suffer to live any longer.

In nature, rattlesnakes have a purpose. It is often said by people who are too ignorant to know better that "the only good snake is a dead snake." These people do not realize that if it were not for rattlesnakes, the human race would be wiped out by plagues and diseases from vermin in just a few years. Rattlesnakes are a necessary creature. We'd be lost without them. But you don't let them into your bedroom where you sleep. Cole looked out through his glasses, and he noticed that they had some specks of blood on them. *Those vipers that get too close and won't go away,* he thought, *you have to kill.* He pulled off the glasses and cleaned them on his shirt.

Perhaps Vladimir had a purpose. He'd never been a good person, or even a morally neutral person. He'd always been purely evil. He was, Cole figured, a rattlesnake that wouldn't leave the house. It had been time for him to die.

Cole was moving slowly, crawling foot by foot towards the rear of the cabin, when he inexplicably heard a voice from some bushes.

The bushes were calling to him using Peter's voice.

But they were calling him using his *real* name.

* * * *

"Do you ever wonder what life might have been like for us if..." Natasha stopped herself before she finished the question.

"If what?" Lang asked.

"...If we'd been from somewhere else... anywhere else... anywhere but Warwick?"

"I do wonder that, Natasha. I've thought about that a lot as we've traveled on this little adventure of ours. But," he squeezed her hand softly as he tried to form the words to say the things he wanted to say. "But, I can't say that I would ask for anything to be different. Not a thing. Not even being here, right now, with you. I've thought about this a lot, Natasha, really I have." Lang reached up and touched Natasha's face, and just then a tear escaped her eye and traced its way down to where his hand rested against her cheek.

"How can you say that?" she asked, but with no hint of agitation or irritation at all. She really and truly wanted to know. "How can it be that you wouldn't change things if you could?"

"Because, I'm free now, Natasha. I realized it back when I got shot crossing Highway 17, a lifetime ago." Lang paused for a moment, and looked deeper into Natasha's eyes. " *'Not everything has a name. Some things lead us into a realm beyond words.'* Solzhenitsyn said that. I don't know that I can explain why I have joy and peace at this moment. I know Volkhov felt the same thing when he was in that prison with Clay in Warwick. When I was shot, I knew then that, for the first time in all of my life, I was moving, and breathing, and deciding, all as a free man. I just wonder... if none of this had happened, if I'd ever have really experienced freedom."

The gunfire from outside had slowed considerably, and Lang hesitated for a moment, afraid that the soldiers outside might be considering a raid on the cabin. He looked up and found that Natasha was still looking at him, as if she expected him to continue. So he did.

"I remember that man Clay. The man who accidentally stumbled into Warwick during the winter storm. He was looking for freedom, too. I'm not talking about political freedom, here particularly. I'm talking about *moral* freedom, the freedom to not be a puppet in another man's game. And I believe that Clay died happy, even if he was confused by all of it. He died saying 'NO' to tyranny and wickedness. Just like Volkhov said. To me, it is okay to die, as long as you are doing it while acting out your freedom.

"So, no, I don't wish things had been different. I'm just glad that things worked out so that I could team up with you and Peter and Elsie... and Cole. I'm just glad that we all made the decision to say 'no.' I'm glad we had the courage to flee the system that was lying to us and enslaving us."

Natasha looked at him and smiled. The mention of Cole's name struck her a bit like a needle pushed into her skin, but she understood Lang's words, and she liked it that Lang said them to her. Another tear ran down her face, and she looked down before speaking again.

"If..." she paused for a moment, gathering her thoughts before beginning again. "If things *were* different. If we'd been born in a regular American town, and if we knew nothing of Russia or spies or any of this mess... well... Vasily Romanovich Kashporov... in such a case, I would love you anyway." She looked up at Lang, and he smiled.

Lang was just about to reply to Natasha, when he saw movement near the back door of the cabin. Cole rushed through the door, and Lang hardly had time to recognize who it was and stop himself before firing at the figure moving towards them. He did hold his fire, but the Missouri National Guard did not.

Seeing the movement in the cabin, the assaulting force opened fire again, and Natasha dove towards Cole dragging him down to the ground as a cascade of bullets smashed through the structure, destroying everything in their paths. Simultaneous with Natasha's dive towards Cole, Lang sprung up again, instinctively, to offer covering fire, and rapidly squeezed off the four remaining shots left in the tube magazine of the squirrel rifle. Once again, his appearance was answered with a barrage of fire through the window, and once again, Lang dropped to the ground instantaneously with a loud thud.

Cole found Natasha on top of him, and he struggled to wiggle out from beneath her. He was worried that she'd been shot, and, as he struggled to get free, her head swung around towards his and their eyes met, and she smiled.

"Hello, brother," she whispered. "You okay?"

"Yes! Are you?" Cole replied.

"Yes. Not hit. Let's get into the kitchen though. It's safer."

The two low-crawled back into the little kitchen area, and there they found Lang—Vasily Kashporov—slumped down with his back against the wooden cabinets.

He'd been shot through the throat, and he was dead.

* * * *

All of the Warwickians, those who were left among the living there on the field of battle, could not have known that they had just participated in a reunion of sorts. There wasn't any time to pause the action to notice. Peter, Cole, Natasha, Mikail, and Steve were still alive. Vasily and Vladimir were now dead. None of them knew the scope of the battle in which they now found themselves.

From high above the battlefield it could be seen that the Missouri National Guardsmen were receiving reinforcements in their positions opposite the tiny little cabin. Panning to the east, one might have seen that a large contingent of the FMA—the Free Missouri Army—was joining the battle against the MNG. A quick calculation would have given you the proper conclusion. *Peter and Elsie were trapped between the two opposing armies.*

Peter and Elsie, for their part, were waiting, hoping, and praying that Cole would bring Natasha and Lang out of the cabin, but as they hoped, they became surrounded by the advancing FMA. Unarmed and not able to fight, they were forced by the FMA units to retreat behind their lines. They implored the soldiers to try to save Lang, Natasha, and Cole inside the cabin, but all they got were assurances that "everything that is within our power will be done."

The FMA tried valorously to hold back the Missouri Guard from taking the cabin. There was a ferocious firefight.

All the while, Ace was off in the distance, doing his best to keep the Guard away from the cabin with his sniper rifle.

* * * *

Shortly after the FMA was forced to retreat back towards Lancaster County, the cabin was taken by the Missouri Guard.

Ace, out of ammo and unable to do anything else to save the people in the cabin, retreated with the FMA. It wasn't a difficult decision to make. He'd seen what the Missouri Guard had done to his hometown of Scranton. There was something in his memory about the way the smoke had curled up in little wisps over the house that had belonged to Irene Ducillo that made him angriest.

* * * *

A WEEK LATER

Peter, Elsie, and Ace reluctantly left the FMA camp, and with beleaguered faces and sad countenances they set off on foot towards Amish country. The days of waiting for Natasha, Cole, and Lang to join them had sapped them of their emotional strength, and Peter finally decided that they could wait no longer.

The men of the FMA had been kind and helpful—at least as kind and helpful as they could possibly be under the circumstances—but it had become obvious that FMA leadership wanted the three travelers to either fight with them, or move along.

They didn't have the materials or resources to keep refugees as pets.

All in all, it was time to move on.

The three said goodbye to their friends in the FMA and thanked them earnestly for their help and support. They left descriptions of their missing friends, and silently hoped that the three would be found safe and sound, and that they would rejoin them in the not-too-distant future.

And so, they walked. As they did, they talked about where they were going, and where they'd been. Well, actually, Peter and Elsie talked. Ace rarely said a word. He was a quiet man, and he talked more with his eyes and his actions than his words. He believed that actions spoke louder than words.

"We have to just keep moving," Peter said, trying to make his voice sound hopeful and authoritative. "If our friends are safe and alive, they'll know where we're headed, and we'll see them again."

"I know," Elsie replied. "I just can't help thinking that we might have all made it out of there *safely*, if only I'd stayed and helped Natasha move Lang."

Peter stopped and looked over at Elsie with a stern look. "We've talked about this, Elsie, and you know what I've said. This is no time for self-recrimination. We've all made decisions we now regret. We all could have done things differently. This world is falling apart and it will only get worse and—"

Just as he said those words, there was a sharp flash of light in the air. The ground rumbled violently. Seconds later, an indescribable wave of sound reached them and it shook through them as they walked. The general brightness in the sky seemed to gather in the east.

Instinctively, they all looked eastward, in the direction from which it seemed the noise had come. They were just above the tiny town of Bloomsburg, and they were approaching Interstate 80 from the north, and they had to move a few steps to their southeast to see it. When they did, they grew silent, and the three of them watched the top of it. It was like life and death personified. The mushroom cloud swelled in the distance to the southeast. It grew and expanded above the tree line.

Elsie shifted Lang's backpack on her back as Peter whispered. He whispered softly, but Ace and Elsie both could hear him...

"Philadelphia."

* * * *

Natasha and Cole stood in line to be processed into the Carbondale prison camp. They'd been captured by the Missouri National Guard and a fluke of circumstance had saved their lives. Rather than be executed on the spot, they'd been saved by the fact that there were no living officers on site to make that decision. Cole had told their captors that he'd only just arrived in the cabin at the very end, and that his sister didn't know how to fire a gun. Subsequently, they'd been arrested, and after they'd been loaded into a horse-drawn wagon full of prisoners bound for Carbondale, the circumstances of their arrests had been forgotten. Now, they were only potential laborers, and no one down the line cared what they'd been doing when they were captured.

"NATASHA JOHNSON!" the clerk shouted over her shoulder as she looked up at Natasha. That was the name she'd been given. No one had identification anymore. For those that did, it wasn't particularly helpful.

Someone behind the clerk wrote down the name, and then handed the clerk a form that explained where Natasha was to be billeted, and what her new occupation would be. Natasha took the form and stepped to the side to wait for her brother.

"COLE JOHNSON!" the clerk bellowed. Again, she was handed a form that she then handed to Cole. He looked at the form...

Barracks 19W
Garbage Detail

Typical, he thought.

* * * *

Cole rejoined Natasha, and they had just turned to leave when they both heard another clerk shout from two tables over.

"MIKE BAKER!"

Cole froze. He turned just in time to see Mikail receive his orders from the clerk.

"STEVE TAYLOR!"

Sergei received his billeting as well.

Natasha and Cole stepped out of the tent and stopped to look at one another. They didn't know exactly what to think about what was happening, but they were both happy to be alive.

Just as the siblings looked down to their orders again, Mikail and Sergei walked up and Mikail smiled sweetly, as if nothing had ever happened between any of them.

"Ahh, look Steve, some Warwick friends. How are you both?"

No answer.

"Where have they assigned you to live, Cole?" Mikail asked, innocently.

"19W," Cole said flatly.

"Fantastic," Mikail, replied. "It looks like we three Warwick men will be roommates. It'll be like home, won't it, Steve?"

Steve just nodded. His face did not betray his thoughts at all.

* * * *

The four Warwickians had just turned to walk away when it happened. They did not feel the ground shake or hear the noise from the explosion. Perhaps the geography was different in Carbondale, or perhaps the terrors of the place blocked out some input from the senses. It is impossible to tell for sure, since a person cannot be in two places at one time.

Someone—they could not recall who—shouted and pointed off to the southeast. The four turned as one and looked up into the sky. They watched as the mushroom cloud bloomed outward, just above the horizon.

Mikail Mikailivitch Brekhunov did not smile and he did not laugh. He just turned to his friend Sergei and said...

"Well, now. It seems that our friends have finally arrived."

An Empty Bed, by C.L. Richter

Rarified hope, in darkness wanting
Vivified breath, breathless by haunting,
In day springs new
the way things do
When light shows false
night's cruel taunting.

Clarified dreams, by reality cleansed
When terrified streams of fear intends
By night to make
thy horrors wake
And strings burned through
bring forth earth's ends.

KNOT FOUR

ONE WORD OF
TRUTH

CHAPTER 35

They decided to set up camp on the lee side of a hill that was covered thickly with trees and brush. As they moved, silently and harmoniously, their activities displayed their growing experience at surviving in this new world. They were now veterans in landscape that showed no quarter to stupidity or inexperience.

Ace grabbed a black, nylon ammo pouch from the stack of gear they'd recently scrounged from a shot-up Humvee. He nodded at Peter, and then disappeared silently down into a small valley to the southeast. Experience told Elsie that Ace was heading out to find a good sniper roost on the opposite hill so that he could stand guard while Peter and Elsie prepared supper. It was a good plan, practiced and perfected, and it worked. An added benefit was that Peter and Elsie would have time to talk. Ace had grown sensitive to Peter and Elsie's growing affection for, and reliance on, one another.

Peter took out a Geiger counter that he'd liberated from the Humvee, and he turned it on and checked their immediate area. He'd informed Elsie and Ace that most of the fallout from both New York City and Philadelphia must have been pushed out to sea by the jet stream and the prevailing winds. Elsie watched Peter move around and through the brush with the Geiger counter. She thought of how he always looked like a bear, the way he hunched over, and she laughed.

"What would you do if that thing went off, Peter? What if it just pegged to the highest reading?" she asked.

Peter shrugged. "When I was just a boy in training, the instructors told us that if that happened, we were to radio the readings back to base, then set the machine down and go prepare for our funerals."

Elsie blinked, but didn't look away. "A boy? In training? What boy trains for this? It seems there is so much about you that I don't know, and don't understand."

Peter stood with the Geiger counter and shifted his weight. He scanned the area again with his eyes, and then looked back at Elsie. He stared into her eyes, trying to communicate what he could not say.

"One day," Peter said, "after we've found a place that is relatively safe—"

"I know, Peter."

"One day," Peter said, and smiled.

"So...," Elsie said, returning the smile, "...as a boy you were practicing for this? That's heartening. My son was riding a skateboard, killing zombies on his iPhone, and talking to his friends with his thumbs."

Peter swept the valley again with his eyes, looking for movement, or anything that didn't seem right. His mind had become practiced at scanning the distance, examining the space for unnatural angles, artificially straight lines, man-made protuberances, or anything at all that didn't fit. He'd learned to listen to the birds and the animals of the forest, eliminating immediately all sounds or sights that fit with what he expected, and quickly cataloging everything else so that it could be compared with tell-tale indications of danger or threats.

"Why does that counter even work?" Elsie asked, "Wouldn't it have been destroyed by the EMP?"

"I can't say. Perhaps it's internally shielded, or maybe they had it in some kind of Faraday box when the EMP went off. Hard to know."

"What good does it do?" Elsie asked.

"Well, at least we know we haven't received any lethal dosages. We've been highly blessed by God, I think. This thing isn't totally useless. If we were to receive a faint reading, you know, just enough to register on the counter but not enough to do any permanent damage, then perhaps we could alter our course and pick a different direction to walk."

Elsie sat down on the ground and looked up at Peter.

"I didn't know you were religious, Peter."

"What?" Peter said.

"You said, 'We've been blessed by *God.'*"

Peter thought of the many nights in that previous life that he'd spent praying for his family. Not knowing where they were or what might have happened to them.

"Of course, I am. I've always been a believer." He waved his hand as if he was dismissing the whole topic out of hand, but he continued. "I gave up on the ikons and the saints and all of that stuff. I've lost a lot of what I used to call 'my faith,' but I still pray. Anyway, I don't pray to saints or pictures any more. Now I just talk to God directly."

"You talk to God? What does he say?"

"He doesn't say anything. He just listens."

* * * *

Shortly after the bombs dropped, the flow of refugees from the east came to a near stop. The stream of humanity from the west and south slowed drastically too, or at least most of it did. There were still homeless people and bandits about, and the Missouri National Guard (MNG)—those who hadn't left to join their enemies in the Free Missouri Army (FMA)—were still a reality and a persistent threat, but the endless hordes of helpless, desperate refugees had finally become only a trickle. At this point, everyone was either friend or foe, and the three travelers had become experts on recognizing foes from a distance.

With Ace off at his roost, Peter and Elsie slipped effortlessly into their friendly and familiar conversation. As they talked, they worked together to set up their supplies and tools for providing supper, but Peter, having learned from the costly mistakes of the past, never let down his guard. His eyes and ears were constantly working, scanning the area for threats.

After they were finished arranging the camp, Peter moved over near a tree to scan the forest again. When he looked back at Elsie, he found her staring at him.

"What?" he asked.

"I'm just wondering."

"What are you wondering?"

Elsie looked down for a moment, and then looked back up at Peter. "I'm wondering if your wife is still alive... somewhere... out there."

"I hope she is," Peter said. He held Elsie's gaze, and he felt like he should say something else, but then the pressure got to be too much for him, and he looked away again.

He scanned the valley again, not wanting to miss seeing anything that might mean danger. It was for this reason that a flash of movement through the trees caught his eye, and when it did, he held his hand out in a practiced signal to make sure that Elsie knew something was up, and that they needed to be silent. Four men approaching. The men used military tactics as they moved through the trees towards the camp from the west. Peter identified the movement as aggressive and not defensive, and he recognized that the men were in assault mode.

Foes.

Snatching up the AK-47 from where he'd left it leaning against the tree, just within reach, he spun around, grabbed Elsie with his free hand, and had barely pulled her down into a small depression in the hill when bullets began to thump into the ground and the brush near where the two had just been standing. He pushed the safety up with his thumb, and he had just raised the rifle to aim when he saw the point man among the attackers fall, struck by a bullet to the head. The other three men dove behind trees but not before Peter was able to pick off the second man with three rapid-fire shots from the AK.

The Russian battle rifle was not configured to fire fully automatic, which was fine by Peter—he didn't want to waste ammo on un-aimed shots—so he took his time and popped off rounds only when he thought he might actually hit a target, or for effect, to keep the attackers from moving any closer.

The two remaining gunmen hunched behind cover, and once they'd located the direction from which Peter was shooting at them, they slowly shifted their position behind the trees in order to protect themselves from his fire. This, it turned out, was a fatal decision for both of them, but their position was such that they couldn't avoid the danger. Trapped in a killing field between Peter and Ace, when they moved to hide from Peter, the battle rapidly ended. With two well-aimed shots fired only seconds apart—just long enough for him to cycle another round and reacquire his target—Ace felled the last two attackers with headshots from the other side of the valley.

Peter and Elsie stayed in their earthen depression. They waited and watched. Peter didn't know if these men were just an advance scouting party for a larger group, and he wasn't going to move until he knew that more attackers weren't coming. Elsie looked at him, and he gathered strength from her glance. She smiled, and when she looked back out in the direction from which the attack had come, the smile remained on her face. It was not a smile of smugness or arrogance. Death was very real, and not something to be scoffed at or enjoyed. It was a smile of complacency—not in its modern definition—but in a way that means 'restful satisfaction.' It meant that all that could be done was being done. For now, things happened to be working out.

After about five minutes of lying perfectly still, Peter pulled a red handkerchief from his pocket and waived it so that Ace would know that all was clear.

Ace's silence was as complete and pervasive from a distance as it was in person. The red handkerchief waving in the distance answered in kind, and Peter saw it. He thought of how some men hear silence, and they see it as a bull sees a red cape. They mistrust it. Peter kind of liked it.

After all, Ace had already spoken.

Three of the four dead attackers testified to Ace's declaration, the red blood from their exploded skulls splashed across the snow like exclamation points at the end of his very efficient sentence.

CHAPTER 38

The Farm. Before the Bombs.

"Somewhere in the jungles of the Amazon or over there in Papua New Guinea—somewhere out *there*—there are uncontacted tribes that, even at this *very* moment..." He paused and looked across the distant horizon and saw the purpling sky. He thought of the dust, the smoke, and the civil war in the distance. "Even now, there are tribes that do not yet know that the world has fallen apart." Clive Darling stopped mid-thought, and indicated with his hand outward, in the direction of the horizon, as if to say *way over there somewhere.* It was only a small flick of his fingers, as if he was conserving his energy. Then he continued, his Savannah accent fully evident as he held court.

"The members of such tribes don't know anything about this tragedy being poured out across this country and the rest of the world. Their daily lives have not suddenly changed. Over the course of the last several days and weeks and years and millennia, they've simply gotten up in the morning just as they always have. They've fed their children, gathered and hunted their food, sang their songs, taught their customs, and protected their territory." He stared out at nothing in particular. "Life, for them, just goes on."

Clive paused and smiled to himself. To anyone else it was only a flash of his eyes, but under his mustache, he smiled. He thought about other moments during his life when he'd told that story—or had told one like it.

Clive spoke and Pat Maloney listened. It was five a.m. The two men were sitting in the drawing room of the farmhouse, talking over the last vestiges of a candle. It was unclear whether they were up early for the new morning or still up late from the night before. It had been unclear for days, in fact, whether these two were coming or going. They simply moved in tandem, and all the while appeared to have been merely passing the time. They talked like old friends would. Clive's Sam Elliott mustache and Pat's red beard. Cowboy and leprechaun.

Pat scratched his red beard and contemplated the thought, too. He said what Clive was thinking. "Life governed by the sunrise. Their only clue on a morning like this that something is different..." He motioned toward the window, and continued, "...is that, at the moment, the sunrise seems more vivid. More dust in the air." Red Beard waved his hand before his face, stirring the dust. He paused.

"Imagine it."

Clive did imagine it, as Pat let the thought hang in the air like the smoke and the dust.

"Life as a kind of perpetual communion with the earth. Somewhere out there those tribes are waiting for the next sunrise, the next day's work. Their only job is to survive and to pass what they *are* along to the next generation," Red Beard said.

Clive reached into a bowl at his feet and fished out an orange. He offered one to his friend, but Red Beard waved it off. Clive massaged the orange as he picked up the thread of the conversation.

"Can you see it?" Clive said. "Passing their mortality and their immortality along through their genes to their children? And their customs? And their languages? And their history? And their very practical survival knowledge?"

Red Beard spread his hands as if to indicate that, although he agreed, there was more to be said. He'd noticed that Clive had not mentioned *the state.* Red Beard finished the thought. "What do such tribes know of war?"

"With nuclear winter coming on?" Clive said, leaning to his right and grabbing a knife from a side table. "Probably more than you'd think, my friend. Probably more than you'd think. They know plenty of war, but war in a primitive state is *explicable.*" He dragged out this word 'explicable,' to emphasize its importance. "Everyone has a very plain and simple reason for fighting. You fight because you want his wife, or he stole your orange, not because someone you don't know wants you to fight some people you've never met over something you could never grasp or hold in your hands. Propaganda and brainwashing doesn't enter in to it."

He began to peel the orange in neat little spiraled strips, beginning each portion by plunging the knife's sharp edge into the wrinkled skin of the fruit, noting how the veins in the rind made the thing look like a fist-sized brain. He carved each strip, and then peeled back the rind. The juice squirted out into the air, and the orange spray smelled nice in the warming air of the drawing room.

* * * *

Clive and Red Beard saw the candle flicker and noticed, in the flickering, their shadows dance on the wall. They looked up, and in the hallway, the figure of Veronica flashed by, going down towards the kitchen to make her morning coffee. Red Beard lifted his chin in the direction of the hallway. "She turned out to be a good one," he said. He thought of how Veronica had seemed to fit perfectly into their little household. Had it only been a week ago? *Only a week?*

Clive reached up, pulled at the corners of his mustache and nodded his head in agreement. "She sure did," he said. His head nodded even more emphatically. "A strong, smart woman."

They listened as she bustled around in the kitchen down the hallway humming to herself as the pots banged in the glow of her camping light. Clive and Red Beard were just about to blow out the candle to preserve the little bit of wick left for some other talk, some other morning, when Veronica called down the hallway to see if either of them wanted coffee. The suggestion in her tone indicated that she had asked this question before and that she knew what the answer would be. She was right.

"No, ma'am. We've got to get moving." The reply was in precise, practiced unison, and with it, Clive and Red Beard were out the front door of the farmhouse.

* * * *

To where? Where were they going? These two had been veritable whirlwinds of activity during the last week. *Had it been a week already?* They'd been inseparable as they went about their work, preparing some business of Clive's—some business known only to themselves—and in their activity they had burned their candles at both ends.

It was never clear to anyone else just what, exactly, the friends were up to. The two were everywhere: directing the militia who patrolled the farm; arranging a number of convoys in and out of the complex; loading unspecified goods and materials onto and off the trucks; leading the convoys along the grid of farm roads and down a ridge of trees to... *who knows where?* No one knew. Or, no one was telling if they did know.

This was what happened every day, this coming and going, and everyone else watching, working, and not knowing.

* * * *

In the evening, Clive and Red Beard discussed philosophy. They cooked meals and organized chores and played hosts to their guests. The two men had also taken to sitting up in the evening, having a scotch, and smoking cigars. That's what they called it. *Having a scotch.* It had become a private joke between Clive, Red Beard, and Veronica. "You 'drink' water, or tea, or juice," Clive was fond of saying, "but you 'have' a scotch, just like you 'have' coffee. It implies relationship, and a time set aside for something more than just refreshment or sustenance."

Last night, they 'had a scotch' well into the night. Veronica joined them, and they'd argued (in a friendly way) about just exactly where one might find the world's Archimedean point. It was the first real conversation the two men had had with Veronica. They found themselves looking forward to more.

They'd reached a happy little moment when preparations were just coming into order. They could see the results of, and perhaps an end to, their work, and they redoubled their efforts. The two men pushed themselves to feats of durability they had not previously thought possible. They didn't sleep much. Truth be told, neither man seemed to notice the strain. They were just two friends, passing time, talking about ideas, going about their business.

The odd little community of Clive, Red Beard, Veronica, Stephen, and Calvin, had formed in a weirdly organic way, in the way that such communities must form in the end times. Everyone naturally fell into a specific role, using his or her own talents, insights, and experiences. Clive and Red Beard had their private business, and they didn't feel the need to talk about it. The others didn't feel the need to ask them about it either. The two odd friends seemed to be directing and steering some larger concern—a global one maybe—and all the time they held firm hands on the tiller of their local preparedness. Veronica, Stephen, and Calvin had their own small little family to contend with—a family within the larger family. Everyone knew that the group was preparing themselves around the farm for something, and knowing that fact gave impetus to their activities. They were all preparing... but, for *what?*

* * * *

During the talk over scotch from the night before, Veronica argued a theory that botany would necessarily play a role in leveraging the future. "Talk about your Archimedean point!" she'd said.

She spoke on like she was giving a TEDTalk, but with nothing to show for slides. She was *convinced*—still—that knowledge of plants held the key to the future. She said that, whether in foraging for food in the forest, or planning a nursery, or feeding a population, all of these things would require knowledge, and an understanding, of plants. She was passionate about this. Clive and Red Beard were impressed by both her ideas, and her passion.

"And also..." Red Beard said, interrupting the thought. "Calvin especially interests me. For some reason I feel very fatherly toward him."

Clive smiled under his mustache. He, too, felt a paternal urge toward the young man. He'd heard Calvin tell stories about his childhood; how his father had come to be persecuted by the Chinese for his participation in Falun Gong; how his father had died rather than take a kidney offered by the state, because he thought it was an organ taken from one of his brethren. Calvin had called his father a "kind of hero." Clive recognized the hurt in the boy's voice when he discussed his father. Like Red Beard, he'd felt the desire to give fatherly advice to a bright young man who'd lost his father.

Last night, finishing off their scotches, Clive had also thought of the church, and the jails, the government, and the state. It had occurred to him that *all* of them, in one way or another, were giving fatherly advice to young men who had lost their fathers. There is a world of difference between advice given by someone who cares for you, he thought, and advice given by an institution interested only in its own preservation.

"Yep. I agree," he had said in reply to Red Beard, and the southern drawl came out. "Jonathan Wall done good when he sent that young'un."

* * * *

Observing that it was 'never clear' whether Clive and Red Beard were coming or going – it should be noted, of course, that this is not to be taken as exhaustively true. If one were watching carefully and paying attention, one might have figured something out.

A person, invisible, watching from the tree line at the crest of the hill, might have surmised things by the movements of the odd-shaped RV on its many ventures in and out of the farm complex. Sitting just above the tree line beyond the northwest fence of Clive's farm, one might have seen that the two friends had, in fact, been coming and going. There, nestled along a stand of trees that started near the river and stretched along the edge of the farm where it rose in elevation, one would have been able to see, without obstruction, the *amount* of activity going in and out of the farm. Standing there in the snow and paying close attention, one would have seen all of the coming and going, and would have known without any doubt whatsoever, that something was about to occur. *Something Big Was Coming.*

Whatever it was hadn't come yet.

Still, all of this is speculative, because there was no one there yet, standing and watching among the trees, to try to put it all together. There was only the buzz of the whirlwind, the military precision of the convoys, the crisp intersecting lines of the field at the fences, covered in snow, as the cold hung in the air like a mystery.

CHAPTER 37

Burying thousands of bodies in the frozen earth by hand had become untenable with only human labor and rudimentary tools, so, instead of digging thousands of smaller graves, the commander of Carbondale had ordered the *planters* to work for days digging one very large one. Then, he'd ordered them to fill the hole with bodies, and then to burn the bodies. This would serve to warm and thaw the earth. The planters would then be ordered to dig both the remains of the bodies, and more of the dirt out again, in order to make the pit deeper. The ashen remains were then separated out, when possible, and formed into smoldering piles to serve as kindling for the next fire. When the warmed earth was sufficiently turned over and dug out, the hole was again filled with bodies, doused with fuel, lit afire, and the process would begin again. Eventually, in this way the commander had built an efficient human incinerator. On the grounds near the burning pit, piles of waiting bodies spread out like spokes from the fire that burned at the center, hot like Gehenna, or hell itself. The bodies of the dead, piled and waiting, sent the stench of decaying flesh across the valley. In addition, there was the problem of the ashes, floating gently down, adding to the air's aroma, sticking in the nostrils.

Most of the planters had become *draggers*, and rather than digging holes sixteen hours a day, they were engaged for the same number of hours in dragging corpses and stacking them in piles where they waited for their turn in the huge burn pit.

Natasha Bazhanov and Sergei Dimitrivich Tupolev worked as a team in body dragging duty. Despite the natural enmity that Natasha had for Sergei (for security reasons she still called him *Steve* when she needed to speak to him), she, strangely, felt more comfortable working with someone from their hometown of Warwick. If she had to make the choice, she would rather work with Steve than with a complete stranger. At least she knew what Steve was, and she didn't constantly have to evaluate his behavior for signs that he would turn aggressive. She didn't have to worry that he might turn out to be some kind of pervert or something.

Besides, Steve hardly ever talked, and when he did, he was all business.

Natasha adjusted her facemask.   The two Warwickians grabbed another corpse with gloved hands and hauled it to the wait pile. Natasha could feel the slip of the flesh against the wet slick surface of her glove.

It was days ago when the announcement had arrived that most of the planters would become draggers. *How many days ago was it?* She couldn't say. The camp commander had simply done what commanders do. He'd commanded. He'd walked to the center of the crowd near the burn pit and announced that they would now stop digging individual graves and begin wholesale burning. Even his guard detail had bristled.

Eventually, there was a lot of gagging and even vomiting among everyone on burial duty, including the soldiers who had to watch over everything. Historic images had come to their minds, and none of the guards desired to be compared or likened unto the monsters of the past. Each guard, though, was able to rationalize his position, because the human mind can rationalize any behavior if it wants to badly enough. *This was nothing like Nazi Germany,* they told themselves. They weren't killing these people (they said to themselves) - at least, not *most* of them. These people were dying from disease, cold, and malnutrition. What the guards did not admit to themselves, was that the people were actually dying of a more deadly contagion. They were dying of spiritual entropy and *unviability,* a condition that evidenced itself in a sense of entitlement, helplessness, and a severe deprivation of the basic survival intelligence that man had developed over the millennia.

Most of the dead had been raised in the modern world to believe that it was someone else's duty to take care of and protect them, and based on this fallacy, they'd decided that life was more dangerous and deadly *outside* the wire. That disease—the disease of dependency and *unviability*—was what was killing these people. But none of the guards admitted that fact to themselves. Instead, they dodged responsibility, no matter how sick the whole thing made them feel.   Any tyranny, any abuse, any apostasy, any atrocity, can be rationalized if those in power can only convince the people that the alternative would be much worse.

As bad as everyone had it, the draggers had it the worst. After all, they didn't have a choice. In addition to the filth and disease that came with the job, the draggers had the certain knowledge that the snapping underneath their feet was the crackling of human bones that hadn't burned in the last fire.

Back when they were planters, they'd only had to worry that if they paused too long to arch their backs from the strain of overuse, the guards would threaten them. Now, as draggers, they had it still worse. While both jobs were physically strenuous, draggers had to contend with the fact that disease was already making headway and cutting the numbers of available draggers day by day. Hour after hour they dealt with the grotesque task of hauling decomposing and rotting human corpses, piling them up to be burned, leaving them in lines as if the bodies were waiting patiently for a bus—in the last queue they'd ever form on earth. The decaying skin of those corpses often pulled free from arms and legs. Sometimes, heads fell off. It was too much to think about, and so, after a while, one didn't.

* * * *

Most of the time, Natasha was able to stop thinking of the bodies as human remains. No matter how good she got at pretending though, the thoughts were always there, just under the surface, waiting to overwhelm her. On those occasions, her mental defenses would slip, and she'd notice a little girl's dress, or a man's tattoo. She would start to wonder who these people were, what their lives had been like before it all came to an end. She wondered that now.

Natasha was glad that Cole wasn't here. Her brother didn't have the make up for it. Dragging duty, if you avoided dying from disease, or crumbling with insanity, was a sure ticket to a lifetime of nightmares, and probably to a permanently damaged mind.

Having been born and raised in Warwick, a Russian spy school in the heart of America, she'd learned to reject the erroneous and dangerous idea that life was supposed to be 'fair.' Still, she couldn't really get her mind around the absolute and complete lack of any vestige of fairness *at all* in the world. As she dragged bodies, she thought about people who had lived their whole lives within the historically rare epoch of American prosperity. So she imagined a nameless, faceless *someone*. The face she summoned was just someone she made up so that she'd have some element for comparison. It was almost exclusively through her imagination that she'd managed it, since she'd been born in a time and place that did not allow for direct experience.

The person Natasha imagined was a woman, born in New York City in 1963. Perhaps she'd died under the mushroom cloud that had recently erased The Big Apple from the map of history. This imaginary woman had lived her entire life in relative prosperity. Period. End of Sentence. Don't even bother arguing the point. Doesn't matter what problems the woman had faced in her life. Doesn't matter if she'd struggled to find a job, if she'd had relationship problems, if she'd developed cancer, or if she'd lost a finger in a trash compactor. In the big scheme of things, her hardships were inconsequential. This woman that Natasha was imagining had *never* been tasked with dragging rotting corpses to a hole to be incinerated. Hundreds of rotting corpses. *Thousands.* That woman had lived in luxury her whole life, and then she was incinerated in a flash of light.

Why were some people subjected to horrors beyond imagination, while others lived in relative comfort, and then disappeared into light, without such suffering? Why were many people still out there somewhere, going on with their lives as if nothing had happened? Natasha could not easily comprehend this detail, this suffering. She wasn't foolish enough to demand fairness, but she did feel like she had a right to ask *why.*

Anyway, she was glad that Cole was not a *dragger.* That bit of unfairness she could appreciate. Cole's billet wasn't easy by any stretch of the imagination, but there was no job worse than that of dragger, and she was relieved that her brother, at least, had escaped death duty. Cole had drawn garbage detail. He was hauling trash (mostly human waste and kitchen refuse.) Not human bodies, though. The stench in Cole's job was bad too, she imagined, but his job had the advantage that he wasn't hauling bodies that would come apart and spill their contents across the ground, causing you to slip in the guts as you dragged the lumps of flesh to the fires. Handling kitchen refuse was worse than the worst day of any job ever held by the imaginary woman in New York City who'd died in the flash of light, but at least Cole didn't end up covered from head to toe at the end of the day with gooey remains of what once were people. Natasha thought about the fairness of that and how fairness didn't even matter when it came to her brother. Humans are capricious and hypocritical that way - always demanding fairness and justice, but never really wanting it.

She wasn't ignorant of this hypocrisy in herself, so she just hauled bodies all day.

Mike, she thought. *Mikail Brekhunov.* Talk about *un*fairness. Mike was another thing altogether. Being a master manipulator, after only a few days in the camps, he'd already wormed his way into a position of power. Cozying up to authority, he'd gotten in with the guardsmen. He'd done it with a pack of cigarettes here, a pretty prisoner girl there. Perhaps someone needed a payback murder or a targeted beating—Mike knew how to get those things done if the right person needed it. His years of practice covering his tracks benefited him greatly now, as he found ways to work his agenda without ever letting anyone know his true intentions. Now, he very nearly ran the place. He was the official spokesperson for the prisoners, even though not a single prisoner trusted him. He'd found that he could do without trust recently. He preferred rather that the people fear him. If the prisoners feared him, he cared not whether they trusted him.

Wait, that word isn't to be used. It is not 'prisoners.'

Natasha laughed to herself as she thought of it. They'd been told over and over again that no one here was a 'prisoner.' Mike was the official spokesperson for the *refugees.* Or the *settlers.* Those terms were officially acceptable. In any case, Mike Baker (that was Mikail's name... for now. Names become fluid when the world melts down.) was the man in charge.

So, they were all now to be called *settlers* because Mike preferred it. Mike reminded everyone that as soon as things were safe, and as soon as order could be restored, the people in the 'resettlement camp' would be 'settled' on land where they could grow crops and live out their lives in peace. *Right,* she thought. That's what they'd all been told. Nobody believed it. No one believed that anyone was going to live long enough to be resettled.

Actually, that part about nobody believing the lies probably wasn't *entirely* true. Ignorant hope still thrived in most of the settlers, even the kind of hope that was pie-in-the-sky. Especially that kind. There were many who, with empty heads filled with fairy tales, thought that things were going to get back to normal. Unhappily, despite promises of land and freedom, hundreds of prisoners died every day from disease, hopelessness, and violence.

Yes, there was violence in the camps. This prison camp was no safer than the chaotic world outside the wires. Still, there'd been no wholesale escape attempts or riots. Victim psychology—a communal Stockholm syndrome—convinced the prisoners that inside was better than outside, even if that statement was objectively not true. Natasha had been outside, and it was no picnic, but life in the Carbondale camp was a nightmare that seemed to never end. Violence in the camps was especially common against women. Natasha shook her head when she thought about it. A man had to be either crazy or criminally ignorant willfully to bring his wife or daughters into a refugee camp.

Still, women were not the only victims. Men were also attacked and beaten, sexually assaulted, and even killed. Such things happen in jails. Gangs of miscreants operated freely inside the wired walls of the Carbondale camp.

Natasha had been kept safe, mostly because she never went anywhere without Steve or Cole by her side. She also suspected that Mike had something to do with the gangs leaving her alone. If it were true that he'd put out a *do not touch* order on her, she hoped he didn't expect her thanks for it.

The two Warwickians grunted and heaved the torso of a young man onto the growing pile. Sometimes they'd handle the same body twice in the same day, once with the dragging, and again when it came time to stack more bodies into the burn hole itself. For now, they were glad to be done with the burden of that particular moment. Natasha had stopped counting individual bodies, but her mind kept track of the size of the piles. She quickly estimated how much more work was left to do. It always seemed, somehow... *endless.* She scowled as she heard the thump of another torso plopped into a pile. More fleshy residue now ready to be combed through by the *pickers.*

Natasha used her forearm to wipe the sweat off her brow. Despite the cold temperatures and the snow on the ground, dragging made you sweat. Sometimes this complicated things, because whenever a rare rest break happened, the sweat would bring on chills, and sometimes the cold would weaken a dragger. Corpses, blood, and waste held diseases that could multiply easily, even in the cold, and sickness often worked to weaken them as well. Dragging duty was not just a ringside ticket to death and decay—sometimes it was a death warrant in and of itself. Natasha personally knew of four draggers—men and women she'd worked with—whose bodies were now either in this pile, or had already been burned into ashes and bone in the bottom of the burn pit.

She looked towards the fence where five guardsmen were overseeing the *pickers*. It was the picker's job to go through the piles of the recently deceased and remove any items of value from the corpses. Wedding rings, earrings, jewelry, necklaces, pocketknives, lighters, etc. Pickers sorted all of these things into rubber bins, and hauled them off to the Commander's office. What he did with the valuables, lowly draggers could not know, but they certainly did speculate. There was no shortage of gossip on the many ways and means available to the Commander for enriching himself with goods looted from the bodies of dead prisoners.

Natasha looked over at Steve and laughed scornfully. She was feeling mean, and when that happened, she usually directed her anger at Steve.

"Why were you stuck with dragger duty, Steve? Isn't Mike your best friend?"

"Mike doesn't have *friends*," Steve replied. "He has supplicants."

"So, why do you put up with it? Why be his stooge when he treats you like this?"

"He said he's teaching me discipline," Steve answered coolly, and with a hint of irony.

"Discipline? Dragging duty is not discipline, Steve. Dragging duty is just another form of the death penalty."

"I know," Steve said. He didn't look ashamed, and he did not look away. He stared at Natasha and betrayed neither thought nor emotion. "You can't say that I don't deserve it though."

"I don't understand you," Natasha said.

"That's because I'm Russian."

"So am I," Natasha replied.

"No you're not. You *speak* Russian, Natasha, but you are something else entirely. I can't say that I've figured you out, but you are definitely not Russian."

"What makes you say that?" she asked.

"Because of *this*," he indicated with his hand everything around them. "This dragging of bodies, senseless war, deprivation, tyranny, authoritarianism, duplicity, horror... acquiescence. This is what it is to be Russian down deep in your soul." He looked back at Natasha, and for the first time that she could remember, he actually smiled. "Everyone from Warwick *spoke* Russian. But not everyone from Warwick *was* Russian."

"Well, I am Russian," she said, leaning into the noun. It was all she could say to that.

"No you aren't, Natasha, but don't take that truth the wrong way. It's not an accusation. Perhaps you have the best parts of being Russian somewhere within you. Maybe you have persistence, and optimism, and poetry, and music. Surely, you have pain and suffering. Those things are truly Russian. But the rest of it, the bad parts, those you don't have."

Natasha looked at Steve and couldn't speak for a minute. She looked down at her boots, covered in mud, blood, and guts. Then she looked back up at Steve. "So why did he punish you this way?"

"God? Or Mike?"

"Is there a difference right now?"

"There is a difference, Natasha."

"Mike."

"I angered him."

"What did you do?" Natasha asked. She felt the sweat beginning to cool her body temperature, and she stomped her feet in the snow, hopping up and down a little to get her blood pumping again.

"He wanted me to work with him—to help him take over the camp."

"He's already done that. And you wouldn't help him?"

"No. I refused. He hasn't done all he wants to do yet. He wants to do more than run things for the people in charge. He wants to *take over* the camp. He's going to overthrow the commandant and take control."

Natasha looked again at the guts on her boots and felt them slip under the soles of her feet as she shifted her weight from side to side. *Did it really matter who is in charge?* She decided to play along. "How is he going to do that? I mean, these National Guardsmen are military people. They are not a bunch of Russian villagers!"

"He'll do it. Don't doubt that. He learned a lot from his failures in Warwick. He's already triangulated the leadership. It's as good as done." Steve stomped his feet and clapped his hands together rapidly. "I've had enough of his posturing and manipulation. I told him that he'd have to move forward without me." He looked around the camp and gestured with his hand as if he were unveiling some exciting prize. "Ergo, I am on dragging duty."

"Well," Natasha said, as she walked over to the stack of bodies the pickers had just finished looting, "with friends like Mike, who needs enemies?"

CHAPTER 38

The mysterious activity at Clive's place seemed particularly fervent that morning. The farm, its winding road lined with traffic whirring out of the complex and onto the grid of curving country roads (headed who knows where,) was abuzz with activity. At the end of a line of military-style vehicles pouring out onto the roads, was the command RV. In the cab of the RV, a cowboy and a leprechaun sat intent on the duty at hand.

The RV lumbered forward on the uneven road. It wasn't much of a road, really, just two dirt slits cut into the field leading out to the county road. From its exhaust pipes, the odd-shaped RV that Clive called 'Bernice' emitted two little trails of steamy smoke. One trail rose from each corner of the back of Bernice, and the puffs lifted up along the sides of the vehicle and out into the inky, fluid light of dawn. The rocking of the RV sent the smoke up in minor turbulences, shaking the trails into tiny little spirals. The wheels peeled through the dug-in trench of a road, and the earth, clay-like and primal, clung to the tires in desperation, or hope, or just curiosity. The smoky spirals rose up like dust devils into the cool winter air.

* * * *

Veronica D'Arcy lifted the plastic lid off the coffee can and stuck her nose down into the aroma, bringing it into her body. She already had a fire going in the black, cast-iron stove, and she sat a pot of water on the grill. She thought about how nice it was to 'have' coffee, even if it was campfire gritty. She ran her tongue across her teeth, thinking about how, during the long bike ride out of the city, and the excitement thereafter, she had lost all sense of time. At one point, she couldn't even remember when she'd last brushed her teeth. The loss of that kind of luxury, of some connection to what once was a 'normal life,' occurred to her, but she did not feel the worse for the loss. She had, very recently, experienced a world of debris—bricks and stones, wreckage, gaping wounds on corpses, and blood running from limbs, and all of *that,* but the indignity of perhaps losing herself in the mix was a new concept for her. The loss of connection to a body in time—*that* was something to consider, so she thought about that.

In this new world, a person grew attuned to *smells.* The eyes are not the only sense used to determine the truth of things, after all. Before this new world, back in the world of Mad Men commercialism and extraordinary excess, brushing one's teeth seemed to be a *duty.* Time was something measured only by a clock on the wall, or the television schedule, or the boss at the office, not by the sunrise or the next meal.

That old world seemed to her to have utterly vaporized. Her old lifestyle was becoming increasingly unimaginable, as if it had only been a dream.

She took a drink of the coffee and really tasted it. It was good because of, not in spite of, the grit. She felt the heat radiate from the stove and was thankful that they were in a secure location. In the old world, security was rarely a consideration because, in the end, it was always someone else's responsibility. The city. The Mayor. The cops. The government. The President. It was their job to see to security. They existed to keep people from panicking. Insecurity leads to panic, so security was necessary to insure that business could go forward. You need business to flow freely if you are going to feed four-hundred million people on the productive capabilities of only a few thousand. Security is necessary to guarantee the free flow of cheaply made goods at market prices. So what happens when those transient forms of security evaporate?

She heard a sound down the hall and wondered whether it was Stephen.

She'd spent a great deal of time during the past week with Stephen and Calvin, watching them grow together like brothers. Every day, Clive and Red Beard went off to their business, she woke the boys, and they went about making themselves useful. Mostly, they'd spent their time picking through the out-buildings on the farm. Looking in sheds, attics, lofts, nooks and crannies, cupboards, anywhere they could think of, seeking to scavenge anything they thought might be valuable.

The barns and sheds were old, but not dilapidated or abandoned. The two young men found many handy items in their searches, focusing on multipurpose things that they could easily carry, along with any materials with specific, useful properties. Old rolls of fencing, chicken wire, screws and nails were particularly valuable. Pieces of old rubber inner tube, aluminum flashing, piles of feathers – all of these things were becoming more and more valuable in a world without industrial manufacturing.

In this world, like the last, they found imagination to be a powerful thing. It was a form of training for them to look at a thing and study it, determining what it was, and what it could be in the future.

They sorted these items and prioritized them. Veronica directed them to find, organize, and lay out tools and materials, and she would teach and entertain them while they worked.

Clive and Red Beard were less than open in sharing any future plans, and she didn't know how long they'd need to stay—to live and prosper—at the farm, so she ran the salvage and re-purposing department like they might be there for the long haul.

"After 9/11," Veronica had told the boys, "I heard some author on NPR or somewhere discussing the skills people need for survival in the end times. The ability to scrounge was at the top of the list."

Stephen had caught her looking at him, and he'd smiled the smile of a son who knows all of his mom's lectures. They'd developed a shorthand way of communicating that rarely required words. He knew then what was coming next.

"Stephen, what do we do?" It was a quiz question. She was testing him.

Stephen had looked at Calvin, and then told his friend what she meant for him to say. "Don't look at what it is. Look at what it can be."

"That's right." Veronica had said.

"Re-purposing is a talent that can be learned. I'm glad to be a scrounger, but in truth all single mothers, artists, and botanists are scroungers. I just happen to be an artist/botanist/single mom, so that means I'm the best expert there is!" She'd flung her hand outward toward the field, and Calvin had followed her gesture with his eyes...

And farmers, he'd thought. *Farmers have to be excellent scroungers. That's why there are all of these out-buildings full of stuff.*

Veronica then told Calvin how she and Stephen used to always search for castaway objects for art projects, or materials for homework assignments, or broken down (but free) furniture that might be fixed up, or neglected plants that could be nursed back to life. "The key is to think about what the thing might do, or become, or adapt to be. An old can might become a small cook stove. A piece of rubber might help you make a slingshot for hunting. Think about the various things you might carry with you in a backpack. Think about things that might have value if you need to cook, to defend yourself, or to use them for barter. Look for value in terms of how it can enhance your life going forward."

Veronica had rambled on like this, as mothers will, for a while. Stephen eventually had cut his eyes towards Calvin and pulled his finger across his throat, as if to say that he would slice his own throat rather than hear another word. It was all in mock fun. Veronica smiled at this, but paused only long enough to begin again. "And so you need to look for materials that are durable and flexible and serve as tools or anything that can be used to increase comfort..." *Blah blah blah.*

Stephen hung out his tongue and cocked his head to the side. He held his hand over his head like a pivot and mock swung his head on a rope, as though he would rather take a hanging. Calvin grinned and they all laughed.

* * * *

Now, Veronica stood alone, drinking her coffee. She thought about all of *that.* She considered that day, the week itself, the trip out of Brooklyn, their newfound home, and the weird duo of Clive and Red Beard, the gracious hosts who had made their farm so welcoming and available. And, the coffee this morning—she thought about that, too. She took a sip, feeling the grit in her teeth. She remembered the broadcast of NPR like it was yesterday. She remembered her son at her feet. She thought about how she once sat and made lists on such mornings of things to do that day. She thought about how Stephen and Calvin told her last night, before they went to bed, that they were going to go on a new scrounging expedition today. "We want to go around the perimeter of the farm," Stephen had said. They'd completed cataloging all of items found in the barn and thought they might find something useful on the far field, adjacent to the next farm over.

Veronica thought of all these things on this morning, how it all had the feeling of normalcy, and how if things could just stay the same, maybe everything would turn out alright.

* * * *

There had been, for most of the week, a preternatural stillness—the kind of stillness that knew ancient stirrings. Not the absence of sirens or the silence of screams; not the sudden awareness of the quiet after closing a door; but a silence that one might feel when standing out under the stars, staring up into the night sky. Such a quiet is not entirely divorced from noise, of course, and this is perhaps especially true in farm country. The silence waxes and wanes with the light in the sky, the pull of the moon. Even the stirring of the livestock is motivated by those gravitational pulls, their motions and life cycles waxing and waning with the moon. The wobbling of the planet against the moon and the sun; all of it works in harmony on some nights.

There had been several such nights recently, disturbed only by the movement of vehicles. She thought of those moments of stillness, when all the forces come into alignment, when the air is just the right temperature, when even the pigs cease their nervous motion, and the farm becomes, briefly, utterly quiet, as if quiet is a state of being and not merely a description of a condition—as *if nature has entered her holy moment and taken a vow of silence.*

This was such a moment. Veronica sat and held her gritty cup of coffee and looked out over the farm. It was winter, and though it was morning, it was also still night, and quiet.

Veronica imagined the farm by day, in spring. She painted the pale grey canvas of the predawn moment with the vividness of her artist's eye. She imagined the rows of corn or cabbage, their striated patterns across the thick green bands of verdure. She imagined the fields beyond it. Her mind considered the fertile land and the crops that exist in imaginative possibility. She thought of other fields, other cups of coffee, and she wondered whether her friend Clay was sitting on his porch in Ithaca, drinking coffee. She thought of her folks back in Trinidad. She listened out across the quiet of the air and she *heard* the quiet, but only for an instant—a butterfly's wings on the air.

Then, the rooster began to ruffle his feathers. The light in the sky began again.

* * * *

The sky was the color of an almost purple. It was the hour of dawn. Clive and Red Beard let the screen door slam as they walked out the door, and it made a sharp crack across the silence of the cool air of the farm complex. The fireball in the sky that heats our planet, and threatens it always with its ever-present violence, had just begun, with the faintest tremors of the slightest waves of light, to push across the lightening atmosphere. It was as inevitable as the tide, really, the light.

The eastern sky began to glow, and the light slowly crept into the outer reaches of the gaseous firmaments, and it crept in and invaded even the night. The earth, Veronica thought, was moving out of its own shadow.

This is a day, she thought, *of import.* She could not say why she thought that.

It was as if the death and destruction taking place in the distance, out beyond the boundaries of the farm, and beyond that the county, and beyond that the country, rising up like smoke into the stratosphere and filling the middle horizon, was just a part of the magical reality of *now.* It was as if all of *that*—the smoke and the dust particles hanging there, filling the sky with a rich purple hue, well... it was all beautiful. Maybe, none of *that,* the thing outside the fence line, had occurred after all. Maybe it had never happened. It was as if the farm was in Clive's Amazon forest somewhere, or in one of those ancient tribal locations where news of the world's end had been slow to reach, or where it wouldn't have mattered if it had reached there.

Such, on that morning, was Lancaster County.

She finished her last swig of coffee and wondered what that portentous day would hold, and if the earth even cared.

CHAPTER 39

Peter and Elsie checked the bodies of their attackers to make sure the men were dead. They were. All four of the slain wore the worn and soiled uniforms of the MNG. Without a word, Peter and Elsie went through their pockets and pouches for valuable items. In this way, over the last few days, the three travelers had steadily upgraded their own equipment. Up until now, Peter, mostly through personal preference, had stayed with the Russian AK-47 that he'd taken from an accountant who had attacked them ages ago. Now, he picked up the AR-15 from the fallen point man. *Maybe*, he thought, *it's time to make a change.* Most of the rifle ammo they were coming across was in the .223 caliber utilized by the AR-15, or a larger caliber, like the .308 used in many sniper rifles. He liked the AK, and felt a bit nostalgic for the weapon, since it was the rifle he'd been trained to use as a young man and in his years as an instructor in the Charm School. Still, wisdom dictated that he use the weapon for which he had access to the most ammunition. The AK would have plenty of value in trade, or as a gift weapon to the FMA.

Ace had taken three lives with perfect headshots from several hundred meters, and the men's deaths had been immediate and without suffering or drama. Ace, the silent sniper who almost never talked, and rarely ate, had become... well... an Ace in the Hole, and Peter couldn't even imagine what life would be like if they hadn't found him.

Peter grabbed a web bag that held seven full magazines for the AR-15 from one of the corpses, and hauled the weapon and the ammo up to the camp.

Elsie gathered up handguns, magazines, and useful gear from the other fallen soldiers and added them to the increasingly heavy bag of weapons and gear the three travelers had acquired in the past few days. She also took the jewelry – the rings and necklaces and watches. Most of the gear would end up with the FMA, once their reconnaissance scouts came around. The other valuables would stay with the group.

This region of Pennsylvania had become home to a cat and mouse war between two opposing forces of former National Guardsmen. Every day or so they'd run across a military unit that was made up of friends and not foes. The Free Missouri Army, acting as a guerrilla resistance force, had patrols out searching, looking for and hoping to engage MNG units. Peter tended to like the men from this group. The FMA had shown themselves to be mostly benevolent. There had been incidents—things that will happen in the fog of war—but for the most part the FMA had proved to be good guys – better guys at least – in the battle that now raged throughout the area.

Nobody wanted to run into an MNG unit. If refugees were spotted by the MNG, the situation immediately became a choice between 'fight' or 'flight.' No one expected good treatment from the Missouri National Guard troops. The MNG soldiers usually shot first and asked questions later, but anyone they did manage to capture they sent by horse cart to Carbondale.

The word "Carbondale" had become a byword among the few refugees that still traveled through the area. When Peter, Ace, and Elsie would run across other folks moving from place to place, the object of universal scorn was the MNG. The two terms had become synonymous with death, both the place where the group was headquartered, and the army that might show up at your door to send you there. "You'd rather be dead than to end up in Carbondale," people would say.

By contrast, whenever the travelers would come upon an FMA unit, they'd barter their excess guns and ammo for food or supplies. If the FMA group didn't have anything to trade, Peter would just give them the guns and ammo anyway. Carrying the bag of weapons had become another burden, but Peter was firmly against leaving valuable weapons on the ground, when he knew the MNG might find them, and he knew that the FMA could use them. The FMA recruited heavily from among survivors they came across, and they were always in need of more battle tools.

* * * *

Kolya Bazhanov, who had taken to himself the name *Cole*, was knee deep in garbage, going through it with stoic disinterest and gloved hands, separating items into different rubber bins. He and ten other prisoners stood yards apart from one another amid the piles, processing the seemingly endless supply of trash and waste. Everything was reused in the camp. Paper, depending on the shape it was in, its type and condition, could be composted, used to start fires, or bundled and hauled to the waste buckets to be used as toilet paper. Aluminum cans were washed out, and the soft aluminum would be re-used for dozens of alternative purposes.

The buckets full of human waste had been composted for a time, but now the sheer amount of the stuff had overwhelmed the garbage detail, and most of it was being burned in open pits dug for the purpose. Human urine was hauled in buckets to a location that was set up for the manufacture of saltpeter and gunpowder. The amount of waste that thousands of imprisoned humans could produce was beyond anything Cole could ever have imagined. This is saying something, since Cole was a man of vivid imagination. He was imagining it now, the sheer amount of it all. *Simply mind-boggling*, he thought. Most of the waste still consisted of consumer goods manufactured before the crash, but there was a lot of it. More, since the MNG was constantly on the move in the area, confiscating goods wherever they could be found. In this way, Carbondale had become like ancient Rome or Athens before those cities had collapsed. Armies were forever on the move, seizing goods *out there* to be used by the people *in here* who consumed, but didn't produce much of anything at all.

Cole threw an aluminum can into the rubber bin marked *cans,* and then turned to the man next to him with a smile on his face.

"Robert! I have a question for you," Cole said.

"It's not going to lead to you quoting Whitman or Emerson is it?" the older man working next to Cole replied as he bundled up some cardboard and tied it with a short piece of string.

In the old world Robert had been a grade school teacher, and during the days spent among the garbage, he would usually work his way until he was somewhere near Cole, because he secretly appreciated the generally higher quality of conversation. He liked Cole a lot, but he always acted like he was frustrated with Cole's constant and humorous banter.

"I assure you, good sir, it will not." Cole paused as if to take a little silent bow.

"Okay, what's the question?"

"Right now, would you rather have money, or a good and honorable name?"

Robert paused and pondered the question for a moment before completing the knot he was tying in the string. "Neither one means much to me in here."

Cole frowned at Robert, and then broke into a smile. "You aren't playing correctly, sir. If you *had* to have one or the other, which would it be? Choose! Money? Or a good name?"

"Money, I suppose."

"Well, your first answer was right. Neither one does us much good in and amongst this trash; but, since we're just talking, and since you have forbidden me to quote from Whitman or Emerson, let's hear from the Bard on the subject..."

Robert rolled his eyes, but smiled. His protest was weak and amiable. "Ahh, man! No!"

Cole dropped the paper he was holding in his gloved hand, and spread his right arm out with the palm facing upward, in the manner of orators of old.

> *"Good name in man and woman, dear my lord,*
> *Is the immediate jewel of their souls.*
> *Who steals my purse steals trash; 'tis something, nothing;*
> *'Twas mine, 'tis his, and has been slave to thousands;*
> *But he that filches from me my good name*
> *Robs me of that which not enriches him,*
> *And makes me poor indeed."*

Robert sighed deeply and Cole smiled.

"That, dear man, is from Shakespeare. *Othello,* I think," Cole said.

"I wonder if Shakespeare ever had to shovel garbage," Robert sneered, light-heartedly.

Cole thought of a few of the minor plays. "I suppose he did on occasion."

Cole did not notice that Mikail Brekhunov, now known as Mike, had approached and was standing behind him.

"Bravo, Cole. I see you're keeping the settlers entertained," Mike said. His eyes did not betray his intent, and his delivery was deadpan.

"Settlers?" Cole spat the word out, sarcastically. "I see you're piping that tune, too."

"I am," Mike replied, and something in his voice suggested that in fact he was doing more than merely piping the tune—that he was also writing the music. "I'm not going to argue with you about it. Words are powerful tools. You of all people should know that. You, too, should call us 'settlers,' *if* you're smart enough to know how perilous your position is here." Mike waived his hand dismissively at the muck covered floor as if to suggest that there was a level even lower than that.

Cole either did not see the implied threat, or did not care, and he pressed his case. "Yes, words are important, Mike, but in the end, isn't it something more that is needed? Something *more.*" He emphasized the words, indicating that what he was saying was actually the something more of which he spoke. "Like the more powerful cousin of words... *action?* Or... well..."

He was about to say "truth" but he didn't get the chance. Mike snapped at him and showed some wit of his own.

"What does Orwell have to do with it?"

Mike patted the gun at his side as he said it, and Cole flinched. "I tire of your quibbles, Cole. It's ten o'clock, and your crew was supposed to be done with this load twenty minutes ago. We get behind, and we get buried in garbage. You do understand, right?"

Cole smiled, as if to offer a silent bow.

"It is ten o'clock: Thus we may see,' quoth he, 'how the world wags:
'Tis but an hour ago since it was nine,
And after one hour more 'twill be eleven;
And so, from hour to hour, we ripe and ripe,
And then, from hour to hour, we rot and rot;
And thereby hangs a tale."

Mike did not smile or laugh. He stepped closer to Cole and stared into the younger man's eyes.

"'All the world's a stage...,' blah, blah, blah. Get it done, Cole."

Mike spit his angry, rancid breath into Cole's face from a distance of inches. Cole noticed that detail because it was the only one that really made him uncomfortable. He could deal with the threats, but that breath...

"You're wearing down my good will and patience, my friend," Mike leaned into the last word.

Cole clicked his boots. There was a slight mockery in the motion. "We will re-double our efforts, Comrade Mike." He said the whole sentence with a smile. He then removed a glove, pulled off his glasses and cleaned them with a small corner of cloth he'd found in the trash. He noticed the smell of urine. *Really, it is mind-boggling, the amount of waste this place produces,* he thought, his mind already turning back to his work.

Mike stood and watched him and glared at him. "One day. One day soon, Cole–," he let the threat dangle before his prey, "– your mouth will get you into trouble that your charm and wit cannot get you out of."

"Yes, Mike. You are undoubtedly correct. And, when such a day comes, I hope to have enough grace to accept it." He spat on the ground and then looked back up at Mike. A small bit of spittle still clung to the corner of his mouth.

Mike wheeled on his heels and walked back towards the administrative tents. His bulldog walk was emphasized by the way he worked his jaw as if rehearsing some argument. The effect made him look like he'd sunk his teeth into something, and his shoulders hunkered over slightly as he tracked his way back down the small slope through the snow.

When he was gone, Cole looked over at Robert and shrugged.

"He thinks I'm charming and witty," Cole said, laughing. He put out his hand again, and this time he spoke with a British accent.

> "Last scene of all,
> That ends this strange eventful history,
> Is second childishness and mere oblivion,
> Sans teeth, sans eyes, sans taste, sans... everything."

* * * *

Peter, Elsie, and Ace were now safely behind the lines of the FMA. A hard half-day's walk brought them to an FMA encampment only ten miles from Lancaster County.

While "safely" had most certainly become a relative word, they knew that they now could feel more comfortable bunching up in a group, talking, and going through their gear. They'd traded their entire stash of extra guns and ammo—including the AK-47— for twenty pounds of dried sausage and a bag of key limes. In the old world, such a trade would have been ludicrous. In this world, Peter almost felt like he'd taken advantage of the FMA officer with whom he'd bargained. The sausage would come in handy as a means of getting protein and quick calories while on the run. The limes would help keep them from getting scurvy, or any of a dozen other diseases and afflictions that are caused or exacerbated by a lack of Vitamin C. Peter had tried to get a roll of baling wire thrown in with the bargain, but the officer had just laughed at him. Peter would have to deliver him a battle tank, the man said, in working order and loaded with fuel in order to get a roll of baling wire. Some things couldn't be had at any price.

Matches, duct tape, aluminum foil, aspirin, and chocolate— these were gotten in dreams, not often in reality.

"Getting that dried sausage was a Godsend, Peter," Elsie said.

Ace just nodded his head in agreement, as he sucked the juice out of a key lime.

"We did well to get so much for those guns. With all the deaths and sickness and so many battles, guns and ammo are going to be easy to get for a while. Someday, they'll be precious again, but right now, they're out there lying around for any scavenger willing to go spend a day looking for them. Glad we found a man who didn't over-value his meat supplies."

"What news did you hear from them, Peter?" Elsie asked.

"They said another ten miles and we'd be rolling into Amish country. There are heavy-duty checkpoints on every point of ingress into the area, even the back roads. Some militia—a well-funded and highly able group—has taken it upon themselves to protect the Amish. Probably it's a brilliant idea, and that's something that Uncle Volkhov hinted at before the crash. He thought that somebody with resources might realize that it was in everyone's best interests to keep the Amish alive and working. Neither the FMA nor the MNG are messing with these militia guys."

"That sounds frightening, Peter," Elsie said. "What will we do?"

"The officer I traded with said that these militia guys are hard core, but reasonable. He said they're letting people in who belong there, who know someone in the area, or who have verifiable business with the Amish."

"You think they'll let us in?"

"I have no idea," Peter said, shaking his head. "He says that from here on in—since they've pushed the MNG to the north—we should be able to travel on the main road and not have to go cross country."

"Do you think that's so? Is that a good idea?"

"I trust him. He says it's dangerous to go cross country into Amish country. The militiamen guarding the area are more nervous about people trying to sneak in than they are about folks who just come up to a checkpoint and make their case."

"That makes sense."

"What do you think, Ace?" Peter asked.

"I'm with you," was all Ace had to say about that. He smiled, though, which was as rare as hearing his voice.

"Okay," Peter continued. "The guy said there is a town up ahead. Only a few miles up the road. It's a mess, but we have to go through it. It's been the focus of a few major MNG offensives, but the FMA holds the town now. To try to skirt the town by going through the forests or the fields is way too dangerous. So we'll just try to get through it as fast as we can."

"I've grown to hate towns," Elsie said. "And don't think I don't get the irony of me, of all people, saying that."

CHAPTER 40

Veronica continued her solitary watch, standing on the porch as the atmosphere slowly turned from purple to blue, then yellow, and then pale white, and then pale white turning golden. These colors splashed across the atmosphere as the morning wore on. The air shimmered in iridescence. Veronica blinked. As the light expanded, the horizon turned brown, green, and red. These colors in the distance slowly came into focus. The red, is the neighbor's barn. The brown, she thought, was the shingled roof of his farmhouse. An Amish farm, Clive had informed her. It was beautiful, in the distance, in the white morning light. The smartly constructed barn and outbuildings stood in crisp relief against the natural elements. She admired how the farm didn't have all the dissecting and diagonal power lines leading up to the house to mar the natural beauty of the objects, and she thought of the farm's value as a canvas, wondering how Van Gogh would have painted it at just that moment. She admired it as a rural landscape, and then wondered if art would even be possible to imagine in this new world. That thought caused her to make a mental note. She'd have to take the boys out in the spring and teach them to pick berries to mix up some paints.

In some of the farthest corners of the field, along the fence line, the slightest dusting from the black soot in the atmosphere sat on the tops of the snow, a distant reminder of what was going on *over there,* beyond this tribal region. The tiny dots along the horizon seemed to stand as if in a snow globe. The smoke kicked into the air from the recent dustups over in the cities, with the civil war and anarchy and lawlessness breaking out in the world - there had been... all of *that.*

Still, the light breaking through on the horizon was beautiful. The earth was now fully out of its shadow.

* * * *

Stephen D'Arcy lay twisted among the sheets of the sofa-bed. He'd slept roughly last night—when he'd slept at all. He kept waking up with his back hurting him. Even at his young age, his back hurt him. He hadn't realized how deeply the muscles in his shoulders had ached from the bike ride and all of the excitement after that. He'd realized it last night, however. So much sleeping on the ground, floors, and tables recently had taken its toll.

The scrounging was hard work too, and had added to the soreness. The tension in his flesh, the little tears in the fibers of his unused muscles, made them tender from overstrain. The soreness radiated out across his young shoulders and down his back, into his deltoids. He was sore even in his bones. The sheets were tangled like vines around his legs as he lay. He'd tossed and turned, trying to find a comfortable place to rest his body against the strange shapes of the fold-out couch that he'd shared with Calvin for the past week. The couch, for its part, didn't care about his comfort, or lack thereof.

Both boys had risen early each day to get ready for their scrounging duties. Today they were making a run to the outer limits of the property line. Stephen stretched his back and yawned, and wondered if Calvin was just as sore. He arched backwards to roll his shoulders forward fully, looking to find the range of motion so he'd know just where the pain would hit.

He looked around and got his bearings. He still was not completely used to living at the farm. Through the open door, he could see that his mother was already up. The rest of the fold-out was empty, and that meant that Calvin was up too. He felt for his boots and sat up on the edge of the bed.

Mom has been sleeping roughly too, he thought as he dressed.

They'd sat up talking last night, just the two of them, as they did at the end of every day. She talked with him about where they might go in the future, and what they might do. He felt that she couldn't bring herself to tell him what she feared was coming. All she'd said was that they should stay put.

This is a good place, she'd said. *At least for the moment.* Even with the weird relationship that they'd established with Clive and Red Beard, it was a good place. His mother liked the men personally, and she'd left no doubt about that. She was concerned, however, that there seemed to be a tension between them all. Stephen had noticed the tension, too. They all had developed some sort of unspoken arrangement, and it must be admitted that the arrangement allowed everyone to live peaceably—that much was certain. However, his mother was still too new at all of this to *entirely* trust the two older men. She wasn't sure she *was* fine with the arrangement, and told him that she wasn't completely comfortable with people who kept secrets. She made motions in the air, putting air quotes around the word "secrets." However, they were guests, after all, and she'd told him that she understood everything that being a guest implied.

Maybe it was just her motherly instincts towards Stephen and now, by extension towards Calvin, who seemed like he was close enough to be Stephen's brother. Stephen could see that. He knew why his mother liked Calvin so much. Calvin had an old soul. There was something in his manner and presence that suggested that he was a man who ought not be slighted or treated like a youngster, merely because of his youthful appearance. He exuded a kind of wisdom born from experience. Where, Stephen wondered, did his new friend get such wisdom? He was clearly too young to have had much experience. It was a mystery.

Veronica had said all of these things, and Stephen had listened. Stephen listened to her and thought that maybe his mother had been saying that Calvin was somehow more mature, more capable than he was. He laughed to himself when he thought of this. He didn't see it that way at all. He saw Calvin as a brother, as an equal. They were two brothers who had lost their fathers - misunderstood, as all youth are.

* * * *

The morning was cool and light and Stephen couldn't help thinking of the way his mother looked as she stood at the fence line while he and Calvin headed out to their day's work. She stood and watched as if she were waiting for something, just as she had on his first day of school, when she'd sent him down the hall towards his classroom. His mother perennially had that look of a mother sending her child off to the danger of the world. Even now, in the midst of catastrophe, she had it.

As the two friends walked off to work, Stephen saw Calvin look back at Veronica over by the fence, and noted that his friend saw the look too. Calvin glanced back at him and smiled. Stephen smiled back and changed the subject that had never been spoken aloud.

The three of them, as a family, bonded as the scrounging project progressed. It was important for Stephen, as a youth still growing in his maturity, to have someone his own age to talk to. Someone who spoke his language. Someone who was member of *his* tribe. He had often leaned on Calvin's guidance. He did that now.

"So what's the plan?" He asked.

"Okay, dude," Calvin said, "you head out along that south fence line over there where it looks like there was a chimney that got burned out." Calvin pointed out shapes across the field to Stephen as he talked. He directed his friend's attention toward the distance. "Usually those kinds of places are picked over pretty well, but sometimes they were picked over in a different time, by people with a different mindset. You might find things that appear useful now that wouldn't have meant anything to people then, back when the last set of looters went through it." He leaned into the word "looters" and pointed across the land as if ironically. He winked at Stephen. "I'm going to go along that ridge over there. I'll circle back down to you. Okay, bro?"

"Cool." Stephen said. He looked up in the direction of the chimney. Like his mom, he saw triangles and boxes of color. He knew there would be bricks, boards, who knows what else...

* * * *

Calvin walked out of the field, then up and along the fence line. He followed the fence for about fifty yards, stopping here and there to mend it when he could, when it poked out of the snow piles occasionally. He came out to a stand of trees at the northwest corner of the field and entered onto a rocky clearing. There, under the trees, he saw a couple of heavy boulders. *Where, in such a landscape, could large boulders like those have come from?* Calvin wondered. He thought of Stonehenge for some odd reason. He thought of the pyramids, and of Easter Island.

The boulders were huge and stacked on each other, and he walked under the trees as his eyes adjusted to the light and to the distance. There was a man sitting on one of the boulders. The man was peeling an apple in the cold morning air. He gave Calvin a little wave. Calvin looked at the craggy features of the man sitting on the boulder, and he knew who it must be. Until that very moment, he had never before seen an honest-to-goodness Amish man. Calvin looked at the man, and the man looked at Calvin, and then they exchanged head nods.

"You must be Jonathan Wall's man."

"Yes, Mr. Stolzfus. Calvin Rhodes. It's nice to meet you." Calvin had heard Clive and Red Beard talking about Henry Stolzfus, and figured that this had to be the man himself.

Henry Stolzfus waved off the offer of a handshake. He made a motion as if to say he would offer an apple if he had another.

"Good to meet yu'uns." He looked Calvin up and down. "Is everything okay with Mr. Wall, then?"

"Yes sir," Calvin explained, nodding his head. "We're managing down in Texas. About as good as can be expected, I guess."

"Good. Well, I appreciate the risk you ran in bringing up this package all that way. The medicines especially were much appreciated. The gold was important too, and you tell Jonathan that we'll store the amount he said for him until he wants or needs it. Tell him we're thankful for the help."

"I will, Sir." Then, Calvin snapped his fingers. He'd just remembered something he was supposed to tell the Amish man if he saw him. "Mr. Darling said he'd bring your shipment over in stages." He paused to get the man's reaction.

"Yes, well..." Stolzfus nodded his bearded chin. "It's true. We've received some already. We need one or two more, I expect. I don't foresee any problems."

Calvin nodded his head and then moved to make his departure. "Okay. Well, then, thanks. We sure appreciate everything you're doing. If you get down to Texas, you know you have a place to stay."

"I know it, yung'un. Y'uns take care." With that, Henry Stolzfus turned his head back toward his own field and rested his feet on the boulder. The conversation was over. He turned again, after a while, and watched the young Chinese man disappear into the shadows. *What an odd choice for Jonathan to have made there,* he thought. He watched as Calvin walked into the field, followed along the fence, and then dropped down into Clive's place. Henry Stolzfus looked across the field toward his own farm again and pushed the last piece of apple into his mouth. He tasted

it, pushing the piece around on his tongue, before standing and
walking back down toward his own valley.

* * * *

Calvin was just coming up along the fence line, across the
field where they'd first sighted the chimney, when he saw Stephen
in the distance.

His friend was standing, shaking his leg, tripping out from
some woodpile or something. As he watched, he began to make
out what was going on. Stephen was hopping, and then Calvin
heard a series of bloodcurdling howls. Stephen fell backwards and
caught himself against the pile, stumbling around, and from a
distance, Calvin finally saw what it was. Stephen had a board
attached to his foot. Sparked into motion, Calvin ran toward the
screams, and as he ran, he stared into the middling distance
watching the drama unfold. He saw Stephen drop like a rock, or
like a man that was dead.

* * * *

Stephen's boot had a board attached to it. There was no
getting around it. Stephen was passed out and Calvin was looking
at his boot curled up under his foot, wrenched at the end of his leg
in an agonizing position. Calvin wondered if anything was broken,
and he saw on the other end of the board another nail, like the one
in Stephen's foot. He saw the gauge of the nail, its rusty length
protruding ominously from the board. *It likely went all the way
through the foot,* Calvin thought. He saw the nasty hook at the
end, where the tip of the nail had broken off in a jagged slice of
rust. He calculated that Stephen had slipped or stumbled
backward and landed on a trashed piece of barn siding that was still
home to the nails that had once attached it to an even older Amish
barn or out-building. No doubt about it. Stephen's foot was
definitely nailed to the board.

Calvin reached down and woke Stephen, shaking him firmly
by the shoulder. Stephen stirred and looked up at him, but the two
brothers didn't speak. The pain hit again just as he helped Stephen

up. Pain gripped Stephen's face, as the two brothers clasped one another tightly and nodded. They knew what they needed to do.

In the old world, they might have secured the board so that the weight of it wouldn't do more damage, tearing flesh, dislocating bone, or maybe cutting a vein. They might have called an ambulance with paramedics on board that could come and immobilize or remove the board more professionally. But this wasn't the old world.

Stephen put his weight into Calvin's shoulder. Calvin placed his arms underneath the shoulders of his younger, new-found brother. Together, they lifted.

There was a vicious sound, unlike any that Calvin had ever heard. What was going on inside the boot—inside the foot—he could not know. Outside the boot, all he heard was a thud and a thwack of rubber and wood and snow. And screams of pain.

Then Calvin felt Stephen pass out in his arms.

* * * *

"Dude, you should have seen yourself."

Calvin was sitting next to Stephen, who was coming groggily back to life.

"You were doing this little dance with this board. I thought you were trying on skis, or waving your arms all James Brown like. I thought maybe you had stepped on a snake!"

Stephen looked down at his foot and began to inspect it while Calvin joked, trying to keep his friend's mind off the pain. Laughter was the only medicine Calvin had with him. Stephen tried to see whether there were any broken bones first.

Stephen stopped Calvin and pointed to the pile of wood about ten yards away. "Yeah, I jumped across that pile over there. I should have taken the time to walk around it. My foot kind of slipped through a rotted piece of wood, and my weight came down directly on the nail."

He looked down again at the foot. "Ouch." *Ouch!* The skin was all blue on the top of the foot. The nail hadn't quite punctured the skin on top, but had gotten... just ... that... close. Blueish-black blood was already coagulating just under the skin, and there was a tiny circle of deepening hues where the nail had nearly come through. The bruise moved outward in concentric circles of purple. The pain, too, radiated outward.

Stephen looked up at Calvin, who tried his best to smile at his friend sheepishly.

"You want to put the boot back on or hobble with it off?" Calvin asked.

"On." Stephen said. "Maybe it will help hold down the swelling." He put the boot back on and they headed back across the field toward the farmhouse.

* * * *

Veronica was standing in a cornfield, thinking about the harvest that this field might bring in the spring. She'd always read about Pennsylvania farmland and its rich soil, and its suitable climate. She looked around and thought, *it has other advantages, too.* She'd read that Pennsylvania has more miles of rural roads than any state in the nation—miles of roads running through cornfields or dairy farms. Back ways. Away from the huddled masses, yearning to... well... to live. Many of the Amish farms were connected, one to another, fence to fence, for miles in every direction.

She looked across the field now, examining it forensically, with her artist's eye. She'd always liked the way snow looks against the line of the sky. The field was white but splattered here and there with broad swaths of color. The fence line cut a grid across the fields, and Veronica was trailing her eye along that fence line, and then along the fence by the river, when she saw Calvin helping Stephen along. She could see that Stephen was hurt. Something in the pit of her stomach made her know that it was bad. The birds in the tree above their head scattered, chirping madly as they flew away in the opposite direction of the two approaching boys.

She ran, her arms outstretched, unconsciously open like a hen wanting to gather in her chicks. She was running toward them, eyes wide open, panic gripping her heart, when there was a blinding flash, as if someone had flipped on a light switch, amplifying the light and making it ten times brighter. Day. No. More than just day. Daylight itself, as if the world had just been put under a magnifying glass. The light was *intensified.*

It almost blinded her with its intensity. Had she been looking just a few clicks further to the right, it certainly *would* have blinded her—at least temporarily. As it was, it knocked her to the ground. She rocked, feeling as if the flash of light had sent a wave under her feet. She heard a boom. No, it was more. It was a BOOM! She was on her knees and trying to get to her feet.

The thing she'd most feared had happened.

She stood up again and continued running toward the boys. She saw Calvin helping his brother along, with Stephen's arm slung over his shoulder. Stephen, her son. He looked like a wounded soldier whose friend was helping him hobble back from the battlefield.

She saw them come over the hill and she was running. When she'd been knocked to the ground by the blast, something in her had changed. There'd been an almost instantaneous realization, as if God Himself had stepped out of the clouds to speak the awful truth.

The world would never be the same. There was no going back. The decision was final. She looked into the assembling clouds and saw the sky open up and the wind rush out, and she ran toward the nothingness.

* * * *

The odd-shaped RV was barreling down a road emptied of military style vehicles for the first time in many days. In the cab, the cowboy was spitting and cursing, and the leprechaun was listening. "Damn it all, damn it all." Clive spat again, angrily. *"Those bastards did it!"*

This was the bomb that took out Philadelphia.

Across the adjacent field, they could see the woman who they'd brought into their home, and she was running towards the boys. The RV had been a hundred yards up the road when the flash split the morning sky. Now, Clive and Red Beard pulled up to the farmhouse and stopped. "Damn it *all*."

Veronica reached the two young boys, and she knew that there wasn't time for explanations. A storm was coming. A new kind of storm. She put her arm around Stephen and threw his left arm over her shoulder. With two of them taking the weight off of Stephen's foot, the three of them picked up the pace.

All five of them got to the house at about the same time. Clive and Red Beard told them to follow, and they all spilled into the farmhouse's drawing room. They pulled back the table, and then rolled back the rug. Clive bent down and picked up a slatted door made as a cutout in the floor. "I was hoping not to have to do this," he said, "but we don't have much choice now."

He pointed to the stairs leading down to a dark steel door.

"In you go."

Calvin went first, and he helped Stephen limp his way down the steep stairs. Clive and Red Beard stood and waited for Veronica to go, both of them looking unsure as to whether she would actually go or not. She did. She didn't even think to ask why.

CHAPTER 41

The Farm. After the Bombs.

Taking a bigger look at things, from space, the planet rolled on. It was now dimpled along its surface by a number of pockmarks, and in its atmosphere was a cloud of dust so thick that, in many places, it might occlude much of the sun for years. Still, the earth rolled along, pushing through the roiling violence of space as if the dimples hardly mattered. It swung its wide arc around the solar system as if the dust was only a hiccup in its calendar. In many places on earth, someone gazing into the nighttime sky would have looked in vain for stars, but still the stars were there. For those seemingly trapped under the darkened blanket, the stars would be seen another night, after the winds would blow in and sweep the skies clean. In some regions, the dust effect would linger, causing drastic temperature drops over the next year, killing crops that weren't already lost to disease and the poisoning of the soil. Other locations would see wild and unnatural temperature swings and difficult growing conditions. Still other places in North America and around the world—areas where the jet stream protected the earth from dust and fallout—would actually benefit from the cooler temperatures that would bring more rains than normal.

From above the eastern portion of North America, the ethereal clouds that hung between earth and space, the clouds that were even now diminishing, were made up of ash and smoke—remnants of The City. Not just a portion of the city, like what had happened at Ground Zero when the twin towers fell in New York - this cloud consisted of the entirety of a cultural and social construct we call *The City.*

Mirroring the reality of the intermittent pyres of global thermonuclear war, from a nearer view, on earth, the phenomenon of fire as a tool and hub of society had returned to the world, spreading outward in webbed fingers into the night. These were the fires of humanity—of *humanness.* Gathering around campfires, people huddled ever closer together. Shell-shocked. The fires stretched across the landscape in waves. Nearer the old population centers, they increased in number slightly and then spread out toward the horizon where they diminished, and disappeared into the unpredictability of the wilderness.

There were many hunks of metal hanging in the pull of earth's orbit. These metal objects once served as communication satellites, but now their only purpose was to bide their time in gravity's tug until they all, in the coming years, and in their turn, would become streaking stars across the earth's skies. Looking at the earth from one of these satellites, we would have seen through the haze of the clouds and dust that, as time passed, the number of fires on the surface of the earth was dwindling. Immediately after the blasts, though, the pockmarks on the earth—those that we mentioned earlier—shimmered like trinkets in the light of heaven, or mirrors reflecting back, flashing a signal code. It was strange, this reflected light. Then, studying it closer, we might have read the code and understood. The blinking was coming from the center of each of the blasts. The superheated gas had turned the surface of the earth in those pockmarks to glass.

* * * *

As the sunlight expanded across the valley, had one been standing along the ridge overlooking Clive's farm, one might have wondered whether the smoke blocking out some of that sun was also made of pulverized human bones. One might consider the possibility of cancer-causing chemicals and radiation in the smoke. One might pause, watch the sunrise, and ask, "Was all of this necessary?"

It is, in the end, a matter of perspective. Some would surmise, not without ample evidence, that humanity's crimes were immense, and that the inevitable justice for such crimes was only now being meted out by some unseen hand. Or perhaps one would have thought that even then, in that moment of most terrible devastation, the earth was bigger than humankind. *"Look what I can do,"* says the child, bending the rules of nature, spreading his havoc. The Earth stands with her hands on her hips, threatening with age and experience. She yawns at the antics, as she yawned at the dinosaurs. She will outlast these tantrums. Earth, in this scenario, simply keeps rolling toward the light in the horizon, as inevitable as the tide. Perhaps one might have considered that both realities were simultaneously true.

Just now, these considerations were just speculations. There was no one there yet, standing on the ridge, to consider them. There was only the farmhouse down in the valley, which seemed for the moment to be protected. Prevailing winds had taken the bombs' immediate toxic cloud out to sea. The farm was peaceful, resting and quiet. The only noise of discomfort came from the barn, from animals that hadn't been fed yet.

The farmhouse, too, was quiet. Occasionally, an electronic blip sounded, emitted from a source in the old farm's drawing room. In that room, in the middle of the floor, just to the side of a hidden floor panel that covered the entry door to the bunker, was a Geiger counter. Clive Darling had left it there as he'd descended the steps on the day when they'd entered the bunker. He'd herded everyone into the cellar, and then he'd placed the Geiger counter on the floor, hastily wiring it up according to his plan.

Completing the task with the counter, he'd then pulled the flooring into place. All of this occurred in only a few moments after the bomb went off. He felt certain that they were all going to be in good shape, but he needed to get some readings before he could be confident. The Geiger counter sent active readings down into the basement.

Now, down in the bunker, Clive sat at an antique oaken table lighted by a wind-up lamp, and fiddled with a slide rule. He made calculations, and occasionally he reached up to grab the lamp to wind the small handle and generate more power. The sound of the lamp's whirring dynamo filled the bunker, echoing off the walls. Despite the noise, Clive sat alone. Everyone else snoozed silently, not even stirring at the sound of the small machine being cranked back to life.

Clive stroked his mustache, leaned in, and tapped the window of the read-out dial on the counter. He waited for a moment and then flipped through a number of sheets in a small spiral notebook he kept in his front pocket. He made a mark on a page and then flipped back to a different page, where he made another kind of mark. On a whim, he thumbed back in his notebook, and his eye caught an entry. He stopped and stared at the page for a moment.

The note was from the day he'd met the traveler—the man he'd called Ned Ludd. Clay was his real name. He smiled at the thought, and he wondered what had happened to old Ned Ludd. *Somewhere in Upstate New York, I reckon, trying to get by.*

* * * *

Now, another man stood his turn at the lonely vigil. He was wide-awake, and his mind raced through a well-worn philosophical maze. He enjoyed these nights alone. He fiddled with his red beard and pondered.

Time will, in future days, become again what it has always been in the past—an ancient and endless thing. Eventually people will come to live by the sunrise again, and that can't happen soon enough for me. People will once again live as ancient man lived. Earth, that changeable mistress, will simply endure. In her heart of hearts, she has always been an unemployable lay-about. Left to her own devices, given time, she always reverts to the most decadent forms of wastrelism. Entropy and atrophy. Weeds growing through pavement in a parking lot. Waves crashing against the Colossus of Rhodes until they sweep it out to the sea. Humankind has spent the last several millennia thinking that they are in control, all the while walking on soil that covers dinosaur bones. Technological man built their whole society on the ancient remains of a larger, heartier species. Hmmm. I wonder what future species will build on the remains of humankind? Perhaps humans, ever the most selfish of all earth's creatures, will leave no remains...

Red Beard paused his thoughts for a moment. He leaned his head against the cool of the concrete and found that he liked the sensation. Soon enough, his thoughts continued...

And all this while they could have been loafing. Not 'loafing,' as in 'doing nothing.' Loafing, as in not worrying. Not working on a treadmill. Not slaving away to own things they don't need, and that can never last. Not straining at a brass ring that will only leave them empty. Now, it will take years to regain knowledge that has been lost in the mists of time. They must relearn skills that will help them beat back decadent, violent nature. In some cases, humankind will literally have to reinvent the wheel. That will all be true in time. But for now, there is the waiting, and that too, is endless. The interminable waiting. The ground has been literally swept out from under the feet of the cities. Ground(s) zero! In New York and Philly, and other places stretching out beyond into the western horizon...

Red Beard was right about one thing, even if he was wrong about others. The systems that had eradicated the importance of concepts like day and night (all except for that most persistent of human requirements... sleep,) disappeared in the blink of an eye. Once again the natural cycles of life would reassert themselves. Day. Night. Seasons. Age. Life. Death. Frailty. All of these realities were rising again to insist upon recognition by humankind. From the hustle and bustle of the 21st Century, in a crystalline moment, the brakes had been applied, and now time would be experienced more purposefully, even down in the depths of a fallout bunker.

Red Beard leaned back in his chair and checked the dial. He made a mark in a notebook. He leaned his head against the concrete again. He thought, somehow, of prisons, of caves.

* * * *

Time passed. Inside the bunker sat a group of people brought together by whatever forces ruled the universe. God, chance, luck. Everyone in that bunker didn't believe all the same things, and individually they conceived of different motivational powers at work in the universe. They did, however, share one commonality: Together, they waited in the bunker for the smoke to clear.

Time is experienced in both small and large increments in such confined, underground spaces. The scenes flashed by in bursts, like blips from the Geiger counter on the floor above them in the farmhouse. Long, lazy hours of conversation coupled with short bursts of emotion. Living underground can be like being in the warm enclosure of a womb, or the cold, dark grip of a dungeon, but, either way, one can only sleep so much. One can only read so many books. The body gets weary in such a prison, such a grave. Time becomes a vanity. Moments are measured by the hunger in one's stomach, the tension in one's legs. There is a feeling of wanting to run unfettered across a field, just as there is a need to sit and explore the inner quiet of one's own nature. Time becomes meaningless in such moments, and it becomes everything.

Here we find Clive and Red Beard sitting and talking. There, Veronica is doctoring her son's foot. Time goes on like this for a while. Now, Calvin is joining Clive and Red Beard in animated conversations and arguments. He is sitting with his back against the wall, polishing some tool he fashions for purposes that only he seems to care about.

Again, Veronica is tending to her son.

There, Red Beard is trying to get her to eat something.

Over here, Clive and Calvin are quietly discussing something in the corner.

The time passed on like this, the intermixing of the people in the bunker, the boredom being embraced, the moments being measured in swirls in the coffee cup. The scenes rolled by in endless succession. Time became both meaningless and endless. The Geiger counter was registering. Its dial showed clear, as it had since they first burrowed into the ground. Still, they were waiting, seemingly forever.

For what?

Only Clive Darling knew exactly what they were waiting for, and as per usual, he wasn't talking.

* * * *

Clive had purchased the piece of property in Lancaster County years before. The property suited his purposes, and it had the added benefit of being a stunningly beautiful piece of Pennsylvania. It rested along the river, which was lovely in its own right, and the river's wide, unnavigable waters served as a kind of natural barrier to the western edge of the property boundaries. Clive had bought the property because he liked it, but he'd also bought it because it was the closest farm in the county to a man he sincerely wanted to know. That man's name was Henry Stolzfus.

Clive had met Stolzfus by placing himself in the right booth of the right coffee spot—one that Henry Stolzfus frequented. This act of buying land next to a man in order to meet him and create a bond with him might be considered particularly manipulative or scheming, and one would be forgiven for thinking that all hidden motivations are inherently guileful. Clive, however, looked at the reality of the situation and excused his own behavior. How else would such a partnership come to be—between a rich worldling and a religious separatist?

The meeting of these two men took place at Smarty's, a shiny, stainless-steel enclosed box of a diner on a shady back road in the southern center of the county. Every Monday at 8 a.m., many of the men from the local Amish community would meet at Smarty's and exchange news. Clive spent some time scouting the area, and it didn't take long for him to notice that the buggies were lined up deep around the diner on Monday mornings.

Clive had goals to be sure. He wasn't *just* looking for friendship with like-minded individuals. Those many years ago, he'd been looking to secure a ready and available food source at a time when the Cold War was raging and the future had looked particularly bleak. Moving forward, Clive would need a sustainable source of food supplies for his men, and for the groups that he financially supported throughout the country. Considering all the factors, and counting into the equation his own long-term geopolitical goals, it seemed to him that collaborating with the Amish seemed like the best plan for getting his needs met. But how to strike the bargain?

On the first day of Operation Stolzfus, Clive walked into the diner to watch and learn. He noticed how the other men treated Henry, as if he was the man to know. The next Monday, he arrived early and sat down in Henry's favorite booth. He'd learned something by watching the Amish man, and had decided the straight-forward approach was probably the best tactic. It turned out that Clive was right.

There was a reason that, in one of the most renowned Amish counties in the country, one of the most respected Amish men lived on the edge of society. Henry Stolzfus lived as far west as one could go and not be in the river or out of the county. Clive decided he might have a friend and confidant in such a man.

* * * *

"You know, the problem is, people came to love the bomb." It was Red Beard talking. Long soliloquies and spoken-word performances had become just another way to pass the time. This conversation happened not long after the nuclear blasts took out Philly and New York. Red Beard was sitting with Calvin and filling the air with words, which was something he loved to do.

"I mean, it goes way back—even before that song about wearing your sunglasses at night. You remember that one? Probably not. Or the one that talks about the future being so bright you gotta wear shades?" He hummed the tune from the song, but it didn't sound like much to Calvin.

"It became cool to love the bomb. The country suddenly became that guy from the *What? Me Worry?* generation. I don't have to look at the military-industrial complex to see some bomb *fetishization* going on. It was all over the media, too. You can go back to Dr. Strangelove at least, but when it happened, it happened. The country fell in love with the bomb, either in an actual way, by wanting more and bigger ones or, ironically, by mocking more loudly and derisively. We loved it or we hated it, but either way we thought about it (that is what love is, after all), and in time we all accepted the bomb as a reality not to be questioned. That's how we became fallout kids, all of us. Besides, what could we do about it, anyway?"

Calvin didn't usually know exactly what Red Beard was saying, but the words passed the time, and sometimes the words were interesting. Not always, but sometimes. Calvin had come to think of Red Beard's dissertations as extended poetry recitations that didn't need to make sense to be art.

Red Beard was talking to Calvin while Clive, who had been napping in the corner, awoke and began shaking off the sleep. None of them had any idea what time of day it was at that instant. Time was irregularly kept by events, and not by machines making declarative statements about subjective concepts. In the morning, or thereabouts, they had breakfast. Then there was the time period known as "after breakfast." There were other periods of the day known by names such as "dinner," and "after dinner," and "reading time." People cleaned up behind a sheet hung in the corner.

Red Beard was talking and Clive was yawning and stretching when they all heard a knock at the door upstairs. Even from where they were in the bunker, they heard the vibrations of sound from the knocking coming from above them. Then there was a bloodcurdling scream. Someone had entered the farmhouse. The person up there had found their way to the trapdoor and now he was pleading for his life. They heard the banging of fists onto the outside shell of the steel door until the thud of the fists made them sound meaty in their return. There was no threat of violence in the pounding, only the sound of pleading. After a while, they made out the reason why.

The person pounding on the door had the voice of one who had come to know the bomb intimately—someone who had survived its blast close up. The person pounding on the door was a temporary *survivor*, one of those stumbling this way from the east, irradiated by a bomb that, Red Beard was convinced, the people had decided to love.

There was no love in the sound of the pounding.

* * * *

Days later...

"Here is what happened in the city at that moment." Now Clive was talking to Calvin. Calvin had been cleaning his tools, and he'd asked the older man about a nuclear blast.

"At the point of detonation—well, imagine that there was a dot on the map about the size of a dime. That dime marks the area where a large hole, three quarters of a mile across, opened up. The devastation within that circle would have been total. Zero survivability. Imagine 9-11, but instead of planes, they had nuclear bombs. Lower Manhattan? All of it vaporized.

"Out beyond that, compare it now with a circle about the size of a nickel—this circle is the *blast radius.* Anyone and anything in its path would have turned to flames. If there were any survivors, they would soon have had acute radiation poisoning. The person out there a while ago? The man knocking on the door trying to get in here? He would likely have poisoned us with toxic radiation if we'd opened the door. How he got here so fast has me concerned, but..." he let his thoughts trail off.

Calvin was starting to get the picture. They weren't in the bunker to escape radioactive fallout. They'd pretty much determined that the fallout cloud had been pushed out to sea. Clive had them in the bunker to escape those who *hadn't* avoided radioactive fallout. He was waiting for those who were irredeemably poisoned, to die off.

In other places, people didn't need a bunker, or didn't have one. Maybe they didn't run into irradiated refugees, or maybe they had fallout suits and just shot strangers... or maybe they didn't know any better, and got poisoned, and would die ten or twenty years hence from cancer.

"Okay, for the next radius, think of a circle about the size of a quarter or a one ounce gold coin. If you placed that coin on a map and looked at the concentric circles and the diagrams of all the blast patterns—that circle is the radius wherein the air is going to be highly toxic, and the soil is going to be spoiled. We're outside that circle, or at least we hope we are. None of us really knows the megatonnage of the weapons that were used, so all of this is speculation, you know? And, we should be happy about that—that we're outside the worst of the problems. Anyway, the fact that we were able to stand and see what we saw, and still get down here to safety in time... Well... We did okay."

Clive flashed his best Sam Elliott smile. "The point is that if you were close enough to survive and you did, you had to keep going. You had to do what was necessary to do."

"Yeah," Calvin said. "It's hard to imagine. I think I've always just thought of it as something that either happens or it doesn't. A bomb going off, I mean. I either survive or I don't."

"Yes, Calvin, but in Dante's deepest pit of hell, it is coldest winter," Clive said. "It's hard to imagine that, too, until you take a look around. Once the money has been accounted for, the imagination of man is the root of most evil." He pointed at everyone in turn, and then tapped on his own chest. "They call that the 'heart.' Desperately wicked. Who can know it?" He nodded his head as if he knew it.

Clive motioned around them. Red Beard was talking with Veronica and Stephen was moaning in pain. The sound coming from Stephen sounded like the noise you'd make when mocking a pain, actually. Stephen was not really giving into it, or, not yet acknowledging it. In fact, it seemed that Stephen was indeed, mocking the pain. As if he could fight it back by mere force of will power.

"How's he doing?" Clive asked Calvin.

"Veronica thinks he has tetanus," Calvin said.

Clive winced. It was just a small movement, behind his eyes, but you could see it if you knew where to look.

* * * *

It should be said here that most of the world has long operated under a misconception about tetanus. This misconception has, in many ways, been a purposeful deception, perpetrated by a few generations of salesmen who have grown very rich by convincing the world to have faith in vaccinations as an answer to every ancient bogeyman. As part of this deception, almost everyone in the world was propagandized into believing that the medical condition of tetanus comes from rusty metal. It does not. Tetanus comes from the production of a highly dangerous toxin produced by the introduction of the tetanus bacterium into the body.

The widespread belief that tetanus comes from rust was encouraged by people in the medical and pharmaceutical professions who wanted to sell tetanus vaccines to everyone in the world. The idea that tetanus is always resident on rusty nails and other rusty items is based loosely on the fact that most rusty items are found outside. Most tetanus cases, especially in earlier generations, happened on farms where animals defecated, and where the tetanus bacteria would often thrive in anaerobic environments (like the pits and deposits on a rusty nail) and in the dirt in areas frequented by animals. The rusty surface of a nail just happens to be a great place for the tetanus bacteria to hide, and when a puncture is made in the surface of the skin, the nail is a handy delivery device that can push the tetanus endospores deep into the wound. It should also be noted that the fatality rate of those who contract tetanus in a full-blown way, and who do not receive treatment, is about 50%. It's a coin toss, if such a thing can be said without it seeming to be too callous.

Everyone doesn't always have all of the information they need to properly treat a medical condition, especially in a situation where there has been a great—even worldwide—calamity, and when the only recourse is found in the colonized minds of technologically crippled people who have relied for too long on chemical drugs and high-tech treatments to maintain a semblance of health through brute force application of money and industry. In short, there are ways to treat someone being afflicted by the toxins produced by the tetanus bacteria. Keeping the wound extra clean; flushing it with clean and sterilized water or saline solution; soaking out the toxin with a drawing solution and with Epsom salts; flooding the body with natural substances that have anti-bacterial qualities; all of these treatments can help, and sometimes even cure, a patient afflicted with tetanus. Whether or not the people in a given radius have that knowledge is what makes the issue problematic.

* * * *

Veronica stood at Stephen's bed and looked down at him. A few hours ago (or was it yesterday?), he'd begun to complain of tightening in his jaw. Not long after that, the jaw had wrenched into uncontrolled spasms. That's why they used to call it *lockjaw.* He almost bit his tongue off because the spasms were so violent and unexpected. Now the convulsions had begun in his feet and arms. She looked down and took his hands into her own. He'd been rubbing them frantically in his sleep. She thought of how, when he was just a boy, she'd held his hands in her own as she taught him to clean the paint from a paintbrush. Those hands were now writhing in grotesque shapes, held there as if frozen in ice, his back arching up and then out, waves of uncontrolled musculature rolling up into his shoulders.

Stephen's face was frozen in pain. Veronica wanted to take the weight from him, but she could not. She felt the helplessness of a mother whose whole world is passing before her eyes. She felt her art slip away into the distance. She hung there over the precipice, over her child.

CHAPTER 42

Just south of Elizabethtown, Peter, Elsie, and Ace joined the few other travelers on the state highway heading southeast towards Mount Joy, Pennsylvania. Peter's contact in the FMA had informed him that they would come upon a large militia checkpoint there, just below Mount Joy.

"They're stopping most everybody from entering the heaviest Amish areas," the man said. The way he said it made it sound as if that answered all that needed to be answered. "If you're lucky, you'll meet up with some other refugees heading into the same country; maybe get in with some party that has a legitimate claim to be allowed in."

Peter liked the way the man didn't stress the word *legitimate.* The tone of the statement suggested that there was social order enough there that one might find someone reasonable in charge to talk to. He didn't know if luck had anything to do with it, but he was silently hoping that just such a scenario might avail itself.

The walk from Elizabethtown to Mount Joy passed uneventfully, and the three travelers spent most of the time in silence, as if they expected a mental onslaught to come upon them at any moment. Perhaps it was the weariness of the journey, or the expectation of still more walking that lay ahead that made them dull. Or, perhaps it was the fact that, as they walked, they were simultaneously scanning the horizon looking for armed bandits. Either way, all work and no play had done its work. The walk through the rural areas was drab and depressing.

By contrast, passing into Mount Joy on a major highway was a traumatic sensory experience when compared to their long practice of walking primarily through the countryside. The destruction of war was everywhere. Off the road to the north, as if they'd been dragged there to rot, piles of bodies laid decomposing in the sun. The decaying fleshy mess was covered with lime or sand, ostensibly to keep down the odor. The whitened bodies looked surreal, and therefore fake, as if they'd been crudely fabricated from picture books of someone else's war.

The remains of fires from the night before, and the debris left behind by disorder and panic, were everywhere. Burned-out buildings lined the streets, and brick edifices were pockmarked with the telltale damage of bullets and bombs. In the streets, blackened cars with shattered windscreens and doors perforated by bullets lay helter-skelter. The shell casings of bullets were swept to the curb where they rested in tiny cylindrical ridges, remnants of stories that may never be told. The scene looked, well, *imaginary*. No one had collected the shell casings yet, but Peter knew that soon enough, someone would. The bodies could be left to rot, but the brass would be gathered because it had value.

There is a strange contradiction in the signatures of urban warfare that can be hard to describe. Since the area had actually *been* a city besieged in battle, it had the texture of a scene put together by moviemakers to resemble an urban battlefield. This made it harder to see the damage and blood and evidences of death as real. And it is precisely necessary to see these things rightly, because they are both real, and immediate. The revolution will not be televised, because the mechanical infrastructure of mass communication will lie in heaps on the ground when the revolution comes. So, when it happens, it is confusing and counter-intuitive. Most people will not have imagined it as it is. They haven't had to, because some set designer has always done it for them. Camera angles and lighting choices have conspired to show them a part, and to present it as the whole. In reality, there was the stench of death coming from bodies covered by lime and sand. There was the weight of the guns in the backpack pulling heavily on exhausted shoulders. A million tiny and violent details assailed the senses. This was not a movie set. This was what Peter and Elsie and Ace were seeing and feeling.

* * * *

Twice within just the first few blocks, our travelers saw men hanging by their necks from light poles. One hanged man, having reached the end of his rope, twisted slowly in the cool breeze, a look of surprise on his face. He never thought he'd end up like this. Pinned to his worn and soiled coat was a piece of cardboard with the word *LOOTER* written on it.

Here and there, FMA soldiers stood in small groupings, smoking valuable cigarettes, huddled around trashcans burning with fires for warmth. Peter noticed that here, in contrast to the few other urban areas he'd seen during the journey, people looked him in the eye instead of at their own shoes. It seemed the *Identify: Friend or Foe* mechanism was at work among most of the survivors now. Indefinable factors and subtle indicators were tabulated quickly as eyes met in brief interludes that were unadorned with movie music or poetry.

When passing groups of men, Peter saw that the males usually looked first at Elsie. This had become a pattern, and he understood it completely. There was nothing nefarious or creepy in it, though he wondered what Elsie thought about the phenomenon. Peter understood it perfectly. He did the same thing whenever his group would pass men traveling with women. Peter would look at the women and children to see if they'd been abused or showed signs of duress. "It's amazing what you can tell of a group's story by seeing if the women are in bad condition," he told Ace.

Ace thought of the fellow he had met once while on furlough. He thought of the blackened eye he saw on the guy's girlfriend once and wondered if he would let that go today. "If women are traveling against their will," Peter continued, "then there is something wrong." He'd said the last word with finality, and then he'd looked at Elsie. She was healthy, bright-eyed, and strong. Peter and Ace were usually given a pass by the men who were sensitive to such things.

In Mount Joy, despite the frightening atmosphere and the collateral damage of war, a few businesses here and there were operating. Here, as elsewhere, organization was already beginning to bubble up in little corners as sharp-eyed opportunists, or strong men, or fast talkers, or, more likely, the best scroungers, were setting up shop. Passing by homes or storefronts, the travelers saw signs advertising goods or services to be had inside. Remarkable. Honest to goodness commerce. A city coming together.

Invariably, armed guards stood by doorways, and the suspicious eyes of entrepreneurs tried simultaneously to woo potential customers and threaten harm and death if they came too close too fast. One merchant had simply posted a sign out front that read *Caveat Emptor.*

There were other signs of business, hand-written on cardboard or pieces of wood, or spray-painted on blankets, or spelled out with charcoal upon the door. The signs advertised things as various as winter root vegetables (mostly turnips, carrots, and potatoes), home-brewed alcohol, AA batteries, and milled flour. Later, Peter would learn that Mount Joy was one of the areas on the periphery of Amish territory where businessmen were getting rich trading in produce, goods, and crafts made by the Amish, or salvaged from a world gone awry. But passing through Mount Joy, Peter didn't know any of that. He'd just walked through the remnants of a nuclear war that made the stores in Mount Joy look like a walk along Park Avenue. He was from Warwick, after all, so he had to admit that what he was seeing right now was remarkable.

Winding their way through town, around abandoned busses and the charred remains of vehicles and men, Elsie noted that the very first signs of some kind of life were returning, like when the first blades of grass or crops poke through the melting snow in spring. They saw children playing in a yard fenced by wrought iron and reinforced by sandbags. A street peddler strolled by with a cart loaded with broccoli, chard, and cauliflower for sale. A guard with an MP-5 machine pistol strolling along behind the cart was the only clue that the peddler was concerned about bandits.

Peter stopped and pointed in amazement at a restaurant that seemed to be open and operating, and he looked at Ace and Elsie in turn to see what they thought of such a thing. The restaurant was in an enormous brick building at the end of a small side block. They could hear it before they could see it because it buzzed with activity. When they did see it, they noticed that it had the faintest remnants of hand-painted signs on the brick edifice indicating that the building had once housed a brewery. It was hard to say for certain, because the sign was flaking off. Little bullet pockmarks punctuated the side of the building, hinting at another story that might never be told.

Ace smiled and nodded his head. Elsie's eyes brightened at the thought of a real meal seated at a real table using real utensils. Peter wept. It was only a brief tear that never crested or ran down his face. He covered it quickly by catching the thought in his throat and choking it down, but the thought had most certainly been there. It was something in the light that glowed along the edges of the building's lines, or the sound of what seemed to be music and dining inside. Whatever the case, he felt the tear rise up in him. He used to take his lovely wife to a place just such as this, back in that old life in Warwick. This place reminded him so much of that. Then he thought of Vasily, his friend. How much he'd love to be walking here with Vasily!

The guards in front of the old brew house looked them up and down but did not search them or demand that they surrender their weapons or gear. That was a good thing, because the travelers were not going to patronize any business that wanted them to be disarmed in order to trade there. The guards waved them in and went back to looking up and down the street for trouble.

Inside the restaurant, a palpable sense of having passed into a fantastical dreamland state immediately overtook them. Except for the fact that everyone in the restaurant was heavily armed, and looked as if they hadn't showered in months, the restaurant itself seemed to be completely unfazed by the drama that was going on in the rest of the world. Candles and lanterns lighted the place, and the delectable smells of Italian cuisine wafted outward from the kitchen. Waiters and waitresses, dressed in aprons, swirled in and through the crowds with trays of drinks (with ice!) and plates heaped with delicious dishes. Luscious green salads, lasagna, spaghetti with meatballs, chicken alfredo, and other sumptuous delicacies steamed past Ace, Peter, and Elsie as they stood and watched with their mouths open and watering.

A maître d' of sorts met them after a moment and showed them to a table covered in a red tablecloth with white cloth napkins. He took their drink orders and smiled when they all ordered Cokes with ice. Before he could walk away, Peter stopped him and asked him what form of money the establishment accepted for the meals.

"Silver coins are preferred, sir," the man replied. "We also take gold or anything else of value, but if it isn't gold or silver coin, you'll need to talk to the owner before you order. I'll get your Cokes though. Should I send the owner over?"

"Yes, sir. Please do," Peter said, nodding his head.

When the maître d' walked away, Ace looked at Peter and smiled again. This was the sniper's third smile in a single day, a new record. "If I'm dreaming, do *not* wake me up!" Ace said. He ran his hands through his hair and felt the rough callouses of his palm scratch the leathery shell of his face.

"I get your point, Ace, but you aren't dreaming."

Peter looked at Elsie; her eyes were bright as the waitress returned with their cokes and sat the small platter down on the table, methodically moving each coke from the platter to the table. The ice clinked in the glasses as the drinks settled, and the gas bubbles fizzled in response. Peter looked at the coke, and then at Ace, and continued, "... unless, that is, we're all sharing the same dream."

"Oh my goodness," Elsie exclaimed. "Cokes, with ice? Parmesan chicken with wine sauce? Where in the world *are* we?"

"Apparently, the owner here has worked out some kind of deal with the two opposing armies, and I'll wager he's being supplied by the Amish somehow, probably via a whole system of underground traders. Commerce is the only creature that will outlive cockroaches and will still be thriving at the end of the world."

"Apparently!" Elsie said.

A tall, dark man with slicked-back hair approached the table and nodded to everyone before speaking. "Paul tells me you might need to work out payment?"

"Yes, sir," Peter replied, looking the man in the eye. "We have gold, and quite a bit of it, but it's not in coin."

"Almost never is," the tall man replied. "What else have you got?"

"That we're willing to part with? Not much else."

"What else you gonna need?"

"Alcohol, if you got it. No dangerous, homemade white lightning or watered down swill, but Vodka or Scotch if it's available. Still in the bottle. Preferably with the original seals intact."

The man laughed. "You don't ask for much, do you? You do know that the world ended, and no one is importing Stolichnaya or Glenfiddich anymore?"

"We could also use vitamins if you have any, a sharpening stone, gun oil, and a gun cleaning kit if you think you might give up any of those items."

"Vitamins? You're on your own on that one. The rest of that I can do."

"Okay, so how does this work?" Peter asked.

"Let me see the gold."

Peter pulled out a small nylon ammo bag and unsnapped the top, opening it so the restaurateur could look inside. Ace made a show of moving his right hand into his lap, showing the business owner that he had a pistol and that he was willing to use it. Ace still had the Glock strapped to his leg, but he'd picked up a .357 revolver that he really liked, and he especially liked the impact it had on anyone who might be considering something evil. The tall man saw the motion and just smiled. He wasn't worried in the slightest.

"Okay," the tall man said, after looking through the gold in the bag, "Here is the way this works. No one else is taking gold that isn't coinage right now. At least no one that actually has anything that you might want to buy. I'll take this bulk gold off your hands and replace it with gold or silver coin—your choice. I take a ten-percent handling fee off the top, and the exchange rate is posted above the bar. If you know gold and silver, you'll be able to tell if the stuff I'm giving you is good or mixed with junk metals. I don't debase the coinage. It's not good for business. I'll tell you plainly that I'd be dead and gone if I was scamming people. I surely wouldn't let strangers," he pointed at Ace, "like your friend here, hold guns on me while I conned them, *if* that is what I was doing."

"So you just take the gold? How does this happen? I mean, *logistically* how does this happen?" It was Elsie who asked this obvious question. She looked at Peter, "He could just walk away with our gold, right?"

The tall man looked at Peter and then at Elsie as if to reassure her. He then motioned to Peter. "You come with me. Bring the gold. My son Charlie there will come and sit here with your silent, but deadly friend." He motioned to a boy in the corner.

"How do we know he's your kid?" This time it was Ace. Again, the question was obvious. The father looked again at Elsie as if the answer was, too.

She looked at the boy, how he sat with his arms crossed and how there was an unspoken argument about this little charade that the father and son had been having. She thought of raising her own son. Then the idea hit her.

"You use your son as collateral?" Elsie asked with shock evident on her face.

"I find it engenders trust. If I try to cheat you or run off with your gold, kill Charlie. He's my only child, though, so be sure.

Don't make a mistake." He let that thought settle and then continued. "I'm not trying to cheat anyone here. I'm doing business, and I'm getting rich. I'm getting rich *precisely* because I don't cheat people. I provide a valuable service."

Peter had heard enough. He pushed back his chair and lumbered to his feet. "Okay, let's do this."

"Easy there," the tall man said, putting both hands up in front of him. Peter sat back down. "I'll send the waiter over with Charlie. Order your food first. Then, after you've ordered, come up to the bar with your bag and we'll finish our transaction. If all goes well, your meal is on me. I'm not getting rich on the food and drinks. They merely add atmosphere to this, shall we say, mutually beneficial transaction."

Peter nodded his thanks to the tall man. He leaned his back into the backrest and felt the strain of the muscles relax into the luxurious comfort of something as simple as... a chair. A few minutes later, a waiter came over. He was followed by a curly-headed boy who was obviously, by all rules of narrative logic, named Charlie.

* * * *

Charlie looked to be about ten years old, and now he didn't seem to be bothered at all that he was being used to expedite a monetary transaction.

The waiter smiled at the three diners and held his pencil and note pad up in front of him. "My name is Paul, and I'm going to be your waiter today. May I take your orders?"

Charlie pulled up a chair next to Ace and plopped down in it demonstrably. "My name is Charlie, and I'm going to be your hostage today!"

"I see you've done this before," Peter said to Charlie while shaking his head.

"Only about a *billion* times a day," Charlie said and folded his feet up underneath him on the chair.

"So it usually turns out alright?" Peter asked Charlie.

"Usually. But don't try any funny business, mister. My Dad has seen it all."

"I'll bet he has."

"Your order?" the waiter repeated with an insistent smile.

Peter ordered the chicken fettuccine alfredo with mushrooms and a garden salad. Ace ordered spaghetti with meatballs and an extra order of garlic bread. Elsie ordered lasagna with a salad and a piece of apple pie. The waiter wrote it all down, nodded his head at everyone at the table, and then disappeared into the kitchen with the order.

Peter got up from the table and took the bag of gold up to the bar. The entire transaction took place out in the open, and there was no attempt to hide what was going on, nor was there any sense that the transaction was out of the ordinary. The tall man went painstakingly through the bag. He carefully examined and tested each item, weighing it before telling Peter what he thought of it, it's eventual meltdown weight, and what he could give Peter for it as part of a wholesale transaction. When he'd gone through the whole bag of gold items, he turned to Peter and asked him how he would like his payment.

"How do you suggest?" Peter asked.

"The gold I can give you in coin, buttons, or bars of different sizes. You've quite a bit of value here, so I recommend that you get half of the value in silver coinage, though. Pre-1965 dimes and quarters. That's what people want now. Then get the other half any way you want. Fact is, not many people out there are able to take or exchange large pieces of gold. You did well to find me. Everyone doing business takes silver, and most people around here take .22 shells or buttons of real copper. Some people take metal wire, spools of thread, or straight nails for small items."

"I'll take it like you recommend," Peter said, nodding his head. "Half in silver coinage, and the other half in gold coins of a quarter ounce or less."

"Okay, it's a done deal then." The tall man went through the process of counting out the silver coins, and then the gold. When Peter nodded his approval, the man put the coins into two separate small pouches made from some kind of leather or skins, and then handed them over to Peter.

"Wait right here," the tall man said to Peter. "I'll get your other items."

When the man returned, he placed a small plastic bottle of gun oil, and a cheap gun cleaning kit on the bar. Then he reached under the bar and pulled out a ceramic coffee mug and two bottles of cheap vodka. "I already charged you for these, so they're yours."

"What's with the coffee mug?" Peter asked.

"You said you wanted a sharpening stone."

Lightning fast, the tall man flipped the mug over while simultaneously, with his right hand, reaching into a sheath hidden beneath a white cloth he wore around his waist like a sash or cummerbund. He'd just started to withdraw a hunting knife, when—out of nowhere—Ace was almost magically standing next to the restaurant owner with the revolver pointed to the man's head.

How Ace had moved so quickly across the restaurant with no one noticing him, Peter could not say. Instantly, though, there were a dozen other guns from all around the restaurant pointing at Ace and Peter.

The restaurant owner, for his part, cut his eyes towards Ace and smiled.

"Everyone calm down!" he said, as he slowly pulled a hunting knife from the sheath.

Ace cocked the pistol, showing no emotion or fear on his face.

"I said, calm down," the man said.

He moved slowly and dragged the knife blade at an angle across the rough bottom edge of the coffee mug several times, turning the blade to do the same on the other side, showing Peter, without words, that this was an adequate way to sharpen a blade. He nodded his head slowly at Peter, and then returned the knife to the sheath. Ace de-cocked, and then holstered his pistol. He turned and walked back over to the table as if nothing had happened. Slowly, the other guns in the room all returned to rest as well, and the noise in the place returned to its previous level. The restaurateur smiled and then put out his hands as if to ask "is there anything else I can do for you?"

Peter looked at the tall man and thanked him, but before the man could leave, Peter asked him another question.

"How do I know that you don't have hired bandits out there who will rob us now that they know we're carrying gold and silver?"

The tall man smiled again, but it wasn't a chilling or malevolent smile. The brief standoff hadn't shaken him a bit. It was a knowing smile, as if he'd heard it all before and now he was just going through the motions of his day like he always did.

"You don't. However, I will tell you this, if you get down the road and you conclude that I've cheated you in any way, feel free to come here and kill us all."

"You seem quite confident that no one is actually going to do that," Peter said.

"I'm a realist," the tall man said.

Peter picked up the things he'd bought, and with full hands, he nodded his thanks to the man.

"By the way," the man said, "my name is Nick. I don't have time or the inclination to worry any more. The bombs cured me of my idealism."

"I was going to ask you that," Peter said. "Why is this place so special? Why isn't it bombed out or burned like most of the rest of the buildings in town? Why aren't *you* being robbed when it's obvious there is so much evil going on around here and in the rest of the world?"

"Well, sir—" Nick said.

"Peter," Peter said.

"Well, Peter, those are a lot of good questions. We aren't robbed here because I pay a lot for security; and I have more security than the average person would be likely to detect without looking for it and knowing what to look for. We aren't bombed out and burned because I've made agreements with both sides in this current conflict, and they studiously avoid damaging my business. In exchange, I handle moving a lot of their plunder—for a fee of course. Morally, it might seem questionable. Practically, I do a lot of good for everyone involved, and I don't harm anyone. Currently this little town is in the hands of the FMA, and to be honest I prefer it that way, but if things turn around again, the town will change hands and we'll be under the control of the MNG. Granted, things are worse under the MNG, and fewer travelers like you are willing to pass through town when the MNG is in charge, but either way, my business goes on. So, whether the MNG or the FMA are in power, I will simply attempt to be my own man until someone runs out of money. Like I said, I'm not getting rich by selling food."

"It seems dangerous to count on the caprices of war," Peter said.

"Damned foolish. But you've been out there. What else should I do? Count on its niceties? Go hole up in a bunker somewhere?"

"I understand," Peter answered. And he really did.

CHAPTER 43

It had been dark for hours. Cole was standing in the back of the meal line waiting to get supper when his new work friend Robert walked up behind him and grabbed a tray from the pile.

Robert snorted. "These trays can hardly be called *clean*," he said aloud.

Cole looked over at Robert, then at his tray, and scraped some dried material of indeterminate origin from it. He shrugged at Robert, then shuffled his feet as he waited. Supper would undoubtedly be some disgusting and watered-down stew comprised of grains and other floating *unknowables*. Still, if you didn't eat, you didn't live very long. Cole and Robert waited patiently, feeling the gnawing in their bellies and wondering what their evening's allotment of calories would consist of.

Robert leaned over to Cole and whispered into his ear, "My friend, you told me to find out whatever I can about your sister Natasha, right?"

"Yes. Yes I did."

"Well, I have some bad news for you, Cole. My brother told me something about that power hungry sleazebag named Mike Baker, the guy you verbally grappled with in the yard today, you know him... kind of personally, right?"

Mikail. Cole winced. "I know him very well. Why? What's going on?"

"I thought it seemed like maybe you two had a past," Robert said. "Anyway, the word is that Mike has been protecting your sister since she's been in the camp. No one's allowed to touch her or do her any harm."

"Yes," Cole said, biting his lip and nodding almost imperceptibly. "I figured as much. Mike's a complete reprobate, but he does seem to have a kind of nostalgia for his home town people. Weird, I suppose." Cole pulled off his glasses with one hand and blew on the lenses one at a time before returning them to his face. "It's a mystery to me why he's protecting her, because he's forced her to work as a dragger. It seems like cutting off one's nose—or simply waiting till it falls off on its own accord—just to spite one's face. Everyone says that being a dragger is a death sentence, but, so far, thank God, her sentence seems to remain an open question."

"I don't know," Robert said, wiping his face with his sleeve. "I can't say what he's doing or why." He looked around and then spoke again in a whisper. "I just know that my brother heard that Mike was going to have your sister brought to his office *tonight*. Apparently, he plans on having her for himself."

Cole turned and stared into Robert's eyes. He did not blink, and his countenance did not change. He refused to allow his face to betray the anger and fear that flared up inside of him. His throat constricted, forcing him to swallow hard before pushing out his words.

"You heard this from your brother?"

"Yeah. Not half an hour ago."

"And who is your brother?" Cole asked.

"He's a picker. He's gotten in with some of the guards. That's how he found out. They were talking about how beautiful your sister is, and one of the guards wondered aloud why someone hadn't already claimed her. Most of the women have been claimed by someone or another—by a guard, or by a prisoner with power in the camp. Another guard told my brother the scoop. The word is that she belongs to Mike, and no one better touch her but him."

Cole shook his head. His heart pounded and he was enraged, but he kept his emotions in check. *Time to think and act, not react.* He flexed his shoulders, trying his best not to show too much emotion. His thoughts, though, were rampaging. *What is this world where humans are traded like fish and treated like dogs?* He could not abide such a world. He thought of the world of his youth. What would Volkhov say of this practice, this trading of people like animals? Cole already knew the answer. Volkhov had sounded the alarms. Old Lev knew what men, deprived of their artificial world of laws and social structures, would turn into, and here was the evidence.

"This is supposed to happen tonight?"

"Tonight."

"What time?"

"What does time mean here, Cole? I don't know. My brother just said *tonight*, and it's already late."

Cole quietly placed his tray back in the stack, nodded at Robert, and then walked out of the dining tent and into the cold and dark of the Carbondale evening. Anyone who had met him on the way and tried to stop him or impede his progress would have received a beating so severe that it would have made that person wish he were dead rather than in Carbondale on that night.

* * * *

Sergei Dimitrivich Tupolev stood in the dark and waited for the soldier to arrive. He kicked a small clump of snow, and, as he did, he thought of the time he'd spent in the camp. He thought of the events that had brought him here, and the adjustments he'd made to just keep going. *Steve.* He hated that name. He spit it out with contempt under his breath. A man does some things during times of crisis or emergency, which he normally would not do. Things not altogether honorable. Sergei had been tallying up the column of his crimes—sins he'd committed under the name of Steve. Since escaping from Warwick, he'd rationalized that *Steve* would do things that Sergei never would. But now, even Steve had found his limits. He'd always been a follower. He'd always let Mikail push him around. He'd done wrong things for what he thought at the time were right reasons. But now he'd had a belly full of it.

No more.

A few seconds later, he handed a roll consisting of all of his pay chits to the man in uniform. The two were in the dark shadow of the infirmary, not far from the dining tent. Their transaction was relatively safe here. No one went to the infirmary, and if they did, they didn't live very long. The smell of death and disease in the air suggested that it was a place to go to die rather than a place to heal and get better. This provided an advantage, as there was little likelihood of this illegal transaction being interrupted by curious persons from within the medical tent.

"It's not enough," the man in uniform said.

"That's what I figured," Steve said. He reached into his coat and withdrew a napkin. He handed the man the folded napkin, then put his hands back in his pockets. Wrapped up in the napkin were four wedding rings and two gold necklaces.

"You stole these from the bodies!" The soldier said, emphasizing his point while still trying not to be heard.

"What?" Steve replied. "Are we obeying the law now? I got these in another, similar transaction to this one, and just as illegal. Are you really surprised at how this black market system works?"

"No," the soldier said with a sly grin, "but... I could take these from you and walk away and there'd be nothing you could do about it. You couldn't report it now, could you?"

"Well, that would make things problematic for you. I'm sure your commanding officers would be upset if they found out that you were selling weapons and other hardware out of the armory. They might ask what I was trying to buy with these *misappropriated* items."

"Nobody would believe you," the guard said. The look on his face told Steve that the guard wasn't sure if he believed that. Steve decided that he didn't.

"Mike Baker and I come from the same town in New York. Warwick, New York. You ever heard of it? You want to check that out?" Steve laughed. "I bet he'd vouch for me against you!"

The soldier stared at Steve awhile before finally handing over the package that he'd held at his side throughout their conversation. Steve opened the package and looked at what he'd just purchased.

"These better be good, buddy. If not, I'll be in really bad shape, but I'll make sure that you are in even worse shape... *if* they're not good."

"They're good," the soldier said. "Took them out of the crate not ten minutes ago and brought them directly here to you."

"Alright then," Steve said with a nod. He looked in the bag and counted the items.

"If you plan on using those things, make sure you stay away from tent 43. That's my tent. My shift is over and I'm going straight there now."

"I'll stay away from tent 43."

"What're you gonna do with those things, anyway?"

"Nothing. Don't worry about it. I'm just using them for leverage. Chances are you'll never hear about them again."

"Whatever you're doing, just leave me out of it, okay? I'm just trying to get by—just like everyone else."

"Yeah, I can do that," Steve said. With that, he walked away, leaving the guard standing alone in darkness.

* * * *

Natasha stood facing Mike who sat in his chair with his feet kicked up on his desk. The light from three kerosene lamps basked Mike's office tent in an orange-yellow glow, and a small kerosene heater clicked rhythmically as it pumped out heat that made the tent comfortable and warm.

"So you want me to be your girlfriend? Are you serious? Are you kidding me, Mike? I detest you! What is *wrong* with you?" Natasha then broke into a long rant in Russian. She emphasized important points in her speech by pointing her finger in Mike's face at the appropriate moments.

Mike just stared at her, unmoved by her outburst. "Just a bit of advice," he said coldly—and in English, "I'd cool it with the Russian-speak, unless you want to start a riot in this place." He paused and let her consider the truth of that. "Nobody—and I mean not one single person in this place—is a big fan of the Russians right now. You'd do well to try to remember that."

"You are an idiot if you think I'd ever throw in with you," Natasha said, now speaking in English with a perfect American accent.

Mike clasped his hands in front of himself, and brought them thoughtfully up to his chin. "It would get you off dragger duty, and probably even save your life. Surely you don't detest me so much that you'd die to make a point?"

"Don't be so surprised."

"Well," Mike said as he reached over on the desk, picked up a pencil, and rolled it slowly between his hands, "things are about to *change* around here, Natasha. I mean *radically* change." He pulled his feet down off the desk one boot at a time, and then leaned forward in his chair to speak conspiratorially, "I'm taking over this place in the next twenty-four hours, Natasha. Maybe sooner." Mike fidgeted with a folded paper that was sitting on the edge of his desk. The paper had rows and columns of numbers on it, and looked official. After a moment of silence, he looked up at Natasha to see whether she believed him. He could tell that she believed just enough to keep listening. "Now that you know *that* little piece of information, Natasha, you will either agree to my proposal, or...," he paused for effect, "...your body will be in that picker pile for your friend Steve to drag tomorrow."

"Why are you even asking me? People like you—people who would threaten to kill a girl because she won't be his girlfriend—they usually just take what they want."

"I'm not a rapist, Natasha."

"So, you'll kill me if I don't become your girlfriend, but you're not a rapist?"

"No. I'll kill you because you know a secret that could harm me and damage our plans. Natasha, I am not going away. We are headed for a worldwide socialist revolution. I am going to see to it that I am at the head of that revolution. This is my reason for existing, Natasha. I only trust you with this secret because I would like you to be by my side."

Mike looked at Natasha and smiled, before continuing. "Listen... we come from the same place. We have things in common. That's all this is. It really is as simple as that. Let's not make this into something it isn't."

"You are a piece of work, Mikail." Natasha spit the words out in anger.

"I'm just trying to help both of us make the best of a bad situation. And, do not address me by that name. One slip like that could get us both killed."

Natasha ignored Mike's answer and pointed a finger in his face. "And what makes you think you can take over this place? You failed with your coup at Warwick." She looked at him and saw that her words cut him. He swallowed before answering.

"I've learned a lot since we left Warwick. I won't make the same mistakes again."

Natasha paused. "But why? Why take over? You have a powerful job right now." She let that hang in the air, not understanding why for some men no amount of power is ever *enough*. "You could help people, Mike! You could do good. These people need help, not another tyrant, so why feel like you need to seize power?"

"I've been biding my time," Mike said, as if he hadn't even heard her speaking. "I had expected that our friends in the new Red Army would be here by now. An invasion was planned to follow the EMP and the nuke attacks." He ran his fingers through his short hair and exhaled deeply. "This has been planned for a very long time, Natasha."

He stood up and walked around the desk, and as he did, Natasha walked to the far end of the desk to increase the distance between them. "Apparently, the invasion has either failed, or it never came off." Mike waved his hand as if it were all water under the bridge now, and of no importance to his plans. "Whatever the case, we're on our own here, and we need to act."

"We?" Natasha snarled. "We? I'm not with you, Mike. I'm not with the Red Army."

Mike paused for a moment and stared at Natasha through narrowed eyes. "You are Russian, Natasha, just like me," he whispered.

Natasha looked away. Her mind flashed back to what seemed like only hours ago, when she'd insisted to Steve that she *was* Russian.

"I'm not Russian," she whispered.

"Yes, you are, Natasha. Yes, you are."

She shook her head, as if she were shaking off the remnants of an old life and an old identity. Strength boiled up in her blood, and hardness returned to her gaze. She clenched her jaw in finality. Only *she* would define who and what she was. She spun around and fixed Mike in her angry glare.

"So what're you going to do, Mike? Operate a death camp? Is that how you want history to remember you? As a Gulag Commander? That is *very* Russian of you!"

"No!" Mike said. "I'm going to liberate this so-called 'death camp.' That is how history will remember me. The Americans built this camp, just like they built the Charm School. I didn't destroy our homes and loved ones with a drone attack. The Americans did that. The Americans killed Lang, Natasha, not me! Don't you blame any of this on Russia!" he hissed. "This prison is being criminally mismanaged for the financial benefit of the one *American* man who is in charge. Hardly a proper socialistic set-up like the one I will soon implement. The commander is also wasting all of his resources in this fruitless war against the FMA. I have almost 100% of the Missouri National Guard officers supporting my takeover. Any officer that does not support me, will be taken care of pretty quickly. They do not know that I am Russian and, of course, I've had to offer them the world in exchange for their allegiance, but we'll see how that all turns out when the time comes. Promises can be *adjusted* once power is consolidated."

"How are *you* going to end the war, Mike?"

"Easy. I just won't fight it any more. Once I am in power, I will negotiate a cease fire, and then I'll withdraw our forces and let the FMA have this useless real estate."

"Oh? And then where will you go?" Natasha put her hands on her hips in frustration. "Your plan is to take over the camp, then abandon it?" Natasha looked at Mike as if her objection was obvious. "That sounds like a brilliant plan."

"You haven't even heard the plan." Mike said calmly, looking at Natasha with no discernible expression on his face.

"So tell me then," Natasha said. "Where will you go? Where will you take all of us prisoners?"

"Settlers."

"Prisoners!"

"I'll be the senior commanding officer of the Missouri National Guard. I will assume the name of the man who currently runs the MNG. I will take his identity. Once that is done, we will go somewhere else. Maybe we'll all go to Missouri. I've heard it's nice there."

* * * *

Just then, Cole stomped into Mike's tent and the wooden door slammed closed behind him. A smile crept across the bulldog's face and his shoulders drew back in amusement. "Oh look, a hero!" he said with a laugh.

"Cole!" Natasha shouted.

"Natasha," Cole said. He glared at Mike. "Time to come with me, sister."

"Glad to," Natasha replied, sneering at Mike as she moved behind Cole and towards the door.

The smile on Mike's face grew, and he raised his hands above his waist with his palms out, as if to show that he'd committed no crime and that he intended no harm. "It's funny," Mike said, "that you two have a way of treating me like some kind of cartoon villain, when I've done nothing but protect you ever since Warwick."

"Oh," Cole said, his eyes half drooping as if he were bored. "We are *so* thankful for all you have done for us, *Mikail Mikailivitch.*" Sarcasm dripped from Cole's lips as he spit out the words in a hard Russian accent. "We'll remember you in our prayers every night. May all of Russia place you in the pantheon of national heroes! May your name be remembered alongside those of Stalin and Lenin, comrade Mikail!"

Mike sighed and his head dropped to register the undeserved abuse. "I should tell you both—" he said, shrugging his shoulders as if he had no other alternative, "—that if you leave this tent without reaching an agreement with me, neither of you will live until morning."

"Yes," Cole said, smiling, "you don't sound a bit like a cartoon villain."

"I'm trying to help you."

"We don't need your help," Natasha said.

Just as she said these words, the door flew open once again, and a cold icy breeze followed Steve into the tent.

"Great!" Mike said, "A Warwick reunion."

Despite the placid look on his face, Steve brought into the tent with him an atmosphere of steadfast determination. The air was electric with tension as Steve quickly moved Cole and Natasha towards the door with his left hand.

None of them saw that in Steve's right hand was a tire iron, gripped tightly and hidden up close to his right pants leg. None of them noticed the two lumps, one in each pocket of the pants he'd worn ever since the day that he, Mikail, Vladimir, and Kolya had first escaped into the tunnel that had brought them out of Warwick.

Steve ignored Mike and spoke directly to Cole and Natasha. "You two go directly to the tool shed at the southeast corner of the camp. Don't run, but walk quickly. Wait there in the shadows until you hear my signal."

"What will the signal be?" Cole asked.

"You'll know it when you hear it," Steve replied. Mike was moving toward him now, and Steve looked away from Cole and Natasha and fixed his eyes on Mike, arresting Mike's movements for a moment. Both men froze and stared at one another.

"At some point, if all goes well, there will be a breach in the fence. That's when you two need to make a break for it," Steve said flatly.

Mike half-stepped toward Steve again before stopping. "Steve, your Chechen blood is rising up in you."

At that, Steve turned fully to square up with Mike. "Shut up, Mikail."

"I always said you could never trust anyone whose people came from Chechnya," Mike said with a sneer on his face. He stepped defiantly towards Steve and this time Steve met him half way and swung the tire iron with all of his might. The iron struck Mike just behind his left ear, and the short, muscular man instantly dropped to the ground. A tiny trail of blood began to pour out from just above his right ear. He was unconscious.

Steve turned back to Cole and Natasha as if nothing at all had just happened. "Listen for the signal, and watch for a breach in the fence. When it happens, you go! Don't try to take anyone with you." Steve now looked directly at Cole. "Kolya, you made that mistake once before. You went back to the tunnel for your glasses and you got caught. Don't make that mistake again. Once the fence is down, RUN!"

CHAPTER 44

"People have always thought that disease would end the world—some bug or some transmuted virus—and it will, eventually. At least that's what I think. Disease *will* end the world. However, it won't be like everyone has imagined. We will have to deal with things like tetanus again, and the rampant and deadly diseases of the middle ages will all return." Red Beard said.

"Rats," Clive said. He spat the word out and turned to look down the small hallway of the bunker.

"Ok, I want to clear up something right now, since we have time, and we're just talking here," Clive said. "Most folks have it wrong about the middle ages. Ignorance and disease killed many people, no doubt about it. But when you hear some historian talking about how industrialism and progress extended the length of human lives in our era, you need to really examine the fallacies in many of their arguments." Clive looked over at Red Beard and smiled. "I'm not arguing with you, Pat, I'm just making a point, since we're all just talking here." Red Beard just nodded, encouraging Clive to continue. Clive did.

"High death rates in the Middle Ages were the product of a combination of about three things. One, the masses of people in Europe had moved to the cities. The cities were teeming with people, most of them trying to escape armies that had been crisscrossing Europe for a couple of hundred years, stealing crops and food and kidnapping young men to force them into military service. So the cities were packed full of people." Clive shook his head and muttered, "It was a recipe for disaster." He looked over at Pat to see if his friend was still tracking with him. Red Beard was.

"Two, the people in those cities were ignorant. Good information was kept from them. They were superstitious and oblivious to even the most basic understandings of cleanliness and hygiene. They threw their bodily wastes out of their windows and into the streets for heaven's sake, and then drank from the rivers that the waste ran into!" Clive acted out this part of his story, and then ended by shaking his head and waving his hand as if something stunk in the bunker.

"This was all in the cities, mind you. Three, there was little to no knowledge of the part played by vermin in the carrying of disease. City people killed all the animals that preyed on vermin, and then the rats and such-like animals, multiplied out of hand in the cities. Just like today. People will kill a harmless snake in their yard because they've been trained to be afraid of snakes, even though humans are about a million times more likely to be killed by a disease that is carried by the snake's natural food! That's the kind of mentality we're dealing with!" Clive threw his hands up into the air. "Have you ever heard a modern urbanite say, 'the only good snake is a dead snake'? Well, *those* are the people who will destroy the world via disease!"

Clive looked at Calvin and Red Beard and realized that he'd raised his voice, and now he was shaking his finger. He put his hand down and started to laugh.

"I don't mean to preach," Clive said, "but it gets me hopping mad that cities and industrialism cause a problem, then they get credit for solving the problems they cause, even if they didn't really solve the problems at all. They just postponed them for a century or two. Listen, an individual, or a family, or an extended family group living on the land *unmolested* in the year 600 would have the same life expectancy as people do now. The trick is to live unmolested. It's a simple thing to grasp, really.

"Walled cities were not places—originally—where people lived. They were once called 'citadels,' and they were places where people went to get away from occasional violence, and also to worship. The citadels stored up food and supplies from the countryside, and eventually people stayed there to trade and do business because it was safer, and of course there were more people there. A lot of those people ended up staying, because it didn't make sense to keep traveling when you could just live in or around the citadel. Once the people got used to the cities though, most of them figured they liked it better than having to work in the fields or forests for their food, so they eventually raised armies to go and plunder other areas, and to defend their own city. The cities became occupied military bases and home to mercenary armies. Rampaging armies have a way of causing... you guessed it... citadels in other places, which is the root cause of more armies, which cause cities. It's a loop. Diseases and a high mortality rate are the result of cities and, of course, ignorance and violence, which are the result of the wickedness in the hearts of men."

Clive stopped again and twisted his mustache between his thumb and forefinger. "Anyway, too many people have these simplistic conceptions about the middle-ages, and they therefore have mistaken ideas about cause and effect." He had his hands in his pockets now, like a professor, and he paced back and forth as if he were lecturing to his students.

"Many people will make it through these critical days only to be killed by tetanus or cancer or hunger, or whatever." Clive looked up and then he froze. He followed Red Beard and Calvin's glances, and looked over his shoulder. He saw that Veronica was glaring at him, and he immediately recognized the insensitivity of his words. The three men all apologized in unison. "Sorry, ma'am."

Clive looked at her and smiled underneath his mustache. "He's a strong boy, Veronica. He'll be all right."

Veronica weakly returned his smile.

They all knew that Clive was lying.

* * * *

After a while, Veronica came down the hallway and sat with them. How long had she been standing over her Stephen? *What is time when your son is dying?* She leaned her head against the cold of the concrete wall and sighed. She sat listening to her own breathing for a moment. The others were content to let her have the silence. Then she spoke. Heartbreak filled her voice.

"Youth and innocence die first in war. Don't let anyone tell you differently," she said.

Red Beard spoke first. "You're right, Veronica. You are surely right."

* * * *

Veronica woke from a deep sleep and the feeling (*was it imagined?*) of cold air rushing across her face braced her. Something left her unsettled. She sat up and looked to her right.

There was her sweet child. He was breathing heavily, and the sweat glistened from his head in beaded droplets. She bent down to brush his forehead with her hand, and he rolled his neck forward. She kissed his cheek and held the face that had looked up at her so many times. Now, his eyes were ablaze with fire and intensity. He was alive, but barely so.

Veronica didn't see or hear anyone else. There was a light from down the hall, and she heard the whirring of someone cranking the lamp, and she called but no one answered. The noise of the dynamo stopped, and after what seemed to her to be only a few moments, she got up to look around, and there was no one to be found. She and Stephen were alone in the bunker. She grew frightened. Anxiety formed in the pit of her stomach and poured out from her towards some unknown point in the future, some obstacle she'd not yet encountered. She thought of the fact that the two of them were locked inside the earth, alone, following a nuclear attack.

She felt, for the first time in her life, like she was in prison. A lifetime ago she and Stephen had locked themselves in the nuclear bunker under the Brooklyn Bridge, but that had been an adventure. This was not an adventure. This was a long nightmare. One from which she could not wake.

* * * *

Stephen's body jerked violently and Veronica wrapped her arms around him and held on tight. His muscles bulged out of his neck, showing the tendons all the way to the shoulder blades and sockets. In an instant, he became all skeleton and sinew. His pelvis arched up and outward. His feet bent back until the bones seemed ready to snap. His fingers looked as if they would pop out of their sockets. Veronica held her son in her arms and whispered in his ear. She rocked him as she had done on those nights when he was just a baby, and as she'd done after they'd learned about his father's death. She held him, swaying with him until the tension relaxed and his muscles released. This scene went on for a while, repeating its own little history as if it were an endless loop.

After a while, Veronica heard a bustling at the door of the bunker, and before she could get up to see what it was, Red Beard came hustling down the stairs. He was wearing a fallout suit. "Are you awake, Veronica?" He leaned his head into the doorway and got his answer. "Good. Sorry for not waking you earlier. We decided you needed some sleep. Come with me for a moment." He motioned with his hand toward the door.

Veronica got up and began moving in that direction. She hesitated, looking back at her boy. *What if?* Then she followed. She didn't even think to ask why.

"We decided that there were things that needed to be done—things that can't wait any longer." He didn't explain what he meant, and she didn't ask. He indicated with his hand to a fallout suit hanging on a hook by the door, and Veronica began putting the suit on without question. Red Beard continued talking while she did so.

"Clive mentioned that he knew someone, a man on the next farm over—the Amish farm."

"Mr. Stolzfus?" Veronica asked. "Clive has talked to us about him before."

Red Beard nodded. "Okay. Stolzfus's old man used to serve as doctor to the whole community. The son, Henry, runs it now, and he learned a thing or two from his daddy, I'm sure. We have to take our doctoring where we can get it now." He finished zipping up his own yellow suit. "Anyway, you don't run a farm or build a barn or raise a roof or clear a field without a cut here and break there. You learn some field medicine by necessity when you're a farmer. The man won't be able to do much, Veronica, but perhaps he can ease the boy's pain." He motioned down the hallway toward Stephen. "We didn't want to see him go on like this any longer."

Pat half-way smiled at Veronica, and she was overcome with emotion. She looked at him standing there in his bright yellow suit, with his head of red hair exploding out over the top, his facial hair spilling onto his chest, and she wanted to hug him. At long last, she smiled. Red Beard smiled back. He wondered whether anyone alive had ever seen such a beautiful smile as hers.

"We're saddling up some horses," Red Beard said to Veronica. "Clive is going to ride over there with the boy in a little bit."

Veronica looked back at him. "I'll come, too."

He frowned. "Oh ma'am, you can't. It's far too dangerous."

Veronica waved him off. "Nonsense. I can and I will."

Red Beard could see that it wouldn't have made a difference to argue with her, so he didn't. He turned on his heel and made a motion toward the door. "Okay, then. I'll have Calvin saddle up another horse." They walked out to the front steps of the house together and waited.

Clive's RV was in the yard. The farm below them was spread out in beautiful rows, all white now and covered in snow that had fallen overnight. This is the way of Pennsylvania in winter. Snow lies on the ground for months, enriching the earth for spring. An imaginative watcher might imagine the scene in spring, rows of corn spread out in the field, lofty stalks pressing up into the lazy blue sky, with the white farmhouse and red barn in the foreground, and the rusty wheelbarrow, and the white and yellow chickens scratching about in the yard. The sun also rises over Amish country, and falls along the trees on the banks of the river rolling just on the western edge of the property. The creative mind could imagine the scene in its entire rural splendor—even now. Even with the smoke.

However, it was not spring. It was winter, and the fields were white, and the sky in the distance was heavy with smoke. Beauty enveloped in ugliness. On top of the strange looking RV blinked the only light that Veronica could see on the immediate horizon, save for the light of the sun and the sky, and the reflections off the water rolling by in the riverbanks. She stopped in her tracks.

On top of the odd-shaped RV was a small transmitter antenna, turning in a slow, robotic fashion to the north. From the lazy and unsteady movement, it was unclear whether the dish was turning by a motor, or whether it gained its motion by a manual, cranking action. The dish stopped for a moment, and the engine revved in the RV.

Clive Darling was on a phone call.

* * * *

They placed the boy's body, racked with pain, onto a stretcher and tied him down firmly with plastic wrap. They could not afford to have the boy jerk in a spasm and fall off either the stretcher or the horse. They would have to move quickly along the roads, though they didn't have far to go. There was no telling what they would find once they got off Clive's farm and headed down the river road. Veronica and Clive fixed the stretcher to a horse that was to going to be led along like a pack mule. As they tightened the straps and secured the litter, Veronica noticed that there were *other* packages tied underneath the stretcher. She noticed them but did not feel the need to ask what they were. She bent forward and awkwardly kissed her son and asked the horse that was carrying him to be careful with her "precious boy."

Clive laughed, but in an affectionate way. His breath rose up in front of his face like a spirit when he did. "You think that animal understands you?"

Veronica stroked the end of the horse's nose and dropped her head to look into its eye. "More than you know, Clive," she said.

The two mounted the horses and pulled off across the snow. At the bottom of the hill, there was a little step-down onto the road. The road was covered by a patch of ice and one of the horses slipped for a moment, its hooves skidding outward, causing the saddle and its rider to slide backward and hang there precipitously for a moment. The horse caught itself, and, steady now, they continued on their way.

The traveling was uneventful. They saw no one on the road, and no dangers presented themselves. Still, the sound of this new world was eerie. There was the clop of the horses' steel shoes on the slush of the pavement, the sound of plastic rubbing, and horses tossing their reins as Stephen tried to yell out, his jaw clenched in agony. These sounds echoed across the snow and rolled into the banks of the river. The riders were lost in the strangeness of it all, noticing the muted noises of the livestock and the sounds of an unexplained and undefined distant explosion. Everything seemed *muffled*, somehow.

As they rode, Veronica couldn't help feeling as if someone were watching them—as if there were eyes peering at them from along the tree line by the river, or from the river itself, or from the ditch. It was as if the hills themselves had eyes. She rode in quiet awareness, watching to her right and northward along the river road. She reached to feel her pistol against her belt and a lightning bolt of understanding shot through her head. In all the excitement to get Stephen prepared, she'd forgotten to pack her pistol.

* * * *

As they entered the road that led to the Stolzfus farm, they stopped.   Clive made a little wave, and then the door to the farmhouse opened up, and Henry walked out into his yard.   He made a little wave back, and the three then proceeded on horseback up into the barn, where the doors closed behind them. There was nothing particularly odd about it in the grand scheme of things.   This was a friendly little neighborly exchange in Amish country, perhaps a visitation on a Sunday afternoon.

No, there was nothing extraordinary about the event taking place in front of Henry's barn, except for the fact that everyone— the two riders on the horses, the boy strapped in the plastic on the other horse, and the man standing in the yard doing the waving, directing traffic—they were *all* wearing nuclear fallout gear.

CHAPTER 45

The explosion rocked the restaurant in Mount Joy, Pennsylvania, just as Ace was wiping up the last of the delectable meat sauce with a piece of buttery garlic bread. Mortars began landing around the area of the restaurant, and Ace could see by a quick-snap look at the owner Nick's face that this attack was not normal. It was something in his eyes. Nick held his smile for the rest of the crowd, but Ace saw the truth in his eyes. He wondered if the others had also.

In seconds, most of the diners had bolted out of the front door and gunfire rattled here and there in the streets outside. Peter jumped up and took Elsie by the arm, pulling her gently but firmly towards the bar, where Nick already stood taking an accounting of the potential danger. Bullets began popping through the front glass of the restaurant, and the three travelers had just crawled along the floor to where Nick stood, when an explosion destroyed a third of the restaurant's seating area. The table where they'd just been sitting was not the dead center of the explosion, but it was close. They watched as the roof collapsed in upon itself, pouring dust and debris on the very plates off of which they'd been eating only seconds before. They looked up at Nick for some reaction, but he only flinched for an instant, and then he went back to assessing the room.

Ace could see bodies falling over as patrons tried to make it through the bottleneck at the front entrance to the restaurant. He tapped Peter on the leg and motioned that they should stay behind the bar along the railing. Bullets began pouring in through the restaurants opening. *Someone is shooting into the crowd.* The plate glass windows that stood on either side of the front door shattered and began to disappear.

Peter saw the small boy crouched behind the bar, and Elsie saw him too and went over to the boy. Peter settled in beside them and saw that Ace was straining to pull Nick down behind the edge of the bar, forcing him to take cover for his own life. Nick struggled against him, but eventually he, too, crouched down. He pursed his lips in anger as he considered what was becoming of his thriving business.

"Those MNG bastards!" he said, barely above a whisper.

"Where's the back way out of this place?" Peter asked Nick.

"You don't want to go outside right now. If they've decided to hit this place, then they'll be coming from all sides."

"What, then?" Peter asked.

"Down." Nick started low crawling along the bar towards the door that led to the kitchen.

"Down?" Peter asked, following Nick and motioning for Elsie and Ace and the boy to stay close.

"Down to the catacombs," Nick said without explanation.

* * * *

Natasha and Cole walked quickly out of Mike's tent heading towards the tool shed. Prisoners wandered here and there, but few people took any notice of the siblings as they moved purposefully towards their goal. A slushy brown-gray mist splashed upwards from their boots as they hustled, and when they arrived at the shed, they ducked into the shadows. They both leaned with their backs against the structure, their chests heaving from the exertion. The air was cold and brisk, and the darkness was almost complete. Here and there, the light coming from inside nearby tents cast long arrows of yellow-gold light onto the slush outside. The breeze howled through the fence in the distance and gave music to their deep and rhythmic, icy inhalations. Neither one of them thought about the possibility of there being cancerous dust or particles in the cold air that they greedily sucked into their lungs. In those moments when there are more immediate and tangible foes in the dark night, the more long-term enemies tend to disappear from the list of frights.

The immediate threat to Natasha and Cole was the guard tower on the southeast corner of the camp. Cole had just begun to wonder why Steve would have picked such a highly dangerous and heavily guarded area for their escape, when a tremendous, earth-shaking blast destroyed most of the upright supports that held up the tower. The structure collapsed in on itself as it fell, and then tumbled outward. A large section of the fence fell flat with a thud.

"Hand grenade," Cole said, barely pushing out the words in his stunned surprise. Both he and Natasha were staring, dumbfounded at the destruction before them. Their ears rang slightly, but through the ringing, they could hear Steve's voice from behind one of the nearest tents. It sounded muffled at first but then they could make it out.

"*RUN!!*"

There was gunfire in the distance, and Natasha pulled on his hand as she began sprinting towards the area where the fence had been destroyed by the falling tower. He felt his legs catch up, and before long, he was running with Natasha, hoping beyond hope that there were no guards with machine guns waiting for them at the fence line.

The two siblings had to slow down to climb through the wreckage of the tower, making certain not to drag a nail or sharp shard of metal across their legs from the broken fence, which had collapsed under the weight of the fallen tower. Cole arrived first, and he pulled Natasha over a particularly tricky section of debris. As she gained her footing, he looked up to assess the situation. He saw Steve standing between the two escaping Warwickians and a large unit of MNG troops, responding to the commotion, were gathering together not far from the collapsed tower. The soldiers, shocked and surprised by the sudden attack, were just beginning to check their weapons, and now they stood and gaped in foggy disbelief. Someone in charge started shouting orders, and the soldiers were in that moment—the milliseconds it takes to make a decision as to whether they should chase, or fire at the escapees.

* * * *

It was the soldier on the far left who saw him first. A prisoner was standing defiantly between them and the destroyed tower with a hand grenade held up in his clenched fist. The pin had already been yanked away, and dangled pointedly from his lips.

One of the soldiers shouted, "Halt!"

Just as he did, Steve spit out the pin and ground it into the ground with the heel of his boot. He turned, locked eyes with Cole, and smiled. He made a motion with the hand that was not holding the grenade. "Run, Kolya! Run!"

Kolya Bazhanov stood and watched his high school friend grinning back at him. He watched as one soldier lost his cool and began firing, the bullets ripping into Sergei's body. "Run!" Sergei yelled as the first shots hit him.

Cole ran.

* * * *

Cole felt Natasha grabbing him by his elbow and pulling him, and he started to run again, but even as he ran, he couldn't tear his eyes away from the drama taking place behind him.

Steve, mortally wounded, dropped to his knees, and the group of Missouri National Guardsmen had started to move forward when the young man used the last of his dying strength to toss the hand grenade into the midst of them. The explosion that followed was terrifying in its intensity.

Now, Cole and Natasha were sprinting without hesitation, and they each unconsciously flinched as the deafening explosion echoed behind them. Their freedom had been bought with a price, and they did not intend to squander the benefit.

"Oh, my..." Natasha said as she ran.

Cole, for maybe the first time in his life, was speechless.

* * * *

The sounds of battle intensified as Peter, Ace, and Elsie, along with the restaurant owner named Nick, and his son Charlie, low crawled deeper into the service areas of the besieged establishment.

"Follow me!" Nick shouted as he crawled. "Stay low and stick together!"

"Where exactly are we going?" Peter shouted back as bits of plaster and brick and other debris filled the air and dropped down on their heads. "The *catacombs*, you said?"

Nick reached a back wall and pulled himself up to his knees. The sounds of battle seemed closer now. The building shook with every impact, and the ground rumbled as Nick began struggling with a long, stainless steel shelving unit. The shelf was seven feet high and ten feet long. It was heavy, and made heavier because it was laden with canned goods and other *barter-able* materials. Nick, without assistance, was only barely able to move it, so he waved for Peter and Ace to come help him, and they crawled forward and began tugging on the shelf until it moved.

"This place used to be a brewery!" Nick shouted over the din of warfare and brutality going on around them.

"I know!" Peter yelled, trying to make himself heard over the constant shelling.

Nick and Peter gave the shelf one last shove, and then Nick pushed his way behind it. Reaching behind a wooden wall panel, he released a lever. The panel slid out of the way, and Peter saw that behind it was an antique door. Nick pulled the door open until there were maybe eight to ten inches of clearance, and then he jammed his ample frame through the gap, waving for Peter and the others to follow.

As everyone pushed in through the crack in the door, Nick squeezed back past them, and pulled the wooden door closed, leaving the group in darkness.

"There are huge, arched cellars under this place," Nick said, as he reached into his pocket and pulled out a Zippo lighter. He lit the lighter and held it up in front of his face. "We'd planned on making them into a restaurant called *The Catacombs*, but that was before the bombs dropped. They've been unused, except for storage, since the 60's!"

He pushed his way back past the group again so that he could lead the way into the catacombs. "Follow me, and hold on close to the person in front of you! We've got about twenty steps, then a landing that doubles back, and then about twenty more steps to the door."

Nick moved slowly towards the first step, hunched over with the Zippo in front of him so he could see. He found the stairs, and began to descend, with the rest of the group close behind him.

"So... what about the rest of your staff?" Peter asked.

"Most of 'em took off when the shooting started," Nick shrugged. "They were loyal, but only to a point."

Nick reached the landing and turned to the left, searching with his foot for the next step down. "A few of 'em got it when that mortar took out the area where you people were sitting. I didn't see any more around, and none of 'em know about this place... only me."

His son cleared his throat. "Me and Charlie," Nick corrected himself.

When the whole group had arrived at the bottom of the stairs, they could see by the illumination from Nick's Zippo that there was a heavy iron door, rusted but very solid, leading into the catacombs. To Peter, the door looked like a movie prop, or the gateway into an ancient dungeon.

Nick produced a heavy, iron skeleton key on a leather strap, and opened the door with a solid push.

"Built in the middle 1800's, the catacombs served as everything from wine cellar and beer-aging vault, to a hospital during the Civil War, to a speakeasy and casino during Prohibition." Nick talked like a tour guide, chatty to take their minds off the rage of bullets that seemed to be pouring into the building over their heads. Once everyone was in the cellar, Nick pushed the solid door closed, and lowered a steel piece of I-Beam into a cradle that received the heavy bar and locked it into place. The barricade served as 'insurance,' Nick said, in case anyone ever managed to find a way to unlock the door.

The subterranean room they were in was cold and dusty, and there were antique wooden shelves laden with goods stretching from floor to ceiling. The shelves curved along their tops, matching the arched ceiling, and the whole of it gave Peter the mental image of a wine cellar in France, maybe back during the Hundred Years War.

The feeling of stepping back in time was shattered, though, when Nick walked over and pulled a tarp off what turned out to be a stainless steel box. Nick flicked a switch, and the box hummed to life with a mechanical whirr, which increased in speed and intensity, until the room filled with the sound.

"What are you doing?" Elsie asked.

Nick ignored her question. He only held up a finger and smiled. He continued his movements, and from under another shelf, he pulled out a device that looked like a World War 2 era battlefield phone. He plugged a cord into the humming stainless steel box, and then he cranked a lever on the phone.

Charlie, for his part, walked around the cellar and lit lanterns. Elsie turned and watched him as he did so. Ace helped the boy reach one lantern that was a little bit out of his reach. The orange-yellow glow lit up the room and gave it a warmth that matched its antiquity.

Ace, Peter, and Elsie watched Nick go through the strange series of motions, and then they glared at one another with a look of intense curiosity. Young Charlie watched the three visitors with unrestrained amusement and just smiled a knowing smile.

A minute or two passed, and the only sound was the whirr of the stainless steel box, and the breathing of the five inhabitants of the basement. Before long, though, Nick spoke into the phone.

"Clive? This is Nick over in Mount Joy. We've had a breech. The MNG have surrounded the place! Heck, they've probably taken the whole town. If you're coming to save the day, now would be a really good time!"

* * * *

As Cole and Natasha sprinted through the snow, the frozen ground and the darkness made their running treacherous.

Still, they ran, darting through the forest and through clearings without any real thought as to what direction they ought to run. Their goal was just to get *away*. *Away* meant 'away from the Carbondale camp.' *Away* was an idea to them, just as escaping from any imprisonment is always an idea. Their escape was no different from that of a man, not long ago, who'd left his Brooklyn apartment to seek freedom from the stranglehold of the city. Or, that of a woman and her son who'd trekked out of the city just to get away from the mayhem.

They ran to save their lives.

Natasha breathed deeply as she ran, and for a moment, she even forgot that Cole was with her. His own strenuous gasping, coming from behind her and to her right, faded for a moment as memories flooded over her. In her mind, she was back with Lang—who was really Vasily—and he was also the man she'd loved, and she was sprinting across the open clearing of Highway 17; sprinting for her life and to escape a world of lies. Tears welled up in her eyes now, and her thoughts tumbled together, and she thought of the other family members and friends that she'd lost. She thought of Sergei, giving his life for her. She thought of Peter and Elsie, and she hoped that maybe they were still alive. *Where could they be? Somewhere out there in the darkness.* She looked out into the rolling hills in front of her and the tree line to the right and ran toward that nothingness.

She ran as if she were running from her bitterest recollections, and running towards all the things she'd loved and lost. That thought brought her mind back around to Cole, the only family she had left. She turned to look at her brother, and that was when both of them stumbled through a particularly deep drift, tripping over something buried under it. Together, they tumbled headlong into the snow, crumbling like Olympic decathletes who'd failed only steps from the finish line.

Lying on their backs and looking up into the darkness, their chests heaved in unison as their eyes flashed around the night sky in a jumbled mishmash of terror, sadness, elation, and hope. They each greedily, and wordlessly, took in the cold, night air—the air of life—and neither of them was prepared when a dozen armed men were suddenly all around them with guns pointed into their surprised faces.

CHAPTER 46

Jay Watkins, former Sergeant in the Missouri National Guard, and now a Staff Sergeant in the Free Missouri Army, squatted down next to a large tree, leaning his back against it as he inhaled deeply from his cigarette. In the distance, there was sporadic gunfire coming from the direction of Carbondale.

"You two may have made it out of there just in time," Watkins said.

"*Time?*" Cole mumbled, shuffling his boots in the snow. The rest of his sentence was a mumble.

"What was that?"

"Time is the father of truth," Cole replied. He glanced up at the soldier, pulled off his glasses, and cleaned them on the filthy sleeve of his coat. He placed the glasses back on his face and snorted in disgust.

"That was Rabelais," Cole said, matter-of-factly.

"Well, ain't that a load of crap!" Watkins said. "And that was Jay Watkins, Staff Sergeant!"

"Time will tell," Cole replied. "That's all I can come up with right now. I suppose I could snort again if you'd like." He straightened his back and looked at Jay Watkins.

Watkins laughed. The laugh was slow at first, but it grew in an increasing way, until the only way to describe the sound would be *guffaws*. Jay Watkins had large heaps of laughter pouring out him, coming from deep in his gut, and his whole body shook.

Cole laughed too, until he looked over at Natasha, and her face—frozen in anger, or maybe it was pain—put an end to the mirth.

Watkins took the last draw from his cigarette and threw the butt down into the snow. "As I was saying, it looks like you two made it out just in time. A dozen more made it out after you, but they got cut down by automatic fire in the clearing. You two beat the rush by a minute or two."

"How do you know all this?" Natasha asked. Her hands were shaking, and her jaw was fixed and set.

"Our guys have been watching the prison for a week. We were in the final planning stages of an assault on the camp when you two blew the fence."

"It wasn't us," Natasha said, looking down at her feet, before looking back up at Watkins. "It was a friend of ours."

"He was a hero then."

"He was."

Watkins looked at the young lady and saw in her eyes that she really meant it. He was touched by such an old-fashioned notion. He could see these two were not ordinary.

"Where are you two from?" Watkins asked.

"I don't suppose it matters anymore," Natasha said, "it only matters where we're going, doesn't it?"

"I suppose."

"We need to catch up with some friends who are headed to Amish country."

Watkins lit another cigarette, took a long drag from it, then blew the smoke upwards into the chilly night air. "Well, our attack is, at the very least, delayed now because of your escape." He jerked his head in the direction of Carbondale. "They know we're here. We might be stuck out here for another week."

Cole reached his hand out to Watkins who just stared at him blankly, not knowing what Cole wanted.

"Gimme a smoke, Joe."

"It's Jay, friend."

"It was a joke, Jay, geez! I'm Cole, and grumpy here is Natasha, so enough of the meet-n-greet and give me a smoke."

Watkins laughed again and popped a cigarette out of the pack, reaching it over to Cole. "Help yourself, Cole. I like you," he said, laughing heartily.

"Do you like Shakespeare?"

"He's alright, I suppose."

"Then I suppose we might get along."

"What if I had said 'no'?"

"I'd have left you here talking to her," Cole said, cutting his eyes towards Natasha.

Jay Watkins caught his breath. She was beautiful, he thought. He was about to say something corny like, "Well, that wouldn't be so bad," but he didn't get the chance. A quick glance at Natasha showed him the impatience of a sister who'd been listening to her brother charm others with kooky bravado, along with her amazement that, even here, in the midst of catastrophe, he was still doing it.

"No," she said. "We're not *getting along* here, because we're not staying, Cole. We've got to try to catch Peter and Elsie." She looked out into the darkness. "If they're still alive."

They heard a quick blast of staccato gunfire from automatic weapons in the distance, probably coming from the prison camp. Natasha wondered if people were being executed because of the prison break, but there was no way for her to know. Maybe Mikail was taking over the camp. She did not speak the words, however. She didn't say a word about the camp.

In retrospect, long after this cold, dark night, sometime in the distant future, she would regret not telling someone about Mike's plan to take over the camp. She'd regret that she was never properly debriefed by the FMA. Those were sketchy times, and a lot of things were not as they should have been.

She tugged at Cole's sleeve.

"Whatever you say, Sis," Cole said. He lit his cigarette and puffed on it happily; the low, red glow of the cherry illuminating his now much slimmer face in the darkness. The glow of the cigarette caught in his glasses and flickered, and he turned to stare out into the darkness, and took the smoke into his lungs.

Cole turned back to look at the people around him, and he saw that his sister was still shaky from the escape—anxious to hit the road. He wasn't so anxious. He felt that it was good to be alive.

A soldier walked up to Watkins and nodded a greeting to Cole and Natasha, who nodded back at him in return. The two soldiers stepped a few paces into the forest to talk, and when they finished, the underling soldier hustled back off into the darkness.

"It looks like you two may be in luck," Watkins said.

"How's that?" Natasha asked.

"We've been called off of this duty for the moment. It seems there's a full-fledged assault going on in the Mount Joy area. We've got wagons and horses, but it'll still take us a day and a half to get there. The MNG is trying to push us out of our territory."

"Or draw you away from here," Cole said. Natasha looked at him, as if to see if he knew anything. He didn't.

Watkins pulled the last cigarette out of the pack, balled up the empty wrapper, and stuck it into his pocket. He pulled a new pack out of his coat, opened it with practiced precision, and then offered another cigarette to Cole.

Cole turned down the cigarette with a wave of his hand.

"I don't smoke."

"But..."

"That one was to keep me from soiling my pants," Cole said, smiling. "I'm okay now."

Watkins laughed and shook his head. "You are a piece of work, Cole."

"That's what they say." Cole smiled when he said it and Natasha watched him smile, and then she looked at Jay Watkins. He motioned toward the darkness.

"Well, we better push off. We have a long trip ahead of us. You two will be safe with us until we get to Mount Joy. I can't tell you what things will be like when we get there, but you'll be a step closer to Amish country."

* * * *

They walked through the snow and darkness until they reached a road where the FMA unit was already packing up for the long haul south. Carts, buggies, wagons, and single mounts lined the road. A hundred soldiers on foot stood stamping in the cold, trying to defy hypothermia, anxious to get moving.

Natasha and Cole followed Watkins and climbed up into the back of an Amish buckboard wagon. When they'd each found their seats, Watkins pulled out a bottle of what looked to be Kentucky Bourbon, and passed it around to everyone in turn. When the bottle got to Cole, the young man grinned from ear to ear.

"Come, gentlemen, I hope we shall drink down all unkindness."

He took a long swig and then wiped his mouth on his coat before handing the bottle to Natasha, who passed it on without drinking.

Cole smiled to Watkins and winked, and then looked over at Natasha, who was glaring at him.

"That's from *The Merry Wives of Windsor*," Cole said with a straight face.

"I don't care, Cole," Natasha replied with her brows furled in mock anger. She stared at Cole for a moment before her own face broke into a smile. She leaned conspiratorially towards the others in the wagon and said, "My brother can get a little obnoxious with the Shakespeare."

"Okay, then," Cole said, "if I have your permission." Then he reached over and slapped his sister playfully on her knee. "Let us every one go home, and laugh this sport o'er by a country fire."

"Indeed," said Jay Watkins, and with that, he turned his horses toward the south and gave a solemn nod towards the moon in the eastern sky.

* * * *

Six hours after Nick had placed his emergency call to Clive Darling, the five people in the catacombs under the restaurant in Mount Joy heard a commotion the likes of which they'd never heard before. They'd been sitting around and talking about the war, and the things they'd seen since the crash had started when what sounded like World War 3 erupted above their heads, and some of the concussions caused bits of mortar and stone to fall down into the cellar.

Nick stared at the ceiling in awe. "It would seem that the battle is joined."

"Ain't no party like an MNG party," Ace said.

"What are the chances this cellar collapses on us?" Elsie asked. There was worry in her voice, and she didn't try to hide it.

"This cellar has been here since before the Civil War," Nick said. "It'll shake, rattle, and roll, but I'm certain we'll be alright."

"I'm fine down here!" The roar of mortars increased, and little Charlie had to yell to make his point.

"We'd definitely rather be down here than up there," Peter said, pointing upwards. The sounds from upside responded to Peter's statement as if to emphasize his point. The violence being unleashed on Nick's restaurant was frightening, and awe-inspiring. "I'm not sure a housefly could live through what's going on up there!" Peter shouted over the noise.

The assault was relentless, and Peter began to worry that—even if the cellar didn't collapse—the damage and debris might take months to clear away, even if someone did know that the party was down in the cellar... which they did not. *How are we going to get out of here?* he thought.

* * * *

What followed, for another twenty-four hours, was a nerve-rending mind siege. The war raged fervently in Mount Joy, and the people in the cellar thought that at any minute, the ceiling was going to come tumbling down on top of them.

The ceiling held, and after a particularly frightening barrage of mortar fire—at a moment in time that became crystalline in their consciousness—everything went eerily silent.

The silence reigned for about twenty minutes, and no one in the cellar spoke a word. Each person just sat stoically, eyes rolled upwards, staring at the ceiling, waiting for another shell to drop, or mortar to shake the earth.

Then there was a sound.

There was a rattling over near the door, and Nick jumped up and darted in that direction. He started pulling some baskets of clothing and cardboard boxes out of the way, and after he did, Elsie, Ace, and Peter could see that a copper pipe, about four inches in diameter, extended down through the ceiling. At about two feet above the ground, the pipe flared open at its bottom.

Nick looked over his shoulder and winked at the travelers. "If I were a careful man, this contraption would be the mechanism I'd use to stash the gold and silver and precious stones, you know, just in case we ever got robbed! The gold you paid me is down in this basket here. I would always drop the goods down the pipe after every transaction."

Now, the travelers watched as a single, folded piece of paper tumbled down the pipe and into Nick's hands. He opened the note and read it, and when he was done he squealed and shouted with delight.

"Woohoo!" Nick yelled. He hugged Charlie, who had a huge smile on his face. "Let me read it to you!" He held the letter near one of the lanterns and read aloud, with obvious glee:

Hey, you Yankee bum! It's over. We won. Quit hiding down in your cellar and get up here, 'cause we got stuff to do!

Love,

Clive Darling.

CHAPTER 47

Mike stood in the open field next to the burn pit in the Carbondale Resettlement Camp. The corpses of the former camp commander and his closest officers lay in a tight line, face down in the snow. Mike stared at the bodies, and then slowly turned to look at the soldiers who were awaiting his next command.

His head hurt, and there was a terrible lump behind his ear. He scratched the back of his head and thought of the blow that Sergei had given him, but he did not wince. He steadfastly refused to show any weakness in front of the men.

He looked up and down the assembled line of soldiers, and he nodded his head. He could see on their faces that they fully accepted him as their leader and commander. *Good,* he thought.

"I want the man brought to me who was in charge of the armory! Bring him to me right now!" Mike commanded. He stood with his shoulders hunched and his jaw clenched. It was slight, but if you knew the man intimately, you would know it. Fortunately, none of the assembled crowd knew him intimately. At least, not yet.

Three soldiers dragged another soldier forward until the man was standing in front of Mike. Mike looked the man up and down with disgust.

"Did you give that prisoner two of my hand-grenades?"

The soldier looked down at his feet. In his mind, he went through a quick analysis of whether or not it would be good to lie to the new commander. He didn't want to be given permanent kitchen duty, or get sent to the brig, but he also didn't want to start out his time with the new commanding officer as a known liar. The soldier straightened his back. He'd made up his mind. He decided to tell the truth. He could deal with a couple of weeks of kitchen duty, or even substantial time in the brig, but he wanted the rest of the men to know him as a man who owned up to his mistakes. He looked Mike in the eye and nodded his head.

"I did."

"You sold two of my hand-grenades to a prisoner, who then used them to kill my men and destroy my property?"

"I did, sir." It sounded worse to him, the way Mike said it.

Mike pursed his lips, but nodded his head. He began to walk slowly around the soldier, and everyone waited—wondering what punishment the new commander would mete out on the wrongdoer.

"I appreciate you being honest," Mike said.

He pulled out his side arm and shot the soldier through the head.

The body slumped to the ground and Mike waved for some of the men to drag the body onto the pile with the others.

He turned to the crowd gathered nearby and told them that honesty was a good policy—that it was like a good deed done to your neighbor.

The soldiers busied themselves around his feet, clearing the body and taking the time to rake the ground so that even any traces of the soldier's blood were removed. The blood served as a reminder to the crowd that good deeds like that would not go unpunished.

* * * *

Stephen was dead. Her little boy. From the time he was old enough to toddle, she'd called him "Little Man." At the end, Veronica looked down into his face, and he looked up into hers. She was reminded that the act of looking into one another's faces, was something that had happened every single day of his life at some point. For Veronica, there had always been a spark in the Little Man's face unlike that in any other face she'd ever seen.

Now, as she looked into that face, she did not see any spark of life left. His body, carefully and lovingly strapped to the bed with long strips torn from Amish sheets, was finally motionless and at peace. The only remnants of the struggle that Stephen had faced in passing on were recorded in the sheets; in the wrinkled ridges where his body had convulsed involuntarily.

There was a creak in the floorboards as someone shifted their feet. The thick ancient planks in the floor rubbed in place.

Henry Stolzfus and his family stood behind Veronica, as she looked down on her boy. For a time, everyone was motionless. The Stolzfus family waited patiently for the next stage in the process. Henry flicked his fingers against the edge of his pants. It was a casual motion, but studiously so, as though he was trying to scratch an itch but didn't want to disturb the scene with so obvious a display. He and his family knew this process well, and none of it was new to them. They would allow time for the mother to grieve and say her goodbyes, and then the Amish women would take the body into the great room to wash and prepare it. They knew the process so well because most of them had performed it many times in their lives. For the Amish, death is a part of life. While it is always sad, it is not seen as extraordinary. Death applies universally, and it must be handled in a way that reinforces this concept to everyone—especially the children. As in life, there is an order to death, and for now, they just stood quietly and waited.

At the end of the bed, looking down at Stephen, Veronica was surprised that, along with her grief, she felt such an overwhelming feeling of relief. Strange, because she'd just watched the life drain out of her greatest love. She stood there and experienced it. Truly experienced it. As she did, she also experienced the unexpected, unspeakable, and contradictory gift of *release*. It was a brief moment, but it was unmistakable. She stood in the room, which was objectively beautiful in its simplicity, and she noticed the palette was blue and brown and white and tan. She noticed the cloth; from the imprinted sheets, to the layers of cloth hanging from the shoulders of these beautiful girls—these strong women. They waited and watched patiently.

Veronica stood there; her long black braids hung in a tied up knot of a rope that draped beautifully over her shoulder, and her dark skin stood in sharp contradistinction to the palette of the room... shockingly so.

To everyone else in the room, her face looked thoughtful, and beautiful, and restful, all at once. It had an angular simplicity. The face echoed in the face of the body on the bed— and both stood in sharp contrast against the paler, whiter faces of the Stolzfus family, and it was all part of the contrast that was impressed upon her mind.

In that moment, Veronica D'Arcy found peace.

A part of her left with Stephen. That's the only way to say it. His body was lying on the bed in front of her, and she stood over him and let go of something. It was as if her art, her view of the world, her argument that simply by breathing in and out and viewing the world through the eyes of artful love that things must go well—all of that, simply *went*. Her belief that looking at everything as merely art, and that this mindset would allow her to live satisfactorily in the world, flew away with her son.

That antiquated view had helped her when John died. Then, she still had Stephen to hold onto, to help her hold that focus. And of course back then, the world was still intact. Whenever she looked into her son's face, she would see John, experiencing her husband anew in Stephen, seeing his habits coming alive in her son, his pleasures. But now, her art failed her. Or... it failed to be sufficient to sustain her. She looked down at Stephen and felt that part of her slip away. That view of life could work—it had worked—if and when an artificial system of life-support could be maintained for most of the world's population. Absent that life-support system, life as *only* art, was insanity. It was dementia.

What she found instead, in its place, was *reality*. She experienced it with acceptance, and strength, and she found peace in it.

For Stephen's sake, Veronica was glad that he'd gone on from this world.

Now, she looked down on her son, and in looking at him she did not analyze his color palette. She didn't remark to herself about the intersecting lines of the sheets with the bed, or note how strange it was to see his musculature in harmony with the Amish severity of the place. Her normal artist's eye was at rest. She looked at Stephen and she saw his father, and the life she'd once lived, and even though she was filled with love for her dead husband and son, she didn't focus on *any* of that.

Instead, from somewhere (who knows where these things came from?), Veronica had a realization. It was as if she came to understand that a page had turned and that it was time to move on. She saw the whole of the page, and she recognized that Stephen's death was a representation of what was going on everywhere in the world. She was not in a position at that moment to exhaustively *understand* the thought, and she could not give voice to everything that Stephen was in that moment, lying there dead in an Amish bed. Nevertheless, an outline of the understanding was there. Maybe Stephen represented naiveté. Maybe he stood for innocence. Maybe he was a symbol of Western, Industrial decadence. Whatever the case, his death represented a particular kind of ignorance; one that comes to be in a world that exists within a framework of artificial ease.

He was her boy, but he was the offspring of a life lived *inauthentically.* She'd tried to teach him to survive, but she'd started too late, and she'd never questioned the fundamental presuppositions of life and living. She'd tried to keep him by her own strength, only to find out that no one living has that power. No one can see all the filthy nails sticking out of all the hidden boards out there in the world.

She breathed in the air and felt relief, and peace, and the realness of the moment. She believed that it would lead to the next moment, and for now, that was enough.

She took a soft step backwards, and the Amish women took that motion as a signal. It was exactly that, a signal. The women moved past her and began their work, untying the boy from the bed. Veronica turned to Henry Stolzfus and nodded her head. The tears were flowing now, but not in an angry or violent way. She was not mad. The tears were marking her place, and she knew that when she stepped out of the room, she was going to be stepping fully into an entirely new world, a world where the veil of superficiality had been rent for her... for good.

Henry Stolzfus put an arm around Veronica and led her out of the bedroom.

She didn't look back.

* * * *

The Battle of Mount Joy had turned into a pivotal battle in the civil war that was now raging across Pennsylvania. This will not come as a surprise to anyone who's been paying attention. For one thing, the detail itself seems positively necessary for the narrative arc of the story. All of the characters must meet up *somewhere* and events must occur *someplace*, and Mount Joy seems as good a place as any. It works from a topographical sense as well a historical one. It also works as a literary one. This will become clear as we go along but, for now, simply note that Mount Joy was *special.*

In this Civil War, the battle had become a high-water mark of sorts. It demarcated a particular line along a larger battlefield map. Some General, looking at a map of the area, might have searched with his finger, and put that finger on the map at a particular place where he could focus his resources in such a way that it would inflict *maximum damage*. That point was Mount Joy. It was central to the conflict.

It had a narrative arc all its own.

* * * *

The collision of forces at Mount Joy was initiated by an intensive MNG offensive that was designed to push the FMA southward, across the Susquehanna River to York, and then, eventually, to push them out of Pennsylvania and into Maryland, and from there, into the South. That is a mind-bending amount of detail to take in.

The battle at hand was representative of a world gone mad with force, and unfolding events, in many ways, would mark the end of that world, at least for a time. During the peak of the battle, there was an uncountable torrent of bullets, and shells, and mayhem raining down on Mount Joy. Someone thought that this piece of real estate was important enough to destroy it utterly, but there was more to it. Much more. Even in the heat of battle, the observer must sometimes stop to smell the roses.

Anyone who has been paying attention, or anyone who knows anything of history or of literature, can appreciate the fact that there is a symbolic war going on between forces centered along the imaginary lines of a map demarcated by the invisible boundaries separating York and Lancaster Counties. One mustn't be a Civil War buff to know that by taking out a pen and marking a trajectory that followed along the path of the extended conflict, the line would eventually pass into Gettysburg, and then dip into the topmost corner of Maryland. It was as if a wall was being constructed by the conflict, forming imaginary boundaries into real ones. As people chose sides, it seemed that they divided out about as they did in the last such conflict. Historically, this imagined line of conflict brings to the mind another high-water mark, in another great conflict that once raged across the land, echoing its ancient voice, seeking our attention.

But that is not all.

One would also not have to be a lover of Shakespeare to notice that the houses of York and Lancaster were at it again. One wouldn't have to be a historian of the Middle Ages and know about the War of the Roses to appreciate the rich irony, and to stop here and *smell* the roses.

One might want to note that in that conflict, it did not come down to a question of whether human beings could be bought and sold. Rather, it came down to a question of whether one should wear a white rose or a red rose on one's lapel. That conflict, the War of the Roses, was ancient even when the last Civil War pierced Pennsylvania. Sometimes, the root and fruit of conflict isn't visible from ground level.

* * * *

Clive Darling, using contacts and means known only to himself, called in substantial 'neutral' forces to fight on behalf of the FMA in their battle to keep the MNG from moving south. He didn't want to do that. He liked to remain aloof—above the conflict—but that was not possible in this situation.

Clive had a vested interest in keeping the MNG away from the front door of Amish country, so he brought all of his power and resources to bear on the problem. It should be noted that he had *substantial* power and resources. It was also notable that he had a very close friend and business associate in Mount Joy. Saving his friend was the motivation that added further impetus for Clive to insert himself into the raging civil war.

One can imagine a world in which Clive wouldn't have cared at all about what happened in Mount Joy and therefore wouldn't have taken an interest in its outcome—but that was not this world. In this world, he did care, and he was interested. The reason Clive was interested was that he was fighting a fight that was older than the War of the Roses. He was fighting to save a friend. In his mind, there was something even biblical about it all. This explains why the battle was so brutal and violent. The MNG didn't know that Clive's forces were coming, so they attacked what they thought was an inferior force, with the thought of rooting them out of the town.

What the MNG *did* know, was as shocking as what they did not know, and contributed further to the ferocity of the battle.

They absolutely *did* know that there was going to be an... overturning... of their own leadership. They did know that the man who was going to be their new commander wanted the way cleared so that the MNG could march south, and then west. For these reasons, the field leadership of the MNG used everything they had—every tool that they could muster—to try to dig the FMA out of Mount Joy. They would have accomplished the task, too, if thousands of well-armed militia, commanded, pre-positioned, and equipped by Clive Darling, hadn't shown up to save the FMA.

* * * *

A young officer crouched down behind a burned out vehicle and wondered whether one of the bullets zipping *by* his head would end up *in* his head in the next instant. Still, he had to work out the details of why he was here, and what he should do next. His new commander, the little bulldog of a man, had gotten right up in his face and made himself, and his demands, known. The new boss wanted the FMA pushed back. That wasn't exactly how he'd said it. What he'd said—exactly—was, *"I want this way cleared!"*

Cleared. The bulldog that now controlled the MNG had made a motion with his hand over the map to indicate that no obstacles were to stop the progress of his army. Then he showed how he would march his army—his "settlers" he called them—south along the line he'd drawn through the territory. In order for this to happen, he needed to control the area.

Because the new commander had been so demonstrative in the way he'd swept his hand across the map, the field officers of the MNG used everything they had, every tool that they could muster. Nobody wanted to be the one who failed. The result was a battle of the ages, both symbolically and literally. The MNG was trying to dig the FMA out of Mount Joy, but the FMA, somehow, was holding their ground. The young officer heard the bullets zing by, and he experienced that singular thought that is so common to soldiers in war. The thought crystallized, and it terrified him more than the bullets did. He now doubted if the objective could be met. He wavered. The resistance, which was stronger than he'd anticipated, was starting to seem impregnable.

* * * *

The man who was the new commander seemed to have an echo about him. It was as though he'd studied the old commander and was now imitating him. He had a way of studying men and exploiting their weaknesses, and now he saw a seam on a map that he could exploit in order to obtain safe passage for his settlement. His plan was visionary. He would simply leave the camp at Carbondale to his enemies, and march his contingent south, protected en route by his friends.

He sat on horseback upon the ridge, watched his army clearing the line in the distance, and enjoyed how beautiful his plan was. His enemy, hiding in the darkness, planning their assault, would come running into the Carbondale camp only to find it deserted, like Moscow left to Napoleon, or the Russian countryside left to the Nazis.

He would have successfully accomplished the task, too, if thousands of well-armed militia, commanded, pre-positioned, and equipped by Clive Darling, hadn't shown up to save the FMA.

* * * *

Clive Darling and Pat Maloney stood with Calvin Rhodes along another ridge, under a cover of trees, and bit into slices of apple. Clive cut the slices with his pocketknife and handed them to Calvin and Red Beard as they stood in the cold morning air. Not long before, Calvin had been walking along with the two men, asking questions about the operations that he could now see unfolding in front of him. Looking through Clive's field glasses, Calvin could see that Clive's army was moving methodically, street by street, commandeering the entire area with the use of a massive amount of force.

"I think it's just about over," Calvin said.

"Then we should head down there," Clive replied.

"It's strange," Calvin said, lowering the binoculars. "I always thought of a war as a meeting of two belligerent opponents. However, here, if you don't mind me saying so, Clive, your forces were more like a kind of a third party. Almost a *disinterested* party. You imposed an end to the battle between two combatants using overwhelming force."

Clive and Red Beard and Calvin walked across the field toward Mount Joy, passing the time, eating apples.

"I don't know, Clive." It was Red Beard. "I'm just uncomfortable with the sheer amount of force, especially when it isn't in self-defense. I mean, nature has forces that could blow up the world and end time. Stuff in space can crash into earth, and put an end to it all in an instant. Then there is all this," he waved his hand in the air, "but there should be a balance in there somewhere." Red Beard was showing his discomfort by shaking his head, and grimacing as they walked.

"Who gets to decide, Clive? Should money be able to impose its will, merely because it can afford to buy power? Isn't that what all of the political parties were doing before the collapse? I mean, you can do this because you have money and you believe yourself to be good, right? Well, it seems to me that all power structures want to limit the power of others, and gather to themselves limitless power—and they think it is okay because they believe themselves to be benevolent. They think that they are good, and everyone else is evil. Democrats, Republicans, Libertarians, Greenies, whoever it is! They believe that their cause is right, so they should make rules for the rest of us. So, Clive, how are you different, if you think that money should be able to impose itself by purchasing force?"

Calvin had been only half following the conversation. He'd been looking at the sky, mostly. He suddenly snapped to, though, when he heard Clive lean into the conversation with an edge in his voice. It was a harsher tone than he'd heard the two men use with each other before. Clive laughed, a bit derisively. "You see that RV, Pat? Do you see Bernice there? That beast cost me twenty million dollars! But that isn't the crazy part. You want to know what is the crazy part? I'll tell you, pardner. I have one hundred of these around the country, and all around the world. I can turn off the power anywhere in the world, any time I want. So don't tell me that money can't buy power. It comes down to what you DO with that power."

"I didn't say that money *couldn't* buy power. It can. That much is obvious. I asked if it should be able to," Red Beard snapped back.

"I just used that power to stop a battle that would have raged for days or weeks and would have cost many more lives, Pat," Clive said. "Personally, I don't mind if these people fight. Really, I don't. But I'm not going to let any of them, as they thrash out at one another, crush the only source of food and productive knowledge that any of us will have in the near future. I'm not imposing my will on people, except insofar as they are heedlessly endangering everyone else. Think of me as a referee."

"I just said I don't feel comfortable with arbitrary power. That's all," Red Beard said.

Clive didn't respond.

Calvin bit into his apple and looked out across the field. He saw the RV roll forward down the street. Clive's army was now moving efficiently toward what had once been the brewery at the end of the block, picking off any remaining opposition with impressive efficiency. It really was a thing of beauty, Calvin thought. He considered Clive and Red Beard's argument for a moment, and decided that it was the willingness to use force that made it priceless... and morally questionable.

To Calvin, Clive and Red Beard's whirlwind of activity over the last few weeks, started to make sense. For the first time he had an inkling as to what the cowboy and the leprechaun had been up to all this time. Even if now, with the fruit of their work made evident, they seemed to be disagreeing about the morality of it all.

* * * *

The group that had weathered the battle down in the cellar emerged from the rubble of Nick's restaurant with smiles on their faces. Clive's men immediately went to work helping Nick and Ace haul the valuables. They removed bags of gold and silver, crates of barter-able goods—a veritable treasury—from the catacomb shelter that had saved five lives.

After the bounty from the basement was loaded into wagons, the group of five joined Clive, Red Beard, and Calvin as they exited the town of Mount Joy, walking the mile to the place where Clive's heavily guarded RV was stationed.

The unified group talked as they moved across the fields, trudging through the snow towards Clive's motorcade, and, as they talked, they caught up on the stories of their lives like old friends or new acquaintances would, like survivors would, with war stories and harrowing tales of terror and survival.

Peter and Red Beard talked as they walked. Calvin and Charlie paired off, with Elsie hovering just over their shoulders, having taken a motherly instinct toward both of the boys. Clive and Nick, old friends, carried on a conversation known only to themselves.

It was only Ace, along with the ever-present armed contingent that served to protect Clive, who was still watching for trouble. That is a critical fact to note.

No one among the group was ever in real danger. That should be noted too. Clive's men were on the job, but they were just a tad slow in spotting two people who broke free from the tree lined rise just ahead, and began dashing towards the group.

The two were running, screaming, and waving their arms. They were two-hundred yards away when they emerged from the trees and began their mad dash, and it seemed that they might be running at a man who had just brought an entire town of opposing armies to its knees as easily as if he gone out for milk.

* * * *

Ace moved automatically, and with no hesitation. In one smooth motion, he dropped his pack and the sniper rifle almost magically swung with his body, rising up into his ready hands. With clock-like precision, he popped up the scope covers, and brought the weapon up to the ready position. He dropped to one knee, and by this time, the whole militia contingent had seen the two strangers sprinting towards the group. They too began moving into position, raising their rifles and pistols towards the onrushing pair.

Ace looked through the scope and raised it until a face filled the lens. His eyes narrowed and he made a few slight adjustments in order to bring the face into clearer focus. That was when he saw her....

Natasha.

He moved the scope over a hair and spotted the other runner. That must be Natasha's brother. The likeness was uncanny.

Cole.

What were they yelling? He could just make out their lips.

"Peter! Peter!"

"Hold fire! Hold fire!" Ace shouted.

The militia unit all reacted immediately, lowering their weapons and repeating the order to hold fire.

Peter and Elsie looked quizzically over at Ace, the unspoken question plain on their faces.

The sniper pointed at the two runners in the distance and smiled.

"Some friends of yours, I believe."

CHAPTER 48

He was no longer Mikail Mikailivitch Brekhunov. He was no longer even Mike Baker. He'd now become someone else altogether different. He was being remade, *reborn*, yet again. He was now on the verge of becoming what he was meant to be. Like, for instance, in the Bible, when men of renown were placed into high office, and God Himself would give such men a new name. Mikail demanded that everyone else treat the affair with that kind of dignity, at the utmost level of seriousness. He had, in the past, been known by several names, but now, with his new office, he was adopting the name and rank that would be his for the rest of his life. He was seizing his birthright.

* * * *

"Gentlemen! Welcome to the new world. That which has passed, is now behind us, and we are moving into the future together. I've spoken to each one of you, and you know what I have promised you. This force is about to rise up and we're going to bring order to this chaos."

He paused for a moment, choosing his words wisely, watching to see how each man responded to the words he chose.

"We have a lot of challenges ahead of us. We're going to have hardships. But, this army is no longer going to be operating for the private benefit of one man!" He paused and looked at the crowd, "From now on, all of us are going to benefit! Everyone will share in everything!"

Mike walked slowly down the line of soldiers, looking each one of them individually in the eye before moving on. He stared into their souls and made contact with the part of them that actually hungered for order, and for recognition, and for improvement.

"A lot of things are going to change, gentlemen. We're all going to change. In the midst of that change, though, there needs to be a continuation of sorts—a *continuity* with the authority that formed us and gave us being. Change. Continuity. Order." He paused again for effect.

"To signify this concept, I am taking upon myself the name, rank, and authority of my predecessor." He motioned toward a solider nearby, indicating the soldier should step forward. The soldier did, nervously.

"Soldier, do you know my name?"

The soldier nervously nodded that he did, unsure if that was what he was expected to do.

"I appreciate your honesty, soldier."

He looked at the soldier and the soldier looked at him. He pulled his pistol out of his holster and asked, "What is my name, then?"

"General Amos Duplantis, sir!"

"Yes," he said. He looked at the crowd of soldiers and they looked at him.

"My name is General Amos Duplantis. I will be known by no other name. To you, that is who I am."

He gave the group one more scan, and then began walking back towards the command tent. After about four steps, he stopped, and turned back to the men.

"Does anyone have a problem with that?"

Maybe, down deep inside, some of them did have a problem with it. But the world had indeed changed. Power was now more fluid. Old habits would have to die hard. Maybe they didn't like a twenty-something year old man taking authority, a name, and an office that didn't rightly belong to him. But they also recognized that the old world may have been something of a meritocracy, however corrupt, but this new world? Not so much. If they wanted peace and an end to the war with the FMA and a portion of the spoils going forward, they were going to have to deal with the new situation as it was—not as they might have wished it to be.

The men all looked at the usual pile of bodies waiting near the burn pit. No one indicated in any discernible way that they had a problem with the name change.

"Dismissed!"

* * * *

Back in the command tent, an officer named Rankin approached General Duplantis and saluted. Duplantis returned the salute, and the officer began his report.

"Okay, General, the team you wanted dispatched south from Mount Joy is on their way. I'm tasked with keeping you informed as information arrives about the mission. Their orders were to travel to the farm of one Clive Darling, a man who we are informed is giving aid and comfort, as well as material assistance, to the FMA. He was the one whose militia troops saved the day for the FMA at the Battle of Mount Joy. The team was ordered to dispatch Mr. Darling, gather intelligence, and then return to their unit which is currently just north of Mount Joy, regrouping after the... setback there."

"How well can we keep informed of the progress of the mission?" Duplantis asked. He opened a cigar box on his desk, and pulled a cigar from it. He rolled the cigar between his thumb and forefinger, and then held it up under his nose. He inhaled deeply, taking the scent of tobacco and cedar into his nostrils.

"Our communications are fine between here and Mount Joy, but once the team is on the mission, they'll be behind FMA lines, and it'll be sketchy at best. We may not hear word until the team returns to their unit," Rankin said.

Duplantis struck a wooden match on the desk and then held the flame up to the end of the cigar. He puffed several times, holding the match still, twisting the cigar in his hand so that the entire circumference was burning properly. He held the match until it burned out upon touching his fingers.

"*If* they return to their unit."

"Yes, sir. *If* they return to their unit."

"It will greatly aid in our extrication from Pennsylvania, if we can push the FMA out of Mount Joy, and eliminate the de-facto head of the independent militias in one fell swoop. If this Clive Darling is dead, we'll sweep through Mount Joy next time like a knife through butter."

"Yes, sir."

"Keep me apprised."

"Yes, General!"

* * * *

"Wow!" Natasha said, as she and the others piled into Clive's RV. "What in the world is this thing?"

"Yes," Cole said. "Quite impressive. I see that someone has been able to avoid the world's current... *difficulties*... in style."

Clive climbed over the console and into the driver's seat. He turned to Cole and nodded his head. "We've managed to do alright, *difficulties* aside."

"I applaud you for your foresight, sir."

Clive laughed. "Napoleon said, 'Forethought, we might have, undoubtedly, but not foresight.'"

A gleam twinkled in Cole's eye. "Oh, so we're quoting Napoleon are we? Well, sir, that's just my game."

It was shaping up to be *that* kind of ride. Natasha punched her brother in the arm. "Would you please shut up? Could the grownups talk for just a minute without you and your word gymnastics?" Cole turned away, trying to look offended. "Why, I am hurt, sister! Hurt, I say!" and they continued like this in their usual way, poking at one another. It was how they knew they were still alright.

The others, too, settled in. Elsie and Peter slid into the plush, leather seats and buckled the safety belts around themselves. Elsie pulled little Charlie down onto her lap, and pretended to tickle him. Due to all of the equipment in the RV, Ace, Nick, and Calvin had to stand up and hold on to cabinets as the RV rocked and rolled along the rural roads of southern Pennsylvania. Bernice was moving at a high speed so no one was doing much talking now.

Red Beard was in his customary co-pilot's seat, and he stared blankly through the windshield as if his mind were calculating the ends of the universe. He'd greeted all of the newcomers warmly enough, but he didn't say much as they traveled back to the farm. Clive could see that there was something still on Pat's mind.

Two well-armed, black APCs escorted the RV from the front, and there were two more coming up behind. A large portion of Clive's local force was still cleaning up at Mount Joy—handing things back to the FMA—and would join the folks in the RV back at the farm. They hoped (they told Clive) to only be an hour behind, but with the snow and the mess at Mount Joy, Clive was hoping that they wouldn't be too delayed. He hated moving Bernice without overwhelming force protecting her. He'd made a pact with himself that he would never let the RV, or any of his *proprietary* equipment, fall into the hands of any enemy force. He had a fallback, if such a thing were ever to happen, but now was not the time to think of that. Clive felt sure that there was no active aggressor—at least no force that he knew about—capable of taking the RV in transit. However, once they returned to the farm, and the vehicle was stationary... well... he worried.

An hour later, when they pulled into the drive at Clive's farm, the light was just beginning to fade to end the day. Driving up near the barn, Clive and Red Beard could see Veronica standing on the porch, looking out across the snowy fields of the farm. Her arms crossed over her chest, and she clutched herself in a way that communicated everything, and nothing.

Red Beard looked at Clive, and the cowboy pursed his lips and lowered his head.

"Stephen," Red Beard said. He clenched his jaw. "Dang it! We should have been here, Clive."

"We can't be everywhere, Pat."

"Well now, isn't that convenient?" was all that Red Beard had to say to that.

* * * *

It was just a moment, just an exchange at the end of a long day. Everyone else had already cleared out from the RV and they were gathering in the yard in front of the farmhouse to talk, and Clive and Red Beard lingered back for a moment, as if something must be said to clear the air.

"Now you listen to me." Clive Darling shook his finger in the air. He had made his fist into a kind of ball and he was pointing out into the growing night. Pat Maloney was listening to him.

"I didn't make the world," Clive said, "but I am damned determined not to lose control of my own. I know you have your limits, Pat, and I have mine. I *do.*" He looked at Pat to see if he believed him, and with the look, there was an overlong pause.

The other man smiled, but shook his head a moment. He let Clive know by the way that he shook his head and smiled that that he *did* believe him, but that the limits they were speaking of were way beyond any he could contemplate for himself.

"You know, Clive," Red Beard said, "I think maybe you had to live down there, down in that prison," he paused, "like I did." He paused again, as if to say *perhaps you needed all those years of research, to know what that really means.*

Red Beard took in a breath, and looked as if he were about to speak out of anger, but then he caught himself and exhaled. A face came to mind—the face of one particular young man he'd met in the city. No one knows why such memories occur in such moments, but they do, and this one did. Red Beard thought of the young man he'd met on the bridge. Clay was his name. He thought of the nice talk they'd had together. It had been such a pleasant time of conversation, but the look in that young man's eyes... Red Beard shook his head. He recalled that Clay looked odd. *So hurt, so defeated.* He thought of the pain in the young man's eyes, and he thought of the authorities and the expression of brute power that had put that hurt there, and he felt a tear rise up in his own eye.

"Clive, I'm not ready to use that kind of power."

Clive was going to argue with him, but he looked at his friend at that moment, and thought that he looked like Tolstoy, or Rasputin, or both. He was just a mad monk—a good friend, but not one built to make decisions.

The two pals had just reached an uneasy peace, when the shots rang out.

* * * *

The APCs opened fire into the tree line that ran along the river's edge. The single rifle shot that had felled Nick, seemed to have come from that direction. Elsie instinctively grasped hold of Charlie, who was pulling and fighting against her, trying to get to his father's body. Peter shouldered his AR-15 and popped off two rounds for effect, hoping to keep any sniper's head down as he pulled Elsie and Charlie towards the farmhouse.

Ace had started running as soon as he heard the first shot. He bolted towards the RV, deciding to use it as cover so that he could make his way behind the house. From there, he hoped to find some high ground so that he could use his rifle and bring some aggression to bear against the unseen enemy.

Running toward the RV, he spotted Clive and Red Beard, and he shouted for them to get down. When he reached the two older men, their only response to the gunfire had been to lean in to one another in a frightened bear hug. They were crouching down in surprise and fear, but they were certainly not under cover. Seeing this, Ace put the full weight of his body to use as he crushed into the two men, collapsing them to the ground.

Red Beard fell into the snowy gravel and he let out a howl—not out of pain—but out of sheer surprise.

"Wow!" he said. "Who is that firing at us?"

No one answered his question. Clive was now sliding backwards across the ground until his back rested against the RV.

"Thanks for the hit, Ace. We owe you one. I... I just froze."

"It happens," Ace said.

"Why would anyone shoot Nick?" he asked. "It must have been a missed shot, or something."

Ace checked his weapon and cycled a round into the chamber. He looked around the RV and fired a round in the direction of the tree line. By this time, there was fire coming in from at least three directions: from the tree line that ran along the river, from a cluster of trees and a high ridge just across the road to the west, and from the north—from an unseen sniper near the woodpile where Stephen had stepped on the nail.

"They didn't miss," Ace said.

"How do you know, son?" Clive said, spitting out the words.

"Because, I do this for a living. They don't miss their *first* shot. That's the shot they had all the time in the world to make."

"Then why would they shoot Nick?" Clive shouted.

"From the age, size, build—I'm guessing that they thought he was you," Ace said. He pulled his pistol and fired two more rounds into the thick trees along the ridge to the west.

Clive looked over at Red Beard, who was now pressing his body tightly against the black metal of the RV's slick sides. Red Beard's eyes were rolled up towards the sky, as if he were praying.

"You two get inside the RV and stay low," Ace said. "If they came here to kill you, Clive, then it's best that they think they got you."

Clive reached up and pulled open the door to the RV. Rising to his feet, he pulled Red Beard up and hustled the man into the vehicle. The RV was armored, and the glass was bulletproof.

Then Clive cursed, because if he'd been thinking, he could have gotten everyone into the vehicle. *Too late now*, he thought. *They've all scattered.*

Ace fired another shot towards the ridge, and then closed his eyes and took a deep breath. He knew what a good sniper could do—even in a low-light situation like this one. Then he ran, sprinting as fast as he could towards the back of the farmhouse. Shots plunked into the snow and earth around him, but they were un-aimed shots, and desperate. The fire coming from the Armored Personnel Carriers was successful at keeping the attacking force busy.

* * * *

Cole and Natasha made their way to the barn. Cole didn't know if the barn was safe or not, but he figured it had to be safer than standing out in the open. When they got inside the barn, Natasha noticed several tractors, some with front loading buckets attached to them. She got Cole's attention and pointed to them, and both of them dove behind the large buckets for safety.

Peter was able to get Elsie and Charlie up to the porch of the house, and Veronica held the door as Peter rushed them all inside.

"Come with me!" Veronica said, as she bolted into the drawing room. She rolled up the carpet, pulled up the flooring panel, and then yanked up the door that led down to the fallout bunker.

"Ah, man!" Elsie said, with disappointment. "I'm sick and tired of being underground!" Her protest was interrupted as bullets pierced the walls and windows, and Peter—not willing to discuss it—hustled them all down into the cellar. Veronica told Peter how to pull the floor back in place, and, when everyone was clear, Peter handed down his backpack to Elsie who took it from him, and then looked up to see that he was closing the door on the cellar.

Elsie looked at Peter and at last it occurred to her that Peter was not coming down into the bunker. "Peter!" she shouted, "you get down here!" It was more a plea than a command.

"I can't, Elsie," Peter replied. Veronica was standing at her shoulder. Peter continued closing the door, only slower now. "My friends are fighting out there. You know I have to go."

Veronica put her hand on Elsie's arm, as if to indicate that it would be foolish to argue with Peter, and also to remind her that there was a hailstorm of bullets pouring in through the windows upstairs. With that, Elsie smiled at Peter in a way that told him to be safe, and he closed the door. He pulled the flooring back over the bunker door and then rolled the carpet back to its place. He made sure it obscured the entire entry to the cellar.

Then he exited the drawing room and ran out the back door of the farmhouse, a bear of a man, facing a conflict he had only just begun to understand.

* * * *

The standoff lasted most of the hour. There was one, brief attempt by the attackers to advance on the farm. It happened just after the APCs had stopped their fire in order to let the gun barrels cool. The opposing force took that opportunity to break cover and move towards the farmhouse.

The gloaming of early dusk was falling, and that made target acquisition harder, but Ace was able to pick off two of the attackers in short order from his perch near the roof at the back of the house. He was glad that there were no enemies to the east of the farm. Of course, they might try a flanking action, and if they did, he'd probably be taken out. Nevertheless, he needed to keep the enemy from advancing. He put their numbers at less than ten men. Now, even if the APCs and other offensive fire hadn't hit any of the attackers so far, they should be down to eight or less.

Just then, the APCs opened up again, taking out three more members of the advancing force. One of the APCs began moving across the farm's yard, heading towards the sniper who was somewhere out in the field towards Henry Stolzfus's place. When the APC got in range, they lit up the woodpile, and the fire coming from that direction ceased forever.

The incoming fire slowed to a near stop after the failed advance, but it picked up again about ten minutes later. Ace was expecting another attack, and was readying himself and his weapon, when he saw to the north a column of military vehicles approaching.

"I sure hope that's Clive's men," he said to himself under his breath.

* * * *

Down in the bunker, Veronica tried to make her guests comfortable, but Charlie was beside himself in fear and anger, and it took everything the two women could do to calm the young boy down. Elsie was finally able to get the boy to lie down, and before long, he curled up on a blanket, sobbing into his arms. Elsie decided to give him some time, so she kissed the top of his head, and went to join Veronica.

Veronica sat at the same desk where the inhabitants of the farm had spent many a day and night, holding long vigils after the bombs dropped. She'd sat at this desk, standing her watch over the Geiger counter readout, making tick marks into Clive's notebook, and sometimes crying—much like Charlie was crying—over the condition of her own son. Now, she was leaned back in the chair. Peter's backpack was sitting on the desk, and she was touching it softly, her mind in another place, when Elsie walked in.

"I think he might eventually fall asleep," Elsie said. "Crying takes a lot out of you. I lost my husband in an attack not unlike this one. What was it? Weeks ago?"

"I'm sorry for your loss, Elsie," Veronica said. "My boy died only a few hours ago. Right next door."

"Oh, my—," Elsie said, and put her hand over her mouth.

"They'll keep his body over there – the Amish will – in a cold room, until spring comes and we can bury him."

Elsie's face was frozen in shock.

Veronica raised her hand in gesture of peace. "It looks like all three of us down here have lost our families."

With that, there was silence for the span of a few minutes. Neither of the two women knew what to say, but they both knew that everything that had happened—all of it—was unspeakable.

After a few more moments, Veronica looked at Elsie and smiled.

"I know this backpack," she said.

Elsie blinked. "Really? Do you know Peter?"

"I don't know Peter, but I know this pack."

"That sounds... impossible," Elsie said, shaking her head.

Veronica pushed the pack over to Elsie. She was still smiling.

"Oh, I'm not accusing Peter, or anyone else, of stealing it. A lot has happened since all of this began, and I don't pretend to know what occurrences have led us all here. I'm just speaking factually. I know that pack." She pushed a stray strand of hair out of her face.

"Do me a favor, Elsie, and unzip it. Unless something has changed, or someone repacked it, or... I don't know... maybe I'm altogether wrong; anyway, there should be a blue box in there. Take it out and open it up."

Elsie was sitting in stunned disbelief. She didn't know what to think. She unzipped the bag and, sure enough, there was a small blue box inside the pack.

"What's in it?" Elsie asked.

Veronica smiled. "When I gave it to Clay, the kind and wonderful man who originally owned that pack, it was just a meaningful gift—a symbol of what I thought he was looking for. Now—," she stopped. She took a deep breath before continuing. "Now, I'm guessing that Clay is dead, and what's in that box could very well save this new world of ours."

"Really?"

"I don't know. You see, it's a special variety of gourd corn. It's a non-hybrid seed corn that grows well in almost any environment. It is disease resistant, and it resists crossing with hybridized and manufactured corn varieties. We're going to need this, Elsie, to save the world."

Elsie carefully opened the blue box, and in it, was a hefty packet of corn seeds. There was a note too.

Clay,

Sometimes we just need to start anew. We need to plow, and plant, and harvest. Maybe that way, we'll get past all that we've lost.

Your friend,

Veronica

"That's you!" Elsie said.
"That's me," Veronica replied.

She smiled. She had found her Archimedean point.

* * * *

"I wonder what happened to Clay?" Elsie asked.

"God knows."

Elsie sat for a moment, looking at the corn. She glanced over, and through the door, she could see that Charlie, indeed, had fallen asleep.

Veronica noticed too, and she nodded at Elsie. "It sounds like it has either slowed, or stopped up there. I'm going to go up and check things out."

"Do you think you should?" Elsie asked.

"I don't know, Elsie, but I'm going to. Do you mind if I take Peter's pack? If I find him, I'd just like to ask him if he knows what happened to my friend."

Elsie didn't mind. She'd lost friends, too.

* * * *

Inside the RV, Clive and Red Beard were talking. The gunfire outside had slowed for a moment, and they were trying to decide if they should do something other than huddle inside the vehicle.

"We should go check on Veronica," Red Beard said.

"You're probably right. She just lost her boy, and now we're in a gunfight. Wouldn't hurt to go check on her."

"Let's go."

The two men slowly opened the RV door. There was sporadic gunfire here and there, as the two friends crouched low next to the RV.

In the distance, they could see the lights of the militia contingent. Clive let out a happy yelp, and he slapped Red Beard on the back. "We're saved!" he said.

"Well, let's get to Veronica," Pat said. "There's Peter, coming around the house, and it looks like Ace is with him. Maybe it's all clear."

It wasn't. More gunfire erupted. Clive watched as the militia vehicles screeched to a stop, and the militiamen started pouring out in every direction. A firefight erupted, just as Clive and Red Beard reached the area where the drive split, with part of it heading towards the barn. Looking to his right, Red Beard saw Cole and Natasha coming from the barn, and he waved for them to stay put.

Ace and Peter were still moving forward towards the RV with their weapons readied, and that was when Red Beard heard Ace shout.

The militia flushed an enemy gunman from the ridge opposite the house, and as he ran from his cover, a militia bullet hit him in the back. He skidded to the ground and rolled and, despite his wound, in one complete motion, he popped up and raised his rifle to fire.

Red Beard saw the gun pointed towards them, and immediately reached for Clive. He seized the older man by the upper arm and, with almost super-human strength, spun him around, tossing him roughly to the ground and out of harm's way. Three bullets thudded into Red Beard's chest and neck, and the leprechaun fell to the ground without drama or pretense. Militia guns finished off the wounded attacker with a short burst, but it was too late.

Clive was already up and running towards his fallen friend. He screamed, "No!" at the top of his voice, but it was a useless and fruitless scream.

The shout echoed around the farmyard, bouncing off the buildings and the vehicles before disappearing into the coming night.

* * * *

The light of the sunset had disappeared into the darkness, and the light of life was fading from Pat Maloney's eyes. Looking up, he saw his friends, new and old ones, bending over him. Clive was clutching him and had pulled him up into his lap, so that his head now rested against the older man's chest.

The world was fading into the fogginess of the surreal dream, and Pat was looking from face to face, and trying to speak, though he could not.

His eyes caught a glimpse of the backpack hanging on Veronica's shoulder, and he reached towards it with his hand, as if there might be in it some savior, some elixir, or some potion that might pull him up from his condition.

He felt himself slipping, as if he were falling into a dungeon, or a prison, and the hand that was reaching towards the backpack was now reaching for anything—anything at all; any strand or rope onto which he might hold that might arrest his fall.

A face appeared to him as he fell, and it was the face of a friend that he'd only met once, and his hand now turned, and opened, and seemed to relax and cease its pointing.

For the others—for Red Beard's friends gathered around him—the scene was tragic and shocking. Clive rocked his friend in his lap, and let out a sob of pain and loss that was surprising coming from a man with such limitless power. Perhaps it is impossible for a man truly to be god-like. Red Beard's right hand reached up, and pointed, and he seemed to strain to say something, so they all leaned in at that moment.

"Clay," was all he said.

Only a few of the team gathered around the dying man heard it, or, if they heard it, knew then what the name meant.

Then there was a release, as if the reason that all of this had happened, going back to the Hurricane that had struck New York City, was only to bring them all to this one moment—for them to be surrounding a man who had minded his own business, who had never hurt anyone, and who only wanted to pass the time with his friends.

The faces around Red Beard looked down at him with sadness. Some of the faces Pat had known for a while, and some of them had been new to him, but now he couldn't see them, because dead men do not see.

Each person had their own thoughts at that instant, as the severity of the moment applied itself to each one of them in turn.

The end of the world is never pretty.

* * * *

It was Veronica, later, who rallied the group, when it seemed that despair and hopelessness might overwhelm them all. She got them moving again, and eventually they could laugh, plan, joke, and argue.

We have work to do, she told them all, *and reality never waits for us, or asks how we feel about the repercussions of our own folly.*

Clive found a truck for Calvin, and the men spent some of their days fixing it up so that Calvin could eventually go home to Texas.

After many discussions, Natasha and Cole decided that, in a few more weeks, when the weather should be better, they would go to Texas with their new, young friend.

Peter and Elsie were going to be sad to see Natasha and Cole go, but they were determined to stay. This was a very tough decision. For Peter, the two young friends were the last connection he had with Warwick, and with his old life there. Peter asked his friends to keep their eyes and ears open down in Texas for news about his wife and child, and to try to get word to him one way or another.

Peter and Elsie adopted Charlie. Not officially, because there was no mechanism for that, but they took him in as if he was their own son, and hoped to help the boy grow into a good man in this new and different world.

Veronica and Ace decided to stay at the farm with Peter and Elsie, to help Clive run things, and maybe to serve as a conscience for the man who seemed to hold so much dangerous power.

The breakup of the team, however, wouldn't be for a few more weeks. For now, they all worked, planned for the future, and lived.

At night, Veronica would read to Natasha, Cole, and Elsie from *The Poems of C.L. Richter,* and they'd talk about the things the poems brought to mind. Ace would listen, but he rarely talked. He liked to look off into the night, and stabilize the world with his silence.

Cole said that he didn't know Clay, but he knew a few men who were very much like him. An old teacher named Lev Volkhov, and another friend named Vasily, reminded him very much of the man that Veronica remembered.

"A great man named Alexander Solzhenitsyn once said that *'One word of truth shall outweigh the whole world,'* Cole said, "so maybe we've all known Clay in one way or another."

Perhaps Cole is right.

THE END

From the Poems of C.L. Richter

The world cycles,
and by that I mean history,
events,
dramas,
civilizations,
they repeat.

And we can learn from that.
If we will.

Patterns develop,
ingrain,
mirror,
showing us,
that what has been,
is what will be.

There is nothing new...

...you know the rest...

A Note from The Author

Due in large part to all of the awesome support from WICK fans along the way, we've arrived here at the end of the WICK story. We hope you have loved it as much as we have loved writing it for you.

Please follow WICK on Facebook so you can keep in touch with me and receive updates about whatever comes next. Also, remember that the WICK universe and story continues in *The Last Pilgrims* – the first part of that saga is now available.

Based on the information that I have right now, there seems to be a lot of interest in reading more of this story. I am considering continuing the WICK storyline with a new series that would take place between WICK and The Last Pilgrims. That would put the new story roughly ten years after the events found in WICK, and ten years before those of The Last Pilgrims. I will leave it up to the readers to let me know if they would be interested in such a series. From the very beginning, this adventure has been a cooperative exercise and I have been talking with you readers all along –that experience has been one of the greatest of my life. This is one of the great things about the modern publishing landscape, readers have more input than ever before into what gets written and whether or not the work is eventually successful.

I hope that you've made it this far because you really have enjoyed the story, and I also hope that you'd like to see it become more popular, so more people will know that it exists. You've heard me say this before, but I really need your help, so I'll say it again...

The *WICK Omnibus* is an independently published work. That is a fancy way to say that I don't have a handy agent or publisher with the means to market it properly. The only way it will ever find its way into the hands of readers is if those people who read it and enjoy it will become a part of the team and help me get the word out that it exists.

The single most helpful thing that you can do to assist me in getting the word out about *The Wick Omnibus* is to review the book. It's free for you to do so, and if you have enjoyed it, it is an excellent way to let other people know what you thought.

Even if you reviewed the individual parts as they were published, The Wick Omnibus is a new book... would you consider writing a short review for the Omnibus? I would greatly appreciate it.

PLEASE, while it is still fresh in your thoughts, go to Amazon.com or wherever you purchased the book and write a review for it. Your review doesn't need to be long, just a paragraph will do. You may not think a single review will help or hurt a book's probability of finding success, but if you think that, you are wrong. It is a fact of the modern market, that books that have more reviews, sell more copies, and have more credibility.

I've been heartened by the wonderful response to the *WICK* story, and it is your feedback and help that has given me the motivation to keep going.

I would also be very pleased if you would share links to *WICK* on Facebook, Twitter, and everywhere else on the Internet where such things are shared and discussed.

If you want to keep up with all things *WICK*, I've made a handy Facebook page for you...

http://facebook.com/wickbook

A *WICK* fan has also set up a WICK discussion page. If you are interested, please check it out:

https://www.facebook.com/groups/543889328956512/

Thank you so much for all of your help and support.
Michael Bunker

To sign up for Michael Bunker's email alert list, please go to:
http://eepurl.com/enJeQ

http://facebook.com/wickbook

The WICK story continues! 20 years after the collapse. Book One of The Last Pilgrims saga... *now available!*

The Last Pilgrims, by Michael Bunker

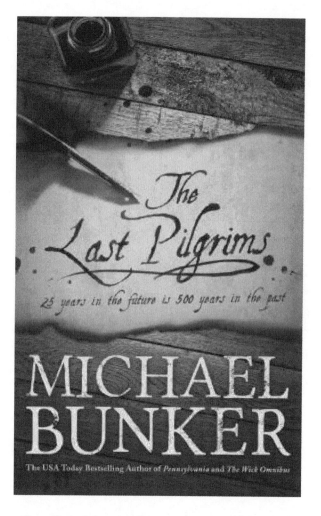

For a limited time, get the sequel to *the Wick Omnibus* for **free** right now! Go to: <u>http://bit.ly/FreeLastPilgrims</u> to get the full novel for free!

About the Authors

Michael Bunker:

Michael Bunker is a bestselling author, off-grid farmer, historian, philosopher, iconoclast, husband, and father of four living children. He lives with his family in a "plain" community in Central Texas where he reads and writes books... and occasionally tilts at windmills.

Michael Bunker on Facebook:
http://facebook.com/michaelbunker

Michael's Twitter:
http://twitter.com/mbunker (@mbunker)

mbunker@michaelbunker.com

Chris Awalt:

Chris Awalt is a middle-aged man who rides a bicycle. He is also the father of two artful young daughters where he lives along the Jersey Shore. He is a freelance writer and a carpenter. His writing can be found on Andmagazine.com, where he writes columns on politics and culture, and chilledart.com, where he and his daughters manage a website on artful living. He can be found on both facebook and twitter.

Chris Awalt can be reached:
lchrisawalt@gmail.com

Other Books by Michael Bunker

The Last Pilgrims, by Michael Bunker (2012).
ISBN 9780578088891

The Silo Archipelago, by Michael Bunker (2013).
ISBN 9781490375915

Three By Bunker (3XB), by Michael Bunker (2013)
ISBN 9781484067987

Michael Bunker constrains most of his communication to _"snail mail"_ (traditional post).   Please write him a letter if you have questions, comments, or suggestions.

M. Bunker
1251 CR 132
Santa Anna, Texas 76878

Or, sign up for Michael's Email List:

http://eepurl.com/enJeQ

Made in the USA
Middletown, DE
08 January 2021